MY HEART LAID BARE

OTHER BOOKS BY JOYCE CAROL OATES

JOYCE CAROL OATES

MY HEART LAID BARE

A William Abrahams Book

DUTTON

DUTTON
Published by the Penguin Group
Penguin Putnam Inc., 375 Hudson Street,
New York, New York 10014, U.S.A.
Penguin Books Ltd, 27 Wrights Lane,
London W8 5TZ, England
Penguin Books Australia Ltd, Ringwood,
Victoria, Australia
Penguin Books Canada Ltd, 10 Alcorn Avenue,
Toronto, Ontario, Canada M4V 3B2
Penguin Books (N.Z.) Ltd, 182–190 Wairau Road,
Auckland 10, New Zealand

Penguin Books Ltd, Registered Offices:
Harmondsworth, Middlesex, England

First published by Dutton, an imprint of Dutton NAL,
a member of Penguin Putnam Inc.

First Printing, June, 1998

1   3   5   7   9   10   8   6   4   2

REGISTERED TRADEMARK—MARCA REGISTRADA

LIBRARY OF CONGRESS CATALOGING-IN-PUBLICATION DATA:
Oates, Joyce Carol.
My heart laid bare / Joyce Carol Oates.
p.   cm.
"A William Abrahams book."
ISBN 0-525-94442-7 (alk. paper)
I. Title.
PS3565.A8M89   1998
813'.54—dc21   98-10531
                                      CIP

Printed in the United States of America
Set in Goudy
Designed by Eve L. Kirch

FOR RANDY SOUTHER

CONTENTS

Part II

Part III

If any ambitious man have a fancy to revolutionize, at one effort, the universal world of human thought, human opinion, and human sentiment, the opportunity is his own—the road to immortal renown lies straight, open, unencumbered before him. All that he has to do is write and publish a very little book. Its title should be simple—a few plain words—"My Heart Laid Bare." But this little book must be *true to its title*. No man dare write it. No man *could* write it, even if he dared. The paper would shrivel and blaze at every touch of the fiery pen.

—*Edgar Allan Poe, 1848*

PROLOGUE

The Princess Who Died in Old Muirkirk

She was not a Londoner by birth, she was very likely not even English by birth, you could hear it in her voice. Sarah Wilcox. Sarah Hood. Nineteen years old, small-boned and ferret-crafty, eyes of no particular brightness, hair of no particular beauty, yet she was her Lady's favored maid, her Lady's most attentive maid, listening at the children's lessons, French, Latin, music, numbers, the Kings of Old England and France, listening at the children's prayers, paying heed to her Lady's friends in the great houses and royal palaces, how to incline the head, how to lift the voice, the eyes rolled delicately Heavenward, as if God on His throne were gazing down: ah, an innocent flirtation! Before her Lady called Sarah knew to obey, before her Lord gave a command Sarah knew to acquiesce, having, as it seemed, no will of her own, surely no cunning, albeit Sarah was not her name and in her voice you could hear she was not a Londoner by birth, very likely not even English.

One day Sarah swept to her Lady's golden mirror, bedecked in her Lady's most exquisite finery—silks, jewels, hairpieces—and made so bold as to inquire, in her Lady's very voice, *Is it little Sarah, or her Lady, who stands here so proud?*—whereupon the mirror laughed, saying, *Your Lady, little Sarah, was never so proud.* And shortly thereafter her Lady and her retinue were summoned to the great palace at Warwickshire to visit

Queen Charlotte, wife of King George III, and now gold coins settled in Sarah's deep secret pockets, and in her small bosom, and she prayed God, *Let me be blessed!*—and God, hearing, could not but obey. Rings flew to her slender fingers, gold chains and pearls and ropes of emeralds, sapphires, diamonds, rubies looped themselves about her neck; velvet, and lace, and silk, and satin draped about her graceful little figure. You looked and she was smiling, you looked and she was weeping for very joy, and her eyes were almond-shaped and sly, and her mouth sweet as bruised plums, and her child's body quick and lithe as any eel's, and every mirror in Queen Charlotte's private apartment proclaimed SARAH, BLESSED OF GOD.

She walked East where no one knew her. She walked West where no one knew her. A great clattering coach took her up and she flew South where no one knew her. Yet, as Venus shone on the High Road of Dover Sarah was apprehended by police in Queen Charlotte's very ermine-lined cloak, and in the tall blond wig and silken gown and pearls of her own Lady, and she wept in fury that coarse hands dared touch her, for was she not of royal blood?—and was she not en route to her beloved father who lay gravely ill across the Channel, and who had summoned Sarah to his bedside, to receive his blessing before he died?

And was *she*, her Lady's favored maid, to be mistaken as a common thief, and trundled back to London and the hangman—?

Now the little gold coins declared themselves, all a-clatter, and the glittering rings slipped from her fingers, and the chains and pearls and precious stones from around her neck (excepting, for Sarah was very quick, a single gold locket of the Queen's on a thin gold chain), and her eyes yielded tears hard and cruel as tiny stones, and her Lady slapped her full in the face for very pique as Sarah had been so prized, till now. She fell to the ground to beg for mercy, she tore at her bosom and repented most piteously, she rolled her eyes Heavenward and spoke of her dying father in France, and at last her Lady intervened in her behalf, that Sarah should not suffer hanging like a common thief upon the Cheapside gallows but be transported to America as a bondwoman. The year, 1771.

Now Sarah sank into the sleep of oblivion blessing her dear Lady, now she woke and her lips were savage with curses. To punish her God placed her at sea, deep in the lightless hold of the *Mayhew*, where the very air quivered with filth, and men and women and children and newborn infants were dying in their own waste. And Sarah Wilcox, convicted thief, died in their midst, aged twenty. Suffocated in her own vomit. Of dysentery she died. Of smallpox, of typhoid, of brain fever, of grain crawling with tiny maggots, of poisoned water. Her lips were covered with sores, her eyelids were crusted shut. She died giving birth to a creature too puny to live. She died, knowing that her breasts were too small to give nourishment, and her baby must die. All her charm had departed her, no man would touch her in her sickness, yet her heart was clenched as a fist, and her eyes glinted mica-sharp even as she knelt, and wept, and prayed, *God, will You not have mercy?—for I am your servant Sarah who has always obeyed You, and who is alone in this Devil's world.*

And I am Royalty, whispered Sarah, *wherever I set my foot.*

And God in His infinite mercy then saw fit to transform Sarah into a shrieking seabird, a great-winged white gull with glaring yellow eyes, pecking in the offal in the *Mayhew's* wake. She was ravenous with hunger, the quickest and cruelest of the great shrieking cloud of birds, she ate her full, did Sarah, and more, and more, *I am Royalty,* she declared, *no matter the filth I must devour.*

And day and night reversed themselves, and sun and moon sped in the sky, and fever raged in her until the air above the *Mayhew* was black with birds, and the many weeks of the crossing were as one long hour.

In Marblehead, Massachusetts, she was sold as SARAH WILCOX to one Jeremiah Hood, a colonial officer, for twenty-eight years' indenture. She bared her meek head and thanked God and Mr. Hood for their mercy. She slept in rags and coal dust, she dreamt of wriggling as a splendid golden-bronze snake into the master's marriage bed, soon the scabs and pustules at her mouth vanished, soon her hair grew full and fair again, soon her small plain eyes were bright with cunning, for was the New World not *new,* as the Old was *old?*—and who might claim royal blood here, where all were transported?

Her mistress Eliza Hood died one frostbound morning in 1773, flames raged at her throat and she died, now sweet pious Sarah slept in the master's great canopied bed, and God oversaw the newlyweds' bliss.

Coins again settled in Sarah's pockets, jingled softly in her narrow bosom, when she spoke she was Royalty, when she rolled her eyes Heavenward she was Royalty, when she read from her Bible to the assembled servants she was Royalty, and all trembled in awe of her. Old Jeremiah was charmed with her high pure faultless soprano voice, a child grew in her womb but it soon turned to stone, now the old man repented of his sin, now the old man begged of God forgiveness, he had no use for Sarah's Latin, or her French, or her fine embroidering, or her tears, and now Jeremiah died of flames raging in his throat, and Sarah fled Marblehead in the late winter of 1775, as York, as Winthrop, as Talbot, her long fair hair bound up tight beneath a gentleman's hat, and her slender body craftily concealed in gentleman's clothes. In Rhode Island she gambled at cards, in Delaware she followed a river south to her father's bedside, *What seek ye, Sarah?—what, and where?*—in Maryland she revealed to admiring eyes that she knew all the dances of the English court, her feet were small, quick, high-arched, her lovely head was high, her eyes ablaze in young womanly beauty. In ballroom mirrors in the great houses of Virginia there was reflected a hundredfold the graceful figure of Princess Susanna Caroline Matilde, and did the sweet English visitor not charm her hosts with tales of her sister the Queen, and her brother-in-law the King, and, ah! numberless intrigues at court? And did she not charm all who gazed upon her with her pure faultless soprano voice, and her skill at the pianoforte, and her pretty French, and her reverent Latin, and her exquisite manners, and her Royal ways?

Though he had already a wife the courtly Governor of the Commonwealth of Virginia wooed Princess Susanna, though he had already a wife and a young mistress the master of the largest plantation in the Carolinas wooed Princess Susanna, and loving no man she loved all, and loving all she loved no man, traveling through 1775 and early '76 as a houseguest in one great mansion after another, hinting at Royal patronage to the happy few who succeeded in pleasing her, *We are Royalty who comport ourselves as such* was Princess Susanna's gentle catechism to all wealthy commoners, who were privileged to offer their guest gifts of a feminine sort (pearls, jewels, and gold trinkets primarily) but dared not offend by offering outright bribes.

Then it happened in the spring of 1776, in one of the great houses in Charleston, Princess Susanna was exposed as "Sarah Wilcox," outlaw bondwoman and suspected murderess.

Now did French avail her?—it did not. And did Latin avail her?—it did not. Nor her pretty little white Bible, nor the locket around her neck (with the likeness of the Queen inside), nor her pure unwavering soprano voice, nor all her tales of court. Yet though she was manacled, and subdued, and weakened, and much abused by her captors, the outlaw escaped while being transported north; and none knew where she had gone, unless it was into the very air—!

Now God had mercy on a poor youth named Durham, now a pale young seamstress named Bethany, now Susanna Shepherd, widow, now Sarah Licht, widow, twenty-six years of age, childless, of Bush Creek, Maryland, engaged in the autumn of '76 to a young British officer, Lieutenant William Ward of the 16th Light Dragoons, soon to perish at Trenton. And did Sarah love him?—she did not. And did she mourn him?—not for an hour. For she had her dying baby to mourn, burning with fever, misshapen head, tiny fingers and toes webbed together, she had crazed weeping Sarah to mourn, running with a drunken mob in Contracoeur, torches and pitchforks and rifles, hunting Tory traitors to the death. She would set the New World to flame, she cried, as if it were the Old! There was Mrs. William Ward, widow, a governess in a Vanderpoel household, dismissed after six months' service for "insolence, impiety, and suspected theft," there was Mrs. Sarah Ward, a country midwife, shrewd and close-mouthed, said to be of the Devil's tribe, who never failed at a birth and never rejoiced at a birth, baptizing mother and babe alike with her black bitter tears.

What seek ye, Sarah?—why, with such passion?—so Sarah's own mother admonished her, appearing one night by Sarah's bedside.

But she paid no heed, for it was not yet her time, she fluffed out her thinned hair, and slapped color into her cheeks, and gave her heart to a dashing young man named Macready, a black-bearded young horse thief from Philadelphia, *Come with me, Sarah Wilcox, and do my will, Sarah*, his eyes sly and slanted as her own, his face flushed with love, he could lift her in one arm if he wished, he could smother her in the bulk of his body if he wished, and Sarah cried *Yes, yes*, and curled like a babe in his bosom.

Would she cut her shining hair for him?—she would. Would she dress in men's clothing for him?—she would. Would she follow him into the countryside, into the hills, seeking plunder where plunder might be sought?—she would, she would, she wept for very joy, she gave him all the gold she had, she followed where he led her, close upon the heels of the British at Valley Forge, close upon the heels of the Americans at Jockey Hollow, where many a stray horse might be haltered and traded for cash. The War for Independence was many wars, the horses knew no allegiance to King or to General Washington, why thus should Sarah and her lover? For it is foolish to starve when one might feast, it is foolish to die when one might live, and why support a war, Macready said, if one might be supported by it? Such fine horses to be had for the taking, albeit starving, and frostbitten, and gun-shy, and wary of mankind—! And Sarah clutched at her tall dashing black-bearded lover as she had never clutched at any man, *Yes, yes,* Sarah wept, Morristown, and Powhatassie, and the doomed British encampment at Port Oriskany, and one day Macready was shot down by moonlight and died streaming blood in Sarah's arms.

Could he die like a dog, in a ditch, streaming blood, though Sarah loved him, and would have died in his place?—he could, he could, in Sarah's very arms, though God looked down and observed the lovers' agony.

Sarah flees to the North, Sarah flees to the South, it is the year 1780, it is the early winter of '81, she is hunted down in Old Muirkirk, she must die in the wilds of Muirkirk swamp, years ago she lost Princess Susanna's gold locket, it has been years since she had gold coins to toss at the horses' hooves, she cannot plead with the soldiers in Latin, they will not pause to hear her pretty lisping French, God Himself is deaf to all her pleas. The first lieutenant fires. The second lieutenant fires. Sarah is a great-winged soaring egret but the terrible shot tears through her breast, she is a leaping doe but the shot tears through her throat, *Will you not have mercy, my Lord, on one of Royal blood,* but the shot tears through her heart, even as the soldiers marvel cursing at the woman's strength, and dare not pursue her into the marsh, on horseback or afoot. How quickly the horse thief runs!—how alive, how desperate!—even as she staggers in agony, her blood cascading from her—even as the shots tear into her back—Sarah Wilcox who cannot be killed, Sarah Licht who cannot be run to earth, Sarah Macready now sinking into the soft black muck—how alive!—how alive!—the Devil's own!—even as the soldiers fire at her fallen body, and fire yet again, and again, with curses of exultation.

And now Sarah *is* dead, surely?—in the spring of 1781?

And the great tractless swamp swallows her up.

PART I

"Midnight Sun"

I

"Do I doubt?—I do *not*. Does my hand shake?—it does *not*. Am I like other men?—*I am not*."

He smiles at his ruddy mirrored reflection, that paragon of manhood, a gentleman in the prime of life, deep-set mica-chip eyes sly with secrets, glowing with interior heat, he smiles and it *is* a smile, it satisfies him, though the flushed muscled cheeks would clench in rage to reveal too many strong wet white teeth. Too many strong wet white teeth.

"Am I to be trusted?—*I am*. Am I a gentleman?—*I am*."

He pauses in his robust lathering of his cheeks and jaws, he examines a three-quarters profile (the left, the truly striking side of his face), hums several bars of Mozart (Don Giovanni in the guise of Don Ottavio), examines the smile again, measured, perfectly calibrated, now a slight modest downturning of the eye, an inclination of the head as well, a gentleman who wears his power lightly, who does not insist, a gentleman-stallion (assuredly not a gelding) who exhibits his charms sparingly, the very essence of "A. Washburn Frelicht, Ph.D."

"Am I like other men?—*I am not*."

He completes his toilet with a flourish and flings down the soapy towel, noting with admiration the light flush of the clean-shaven cheeks, the perpetual fever of the cheeks, noting with awe the hard, hard bones, his inheritance, that press against the flesh: *his*. Why, *it is all his*.

"Do I doubt?—I do *not*. Does my hand shake?—it does *not*. Am I eager for it all to begin?—yes, yes, a hundredfold *yes*."

II

This day of legend, or of infamy.

To be spoken of, written of, speculated upon, recalled with perennial controversy in the annals of American horse-racing (and gambling) circles well into the twenty-first century: Derby Day of 11 May 1909 at resplendent Chautauqua Downs, one of the first of the "playing fields of the rich."

At Chautauqua, at that time, speculation in the clubhouse centered as much on the mysterious gentleman gambler, the "astrological sportsman," one Frelicht, "Doctor" Frelicht as he and his associates insisted, as of which of two great horses, Stone Street or Xalapa, would win the cup.

Frelicht. A. Washburn Frelicht, Ph.D. A stranger to Chautauqua Falls, New York; but wasn't his name dimly notorious in racing circles back East: wasn't he, or an individual with a name very like his, the inventor of the "tipster sheet"? . . . beloved of gamblers and despised by honest horsemen, and just this past season outlawed from the Chautauqua track as from Belmont and Saratoga. Wasn't Mr. Frelicht in some ambiguous way associated with "Baron" Barraclough of Buffalo, the railroad speculator; and with the seemingly disgraced congressman Jasper Liges of Vanderpoel; hadn't he, or an individual with a name very like his, been involved in the secret selling of shares in the "newly discovered" estate of an heir of Napoleon, descended by way of an unclaimed illegitimate son?

These rumors, amounting in essence to character assassination, circulated freely in Chautauqua Falls in the days preceding the race. Many persons had opinions of A. Washburn Frelicht who had never set eyes upon him, including the very owner of the Chautauqua track, Colonel Jameson Fairlie, who dared to speak of him to the Warwicks (brother and sister, the elderly bachelor Edgar and the widow Seraphina, former wife of the Albany banker Isaac Dove), who were Frelicht's friends and staunch supporters. To Seraphina the Colonel spoke with his accustomed bluntness, warning her against involving herself in matters that might have been repugnant to poor Isaac, causing the widow to snap shut her black-lacquered Japanese fan, and fix her old friend with a glacial eye, and say, in a voice usually reserved for slow-witted servants: "Mr. Dove, being dead, is hardly 'poor,' as he was hardly 'poor' in life; and has no more stake in my current affairs, Colonel, than do you."

And this exchange, too, quickly entered the lore of that day of legend, or of infamy.

III

"Stone Street," and "Xalapa," and "Sweet Thing," and "Glengarry"; "Midnight Sun," and "Warlock," and "Jersey Belle," and "Meteor," and "Idle Hour" . . . nine handsome Thoroughbreds in descending order of presumed merit, competing in the Twenty-third Chautauqua Downs Derby; nine Negro jockeys in gaily colored silks armed with little whips and spurs and every manner of jockey trickery, the smallest of the riders weighing in at eighty-eight pounds and the heaviest at one hundred twelve. The public stakes are $6,000 ("The Highest Stakes in America") and a costly engraved silver trophy, to the winner; $1,000 to second place, and $700 to third. The serious money, however, is as usual in the betting, for what is any horse race, what is *this* prestigious horse race, without the exchange of cash?—and without clubhouse rumors of Glengarry's swollen knee, and Jersey Belle's colic, and Warlock who started so poorly at the Preakness, and Midnight Sun whose owner has been racing him too frequently, and the hairline crack in Meteor's left rear hoof—or is it Xalapa's? And Sweet Thing is said to have been "coked to the gills" last month at Belmont—or dosed with a mild painkiller for an ear infection; and there remains the bitter rivalry between the jockeys Parmelee (on Midnight Sun) and "Little Bo" Tenney (on Xalapa), and the strange flurries of betting, now Stone Street is the favorite, now Xalapa is the favorite, now Midnight Sun is up to 2–15, now Henley Farm's Idle Hour has dropped to 1–30. . . . If the Derby betting is too eccentric—if there's suddenly a run on any but the two favorites—the overseeing judge has the privilege of declaring all bets off, switching the jockeys around, and an hour set aside for the hasty remaking of book: which many a horseman and gambler prays will not occur. For, the vicissitudes of chance aside, a Thoroughbred is but a horse while a race is—performed by jockeys.

(Yet the Colonel has satisfied himself that *these* jockeys, *this* Derby, will be absolutely honest.)

Is Washburn Frelicht, seated in the Warwicks' clubhouse box with his hosts, one of those gamblers who fret as the hour of the race approaches, and suck at their cigars, and consult their gold pocket watches another time, and make only a polite show of attending to the band's spirited "Blue Danube"? A neutral observer could not have said whether the handsome gentleman with the black satin eye patch over his left eye, and the meticulously trimmed salt-and-pepper goatee, and the jaunty straw hat, and the air of patrician confidence, was betraying now and then a just-perceptible apprehension, or whether, like numerous others, quite naturally in these heightened circumstances, he is merely anticipating the contest to come. A neutral observer would have guessed that so sporting a gentleman, with that steely-smiling gray gaze, those moist white teeth and ruddy lips, has placed a sizable bet; just possibly, on a "dark" horse; but could not have guessed that the gentleman has secretly made book with $44,000 of his and his clients' money on the rangy black colt Midnight Sun—whose odds are presently 9–1.

(That's to say: if Midnight Sun wins the Derby, as Dr. Frelicht believes he must, he, Frelicht, will collect an unprecedented $400,000 from a half dozen bookmakers and private parties, to be divided not quite equally among himself and the Warwicks; Frelicht's share being understandably disproportionate to his modest $1,000 stake. And if Midnight Sun betrays Dr. Frelicht's astrological prognosis, if the very Zodiac has misled him, then Frelicht will lose his $1,000 and the Warwicks will lose their $43,000 . . . a prospect that doesn't bear contemplation; so Frelicht refuses to contemplate it.)

No, *he* betrays no sign of worry. Only the vulgarian worries in public.

A tumultuous day of brisk chill winds, and high, fast-scudding clouds like schooners, and a slate-blue sky far, far overhead!—and here below, on time-locked Earth, an amiable confusion of handsome carriages, and motorcars gleaming with newness, and spectators afoot, crowding the narrow streets and lanes leading to the Colonel's racecourse. Here are splendidly dressed ladies and gentlemen in the clubhouse area—terrace, lawn, shaded boxes—white clapboard and dazzling white-painted stucco—a lawn fine and clipped as a bowling green, edged with rhododendron shrubs and vivid red geraniums. In the grandstand, newly painted dark green, sits the noisy majority of citizens, while the "common-folk," quaintly so called, of both mingled races, settle themselves in the infield or on low roofs and hills abutting the track. For all are Thoroughbred fanciers on Derby Day in Chautauqua; no one so poor, or in debt, that he, or she, can't afford a bet of at least $1 on one of these fine racing horses; even children are caught up in the betting frenzy. *For all who live humanly are wagerers* as Dr. Frelicht is in the habit of murmuring, with that inscrutable expression to his strong-boned, ruddy face that some observers have described as philosophic and stoic, even melancholy, and others have described as childlike in yearning. *And Americans are, of the Earth's population, the most won-drously human.*

The band strikes up an exuberant polka, mule-drawn watering wag-ons make their slow, stately way around the track. By Colonel Fairlie's proud estimate some forty-five thousand persons are attending this Twenty-third Derby, having converged on Chautauqua Falls from such places as New York City, Chicago, St. Louis and Kansas City, and of course Kentucky, as well as Texas, California and abroad; by highways, waterways, and rail. The Kentucky Derby having lapsed into a decline, the Chautauqua Cup has emerged as the most prestigious of American Thoroughbred races, for a record one hundred eighty-four horses were originally entered for the race, of which nine, from the finest stables in the country, are to start. Every hotel in town is filled, including the palatial Chautauqua Arms, where Lord Glencairn of Scotland (a racing enthusiast rumored to wish to purchase the beautiful chestnut Xalapa) has taken an entire floor; the Pendennis Club is given over to officers of the Eastern Association for the Improvement of Breeds of Stock, and their wives and companions; such famous sporting gentry as James Ben Ali Hagin of Kentucky, and Blackburn Shaw of Long Island, and Elias Shrikesdale of Philadelphia are here, having chartered private Pullman cars for themselves and their retinues. Every bookmaker is happily occupied (though the Colonel has raised their clubhouse fees to $140 for the occasion), as are the Pari-Mutuel betting machines;

milling about in the half hour before the race are newspapermen, "amateur experts," owners, breeders, trainers, jockeys, grooms, and veterinarians. Unattended young boys, both white and colored, run wild in the infield and beneath the grandstand, pursued by security guards. Though "tipster sheets" have been disallowed at respectable tracks, it seems that some persons have them, and that they are being surreptitiously sold; as are Derby Day cards, and frothy pink cotton candy, and lemonade in paper cups, and bright-colored ices. Beribboned parisols and sunshades, gentlemen's straw boater hats, shoes polished to a piercing high sheen, starched white snap-on collars, watch chains, walking sticks, gloves, ladies' veiled hats, gentlemen's white flannels . . . A. Washburn Frelicht, Dr. Frelicht as he prefers to be called, gazes upon the crowd with his single good eye. *And God saw everything that he had made, and, behold, it was very good.*

Dr. Frelicht, keen-nerved as a stallion, would take a quick nip from the silver flask concealed inside his blazer but no—he will have an English toffee instead, how kind of Mrs. Dove to pass the tin, with a smile; both Warwicks are fond of sweets, as indeed is Dr. Frelicht, but sweets do the teeth ill; wreck the smile. The hard bared grin of Teddy Roosevelt, a thousand times pictured, brought teeth, muscled cheeks, and impassioned fists into style among the populace, but so energetic a style displeases ladies and gentlemen. For is not Teddy R. something of a boy, a boy-man, and thus laughable, contemptible? Not a blunt bold baring of the teeth is desired, but a slow, measured smile of manly intelligence, thinks Dr. Frelicht. *Like this.*

The band's spirited playing of "Tramp, Tramp, Tramp," the old Civil War favorite, is interrupted by the announcement that the race will not start at 4:30 P.M. as planned, but at 4:50.

And why? No explanation offered. A wave of disappointment, curiosity and apprehension washes over the racecourse.

Stroking the neatly trimmed salt-and-pepper goatee to which he has only just recently become accustomed, dabbing lightly at the forehead with a fresh Irish linen handkerchief monogrammed AWF. The noble uplifted profile, the glint of the gold watch chain. Dr. Frelicht has not wished to cultivate a reputation for wit in these circles, where he is known as a mystic student of the Zodiac, but he sees no harm in saying, quickly, in a general voice, that others in the clubhouse seats might be amused as well as his hosts the Warwicks—ah, the need of *nerves*, to perfectly express the mood of a moment—" 'If it were done, when 'tis done, then 'twere well it were done *quickly.*' "

And the ladies and gentlemen respond with delighted laughter at this clever allusion to—"Shakespeare, yes? I believe it must be Hamlet?" Mrs. Dove cries, with the air of a giddily bright schoolgirl of stout middle age; for even the rich are touched by anxiety, when matters of chance and cash are at stake.

IV

Not the wealthiest citizens of Chautauqua Falls but well-to-do, indeed, Edgar E. with his inherited fortune in asbestos, ink and sugarcane (Hawaiian), his sister Seraphina with a similar inheritance in addition to her deceased husband's portfolio. The gentleman, only sixty years of age but looking distinctly older, with a hairless skull, sunken eyes, squat nose and cavernous nostrils—the nostrils darkly alert as the eyes, lost in fatty ridges of flesh, are not; the lady, the widow, well corseted, flushed with health, yet possessed of a cold pale eye and very small pursed lips. Edgar E. Warwick is known for his Lutheran zeal (did he not lead a successful movement to defrock a Contracoeur minister in '88?), Seraphina Warwick Dove is known for her litigious zeal (did she not, only the previous June, bring suit against her own newly widowed daughter-in-law, to break her son's "disgraceful" will?) . . . How the parsimonious Warwicks became acquainted with A. Washburn Frelicht, a stranger to the Chautauqua Valley and a person of some ambiguity, no one in their social set knows; why they became disciples of a sort, fervent believers, eager to finance Dr. Frelicht in his astrological stratagems, is somewhat less mysterious: they scented profit, the greediest and most gratifying sort of profit. For it was Dr. Frelicht's artless contention that they could not lose. His method, which was a scientific one, could not lose. The Derby winner of '09 was as clearly inscribed in the Zodiac as were the Derby winners of past years, if one but knew how to read the celestial hieroglyphics. "For, in the heavens, 'future' and 'past' do not exist," as Frelicht explained enthusiastically, "but all is a single essence, a *continuous flowing presence.*"

Edgar E. and Seraphina, hearing such words, exchanged a glance. A twitching of the lips meant to signify a smile. Brother-sisterly complicity. Since the Warwicks as a family strongly disapproved of gambling, they needed to be convinced that, in truth, this was not gambling; it was, however, a delicious opportunity to beat gamblers, as Dr. Frelicht said, at their own game. Could anything be more just—?

Where the Warwicks went, in spring 1909, there the "astrological sportsman" must be invited as well. Else Seraphina in particular would have taken offense.

Colonel Fairlie, reluctantly giving way and including Frelicht in a clubhouse dinner honoring Lord Glencairn, complained that his nerves were rubbed raw by the man's very presence. Who was this Frelicht, what was his background, had he any decent occupation other than that of self-ordained gambler-mystic? Was he the fool he seemed? Was he simply very clever? Edgar E. and Seraphina teasingly pricked their acquaintances' curiosity by hinting at coups Frelicht had accomplished at other racetracks, but the details were scant, for the success of Frelicht's method depended upon its secrecy; and, being but human, brother and sister wanted to keep their find to themselves. Yet there were hints, elliptical and tantalizing, that he had once been a Shakespearean actor, perhaps a singer (hence the power and range of his voice), he had pursued a career in science (hence the Ph.D.); he might have been a seminarian in his youth; a musician; a tiller of the soil; a railroad agent; an explorer; a journalist. (Assuredly he had been a journalist. For, at Colonel Fairlie's dinner, when the gentlemen retired for brandy and cigars, Frelicht fell to talking confidentially with old Blackburn Shaw and told him, in a sudden rush of emotion, that he had lost his eye to the "Spanish enemy" in the *Maine* explosion. . . . The *New York Journal* had commissioned him to write a series of articles on the Cuban revolution, along lines sympathetic to American interests, and, as a special friend and advisor to Captain Charles Sigsbee, he had been aboard ship when the *Maine* anchored in infamous Havana Harbor. Only imagine, two hundred sixty-six American lives lost! To this day, Frelicht said, he feared for his own life since certain Spanish agents had vowed to kill him.)

Had he a wife? No. Not living.

Had he children? No. Not living.

And where, customarily, did he make his home?

"Where I am honored and respected," he said, looking his interlocutor full in the eye, "and where I can be of service."

A bower of tropical flowers, orchids, descending from the ceiling: purple, lavender, pearly-white, black. Linen-draped tables in a horseshoe pattern overlooking a pond in which small golden carp swam and cygnets, black and white, nervously paddled. A young woman harpist from Dublin; rose-tinted shades over candles set in antique candelabras; Negro waiters in red jackets with gold brocade, red fezzes with black tassels, immaculate white gloves, serving the Colonel's sixty-odd guests from seven until midnight. . . . Lord Glencairn and his Lady, the guests of honor; the beautiful Polish actress Alicja Zielinski and her gentleman companion; the L. H. Vanderbilts; the James Ben Ali Hagins; the Blackburn Shaws; Senator and Mrs. Gardner Simms; Elias Shrikesdale; the Cone-Pettys; Edgar Warwick and his sister Seraphina, the widow of Isaac Dove; and many another party including "A. Washburn Frelicht" in white tie and tails, who, to his credit, guessing himself not fully welcome in the Colonel's clubhouse (being the only gentleman present not a member of the Jockey Club—the only gentleman who did not sport a diamond stickpin in his lapel, a gift of the Colonel's), ate and drank sparingly, and inclined his handsome head to listen, rather than to speak. Did he, amid the numerous champagne toasts, amid courses of fresh clams, and vichyssoise, and salmon, and squab, and roast beef, and Virginia baked ham, and, at the very end, colored ices in such artful equestrian shapes (Stone Street, and Xalapa, and Sweet Thing, and Glengarry, and Midnight Sun, and Warlock, and Jersey Belle, and Meteor, and Idle Hour, ingeniously rendered at four inches in height) everyone lamented that they must be eaten—did he sense how roundly he was being snubbed by the other sporting men?—how idle and mocking were the questions put to him of his "astrological science"—?

Not at all. For here, in A. Washburn Frelicht, we have a gentleman. Charming. Amiable. Well informed. Imperturbable. A holder of moderate opinions, political and otherwise. No admirer of Taft—no admirer of a lowered tariff. No admirer, assuredly, of Senator La Follette—the insurgent Wisconsin warrior much vilified in the Republican press for his campaign against the railroads. Dr. Frelicht is well-spoken and witty with the ladies; cultivated, yet not so cultivated to offend; with the men, he is shrewdly deferential. Seeming to suspect no drollery, no scorn, no scarcely suppressed laughter behind his back. If the muscled shoulders tighten beneath the handsome fabric of his blazer, if the goateed underjaw extends itself as if to block an improvident word, if the single good eye emanates chill even as the ruddy cheeks burn with an impassioned fever, is there anyone in this company equipped to *see*?

The solitude of the pilgrim. Depend upon it, we are invisible in this world.

Gradually, at Colonel Fairlie's table, it becomes clear that Frelicht believes in his own betting stratagem—"In the infallibility of the Zodiac," as he several times, portentously, declares. The man is a fool—yet a gentleman. A mystic of sorts. The specific details surrounding his and the Warwicks' betting, the amount of cash involved, the *horse to win*, are naturally not revealed; but Frelicht speaks freely, even rhapsodically, of the Heavens, the astral plane, the "star-consciousness in which Past, Future and Present commingle like flame absorbing flame, or water, water." It is stirring to hear the man speak, his words are beautiful if purely nonsensical and self-delusory, yet so poetically expressed that many a lady (the Colonel's own Belinda, in truth) might well be swayed, for suddenly the company is hearing of the Great Nebula of Orion . . . the reign of the Pleiades . . . how Andromeda inclines to Pisces and to the bright bold star of Aries . . . how the rings of Saturn quiver with electric charges . . . how the Moon exerts its secret tides upon the human psyche.

Frelicht concludes by saying with a deferential smile that he sympathizes with those who are doubtful of his beliefs, as, until very recently, he was a doubter himself; a kinsman of Shakespeare's Cassius, who so arrogantly claimed that man's fate lay not in the stars but in himself. "Now, however, it has been revealed to me that any man, or woman"—with a glance at the beaming Seraphina across the table from him—"sufficiently initiated into the science of the sky is at the same time initiated into the science of the Earth. 'As above, so below'—this is but ancient wisdom."

Luckily, Colonel Fairlie changes the topic before one of the scowling gentlemen at the table can ask Frelicht a rude question, such as why the Heavens were to be interpreted through *him*, and risk insulting Seraphina.

* * *

Yet after dinner, when the gentlemen gather together in the Colonel's oak-panelled smoking room, over brandy snifters and Cuban cigars, things look up for Frelicht, indeed yes.

For there is ninety-year-old Blackburn Shaw, of the famous Shaw Farm, a patriarch of the racing world, revered by all, laying a proprietary hand on young Frelicht's arm, angrily lamenting the decline in Thoroughbred racing and breeding since the War, no horses like the great horses of his grandfather's day, Diomed, Arisides, Ten Broeck, Lexington, Hindoo ("Hindoo!—there was a horse!—did you know, Dr. Frelicht, that Stone Street is sired out of Hindoo, the greatest stallion of all?")—now times are changed, even gentlemen are breeding horses not for sport and beauty but for the market, in fact there are fewer and fewer *gentlemen* remaining in America—why, did Frelicht know that in the old days the highest qualities in a Thoroughbred were vigor, stamina, courage, sheer stubborn *heart*—if an animal couldn't do three four-mile heats in less than eight minutes, why sir he would be turned out to pasture and his trainer with him—but now—since the War— since the turn of the century—now all that matters is "dash"—and a race is no sooner started than it is over. In the early years of the sport, too, stallions were far more virile than they are now: Hindoo, for instance, put out to stud at the advanced age of twenty, was so unquenchable in his appetite, so fired with lust, he would gallop out of his stable as if at the starting post!—serving all mares at his disposal with unflagging zeal, and siring one prizewinner after another. Whereas now, Shaw says pettishly, while his companion frowns in sympathetic disapproval, "Foals are half the time aborted in the womb, it seems; and stallions lose their virility almost as soon as they lose their racing legs."

Frelicht, stroking his goatee, murmurs sadly that he had not known, sir, things were at such a pass.

What is even worse, jockeys can no longer be trusted: those agile little colored boys who'd performed so well in the past! Nor could grooms be trusted, white or black. Nor trainers. It was common knowledge that races were being bought and sold every day—horses, poor dumb innocent beasts, were being fed drugs to slow their heartbeat, or stimulate it—any low trick to upset the "odds"—as if "odds" were king!—jockeys cunningly held their mounts back, the more skilled jockeys the more likely to pass off such trickery undetected—or they set their mounts too cruel a pace—threatened one another—sometimes assaulted one another—turned up at the stables drunk, or themselves coked to the gills. Worse yet (here the old man tugged at Frelicht's arm, whispered fiercely into his ear), owners could not be trusted, even those who prided themselves on being gentlemen—"Even certain members 'in good standing' of the Jockey Club."

At this charge, however, Frelicht respectfully demurred; though he wasn't a horseman himself, and not a member of this prestigious club, yet he could not allow himself to believe . . . (Speaking earnestly, quietly, with no sign that he guessed how most of the gentlemen in the room were listening. Stroking his goatee with meditative fingers.)

This, the deaf old patriarch chose not to hear; and continued for several minutes more, lamenting the passing of the old days, the stability of the Union, before the rabble-rouser Lincoln went to war, and men were confounded to be told, like it or not, that they were but descendants of apes! In the end, though, smoking the heavily fragrant cigar his host had given him, pleased by the avid attentiveness of A. Washburn Frelicht, Mr. Shaw pressed upon that young man one of his business cards, and extracted from him a promise that, when Frelicht's affairs next brought him to New York City, he would be a guest of Shaw's at his Long Island farm, to stay as long as he wished.

Thank you, Mr. Shaw, thank you very much, perhaps I will.

V

Now all transpires swiftly as if, indeed, preordained.

And time-locked Earth where mortals abide but a *remembering-forward.*

The band ends "The Star-Spangled Banner" with a solemn military flourish; the white silk purses heavy with prize money are hung at the finish line, for the winning jockeys to seize after the race; promptly at 4:50 P.M. the bugler blows first call; and here are the horses—at last, the nine Derby horses!—trotting out of the paddock to the track, parading ceremoniously to the right, then, at the clubhouse turn, wheeling slowly around to trot to the starting post, ears erect, tails flicking with nervous excitement, the jockeys in their bright silk costumes standing in their irons, here is Shep Tatlock on the tall bay colt Stone

Street, here is Bo Tenney on the beautiful chestnut-red Xalapa, here is Parmelee on Midnight Sun, horse and rider both black as pitch, here is little Jenk Webb on Glengarry, little Moses White on Sweet Thing. . . . The jockeys are told their positions, the horses are assembled at the starting line, milling, crowding, jostling one another, Stone Street visibly nervous, Midnight Sun stamping the dirt, so unruly he has to be held by his tail, Idle Hour misbehaving, tossing his head. . . .

(Frelicht's companions sit quietly and calmly as he. Though doubtless their hearts beat, quickened, like his. For *is* the race preordained? *Is* it written in the Heavens that an investment of $44,000 will yield some $400,000 in a scant five minutes of earthly time?)

Sunshine harshly bright as if diamond-refracted, cold May winds from the Chautauqua Mountains north of the racecourse; a hard dry track, an ideal track; now the horses are assembled behind the elastic web barrier; now—but now Midnight Sun, prancing excitedly, breaks through the webbing and has to be led back; and all the horses quieted; and now the red flag is waved, and the webbing flies violently up, and the race has begun—

Stone Street in his inside post position breaks away at once, Xalapa nearly beside him, Sweet Thing close behind, the others are caught briefly in a jam-up, cagey little Parmelee on Midnight Sun pushes free (has Parmelee, in a gesture so swift no one has seen, yanked at Glengarry's saddle cloth to throw the horse off stride?), Warlock is being nudged into the rail, Jersey Belle and Meteor and Idle Hour are already lengths behind, out of the race. Now the leaders are passing the grandstand, now the clubhouse, but isn't Stone Street being ridden strangely, isn't he beginning to weave . . . Xalapa and Sweet Thing rapidly gaining, overtaking . . . and Midnight Sun on the outside, Parmelee using his whip, Parmelee and Sweet Thing's rider involved in some sort of altercation. But Xalapa, at the front, is suddenly the crowd's favorite, passing Stone Street on the inside as they come into the backstretch; and suddenly it is clear that Shep Tatlock is drugged, or drunk, or sick, pulling his horse's head from side to side, dropping back to third place, to fourth, to fifth, weaving across the track . . .

The race is half run, the race is three-quarters run, chestnut-red Xalapa in the lead, Glengarry a half length behind, then silky black Midnight Sun, long-legged deep-chested Midnight Sun, the white bandages on his legs flying . . . now past the starting post, now past the cheering spectators in the grandstand, Midnight Sun with a warhorse's powerful stride . . . and then, suddenly, is it possible? . . . suddenly it seems that Xalapa has stumbled . . . yet keeps running . . . momentum keeps him running though he is clearly injured . . . while Glengarry pounds past, Midnight Sun pounds past, Parmelee hunched low over his neck, whip and spurs in use, Parmelee making his move, looping wide on the outside to avoid the falling Xalapa; to pass Glengarry, to break in a wild burst of speed away from Glengarry, to cross the finish line in the first position by a length and a half.

Midnight Sun, Glengarry, Sweet Thing . . .

(Stone Street, in the home stretch, weaves drunkenly into Meteor's path, the two horses collide, Shep Tatlock—drugged, drunk, sick?—to be banned from the turf for the rest of his life—tumbles from the saddle onto the track and lies insensible.

And what of the chestnut-red beauty Xalapa?—the crowd stands silent, stunned, as an announcement is made that he snapped his left foreleg above the ankle; as the horse ambulance picks him up from the track, to take him around to the dump behind the stables, where, in as brief a time as it takes to record the melancholy fact, he is destroyed— by a single bullet between the eyes.)

VI

We have won! We have won! We have won!

Where so many thousands of persons are dazed with sorrow, it is unseemly to show rapturous delight; where sentiment runs so powerfully in one direction, only the ill-bred would gloat.

Being extremely well-bred, therefore, Edgar Warwick and his sister Seraphina keep their gleeful smiles to themselves; but cannot help tugging like children at Washburn Frelicht's arm, and whispering again and again, and yet again—

Why, we have won!

Frelicht smiles his composed smile, Frelicht dabs lightly at his forehead with a fresh handkerchief, Frelicht says quietly: *Of course.*

VII

The talk for weeks, for months, will be of Midnight Sun and that wild, wild ride.

The talk will be of the beautiful Xalapa who (it was afterward reported) had had a hairline crack in his left forefoot, detected but not taken seriously by his owner.

The talk will be of the disgraced Shep Tatlock, thirty-two years old, banned from American racing for life: drunk on the track (it was charged against him), or drugged (as he himself claimed) against his knowledge.

And the talk—for months, for years—will be of the mysterious gambler "A. Washburn Frelicht" who won for himself and his clients a record $400,000 on 11 May 1909; and then, on the very night of the Derby victory, while celebrating in a private dining room in the Chautauqua Arms . . .

VIII

The robber was a young black man.

The robber was a young black man wearing a black domino mask and carrying a long-barreled pistol.

The robber entered the room silently by way of a balcony and French doors opened to the night air.

A sudden leap and there he was, a few yards from the table where Frelicht and the Warwicks were seated . . . slightly bent at the knees, dark skin exuding moisture, eyes showing rims of white inside the black mask: *Gentlemen and lady, thank you please, you will remain where you are please, you, lady, and you, sirs, your money please, thank you for your kindness please:* a low soft mocking voice, an accent suggestive of the West Indies: *Only do not distress me, gentlemen and dear lady!*

A slender young black man, pistol raised calmly aloft, aimed at Dr. Frelicht's chest. He knew precisely why he had come, knew what the sweet-scented rosewood box contained, betrayed no agitation, managed an insolent smile, a flash of gold in his left incisor, *Thank you gentlemen and lady for your cooperation!*

Black domino mask, a wide-brimmed straw hat with a red polka-dot band, creamy white blazer and trousers, white starched shirt, red and white striped tie, was there ever such a *colored boy* in all of the Chautauqua Valley? A dapper little moustache riding his pert upper lip (as Edgar Warwick afterward recalled), a thin twisting scar in his right cheek, the mark of the Devil (as Seraphina Warwick Dove recalled), the terrible weapon held unwavering in his hand, pointed at Dr. Frelicht's heaving chest. *Now quiet! Now no alarm! Gentlemen and lady—you have my warning!*

Not five minutes before Frelicht had led the others in a toast, victory champagne, glasses held high over Seraphina's rosewood box—" 'Thou visible god!' " Frelicht intoned in a luxuriant baritone—and now the black man in the dazzling creamy white clothes was aiming death at his heart, *his* poor pounding heart, and where were the words, where the breath, to protest? *You sir,* the robber said to Frelicht, hunching his slender shoulders in a sudden childish spasm of pleasure—*you, sir, are not to arouse my ire!—but will please obey!*

Frelicht tried to speak but could not: his lips, drained of blood, were suddenly flaccid.

Edgar E. Warwick tried to speak but could not: a wave of sheer animal panic rose from his bowels, and he knew he was to die.

Poor Seraphina, more agitated than she'd been at the deathbed of Mr. Dove, tried to speak but could not: her words of angry protest broken into mere sounds, stammers, breathy sobs, for here was a young black man *not a servant*, not one who must obey her but one *whom she must obey.*

To be robbed by a mere nigger of their prize—!

Yet it was to be, as if ordained by the Heavens: an outrageous black man in a domino mask and cocky straw hat, $400,000 in bills deftly transferred by chocolate-brown fingers into a smart crocodile-hide suitcase as the cowering victims stared . . . the victims and three other witnesses, belonging to the hotel staff: two waiters (black) and a wine steward (of French origin, but white), none of whom dared offer resistance.

The miraculous money—the highest recorded winnings in Chautauqua's history—in bundles of $100 primarily though there were also some $500 and $50 bills—stolen away by an outlaw's hand, 11 May 1909, 9:25 P.M. in the Crystal Room of the grand old Chautauqua

Arms, the victims surprised in the midst of a victory feast (oysters on the half shell, pheasant *au vin*, truffles, French champagne), Edgar E. Warwick, sixty, lifetime resident of Chautauqua Falls, Mrs. Seraphina Warwick Dove, fifty-eight, lifetime resident of Chautauqua Falls, A. Washburn Frelicht, Ph.D., age given as forty-eight, various addresses offered to police (most recently, Mrs. Dove's residence), *Thank you gentlemen and lady, you are indeed wise to save your lives*, insolent dazzling-white smile, soft mocking melodious voice, bright dark gaze showing a rim of white inside the tight-fitting mask. *Now you will please to keep your places, not to stir for many minutes!—not to summon aid!— not to dare!—not to arouse my ire!—not to follow after!—not to be the temptation, to make of me, who has never yet spilled a drop of blood, a murderer!*

This speech so froze the company, all stared at the robber as if turned to stone, as he, agile as a dancer, assured as one who has had a long apprenticeship on the stage, turned, and with a final (taunting? playful?) sighting of his long-barreled pistol at Washburn Frelicht's chest, *leapt into the very night outside the window and disappeared.*

Seraphina fainted, fell heavily forward into her melted crimson sorbet, Edgar E. tried to rise from his chair but lacked the strength, ashen-faced Dr. Frelicht, of whom more might have been expected, merely *sat*—like a suddenly aged, broken man—his "good" eye glassy in disbelief—staring after the unknown agent who had made off with his Zodiac prize, the culmination of his astrological speculations as, witnesses afterward surmised, it was perhaps the culmination of his life—staring at the empty window, the flung-open French doors, as if, poor fool! poor coward! he hoped for Fate to reverse itself, and his hard-won money to be returned, by the very agent who had carried it off into the night.

IX

Now it is all history, the improbable no less than the probable.

Little Shep Tatlock maintained to the day of his death (soon, in 1914) that he was "poisoned" on the morning of the Derby.

Xalapa's beautiful corpse was shipped to his grieving owner's farm in Aylesbury, Pennsylvania, where it was interred with great ceremony, including a five-gun salute.

Midnight Sun, to earn a fair amount of money for his controversial owner, was never again to run quite so *spirited* a race; nor would his rider Parmelee enjoy so spectacular a victory.

The Warwicks, Edgar E. and Seraphina, publicly humiliated by their Lutheran God, as punishment (so Seraphina believed, stricken with repentance) for gambling, withdrew abruptly from social intercourse. And the "astrological sportsman" A. Washburn Frelicht, a broken man, a disappointment to all the ladies, disappeared from Chautauqua Falls within a day or two, after having given testimony to police, never to be glimpsed again in American racing circles.

What of the "Black Phantom"—as he was dubbed by excitable journalists, particularly execrated in Mr. William Randolph Hearst's papers as a "Negro Devil"? This amazing figure apparently disappeared as well, despite enormous publicity, police efforts ranging over five states, and the vigilance of all.

And the $400,000 was never returned to its rightful owners.

"The Lass of Aviemore"

I

It was eight days after the shock of Mr. Stirling's death, when the house at Greenley Square was still steeped in grief, that the girl in the worn black velveteen cloak came to the front door—knocking so faintly with her small gloved fist (did the poor child know nothing of doorbells, or of the use of the wrought-iron American eagle knocker?) that the downstairs maid failed to hear her for several minutes. And what a wild gusty May morning it was, the air so agitated, the sunshine so chill, the season might well have been late winter, and not spring. . . .

Who was she? Yet another mourner, arriving belatedly? (For the elaborate wake, the yet more elaborate funeral services and burial, the several crowded days of visitors, were just past.) Or had she nothing to do with Mr. Stirling's passing at all? And why, being so young, surely no more than seventeen, was she alone, unaccompanied, in a city the size of Contracoeur? Strange, too, how long she hesitated before finally, and rather timorously, unlatching the front gate, to proceed up the brick walk to the front door; her face all but hidden by her loose-fitting hood, as if she feared someone might be watching her, and dreaded being known.

As it happened, by chance someone was watching her from an upstairs window: nineteen-year-old Warren Stirling, the deceased man's younger, romantically inclined son, who, exhausted and sluggish with grief, had fallen into the habit of staring down into the square for long minutes at a time; watching hackney cabs, motorcars and pedestrians pass by in a sporadic, monotonous stream, his thoughts, too, wayward, melancholy, tinged with the anger of loss, passing in a monotonous and ungovernable stream. Why could he not think of his father but only, obsessively, of Death? And why, trying to envision his father, whom he had respected and loved, could he recall only the shock of that ghastly wax-faced corpse, that mimicry of a living man in its false slumber amid white satin cushions and smothering banks of dead-white lilies? The wake; the funeral; the burial in the cemetery; so many mourners; so many tear-streaked faces; embraces, handshakes, faltering words of commiseration—! And now, these days of mourning: each hour capricious in its emotions, each hour perilous, for sometimes Warren Stirling contained his grief like a mature young man, and sometimes he succumbed to it weak as a child. Why had God struck his father down? Why so suddenly, so cruelly? At only fifty-two years of age, seemingly in good health; happy in his family, in his work, and in his religion. Mr. Stirling had been an uncommonly good man, loved and admired by many; yet, stricken by a heart attack, he'd died before Warren had arrived home from Williams College, summoned by his mother; this abruptness seemed to Warren God's most wanton cruelty.

"Before, even, I could say good-bye to Father!"—Warren spoke aloud, in an anguished young voice. "I cannot forgive God—though I know I must."

Away at college in Williamstown, Massachusetts, Warren had fallen under the spell of certain freethinkers and Darwinists among his professors, and had been reading, of his own, such disruptive influences as Thomas Huxley, Walter Pater, Samuel Butler and the sickly versifier Algernon Charles Swinburne; he'd been morbidly excited by Thomas Hardy's *Tess of the D'Urbervilles*, and yet more by *Jude the Obscure*; instead of taking exercise in the open air, he spent days sequestered in his room, brooding at the window, contemplating the cobbled street and the little park beyond, where, in his childhood long ago, he'd run in innocent delight under the watchful eye of his nursemaid. "May God strike me dead," Warren brashly declared, "if ever again I am so unthinkingly happy."

Yet this morning, as if against his will, he felt his interest stirred by the mysterious presence of a young girl in the park. She was no one he recognized; not a governess or a nursemaid (for she had no children with her) or a servant girl (for no servant would be free at ten o'clock of a weekday morning), yet judging by her modest dress and her hesitant manner, and the fact of her being so conspicuously alone, clearly not a young lady of his own social class. For some ten or fifteen minutes she walked slowly along the paths, steeling herself against the chill wind and glancing, shyly it seemed, in the direction of the Stirlings' house. Did she intend to cross the street, to ring the door? Warren found himself pressed close against the windowpane, watching. Though he had but a glancing notion of women's fashions he suspected that the girl's long hooded cloak was no longer in style; moreover, it fitted her rather gracelessly, the hem trailing along the ground. The hand-me-down costume of a country girl, perhaps, charming in its own way, but out of place in Greenley Square. As the girl's shy manner seemed out of place, quaint and old-fashioned. At last, she made up her mind to cross the street. Warren, excited, drew back from the window to avoid her glancing up and seeing him. His impression of her was that she was very young; very pretty; very frightened. Like one stepping to the edge of a precipice. In the ill-fitting velveteen cloak, the hood lifting in the wind, she reminded him painfully of one of his father's favorite paintings: an oil by an eighteenth-century Scots artist that hung in his grandparents' drawing room called "The Lass of Aviemore," which depicted a tempestuous sky, a rocky wooded landscape, and in the foreground, in a voluminous ink-black cape, a slender young girl standing with eyes uplifted and hands clasped in passionate prayer. Exceedingly pale, even ethereal, the girl had an innocent, angelic beauty; the artist had given her eyes an unearthly glisten, and her cheeks a light feverish touch; the velvet hood had slipped from her head so that pale blond tresses streamed in the wind. In the near distance was a gray stone cross. What was the tale "The Lass of Aviemore" meant to tell?—an old legend, a ballad, a Highland tragedy?

No one among the family, even Mr. Stirling, an amateur collector of Scots artifacts, had seemed to know.

II

Mina Raumlicht?—from the village of *Innisfail?*

She was clearly a country girl, intimidated by the elegance of the Stirlings' house—so the downstairs parlor maid took her measure at once, reasoning that, with this visitor, she need hardly be courteous.

Asking for Mr. Stirling!

In that frightened child-voice!

Since Miss Raumlicht, as she called herself, knew nothing of the master's death, she could not be anyone of significance; no relative or acquaintance of the Stirlings'; no former employee; no one to be taken seriously. So the maid informed her brusquely that it was not possible, no she could not see Mr. Stirling; nor could she see any other member of the household at the present time, for they were all "indisposed." But she might leave a calling card for Mrs. Stirling, if she wished. Or, she might write and post a letter. . . .

The girl who called herself Mina Raumlicht shrank slightly backward at the unwelcoming tone of the maid's voice, yet placed herself, with childlike stubbornness, in front of the door. Her eyelids fluttered with daring, her lips trembled, yet she insisted she must see Mr. Stirling, Mr. Maynard Stirling, for it was a matter of the gravest urgency, and she had come a long distance.

A long distance?—from Innisfail? The parlor maid's voice was edged with scorn. For Innisfail, a tiny settlement in the foothills of the

Chautauqua Mountain range, could not have been more than twelve miles west of Contracoeur.

The girl's eyes brimmed with tears. She had grown breathless; agitated; like one who has steeled herself for a grand, brash exertion requiring all her strength and courage—and cannot now retreat. She asked again if she might see Mr. Stirling and was told again, curtly, no she might not. Wringing her hands, she asked if "Maynard was at his place of work"—the expression quaintly rendered—and was told, in a harsher tone, that, no, he was not. Was he then traveling?—for she knew (she murmured faintly, with downcast eyes) that he traveled a good deal—but was told, emphatically, no—"Master is *not traveling.*"

Then might she leave him a message?—for him alone?

By this time, the girl in the black velveteen cloak was nearly sobbing in desperation, and the parlor maid hesitated, worrying that she might have gone too far—been too bold; though "Mina Raumlicht" of "Innisfail" could be a creature of no importance, a shopgirl or a servant girl at best, and could not get her into trouble with the Stirlings. Yet, making up her mind, with the imperviousness of an older sister sweeping away the claims of a younger, she moved forward as if to force the girl outside onto the stoop, saying, no she *might not* leave the master a message, for it was not allowed.

"Not—allowed?" Miss Raumlicht whispered. "But how can that be?"

"Not *allowed*, miss."

But, so strangely, the girl surrendered not an inch; refused to budge from her position in front of the door; turned her delicate, childlike face at a defiant angle, and said in a whisper, words which so utterly shocked the other young woman she would recall them through her life: "You lie. You lie, and you know it; *and I shall tell Maynard how rudely you have treated me.*"

At this the haughty parlor maid suddenly lost her composure, recognizing that, perhaps, this girl was not a younger sister of hers, after all; but someone who might be important; one not to be trifled with, despite her youth; she relented, saying that Miss Raumlicht might come inside and take a seat in the drawing room, and she would, she said, see if the mistress of the house might speak with her.

"But it is the master with whom I wish to speak. . . ." the girl said in a softer voice.

III

Surely it was an error. A miscopying in a document. Attributable to a clerk, or a secretary, or one of the junior attorneys, that he, Maynard Stirling, should—*die?*

Though the firm of Stirling, Stirling & Pedrick dealt daily in the anticipation of, the fact of, and the consequences of death among their clients, and though Maynard Stirling had years ago drawn up his will, as a responsible head of a household and a professional man of some accomplishment, it had never been very real to him except as a theoretical proposition: *Ashes to ashes, dust to dust.* But was that not mere metaphor, a poet's turn of phrase?

And to "die" at such an ordinary, inauspicious, and inglorious moment: on a weekday morning, in the midst of the devising of a codicil of tedious complexity, in the eleventh month of contract negotiations in which Stirling, Stirling & Pedrick (representing a Chautauqua manufacturer of enormous wealth, one of the founders of the National Association of Manufacturers) were locking horns with their old rivals Bagot, Bushy & Greene (representing downstate copper-mining interests); in the midst of uttering a single choked Latin term—was it *pro tempore?*—it became the essence of his life to articulate, as if, in the midst of an attack of angina pectoris that threw him forward onto the conference table, and was to kill him within a few hours, he might yet save himself, save all of the universe, by successfully uttering *pro tempore.*

But he failed. Ignobly, choking and writhing in agony, he failed. Exactly as if he, Maynard Stirling, were not one of the most prominent attorneys in upstate New York.

What was Mr. Stirling trying to say, so desperately?

A message to his family, I think.

No, surely it was a prayer. A prayer to God, to save his soul.

At the time of his sudden death Maynard Stirling presented a striking figure to the world: solidly built yet not portly; with a solid moon of a head about which his hair, faded to a silvery hue, seemed to float; close-set, hooded eyes both kindly and shrewd. He was one of those gentlemen in whom life throbbed quick and urgent in his breast, for he knew, and had always known, who he was; and the nature of his mission on earth, as a devout Christian (he was a deacon in the First

Presbyterian Church of Contracoeur), and a member of the hallowed legal profession (like his father and grandfather before him). He was an ardent Republican who yet believed, with ex-president Teddy Roosevelt, that the alarming spread of Socialism at the present time was the result of the "purblind folly of the very rich"; though, in general, Mr. Stirling was obliged to represent the rich, and to profit from his association, he did not shrink from voicing certain moderate views . . . of course condemning Socialism as the enemy, if it came to outright war. Above all he was a devoted husband and father, a loyal friend, a man of impeccable good manners and probity and God had always seemed to favor him and . . . surely it must be an error, that he should die? stricken in the midst of a mere codicil? and in the very prime of his life, in his fifty-third year?

A life of matchless integrity. Yet there was to be, kept secret by his family, something distressing . . . mysterious . . . a hint of . . . what, precisely? . . . which came, not exactly to light, then to a sort of miasmic glimmer on the very morning of Mr. Stirling's funeral, delivered by the postman amid a stack of condolence cards:

> Mr STIRLING please do not be angry again with yr. Mina that she has disobeyed one of yr. comands—but I am so fearfull of late I am so FEARFULL of a change in me I dare not reveal to my Aunt & MUST SPEAK WITH YOU SOON. O PLEASE do not be angry at my weakness for I am scarcely myself of late & KNOW NOT WHO I AM so craven in fear.
>
> Y^r adoring Mina

This brief message was written in midnight-blue ink in a large looping childlike hand, on a plain sheet of white stationery, the envelope postmarked "Innisfail, N.Y."—a country village on the Nautauga River a short distance west of Contracoeur. But who was "Mina," let alone "Y^r adoring Mina"—?

This mysterious and disturbing letter was delivered to the house in Greenley Square in the morning post, and opened by the distraught Mrs. Stirling in the late afternoon; read, and dazedly reread, if not fully comprehended, as she stood in her late husband's rosewood-panelled library in the handsome, black-laced mourning dress she had been wearing most of the day, her veiled black hat not yet removed. Seeing that his sister-in-law had suddenly stiffened, with an expression of baffled fright, Tyler Stirling, Maynard's younger brother, quickly approached her to inquire what the letter was; yet even as Fanny Stirling stammered anxiously that *she did not know what the letter was*, Tyler drew it discreetly from her trembling fingers. With a rapid, practiced eye he scanned the offensive note, betraying no surprise or upset or incredulity; and, acting with the judicious calm for which the Stirling men were known, he folded the sheet of paper and slipped it into his inside coat pocket for safekeeping. (With similar composure Maynard Stirling had once received a note in court informing him of the birth of his son Warren, just as he was about to address a jury on behalf of his client, the plaintiff in a bitter lawsuit: betraying no hint of emotion, the attorney proceeded with his usual vigor and confidence, winning the case for his client.)

"What is the letter? Who is—'Mina'? How dare a stranger speak with such intimacy, to—Maynard?" Fanny Stirling asked anxiously, and Tyler said, as if concluding an argument, "The letter was incorrectly addressed, and misdelivered. I suggest that you banish it from your thoughts, Fanny, at once."

IV

Yet what a riddle it was, and how it tormented her: Y^r *adoring Mina of Innisfail*.

In the midst of her grief, Fanny Stirling's thoughts seized upon that childlike message, which Tyler had taken from her, and of which he would not speak. Nor did anyone else in the family know of it. *It is an omen. An evil omen. God help me!* The shock of Maynard's death had rendered Fanny nearly incapable of coherent thought and speech; her doctor had prescribed liberal dosages of "nerve medicine" which left her groggy and disoriented, as if struggling to retain consciousness in the midst of a dream; and what a battalion of Stirling in-laws, relatives, friends and social, business and political acquaintances the family had to contend with—! Even as her sons Warren and Felix believed they were comforting her, Fanny felt obliged to comfort them; this was the case with Maynard's elderly mother and aunts as well, who had adored him. The widow knew herself closely observed by female acquaintances in Contracoeur, and worried that she was being found wanting in certain particulars: the horror of Death had gradually become obscured by the more immediate anxiety that Fanny was inadequate to the social demands of her position. Fanny Stirling was one of those well-to-do but insecure society women who agonize more about being *talked about* behind their back than about even illness or death.

Fanny Stirling, née Nederlander, a daughter of the barrel-manufacturing family of Buffalo, New York, was a girl of fifty at the time of her husband's unexpected death. Her personality was girlish, rather than womanly; her mannerisms—a way of ducking her head, a way of smiling, a way of fluttering her fingers in conversation—were meant to suggest girlhood, and not maturity; for the Stirling men had not admired, in women, forcefulness of manner or any suggestion of a restless, critical or speculative intelligence approaching their own. It had always amused Maynard, and made him love her the more, that she should try repeatedly to grasp the nature of his work, and repeatedly fail—"I swear, Fanny knows less about the law now than she did when we first met," Maynard had liked to say with a smile. Nor was Fanny quite able to share Maynard's other interests—in billiards and golf, at which he excelled, and in the collecting of English and Scottish paintings, rare stamps, coins, and old manuscripts (in Latin and Old German primarily) pertaining to the law. As Maynard was large-bodied and assured, with a lawyerly habit of speaking slowly, yet with forceful logic, like a locomotive pulverizing anyone or anything who stood in its way, so Fanny Stirling was high-strung by temperament, both vain and self-effacing. She was very like her good-hearted but nervous mother, who had so dreaded exposing herself to the judgment of society, she'd died rather than acknowledge a malevolent growth in her "female anatomy," fearing gossip, and, under the anesthetic, the possibility of unclean words issuing from her lips; for all good, decent Christian women feared such exposure. *If I am known for what I am, I cannot be loved. God help me!*

So, on that May morning, eight days after Maynard's death, when the downstairs maid hurried to Fanny Stirling with a most peculiar expression on her pert little face, saying that a young woman named Mina Raumlicht was asking to see Mr. Stirling, in fact demanding to see him, knowing nothing apparently of Mr. Stirling's death, Fanny shut her Bible at once and rose stiffly knowing only that, at all costs, *scandal must be avoided.*

V

Here was a mild shock: as Fanny Stirling descended the stairs, her hand gripping the banister to guide her, she saw her son Warren standing in the hall just outside Maynard's study, staring at the visitor just inside. *How does he know of her? So quickly?* Fanny felt a stab of maternal panic. When Warren glanced up at her, his expression showed embarrassment, yet excitement. "Who is she, Mother?" he asked in an undertone. Fanny said, frowning, "This is not your concern, Warren. This has nothing to do with you." Her brother-in-law Tyler approached, exchanged a glance with Fanny—how quickly the two understood each other—and slipped into the room without a word to Warren. "But, Mother—" the boy protested, as Fanny said, with more harshness than she intended, "She is no one we know, or wish to know," and Warren said, "Then why is she *here?*—I saw her approach the house, she looks so frightened," and Fanny said, her voice rising with a threat of hysteria, which never failed to intimidate the men of the family, "Warren, go away. I forbid you, in your late father's name, to speculate on matters that do not concern you."

VI

A seamstress's assistant. Seventeen years of age. Who had come to Contracoeur to work the previous year, and had taken lodgings with an elderly relative of her family, across town in East Contracoeur—"The far side of the Chautauqua & Buffalo tracks."

Their initial interview lasted well into the afternoon. The three of them shut away in Maynard's rosewood-panelled study, the shutters partly shut against a too-bright, too-intrusive spring sunshine that hurt

Fanny Stirling's swollen eyes. Within minutes the situation became
clear, in its horror, to the adults; the worst part of it being that the
naive young girl was no less dangerous to the Stirling household and
to Maynard's unblemished reputation for being, as it so painfully appeared, wholly *innocent*.

Self-conscious, shrinking, out of her element, as out of her social
class, in trying to converse with these imposing adults, Miss Mina
Raumlicht seemed incapable of comprehending, at first, that Mr. Stirling had "passed away"—she seemed in fact not to hear, staring, blinking, smiling with a peculiar intensity at Tyler, who was obliged to
repeat his words. As Fanny, in a haze of migraine and despair, tried
to harden her heart against the intruder, a shy little wren of a country
girl for whom, in other circumstances, Fanny would have felt Christian compassion. (For years, Fanny Stirling and certain of her women
friends had been active, to a degree, in the founding and funding of the
Presbyterian Home for Unwed Mothers in Contracoeur.) Mina Raumlicht had large deep-set bluish-gray eyes, threaded with blood and
ringed with fatigue; there was a hectic flush to her cheeks, a symptom
of fever—or worse; her small, doll-like features were pinched and
sickly. Her hair was a fair silvery brown neatly plaited and worn about
her head like a crown. Her cloak was well worn, over-large for her slender figure; made of some cheap velveteen material of a magenta hue so
dark as to appear black, neatly hemmed, but beginning to fray. Beneath
it, the girl wore a simple dark cotton frock with a square yoke, tight
sleeves and a wristfrill that fell despondently to her somewhat raw-
looking knuckles. The skirt was full and stiff and rustled unpleasantly,
like muffled whispers; the jacket, drooping in the shoulders, tied rather
than buttoned across the front. Sensing how ill-dressed she must appear
in the eyes of a rich Greenley Square matron, Miss Raumlicht sat
hunched in her chair, arms loosely folded across her waist, and fingers
tightly clasped. It struck Fanny Stirling's eye that the girl did not wear
gloves; her fingers were without rings, and her nails were painfully short
as if bitten. *As once I bit my own nails, in terror of the male mystery that
surrounds.*

At last, Mina Raumlicht seemed to comprehend that Mr. Stirling, to
whom she'd recently written, and whom she now so daringly, desperately sought, was dead. "But—how could God allow it?" she whispered.
"*At such a time—?*"

With a warning glance at his sister-in-law, Tyler said, in a cooler voice than he might have wished, "I'm afraid, Miss Raumlicht, that God allows many things in His world, and in His time."

There was a silence. At a near distance, the somber yet surpassingly beautiful bells of St. Mary Magdalen's Church began to toll the hour. As in a sick, sliding dissolve, as if on the verge of illness, Fanny Stirling was weeping unrestrainedly, and now Mina Raumlicht began to weep. The one haggard with grief and the other, so many years younger, with a child's gasping sobs, her beautiful eyes spilling with tears that glinted like acid and her hard little knuckles jammed against her mouth.

Tyler moved to comfort the women, with an air of both gallantry and vexation. How quickly a man tires of female weakness, especially female grief for another man! As he rose from his chair, the little seamstress's assistant seemed to shrink from him, as if fearing a blow; her eyes rolled upward in their sockets, her skin drained deathly white; she moaned, "Oh!—help me!" and fainted, falling heavily to the carpet before either of the Stirlings could prevent her, revealing, to their horrified eyes, the small but unmistakably rounded, swollen belly inside the shapeless clothing.

The more grotesque for being as Fanny Stirling would recall for the remainder of her unhappy life *so disproportionate to the child's body, only a fiend would have inflicted it upon her.*

Of course they dared not summon a physician, or even one of the household servants, for fear of scandal.

Though Fanny Stirling, loosening the girl's tight bodice with trembling fingers, and holding a small vial of spirits of ammonia beneath the girl's nose, worried aloud—"God help us if she dies!"

Tyler said, half-angrily, his lower jaw trembling, "*This* sort of female doesn't die for a trifle, I'm sure."

Awkwardly, Fanny and Tyler carried the stricken girl to a sofa where by slow degrees she revived, though it was nearly an hour before she came sufficiently to her senses to recognize her surroundings and to recall who the Stirlings were, and why she had come. With numbed lips she whispered she was sorry, so sorry, so frightened, she knew she must leave but she had nowhere to go, how could she return home to Innisfail, or even to her aunt's house, she had hidden her condition from her aunt but could not hide it much longer, Maynard had promised her he would assist her, what a good man Maynard was, how wicked of God to have taken him away!—so that Fanny was obliged to interrupt, with the alarmed caution with which she might have spoken to one of her own children, "My dear, no!—never say such things. We must believe that God is *good*."

"But God is *not good*," Mina Raumlicht wept, writhing on the horse-hair sofa, her plaited hair coming undone, her small, distended body exuding a damp disagreeable heat. "—God has hurt us all, so cruelly."

Tyler went to fetch a glass of brandy for the girl, but she lapsed into a sudden sleep, or trance; her reddened eyes only partly closed; her mouth, that looked hurt, slack as an infant's. The Stirlings stood over her, uncertain what to do. Tyler, who knew far more of the world's ways than did his sister-in-law, was yet stymied; in his soul, deeply shocked, and angered, by his late brother's behavior—what a hypocrite, that Presbyterian deacon! How incensed Maynard had been, in public at least, two decades ago when the Democratic candidate for president Grover Cleveland had been exposed in the public press for having sired an illegitimate child—as if such creatures were not being sired daily, by so-called gentlemen like Maynard Stirling and Grover Cleveland.

"She is correct," Fanny Stirling said wearily. "God has hurt us all cruelly."

"But God will show us a way out, Fanny. Never doubt Him."

VII

Tyler Stirling, too, was trained in the law; lacking his older brother's reputation, forever in the shadow of the formidable Maynard, yet not without gifts of his own. During the brief hour that Mina Raumlicht slept deeply, Tyler conferred with his sister-in-law in a far corner of the study, deciding what must be done. "The remarkable thing is, the girl makes no accusations. She makes no demands. She seems almost not to know her advantage. She leaves it to us, it appears. Almost, one could take pity on her," Tyler murmured; and Fanny said vehemently, "I do take pity on her, and on us. It's Maynard I cannot forgive." "Possibly, the girl is lying," Tyler ventured uncertainly, "—or there is another man involved. If Maynard were here to—" "But Maynard is *not here*," Fanny said, with surprising feeling. "And if he were, you see, we would not have met Miss Raumlicht; we would know nothing of Miss Raumlicht; it would have been very quietly, very discreetly settled. Ah, I am beginning to see how such things work out, in the world of men!" Tyler and Fanny were sipping brandy to steady their nerves; Fanny, unaccustomed to strong drink, and at such an hour of the day, refilled her own glass, and raised it to her trembling lips. The fierce, astringent fumes cleared her head wonderfully. The effect was like a windowpane long dimmed with dirt, wiped clean. Almost, she felt exhilarated: freed! For truly, had she loved Maynard Stirling at all?—except as she'd been, by law, his wife? Dimly she was recalling the hurts and slights of long ago, following the birth of Warren, when Fanny was yet a relatively young woman, and her husband had ceased to "approach" her in their bedroom as once he'd been in the habit of doing; not that Fanny, being a decent Presbyterian woman, had not been relieved, for of course she had been, of course she'd even thanked God to be spared; yet at the same time, hadn't she felt . . . slighted? rather hurt? resentful? Knowing her husband a man of vigorous physical appetites, she had even tormented herself that Maynard might have looked elsewhere for that balm to which such manuals as *The Wife's Medical Companion* referred to discreetly as "marital satisfaction."

She had told no one of this torment, of course. Even among the other Stirling wives, and her own married sisters, there were shamed subjects of which a woman could not speak.

Seeing that Fanny was in a state of unpredictable emotions, Tyler told her he preferred to speak with the girl in private when she recovered sufficiently. He would make a financial arrangement with her; he would see that she signed a document legally binding her to silence. "A cash settlement. A fairly generous settlement. And nothing more— nothing for the future. No future contact. That must be agreed upon." Fanny said, gazing across the room at the sleeping, now rather angelic-appearing girl, "And yet, if it's Maynard's child . . . We had hoped for a daughter, you know." (Though, was this true? Fanny had hoped for a daughter, a third child; Maynard had seemed quite content with two strapping healthy sons.) "It's like a fairy tale, the princess has come home. She is both the missing daughter and will give birth to the daughter. Oh, Tyler, do you see? Is it possible, this is *God's secret will?*"

Tyler had never much respected his sister-in-law's intellect and general character, though he had always liked the woman well enough, with some of the affectionate condescension he felt for his own mother and sisters; now, he sensed that Fanny was on the verge of another fit of female hysteria, and quickly comforted her by grasping her icy hands and assuring her that God's will was simply that the Stirlings behave in a decent, Christian manner toward the girl—"Hardly that we martyr ourselves on her behalf, for that would only bring unhappiness and shame upon the entire family, including the Nederlanders."

Fanny shuddered. Fanny drained the little shot glass of the last of its brandy. Yes, it was so. Martyrdom was not for her, as it had been for her poor mother. "So long as we are generous, Tyler," she said in a wistful voice.

VIII

The remainder of the afternoon and early evening were taken up with Tyler Stirling's consultation with Miss Raumlicht, and his success, at last, in persuading her to sign a document of his devising in exchange for a "lump sum" of money.

The exact amount, Fanny Stirling was never to know.

Tyler had banished her upstairs, to bed with a blinding migraine.

Tyler had set about the task of cleansing, as he irritably thought it, his elder brother's soiled linen—"For which I will get no credit, since no one except Fanny will ever know. And even Fanny doesn't *know.*"

For it wasn't an easy task to persuade the little seamstress's assistant to accept money from him "in the name of Maynard Stirling," and to sign the document promising not to contact any member of the Stirling family ever again; Tyler was astonished at Mina Raumlicht's stubborn virtue, so unlike any he had ever encountered in his experience as a lawyer. "She is impossible! Ridiculous! Yet so pretty, even in her condition, it's clear why Maynard was taken with her."

Mina Raumlicht declared she did not want money. She did not wish to soil herself by accepting money. She had not come to Greenley Square to "sell her honor" but simply to see Mr. Stirling, her beloved Maynard, one final time; only out of desperation that he had not contacted her for the past eight days, where never before had he allowed more than three or four days to pass without sending her a message, or a little gift, or coming to see her during the thirteen months of their acquaintance. "Thirteen months!" Tyler thought with envy. His gaze lingered on the girl's strained but doll-like face; those bluish-gray, deepset eyes that were, for all their woe and perplexity, intelligent eyes. Though her slender, distended body was now hidden inside the velveteen cloak, Tyler felt a stab of excitement imagining . . . the young, vibrant flesh his lustful brother Maynard had had no need to imagine. "A convenient arrangement on his side," he said, an edge of bitterness to his voice, "—yet not so convenient, I should say, on yours."

But Mina Raumlicht emphatically disagreed. "No, Mrs. Stirling was right, he was *good*. It is I who am *bad* in the eyes of God and of the world, and should not be rewarded for my *badness*."

Tyler all but ground his teeth, that his elder brother had somehow earned this beautiful young girl's unquestioned devotion. *He* had married reasonably well, in the world's eyes; yet he was capable of forgetting his wife when he was not in her company, and could not claim that he had ever felt passion for her, even when they were newlyweds. Tyler told the girl that he understood her feelings, and respected them. But in the present circumstances, she was obliged to think of the future; surely, his brother would have wished it this way. (Tyler wondered if, hidden amid the intricate codicils of Maynard's will, a document of numerous pages, there might not be a generous sum set aside for Miss Mina Raumlicht, by way of a third party; but there was no way of his determining this, without arousing suspicion, since he was not Maynard's executor. In any case, the will would require months of probate before it was settled.)

"Wished me to sell my honor?—*that* I can't believe," the girl said sadly.

Tyler protested, choosing his words with care: "Miss Raumlicht, you must think of it as making provisions for the future, assuring the well-being of your child soon to be born."

Your child soon to be born. Again, gazing at the girl, Tyler felt a powerful stab of excitement; almost, a swooning sensation in his bowels; for if he wished, he might place his hand against the girl's pregnant belly, and feel her inner, secret heat. . . . "But no, that's absurd," he thought, reproving himself. "I am not my brother, I am a man of integrity."

He summoned a servant to bring tea for Miss Raumlicht and himself; the sharp, tart English stimulant refreshed them both.

By this time, late in the afternoon, Tyler had removed his coat and was, in his shirtsleeves, pleasantly warm, if agitated. At 4:40 P.M. Tyler at last succeeded in getting the girl to take up a pen, to sign the brief document he'd devised; she brooded, and frowned, and seemed about to sign, but did not; at 4:48 P.M. she pushed the pen from her like a stubborn child confronted with a plate of repulsive food. There followed then another patient, kindly appeal on Tyler's part. A moment when by accident his hand brushed against Mina Raumlicht's shoulder; another moment, when in an unthinking avuncular gesture, he brushed a wisp of hair from the girl's warm forehead.

How quaint, Mina Raumlicht's crownlike plaited hair, a fair, silvery brown of the hue of late autumn; how pert her brave upper lip, though beaded with perspiration. How rare a sight, Tyler thought, marveling, to see a female *perspire*; he was sure he'd never seen any female of his acquaintance *perspire*; but, perhaps, he'd never noticed.

By 5:12 P.M. Mina Raumlicht again took up Tyler's pen, and reread the document with painstaking care, dipped the quill point into ink, and seemed about to sign; then, in a gesture of anguished conscience, winced, and shook her head, murmuring, "Oh! I cannot. This is wrong."

Now Tyler did grind his teeth; deciding, impulsively, that he would double the sum of money he was offering her. He took the document from her, crossed out the former sum and hastily wrote in the new, seeing with satisfaction the girl's widened eyes. "Miss Raumlicht, for the good of us all, you *must*."

Yet at 5:35 P.M., Mina Raumlicht again laid down the pen and, hiding her face in her hands, wept; saying, in a near-inaudible voice, "—but in accepting so much money, I am compounding my wickedness . . . am I not?"

"Assuredly, Miss Raumlicht, you are *not*." Tyler's face flushed with excitement; an artery beat hard in his throat, on the verge of triumph. "I am the man to tell you that. You must listen, no longer to Maynard, for he cannot help you in the slightest, but to *me*."

Still, it would not be until 6:13 P.M. that the little seamstress's assistant from Innisfail again took up the pen, and bravely signed her name, to Tyler's surpassing joy.

Mina Raumlicht   13 May 1909

IX

Though Tyler was elated, and fairly bursting with enthusiasm at the conclusion of this long session, yet how drawn and defeated Mina Raumlicht appeared. *As if we have been engaged in a physical, and not merely a mental, struggle. And I have won.*

Still, Mina Raumlicht managed to thank her benefactor, in a courteous voice, and to accept from Tyler's hand a considerable quantity of cash ($8,000 in varying, mainly large denominations, taken from the Stirlings' safe, for the family did not trust banks after the local panic following the sinking of the *Maine* in January 1898), which she carried away in a handsome kidskin traveling bag belonging to Fanny Stirling (which was happily donated by Fanny, whose relief at the outcome of the consultation with Mina Raumlicht may have exceeded Tyler's). "Thank you, Mrs. Stirling," Miss Raumlicht said, making a charming if awkward little curtsy, in the foyer of the town house, "—and thank you, Mr. Stirling. I will always remember you with the high regard with which I will always remember—*him.* 'As above, so below'—it is said—which gives me courage, for what we must endure on Earth is ordained for us in the heavens, and, in the heavens if not on Earth, we who dwell in darkness shall be justified."

A remarkable little speech to issue from the lips of a seventeen-year-old seamstress's assistant, especially one who staggered beneath the weight of an eight-month pregnancy! Rendered quite speechless themselves, Tyler Stirling and his sister-in-law Fanny exchanged a perplexed glance.

By this time, however, the hackney cab had arrived which would deliver Miss Raumlicht, prepaid, to the Contracoeur train station. Tyler lost no time in escorting the girl out to the curb, and out of the lives of the Stirlings, forever.

And so God spared us Fanny would exult in secret *from the horror of public scandal beside which the very fires of hell seem benign!*

X

Who is she? Where has she come from, and where is she bound?

Unknown to his mother or his uncle, Warren Stirling slipped from the house at Greenley Square to follow the cab, on foot, for many blocks, keeping a vigorous pace until, at Highland Boulevard, he saw to his surprise that the cab stopped; the mysterious girl in the dark traveling cloak, with whom his uncle had been shut up for most of the day, in what must have been a secret conference, climbed gracefully down, and sent the cab away. How lovely she looked, the velveteen hood now removed from her head, her silvery-brown plaited crown shining! Carrying what appeared to be Mrs. Stirling's kidskin bag, the girl made her way, unescorted, yet with no suggestion of hesitation or shyness now, briskly along the crowded sidewalk, past the somber portico of the Presbyterian church, where generations of Stirlings had worshipped; past the handsome Neo-Grecian facade of the Contracoeur Hotel; and finally, again to Warren's surprise, into the hurly-burly of lower Commerce Street. There, suddenly, she was joined, or approached, by an unexpected individual, indeed: a tall, lean, neatly dressed Negro gentleman of middle age, it appeared, judging from his powder-gray hair and goatee, and the stoop of his shoulders; he wore rimless glasses, and a black bowler hat, and walked, stiffly, with a cane. How very different this well-bred Negro was, from the common Negro laborers and servants one saw constantly; he must have been, Warren thought, a minister. Yet how strange it was: the girl in the traveling cloak and the Negro appeared to be walking at precisely the same pace, without glancing at each other; the Negro followed the girl at a discreet distance of about five feet as they headed swiftly on Commerce—so swiftly that Warren, a football player, long-legged and in excellent condition, had difficulty keeping them in sight.

Earlier that day, Warren had been reading in the *Contracoeur Post* about the "Black Phantom" who'd committed a sensational robbery in Chautauqua Falls a few days previous, and had disappeared with an undisclosed amount of cash (rumored to be several hundred thousand dollars); he'd studied a crude pen-and-ink drawing of the robber in the paper, a young simian-faced Negro with a moustache, in a black domino mask, his long-barreled pistol raised, for effect, beside his arrogant countenance. $12,000 REWARD! WANTED 'BLACK PHANTOM'! BOLD NEGRO ROBS CHAUTAUQUA FALLS LADIES & GENTLEMEN AT GUNPOINT! Seeing now this older Negro in the apparent company of the girl in the traveling cloak, Warren naturally thought of the "Black Phantom"— but of course there could be no connection, for this Negro was a well-bred individual in his early fifties, and the "Black Phantom" was a mere youth in his twenties.

Yet were the two, the girl and the Negro, really together?—Warren couldn't decide. Surely, no one else, glancing in their direction, would have thought so. Warren was fascinated; aroused, as invariably we are in the presence of mystery; staring so avidly, he took no notice of colliding with other pedestrians, and at Grant Street, by the train station, he was almost killed stepping into the path of a clanging streetcar.

To his surprise, and dismay, Warren lost the two in the milling crowd at the train station, and had to give up his pursuit. He'd had a glimpse, and more, of *her* haunting face which he would cherish for decades; which he would seek, in his romantic relations with young women, always in vain; but which would never fail to stir a sense of exhilaration and hope in his heart.

" 'The Lass of Aviemore' "—his numbed lips moved in reverence. How much more beautiful the girl was, to Warren's way of thinking, than any mere painted beauty hanging framed in gilt in his grandfather Stirling's house these many years.

"A Bird in a Gilded Cage"

I

What is the source of this daring, this giddy springtime bravado, and Eloise Peck née Ingram the granddaughter of the renowned Episcopal bishop?—French champagne at midnight on the terrace of the Saint-Léon Hotel, in Atlantic City, New Jersey; and here in the suite, in the sumptuous bedroom, more champagne at noon; and Russian caviar lavishly spread on toast (though *he*, with an overgrown boy's appetite, prefers marmalade or peanut butter); pheasant-brandy pâté, rum-butter-balls, croissants greedily devoured in bed . . .

Christopher! . . . are you asleep?

. . . No ma'am.

Did I wake you?

Oh no ma'am.

I *did*, didn't I? . . . I'm so sorry.

Oh no ma'am, I was awake. . . . I was waking.

But, dear Christopher, why do you say "ma'am"? . . . Haven't I begged you to call me "Eloise"? . . .

. . . *Eloise.*

Don't you love me, Christopher?

Oh yes . . . *Eloise.*

Then why are you so shy, you silly boy? . . . Why *now*? . . . after these many days of happiness . . . when you know how I adore you?

. . . I am sorry, Eloise.

. . . now that I am your fiancée, and we have only to wait until the decree, and then, oh sweet Christopher! . . . *we will be married.*

Yes Eloise . . . ma'am.

* * *

Why, is she not *young?* . . . Eloise Peck née Ingram so very *young?* . . . to have been married twenty-three years to an old man *who will not die?*

Christopher!

Yes ma'am.

. . . We *will* be wed when I am free, it is not a mere dream? . . . a champagne fancy?

Not at all, ma'am. Which is to say . . . *yes*.

And you love your Eloise?

Oh yes.

And you will be tender with her?

Oh yes.

And you don't care a fig for the world's censure?

Not at all, ma'am.

And you have no fear of my vindictive husband?

Not at all, ma'am.

And you don't regret your lost vocation? . . . for you would have made, dear Christopher, so very handsome, so very . . . so very powerful a man of the cloth!

. . . Why yes ma'am, Eloise I mean, I do regret . . . some things.

But your heart is not broken?

Oh no.

Your heart is whole . . . *wholly* . . . mine?

Oh yes.

We will be wed till death do us part? . . . in sickness and in health, whether rich or poor?

Oh yes certainly, ma'am.

And you do love your Eloise? And no one else?

And no one else . . . ? Oh *yes*.

On the Sunday-thronged boardwalk, on the wide windy splendid beach, Eloise Peck and her strapping young blond lover (said to be a former farm boy?—a former seminarian?), Eloise Peck and her twin Pomeranians (Princess and San Souci—so sweet), Eloise Peck causing heads to turn in her aigrette-adorned silk turban, her sapphire-and-diamond choker, her printed silk Poiret frock (Empire waistline, loose flowing sleeves, tight "V-necked" bodice) . . . She carries a white chiffon sunshade, wears white net gloves (showing stark little rhomboids of flesh), her face is hidden by a white tulle veil but everyone in Atlantic City knows who she is: who else but old Wallace Peck's runaway wife?

Christopher!

Yes?

Give me your arm, dear, and don't take such long strides. . . . I am quite out of breath in this *wind*.

Sorry ma'am. Yes ma'am.

. . . *Eloise*, dear.

Oh yes: *Eloise dear*.

. . . And you are tugging too hard on Princess's leash, the collar is cutting into her throat, *do* take care, dear.

Yes certainly Eloise dear.

Ah, that's better!

Yes?

After twenty-three years of being *good*, whence comes, and so suddenly, this delicious *badness*; after twenty-three years of being *Mrs. Wallace Peck* in her gilded cage, whence comes, with such exhilaration, this certainty in being . . . *Eloise?* Glasses of champagne, and French burgundy, and Swiss chocolate almond liqueur, and, in the candlelit Crystal Room of the Saint-Léon, squeezing, sub rosa, the blushing young Christopher's knee: *Do* you love me, Christopher dear, or is it all a . . . fancy? In the airy vestibule of St. John's Episcopal Church the renegade Mrs. Peck snubs, before they can collect their wits, and snub *her*, the dowager sisters Vandeventer; in the clubhouse at the Atlantic City racetrack Mrs. Peck manages a coolly blithe flirtation with old Elias Shrikesdale, a friend of her late father and her yet-current husband. She drinks a good deal these days (as she is the first to admit!) but she is always in control, perhaps too generous in her tipping, too lavish in her confidences, telling dressmaker, masseuse, hotel manager, telegraph operator, tearoom proprietress, most of all her Filipino maid . . . certain ecstatic plans for the future (honeymoon voyage to the Greek Isles, renovation of the old Ingram estate in Newport) once she is, legally, *Mrs. Christopher Schoenlicht*.

Sometimes she weeps, it's true. But only out of joy. For she is shortly to inherit a great deal of money (by way of a long-delayed court settlement following her father's death) and she is shortly to be freed of her marital bond to the dyspeptic old tyrant Wallace Peck (who visited upon his young bride two miscarriages, one stillbirth, and a nameless infection eventually cured by way of hydrotherapy and mercury treatments).

But why should Love hide its face?

Why should *she* hide her face? . . . coldly explaining to cousins, to friends, to skeptical Manhattan acquaintances, that she and young Christopher love each other, she and young Christopher honor each other, it matters not at all that, yes, he is nearly twenty years her junior, that he is from a modest rural background in upstate New York, that, apart from a year at the Mount Chattaroy Bible Institute, he has had very little formal education; it matters not at all—this said with an angry flaring-up—that the world professes doubt as to the charity of Mrs. Peck's behavior in taking up with, or taking advantage of, a sweet but somewhat simpleminded farm boy.

Whence comes, with such force, the conviction that she is mad with love for the boy, that she would die for the boy, that though he is not the first, nor the second, nor even the third, of her "enthusiasms," he has replaced them all in her heart—in truth, obliterated their memories altogether? Whence comes this defiance, so uncharacteristic of the Ingrams, or of anyone, female particularly, in their circle, that she *is not* ashamed and she *will have her way* . . . though discreet enough here in Atlantic City, where of course she is known, to have taken two rooms, a suite for her and an adjoining room for him, to forestall wagging tongues, and the censure of the Saint-Léon management? Whence this delirium of desire? . . . an intoxication of brawny sprawling limbs, hard-muscled limbs, limbs covered in fuzzy blond hair . . . a slow shy crooked smile . . . a deep flush rising from the throat to the cheeks when Eloise, slightly tipsy Eloise, admires him too ecstatically, or caresses him with too-eager clumsy hands: *dear* boy! *dear* innocent boy!— *do you love me above all the world?*

II

The talk in fashionable Atlantic City in the summer of '09 was of nothing but scandal: scandal in politics, scandal in horse racing, scandal in the behavior of Wallace Peck's "estranged" wife.

Was there ever a woman of good family who behaved, in public, with such defiance?—glimpsed on the boardwalk, on the beach, in one or another dining room or salon or restaurant, in the company of the lanky rawboned youth she called her fiancé: a boy young enough to be her son, as the ladies angrily observed.

And her elderly husband back home in Manhattan, said to be in ill health ... (It had come to the point, as the gentlemen whispered among themselves, that the expression *Wallace Peck'd* was beginning to be heard, bandied cruelly about in clubs and drawing rooms: for to be *Wallace Peck'd* was to be most conspicuously and shamefully *cuckolded*.) A divorce was in progress, it was known, and Peck had allegedly washed his hands of her, but still!—what scandal!—Eloise Peck in her costly designer clothes (favoring, this season, the controversial Parisian Poiret, who preached the abolition of the corset), her chestnut-red hair too fiercely hennaed, her face powder and kohl too much in evidence, and didn't she make a spectacle of herself, smiling and simpering at everyone in sight, as if she imagined they might wish her well?

Eloise Peck, married off at twenty, had grown into a plump coquettish woman with startled eyes and a busy, bustling, rather too sunny nature, quicker to smile than was absolutely necessary, and given to distracting peals of laughter ... as if (as her detractors said jeeringly) *she found much in the world to cheer her.* Until recent years, when her slender waist began to thicken, and the flesh about her jowls and throat slackened, most of the gentlemen in her circle found her charming enough; the ladies were more ambivalent, as ladies invariably are judging one of their own—for was Eloise Peck a silly, vain, shallow woman, the very epitome of the Gay Nineties, or was she a woman of mysterious depths, injured in her girlish spirit by a bad marriage and marked, perhaps, for a tragic fate?

Harry von Tilzer's wildly popular song of 1902 was rumored to have been penned with Eloise Peck in mind—

'Tis sad when you think of her wasted life,
    For beauty cannot mate with age,
And her beauty was sold
For an old man's gold,
    She's a bird in a gilded cage.

And now—was the bird to flee her cage?—to spread her brave wings and fly, and fly, and fly?

She is a fool, says one observer.
She is a common adulteress, says another.
A harlot—but to be pitied.
A slattern. A doxy. A traitor to her class.

III

In politics the fresh scandal was: Senators Zalmon Briggs (Republican, Ohio) and Denver Cosby (Democrat, New Jersey) were exposed as hirelings of Standard Oil!—certain incriminating letters having been published on the front page of Mr. Hearst's crusading *Journal*. (For now it was William Randolph Hearst's turn to retaliate for his having been exposed only a few months before by the *New York World* and *Harper's Weekly* for his own cloudy deals in Wall Street.)

In Thoroughbred racing the fresh scandal was: the much-acclaimed winner of the Preakness, a three-year-old filly named Belladonna, was believed to have been injected with cocaine before the race, a charge bitterly denied by her owner, who threatened to bring suit against Preakness officials for "slander and character defamation." And sporting gentlemen were still shaking their heads over the debacle at Chautauqua Downs, where so many had lost their bets, and the beautiful Xalapa was put down, and the armed robber the "Black Phantom" ran off with hundreds of thousands of dollars—despite an intensive manhunt and the posting of a $12,000 reward, he was still at large.

"A topsy-turvy world!"—Mrs. Eloise Peck was heard to observe laughingly at the Broadway opening of the operetta *Mademoiselle Modiste*, where she was clothed in stylish finery including a summer ermine and several strands of costly pearls; and as usual attracted a good deal of attention for herself and her handsome young escort Christopher. A sharp-eyed woman, Mrs. Peck didn't fail to observe how certain of her acquaintances snubbed her, yet in this new phase of her life, enlivened by champagne and by love, she seemed not greatly to care. In the theater lobby she spoke intimately yet rather loudly to her young man, as if they themselves were performers, deserving of others' attention.

So Eloise Peck declared with a tinkling laugh of both bemusement and sorrow that the world had lately become "topsy-turvy"; and her fiancé was heard to reply, shyly, in a voice that betrayed a rural up-state accent, "Ma'am, it is said 'As above, so below'—which means that, however wicked things seem to our eyes, they are ordained in the heavens."

Mrs. Peck ceased to smile, and stared at her husky blond escort in his formal attire, as if she had never seen him before. "Why, Christopher," she said at last, laughing, "—you are a philosopher and metaphysician, too?"

IV

Eloise Peck had met Christopher Schoenlicht at—was it Saratoga Springs? or another fashionable watering place—where he'd been a stable hand, or a bellboy, or a waiter, or . . . a chauffeur? A social acquaintance of Eloise's claimed that Eloise had confided in her that Christopher had "dropped out of Heaven one day in answer to my prayer that my life be saved"—helping her climb down from a hackney cab at the Waldorf-Astoria. Yet another female acquaintance claimed that Eloise had confided in her that she'd been introduced to Christopher by the pastor of her church—Christopher being a luckless Christian youth forced to terminate his studies in Bible school when his father died a bankrupt. "Someday, we hope, Christopher will resume his studies," Eloise said, with a mischievous wrinkling of her nose, "—but not, we hope, too soon."

Soon it was whispered that Wallace Peck's wife was separated from him, and traveling about openly with a mysterious young man; not a nephew, nor any blood relation; nor yet a member of her extravagant retinue, which included, from time to time, a Parisian hairdresser, a Canadian "nerve doctor," and a Jamaican masseuse in addition to a Filipino servant. At first it was hoped by Eloise's friends that young Christopher was an errand boy (for Eloise frequently sent him on errands to deliver telegrams, fetch a shawl or a fur wrap for her and, in disagreeable weather, to walk the yapping Pomeranians), but in time this fiction dissolved as the lady herself, gaining courage with the passage of weeks, began introducing him as her fiancé. And Eloise Peck not yet divorced from her husband!

Though clearly not a youth of sophistication or exceptional intelligence, Christopher Schoenlicht was sensitive enough to know very well how people talked; how eyes fastened covertly upon him and the glamorously dressed Mrs. Peck, in public; how whispers and innuendos were exchanged sub rosa. At such times, he blushed fiercely and tightened his jaws, enduring in silence what Eloise Peck, if she knew of it, would have remarked upon with her sharp, shrill laughter. The young man was in his mid-twenties, though still boyish; about six feet two inches, with broad shoulders, a frank strong-boned face, and the sort of rapidly growing beard that requires shaving twice daily. ("At the State Fair at Syracuse, such a specimen would win a blue ribbon," one of Wallace Peck's friends dryly observed.) Christopher's hair was white-blond, like his eyelashes and brows; his eyes were a pale bluish-gray; he carried himself with an awkward sort of grace, rather like (as a columnist for the *New York Post* slyly commented, alluding to the "Bird out of her Gilded Cage with her new companion") a bear walking on his hind legs.

Mrs. Peck, who'd never had children, dressed her young friend with flair, yet with taste: in tailored blazers, white flannels, ascot ties, narrow-pleated silk shirts, smart Panama hats of the kind made stylish by Broadway's George M. Cohan; yet it couldn't be said that the young man wore them with ease, and more than one observer, introduced to young Schoenlicht, noted that his nails were ridged with dirt and his linen, though presumably fresh that morning, was fresh no longer. Whether in shyness or in shame, his gaze was often downcast; he had the guarded manner of one who, in childhood, has been the butt of cruel jokes.

Even so, Christopher Schoenlicht wasn't so backward as Mrs. Peck's critics wished to believe. He could exert surprising authority when sent about town as her emissary: speaking firmly with shopkeepers, tradesmen, hotel employees and the like, when the situation required. Mrs. Diggett, the admiral's widow, reported having seen him smoking a cigar on the beach while walking the twin Pomeranians, at dusk; and reported too that the young man spoke harshly to the dogs, when their yapping grew frenzied and their leashes became wound around his ankles. "He is no fool, it seems, when he's alone." Mrs. Amos Sellick, a young Manhattan matron, reported that Christopher was "kindly" and "gentlemanly" in her presence; when Mrs. Peck was elsewhere, Christopher took time to set up a beach umbrella for the Sellick children and to play with them for hours, splashing in the surf, carrying them on his strong shoulders, building elaborate sand castles. Within a few days of their acquaintance, Christopher was like a big brother to the Sellick children; a decent, sweet-tempered, honest Christian youth and hardly an immoral gigolo living openly with a woman old enough to be his mother. "He is her victim—the shameless seductress!" Mrs. Sellick whispered. "And what a pity, he seems not to have any family to rescue him from her."

V

Christopher! . . . are you listening?

. . . Yes ma'am.

Yes Eloise.

Yes *Eloise*.

Are you listening, dear, or daydreaming? . . . I swear your mind was miles away!

Not at all Eloise.

Are you bored here in Atlantic City . . . *Are* you happy? . . . Is it time for us to move on?

Whatever you wish, Eloise.

. . . time for us to wed, surely!

Yes surely.

And you *do* love your Eloise, above all the world?

Oh yes.

And you have no worry of the future . . . of the world's cruel censure?

Oh no.

And you don't regret your lost vocation? . . . Please tell me, dear, that you *don't*; for it would be very wrong of me to come between you and God's wishes for you.

God's wishes for me?

That you were meant to be a man of the cloth . . .

But God's wishes for me, ma'am, must be that I would *not* be a man of the cloth . . . since He caused my father to die, and my studies to come to an end.

Oh yes dear! . . . I suppose you are correct, dear.

And it can't be that you, ma'am, could come between me and God's wishes for me . . . for God has told me you *are* His wishes for me. If not, I couldn't be here in such a place.

Yes sweet Christopher: I suppose you are correct.

But how, ma'am, could I be anything other than correct, if God has sent me to you? . . . if all that we do or say or think or wish is prescribed by Him?

It's true: sometimes Christopher frightens Eloise. Just a little.

Makes her shiver. The fine hairs stirring at the nape of her neck.

When he speaks so matter-of-factly of God, and God's wishes.

As if he believes! Eloise confides in a divorcée she has casually befriended. *As if what to others is mere prattle, to him is God's very word.*

Mid morning in the hotel suite sharply fragrant with yesterday's flowers, and a commingled scent of stale champagne, liver pâté and scattered crumbs of Gorgonzola cheese. Yet: a delirium of satin sheets, and lace-edged pillowcases smeared with Eloise's makeup, and gilded mirrors holding no reflections, and in the near distance, rooms away, the petulant whimpering of Princess and San Souci mad with jealousy of their mistress's new love. A delirium of brawny sprawling limbs, hard-muscled limbs, limbs covered in fuzzy pale-blond hair . . . patches of darker hair, wiry, kinky, at armpits, belly, groin. No matter that there is a patina of grime between Christopher's toes, no matter that his fingernails are permanently ridged with black, no matter that the ignorant world cries Fool! . . . and Harlot! . . . and Adulteress! . . . and Seductress!

For Eloise Peck would fling in their teeth just one word: *Love.*

Does she dare, now that he sleeps? . . . now that his breath has become a rasping snore, and his body gives off a warm rank damp heat? Does she dare, now that she has drained the bottle of champagne, and the world is a-tilt, to kiss her lover in that most forbidden and delicious of places?

A secret kiss; yet, at the touch of her swooning lips, the blood-warmed flesh at Christopher's groin begins to stir like a very snake roused from sleep.

VI

Father has taught: The Game is never to be played as if it were but a game.

And the spoils we reap, but spoils.

So Christopher sleeps truly, exhausted from love; and, when he wakes, wakes truly; and "loves" truly . . . for it would be cruel of him to come between Mrs. Peck and God's wishes for that improvident lady.

VII

Except: on the evening of 23 June 1909, in the space of a quarter hour, the lovers' plans are as completely devastated as if an earthquake had struck Atlantic City, and the elegant Saint-Léon razed to the ground.

And what glorious plans the lovers had had: to be married in the eyes of God, as soon as the divorce decree from old Mr. Peck was finalized; more immediately, to dine early on the twenty-third, and to attend a musical evening (the much acclaimed operetta *The Fortune Teller*) at the new Gaiety Theatre.

Grown fatigued by an afternoon of indolence on the beach, Mrs. Peck lay down in the sumptuous four-poster bed for a brief nap; slept fitfully; woke, and slept again, and woke, or seemed to . . . disturbed by raised voices in the adjacent room. "Christopher? Is that you?" she whispered. The voices ebbed, and she lay for a while in a pleasurable trance not knowing if she'd heard accurately or had been dreaming; lazily calculating whether it was too early for her to summon a maid, to draw her bathwater. The evening at the Gaiety would be festive and public, covert eyes moving upon her and Christopher, and so her toilette must be impeccable.

Again the voices were raised: masculine voices. One of them was Christopher's, unmistakably. But whose was the other?

"My dear boy, in an argument of some sort? Can it be?"

Excited, thrilled, Eloise quickly wrapped herself in her new emerald-green crêpe de Chine robe; powdered her unfortunately puffy face; made an attempt to smooth down her matted hair. No time! no time! At the door she paused to listen, for Christopher did sound angry, as she'd never before heard him; and who could it be who dared to answer him in such a provocative tone? Not a hotel servant, surely?

Eloise listened. Christopher was being threatened?

Or, no: Christopher was threatening another person.

. . . Another young voice, whining, childish, slurred with drink, a bullying intimacy; a brotherly tone alternating with one of crude malice.

Money, evidently, was the issue.

Someone was demanding money of her Christopher.

And Christopher was saying in a lowered voice that there was no money to be had, damn it. *No money to be had—yet.*

The other, unknown party laughed harshly, saying he didn't intend to leave this damned hotel without some cash; no less than two hundred dollars. He was flat broke, his Baltimore plans had gone bust, he'd been lucky to have escaped with just a beating! . . .

Eloise was shocked to hear how Christopher cursed his companion, and commanded him to leave at once *before the woman overheard, and everything would be ruined.*

. . . two hundred did I say, shit three hundred's what I meant.

Christopher stammered *there was no money to be had yet!* . . . *no money of any significance.*

The old bitch's got jewels, don't she? Come on. Before I lose my fuckin' sand-frawd.

In this way, recklessly, the two young men quarreled with an old, heated intimacy; even Christopher seemed to have forgotten where he was; and, on the other side of the door, Eloise Peck stood paralyzed, her pretty crêpe de Chine wrapper fallen open to reveal her sad, slack figure, and her eyes filling with tears in one of those intervals of horror that mimic, and sometimes augur, the termination of a life.

VIII

Here is how the catastrophe occurred.

Christopher, as he was known to Mrs. Peck, had gone swimming, alone, in the late afternoon, along a stretch of windy deserted beach a quarter mile from the Saint-Léon; returned to the hotel suite, and since Mrs. Peck was asleep, enjoyed a cigar, and one or two small glasses of Swiss chocolate almond liqueur, out on the balcony overlooking the frothy, winking surf; was roused from his reverie by a surreptitious knocking at the door, at 5:25 P.M., and giving no thought who it might be, suspecting it was one or another flunky of the Saint-Léon bringing Mrs. Peck some trifle she had ordered, went to open it; and saw to his astonishment *his younger brother Harwood*, in a disheveled state.

Before Christopher could speak, Harwood pushed his way inside, and, seeing they were alone, began to demand money from him. He was in a bad way, Harwood said; his life was in danger; he needed money, and he needed it immediately; *and Thurston must provide it.*

Christopher was so rattled at the sight of this brother of his, of whom he'd never been fond, whom he'd never trusted, in this place where his brother should not have been, he could only stammer that there must be some mistake: he wasn't Thurston, but Christopher—"My name is Christopher Schoenlicht."

Harwood said contemptuously he didn't give a damn what Thurston's name was or wasn't; he needed money; and it was obvious that, here, money was to be had. He knew all about Thurston's liaison with some wealthy old female and he wanted his share. "My luck has temporarily run out," he said, "—and now, 'Christopher,' I want some of yours."

Still Christopher stammered that there must be some mistake: he wasn't Thurston, but Christopher: and unless Harwood left at once, he would be forced to eject him.

" 'Eject' me, eh! Will you! Oh will you!—just try it, fancy boy!" Harwood laughed, lowering his head like a bulldog about to leap to the attack, and clenching his fists. "Dare to touch me, and see what happens."

In the course of his precocious career, the young man who currently called himself "Christopher Schoenlicht" had encountered a number of upsetting situations, and calculated his way out of several tight spots;

even at panicked moments he recalled a favorite epigram of his father's—" 'The worst is not so long as we can say, *This is the worst*' "— though he couldn't have named its source, whether the Bible, or Shakespeare, Homer or Mark Twain. Yet, his drunken brother Harwood standing belligerently before him in a place and at a time where Harwood was, by all the rules of The Game, *not to be*, these words ran rapidly through his head—"This is the worst!—*this*."

For it had never happened before, that any of the Lichts had put another so at risk.

Brothers by blood are brothers by the soul.

Control, and control, and again control: and what prize will not be ours?

Christopher, or Thurston, had last spoken with Harwood several months ago at the old country place, as the family called it, in Muirkirk, in the Chautauqua Valley of upstate New York, around the time of Harwood's twenty-second birthday. Afterward, as usual, the brothers had gone in separate directions, for they had quite separate destinations: Harwood to Baltimore, to attach himself to a relation of some sort, a "cousin" of their father's, with whom he was to organize a racing lottery, and Christopher, or Thurston, with his very different gifts, to return to Manhattan and to his quick-blooming romance with the wealthy Mrs. Peck. When he was apart from his brothers and sisters, Thurston rarely gave them much thought, for how could thinking along sentimental, familial lines be productive?—as Father might say. He did allow himself moments now and then of reverie, smoking a cigar, sipping a rare liqueur, as he'd been doing on the balcony of the hotel suite just now; at such times he contemplated the Muirkirk home as one might contemplate a place of refuge; he might indulge himself in a mental colloquy with his father, whose spiritual presence he required to get him through knotty times. (Like "making love" with Mrs. Eloise Peck.)

As Mr. Licht had instructed his children, it was always wisest to say *How would Father deal with this?*—not *How should I deal with this?*— when they were faced with difficult situations.

But how would Father deal with *this*?—Christopher, or Thurston, asked himself, as his unwanted brother Harwood prowled about the luxurious room, sniffing doglike at vases of Mrs. Peck's favorite flowers, pearl-pink roses; picking up items (a cashmere net scarf of Mrs. Peck's, from India) as if to appraise them, and tossing them down; repeating, like a demented parrot, that he needed money, he needed cash, wasn't going to leave until he got cash, he knew that the "wealthy old whore what's-her-name—'Peek?' 'Poke?' 'Pig?' "—gave Thurston money, for certain she gave him presents, *and he wanted his share.*

Had Thurston, or Christopher, happened to have seen his brother on the street in Atlantic City, he would probably not have recognized him at first: the stocky young man hadn't shaved in days, and seemed to have suffered a beating—his upper lip was swollen, and his left eye luridly discolored. He was wearing a soiled golfing cap Thurston had never seen before, and a rumpled navy blue gabardine suit that fitted his muscular shoulders tightly; his white shirt, poorly laundered, was open at the throat, and missing a button. It was clear too that he'd been drinking.

Of the Licht children, Harwood had long been acknowledged as the least gracious, the least talented and, certainly, the least attractive: he had a face (as Mr. Licht had once half-admiringly observed) like the blunt edge of an ax; and small close-set suspicious eyes of no discernible color, moistly alert as the eyes of a large predator frog. Harwood had grown rapidly and prodigiously until the age of twelve, but then ceased to grow; he was now several inches shorter than his handsome blond brother, squat-bodied, rather clumsy, yet, if it came to a fight, Thurston knew from past experience that the wily Harwood would win: his tactics were improvised, wild, manic and lawless, no blow to the kidney, groin or throat, no gouging, or biting, or stranglehold forbidden. *The law of the beast* was Harwood's unarticulated law. The last time the brothers had fought, at an edge of the Muirkirk swamp, Thurston had been able to save himself only by holding his brother's head under water . . . until, after what seemed like a very long time, Harwood's steel-like fingers relaxed their death-grip around Thurston's throat.

Now Thurston relented. "All right, I'll meet you somewhere tonight. But, damn you, you must get out of here now."

"Bloody hell will I 'get out of here,' " Harwood said loudly, his hands on his hips, "—you think I'm a bellboy, to take orders from *you?*"

So, fatally, it continued. Harwood, drunk and blustering, making his demands; Thurston, trying to placate him; the brothers' voices more reckless, louder; until they were shouting, and the heavy gilt-framed mirrors on the walls began to tremble. It was a curiosity of the episode, as both would recall afterward, that neither dared to so much as touch the other's sleeve . . . for fear of the murderous violence that might ensue.

And, in the adjacent room, Eloise Peck stood rooted to the spot, listening.

IX

It was unfortunate for all that Mrs. Peck lacked the cunning, or the simple presence of mind, to flee such a humiliating scene at once; to summon help from the hotel management, or to seek out her Filipino maid, that she might run for help.

And that the deluded woman lacked the wit (being, perhaps, as madly in love as she was habituated to claiming) to perceive that "Christopher Schoenlicht" did not exist; still less that, had he existed, he would not be *hers*.

Instead of acting with caution, however, as she would have done in her former respectable life, Mrs. Peck sobbed aloud, like a heroine in a Broadway melodrama, "I am betrayed—he does not love me," and in a paroxysm of wounded pride flung open the door between the rooms to dramatically reveal herself; and rushed inside with a choked cry that "Christopher"—"my Christopher"—had deceived her. In a wild voice she ordered her fiancé and his brute brother (for even in her agitation it was self-evident to her that the two young men, for all their differences, were kin) out of the suite at once.

"Or I'll call the police! *The police!*"

Eloise Peck's indignation, hurt, female fury were surely sincere, like her hot gushing tears, yet even as she threw herself at her terrified fiancé, to rake his handsome face with her nails, she might have had the idea that this lurid event was but a "scene" of some kind; and that, like any glamorous heroine, she would be protected from actual harm. For hadn't that been her experience through life, as a child, a young girl, a married woman? And didn't such flamboyant emotion carry with it its own sanction?

So it was a total surprise that Christopher, who had always seemed so sweet-tempered, and so devoted a lover, should defend himself roughly

against her attack; gripping her wrists hard, and telling her to be still—
"Mrs. Peck, shut your mouth."

It was more of a surprise that Christopher's churlish brother, face
swollen and discolored, narrowed eyes glistening like acid, should turn
upon her a look of sheer loathing . . . in which no particle of sympathy,
or respect, or alarm for her threats could be discerned; and that, with
no more than a moment's hesitation, and silently, he should wrench
her from his brother, and press his hard gritty hand against her mouth
to stifle her screams—"You heard him, lady. *Shut your mouth.*"

So they struggled. Mrs. Peck and the brute Harwood Licht. A table
was overturned, a porcelain lamp smashed, the crystal chandelier swaying, the very walls swaying, a ruffian's hand pressed so tight against her
face, she was in danger of suffocating. Why, was he murdering her?—
the beast murdering her?—as, frenzied as a wildcat, she jabbed at her
assailant with her elbows, tried to claw his face, butted at his head with
her own.

How degrading!—how preposterous! Eloise Peck, only partly dressed,
hair disheveled, rouge with its subtle silver base streaking her teary
cheeks, grappling with a stranger who threatened, dear God, *to wring
her neck!*—while Christopher, sweet Christopher, her Christopher whom
she had loved with such passion, tried to wrench him away, crying in a
child's voice, "Harwood, no. Harwood. Harwood. *No.*"

But within five seconds Mrs. Peck's neck was snapped: she was to die,
within minutes, an excruciatingly painful death.

X

The woman fell heavily to the floor, her silky emerald-green dressing
gown undone, revealing a soft, flaccid skin of the hue of curdled cream.
For several seconds there was silence except for the brothers' labored
breathing and, in a room close by, a sound of—weeping?—laughter?—
childish high-pitched prattle?

Harwood's blood-threaded eyes snatched in panic at Thurston's; but
before he could speak, Thurston said simply, in a voice of infinite resignation and contempt: "*Dogs.*"

XI

While Harwood moves about the room plundering what he can find that can be shoved into his pockets, daring even to venture into the adjoining boudoir in search of cash, Thurston, once "Christopher Schoenlicht," kneels beside the dead woman, staring.

Thurston whispers, ". . . This hasn't happened."

Thurston whispers, a sob in his throat, ". . . This can't have happened."

Harwood returns, impatient, panting, giving off a rank ripe fleshy odor of animal excitement; carelessly stuffing jewelry (a pearl necklace, a sapphire-and-diamond choker, a handful of rings) into his pockets, and pawing through a wad of bills . . . twenties, fifties, even several one-hundred-dollar bills.

Thurston doesn't respond as Harwood slaps him in the arm, tells him they must leave, must leave the hotel separately, by different doors, the woman is dead and isn't going to come back to life. . . .

Thurston says slowly, "Harwood. You *didn't* do this."

Harwood says quickly, "Did you?"

Harwood has cunningly dusted his face with the deceased woman's face powder, a peachy-beige hue, but has neglected to powder his neck, which is none too clean; he's grimacing to himself, grinning and frowning and muttering and licking his lips compulsively; dying for a drink; hastily knotting a silk paisley ascot tie (belonging to "Christopher Schoenlicht") around his neck; though completely sober now he sways like a drunken man, perceives that the walls of the room are a-tilt, laughs and, as he backs toward the door, tosses a handful of bills at his brother. Harwood's moist eyes glisten in panic that is also a kind of wisdom, for he knows that at last he has crossed over: he has committed a murder.

And what ecstasy in it, he'd never guessed: the need *to flee for his life*.

In Old Muirkirk

I

◆ ◆ ◆ The place that is haunted, the place that smells of sweetness and rot, the place where the marsh gas bubbles, the spider-trees lift themselves on their roots, the talons, the teeth, the shrieks, the rippling tawny snakes, the mayflies that brush against your face, the soft black wood teeming with ants, the eating, the gorging, the hollow trees gray with excrement, if you wander too far you will be sucked down, if you wander too far you will be drowned, your life will be sucked from you, do you think your breath is your own, do you think you can find your way back, don't listen to the singing, the voices, her voice, the shriek of the owl, the cry of the hare, the mayflies' droning, it is not singing but the voice of the woman at the bottom of the swamp, you must not heed her, you must not go to her, Katrina forbids it.

. . . the place of summer heat rising in waves, the stink of scummy green water, the puddles rich with Death, the wings and glittering eyes darting through the air, the place that has lured in children who have never returned, their bones ground down fine, their bright shining hair adrift in the marsh, their eyes sewn into the hides of snakes, their teeth given to the baby weasels, the baby foxes, that music? it is not music, it is the cries of the children, it is their souls caught in the roots of trees, in the roots of the lilies, in the soft black muck, waiting, waiting for you, waiting for you to drown, you must not heed their cries, you must not go to them, Katrina forbids it.

. . . the place where sunlight ages and withers to Night, the place where the trees are Night, beneath the sticky wet leaves there is Night, inside the silky cobwebs there is Night, the vines covered in babies' hair, the grasses, the whispering, the pondweed, the rain pelting like gunshot, the rising mists, the woman who walks in the mists, the woman who brushes her long hair in the mists, it is a tall white lily, it is a tall white poison lily, it is the Night brushing its hair, it is the Night singing, Katrina forbids you to listen, it is the place of pestilence, it is the place of lost children, the flies will cover your eyes if you go, the flies will fill your mouth and crawl up your nostrils and eat out your skull if you go, Katrina knows, Katrina has seen the doe gutted of her baby, the torn belly, the grass trampled in blood, Katrina has heard the cries of the children, Katrina knows the woman's trickery, Katrina knows.

. . . the place of hunger, the place of feeding, the place of quick-jabbing beaks, the talons, the sticky tendrils, the tiny sucking mouths, the mosquitoes ruby-bright with blood, the leeches swollen with blood, the gassy bubbles, the rot, the stench, the pale brown speckled eggs smashed and licked clean, the fruit you must not eat, the delicious black fruit you must not eat, if you bite into it the hot black juice will burn your mouth, if you swallow it your throat will close, do you hear the sound of drinking, do you hear the sound of lapping, it is the sound of terrible thirst, it is the sound of shame, you can't see its shape in the dark, you can't see her yellow eyes, her hair is twining in the trees, her feet have turned to roots, her song is hunger, her song is Night, do not listen, she has no name, it is only the steaming rain, the heavy pelting rain, the rain that turns to ice as it falls, Katrina has warned you.

. . . the place of fat green leaves, of slugs, puddles teeming with Death, tiny white worms, tiny white eyes, the place of yellow iris, Muirkirk violets, the hot rich smell of green, the dappled backs of snakes, do you think your breath is your own, do you think your thoughts are your own, the woman at the bottom of the pond is listening, that is the sound of her sorrow, that is the sound of Night, the larvae eating the leaves, the white cocoons being spun in secret, do you hear the soldiers' shouts, the soldiers' laughter, the gunfire, the screams, the flapping wings, the wild darting eyes, the bones sifting to ash, falling from the sky to melt in the swamp, to turn to vapor in the swamp, her voice is muffled in snow, her blood has frozen white, Katrina knows.

* * *

. . . the place of your father's blessing, the place that will be your father's grave, the teeming water in which he secretly bathes, the bubbling laughter that runs down his chin, the grasses, the sickle moon floating in the marsh, the cries of summer insects, whose name? whose name? it is not your name, it is not your music, it is Night, it is Death, it is the sound of the woman in the mist, her hair twining in the trees, her feet tangled in the roots, it is the sound of the woman at the bottom of the swamp, you must not heed her, you must not go to her, Katrina loves you and Katrina forbids it.

II

Esopus, the lost village.

Settled in 1642 on the curve of the river where Muirkirk now stands. A small Dutch outpost of approximately seventy-five men and women who made their way upriver, from the more populous settlements south of the Chautauquas. According to one Claes van Hasbroeck, who kept a personal daybook, in addition to filing systematic and meticulous reports for the Dutch West India Company through the 1640's, when agents for the Company explored the area of Tahawaus Pass, above the great Nautauga River, it was discovered in 1647 that the little settlement of Esopus no longer existed. All traces of it had vanished from the river's bank: no houses, or farming plots, or human artifacts, *or even any graves*, were to be found. The wilderness had not entirely grown back, a clearing of sorts remained, though overrun with vegetation at its edges.

In his daybook Claes van Hasbroeck asks eloquently what had become of the brave settlers of Esopus: had they been killed by Indians, or sickness, or a bitterly cold winter; had they been frightened away into the wilderness to die; had their God simply abandoned them in this remote spot? But why did no human artifacts remain, no sign of human habitation?

So it happened that Esopus vanished; and vanished yet a second time in memory; for this was the heady era in which Dutch adventurers were intrigued by the prospect of "prodigious" and "fathomless" copper mines in the more southerly part of New Netherlands; and Esopus was soon forgotten, a mere notation, a curiosity in the historical records of the time.

Robin, the miller's youngest son, was treated cruelly by his father, and mocked by his three older brothers, and, as his mother had died, and there was no one to love him for his quiet ways, he said to himself, I will leave home and live alone in the marsh. And off he went afoot to the edge of the marsh, and for an hour or more pondered how to proceed; for many a luckless wanderer had died in this place, lured by the beauty of the smooth waters, and the swamp flowers, and the great trees, and the shimmering birds and butterflies that dwelled there. Until finally a snowy white bird approached, of the size of a swan, yet possessed of long legs and a long sharp beak, and the bird asked of him where he meant to go, and Robin told him, and the bird flew off to lead him to firm ground, by which he could hurry across, into the depths of the marsh; and he was cunning enough to disguise his path behind him, so that no one could follow to bring him back home.

For three days and three nights he wandered in the marsh, seeing many wondrous sights, and, on the fourth day, he saw an old woman walking in the mist, with white hair, and white skin, and white lace on her head; and carrying in her hand a tall white candle. To Robin the old woman was young and beautiful, so he followed without hesitation when she led him to her home in the marsh, to give him food and shelter. The old woman said, Am I to be your bride, dear Robin? and Robin answered at once, Am I to be your bridegroom? for he had fallen in love, and took no note of her strange hooded eyes, and long curving fingernails, and fine-wrinkled skin like the striations on ice; nor did he see that her dwelling place at the heart of the marsh was dank and cold, for to him it was warm, with a glowing fire, and polished floorboards, and smelled of rich heated broth. So it was, Robin the miller's son became the old woman's husband, and wanted never to leave her side.

One day it happened that his brothers sought him out, for his father was old and ailing, and wanted his youngest son by his side. Like Robin they were perplexed as to how to enter the marsh, for they knew of the many wanderers who had died there; until the great white bird flew to them, and asked of them whom they sought, and did they mean harm, and the brothers said only that they sought their dear brother Robin, and meant no harm. So the bird spread his wide wings and led them to the place where Robin had crossed over, and which he had so cunningly disguised. And like Robin they wandered for three days and three nights, and on the fourth day they came upon the old woman's dwelling-place at the very heart of the marsh; and saw to their astonishment that their brother was the loving husband of an old woman, known as the White Witch of the Marsh. How is it possible, they asked, that Robin has wed her, and that he sleeps by the fireside oblivious of her evil?

As there was no way to break the enchantment save to kill the witch, Robin's brothers rushed into the house, and fell upon her at once, with no warning; striking her to the heart with their sharp knives, and killing her; and rousing poor Robin from his slumber. He struggled with them as if they were enemies, crying, Why have you killed my young bride?—for there is no one so beautiful in all the land. His brothers overcame him, and threw him down; and explained that the White Witch of the Marsh was not young and beautiful as he believed, but an old wicked woman. In scorn they showed him her corpse that he might see her white hair, and her white wrinkled skin, and the talons that grew from her fingers; yet Robin in his enchantment continued to lament the loss of his bride; and begged his brothers that they strike him to the heart as well.

Against his will, and in great sorrow, Robin was brought out of the marsh by his brothers, and restored at last to his father, who was lying on his deathbed. Seeing how he had wronged his youngest son, the miller gave him his blessing, and instructed him that the mill was henceforth to be his, and his brothers merely his assistants; and that there was a young maiden who lived close by, whom he should marry within a year. These matters Robin complied with, as his soul was shrouded in mourning, and he cared not what the remainder of his life must be.

Though Robin's bride was fair, she never conceived a child; and Robin the miller was known through the Valley for the iciness of his touch, and the frost-glitter of his skin, and the fact that, despite the modest riches he accumulated, he had no care for worldly matters, nor any wishes, it seemed, of his own.

Once, long ago, in Old Muirkirk, in the last years of English rule, the Crown Governor Sir Charles Harwood had a beloved daughter he named Mina, who was dearer to him than anyone else on earth. So comely, and graceful, and gay was Mina Harwood, very few persons held it against her that she was the Governor's daughter, and inclined at times to pride; or that, as a result of her playfulness, one could not always judge whether she spoke in earnest or in jest.

If Sir Charles or his wife approached Mina with the kindly intention of wiping away her tears, she surprised them with a bright smile, and the admonition that they took too seriously what was but a whim; if they, or Mina's fiancé, or one or another of her cousins, dared to smile at her outbursts, she charged them with cruelty, and not caring to know what was in her heart. Even as a child Mina threatened those who loved her with running away, as she called it, to her true home, but no one understood what she meant by these strange words; nor could Mina herself explain. *Where was her true home, if not in Muirkirk?*

One midsummer day when Mina was eighteen years old, she and her fiancé and a small party of friends went picnicking on the riverbank, in the vicinity of the great Muirkirk marsh; and somehow it came about that Mina wandered off, being nettled, it was thought, by an inadvertent slight on the part of her fiancé . . . and disappeared for hours. Her friends called out her name, and searched for her, to no avail; not knowing if the headstrong young girl had lost herself in the marsh, or whether in a pique of childish temper she was simply hiding in order to frighten them.

Finally Mina returned, appearing suddenly out of nowhere, flush-faced and smiling, saying in a chiding voice, "Why are you looking at me so strangely?—don't you know your Mina?" If she had truly been hurt by a stray word or gesture of her fiancé's, she now forgave the distraught young man (who indeed adored her); her arms were filled with things for her friends—violets, swamp lilies, purple lobelia, a strange pulpy fruit (of the size of a large apple, but a dark orangish-purple in hue, and disagreeably soft to the touch), which she pressed gaily upon them. For the remainder of the afternoon, and, indeed, for days afterward, Mina prattled with delight of the "secret wonders" of the great marsh. How unjust it seemed to her, that the swampland was feared and loathed, when it was a place of such exquisite beauty. . . . From childhood on Mina had heard ugly things whispered of the Muirkirk swamp: that it bred pestilence; that it was a place where unwed mothers might dispose of their infants; that, in former times, it had been the ceremonial ground for unspeakable tortures and executions practiced by the Mohawk Indians. But all she had glimpsed were wonders, like the flowers and fruit she had brought back, and the tall straight leafy trees she had seen (so very tall, Mina claimed, their tops were obscured in cloud), and the black and gold butterflies large as a man's fist (in whose delicate wings glinted "eyes" of a sort), and the nameless birds whose songs were infinitely sweeter than any she had ever heard (a bird the size of a sparrow, but beautifully marked in crimson, gold, and blue, had perched on her forefinger, Mina claimed, and had showed no fear of her), and many another remarkable sight. . . . She had been able to walk on the surface of the plankton-encrusted water, she said, for a brief distance, a most uncanny sensation indeed, as if for her, *and for her, Mina Harwood alone,* the laws of Nature had been overturned.

(Of the persons who had eaten the dark pulpy fruit, including Sir Charles and his wife, all reported disagreeable symptoms, vomiting, malaise, loss of appetite, which Mina dismissed with a wave of her hand, insisting that the fruit was a secret "love fruit" whose juice would have a beneficial effect upon them, in time.)

Weeks passed. It was observed that Sir Charles's daughter wasn't wholly herself: for she either shrank from the touch of those she loved, or pressed herself too anxiously upon them; her manner was often arch and strained, and feverish; too relentlessly merry. She quarreled with her fiancé over trifles, and declared tearfully that she would never marry him, or any man. Who was there, she asked boldly, in *this* world, fit to be her bridegroom? Though Mina was no less beautiful than ever, her beauty was of a wild, unsettling sort: her long dark hair was snarled and matted and smelled of brackish water; her skin was damp, clammy, very pale, like the skin of a certain species of swamp mushroom; her eyes had faded to a silvery-pale lustre in which the pupils were tiny pinpricks; even her fingers were white and puckered, as if resting too long in water. . . .

Is this my daughter? or a changeling? Mina's mother thought one day, as the girl spoke in her bright, gay, oblivious manner, for wasn't there something in the cast of her eye? the quirk of an eyebrow? a momentary frown that caused her entire smooth face to be encased in ghost-wrinkles?—as if an elderly female face were beneath, cunningly hidden. Yet in the next instant, Mina laughed, and became herself again. "Why do you look so grave, Mother?" She took up Mrs. Harwood's warm hands in her own cool ones, and squeezed them reproachfully. "*I* am here, after all."

More disturbingly, Mina began to behave coquettishly with nearly every man she encountered, including the minister, the elderly bishop, the chief justice and the lieutenant governor, and most disagreeable of all, Sir Charles himself!—as if an animal wildness were stoked in her by the mere presence of a man. At first this behavior was supposed harmless enough, if disconcerting; then it began to be whispered of the girl that she sought out even servants, and cajoled them into meeting with her at night; that she'd gone so far as to "give herself" to several young men in her social circle—yet not, out of sheer wantonness, to her fiancé, whose very touch Mina now claimed to abhor. By one or another mannerism she was perpetually drawing attention to her physical being, and didn't hesitate, even in public, to yawn with her pretty mouth open, revealing a shocking moist redness like the interior of a snake's mouth; nor did she hesitate, in the most innocent of conversations, to give to ordinary words a lewd color by an insinuation of her voice or a suggestive movement of her body. Then again, only a while later the Mina of old would reappear, sweet, vivacious, playful in a childlike way, and perplexed that her family should regard her with such unease . . . as if this Mina didn't comprehend what the "other" Mina was about, or even that she existed. Or what disturbance she was wreaking not only in the Harwood household but through the small community.

"Why are you all looking at me so strangely?" Mina frequently asked, with a baffled, hurt smile. "Don't you know your own Mina?"

At last, in early winter, it was discovered that Mina was with child.

In fact, several months with child. So cleverly had the young woman kept her secret from even her mother.

This revelation rocked the household, and threw all the Harwoods into grief; except the guilty Mina herself, who owned the fact with an astonishing arrogance, as if it were no more than a child's prank at which she'd been caught. "Why, you are all very silly," she told her family, who stared at her appalled, "to suppose that Nature can be guided according to your narrow wishes." And she laughed, showing the moist red interior of her mouth.

From time to time, over the weeks, Mina did seem to repent, shutting herself away in her room; then, haughtily wiping away her tears, she insisted upon coming downstairs as if nothing were wrong; or, rather, as if the Harwoods were at fault with their attitude of despair and anger over her. Of course, Mina was questioned repeatedly about the child's father, and always claimed with a cool smile that the partner of her "sweet sin" was—why, someone very close; well known to the Harwoods; perhaps even a member "of austere reputation" of the Harwood household.

Quickly it was whispered through the Colony that Sir Charles's beautiful daughter Mina was with child, and unrepentant; that the father was rumored to be a man of her own social set (yet not, perversely, her fiancé—on that score, everyone was agreed); unless it was a servant of the Harwoods (the lowest caste of whom were indentured Irishmen known for their promiscuous ways); even a Negro slave, or an Indian; or (it began to be whispered) an emissary of the very Devil. What was most remarkable was that Mina appeared to be drawing strength from the heartbreak and disorder she provoked on all sides; even as her father languished in ill health, the despoiled young woman thrived. Her cheeks were full and flushed, her silvery eyes unnaturally bright. Where the delicate Mina of old had had to be coaxed into eating properly, this Mina now devoured everything placed before her with appetite; playfully ate off others' plates; laughingly commented that it seemed, overnight, her "physical being" had become a fathomless pit which it fell to her to fill.

Stubbornly, Mina refused to name the father of her child. No matter if Sir Charles angrily locked her away, or allowed her a measure of freedom as a kind of bribe; no matter if Sir Charles denounced her, or pleaded with her, or prayed for her, or refused to speak of her. As her pregnancy progressed, and her belly grew more and more swollen, Mina pouted that so much was made of it, and that she was being persecuted. "Why, when it's only Nature?—when 'Mina,' like any of you, is only Nature?" At times, strangely, she seemed to awaken to the enormity of her sin . . . struck dumb with shock and grief when she hid herself away to pray on her knees, begging God for help. In one of these queer repentant states Mina told her mother that she should be banished at once—driven into the wilderness—wrists and ankles bound and her sinful body thrown into the swamp; yet, within an hour, the other Mina returned with greater vehemence, screwing up her hardened face in scorn, that fools should have taken her "silly remarks" seriously.

Mina began to hint that, when her baby was born, she would hand it over to the father, for the secret would be immediately revealed. "Everyone will see, at once, seeing *it*." And again she laughed, her cruel cutting laugh.

Yet the outcome of the mystery was to be, tauntingly, *no outcome, no resolution*; for on the eve of giving birth (as her physician calculated) Mina slipped away from the Governor's mansion high above the river, and fled alone, or with an accomplice, never to be seen again in all of the Chautauqua Valley.

For a long moment the children were silent, rapt with listening. Millie, Darian, and six-year-old Esther. Then, in a sudden temper, as if old Katrina had willfully deceived them, Millie cried, Why Katrina, that's no proper story, I hate that story! (For though Millie was now seventeen, almost grown, and had been told the tale of the Crown Governor's daughter a hundred times since she'd been a baby, her excitable nature was such that she never failed to anticipate an ending, a real ending. The ending that must have been.)

But Katrina, offended, rose with dignity from her chair beside the hearth, and wrapped her warm-knit shawl about her thin shoulders, and said, in her typically enigmatic way, leaving Millie, Darian and little Esther to puzzle over her words among themselves, It is hardly your privilege to hate any such story, miss—as if you were not a Licht, and that fated girl's blood your own.

"In Adam's Fall . . ."

In the village of Muirkirk few indisputable facts were known of Abraham Licht and his mysterious family (if "family" they were, indeed); but, beginning with that autumn day in 1891 when Abraham Licht first appeared, on horseback, to make his unexpected bid at the auction of the Church of the Nazarene, so many theories were aired, debated and sifted through and promoted as truth, hardly an inhabitant of the region was without an opinion.

(Some even argued that the dashing Mr. Licht *reappeared* in Muirkirk that day. That he was in fact a native of the countryside, born there, returning home after years of absence.)

So many tales told of Abraham Licht: so many fancies spun of his women, his children, his "profession"—!

For instance:

He had a wife named *Arabella*, mother of his two eldest sons (discounting his dark-skinned son Elisha, whose mother was unknown); he had a wife named *Myra*, or *Morna*, whom no one in Muirkirk ever spoke with except Dr. Deerfield, who delivered her of an infant girl in the summer of 1892; he had a wife named *Sophie*, delicate, blond, withdrawn, the mother of the youngest son Darian and of little Esther, whom Dr. Deerfield delivered in March 1903. (And what of these fated women? Arabella disappeared from Muirkirk and was never seen again, abandoning her sons to their father; Myra, or Morna, disappeared from Muirkirk and was never seen again, abandoning her little girl to her father; poor Sophie died of childbed fever within two weeks of her baby girl's birth and was buried by a distraught Abraham Licht in the old churchyard behind the rectory in which the family lived.)

Of course, the most speculation centered upon dark-skinned Elisha. Who was the boy's mother?—was Abraham Licht truly his father? For here was a Negro boy who behaved as if he was "white"—who behaved, indeed, as if he were of royal blood, arrogant and "uppity" like no other Negro the inhabitants of Muirkirk had ever glimpsed. Mr. Carr, the banker with whom Licht dealt, claimed that Licht had once indicated that Elisha was a "valet" of his whom he would "trust with his life"— and with sums of cash. Reverend Woodcock, the Methodist minister who tutored Darian and Esther, and taught Darian to play the foot-pedal organ, was convinced that Elisha was a foundling, an orphan, brought home by Abraham Licht as an act of Christian charity; for Darian claimed that "my brother Elisha" was born in a storm and a flood "on a great river thousands of miles away." If the dark-skinned boy grew to resemble Abraham Licht by adolescence, it was less a matter of physical appearance (for Elisha had distinct Negroid features: a smooth mahogany-dark skin, very dark thick-lashed eyes, wide nostrils, an upper lip thick and broad as the lower) than of the acquired: as Abraham

Licht was accustomed to walking briskly in all weather, with a military bearing, head high, so was young Elisha; as Abraham Licht smiled happily, and brightened, whenever he caught sight of another person, like an actor striding out on stage to confront his audience, so too did young Elisha; as Abraham Licht was always impeccably groomed and stylishly dressed, exuding an aura of virile self-assurance, so with young Elisha.

Despite the fact that the boy was after all *black*; which is to say, *not-white*.

Fortunately, Elisha Licht was rarely glimpsed in Muirkirk, now that he'd grown up. For years it was believed the youth was "away at college" somewhere in Massachusetts. When he returned, it was for brief periods, sometimes no more than a week, so that his cocky airs couldn't cause much harm; and if he was entrusted with business errands in the village, making a deposit at the First Bank of the Chautauqua, for instance, or paying Reverend Woodcock his fee for the children's lessons, or spending within an hour $500 at the saddlery in a purchase "for Mr. Licht"—the handsome youth was so charming, so well-spoken and congenial, even the most rabid Negro-haters felt compelled to comment, in his wake, "Elisha Licht *is* different."

Except: there was one occasion, about eighteen months before the time of this narrative, when Elisha and his white brothers Thurston and Harwood were observed at the Sign of the Ram, a popular tavern on the Innisfail Pike, drinking ale together at the bar, talking earnestly, laughing loudly, seeming oblivious of the attention they drew; and in response to a remark made to him by a fellow drinker, apparently in reference to his racial ancestry or the color of his skin, Elisha flashed his dazzling Licht-smile and said, "True, my skin is *black*; and my soul— well, in fact, *my soul is black as well.*"

Since the gentleman who called himself Abraham Licht had bought the abandoned property belonging to the Church of the Nazarene in 1891, there were periods of time when he not only indicated he'd retired permanently to the countryside ("So blessed an atmosphere," he told his neighbors, "—set beside the polluted city") but gave every sign, by his zeal in becoming acquainted with Muirkirk's most influential citizens, that he planned a local career of some sort, probably in politics. So congenial was Abraham Licht, so animated and well-spoken, both Republicans and Democrats (a minority in the Chautauquas) believed he would surely go far, if he wished. But then, with no warning, Licht would break his connections by vanishing from Muirkirk for months at a stretch. Some of his family he left behind, and others he took with him; but never in any pattern that his neighbors could discern. And when he returned, he often made no effort to reestablish his old connections, as if he'd forgotten them.

What was more curious, when Licht reappeared he often looked subtly changed: having gained or lost weight; having grown a beard, or having shaved one off; now older, or more youthful; now in robust good health, or slightly sickly; and so forth. Sometimes Licht dressed in the very height of fashion, and sometimes with the austere plainness of a well-to-do Quaker businessman. Sometimes he drove a handsome new motorcar, sometimes an old Selden buggy, sometimes he rode on horseback, exposed to the elements like a figure out of a Wild West illustrated tale. Always, he was triumphantly *himself* and could never be mistaken, as observers said, part admiringly and part critically, for anyone else.

How many children has Abraham Licht?— was a question frequently posed in Muirkirk, in the bemused tone of a riddle. And what was the man's relationship with the old woman Katrina who had long managed his household?

Over the years, so many were the comings and goings in the Licht household, it was claimed that Abraham had ten or eleven children. Then again, it seemed he might have as few as four. By the summer of '09, a consensus was reached that there were six young people in his household, no more and no less. These were Thurston, the eldest (blond and fair-skinned as a Viking, grown taller than his father); Harwood, who was two or three years younger than Thurston (stocky, muscular, with hair the color of ditch water, of middling height); the enigmatic Elisha (believed to be about twenty years old); Millicent, or Millie, seventeen years old (as fair as Thurston, with a delicate, porcelain beauty and striking bluish-gray eyes); and the younger children, who never left Muirkirk—Darian, who was nine, and gifted musically; and Esther, who was six.

And what of Katrina? It was she who shopped in Muirkirk, and she whom tradesmen and other women knew. A formidable presence, in her mid-sixties, fierce-eyed and dignified, a woman who spoke with a distinct German accent and who wore her pewter-colored hair in braids like a helmet. "Yesss thank you"—"Nooo thank you"—"That is enough thank you": so Katrina spoke, when obliged to speak, rarely smiling at anyone outside the family, even shopkeepers with whom she'd dealt for years. Generally it was believed that Katrina was Abraham Licht's housekeeper (though entrusted by him with much autonomy in his absence) but there were those who believed, or out of mischief claimed to believe, that Katrina was *Abraham Licht's own mother.*

And what was Abraham Licht's business, or profession? How did he support himself and his family, seemingly so well?

It had long been a matter of curiosity that a gentleman of Abraham Licht's self-evident talents and background should wish to bury himself away in a remote corner of the Chautauqua Valley, at the edge of a marsh; and to make a home for himself and his attractive children in an abandoned stone church of all places. (This had been the church of the evangelical Nazarenes whose faith had died out in Muirkirk decades ago. The Church of the Nazarene, however, whose original foundation dated back to 1851, was no ordinary clapboard country church but was built of irregularly matched fieldstone, stucco and untreated timber; it had a steep roof at the peak of which was a crude, dignified stone cross; its windows were tall and narrow; its rectory consisted of four small rooms; to the rear was a churchyard of weatherworn gravestones and markers, long allowed to grow wild. The main interior of the church was plain, spartan, of "Protestant chill" as Abraham Licht described it: twelve oak pews, a pulpit of modest proportions, a foot-pedal organ, a carved hickory cross that was imposing though but three feet in height. This interior was more spectral and aqueous than holy, as a result of the atmosphere, laden with moisture from the swamp close by.) Over the years Abraham Licht had greatly improved the property, expanding the building at the rear, creating sizable living quarters adjoining the rectory, adding a stable, and the like. *But why sink cash into such a property, why not buy a new house?—invest in more valuable land, in a more prestigious part of the Valley?* Such questions, common in Muirkirk, were never addressed to Licht himself.

Because of this eccentricity it was vaguely believed that Abraham Licht must be a defrocked minister, possibly of an evangelical sect. For there were occasions when the public tone of his personality suddenly changed; even his voice, so rich, deep and self-assured, grew somber. He might allude to pessimistic passages of what he called the Hebrew Bible ("And what is that, Mr. Licht? Do you mean the 'Old Testament'?" he was asked in genuine bafflement), particularly the teachings of the prophet Ecclesiastes; he murmured such Latin expressions (*vae victis, tempus fugit, caveat emptor, fiat justitia, ruat caelum*) that seemed to signify an immense sorrow tinged with anger. Speaking with Reverend Woodcock in the Methodist minister's office, Abraham Licht was likely to make reference to one or another of the Church Fathers, American Puritan preachers like Cotton and Increase Mather, and to quote, in a tone of seeming sincerity:

*"In Adam's fall
    we sinneth all."*

Reverend Woodcock would then counter by saying that such a pessimistic vision had been modified by the sacrifice of Jesus Christ, surely; the New Testament had modified, if not entirely erased, the dour claims of the Old; just as the New World of North America had surged far in advance of the Old World of Europe. "Our Savior entered history to alter it," the soft-spoken yet impassioned Woodcock insisted, "and bring us the 'good news' of salvation." Abraham Licht would murmur, staring at the older man's face as if he hoped there to see the promise of his own redemption, "Ah, *did* He! *Is that it!*"

More worldly Muirkirk citizens were scornful of the mere idea that Abraham Licht, one of their own kind, might have once been a minister! Instead, Licht had obviously been a man of the world, possibly an actor; trained in the classics, and most of all Shakespeare; possibly he was an actor at the present time who for reasons of privacy hid away periodically in the country incognito. For on the dreariest midwinter day when the sky above the Chautauqua Valley glowered a soulless white like dirty snow, and all of Earth seemed flat and stale, didn't Licht carry himself with the arrogant self-confidence of a Hamlet, an Othello, a Lear?—wasn't his broad, handsome face flushed with good health as if illuminated by footlights? Didn't he seem, pausing after certain of his remarks, *to be awaiting applause?*

And there was mysterious Elisha (valet, adoptive son, bastard son!) with the bearing and personality of an actor too, like P. T. Barnum's famous Master Diamond, who'd been the most celebrated Negro performer of his day. And there was pretty, volatile Millicent with the airs and fetching, if unpredictable, ways of a Broadway ingenue. The wife of the owner of the *Muirkirk Journal*, who loved opera and traveled by train to New York City expressly to attend openings at the Met, claimed that Abraham Licht had "obviously been trained in opera": for it happened that one fine June day when she was working in her rose garden in Muirkirk, imagining herself alone and singing a few bars of *Tannhäuser*'s Venus in her bower, she was answered by a rich baritone voice out of the very air!—the rogue Tannhäuser himself stealing up behind her with hands clasped in mock gallantry, eyes bright with pleasure, in the guise of Abraham Licht.

And it didn't go unremarked how musically gifted the child Darian was. At the age of four, this amazing little boy with his father's dark, brightly alert eyes was already composing melodies in his head, and he'd learned to play both the piano and the organ, so far as his small hands allowed him, by the age of eight. "A prodigy"—as Reverend Woodcock called him.

But other observers scoffed at the notion that Abraham Licht had ever been a "mere actor . . . entertainer." A certain sobriety in his manner, his forceful personality and his habit of seemingly firsthand war reminiscences (one of his favorite subjects was the recent War with Spain and the "filthy little war" with the heathen Filipinos) argued that he was obviously an ex-military man, of officer status. Yet if questioned closely, Licht grew evasive and changed the subject; which led a contingent of Muirkirk veterans, the oldest of whom had fought for the Union in the War Between the States, to suspect the man of having been dishonorably discharged from the Army, or a deserter. ("For what ex-military man will deny his past except if there is something in it to shame him?"—so their reasoning went.)

Dr. Deerfield, the only Muirkirk resident to have ever set foot in the mysterious Licht household, disagreed with all these theories, insisting that Abraham was some sort of collector or dealer of antiques of all kinds: furniture, arts and crafts, clothing, costumes, aged books and maps. Though Deerfield had seen little of the Licht residence apart from the room in which Abraham's wife Sophie was bedridden, he'd had a distinct impression of a household crammed with odd, miscellaneous items—"Some of them fairly ugly, in my opinion. But then, what do I, a country doctor, know about 'antiques' and 'objets d'art'?"

But there was the opinion of Edgar Carr, president of Muirkirk's First Bank of Chautauqua, who, claiming to know firsthand of Abraham Licht's "wildly fluctuating" finances, believed that the man was either a professional gambler (his specialty Thoroughbred racing) or one of the notorious new breed of Wall Street speculators, capable of making, and losing, and again recouping, hundreds of thousands of dollars in a day's trading, by abstruse manipulations Carr himself could not fathom. Such gentlemen, Carr said, were spiritually descended from the "dark geniuses" of Jay Gould, Lord Gordon-Gordon and their brethren— individuals we can't help but admire yet would never wish to do business with.

"Depend upon it," Carr would say, with a wink, "—Abraham Licht is first and foremost an American capitalist, whatever his self-definition, his product or his services! He worships one thing, and one thing only: *money.*"

The Pilgrim

The tragic history of the Church of the Nazarene, Risen (for such was the sect's full name), had much to do, all of Muirkirk agreed, with the unwholesomeness of its setting: for, unwisely tempted by the cheapness of land bordering the Muirkirk swamp, the sect's young minister decided to erect his church building on a dirt road a quarter mile off the Innisfail Pike, scarcely more than a rutted cattle trail at the time; and so very near the marsh, residents of the area joked that the church was *in* it.

The life span of the church was approximately nine years, counting the two years it took to complete the building, during which time the minister and his family, and any number of his followers, were laid low by so many flus, fevers, bone-aches, malaises, and the like, that it seemed to some that God Himself was putting their faith to the test (as, indeed, He had put Job's, to Job's great glory); yet to others, that Satan dwelt near, and resented any incursion upon His domain. For, in late spring, and continuing well through October, a sickly sort of atmosphere pervaded the church buildings, a tropical, damp, lugubrious air that seemed very nearly visible, and tactile, a wild commingling of odors, rich, rank-smelling pollen, and animal decay, and brackish water, and gases of a feculent nature, all wafted sluggishly about, and weighed down, it seemed, by an unnatural heat that had the power to attach itself to human flesh.

"But God has set us down in the wilderness, to conquer, and to thrive"—so the impassioned young minister preached, in the very face of any number of afflictions.

Despite his faith, however, and that of his followers, God showed, it seemed, very little mercy for the Church of the Nazarene, Risen: for the building was beset by dry rot, and mildew, and beetles, and termites, and slugs, and leakage, and that sickly oppressive malaise of the air; wind-funnels tore at its roof, and floods destroyed its floors; poisonous snakes invaded the rectory; the well was contaminated by seepage from the cemetery; the congregation dwindled from sixty members, to forty-five, to thirty, to ten. . . . At last, in the summer of '90, the minister himself succumbed to a virulent strain of influenza, and died, it was said, an agèd man though not yet forty; deranged, and raving, and cursing God. For had not God betrayed His Covenant, in this accursed corner of the world?

The Church of the Nazarene, Risen, was therefore declared in bankruptcy; and given over to its numerous creditors, land, buildings, and fixtures, to be sold at public auction as quickly as possible.

At which time, on a warm October afternoon, a small crowd of less than thirty men gathered, as much out of curiosity and idleness as interest; for it was thought unlikely that anyone in Muirkirk, knowing the church's history, should wish to make a bid on it. Lichen thickly encrusted the stone, the roof shone emerald-green with patches of mossy rot, puddles of brackish water lay on the floorboards; large white cocoons damp with spittle had been spun about the hickory cross, repulsive to see. On all sides the air was aqueous and unmoving, as if concentrated in thought: yet what might such a *thought* be!—and *who*, or *what*, empowered it!

No sooner had the spiritless bidding begun on one or another portable item, a three-legged stool, a water-stained hymnal, a canopied baby carriage, than a dashing young man, a stranger, appeared on horseback, at a gallop; astonishing the gathering by declaring, in a ringing, breathless voice, that he was making a bid for the entire property—"I offer you eighteen hundred dollars cash."

Which sum was held to be in such excess of the damnèd property's worth, no one would have cared to challenge it.

And so, by a miracle, within the space of twenty minutes, the Church of the Nazarene, Risen, buildings, fixtures, land, was sold to the highest bidder: one "Abraham Licht," resident at that time of Vanderpoel.

True to his word, the gentleman paid in cash. One-hundred-dollar bills, that seemed to staring observers far larger in size than any American minted bills they had ever seen, yet were, as a banking official declared, wholly legitimate.

Abraham Licht smilingly described his profession as "land speculator."

What an amiable, attractive young man, broad-shouldered and in excellent physical condition, like a soldier, or an athlete, or an actor; probably not more than thirty-one or -two years old, but with a mature, reassuring manner. Licht stood slightly above six feet in height, yet seemed taller; with thick wiry lustrous hair, a mahogany-brown threaded with blond or silver; his shrewd, quick-darting, friendly eyes were described by some as brown, by others as black, by others as sky-blue. His cheeks were partly covered by precisely trimmed whiskers and moustache in the style of the late James G. Blaine, the "Plumed Knight" of Congress; what one could see of his jaws suggested strength, steeliness, resolution. His handshake was vigorous, if slightly cool; beneath his social poise, there was an air of excitement, or fevered strain; his fedora was cocked back on his head in a way that could be interpreted as casual, or careless; his dark gabardine "city clothes" were of a stylish cut but soiled from perspiration and the dusty effects of travel by horseback. Licht's horse was a deep-chested black gelding with a blade of white between his eyes, a beautiful specimen badly lathered from the run and no longer in the prime of life.

Why had Abraham Licht ridden out ninety miles from Vanderpoel to this unpublicized auction, why his particular interest in Muirkirk, a village at that time of less than two thousand inhabitants?—Licht answered all questions put to him frankly, with a guileless, friendly smile, yet afterward, everyone realized, he managed to answer none; and had only one urgent question to put to them: *Was the Church of the Nazarene, Risen, properly deconsecrated?*

The Forbidden

W ho is he, with the almighty eye, the voice of a bugle!—why does he pursue them!

They have clambered to the highest peak of the roof to escape— they are crouched behind the crumbling brick chimney where the starlings nest—now they will step off into space, now they must spread their wings and fly, fly to the top of the highest tree—

'Allo, 'allo, my little ones—'allo I say!

Who is he, has he only one eye, glassy and glaring, puckered in sunshine, and the other an empty socket (have the crows picked it out) hidden by a leathery black patch?—tramping after them, a giant, big booted feet, ivory-headed cane rapping rapping rapping, *'allo my little ones, 'allo my sweet little birdies,* bewhiskered and solemn, rubbery red lips, clenched white teeth, black riding coat bunched at the shoulders (is he a dwarf grown to the size of a giant, is he a troll dressed in a gentleman's costume), handsome black Western hat sloped low over his forehead, *'allo little birdies, where will ye fly, Old Sir Ebeneezer Snuff has y'r number, Old Sir Ebeneezer Snuff knows both y'r names, what-ho Master Darian, what-ho Mistress Esther, where will ye fly, my sweet little birdies, Old Ebeneezer Snuff sees all in Heaven, and Earth, and the Darksome Regions Beneath, with his one all-mighty eye!*

Has he only one eye, and the other picked clean by crows?

Is his voice, slicing the air, meant to hurt?

They have flown to the topmost branch of the oak tree to escape him—they have flown to the topmost branch of the tallest tree in the marsh—and now that ridge of cloud overhead, ribbed and shadowed, like steps, and they *are* steps, steps leading up—up and up into the sky—

But Old Ebeneezer is too quick, Old Ebeneezer scoops them up in his arms, snorting, clacking his teeth, did they think they might escape? did they think they might fly away into the sky? Old Ebeneezer gives them wet smacking whiskery kisses, *What-ho, Master Darian, what-ho, Mistress Esther,* squirming like eels, wild and frenzied and hot, shrieking with laughter, it isn't good for little Darian's jumpy heart (Katrina has warned), it isn't good for little Esther's delicate nerves (Katrina has warned, has warned), but this is Old Ebeneezer who loves them, Old Ebeneezer who adores them, *My sweet ones, my darlings, O my darlings I am home!*—and today the honor falls to Esther to peel away, with trembling fingers, the silly scratchy beard, the Distinguished Silver Goatee, and, ah! what a fit of giggling just to see the sudden clean-shaven chin, the familiar chin, big strong snapping jaws and clackety-clackety teeth, *Where did you think you might fly, sweethearts, where were you headed, my darlings?*—the hot tender kisses, the heated love, *O my darlings, I am home!*—the hat whipped from his head to sail, to sail where it would—the thick-waved hair scented with powder, whitish-silver dust (to make them sneeze)—and now it is Darian's privilege to peek beneath the eye patch, the terrifying black eye patch, to see at last if the socket is empty (but it cannot be empty), if the socket is picked clean (but it cannot be picked clean), and, ah!—what relief, what heartstopping joy, for of course Father's eye is there as always—Father's eye has been there (*must* have been there) all along—winking out now slyly, brightly, blindingly—

The children bucking about on Father's strong shoulders, Father's high, high shoulders—so high!—their heads brushing against the ceiling, their heads brushing against the sky, *My angels, my sweetest sweetest innocents, do you love your poor old Sir Snuff?*—the center of all the world, here. So long as Father is home.

(*But will you go away again?—Oh, never.*
And will you take me with you when you go?—Oh, never.)

And there are presents for all, of course there are presents, that is part of the reason, isn't it, for Father being away so long, so very long this time, March, April, May . . . well into June?

No matter. Father is home *now* and home is the center of all God's world *now*.

For Esther a pretty French doll with blue paperweight eyes, wood and papier-mâché body (a doll of high degree, boasts Father, signed by one "Jumeau, Paris 1883"); for Darian a shiny black-and-ivory harmonica which he can play within minutes; for Katrina, doubtful Katrina, a new coffee grinder, look here he'll unscrew the old and screw in the new, right here beside the sink, just at the height Katrina requires.

But there is more, of course there is more—

For Esther, sweet shy Esther, a pair of white eyelet gloves trimmed with embroidered violets; for Darian a glossy-covered songbook, *Gems from Erin, Book II*; for Katrina an enormous black silk umbrella with a carved ivory handle, look how it opens with an explosive *snap*—!

And, again for Darian, a "pocket sundial"; and for Esther a keepsake box (enamel, mother-of-pearl, chips of colored glass like demented winking eyes); and for Katrina a potpourri jar of wavy glass—which at last melts Katrina's mask of a face into a smile.

And we all applaud! Squeal, stamp our feet and applaud!

For Father is home *now* and it is time to be happy *now*.

(It's proper clothes and provisions we need, it's mending the roof we need, Katrina says, and Father says in an undertone, But Katrina you know I will provide, haven't I always provided, O Katrina we're rich again, rich as kings, don't fuss! And Katrina says, We've been rich before haven't we?—which is why I know enough to fuss.)

Where is Millie? the children ask.
Coming home soon, darlings: tomorrow! Father says.
Where is Elisha? the children ask.
Coming home soon, darlings: day after tomorrow! Father says.
And where is Thurston, where is Harwood—?
Soon, soon! A victory banquet, soon!

My darlings, my dear ones, what have I missed?
Father's white shirt open at the throat, Father's shirtsleeves rolled up

past his elbows, Father's cigar and the laughing expulsion of Father's
smoky breath, now it is time, it is time, it is time to explore the property, now it is time to examine everything anew, the garden that belongs to Katrina, the damage done by porcupines, the damage done in a
windstorm last month, spiky thistles everywhere amid the graves, briars
grown so high, so high, snails, slugs, the crumbling stone wall, the blue
heron and his mate at the edge of the pond, the owl's nest in the dead
tree, a wasp's nest under the eaves, the lichen encrusting the gravestones, Father is tall, a giant, his hat tilted back on his head, they cannot see where his restless eyes shift, they cannot hear his every word,
amid the graves, the old churchyard, Mother's grave, pausing to brush a
cobweb from the granite, pausing with cigar clenched between his
teeth, head bowed, eyes narrowed, Ah how he loved her! and promised
her never never to take *her* children away with him into the world!—as
Darian squats to pluck nervously at tiny weeds, as Esther burrows trembling against his trousered leg (knowing it is her fault, as cruel Katrina
has hinted, that Mother died and is buried here in the churchyard, she
must be blamed, all the world will one day blame her), the sudden expulsion of tobacco smoke, the angry sob, the abrupt alteration of mood,
Father hauling Darian to his feet, Father seizing Esther's frightened little hand, stepping high in the grass, marching, singing, swinging their
arms in their old noisy song—

"Tramp! Tramp! Tramp!
  The boys are marching!"

Father lays a finger alongside his nose, winks and confides in these,
his youngest children, his angel-children, certain secrets he would not
wish Katrina to overhear. *Children, the earth is owned by the dead! There
are many more dead than living, children! Count 'em up, children, should
you doubt your father!—count 'em up!—the earth is theirs, dear children
and, ah! the world is ours.* A vast breath, his chest deepening, swelling,
eyes grown bright, hard-muscled jaws relaxing finally in a smile.
  The world, dear children, is ours—so long as we claim it.
  So long as we have the courage, dear children, to claim it.

Later, Father's mood changes abruptly and he wants to be alone.
Wants to wander in the marsh, alone.

As always, alone.

(He has been quizzing them playfully yet seriously on their studies, posing little mathematical problems; listening with interest to Esther's singing, her thin wavering sweet little voice; listening to Darian playing a Mozart rondo on the organ, but more severely, snapping his fingers to scold when Darian's small hand fails to stretch an octave and a wrong key is struck—"Shame on you, son. When Amadeus Mozart was your age, he wasn't just playing music like that perfectly, *he was composing it.*" Disgusted now suddenly he's had enough of children, even angel-children, Sophie's darlings, he wants to be alone, to wander in the marsh alone, to vanish from their sight, to elude even Katrina's sharp possessive eye, to have no one trailing after him and adoring him calling him *Father.*)

It is forbidden to follow so of course heartsick Darian does not follow.

At the keyboard, left behind. Abandoned. A nine-year-old with a peaked narrow face, large glistening-brown eyes, a fluttery rheumatic heart. Slender fingers trailing over the yellowed ivory keys. The distinctly flat C above high C. The F-sharp that grates on the ear. Keys that stick in the humidity, keys that no longer sound, the crude pumping of the pedal, flies buzzing high overhead, trapped against the windows, the airless heat of the church interior, jammed with old furniture amid the pews, rolled-up carpets secured with baling wire, piles of aged leatherbound books with gilt titles . . . Music is Darian's solace, music is Darian's companion, the foot-pedal organ like the spinet piano is but a vehicle to render music audible; music which would otherwise exist solely in his head, yet how beautifully there, with what purity, precision; his small clumsy hands can't violate such music, such music can't be betrayed by any mortal failing. *I who have never lived will outlive you* the simple notes of the Mozart rondo promise, *in such is the highest happiness.* Though Darian is only nine years old, and small for his age, a "runt of an angel" Father has sometimes teased, he knows that this is so; and he is happy. As treble notes, bass notes, inverted scales, powerful chords range up and down the creaking keyboard. His hands moving with their own antic life. Their own volition, desire. The woman at the bottom of the marsh is singing, the woman at the bottom of the marsh is calling, the woman at the bottom of the marsh commands *Come to me! come to me! come to me!* he hears, he does not hear, his fluttery heart beats panicked as a bird trapped inside his ribs like those occasional birds trapped inside the church flinging themselves against the windows, but he hears nothing, he is responsible for nothing, he is not even responsible for his little sister whom he adores, like magic his fingers move where they will, as in one of Katrina's tales something will happen as it will, no one can stop it, no one can guide it, no one can predict it, how Darian's small aching hands leap and strike and frolic where they will, he hears the woman singing in the marsh and knows that Father has gone to her but it is forbidden for Darian to go to her, it is forbidden for him even to know of her, to have such intimacy of her, hunched as he is at the keyboard of the old organ in the Church of the Nazarene, Risen, in Darian Licht's long dream of childhood.

II

The cruelest dream is not Darian's alone. It is a dream of the household. A dream shared by all the children, in turn—that *Father has children elsewhere.*

And there will be a time (if they disappoint him, if they are clumsy, or slow, or cowardly) when he will not return to Muirkirk.

For hasn't Father hinted of such, himself?

For there is evidence: daguerreotypes, cameos and drawings of other children they have discovered . . . children like themselves, and children near-grown, and mere infants, swaddled in white, on their mothers' and nursemaids' knees. . . . Millicent once declared in her bright angry voice that it didn't matter who these children were, *they weren't Lichts.* Yet another time, on another day, examining a faded cameo she had discovered in a trunk of old clothes, the likeness of a child with eyes wistful and lovely as her own, curly blond ringlets as charming as her own, she said, sighing, "Oh, but suppose she *is* my sister, somewhere! And one day Father allows us to meet. . . ."

Elisha snatched the cameo from Millie's fingers and regarded it with a queer little smile, not quite derision and not quite sympathy. He said, "*This* girl is most likely dead and gone by now, how old do you think she'd *be* in real time—!"

(Elisha has said that nothing of Father's—nothing that is stored in the church, at least—belongs to "real time.")

But he is mistaken, isn't he?—for one of the oil portraits, the most beautiful portrait of all, is of Darian's and Esther's mother Sophie.

Father keeps the portrait hidden in a locked room at the very rear of the church, his "vault" as he calls it. He allows Darian and Esther to look at it only in his presence, perhaps he fears they will ruin its delicate cracking surface with their fingers, their furtive caresses. . . . When it is time, and only Father knows the correct time, he takes them into the secret room, he draws off the dusty velvet cloth with reverent fingers, crouching solemn and transfixed before the painting, Darian in the crook of his left arm, Esther in the crook of his right, Why, *is* this their mother! *Is* this poor Sophie, who lies buried now in the churchyard! Their eyes mist over with tears and at first they cannot see clearly. In the painting Sophie is alive again, as they cannot remember her, a girl again, no more than twenty years old; younger than Thurston and Harwood are now. As the artist has rendered her she is extremely handsome, with fair creamy skin, lustrous dark eyes, gleaming black hair pulled smartly away from her forehead; a small pensive smile playing about her lips; yet a mature, composed tilt to her head, an air of startling self-assurance. How easy to imagine that this woman, their mother, is gazing at *them*; she sees and recognizes *them*; that glisten of interest in her beautiful eyes is her love of *them*. Darian and Esther marvel that their mother has scorned to costume herself in the stiff, fussy clothes worn by other women portrayed in other paintings stacked carelessly about the church; Sophie wears a smart riding habit, dove-gray, with pert, mannish, raised shoulders, black velvet trim at the collar, a ruffled white blouse. Beneath her left arm she carries a riding crop as if, only a moment before, she'd strolled casually into the room . . . and has turned her head, casually, to glance in their direction.

You? Of course I know you. You two children are my secret, and I am yours.

Father tells them quietly that of course their mother was of aristocratic birth. "Her maiden name was Hume. The Humes of New York—Old New York—English-Dutch-German stock. One of the great shipbuilding fortunes. Of course, they disowned Sophie for marrying me," Father says, staring at the portrait with such intensity the children begin to be frightened, "as if Abraham Licht were not their equal! As if I, an American, am not the equal of any living man! But I stole her from them," he adds, laughing. "And I broke their hearts."

Father is breathing audibly, as if he has just run up a flight of steps. Impossible to tell if he is angry, or deeply moved; or behaving in this way for their benefit. *To educate us. In the cosmology of that mysterious time before we were born.*

Esther has begun to fidget; Darian has begun to find his mother's face too terrible to gaze upon; those eyes! Mercifully, the visit is over. Father draws the black velvet cloth reverently back over the canvas.

It is forbidden to ask questions but it is not forbidden to play (if they are careful) in the storeroom, in the old church, among Father's inheritances.

(Not all the items are "inheritances," however. Some are called "payment for debts." Others are called "gifts.")

Here, amid the battered oak pews, pushed into the corners and crowding even the pulpit and the hickory cross, are trunks, and wardrobes, and stacks of china, and tarnished silver plate, and crystal, and panes of stained glass; furniture of every kind—divans, and S-backed chairs, and tables, and lamp stands, and settees, and desks, and giant sideboards, and chandeliers with dripping prisms; marble statuettes; carpets of various lengths, rolled up cruelly and bound, tight, with fraying twine; sextants, and astrolabes, and telescopes, and great framed maps of North America; globes of the Earth, where entire continents have faded to near invisibility; gentlemen's and ladies' and children's clothing—top hats, tuxedos, traveling cloaks, chesterfields, boiled shirtfronts, detached collars, women's gowns, feathered boas, capes, cloaks, fur stoles, fur hats, even a riding habit and smart curved hat; wigs—ah, what a variety of wigs; and jars and tubes of theatrical makeup; election campaign material for one JASPER LIGES (said to be a "remote uncle," whom the children have never met) who unsuccessfully ran for Congress on the Democratic ticket out of Vanderpoel, New York, in 1902; cigar boxes elegant as jewel boxes stuffed with tickets and ticket stubs (lotteries, racetrack, railway, steamboat, the Metropolitan Opera); a stack of yellowing copies of a five-page newspaper, *Frelicht's Raceway Tips*; soiled, dog-eared "shares" in such companies as The Panama

Canal, Ltd., North American Liberty Bonds, Inc., Banting Cotton Goods Co., X. X. Anson & Sons Copper, Ltd., The Society for the Reclamation & Restoration of E. Auguste Napoleon, The Byrd Expedition, and Hollowell Aerocraft; a single handsome golf club; a pile of mud-encrusted croquet mallets; an agèd, discolored drum; a tarnished bugle, *property of U.S. Army*; a violin with three snapped strings; a flute in poor condition; a carton of mounted and stuffed creatures—snakes, pheasants, raccoons, rabbits; shelves of worn leatherbound books— Hugo, Dumas, Hoffman, Poe, the entire works of Shakespeare, the entire works of Milton, *The Illustrated Don Quixote*, dog-eared books on medicine, agriculture, necromancy, the settlement of New Netherlands, horse breeding, cabinet making, a tattered pamphlet on mesmerism, studies of phrenology, vegetarianism, astrology, *Home Cures & Emetics, The Complete Poems of Longfellow, Tales of the North, Memoirs of Ulysses S. Grant, The Dictionary of the English Language (Including a Rhyming Index)*; a squat wooden barrel filled with every variety of footwear—mens and ladies' and children's shoes, formal shoes, work shoes, high-top boots, slippers, etc.; and immense gilded mirrors, propped haphazardly against the walls, reflecting, it seems, bygone times—in which poor Darian and Esther tiptoe diaphanous as ghosts, fearful to look too closely at their own images.

What a curious world it is, Darian thinks. Already, he has tried to speak of it in his little musical compositions. Or rather to hint of it. Father's world of inheritances, payments for debts, gifts from mysterious admirers. For, as Father is in the habit of saying, with a wink, "The man or woman who doesn't adore you is the man or woman who hasn't— yet—made your acquaintance."

And there, against the front wall of the old church-interior, is the foot-pedal organ which Darian has been able to play this past year, wearing Father's boots so that he can reach, just barely, the pedals; it's a crude, hearty, boisterous musical instrument very different from the spinet piano that had been Sophie's, in the parlor; Darian loves the noises that ring out with a wild, deranged glory, as if God were shrieking through the pipes. Darian has mastered most of the hymns in the books Reverend Woodcock has given him: "A Mighty Fortress Is Our Lord," "Rock of Ages," "Soldiers in Christ," and his favorite for its treble runs like crashing icicles, "For the Sound of the Lord is Joy, Joy."

Hearing her brother play the organ, Esther stands transfixed, her small cameo of a face radiant with wonder; at times, when the notes crash noisily, she giggles, presses her little hands over her ears and begs him to stop. (If Darian knows how to play nice, Esther says, why doesn't he play *nice*? He knows how much she likes "Chirping Crickets" on the parlor piano, "Fire-Balls Mazurka," Father's favorite marching songs, and "The Lass of Aviemore," "Carry Me Back to Old Virginnie" which Father and Elisha sing in bawling unison, like old black slaves . . . why doesn't he play *nice* if he knows how? And Darian says coolly, his child's pride stung, "Music isn't meant to be *nice*, it's meant to be—*music*.")

Father's youngest children, his angel-children as he calls them, share a peculiarity: they are afraid to be alone.

And there is no reason for them to be alone when they have each other.

It is forbidden to ask too many questions but it is never forbidden, in fact it's encouraged, for these bright, inquisitive children to read aloud to each other from Father's library of old mildewed leatherbound books; to take as many parts, "voices," as they wish. Such activities delight Father. It is encouraged, too, that they dress in certain of the clothes, or costumes, in the closets. And the wigs. And the shoes, the boots. There is even an antiquated makeup kit, paints hardened and cracked, brushes stiff as sticks. How Father laughs in delight, seeing his youngest son in a spiky black wig, and his younger daughter in an enormous flower-festooned hat; seeing the children in drooping silk vests and beaded satin jackets, in petticoats stiffened with dirt . . . a moustache painted inexpertly on Darian's upper lip, flaming spots of rouge on Esther's round little cheeks . . . what waves of childish hilarity, waves of sudden panic, for *who* are they now? *whom* have they become? as in a silken top hat Darian prances about, an ebony cane slung through his arm, and in a beribboned lace frock little Esther stumbles after him, humming, clapping her hands like a Broadway ingenue . . . *who* are they now, *whom* have they become?

"They're not fit for The Game. Even if I hadn't promised their mother. I have an instinct for such things."

They'd overheard Father tell the older children this, one winter evening by candlelight. Father's pungent-smelling Cuban cigar settled in the corner of his mouth. Father's expression was somber yet affectionate. No one, not even Millie, who loved to contradict, wished to contradict Father on this point. He'd been discussing plans with the others, his plans for them, the "projects" they would be pursuing in the months ahead, the "investments," the "dramatis personae"—handsome Elisha in shirtsleeves sprawled by the fire like a lazy ebony-dark panther; Millie in silk slacks and an aqua brocaded kimono, languidly brushing her waist-long hair; Thurston in rumpled riding clothes, smiling and dreamy, smoking one of Father's cigars; and scowling Harwood sipping at a tankard of ale, his glance flicking briefly onto Darian and Esther as if he'd never seen them before, and took not the slightest interest in whether they were fit, or not fit, for The Game.

Father pursued his line of thought as Father had a way of doing, speaking of certain of his children as if they weren't present and avidly, anxiously listening; one day, Darian would think *It was as if God spoke His thoughts aloud, and we were inside them.* Stroking sleepy Esther's baby-fine hair, drawing a forefinger along Darian's jaw, musing philosophically, "No. They are unsuited. It can never be. Though they are children of Abraham Licht, they are not such robust children as *you.*" For Father was addressing the elder children, who basked in the pleasure of his pride, even Harwood, sipping ale, not so scowling now, though the creases remained in his brow.

"Katrina? What does Father mean—we're unfit for The Game? What is The Game? Katrina?"—so Darian and Esther plagued Katrina, in the months to come when Father, as well as the others, was absent from Muirkirk. And Katrina would say, with a shrug, "There is no Game, there is only life itself. Your father knows, but doesn't wish to know." "But, Katrina," they begged, plucking at her sleeves, "—The Game, what is *The Game?*" But Katrina turned away with a dismissive wave of her hand. And they gazed at each other in exasperation and hurt, that they were silly little children, and never to know what their elders knew, and never to play The Game their elders played, whatever that Game was.

III

"Here I am. But no, no—I prefer to be alone. Thank you, dear Katrina. I said *alone.*"

Mud-splattered, bleeding from a dozen nicks and scratches on his face, one side of his throat inflamed by insect bites, Father returns at last after three hours tramping in the marsh. He slams through the rear of the house, locks himself in the bath, sits down at 9 P.M. for supper with so ravenous an appetite, poor Katrina can't serve him quickly enough, or plentifully enough, though she's been preparing food much of the afternoon. Father eats, and drinks several tankards of cold dark brimming ale; lights up one of his cigars; and feels, suddenly, an overwhelming wave of fatigue.

He had not wished, truly he had not wished that Xalapa, beautiful Xalapa would be put down, that hadn't been his plan, truly it hadn't been his plan, *may God have mercy on my soul if there be a God and if I possess a soul.* Such fatigue! It's a mercy, he can't brood upon mistakes for very long. Abraham Licht isn't a man to brood for very long. His head nods, wily Katrina removes the drooping cigar from his fingers. Since his itinerant boyhood, when alertness and alacrity kept him alive, Abraham has had the gift of sleep when he knows himself safe; sleep doesn't steal upon him by degrees, but overpowers him at once. He is a Contracoeur pine, he has boasted, the magnificent tree that is rumored to have no natural ceiling to its height, nor depth to its roots; the Contracoeur pine is a tree of exquisite beauty and strength that can grow forever—and live forever. (If no circumstances intervene.) Just as Day beckons to Abraham Licht, stirring his imagination like a lover's, so does Night draw the man down, down, down to a voluptuous consummation in sleep. *So that I must wonder who I am: if the Abraham Licht who dwells in shadows isn't the supreme self, and the Abraham Licht of day the imposter.*

He sleeps for ten hours. For twelve hours. For fourteen.

Waking at last refreshed, and smiling again. Kissing little Esther and little Darian, who squeal with delight, that Father is returned to them yet again.

IV

From four o'clock until six on weekday afternoons, and from nine o'clock until noon on Saturday mornings, Darian and Esther are tutored by the village schoolmaster. For Abraham Licht can't tolerate the thought of his sensitive angel-children attending the Muirkirk school, a one-room schoolhouse attended by eight very disparate (and often rowdy) grades. Of course, he tutors them himself when he can, as he did with the four elder children: he lectures them on Science, Grammar and Elocution; on History, Art, Music, Etiquette and the Ancient World; on Mathematics (both applied and pure). He assigns them the great soliloquies of Shakespeare, in which, in his estimate, all the natural wisdom of the world is contained, in miniature.

"For if you know Shakespeare, children, you know all."

What a boon it would be, if one of Abraham Licht's children had a natural talent for the stage! But Thurston, years ago, was slow to memorize lines, and recited them so woodenly it was painful to hear; Harwood, being Harwood, was surly and stammering; Elisha could memorize lines of difficult verse with no trouble, as if imprinting them in his mind's eye after a single reading, but he spoke with an annoying glibness, mocking the elevated poetry. (For Elisha was destined for satire, it seemed. "Inside my black skin, my black soul.") And there was Millicent, lovely yet exasperating, who recited verse as if she were reciting popular song lyrics, pursing her mouth in mock sobriety, crinkling her smooth brow, wringing her hands as she murmured "Out, out damned spot!" in the throes of conscience as Lady Macbeth, then lapsing, with a wink at her audience, into a Paul Dresser tune—

"A wild sort of devil,
  But dead on the level,
  Was my gal Sal."

Now Darian and Esther were made to memorize passages of demanding, riddlesome verse, as Abraham Licht listened frowningly, without much pleasure; for, as he's suspected, these two of his children are not suited for The Game; with no talent for making of themselves ventriloquists, no aptitude for the most innocent sort of duplicity. Darian, trying so hard to please his father, stumbles over lines repeatedly; Esther, only six years old, is perhaps too young for the exercise. Yet, for all her prettiness, she seems to lack the spirit for self-display that is so natural in Millie, a certain glisten to the eyes, an animation like flame. "No matter, I suppose," Father says, sighing, "—for neither you, Darian, nor

you, Esther, need ever leave the protection of Muirkirk, if you don't
want to; and life will spare you its grim trials."

It's a surprise, then, that the children fare so much better with
their tutor (whom Abraham Licht is rumored to pay generously); as
pupils, they're eager to learn, and love reading—"I'd rather read than
anything," little Esther declares with childish passion. And Reverend
Woodcock continues to marvel at Darian's gift for music. Is this an inherited talent?—is the slender, shy child but the father's son? Darian
has had a little difficulty learning to read music but he plays with remarkable intuition, "by ear"; Woodcock tells friends that the child
doesn't seem to pick out notes, like most keyboard musicians of his
acquaintance, including himself, but plays "as if the music already exists in his head—as a stream of water is but a continuous stream, from
its source to its destination." In Muirkirk there are a number of moder-
ately talented pianists and organists, most of them female, and Woodcock himself is a competent musician, but nine-year-old Darian is
altogether different. Already he has mastered such favorites of the amateur's repertoire as Gottschalk's "The Last Hope" with its glimmering
arpeggios, Chwatal's "The Happy Sleighing Party" with its merry twinkling bells, Lange's "Crickets," Behr's feverish Mazurka and a number of
stalwart, thumping Christian hymns; and works by such masters of the
keyboard as Spohr, Meyerbeer, Mozart and Raff.

It is Bach's Two- and Three-Part Inventions, however, which Woodcock was reluctant to assign, that most intrigue the boy, and draw forth
every reserve of his precocious talent. How he strains himself, quivering at the keyboard of the old upright piano in the Woodcock parlor;
how his small hands strain, and stretch—for Darian has a reach of only
six notes in his left hand and five in his right, and hasn't yet mastered
the trick of eliding octaves with grace. Still, Darian plays, and plays,
and plays; if he makes mistakes, he insists upon beginning from the
start, and playing through; a child-perfectionist, amazing to see. (Abraham Licht has warned Reverend Woodcock that Darian shouldn't be
allowed to overexcite himself, he isn't a strong boy, he suffered rheumatic fever when very young, his health is problematic.) Unlike any other
pupil of Woodcock's acquaintance, Darian begs his teacher to give him
difficult assignments and to insist that he play them not just "well" but
"*very* well—as they are meant to be played."

Sometimes Darian brings Woodcock musical compositions of his own. Woodcock is charmed by these, if baffled. The musical scores are neatly written in ink, with no erasures or emendations; they are pastiches of Mozart, Chwatal, Meyerbeer, Bach—but very oddly designed, and in the playing illogical to the ear. Woodcock's response is always, "Promising, Darian! Very promising. But you should know, son, to save yourself grief, that the great music for the piano and organ is European, and has largely been written by this time in history. American music is 'popular'—for childlike tastes exclusively."

Darian broods, and gnaws at his lower lip; seems about to protest, but finally does not. Yet he continues to write his queer little compositions and to show them, bravely, or perhaps boldly, to the bemused Woodcock.

V

It is forbidden to inquire of (Death) . . . for Father, as Katrina warns, is not on friendly terms with (Death); and *she* has not the time.

Yet it isn't forbidden, in fact it's greeted with delight, when Darian composes a lovely little dirge for Old Tom the barn cat when he dies; Darian leading the funeral procession playing a flute while Esther shakes a strip of tiny bells, and Katrina herself carries the body wrapped in red silk and placed in a box, to be buried at the edge of the churchyard. Father, who loves all things theatrical, puffs on his cigar and applauds—"Bravo! That's the attitude to take, my dears."

It is forbidden to inquire of (God) . . . for Father, as Katrina warns, is not on friendly terms with (God); nor has *she* had much encouragement along such lines.

Yet it isn't forbidden to Darian and Esther to attend Sunday school and church services at the Methodist Church, where kindly Reverend Woodcock is minister; nor is it forbidden, so long as Father doesn't explicitly hear of it, to Darian to hike to the far side of Muirkirk to attend prayer services at the Lutheran church, and at the Episcopal church, and, several miles beyond, the clapboard Church of the Pentecost, where the smiling perspiring Reverend Bogey leads the congregation in song, in hand-clapping and foot-stomping—"What a Friend I Have in

Jesus," "When I Looked Up, and He Looked Down," "This Little Light
of Mine." Darian listens, enthralled. His heart beats rapturously. *Almost
I could believe in Jesus my savior, the music was so joyous.*

VI

What a handsome, mysterious couple: is the young woman—Millie?
And the brown-skinned man—Elisha? Millie with her hair elegantly
braided and an ostrich-feather hat on the plaited crown, laughing at
their amazed faces, leaning out of the two-seater motorcar to greet
them *Why, don't you know who I am? Your own sister who adores you?
Come give Millie a kiss! Two kisses!* And there beside her is a man they
can't at first identify though surely it must be Elisha, who else but Elisha, yet looking so much older than his age in prim wire-rimmed
glasses, wearing a humble cloth cap and plain drab-brown clothes, and
his hair gone gray and his shoulders stooped . . . *is* it Elisha? Esther has
jammed a finger in her mouth, blinking, shy and indecisive, Darian is a
little more confident, even as Father gives the game away striding down
the walk roaring with laughter, and the brown-skinned man leaps out
of the driver's seat of the motorcar with the agility of an acrobat, tosses
away his wire-rimmed glasses and cap and flashes his dazzling Elisha-
grin reaching for them. *You! Darian and Esther! Don't you know your
own brother 'Lisha?*

The Catechism of Abraham Licht

Crime? Then complicity.
Complicity? Then no crime.
No crime? Then no criminal.
No criminal? Then no remorse.

All men are our enemies, as they are strangers.
Brothers and sisters by blood are brothers and sisters by the soul.
Do you doubt, children? You must never doubt!

To doubt is to already lose The Game.

Covet where you wish, but never in vain.
Would this earthly globe were but the size of an apple, that it might be
*   plucked, devoured!*
(By one who has the courage to pluck, and to bite hard.)

You cannot measure a live wolf.

Past?—but the graveyard of Future.
Future?—but the womb of Past.

It is never enough to have confidence in oneself; one must be the means of
*   confidence in others.*

The first refuge of the clever man is God—their God.
The final refuge of the clever man is God—our God.

Never discover a strategy if another can be made to imagine he has
*   discovered it.*

The world has been divided into fools and knaves?—yes, more precisely
*   into fools, knaves, and those who so divide the world.*

To penetrate another's heart is to conquer it.
To penetrate another's soul is to acquire it.

Pity?—why, then cowardice.
Remorse?—why, then defeat.
Guilt?—the fool's luxury.

A gentleman will not soil his gloves, but will soil his hands.
A lady will not reveal her secret, except for the right price.

To us who are pure, all things are pure.

No success without another's failure.
No failure without another's success.
To feel another's pain is defeat.
To turn the other cheek, a betrayal.

In Aesop, the foolish vixen boasts of her numerous progeny and
challenges the lioness how many offspring she has had. The proud
lioness says, "Only one—but a lion."

The Game must never be played as if it were but a Game.
Nor the Game-board traversed as if it were but the "world."

Out of Muirkirk mud, a lineage to conquer Heaven.
To suck marrow, children, is our nourishment.
To suck marrow, yet be heaped with gratitude.
Yet never seduced, children, by the music of your own voice.

Control, control, and again control: and what prize will not be ours?

Die for a whim—if it is your own.

Honor is the secret subject of all catechisms.

For where there is love there can be no calculation.
For where there is calculation there can be no love.
And where The Game is abandoned, mere mortality awaits.

"As above, so below"—all on Earth is ordained.
And where ordained, blameless.
For, children, I say unto you—
Crime? Then complicity.
Complicity? Then no crime.

And the light shineth in darkness, and the darkness becomes light.

"The Mark of Cain"

I

A day, and a night, and no word from Thurston. And no word from Harwood. And Abraham Licht hid the dread in his heart. Thinking, As I am a man, I must accept disaster no less than triumph.

Thinking, One day I will record it all. *My Heart Laid Bare; a Memoir of Abraham Licht, American.* I will shrink from no fact however shameful. I will speak in frank, forthright language. I will spare no one, especially not myself. A posthumous work perhaps. The royalties to go to my children. Not a pseudonymous work, for I am a man of pride. What I have done, I have done. What has been done to me, I have also done.

Yet not knowing how swiftly disaster would sweep upon him, though he prowled the marsh, sucking at his cigar for courage, rehearsing certain dramatic scenes of the memoir. *And then there came a time when the family was in jeopardy, owing to a stupid blunder of the least talented of my sons. . . .*

Past nine o'clock of a warm, sulfurous midsummer evening, and the family still seated at the dining-room table; Abraham Licht at the head, and Katrina in her apron close by; little Darian and Esther allowed up past their bedtimes yet another night (for this was still a time of celebration); Millie's beautiful face aglow in firelight, and her hair no longer plaited but cascading over her shoulders; and Elisha, buoyant Elisha quite the dandy in a wing-collar shirt, tieless, his handsome face gleaming in firelight as for the benefit of Darian and Esther he recounted the sensational exploits of the notorious Black Phantom of Chautauqua Falls whom police in a half dozen states were hunting for his "Negro audacity" (as the Hearst papers described it) in boldly

robbing three white persons of more than $400,000. The children lis-
tened wide-eyed, looking to their father to see how he reacted; for they
knew that robbing was wrong—wasn't it?—yet, perhaps, there were
times when robbing was admirable—was it? Even Katrina, who disapproved of such exaggerated tales, as she called them, couldn't help
laughing, hiding her face in her apron. And Millie interrupted with little cries of delight, clapping her hands and declaring that she would
have loved to be a witness to such a crime—"That is, if the Black
Phantom wouldn't have robbed me of all my possessions."

Elisha, basking in the family's attention, said, frowning, "The man
was said to be a gentleman, despite being Ne-grow. Apparently such is
possible. De facto, it is not only possible, but *is*. So he would not have
asked a thing of you, Millie." Saying to Father at the head of the table,
"Isn't it true, Father, the Black Phantom robs only those who deserve to
be robbed?"

Abraham Licht said, with satisfaction, "Certainly. But there are
many so."

"*Many* so!"—Elisha grinned, and clapped his hands.

At this point Darian asked innocently, "But how do you know who
deserves to be robbed?—how can you *tell*?"

All the adults laughed, though not cruelly.

"Yes," said Esther, anxiously, "—how can you *tell*? And do you *shoot*
them? Is there a *gun*?"

"Why, Esther, what a thing to say," Abraham Licht exclaimed, not
knowing if he should laugh, or frown, "—what a thing for a sweet little
girl to *imagine*. Who has been talking of guns?" (In fact, Elisha had
been talking of the gun the Black Phantom had used, demonstrating
how it must have been brandished—according to accounts he'd read in
the papers.) "Who has been talking of *shooting*? Unburdening fools of
their excess cash is a very different matter from shooting them; for,
after all, not even a fool deserves to be *hurt*. You can argue that a fool
deserves our protection. A fool, like a sheep, is to be cherished."

Elisha said, continuing his own line of thought, "It *is* a tricky procedure, Darian, and Esther, for the problem lies in the fact that, of
so many who deserve to be robbed, which in the United States of the
present time is a considerable number of 'the wealthy'—the 'ruling
class'—only a small percentage ever are robbed; there are not enough

trained robbers to execute the task. Mainly, these individuals are the ones who do the robbing. Not at gunpoint but through 'business.' So there's injustice. There's disproportion. Of the hundreds of persons at Chautauqua Falls who richly deserved to be robbed, only three were robbed. That's unfair!"

Again, the adults laughed. But Darian and Esther only glanced worriedly from face to face, their eyes ringed in fatigue from the late hour, and so much excitement in the normally quiet Muirkirk residence, and this sense of—what?—playful confusion, a complex and protracted joke or game they could not comprehend? *Unfit for The Game.* Seeing Darian's hurt, baffled expression, Millie leaned over to kiss him, saying, "Don't mind, Darian, if they tease. They are always teasing. One day, just you wait, *you* will do the teasing."

Since Millie's arrival home she'd been impressed, as she said several times, by her youngest brother's "prodigious gift" for music. She believed he should be trained professionally, brought to New York City and enrolled in a music school. Why, he might be launched upon a stage career as a sort of music-genius Tom Thumb—"Audiences would adore him." (Abraham Licht did not like this idea at all. Tom Thumb, he said, was a genuine midget—"And my son, I hope, is a normal child.") In any case, Millie said, she'd heard many professional pianists who played no better than Darian, and many who played much worse. And Darian would be only ten years old, and could easily pass for seven or eight. "I could present him on stage. I have just the idea for candle-light, and his costume," Millie said.

(On the first evening of Millie's and Elisha's arrival home, Darian had played the spinet for them, in the parlor; a number of the compositions Reverend Woodcock had assigned him, and Bach's "Inventions"; on the second evening, at their request, he played one of his own compositions—"Welcome Home." This was a strange piece with lengthy arpeggio flights, a crashing of chords up and down the keyboard, spirited, yet solemn; noisy, yet subdued; clearly, Millie and Elisha didn't know what to make of it, any more than Father or Katrina knew, but they applauded enthusiastically just the same. On the third evening, Darian played another of his own compositions, titled "Now We Are Happy," this time on a harmonica and an ingenious foot-operated drum of his invention, while Esther stood beside him humming several eerily high-pitched notes, wordless. In contrapuntal design rivalrous melodies rose and fell, rising out of nowhere and trailing gradually into silence . . . as if the final note could not be found. "Darian, how strange! How wonderful," Millie said, vigorously applauding, though with doubtful eyes, "—but when you begin your stage career, you know, you will have to play real music, by real composers. Music that pleases the audience's ear, not just your own.")

Next day, to his relief, Darian was taken aside by Father, who told him to pay no attention to Millie. "The girl means well, of course. But things come so naturally for her, as for Elisha, she confuses you with herself; she imagines that a career as a musical 'Tom Thumb' would suit you, as it might have suited her. But don't worry, son, your father doesn't intend to expose you to the rigors of any profession, at least not without your consent, and not for a long time. For I've promised your mother . . . I am a man who does not go back on his word."

II

And then, Harwood arrived home.

They were seated in the cozy firelit dining room at the old oak table, the only table in the world, as Abraham Licht said, at which he felt entirely *safe*, when suddenly there was a noise outside, at the rear of the house, and a pounding at the door, which Elisha leapt up to open, for the Licht residence was the only residence in Muirkirk in which doors and windows were customarily locked, and, there, looking exhausted, starved—there was Harwood, staggering into the kitchen.

Staring at Father. His wild bloodshot eyes fixed upon Father.

As if no one else was in the room, only Father.

And Father on his feet, shocked by Harwood's appearance; not, at first, moving to him.

Harwood stammered he'd come a God-damned long distance on foot.

He'd had, he said bitterly, some God-damned bad luck.

Not his fault. None of it. Thurston was to blame—partly. And Father's "cousin" who'd betrayed him, in Baltimore.

Didn't want to talk about it right now, God damn.

No he wasn't injured.

No not sick.

But tired.

And starved.

God-damned starved.

Elisha would have helped his brother to the table but Harwood shrugged away from him, began eating while still on his feet, by hand; poured himself ale, which he downed like a thirsty horse, in prodigious quantities. In stunned silence, the family stared at Harwood. Father was still on his feet, and fumbling to relight his cigar. The younger children weren't certain—at first—that this disheveled man was their brother Harwood, except his voice was Harwood's, and that angry mirthless laugh. His beard had grown out like a porcupine's quills, there was something mashed and furious about his mouth, his left eye was bruised and swollen, he'd sat down at a chair Katrina had provided for him, and was eating, head lowered toward his plate, warmed-up supper which Katrina placed before him, with that look of fearful affection she'd directed toward Harwood since boyhood; as if, of Abraham Licht's progeny, Harwood was the one fated for hurt, both to commit and to suffer. Yet, unlike his brothers, Harwood paid the old woman little heed, and seemed scarcely to know whose hands fed him, so long as he was fed.

Elisha regarded his brother with an expression of disdain: they were not friends, it was enough they must be brothers. Millie made an effort, as it seemed she could not help doing, to charm him—"We were missing you, Harwood. And—here you are."

But Harwood, eating noisily, biting off the heel of a loaf of bread with his strong teeth and washing it down with a large mouthful of ale, only shrugged.

Still, Millie persisted. For Father's silence unnerved her.

Asking Harwood what news he had of Thurston, and Harwood now glanced up at her, and scowled, saying he hadn't seen Thurston in a long time.

Since March, maybe.

Maybe February.

"Why ask me of Thurston?—I don't know God-damn nothin' of Thurs-ton."

Chewing as he spoke, sarcasm like pulpy food in his mouth.

Millie began to say, hadn't he just now spoken of Thurston?—blaming bad luck on Thurston?—but, seeing the blood-blackened look in her brother's face, shrank back in silence. A pretty fair-haired princess of a girl is no match, even in Muirkirk under Father's watchful eye, for a "roughneck" American youth like Harwood.

Still, Abraham Licht had not spoken.

For he knew. He knew. He knew. *Owing to a stupid blunder of the least talented of my sons . . .*

Harwood, seeing how everyone watched him, with a bold, fearful look at his father, began to snort with laughter, saying maybe Thurston eloped with his fancy lady, maybe they were on their honeymoon, sailing the high seas to Baby-lon, or Mad-a-gask-kaw, wherever you go on your honeymoon, maybe nobody would ever hear of Thurston again: how's it Harwood's fault?

Wheezing-snorting laughter. Suety juice trickling down his chin.

Seeing Father's expression, he fell silent. Fumbled for his fork, which clattered to the floor.

Jesus he was tired suddenly. So tired.

Nearly collapsing as Elisha, quick on his feet, helped him from the table. With a glance at Father, for Elisha and Father are close as Siamese twins it sometimes seems, their brains a single circuit, surely they share identical thoughts, but Father was occupied in lighting his cigar, face like stone. Elisha and Katrina helped Harwood to his room, Harwood's spiky-haired head lolling on his shoulders, knees buckling, half-sobbing he was saying O Jesus O God so tired, wasn't his fault not his God-damned fault . . . nobody could blame him.

Abraham Licht succeeded in relighting his cigar, and tossed down the match onto the table.

Esther whispered, "That isn't him . . . is it? Who is it?"

The boy had committed an evil act, yes, but more reprehensibly he'd lied to his father. *He'd lied to Abraham Licht.*

He hid his distress. That kick of his heart. Murderous rage.

Yet: it could not be rage. For Harwood with all his imperfections was a Licht, unmistakably; flesh, blood and bones; though his elder sons' mother had betrayed Abraham Licht long ago and he would never forgive her, yet Abraham Licht loved them as much as he loved the others. *For that is my vow. As I am their father.*

So next day when finally Harwood crawled from bed, still unshaven, unbathed, smelling rank as a horse, beset by spasms of nausea, but unable to vomit, Abraham Licht called him into the room at the rear of the house that was Abraham Licht's "rectory"—his office and library, containing stacks of files, and boxes of documents and correspondence, and a three-foot safe with a combination dial. Bluntly he asked, "All right. What has happened between you and Thurston?"

Harwood said quickly, with a guilty duck of his head, "What—what d'you mean, Father? Has something happened—?"

"Tell me."

Harwood, groggy from his stuporous sleep, steadied himself against a chair. His greasy hair fell in quills into his face and he brushed them back nervously. His puffy lips twitched in a kind of smile. "Did I say last night I saw Thurston?—because I don't guess I did. It was a mistake if I did. I mean—if I said I did."

"Harwood. I've asked you if something has happened between you and Thurston."

Harwood shook his head like a baffled dog.

"Has something happened to—Thurston?"

"I don't know anything about God-damned Thurston," Harwood said irritably, "—all I heard is, he's in some kind of trouble. In Atlantic City, at that fancy hotel. Where I didn't get to go 'cause I had to go to God-damned Baltimore to operate the God-damned lottery."

"In trouble?" Abraham said sharply. "Thurston? How?"

"'I don't know!'"

"Tell me."

"Father, I said—"

"Do you imagine, Harwood, you can lie to *me*? You are my *son;* you are my *creation*. Even as a lie forms in your brain, d'you imagine I can't sense it? *hear it?*"

Harwood stared in terror at Abraham Licht. In the act of wiping his mouth with a beefy forearm he froze, and began to back away as, on his feet now, Abraham Licht advanced. Harwood swayed as if faint, his eyes showing white above the rim. "Look at me, son," Abraham Licht said, calmly. "Tell me what's in your heart."

And now Harwood began to sob, visibly trembling. It was as if his very backbone had become unhinged. Saying in a faltering voice, "—don't know, I never saw him—God damn I was on my way to see him, and he wouldn't let me in—wouldn't lend me money—*denied that we were brothers.*"

Abraham Licht gripped his son's hunched, muscular shoulders to prevent him wrenching away. He said, still calmly, "Tell me."

"Father, I did nothing wrong—it was his fault—"

"What was his fault?"

"—he denied we were brothers, Father!—made me beg for crumbs—"

"*Tell me.*"

Harwood stood mute, his bruised face turned aside in an attitude of shame. An odor lifted from his cringing body that Abraham Licht knew well, of rank animal distress. *Even then, though I knew, I could not believe. For we had reaped such a harvest, until then.*

It was then that Abraham Licht saw a curious shadowed or indented mark on Harwood's forehead. Forcibly he drew him to a window, the better to examine him in the light. "Harwood, what is this? This mark? Since when have—" Harwood panicked, pushing away from his father; not daring to flee, but sinking to his knees on the floor; raising his hands in a childlike gesture of piety. His face was puckered; he wept in harsh, heaving sobs; clutched at Abraham's hands, stammering, begging for mercy—"Father, it was Thurston's fault, not mine! Thurston is the murderer, not me! *It was Thurston who strangled her.*"

The Mute

He fled to the north, along the wide bleached sands, past Oyster Creek, and Little Egg Harbor, and Barnegat Bay; he fled to the west, to the trackless wilds of the Pine Barrens, where he might hide for days, years; unwisely (now starving, near-delirious) he fled south, by Batsto, by Makepeace Lake, by Vineland . . . where, at last, on the fourth day following the murder of Mrs. Wallace Peck, he would be run to earth.

And so ignobly, like any common criminal!—tracked down by blood-

hounds, pursued by police, shot and wounded, beaten, kicked, manacled, brought back to Atlantic City in triumph.

CHRISTOPHER SCHOENLICHT the "fiancé" of MRS. WALLACE
PECK.

CHRISTOPHER SCHOENLICHT the murderer of MRS. WAL-
LACE PECK.

CHRISTOPHER SCHOENLICHT standing mute at his arraignment, nodding just perceptibly when asked if "Christopher Schoenlicht"
is his name, shaking his head no, just perceptibly, when asked if he had
any accomplice in the heinous crime.

CHRISTOPHER SCHOENLICHT (unrepentant? in a daze of terror and grief? weakened by the gunshot wound in his left shoulder?)
standing mute as testimony is given . . . by the little Filipino maid (who
had been hiding in a wardrobe in the adjoining room, paralyzed with
fear, "For next, I knew, he would have strangled me"), and the manager
of the Saint-Léon (who had behaved so very unctuously to Eloise and
Christopher in the past), and many another witness, including sweet
Mrs. Amos Sellick, who had seemed, at one time, to have been attracted to him. . . .

CHRISTOPHER SCHOENLICHT about whom much official and
unofficial speculation soon rages—for who *is* he? how had he and the
wife of Wallace Peck met? where does he come from, why can no
county supply a birth certificate, has he no family he wishes to contact?

CHRISTOPHER SCHOENLICHT standing mute, sullen, declining
to confess or to deny the charge that he murdered ("by an act of wanton and willful brutality, with robbery as the motive") the unhappy
woman, the supremely foolish woman, who had publicly declared herself, only a week before, his "fiancée". . . declining to enter a plea of *Not
Guilty* and forbidden by law to acquiesce to the charge of *Guilty* since
the plea of *Guilty* is tantamount to suicide, which cannot be allowed
under the New Jersey statute.

CHRISTOPHER SCHOENLICHT, mute, unmoved, doubtless "cal-
loused," "hardened," "defiant," when told that the penalty for his
heinous crime is death by hanging.

CHRISTOPHER SCHOENLICHT, mute.

The Grieving Father

I

For the next eleven months, from the time of Thurston's arrest and arraignment, through the four-day trial, and the long months of his imprisonment, up to the very hour of his "execution" at the State Correctional Facility at Trenton, New Jersey—Abraham Licht was to think of nothing else; no one else.

It was the great challenge (as it threatened to be the great sorrow) of his life.

For Thurston was as dear to him as his own breath, his very heartbeat, *and must be freed.*

For Thurston, being a gentleman, could not be guilty of the vulgar crime charged against him, *and must be freed.*

For, guilty or no, he was a Licht, and Abraham's firstborn, and therefore innocent, *and must be freed.*

Within an hour of his interview with Harwood he left Muirkirk, alone, telling no one where he was going; and was away for several days.

During that time he ascertained these terrible facts: a woman by the name of Eloise Peck had been murdered in Atlantic City; one "Christopher Schoenlicht," her twenty-five-year-old fiancé, was suspected of the crime; "Schoenlicht" had already been arrested, booked on charges of murder, arraigned for a trial; he seemed to have no prior record, and nothing was known of his background; he was reported as "uncooperative" with authorities and "clearly guilty" of the heinous crime.

Abraham Licht subsequently made no attempt to see his son in jail (for reasons having to do with his own past record); but, acting swiftly, he contacted a lawyer acquaintance by the name of Gordon Bullock, of Manhattan (a business associate from the era of X. X. Anson & Sons Copper, Ltd.); and allowed it to be known in Atlantic City courthouse circles that a generous defense fund had been established for "Christopher Schoenlicht," by way of an anonymous donor.

He then returned at once to Muirkirk, knowing himself, for the first time, a man no longer young.

"Do I doubt—I do *not*. Does my hand shake?—it does *not*. Am I like other men?—*I am not.*"

Now he must plot strategy, now his son's life depends upon his genius, and *his* life depends upon his genius; now that all that Abraham Licht *is* must bear fruit in what he *does*.

The door to his room is kept locked, the blinds drawn against the shimmering white heat of August. He is able to eat only one meal a day, late in the evening, brought to him by Katrina, who can be trusted to ask no questions; not even to glance, that sharp-eyed old woman, at the newspapers he has spread across his desk. When he questions her (about Millie, Elisha, Darian, Esther, but especially Harwood, who will be leaving again soon) she answers succinctly, without reproach. Have they lived through a terror before, he and she?—the protracted dying of poor Sophie, perhaps?—Abraham Licht's own ill luck with the law, and his subsequent (secret) imprisonment? No matter, no matter, Katrina can be trusted.

"Does my hand shake?—it does *not*."

Bloodshot eyes confronting their own filmy mirror image, beneath eyebrows grown grizzled and queer; fingers plucking at the beardless chin; lips that have acquired the habit, it seems, of moving of their own accord . . .

How could Thurston have forgotten, a gentleman does not soil his gloves, raise his voice, lift his hand! . . . How could Thurston of all people have committed so vicious a crime! . . . *breaking a defenseless woman's neck*.

Assuming of course that this time Harwood has not lied.

But Harwood would not dare lie, would he, to his father?

* * *

These had been weeks of triumph, coups to be recorded at a later date in *My Heart Laid Bare*, that readers eat out *their* paltry hearts in envy and outrage: the adroitly "coked" Midnight Sun ridden by that most professional of jockeys Parmelee (with whom A. Washburn Frelicht had never once spoken directly); the mysterious poisoning of little Tatlock (by way of an herb of the family *Atropa belladonna*); the felicitous accident of Xalapa's fall (with which Frelicht had nothing, nothing to do—ah, the poor beast!); the honest winnings, in excess of $400,000, now kept in absolute *safety* in Abraham Licht's master bedchamber, until such time as investment seems providential. And there was "Mina Raumlicht" in her brilliant debut; and Elisha, proving as clever at the age of twenty as Abraham Licht had been at that age.

And now it seemed that the Wheel was reversing itself, to destroy all that Abraham Licht had forged out of very nothingness.

Honor is the subject of my story.

For God is theirs; and The Game, ours.

For years, for a quarter century, since the very morning of Thurston's birth, Abraham Licht had tormented himself, in idle hours, with dread of catastrophe involving one or another of his children. When he was caught up in his work, in the intricacies of The Game, why, *then* he had no time for such feverish imaginings!—*then* he had scarcely time for "Licht" itself!—but in the interstices, so to speak, of his professional life, it seemed he was prey like any man or woman to certain ignoble fears. For these children were hostages to Fortune, indeed. For he had not counted on loving them so much.

"I suppose I do not care greatly about myself," Abraham Licht mused, "—for there is some doubt as to the existence of 'myself.' But no doubt, certainly, about the existence of my dear ones!"

(And though it could not be said, in the most precise terms, that the adopted Elisha was "his"—flesh of his flesh, blood of his blood—he loved the boy as deeply as the others.)

As a younger man, as an impassioned lover, Abraham Licht had often fancied himself at the mercy of Woman's caprices; but with the passage of years he had come round to believing that it was but his *idea* that rankled his heart, and not the women *in themselves*. For did a woman, even the loveliest of women, exist, apart from the aroused imagination of a lover? . . . had Arabella, and Morna, and poor Sophie, and one or two others, been as potent in the flesh as in the heated confines of Abraham Licht's mind? Two of the women, Arabella and Morna, lived yet, so far as Abraham knew; yet they seemed to him no more immediate, and distinctly less worthy, than Sophie who was dead. Ah, they had betrayed him so cruelly! . . . and Sophie as well! . . . and one or two others, harlots best forgotten.

Yet the women, Abraham Licht's "wives," had given him splendid children; which argued, however fleetingly, for their existence. And if he lost Thurston, whether to the hangman, or to exile, might he not *father* another son?—might he not acquire a new wife, as beautiful as any of the others, and *father* another miraculous being? For Abraham Licht was yet in the prime of life, no less handsome and vigorous than he had been in the days of his early manhood, arguably *more* handsome, *more* vigorous, the wisdom of the years upon him—the natural graying of his yet abundant hair—the natural weathering and creasing of his skin— the deepening of his voice—the sorrow glinting like mica chips in his gaze—*Spirituality* suffused throughout his well-proportioned figure.

Was he not Abraham Licht, most remarkable of men?—and might he not be again a lover, a bridegroom, again a *father*, holding his infant aloft, as if daring the hand of God Himself to strike it from him—?

II

"Father!—look here!"

How is it, so very suddenly?—here is Thurston, but a child again, in short pants, jacket, and striped school tie; his white-blond hair ablaze in innocent sunshine; his face healthily tanned, his eyes light, his smile dimpled and sweet. . . . He has trotted up quietly behind the Irish nursemaid, that he might, in a twinkling, wrest the handle of the baby carriage from her grasp . . . that pretty carriage, of the subtle shade of mother-of-pearl, bedecked with pink ribbons and Belgian lace, in which, in infant glory, beautiful Millicent rides! . . . and now, calling out to his father, his face uplifted, he pushes the carriage along the sidewalk, to Abraham Licht who awaits him. . . .

What a shock, to see the boy so young again, and so small: no more

than nine years of age: which means that the family is living in the
three-story brownstone in Stuyvesant Square, in one of the finest residential neighborhoods in Vanderpoel; moneyed again—at least for the
space of ten or twelve frenetic months; and able to afford clothes of the
highest quality, and travel by Pullman car, and evenings at the opera,
and a personal maid for Morna, and an Irish nursemaid for the baby, and
a private Episcopal boys' school for Thurston and Harwood, and an elegant house in which Abraham Licht can entertain business associates
and potential investors . . . in the copper mine, is it? or, by the time of
Millie's birth, in '92, has he already launched the problematic Santiago
de Cuba Sugar Cane Plantation?

Faithless Arabella, the boys' mother, is gone from Abraham Licht's
life; and Miss Morna Hirshfield, the parson's daughter, has taken her
place; the feckless young woman who has vowed, weeping, that *she* will
love Abraham forever, and follow him wherever he wishes to go, and
be a true Christian mother to his sons. . . . So little Thurston, dimpled
and husky, rushes up to his father to claim his father's full attention: so
happy in his prank, he appears oblivious of the fact that Abraham Licht
is not *bodily present* on that sun-splashed sidewalk, but only regarding it,
as it were, from an eerie pleat or tuck in time.

"Father!—look *here*!"

And now time has shifted abruptly, and Thurston is still younger,
held aloft in Arabella's arms, to shout at the jailhouse window at which
Abraham Licht, or a gentleman who very much resembles him, stands
shivering (for the wretched place is unheated, and Abraham is suffering
from a chest cold, and his cousin "Baron" Barraclough will not post
bond for another forty-eight hours); the scene being Powhatassie Falls,
is it? Or Marion, Ohio?

How is such a thing possible?—Arabella, bareheaded, defiant, a
young woman again, tears glistening on her cheeks, her feet set stolidly
apart, brandishing aloft the kicking child—*their* child, in reproach?—
while the younger boy, Harwood, clutches at her skirt, wailing, and
scarcely able to stand. Mrs. Abraham Licht, slightly drunk, come to
visit her husband. Standing down there in the muddy courtyard, in the
chill spring drizzle, that any idle jailhouse inmate might contemplate
her in derision, and know her for what she is. Abraham vows: he will
never forgive her, he *cannot*.

"Father!—*help!*"

Suddenly they are in the dim-lit parlor of the rectory, here, close at hand, Thurston and Harwood, mere boys, playing rather roughly together—now on the floor, and wrestling—striking each other swift savage blows—cursing like grown men—gasping for breath—rolling over, and over, and pummeling each other, panting, amid the furniture— now Thurston, red-faced, on top—now Harwood—crashing against the spinet piano—overturning one of Sophie's little tables—"Father! help! he is killing me, *help*!"—Thurston's cry of pain as, enraged, Harwood sinks his teeth in his throat, just below the jaw, and, like any bull- dog, will not release his bite, will not, will *not*! until Abraham Licht seizes him by the hair and thumps his head against the carpet.

So thoroughly repulsive an episode, he forgets it immediately upon waking; as, in life, he managed to forget it, many years ago.

III

Why was handsome young Abraham Licht so angry, now that he knew himself in love for the first time in his life?

The year was 1884, Abraham Licht was twenty-three years old, an agent for Pyramid Mail-Order Watches & Jewelry, Ltd. (headquarters and "warehouse" in Port Oriskany, New York); a fledgling journalist for the *Port Oriskany Republican*, whose publisher was his mentor; an actor of amateur status, yet "considerable histrionic gifts" (this, to quote from a review that appeared in the *Republican*, following a local production of the popular melodrama *The Wayward Husband*, in which Abraham Licht played a supporting role); a high-spirited well-bred gregarious fel- low, mature for his years, a graduate, it was said, of Harvard College (or was it Yale?), who knew wines, horses, poker, music, politics—or, in any case, could speak zestfully on these subjects, and on numberless others.

What, precisely, were Abraham Licht's origins?—the organizer of Pyramid Ltd. (himself a youthful thirty-two years of age) believed his young friend hailed from "somewhere in the East"—Massachusetts or Connecticut, perhaps; the publisher of the *Republican*, being originally from the Chautauqua Valley himself, believed he could hear, in curious dissonant tones, the nasal accent of the Valley; Mrs. Arabella Jenkins, whose lover he became, was entrusted with his secret—that following an alcoholic breakdown of his wealthy father, a Boston banker, of high social prominence ("Licht" being but an approximation of his Teutonic name), the young man had been *disowned*: a fortune held in trust for him, prized away by devious lawyerly means; his health so severely, if temporarily, shattered, he had been forced to his shame to withdraw from Harvard Divinity School with but a single semester remaining before graduation.

When he arrived in Port Oriskany by day coach, in the fall of '83, he knew no one in the entire city of twenty-eight thousand persons, and had no letters of introduction or recommendation. Yet within six months, it might be said that he knew everyone worth knowing. The attractive young bachelor dined as a guest at the Coliseum Club, and in numerous private homes (among them the homes of the mayor of Port Oriskany, and the pastor of the First Congregational Church, and the most prominent funeral director in the city, and the publisher of the newspaper); he sang in the choir of the Congregational Church, and attended all services and rehearsals faithfully; he participated in amateur theatrical and musical evenings, content to assume minor roles, and not to upstage local talents; he soon displayed his amiable gifts for poker, as one who lost as cheerfully as he won, and did not win *too* frequently; he knew Thoroughbred horses, though he rarely allowed himself to place bets, as, in his eyes, doing so degraded the Sport of Kings; while basking in the attentions of charming young women, he did not slight their mothers, or elder sisters; he so impressed the publisher of the *Port Oriskany Republican* with his shrewd good sense as to ways and means of drumming up more advertising revenue, and presenting favored politicians in as human and seductive a light as possible, he might well have had a career there, had the Pyramid Mail-Order business been less challenging, and his own temperament less restless. . . .

(Though too young to be taken seriously by the party, yet Abraham Licht was approached upon several occasions as to his plans for the future: did he intend to remain in Port Oriskany, did he hope to marry a local girl and settle down, had he any interest in . . . serving the public? The Republicans had lately suffered considerable losses, following the surprising election of Cleveland, a Democrat, as governor of the state, on a rabble-rousing "reform" ticket; fresh blood was badly needed. The chairman of the state Republican caucus took him aside, and clapped him on the shoulder, and confided in him that, if he had a penchant for The Game—"and that is all there is in politics, son, 'success' being but Dead Sea fruit"—he might well make his way up the ladder of county and state offices; for vacancies regularly appeared from year to year as men died off, or were retired, or slipped from favor with the public. To this friendly overture, as to numerous others made to him, young Licht replied with great enthusiasm and pleasure, though with an air of evasiveness; for, as he admitted, his temperament *was* restless, and he hoped for more travel and adventure in life, before settling down with a wife and family.)

Then, whether by Destiny or crude Accident, it happened that Abraham Licht fell passionately in love with Mrs. Arabella Jenkins, the young widow of one prominent Port Oriskany attorney, and the suspected mistress of another; and his flourishing career in that city came to an abrupt end.

The occasion of their meeting was a musical Thursday evening at the Coliseum Club, where German lieder were being sung with melancholy spirit, and such perennial favorites of the drawing room as "The Angel's Whisper," "Come Back to Erin," and "Jeanie, with the Light Brown Hair." The most applauded event of the evening, however, was a piece by Schubert, for mixed chorus (three male voices, three female), piano, and violin, in which the brunette beauty Mrs. Jenkins shone to advantage, singing in a deep, rich, full, unfaltering alto voice, and, with seeming artlessness, commanding the attention of the entire room. Was she not, with her thick-lashed brown eyes, and her gleaming black hair, and her Junoesque proportions, a splendid woman indeed?

Abraham Licht stared, and stared, at Arabella Jenkins; and listened so intensely to her, the voices of the others faded.

Why, what could it mean—that her eyes moved so carelessly upon him, and drifted past?

He did not know her, but knew of her: knew certain romantic tales and rumors of her: that she had lost her well-to-do husband after only a few years of marriage, that she was childless, and showed little inclination to remarry; that she had lately become the secret beloved of a middle-aged Port Oriskany attorney, whose influence in the city was considerable.

A fallen woman, then, of a sort; yet, very clearly the undisputed queen of such gatherings as these; and one who, if Abraham Licht judged her correctly, thought rather highly of herself, basking in the applause she made a pretty show of disclaiming. (Yet, how sweet the hand-clapping and shouts of "Bravo!" surely were, to a woman un-fettered by tiresome notions of modesty: knowing herself supremely *herself*: and calibrating her value by way of the admiring faces that sur-rounded her.)

Abraham Licht, standing apart, continued to stare, unsmiling, at Mrs. Jenkins; joining but mechanically in the applause; feeling for her so ambiguous an emotion, or sensation, he could not have said if it was resentment, or tenderness, or confused anger.

And what did it mean, that she dared to glance so casually at him—and then away?

(As to young Licht's previous emotional life, his love-experiences, romances, courtships, et al.—it seemed that he had had none; or did not remember them. For he remembered very little of his past, other than the fact that it was comfortably *past*, and could have no hold upon the present, let alone the future; and it was his assumption that all men and women shared identical inclinations. Had he made the conscious attempt, which he was unlikely to have done, Abraham could not have recalled any distinct events from his childhood: knowing only what he had been told, by a blacksmith and his family who took him in, that, at the approximate age of ten, he was found wandering sickly and deliri-ous, and evidently amnesiac, on a country road south of the great Muirkirk marsh; in so confused a state, he could not even provide the blacksmith with his name, for several days.)

Abraham Licht stared, and stared, and suffered a humiliating wave of heat that rose, it seemed, from his very bowels, to suffuse his face in a mottled blush; followed, within the space of a few minutes, by a warring sensation of chill—of cold so *very* cold, he feared his teeth would begin to chatter. Why, was he ill? Was he mad? Was he *himself*, to succumb to a schoolboy's infatuation, for a woman several years his senior, and the possession of another man?

Ah, how he resented her, beforehand; how bitterly, how proudly, he resented Desire, that it rendered *him* so very suddenly, incomplete!

As for the woman—the evening's exertions had visibly warmed her, flesh and spirit alike: her rosy skin glowed with an interior heat, her pert upper lip gleamed with moisture, her ample bosom strained against the delicate silk of her bodice, she did, indeed, fairly bask, like a cat, in the effusive praise that lapped about her. And the well-to-do gentleman, her rumored lover, standing close by, with his unknowing wife at his side—he too basked in Arabella Jenkins's success, as if, by some oblique logic, it were his own.

"But *he* is not man enough for *her*," Abraham Licht thought, in a spasm of rage. "I shall show him!—I shall show *her*!"

Near the end of the evening Abraham Licht approached Arabella Jenkins, to compliment her like all the others on her exquisite alto voice; while staring at her so raptly, without even the formality of a smile, that, being of a sensuous temperament herself, and hardly a fainting virgin, Arabella could not fail to sense the drift of his intention; indeed, the peremptory beat of his desire.

He informed her in a lowered voice that he would come to see her the next day, and Arabella, rapidly fanning herself, said at once she was sorry, he could not; and Abraham amended, that he would come to her later that night, when the gathering of tiresome old fools and humbugs was dispersed, and the two of them might discuss the subtleties of Schubert's musical genius in greater privacy.

"I am very sorry," Arabella said sharply, with a look of genuine fright, "—but you *cannot*."

("Ah, can I *not?*" says Abraham Licht, "—what is it, dear lady, Abraham Licht *cannot* do? Is it *this*—and *this*—is it *this*—and yet again *this*, dear lady, that Abraham Licht of all men *cannot* do?")

In that way young Abraham Licht succumbed to the violent passion of love, for the first time in his life; his resentment overlaid, for the most part, by an emotion so intense as to approach delirium—for the woman *was* infinitely desirable, and the woman *was* his.

For, in the very early hours of a March day of 1884, they did become lovers, and unbridled lovers indeed, without an excess of ceremony.

For, it soon ceased to matter that Abraham Licht was but a youth of twenty-three, and near-penniless; and that Arabella Jenkins was twenty-eight, and possessed of a house and furnishings, and a small bank account.

For, being besotted on both sides equally, they soon gave no thought whether all the world—which is to say, a select scattering of Port Oriskany citizens—knew of their liaison and condemned it; or marveled at it in secret, as the match of two godly persons, of unusual physical beauty, and personal magnetism, and intelligence, and talent, and rare good luck. . . .

For, with the triumphant appearance of a *man* (Abraham Licht), the *half-man* (Arabella's middle-aged "protector") was banished forever; and could make no claim upon her. ("Though it fairly sickens me," Abraham said to Arabella, in a moment of chagrin, "—to think of a man, any man, even your former husband, touching you as I have touched you." "Why then, my dear, my darling, *please do not think of it*," Arabella begged, covering his warm face with kisses.)

At length, Love so roused them to defiance, why not declare themselves lovers?—why not, scorning custom, publicly declare themselves not *two*, but *one*?—a matching of a sort never before seen in provincial Port Oriskany?

Why not elope?

Why not sell Arabella's property, and move to Manhattan, where each might pursue a career on the stage?—Arabella being gifted in both singing and acting, and Abraham being gifted in acting, and diverse sorts of showmanship? (And his promising baritone voice *might* be trained.)

So the lovers planned, and plotted; and saw that Destiny lay all before them, had they but the courage to strike out for new territory. In a voice quivering with emotion, Abraham Licht one evening recited Mark Antony's great speech to Egypt's queen—

> *Here is my space,*
> *Kingdoms are clay; our dungy earth alike*
> *Feeds beast as man; the nobleness of life*
> *Is to do thus,—when such a mutual pair*
> *And such a twain can do't, in which I bind,*
> *On pain of punishment, the world to know*
> *We stand up peerless.*

—even as he embraced his beloved Arabella, as if in defiance of their enemies. She was greatly moved, and asked Abraham where he had learned Shakespeare's verse with such accuracy and feeling; her young lover told her he'd succumbed to Shakespeare's genius as an undergraduate at Harvard, having fallen ill with an influenza for several weeks one winter, and being confined to his room, with the opportunity of submerging himself in the great tragedies. "For when one is confined in a small space, with no promise of freedom for many days," Abraham said, with a stiffness of his jaws, and a steely-melancholy glint to his eye as if he were recalling an incarceration more onerous than merely the flu, "—there's no salvation quite like poetry, and no poetry quite like Shakespeare's."

So it happened that, one April day, the young lovers left Port Oriskany, eloping to Manhattan; and there experienced numerous adventures—as Abraham Licht might one day reveal in his memoir, these were too many, and too motley, to be described in a small space. *The essence of it was, Fortune did not smile upon us. Though we shook, and shook, and shook the dice, our lucky number never came up.* How was it possible, their hopes for success on Broadway were thwarted repeatedly?— if Arabella was cast for a musical evening in which she excelled, it nonetheless did poorly and closed within a few days; if Abraham succeeded in winning, at last, a supporting role in a play—why, the actors were certain to be betrayed by their producer, and even the "stars" went unpaid. A highly regarded Broadway talent agent took them on—and was exposed by Hearst papers within a few weeks as an exploiter of youthful talent, wanted for bigamy in another state. Within six vertiginous months Arabella's money ran out and Abraham was forced to swallow his pride and take whatever employment he could, being too proud, as he told Arabella, to cable his family in Boston for aid, even as the couple moved from hotel to hotel, each less sumptuous than the former, and farther from their early euphoric dreams.

So they found themselves quarreling. And forgiving each other— passionately, tenderly. Yet again quarreling. And again forgiving each other—with an air of desperation. "Hardly a stranger to misfortune, I'm not accustomed to making another share it with me," Abraham confessed to Arabella. "I feel sickened, ashamed. I feel—less a man." He might have said, too, that he was accustomed at times of misfortune to moving swiftly, leaving town without a backward glance; he would simply "plot" his way out of difficult financial predicaments; sometimes, when necessity forced his hand, he would disguise himself so casually, yet so ingeniously, "Abraham Licht" was never to be detected. But now, living with Arabella, a woman of pride, integrity and character, and in such intimate, cramped quarters, he couldn't escape seeing his misery mirrored in her beautiful eyes. And it began to upset him, that Arabella should be passing judgment daily on *his* worth.

They quarreled about finances, and where next to move, and why Abraham didn't humble himself and ask his wealthy family for help: for, as Arabella tearfully pointed out, they could use the plea of her pregnancy—surely Abraham's father, a gentleman, would take pity on them? Surely he, and Abraham's mother, a gracious wellborn lady, wouldn't be so cruel as to reject an unborn grandchild? "Arabella, please. Say no more on this subject," Abraham said quietly, clenching his jaws. "You know nothing of my people—nothing of our tragic history."

Arabella replied, with an air of startling cynicism, "But what 'history' isn't tragic, if you look closely enough?"

Yet their most bitter quarrels were over what Abraham called Arabella's faithlessness: her moods of caprice and idleness when, to upset him, she smiled with easy favor upon other men; and always, in Arabella's vicinity, there were other men. As if any stranger should be raised to her lover's rank by a warm glance, or a sweet murmured word, or a charming quirk of Arabella's eyebrow.

Like many another lover in such a circumstance, Abraham chastised himself for his weakness. "If only I didn't love the woman so much! Surely the fault is in *me*, rather than in *her*."

For Abraham Licht had been born with the acuity of perception that allows us to know that our anger at another is probably nothing apart from our unexpressed anger at ourselves.

And, as a sexual being, a man must know that while "manliness" is provoked by the female's physical charms, it is also, consequently, depleted by these charms. *The power of Venus Aphrodite. The pagan goddess who tempts men, and exhausts them, through mortal women.* The goddess is a ray of brilliant sunshine animating an otherwise lifeless, colorless landscape, gazing out of an individual woman's eyes, and arousing passion in men which can never be fully satisfied. And, like the ray of sun-shine, she passes steadily and inexorably by; bodiless; without sub-stance; without fidelity.

"And in this crime," the wounded lover muses, "—is there complicity?"

In early summer of '85, Abraham decided that he and Arabella must quit Manhattan to live in the Chautauqua Valley, that their child might be born in more congenial surroundings; and he himself might make a fresh start in business. "After all," he told Arabella, with an air of mild bafflement, that his early promise had come to so little, "I'm not yet twenty-five."

Arabella said, with her air of subtle reproach in which (unless Abra-ham imagined it) a sexual invitation lay coiled as a snake, "Twenty-five! Many a human being has been long dead and buried in the earth, and their bones dissolved to dust, by the age of twenty-five."

So the tempestuous couple moved to the crude village of White Sul-phur Springs, where in the early, harsh winter of '85, a son, Thurston, was born; from there they moved to Contracoeur; next to Mulligar, where their son Harwood was born; then, as bad luck would have it, to the small city of Powhatassie Falls, where Abraham Licht suffered an embarrassing setback in his promising business career.

(Except, though Abraham was arrested and made to spend forty-eight repugnant hours in the county jail, he was not to be convicted of any crime. *As records will show.*)

In all, he and Arabella lived together for five turbulent years. They were never officially man and wife, though Arabella gave birth to two strapping boys and their neighbors generally supposed them married. It had been an early, ardent hope of Arabella's that they would marry; but with the passage of time, and the gradual escalation of their quarrels, her hope faded until she thought no more of it. And perhaps she wouldn't have wished it, in any case. For if she were Abraham Licht's *wife* under the law, the law that so definitely favored men, she would not be able to escape him, should she wish to escape him, quite so easily.

For though Arabella loved the fierce young Abraham Licht, a man so handsome women would stare after him in the street, she believed that for the sake of her soul as for the sake of her physical being (which could not tolerate another pregnancy—not in such impoverished cir-cumstances) she felt she must leave him.

Their life together was wayward and unpredictable, and gave her little sustained happiness. Nor did motherhood appeal to her: her hungry babies were always "at" her, like her husband himself.

"Such hunger," Arabella thought, a panicked fluttering in her heart, "—can I satisfy it? And at what cost?"

If at times they were poor and transient, and objects of community suspicion, at other times they were unexpectedly flush with money from one or another of Abraham's business transactions, or gambling triumphs—and objects of community suspicion as well. They dined extravagantly, it seemed to Arabella, or they did not dine at all. They costumed themselves in fine clothes which, within weeks, ill became their diminished station in life. They traveled by first-class train or carriage, or they did not travel at all—except to steal away, usually by night, from one or another residence. Sometimes Abraham adored her; sometimes, with no warning, he seemed to despise her as a temptress who allowed other men "to court her—to caress her—and to make love to her with their eyes" and who even deceived him, in a subtle way, with their sons. For didn't she love Thurston and Harwood more than she loved *him*?—when he spied upon his family, didn't it seem self-evident, they were happier without him, more relaxed, more inclined to laughter? "Born of her flesh, far more closely bound to her than ever a husband could be, a woman's children must usurp his place," Abraham reasoned, tormenting himself. "For if I could give birth, out of my loins, I know that would be true, for me."

Arabella denied such fancies, as she called them. If, having drunk too much, Abraham persisted, she lost her temper, saying what never failed to upset her young husband: "D'you know what you are getting to be?—*mad*."

Which was the deepest insult to his soul. And how to reply to such a charge, without flushing hot and chagrined, or lashing out in stinging words of his own?

(Yet, Arabella was devious. As Abraham would one day discover. Hiding away what money she could, from unknown sources, over the months and years; encouraging Abraham to buy her expensive jewelry when he had money and the "spending fever" was on him. As if she'd planned to be female indeed, when the opportune time came.)

* * *

Five years of turbulence and passion; waxing, and waning; and waxing again; by no logic Abraham Licht could comprehend.

And bitterly I resented it, that I could not comprehend.

That life is a riddle, I could not comprehend.

That to be the teller of riddles is a destiny, while to be the one to whom riddles are told is but fate.

It infuriated him that Arabella was a beautiful woman who was *his*, and the mother of *his* children, yet so independent in her thoughts and emotions. "What do you want of me, Abraham, and of the world?" she frequently asked him, with a pretense of female bewilderment. "What do you want, why can't you settle down to one occupation, to one residence, to one life?—why, for God's sake, must you want *so much*? Like a giant baby at the nipple, too famished to be *fed*."

This so wounded Abraham, and enraged him, he saw himself in an instant in fine clothes, bathed in light, on a Broadway stage, confronted with a glamorous young woman, beguiling, seductive yet (as the audience well knew) duplicitous. With the ease of the matinee idol who understands how much, how uncritically he's adored, and quite shares in the adoration, Abraham laughed gaily and said, "Then will you marry me, my darling? Tomorrow morning? Yes?"

"Are you serious, or joking?"

Abraham laughed again. He heard, at a distance, the murmured approval of the audience, invisible to him but palpably *there*.

"Surely a man may be joking, yet serious? Serious, yet joking? If you know me at all, Arabella, you must know that."

Arabella gazed searchingly into his eyes. As so many others had, and would. *And how futile, such a search. For my soul is not to be had cheaply.* "Yes," she said finally, with an odd melancholy smile, "—I know."

The next night, in November 1888, Arabella slipped away from their boardinghouse in Vanderpoel while Abraham was out of town on business; leaving four-year-old Thurston and year-old Harwood behind, attended by a young neighbor girl, whom she'd befriended, and a brief, cruel message.

Farewell. Do not follow. Your "love" is too hungry. I am not to be consumed!

A.

Arabella took with her only her finer clothes, and her jewelry, and about $300 in cash of which Abraham knew; the word on the street was that she hadn't run off alone, but Abraham in his pride and fury refused to make inquiries. Nor would he hunt Arabella down.

"Your mother has left us. You must not ask of her. She has behaved badly, yet is not a bad woman. 'Crime? Then complicity.' We trusted her, we were fools, we are to blame. *But not a word of her, ever—d'you understand?*"

Wide-eyed, little Thurston nodded mutely, and one-year-old Harwood blinked and gaped with a baby's sweet acquiescence. For they were their father's sons after all.

Of those five years of Abraham Licht's young manhood and the first flowering of his genius he cares to recall primarily the wondrous hour of his eldest son's birth. In a rooming house in White Sulphur Springs, in a bed smelling of must and mildew and very shortly of the laboring Arabella's sweat, and finally of her blood; when after eleven agonizing hours the midwife at last shouted for him to enter the room and dazed, frightened, his heartbeat sounding in his ears, the young father stepped inside to be presented with a red-faced gasping infant boy, so heated, so perfect in all his proportions, so magically alive, wailing and squirming with life, tears ran freely down Abraham's cheeks. "My son? *Mine?*"

Arabella, her face drained of blood, gaunt as a death's-head, tried to smile at him, as in his astonishment he tried to smile at her. Yet for that instant they might have been strangers. For it was the squirming baby that drew all attention, as if a bright beam of light were shining upon him. "Thurston. Thurston Licht. My son." Abraham was holding the baby in his awkward arms, trembling violently. The midwife smiled broadly at him, bemused by his youth, his handsome face, his new-father's look of commingled pride and terror. *A shrieking hairless monkey, a beautiful creature only minutes old, with his father's features and spirited energy—obviously!*

For wasn't the baby a form of Abraham Licht's very self, reentering the world, like an act of Hindu reincarnation, to conquer the world again? *and yet again?*

The Fate of "Christopher Schoenlicht"

I

It could hardly be held against the bookmakers of Atlantic City and their sporting clients, that hundreds of bets were placed on the outcome of Christopher Schoenlicht's trial for first-degree murder, in December 1909, in the Atlantic County Courthouse: not whether the defendant would be acquitted (for that was never an issue), but whether he would be hanged by the public executioner, as the county prosecutor passionately urged; or sentenced to life imprisonment, as Bullock, his attorney, yet more passionately urged. For neither the prosecution nor the defense doubted that Schoenlicht, and Schoenlicht alone, was guilty of the murder of his "fiancée" Mrs. Eloise Peck; nor did young Schoenlicht himself deny the charge.

The interest of the trial, then, lay exclusively in its outcome; and its mystery, or mysteries, in several isolated elements—the background of the defendant (if, indeed, he had any: for no one could discover anything about him); his motive for the brutal murder, in circumstances in which he could not fail to be apprehended; what had become of the money and jewels he had taken from her room; why did he stubbornly refuse to speak to police, or even to defense counsel, when his life was at stake; and so forth. Though, being an open-and-shut case, with no courtroom surprises or reversals, the trial ran its course in four swift days, newspapers in Atlantic City and New York City sought to enliven proceedings by publishing interviews with persons who claimed to be acquainted with the "Doomed Heiress" (as the papers called poor Eloise), and others, mainly employees of the Hotel Saint-Léon, who claimed to have known "Christopher Schoenlicht." Photographs of the deceased woman were run daily, as were companion photographs of the young man charged with her murder: though Schoenlicht now looked so drawn and fatigued, and carried his tall frame with such lethargy, it might be said that he was no longer a young man at all.

And in the courtroom itself, exposed to all eyes, with nowhere to turn that he might hide his face, Schoenlicht was the very image of sorrow: yet a sorrow of bone-weariness, and indifference: his skin grainy and flaccid, the flesh beneath his eyes puffy, and the eyes themselves glazed over, like those of a somnambulist. Was *this* Eloise Peck's dashing young lover, whom she had loved with such fatal results?—so observers wondered.

It was the wily Bullock's strategy, in the face of a succession of damning witnesses for the State (for who, in fashionable Atlantic City, had not seen Mrs. Peck hanging on the arm of Mr. Schoenlicht?), to argue to the court that his client was mentally infirm; mentally deficient; with no volition of his own, and no "free will"; sunk at the present time (as the gentlemen of the jury were invited to observe) into so pathological a torpor, very likely he did not *see* or *hear* distinctly; and could have no interest in his own fate. "To condemn a human being so helpless, and, indeed, so *harmless* now to society, would be an act of greater cruelty than the unpremeditated crime for which he is being tried"—so Bullock charged with such evident passion, and such finely calibrated drama, Abraham Licht himself (who was paying the attorney his customary handsome fee) felt forced to admiration.

A Boston alienist of "unassailable reputation" took the stand, to argue, for the defense, that Schoenlicht was of a *catatonic disposition*; he had long, it might be inferred, exhibited symptoms of acute mental disease, which went unrecognized by persons about him, or were interpreted as but *traits of character.* He had examined the defendant closely, he said, and was satisfied that the man was distinctly abnormal; of a temperament that might well crack under emotional pressure; go berserk; commit a savage crime under compulsion, without being aware of what he did, or remembering it afterward.

This, the prosecution handily countered with the testimony of an alienist for the State, who argued that all criminals might be said to suffer "mental disease"—the proof of it being, *they are criminals.* And, granted the compulsive nature of most violent crimes, and the lack of conscious volition on the part of the criminal, was it not a felicitous thing indeed, that capital punishment *was* the law of the land?

Yet more damningly, the prosecuting attorney called attention to the fact that, long before Schoenlicht had "gone berserk" and committed his "savage crime," he and the late Mrs. Peck were widely known to have been behaving in an immoral manner: cohabiting together (with all that implies of the violations of Christian morality, the standards of decent society, good taste, and the like) with no discretion or shame. And if, as it was rumored, Schoenlicht had once studied for the ministry, surely his public embrace of sin must be judged the more reprehensible; for he *knew* what he did, and might have known what a price would be exacted from him.

In all, the prosecution called thirty-five witnesses, of whom only a few were cross-examined by Bullock, to avoid testimony further damaging to his client; and of these only one, Mrs. Peck's personal maid, evinced any doubt on the witness stand regarding her statement to the police. She had said that she heard the voices of Mrs. Peck and Mr. Schoenlicht, in a room adjacent to her own; yet, some minutes before that, she believed she had heard the voices of two men . . . although she could not swear to it. "And who was the second man?" the prosecuting attorney asked skeptically. But the shy young Filipino woman, who spoke English haltingly, could not answer, and the subject of the "second man" was dropped. Next morning when Bullock tried to pursue it during his cross-examination of the witness, the young woman denied she had heard any such voice—only the voices of Mr. Schoenlicht and Mrs. Peck, which she knew well.

The tragedy of one son convicted of murder, and taken forcibly from me might only be compounded by the tragedy of two sons taken from me.

A gamble this veteran gambler dared not take.

(Behind the scenes of the trial things progressed as badly. By degrees Abraham Licht's money was being drained away in desperate stratagems overseen by the wily Bullock and executed by his secret, unnamed assistants: the attempted bribery of key prosecution witnesses, those members of the jury who appeared most susceptible to persuasion, the examining physician, the county coroner, and so forth. The manager of the Saint-Léon accepted a generous sum of money to be used on "repairs" in the damaged room in which Mrs. Peck had died, yet on the witness stand spoke distastefully of the defendant as a "cold and calculating youth" who had pretended to be good-natured and charming while doubtless planning his crime for weeks. One of the jurors expressed an initial interest in an arrangement by which, in return for his promise to abstain from voting, and thereby hang the jury, he would receive a generous sum of money as a "donation" he might then give to charity; but when a fellow juror suspected the plan, he hurriedly backed away saying he would vote "as God, and not the Devil, directed." Several "character witnesses" were found by Bullock, and coached and rehearsed in praise of the defendant, but were such poor, unconvincing actors, Bullock conceded it would be a mistake to bring them into court to be cross-examined. The idea of involving Elisha in some way was considered, but finally dropped, for Elisha, even in an ingenious disguise, might be linked by police or newspaper reporters with the Black Phantom of Chautauqua Falls, which would be unfortunate indeed.

The trial proceeded swiftly. The day of summation approached. Abraham Licht's heart was wrung by the pitiful spectacle of his eldest, beloved son a prisoner in the courtroom, in shackles as he was led in and out of the building by uniformed guards; his handsome face ravaged with sorrow, lost to all hope; his gaze steadfastly averted from his father's, in despair and shame. *For one Licht must never betray another even to save his own skin. For what could be done in such circumstances?* Abraham Licht urged Bullock to try a higher, more idealized philosophical defense, in the manner of the celebrated Clarence Darrow, where the issue of capital punishment itself would be tried—for in these years, a number of liberal-minded persons opposed execution as a punishment in violation of the United States Constitution. But Bullock countered by saying dryly that he had tried that ploy too often, finding to his chagrin that while an individual judge might be swayed by such humanitarian pleas, juries never were. For a jury was a microcosm of the public and the public wanted hangings.

"Even if the defendant is innocent?" Abraham asked in so plaintive and sincere a tone that Bullock stared at him, embarrassed, and could think of no reply. *For of course he believed that his client was guilty.*)

So it happened that the sensational, much-publicized murder trial, the *People of the State of New Jersey* v. *"Christopher Schoenlicht,"* ended

within four days; to the disappointment of all, particularly the platoon
of newspaper reporters crowded into the front rows of the courtroom,
the somber young defendant declined to take the witness stand to plead
on his own behalf; the judge, visibly disdainful of both defendant and
defense counsel, as if a bad smell permeated his courtroom, gave brief,
perfunctory instructions to the jury, without troubling to lay particular
emphasis on the principle of "reasonable doubt"—for was any doubt
reasonable, in so lurid a case; the twelve frowning jurors retired to de-
liberate, and vote; and were out of the courtroom, as newspaper banner
headlines excitedly reported next day, only eight minutes—a "record-
breaking" brevity of time for any murder trial, in any known United
States court of law.

II

Before and during his trial there came to visit Christopher Schoenlicht, in his solitary cell in the Atlantic County jail, a gentleman legal
consultant of Mr. Bullock's named "Murray M. Kirk" of Manhattan. An
optimistic middle-aged fellow with a habit of pressing his pince-nez
against the bridge of his nose, and speaking loudly and clearly (so that
the prisoner's guard would not become suspicious); with a handsome,
tired face, and shadowed eyes, and a head of thick, fawn-colored hair
always impeccably combed; in a three-piece gray woolen suit, a white
shirt with a stiff wing collar, a bow tie with ends tucked neatly beneath
the collar and a smart black homburg hat. Mr. Kirk carried black gloves
and an ebony cane and had folded a fresh white linen handkerchief
into his lapel pocket. The very image of legal propriety; and authority;
yet how odd, that he should stare with such baffled yearning at the
young Schoenlicht, who shifted uneasily on his hard-backed chair, and
sat with bowed head reluctant to meet the elder man's gaze.

Son? Don't you know me? Look me, my darling boy, in the eye!

Though Schoenlicht and Kirk were seated not three feet apart, on
either side of a narrow pinewood table, yet the younger man continued
to avoid the elder's gaze; sighing often, and passing a hand over his
eyes, as if in a state of extreme agitation. This was apparently quite
different from Schoenlicht's normal behavior with others. Though

indicted for the most serious offense, except for treason, that could be-
fall him in the United States, the young man was in the habit of staring
stonily into space; not listening to his attorney's words; showing indifference to his circumstances, and to his imminent fate. If required to
answer a question (as, for instance, Bullock's exasperated, "Son, do you
want to *live?*") he might shrug silently; then revert back into his stony
trance. Abraham Licht had told Bullock that in his presence Christopher would "come alive—to a degree" but in fact this had not happened.
Not to the degree that Abraham wished.

At one of these meetings, "Mr. Kirk" whipped his white linen handkerchief out of his pocket, dabbed at his perspiring face, and said, in a
voice edged with avuncular impatience, "Young man, I command you
to sit still. I am your legal counsel's assistant and you must answer my
questions. *Otherwise you will be lost.*"

At this, Christopher froze. In a most awkward position, one shoulder
hunched forward and his head inclined to the right, as if gravity were
dragging him down. Did he hear? Did he comprehend? Something glittered in a corner of his eye but did not spill over. Tight as a fist his face
was clenched as if the spirit, the stubborn Licht spirit, had retreated far
within.

Abraham was reminded, with a shock of fierce tenderness, how,
during his eldest son's single year of college at Bowdoin, he'd had the
opportunity to travel north to Maine, to visit the boy; discovering
the lad in a tavern near campus, in the company of several friends.
Abraham Licht had stood at a short distance listening to the boys' artless speech, punctuated by laughter; he'd surprised himself with the
thought *How like the others my son is!—if I did not know he was mine, I
would never identify him as a Licht.* Later, father and son had quarreled
over this issue, that Thurston should be on such easy, friendly terms
with strangers; that he should be accepting invitations to visit their
homes, which Abraham hadn't known; that he should risk exposure,
and at the very least a serious diminution of his powers. For how could
Thurston perceive these individuals as enemies, if he allowed himself
to befriend them in such a way? *All men are our enemies,* then and now
was the ethic by which Abraham Licht lived, and the ethic in which he
had trained his children, and how came Thurston, obedient Thurston,
his Thurston, to contest it?

The disagreement, like so many between Abraham Licht and his children, wasn't so much resolved as simply dropped. For Abraham arranged for Thurston to be "expelled" from Bowdoin—a discreet bribe to a residence proctor, a discreet bribe to a dean, and the undergraduate was discovered "in a state of alcoholic inebriation" while returning to campus one night; the only young man of a dozen revelers to be so discovered, apprehended, and charged. It was a measure of Thurston's extreme innocence, Abraham realized, that the boy had never guessed what, or who, lay behind his expulsion. He had simply accepted his fate—"My grades were not so very good, Father, in any case," he'd said sheepishly. And how readily he'd pleased his father by agreeing that it was time to begin his professional career under Abraham's tutelage, and break off his trifling friendships forever.

"Do you hear me, Christopher?" Abraham Licht asked, in a wonderfully controlled voice. "Will you do me the honor of looking at me? *I command you.*"

Slowly, reluctantly, shamefacedly, the young prisoner turned to his visitor. His lips trembled wetly. His gaze wavered. *Yes I am your son. Yes I love you. But, Father—* So strained was the atmosphere in the airless space, the uniformed guard dawdling in a corner took a sudden unwanted interest in them, and Abraham had to temper his speech and govern his manner carefully. For now that his unhappy son was facing him, and looking at him, tears gathering in his eyes, a slip of the tongue or a sudden inadvertent gesture might cause him to break into sobs and to throw himself, like a child, into Abraham's arms.

So Abraham spoke judiciously, and calmly. Asking why did "Christopher" refuse to cooperate with his counsel? Why did he show so little interest in his fate? And who was the true murderer of Eloise Peck?— "For if you know, son, you should tell. You should tell me."

For a long moment Thurston stared at him. His young face was drawn, and curiously lined, as if a mask of age had been fitted onto it. When he seemed about to speak, but did not, Abraham whispered, "I command you to speak. *Otherwise you will be lost.*"

Was the guard listening? Could the guard, an ignorant, loutish man, have understood? Yet Thurston, being a Licht, could not trust him; and shaped with his lips the heartrending plea *Father, I am lost in any case. Better die one than two. For it must be two if not one. Forgive me, Father! I am lost, Thurston is lost.*

The distinguished visitor from Manhattan pressed his pince-nez sharply against the bridge of his nose, and rose to his feet. With an abrupt farewell to the prisoner, he turned away; and asked the guard please to escort him out. He would visit him again, in the interest (or so it would appear to observers) of proffering moral support; but never again would the young prisoner so frankly face him, and never again would the air of the visiting room be so highly charged.

III

For of course "Christopher Schoenlicht" was found guilty of murder in the first degree.

And no recommendation was made by the jury for mercy.

It was on a bitterly cold January morning, nearly six months to the day after the death of Eloise Peck, that the young murderer, manacled, hollow-cheeked, appeared before the judge who had presided over his trial, to be told the specific details of his fate.

Had he anything to say to the court, the judge inquired, before sentence was passed?

"Christopher Schoenlicht" stood hunched, between his attorney and a bailiff, hearing the judge's words, yet not hearing them; his expression stony; his eyes resolutely downcast; his lower jaw slightly extended beyond the upper, and held rigid.

He had nothing to say.

So it was, nettled, the judge read off his prepared statement, slowly enough so that Schoenlicht might absorb every syllable of every word, to the effect that, his crime being one of inordinate savagery, and his state of mind since his arrest that of a thoroughly unrepentant man, he was thereby sentenced to be hanged by the neck until dead, in accordance with the statute of the state of New Jersey, on a date to be determined by the public executioner, such sentence to be carried out on, or before, 1 June 1910.

"Little Moses"

I

Crime? whispers Father.
   Then complicity.
Complicity?
Then no crime.

"Little Moses," husky for a child of ten, isn't he, sweet-tempered and dim-witted, obedient, faithful, uncomplaining, yes, black as pitch, yes, able and willing to do the work of a near-grown man, and, yes, he will grow, and grow, and grow, and he will work, and work, and work, and, being sweet of temper and dim of wit and black, black as pitch, he is faithful as a dog, he will be loyal for life, he has no *thought* of anything save work, he has no *thoughts* as you and I do, as white folks do, and, being of course the son, that is the grandson, of Alabama plantation slaves—will he not repay his cost numberless times over the next fifty years?

And his cost, sir, is so reasonable, sir, I will whisper it in your ear so that he cannot hear: $600 cash.

Lemuel Shattuck, farmer, of Black Eddy, Michigan; Alvah Gunness, farmer, of La Porte, Minnesota; Ole Budsberg, blacksmith, of Dryden, Minnesota; William Elias Schutt, candymaker, of Elbow Lake, Illinois; Jules Rulloff, farmer, of Horseheads, New York; the Abbotts, dairy farmers, of Lake Seneca, New York; the Wilmots, cotton manufacturers, of North Thetford, Pennsylvania . . . *And his cost, sir, is so reasonable, sir, I will whisper it in your ear so that he cannot hear: $600 cash.*

Though the prosperous Uriah Skillings, stableowner of Glen Rapids,

Ohio, paid $1,000. And Estes Morehouse, retired classicist, of Rocky Hill, New Jersey, paid $800.

For these gentlemen, and for some others, "Little Moses" strutted, and cavorted, and grinned, and rolled his white, white eyeballs, and sang:

"Come listen all you gals and boys
I'm just from Tuck-y-hoe
I'm goin' to sing a lee-tle song
My name's Jim Crow!

Weel about and turn about
And do jis so
Eb'ry time I weel about
I jump Jim Crow!"

In the autumn and winter of '98, through the spring of '99, they criss-crossed the countryside, frequently by night, frequently by back roads, Solon J. Berry and his obedient "Little Moses," Mr. Berry possessed of a broad heavy melancholy face, close-trimmed salt-and-pepper whiskers, wire-rimmed glasses, a farmer who had lost his eighty-acre farm, a mill owner who had lost his mill, a former railroad agent for the Chesapeake & Ohio, a former druggist of Marion, Ohio, a casualty of the recession, once proud now humbled, once a man who owned property free and clear now a man hounded by creditors, ashen skin, pouched eyes, queer nicks and blemishes in his cheeks, forced to certain actions, compromises, pragmatic measures which, in his prime, he would never have considered—being a Christian, after all, of stolid Calvinist faith.

Solon J. Berry, or Whittaker Hale, or Hambleton Fogg, but always "Little Moses," for he was plucked from the bulrushes, yes, more or less, yes indeed, an Act of God, saved from certain drowning when the mighty Wabash River overflowed its banks in April '89 in Lafayette, Indiana, a howling black baby discovered amid drowned dogs, drowned chickens, drowned rats, snagged by an iron hook and pulled to shore, lifted from a nest of matted grass and filth that teemed with spiders, a living infant!—a black infant!—abandoned by his mother yet living, still, thrashing with life, mouth opened wide to howl, to shriek, a vast O of a mouth, wailing, wailing!—*why, the pitiful thing yet lives.*

And has grown husky, hasn't he?

And uncomplaining, and zealous, and patient, *and doesn't eat too much*, and can work twelve hours a day, farmwork, lifting and carrying, scouring pans, digging ditches, did I say twelve hours?—fourteen; sixteen; as many as a task requires. And doesn't need to sleep more than three, four hours, most nights, yes it is the black blood, yes his people were Alabama plantation slaves, the best West African stock, pitch-black, strong as horses, never sick a day until, at the age of ninety-nine, they drop over dead, why that won't be till the year 2000, almost!—and here he is grinning, strutting, obedient as a puppy, clever as a little monkey, dull-witted as a sheep, reliable as an ox, and, when the mood is on him, a genuine entertainment right in the home, rolling his eyes, and snapping his fingers, and kicking up his heels, here is "Zip Coon," here is "Poor Black Boy," here is " 'Possum Up a Gum-Tree," but the *pièce de résistance*, the *ne plus ultra*, the *flagrante delicto*, stand back, give him room, it's wild "Jim Crow" himself!

And all for $600. And no one ever to know, *precisely*, the terms of the orphan's contract.

Sometimes "Little Moses" slept for an hour or two in his new master's house, in a corner of the woodshed where rags had been tossed, in the back room in Grandpa's old urine-stained bed, once in a hayloft with mice and rats, once in a cardboard box beside a woodburning stove whose embers smoldered with a slow dull cozy heat, sometimes, more often, "Little Moses" didn't risk sleep at all but lay awake, waiting, quietly waiting, for the white folks to settle down for the night.

Then he would slip away, not a creaking floorboard to betray him, not a barking dog, "Little Moses" running hunched over, head down, crawling if need be, making his stealthy way from one shadowy area to the next, in case his new master was watching from a window (but how could he be watching, the fool was fast asleep with the rest), trotting out to the moonlit country road where, in the two-seater gig, "Solon J. Berry" waited, napping, as he liked to say, with one eye open.

"Is it true, Father," Elisha asked doubtfully, "—that you found me in the Wabash River?—*in a flood?*"

Abraham Licht smiled, and lay a warm protective hand on the boy's woolly hair, and said, after a pause of perhaps ten seconds, "No, 'Lisha. It was the Nautauga, back East, but folks hereabouts might not have heard of it; and I don't want to arouse their suspicions."

"Is it true, Father," Elisha asked, "that the white folks is *devils*, and all of them *enemies*? Or is some of them different, like you?"

And Abraham Licht smiled, and sucked zestfully on his cigar, and said, "Now look here, 'Lisha—*I'm not white*. I may look white, and I may talk white, but I stand outside the white race, just like you, and all of my people stand outside the white race, because they *are* devils, and they *are* enemies, each and every one."

But none of the enemies reports Mr. Berry, or Mr. Hale, or Mr. Fogg to the police.

And none of the enemies reports "Little Moses" missing.

"Nor will they ever, the wretches!" Abraham Licht says, baring his big white teeth around his Cuban cigar, counting his cash, "*that*, Baby Moses, we are assured of."

So they crisscross the countryside, keeping to the back roads, upon occasion traveling fast—very fast—along a main artery—no time to dally, no time to browse—but for the most part ambling along in no great hurry: for the land *is* beautiful, the North American continent *is* beautiful: no matter (as Abraham Licht says with an upward twist of his lip) that human beings have begun to foul it.

(Does Elisha sometimes doubt that people, white *or* black, are devils?—and only the Lichts can be trusted?—Father then reads him tales from the newspapers, the confessions of the hard-hearted murderer Frank Abbott-Almy of Vermont, the "true story" of the monstrous Braxtons of Indiana, and, most ghastly of all, the saga of Widow Sorenson of Ohio, who acquired twenty-eight husbands by way of matrimonial journals, and, over a period of two decades, killed them for their money, and fed their remains to the hogs.

The lesson being, as Elisha learns to shape with his lips, while Father speaks: *All men are enemies, then or now*; but, *Brothers by blood are brothers by the soul*.)

Then one day Abraham Licht declares that he is *Licht* again, and Elisha is *Elisha*; and very suddenly he is homesick for Muirkirk; and his beloved Sophie; and dear little Millicent, whose seventh birthday—*is it the seventh?*—he has missed, laboring here in the vineyards, casting his pearls before swine.

So, within an hour or two, he sells the two-seater gig, and the sway-back horses, and buys some new clothes for himself and his boy, and arranges for them to travel to Chautauqua in a private Pullman car, now he is Licht again, now he can breathe again, now he can hold his head high again, $4,500 in clear profits, $6,200, perhaps it is as much as $9,000, and not one of the enemies reports the affair to the police, not Shattuck, nor Gunness, nor Budsberg, nor Schutt, nor Rulloff, nor the Abbotts, nor the Wilmots, nor the others, the many others, the contemptible execrable *fools*, not a one! not a one!

"And do you know why, 'Lisha?" Abraham asks.

'Lisha grins and nods; 'Lisha knows; in mock solemnity wheeling, and turning about, and mouthing the words, the terrible words, *I jump Jim Crow!*

II

When, in the spring of '89, Abraham Licht brought the squalling black baby home with him, the red-haired woman with whom he was living—*not* Arabella, who had run off the previous year, and *not* Morna the minister's daughter, whom he wasn't to meet for several months—this woman, this ignorant woman, what did she do but push at Abraham and the baby both, laughing, incensed: "What is it! Keep it from me! *I can't be that thing's mother.*"

He turned the woman out that very day.

Forgot her name within a week.

And soon Elisha, sickly little Elisha, was as dear to him as his own boys, or very nearly: for the pitiful creature had no mother, or father, or name, or place of birth: as damned by the black God, it seemed, as by the white.

In neither of whom, Abraham Licht boasted, *he* believed.

Was it true that Elisha had been hooked and snagged out of a flooded river, pulled to shore, saved from drowning? . . . was it true that Abraham

Licht, returning to his hotel room in the Nautauga Falls Arms, saved the baby himself?

Indeed yes.

Very certainly—yes.

Though it had not been the Nautauga River but a rain-swollen ditch that ran beside a wooden sidewalk, just down the hill from the hotel, a filth-choked ditch three or four feet deep, the dark water swirling and gurgling and rushing along, as noisy, or nearly, as the great Nautauga itself.

So the little black thing was snatched up, and saved.

So the little black thing, howling, mouth opened to an enormous O, was snatched up, and saved, and hugged to the breast of the fashionably dressed white gentleman (chesterfield coat with black velvet collar, silk top hat, ivory-headed cane) whose cheeks were flushed and spirits gratified by a long evening of poker, at worthwhile stakes, at a private Nautauga Falls men's club.

"Why, the devil—!" Abraham Licht exclaimed, as the wailing creature soiled his coat sleeve, and thrashed about with a remarkable energy, "—it *is* the Devil! *And am I to be its father?*"

At this problematic time in Abraham Licht's life Thurston was five years old, Harwood two, motherless boys for whom Abraham must find a mother, a decent mother, and *soon*: and he yearned, too, for a daughter: for would not a daughter complete his soul, indeed?—and help to make amends for the cruel treatment he had received at the hands of Arabella. He was obliged, too, to resume his business, or businesses, being not overly flushed with cash; most eager to launch the secret Society for the Reclamation & Restoration of E. Auguste Napoléon, the "true heir" of the Emperor. (To this end, Abraham had prepared for the printer certain genealogical charts, certificates, and model shares pertaining to the Society; and had scattered the vague hint, to credulous newspaper editors in the East, that the French government was conspiring to cheat a number of American citizens—some two hundred, or five hundred, or more—of their rightful inheritance as descendants of the bastard heir.)

So it was not a very felicitous time for him to take on a Negro infant, no matter that there is a special providence in the fall of a sparrow!

Yet Abraham Licht wouldn't give up the pitiful creature, to turn it over to the tender mercies of the township. Instead he took it home with him, determined to love it, and make it his. " 'Poor, bare, forked animal!'—I baptize these *Elisha*, my 'salvation,' " he whispered, bent over the baby, which slept now peaceably as a kitten atop his bed, and kissing its forehead.

And never would Abraham Licht regret his decision.

And never, until Elisha's twenty-first birthday in the early winter of 1910, when the black foundling dared challenge *him*, would he love the boy less than he loved the children of his own loins.

III

And it happened that, shortly after Elisha came to live with him, as if by magic Abraham Licht's uncertain luck changed for the better. He acquired the wonderfully capable Katrina as a housekeeper—this mysterious, formidable woman who was a great-aunt of his, or a cousin several times removed, from the remote area beyond Mount Chattaroy; and he met, and at once fell in love with, Miss Morna Hirshfield, pursuing the lovely young woman with such ardor that she was won within three weeks; and, in the early euphoria of her love for Abraham Licht, vowed she would love his sons, *all* his sons, the Negro no less than the white, as well. (For Morna Hirshfield, daughter of a Unitarian minister and granddaughter of fervent Abolitionists, believed herself a paragon of Christian and womanly virtues; and yet, the year being 1890, a bravely modern person—independent enough to live with a man she loved "bereft of clergy" and even to bear him, in time, a child.)

And, too, Abraham was able to purchase the auctioned property of the Church of the Nazarene, Risen, for a mere pittance; and to move his now-large household there, to the beautiful wilds of Muirkirk, for greater safety, as he believed—"and safekeeping."

Did it seem puzzling, and vexing, and somewhat shameful to Thurston and Harwood and, later, to Millie, that they had a Negro brother?—*it did not.*

Of course, Muirkirk observers must have gossiped. There must have been cruel, outraged speculation. There must have been coarse jokes, at least initially, before Abraham Licht became well known and well liked in the region. Whenever the children appeared together—Thurston in particular so fair-haired, so handsome a boy, in stark contrast to the swarthy-skinned, woolly-haired Elisha—you could depend upon it, people would stare. "For Homo sapiens is by genetic inheritance xenophobic," Abraham Licht explained to his family, "—I would not doubt that there is, in the brain, some tiny cog that triggers 'fear'—'distrust'—'loathing'—'threat'—upon seeing another whose features and skin color seem *foreign*. So we must accept the foibles of others, who are our enemies in any case; but it would be well for us to contemplate how such foibles might be pressed to our advantage, rather than attempt to overcome them. All we need to know is, *We are Lichts. Out of Muirkirk mud, a lineage to conquer Heaven*."

The white-skinned children of Abraham Licht didn't require such wisdom from their father to feel affection for Elisha, or 'Lisha as he was called. For of all of them, 'Lisha was sweet, funny, and sly; a natural mimic, clearly bound for the stage or for public oratory of some kind; a "wily little Devil" as Katrina (who rarely indulged in such commentary on her charges) said; the smartest of the boys; hot-tempered, and quick to repent; quick to burst into tears, and quick to wipe away his tears and smile; a congenial household presence as "Little Moses," and a good deal more intelligent. Also, it was always the case that Abraham Licht, as Father, determined how his progeny should think and feel and, to a degree, behave; and "feelings" not granted a vocabulary by him had not much existence, or at any rate could not be expressed. Abraham explained this simple psychology to his bride Morna, who laughed at its logic—"Why, if we had no word for sorrow, melancholy, wickedness, evil, would these not exist?" Abraham merely smiled, and laid his finger alongside his nose. *To adore a woman is not to respect her intelligence. To find a woman infinitely desirable, we need not lay bare our souls to her.*

Upon one memorable occasion, eight-year-old Harwood inquired frowningly of Katrina why 'Lisha, then six, was "dark-skinned like mahogany" and his hair "so fuzzy-strange," and the insides of his hands "pinker than mine"; but Harwood's childish questioning carried no evident suspicion or rancor, and Katrina's reply, much repeated in the household, seemed to satisfy him completely: "Because Father wishes him so."

Elisha himself, sly Elisha, thought well enough of 'Lisha, and "Little

Moses," or any of the black boys of Abraham Licht's creation, to have no fear that *he* was inferior—not him! Nor even set aside from the others by any peculiarity of being. He loved to contemplate his image in any mirror: for was he not handsome with his tight-curled, glistening hair trimmed close to his skull, or allowed from time to time to fuzz out splendidly, like dandelion seed; and his wide-set dark eyes, liquid-bright, and flecked with hazel like glints of mischief; and his slightly flat nose, and deep, dark nostrils, and chiselled lip? When 'Lisha was lazy, it seemed ideal to be lazy; when he leapt and pranced about, and kicked up (as Katrina fondly scolded) a "ruckus," then that seemed ideal. If Father was at home Father closely observed whatever 'Lisha did, took note of whatever he said, as, indeed, Father was inclined to do with all the children, not to censure or scold, but, it seemed, simply to *observe*: that he might, perhaps, discover where Elisha's best talents lay, and which traits in him were weak. ("*You* are the chameleon of the household," Father declared, laughing, "—and so very quick, one would not be surprised to see you slip out of that skin, and into another.")

It might have distressed Elisha that his brothers, and, in time, his pretty sister Millie, were sent away to expensive private schools (at least intermittently: for Abraham Licht's fortunes continued to rise and fall with less predictability than the moon's tide), while he was kept at home; but, as Father chose to tutor him himself, in such subjects as French conversation, and mathematics, and Shakespeare, and the manners of a gentleman, and declared him his "right-hand man," even at so young an age, Elisha could not forbear feeling pride, if not outright vanity: for he sensed himself—indeed, did he not know himself?—Father's favorite. "You are all loved equally, as you are all deserving of the same degree of love," Father sometimes said, staring, with a kind of wonderment, at his children, and approaching them each in turn, to kiss them, or embrace them to his bosom, "—for it is the irrefutable truth, *you are all marvels.*" Such declarations had the effect of fairly mesmerizing the children, and bringing tears to their eyes; for they had no doubt but that Father spoke the truth; for that which Father spoke—was it not Truth? Yet, afterward, regarding his reflection in a mirror, or even, hazily, in a pool of marsh water, Elisha murmured aloud in elation, "He loves us all equally—*and 'Lisha most of all!*"

Nor was he jealous when Darian was born, and then, not long afterward, Esther—these little ones, Sophie's children, being so very *little*, it was hardly reasonable to think that Father would ever care to love them; or even to observe them with much interest.

When Father was away on business that did not involve him, and Elisha was left behind in Muirkirk, he hid his disappointment and impatience, and set about completing tasks assigned by Father: for instance, studying the latest edition of *The Young Christian Gentleman's Guide to Perfect Etiquette* so very meticulously, he could pass a quiz on the correct employment of visiting cards, and every manner of fork, spoon, and knife, to be encountered at a formal dinner party, and how precisely one must behave when presented to Royalty; he learned to sing, from memory, a Bach cantata, "Brich dem Hungrigen dein Brot," which Father had assigned for mysterious, yet urgent, reasons; and he learned to recite, in faultless French, an exquisite poem about angels by a poet name Rilke. It fell to Elisha, for the most part, to do an inventory of the various items stored in the church, which, someday, Father hoped to sell at auction; these mismatched items of furniture, artwork, clothing, musical instruments, etc., being articles "in lieu of cash settlements," given to Abraham Licht by his debtors. And, though unbidden to do so, he spent a strenuous morning cleaning the hickory cross of cobwebs and grime, and polishing it to a high sheen, in which his own adolescent face (might he have been about fourteen at the time?) was reflected, with a ghostly sort of beauty. As to the human figure nailed to the cross—made of pewter rather than wood, it could not be salvaged, but had become so badly tarnished by the passage of time, it might well have represented a personage as black as Elisha himself—!

Of the "Savior, Jesus Christ," Elisha knew only what Father had told him and the other children: that, like "God, the Father," and any number of fraudulent deities throughout history, this "Savior" was nothing but an inspired lie told by crafty men to their simple-minded brethren, that they might cheat them of the pleasures of this world, in exchange for the pleasures of the next. Elisha had been puzzled by the notion of a *next world*: was it *next* in time, he asked Father, or *next* in space, many thousands of miles away? Amused by the boy's question, Abraham Licht laughed heartily; but pondered awhile; and finally said that what the majority of men meant by any of their ludicrous beliefs and fancies, *he* did not know, and could not care. "For, Elisha, it is only the meaning we Lichts assign," he said, "that has merit for *us*." Elisha had felt the rightness of the answer; yet, one day not long after, studying the contorted pewter figure closely, and peering at its corroded face, Elisha felt a curious tug of pity for the "Savior," and sympathy. For if "Jesus Christ" had been a lie these many centuries, had He ever known it Himself?—had the terrible truth ever been revealed to *Him*?

Left happily to his own devices, Elisha learned to play a drumroll; and taught himself simple melodies on the piano; and read voraciously, hour upon hour, in haphazard volumes of the *Encyclopaedia Britannica*, *A History of the Penal Code in the United States*, *The Art of Mesmerism*, *Poor Richard's Almanack*, *Home Cures & Emetics*, *Selected Sermons of Rev. Henry Ward Beecher*, *P. T. Barnum's Illustrated News of 1877–1881*, etc.; he outfitted himself in splendid silk-lined evening capes, and ruffled shirts, and brocaded vests, and top hats, and even certain articles of women's clothing—organdy gowns, swans'-feather boas, fox-pieces, turbans—that set off his glowing mahogany skin to great advantage, and brought out a subdued lustre in his eyes. The door to the rectory shut tight against any unwanted intrusion, Elisha whiled away many an afternoon in languid contemplation of his own exotic image; or danced about—kicking up his heels, flinging his arms about, learning to leap from a stationary position, even to "fly" through the air as if weightless! So agile did Elisha become at these secret times, so possessed by an unknown Spirit of elation, bravado, and cunning, he laughed aloud, to think of what he might do, one day, to Father's great approval, in that world of contemptible *enemies* that surrounded them.

IV

The tragedy that befell Thurston struck nearly as deep in Elisha as it did in Abraham Licht himself: for of all the persons in the world, after Father, it had always been his eldest brother whom Elisha most admired and loved.

Not that Thurston was especially quick-witted or inventive (for Millie was sharper—indeed, nearly as sharp as Elisha himself); and not because Thurston was so remarkably attractive a youth, causing, at times, heads to turn in the street (for Elisha was confident that *he* was more striking); but rather, because Thurston maintained so placid a temper, and seemed so artlessly to inhabit his skin, not minding a defeat now and then, and not overly glorying in his successes, as Elisha was inclined. (Ah, Elisha!—as he passed into adolescence, and then into young manhood, it became ever more difficult for him to predict a mood of his own, from one hour to the next, unless of course he was under Father's guidance. Successes like that of the "Black Phantom of Chautauqua" he positively revelled in; defeats wounded him to the quick, and haunted him for months, though, as Father consoled them all, "Failure is but a crafty rehearsal of Success: have faith!")

When, one somber midsummer evening, Father at last summoned Elisha to his room to inform him of Thurston's arrest in Atlantic City, the capital charges brought against him, etc., Elisha could not at first believe what he heard; felt the blood drain rapidly away from his head, and the strength from his legs; he knelt before Father, clasping his hands like a small child, and begging to be allowed to help—for surely *he* might be of special aid in saving his brother?

But for the first time in memory Abraham Licht seemed to have no ready reply, and to be as much in need of comforting as Elisha himself.

"Yes, surely—you will help us with Thurston—he will be saved—he cannot *not* be saved, as he is my son—we will do it, somehow—we will free him," Father said, in a voice that, to Elisha's surprise, faltered. "I know not how, precisely, at the moment—but *we will do it: we must.*"

Elisha fantasizes, these sleepless nights, an extravagant drama in which he (alone? or leading a contingent of armed men?) rescues his eldest brother from the gallows: so terrorizing the armed guards, and the gawking populace, that not a hand is raised against them; and within the space of a few minutes Thurston is freed—riding away on a fiery stamping snorting stallion.

Yet another fantasy, of heart-quickening poignancy: Elisha sacrifices himself for Thurston: stepping between Thurston and a bullet meant to kill him: with the consequence that Father, and sweet Millie, and all the world, indeed, celebrate his courage.

That such astonishing dramas *might* be performed, raises hope in the heart of the "Black Phantom" that they *can* be performed.

Less extravagantly, but more reasonably, Thurston might well be freed from prison beforehand, following one or another of the provisional sketches Father has drawn up; these plans involving an escape by tunnel, or over the wall; and necessitating the cooperation (which is to say, the *paid* cooperation) of various guards, fellow prisoners, perhaps the prison physician, perhaps (if Abraham Licht's money is not too severely depleted by this time) the warden himself. "For men have been escaping from prison as long as there have been prisons," Father has pointed out with faultless logic.

Yet further, Father has broached the subject of a certain herbal medicine, or drug—derived from a species of marsh nightshade (*Circaea quadrisulcata*) with which Katrina is said to be familiar. So potent is marsh, or enchanter's, nightshade, a single dram will cause a full-grown man to fall down in a stupor; and, for a period of twelve hours or more, to so mimic death, no heartbeat can be detected, nor any breath, or bodily warmth. The primary danger of the drug, Elisha gathers, is that it might also cause death, if administered to a man in ill health . . . and that, as Katrina has warned, the precise dosage required for the trance, and not Death, is difficult to calibrate.

"Perhaps Father might experiment with the dosage, using 'Little Moses' as a subject," Elisha thought uneasily.

But, whether out of prudence or simple forgetfulness, he was never to pursue the notion further.

Thirteen years before, Thurston had saved *his* life.

Taking advantage of Father's absence from Muirkirk, the three boys—Thurston, Harwood, and Elisha (seven years old at the time)—went exploring in an area of the great marsh unknown to them; crossing into the dense interior by way of a ridge of earth that formed a natural bridge, wildly overgrown with vines and suckers; and making their way forward with extreme difficulty. Asked where they were headed, and why, they could have supplied no answer: only that Thurston had felt idle and restless at home, and Harwood was in the habit of following Thurston about; and little Elisha had pleaded to be taken along.

Once in the swamp, however, Elisha soon outdistanced his brothers, being so much smaller than they, and wiry and clever as a monkey; and gripped with a sudden fever, that *he* might go where he would, no matter that Thurston called worriedly after him.

"Let them catch up with me, if they can," he thought, "it is only 'Little Moses' after all!"

Unsurprisingly, the reckless child was lost within a half hour, and had not the faintest idea of where he was; whether he was still pushing forward, or had turned about in a circle. His face and hands were reddened with insect bites, he was wet past the knee, and stinking of swamp mud; his breath was ragged and sharp.

How strange, and how terrifying, to be, so suddenly, *alone*.

As if Father had never snatched him up from the flood, and saved him, and brought him home . . .

By now he could no longer hear Thurston's voice, and was too stubborn, or too ashamed, to shout for help. On all sides a pale luminous whitely glowering mist hung low, smelling of chill stagnant water and animal decay; nothing looked familiar; yet he half ran, stumbled to his knees, rose, and ran further, in another direction, instructing himself that *this* was the way back, and that he would be in sight of the church tower shortly.

Though, earlier that day, the temperature had been warm and the air mild, now it seemed that, far overhead, the tops of the marsh trees were shaken by fierce gusts of wind, that rose out of nowhere, and quickly subsided. What was it that splashed in the water close by? . . . or, spreading its wings, flew violently upward, crashing through the sinewy vines? . . . Elisha's heart leapt in his breast as he saw a female figure drifting ahead (but it was only the mist, forming and dissolving) . . . and heard faint ripplings of laughter. A gigantic butterfly floated near, or was it an immense lily? . . . covered, it seemed, in bright-glaring eyes, eyes very like his own, focused sharply upon him.

He shouted for help, running and staggering.

He shouted for Thurston—Thurston!—until his throat was raw.

Now he was ravenous with hunger, and so thirsty his mouth ached. He had been gone from the rectory—from home—for hours; for days; he would never get back safely; they would tell Father that he had wandered off into the swamp, that he had run away, and Father would say, *Then he is no son of mine any longer.* . . . A cloud of mosquitoes surrounded Elisha, sucking blood from his face and throat, his exposed arms, if he did not energetically brush them away. To elude them he must run, run, yet he was exhausted and could *not* run, and so hungry, he found himself desperately plucking at berries . . . tiny white berries, shrivelled, and bitter to the taste . . . and then, by chance, to his delight, a curious plumlike fruit that grew from a gnarled tree resembling a wisteria . . . he bit into it hungrily . . . as delicious a fruit as he had ever tasted . . . though *very* curious: being the size of an apple, but heavy, and pulpy, and unusually juicy, of the color of dusky purple grapes, so richly dark as to seem black.

Poor Elisha!—he could not stop himself from devouring the fruit in ravenous mouthfuls, the juice hot and stinging down his chin; until, with no warning, the back of his mouth burst into flame—and his throat closed up tight—and he choked, and gasped for air—gagging, and retching, and throwing himself frantically about, until—

" 'Lisha! There you are."

He was being nudged awake. Tenderly lifted. His tall fair brother Thurston had discovered him, saved him. Yet with no word of reproach or chiding, still less anger. Thurston, freely perspiring, short of breath, holding him in his strong arms, bringing him back to firm ground and safety.

And Elisha grasped his brother tight around the neck, and wept in gratitude, exhaustion, belated terror. For Thurston was his elder brother who loved him, and would always love him. (If this poor wretched creature stinking of swamp muck, eyes swollen nearly shut from insect bites, skin abraded and bleeding, was in fact Elisha and not a changeling.) Elisha surrendered all pride and clung tightly to his brother as if he were a small child, lacking all strength, volition and self-definition. O *Thurston!—one day I will do as much for you.*

V

And there is Millicent.

Beautiful Millie, his sister.

Of whom, these troubled days, Elisha cannot allow himself to think; nor remain in a room with for very long, especially if they happen to be alone together.

"Gaily Through Life I Wander"

M illicent Licht breaks hearts but it is not *her* fault, if hearts there are, in plenty, to be broken.

And so many very silly people in the world!

Her schoolgirl classmates have always adored her, at the Husebye School in Albany, at Miss Metcalf's in Hartford, at the Lake Champlain Academy for Young Christian Ladies, they court her, shyly, aggressively, they compete for her fickle attention, leave little gifts for her in secret, for Millicent Licht *is* the prettiest of the lot, and Millicent Licht *is* by far the most clever (as even the schoolmistresses are forced to agree): and those who have been fortunate enough to meet Mr. Licht, and to exchange a few words with *him*—how impressed they are! (For, set beside their own fathers, is not Millicent's father a paragon of manhood, indeed? And so very solicitous of *them*.) Some particularly privileged girls have even been shown photographs of Millicent's elder brother Thurston, with the vague smiling hint . . . the merest whispered murmured soupçon of a hint . . . that one day, perhaps, they might meet. (One fifth-form girl, who had formed an especially passionate attachment to Millicent, declared, looking from Thurston's photograph to Millicent, and back again: "Why, he is your equal in beauty!—you are Greek gods!" And Millicent, smiling but faintly, and showing none of the amused contempt she surely felt, said quietly: "Please!—it is all we have to do, being *mortal*.")

It has sometimes been whispered of Millicent Licht that she breaks hearts because she is cruel, and wanton, and selfish, and manipulative, and because she delights in hurting (did she not laugh when told that little Edie Saxon tried to drown herself one rainy March night, after being snubbed by her?—or that, just last year, at the Champlain school, both her roommates lied to save her from expulsion in a matter of suspected cheating on a French examination, and were themselves expelled and sent home in disgrace?); but the truth is simply that she forgets; forgets their existence from one hour to the next; as if it's a matter of vague astonishment to her that creatures so silly and childish *do* exist from one hour to the next.

"And they take themselves so seriously," Millicent marveled to herself, "as if their little griefs and jealousies and heartbreaks are a matter of cosmic concern. As if I am to blame for their being 'hurt' over my inability to return their affections."

Indeed, how could blame be laid on Millicent Licht's comely head, that in pressing unsought gifts upon her, certain of her classmates should be wounded to the heart that Millie might politely accept the gifts but decline the offer of friendship?—that they should mistake vague murmured promises for actual vows?—as if Millicent Licht had nothing more important to do than remember such childish transactions from one day to the next.

So it seemed she often found herself uttering the identical words, like a Broadway ingenue in a popular, long-running play, with innocent widened eyes and an expression of startled compassion on her porcelain-doll's face, "Why, whatever do you *mean?*—what on earth is *wrong?* Please don't cry!" while trying not to laugh in angry ridicule that some silly girl should presume to shed tears in her presence, and attribute them to *her.* The most upsetting incident took place during Millie's second year at Miss Metcalf's when a thirteen-year-old girl in the form below hers, a granddaughter of Andrew Carnegie, tried to slash her wrist with a dull penknife when Millie inadvertently snubbed her at chapel. There was much fuss and flurry and scandal, the hysterical little Carnegie heiress was shuttled off home and Abraham Licht was summoned to the school to take Millie away with him—"As if *I am to blame. And I am not, Father!—I am not.*"

"Of course you're not to blame, darling," Abraham said, kissing his vexed daughter on the forehead, "—but it might be politic, you know, to express some regret."

" 'Regret'?—for what?"

"That this silly little girl imagined she should die over you, and take up arms against herself, in violation of all common sense. That, you know, she was *hurt*; and her life, and her family's, is in a turmoil."

"But how is that my fault, Father? What had I to do with it? Everyone has been so unfair!" Millie cried, wiping at her eyes. "They look at me as if I'd given her the knife, myself. A ridiculous little dull penknife that wouldn't cut butter. If *I* had—"

"Now hush, darling," Abraham said quickly, squeezing his daughter's shoulder just hard enough to capture her attention, "you must not speak words that might be misunderstood, and misquoted."

But there was nothing to be done. Miss Metcalf herself, the venerable headmistress, would not hear of Millie's staying on at the school. Nor did Abraham think it a very good idea under the circumstances, though Millie's grades were quite good, and her relations with her instructors excellent. "At least, Father, they should refund you for the remainder of the school year," Millie relented; and Abraham said, with a wink, "The remainder of the year?—my dear, Miss Metcalf has agreed to refund the entire amount, dating back to September; and, in addition, the trustees have agreed to pay me a generous little sum in 'damages'— to compensate for the upset you and your family have endured."

Which made Millie laugh gaily, as if she'd been tickled.

Which made Millie stand on tiptoe to kiss her handsome bewhiskered father on the cheek, and tug in a frenzy of delight at his arm.

A tale to be recounted many times, in Muirkirk. A tale Millie loved to tell to 'Lisha in particular.

Precocious girl! As, in childhood, she possessed certain startling qualities of adolescence, so in adolescence, well beyond her sixteenth year, she retained certain charming qualities of childhood. As all wellbred ladies of the era were trained, but very few succeeded in doing.

In her sweet bell-like slightly wavering soprano voice Millie sings, for Father's admiration, that delicate air from *The Bohemian Girl* that is one of his favorites—

> *"I dreamt that I dwelt in marble halls*
> *with vassals and serfs at my side . . ."*

and the rapid clipped patter, in compound meter, of "It Is Better to Laugh Than Be Sighing," from the splendid *Lucrezia Borgia*; and *La traviata*'s "Gaily Through Life I Wander"; and, with the coquettish mannerisms of an accomplished performer, the irresistible "La donna è mobile" from *Rigoletto*. When Millie was seven years old, and recently bereft of her faithless mother, Abraham saw to it that she was diverted by Broadway musicals and spectacles, among them Rossini's *Cinderella* at Booth's Theatre; so for months and years afterward Millicent sings Cinderella's arias and dreams of herself as a prima donna . . . making her debut in Booth's Theatre with Father, 'Lisha and the rest of the family proudly looking on.

Her praises, and her smiling face, lavishly displayed in all the papers.

For six arduous months Millie takes singing lessons with an elderly Neapolitan who'd made his operatic debut in *Il trovatore*; she attempts piano lessons, harp lessons, ballet—with initial enthusiasm, and a modicum of talent, before losing heart. *For it is so much work! So much damned, tedious work.* Millie is certain that acting on the stage isn't at all demanding, except for memorizing dialogue; but, for some reason neither she nor Father can comprehend, considering her excellent auditions, Millicent Licht is never chosen for any play. When, for reasons having to do with one of Abraham Licht's projects, the "Santiago de Cuba Plantation," she, Father and 'Lisha are living in New Orleans, Millie takes elocution lessons with the Parisian Madame LaTour of Bourbon Street; another time, when the family is living in Philadelphia, she takes lessons in watercolor- and silhouette-painting, lessons in "gracious deportment" and, so long as she has the use of a spirited Thoroughbred mare owned by a woman friend of Father's, riding lessons given by a handsome young Brazilian instructor. She is fourteen years old and has quite forgotten her mother; she is fifteen years old, she is sixteen—by this time utilized by Father upon a number of occasions as a "daughter" of his—that is, a daughter of Mr. Anson, or Mr. Berry, or Mr. Frelicht, or Mr. St. Goar. Depending upon the venue, and the project. Despite her age, Millie can even play hostess for her father if required. She wears the loveliest silks, velvets and wools money can buy when, as Father quips, there *is* money to buy them; her hair is charmingly fashioned in braids, or sausage curls, or queenly plaits wound about her head, or is brushed smooth and glittering on her shoulders. She has kept nothing of her mother's, for, acting in a fit of childish temper one day, she cut up most of her mother's possessions (clothing, linen, correspondence, books) with a scissors; but she has a beautiful little ermine muff and matching hat, and a red mohair coat with a mink collar; she had a darling Persian kitten (named Cinderella), until it died suddenly; her brothers are not jealous of the fact that Father so clearly loves her best . . . excepting perhaps Harwood, who is jealous of everyone. (Though she has never told anyone, Millie is sometimes frightened of Harwood, for he seems so resolutely uncharmed by her. In his small close-set unblinking eyes her china-doll prettiness counts for very little; her ploys, her mannerisms, her habits of speech and gesture provoke in him, at the very most, a mirthless grin. When they were younger he frequently pinched her, shoved her, tugged at her braids, whispered disagreeable things in her ears . . . but no matter, no matter, for *he* does not count: the remainder of the world is there to adore Millicent Licht, and to be heartbroken by her.)

In short, Millicent lacks for nothing; and wants nothing she does not have; only that (but this is mere girlhood fancy, not to be voiced to Father) Time come to a halt . . . *and Millie remain the daughter she is, and Father continue to love her as he does, forever and ever, Amen.*

II

Yet now, with no warning, so suddenly, in Millie's eighteenth year, with the triumph of "Mina Raumlicht" fresh in her memory and so applauded by the family, and other ingenious projects surely to follow— now the bliss of childhood seems to be coming to an end.

For Thurston has fallen into the hands of their enemies, and has been sentenced to death. And Elisha, her 'Lisha, has begun to behave strangely.

And Father now neglects her. He's away most of January and February on business (for Bullock is appealing Thurston's case before the New Jersey State Supreme Court, and more money is needed, *more money is always needed*, to do the job properly); and when Father is at home in Muirkirk he's exhausted, melancholy and distracted, and only vaguely aware of his elder daughter.

"Am I imagining it," Millie frets, "—or is Father mourning Thurston already? That cannot be!"

Certainly Millie isn't imagining this: in the altered atmosphere of the household, Miss Mina Raumlicht, like her sisters Delphine St. Goar, Arlina Frelicht, etc., no longer has the power to make Abraham

Licht smile and laugh in delight; no longer has the power to arouse in him that mysterious scintilla of energy that might take root, and smolder, and spark, and eventually flame forth in ideas—plans—plots—stratagems of The Game. Father's brow is anxiously knit, his eyes brood, the poor man is thinking, almost palpably thinking, but his thoughts yield little evident pleasure. Where, in the past, the children were accustomed to Father brooding in this way, and at last snapping his fingers and shouting in delight, "Eureka! I have found it!" now they must grow accustomed to brooding without relief, without end.

Of his plans for Thurston's rescue, should the appeal fail, Father is disturbingly vague. He consoles Millie with the unconvincing promise that "when it's all over" they will join up with Thurston in Canada, or Mexico, or Cuba . . . maybe Abraham Licht will shift his base of operations to this foreign site where he might enjoy complete anonymity, and begin his career afresh.

"There is something so appealing, isn't there?—so American—about beginning afresh," Father says, in a curious, yearning voice. "What will be a necessity for Thurston might be a fine idea for us all."

Millie makes an effort to comfort her father, lashing out bitterly at their enemies who dared to find her brother, her innocent brother, guilty of a crime no Licht would lower himself to commit. *If only the true murderer were found!* Millie rages. *If only the police would do their duty and arrest him!* Yet even that wouldn't erase the supreme insult, the insult against their family, Millie says breathlessly, of Thurston being found guilty *as if he were guilty.*

Abraham listens to his daughter's words, as her eyes flash damp in the firelight. And makes no reply, when she speaks of the *true murderer.*

For Millie knows nothing of Harwood's involvement. Like all of the household, excepting Father, she suspects nothing.

"But you will save Thurston, Father, won't you?—he *will* be saved?" Millie pleads, in a lowered voice so that the younger children won't hear, and be frightened; and Abraham Licht is roused from his fireside reverie, saying gently, "Yes, Millie, of course. *Thurston* will be saved," with a curious, almost imperceptible emphasis on the name, as if they'd been speaking, half-consciously, of someone else as well, unnamed.

III

How many years ago, more than a decade, when Millie was a very small child, the baby of the family, and the church-dwelling at the edge of the marsh wasn't nearly so habitable as it is now, she'd crept along a corridor wide-eyed, frightened, imagining she heard . . . adult voices raised in anger: Father whom she adored explaining (annoyed, amused) that there was nothing, absolutely nothing about which Morna should concern herself, for all business was his business, and not hers; and Mother whom she adored protesting in a voice like shattering glass, But I must know, Abraham! I demand to know, it is my life as well as yours . . . mine and my daughter's.

And Father replies sharply: I don't discuss my business affairs with women.

And Mother laughs suddenly, and says: *Women! Am I women! I'd de-ceived myself that I was your wife!*

And now silence, silence, silence . . .

And now great waves of silence . . .

For Father does not reply. Father does not condescend to reply.

And the shivering little girl crouched in the hallway, fingers thrust in her mouth, hears nothing further save the sound of a woman's heartbroken sobbing.

(*Mine and my daughter's:* what extraordinary words!)

(Is this pain *daughter*, this anguish *daughter*, this paralyzing suffocat-ing fear *daughter*?)

Mother insists that Katrina and the boys address her as "Miss Hirsh-field" ("For I am not Mrs., it seems—God has spared me that blessing") and that little Millie address her not at all.

For *daughter* is to be explained as shame; as error; as sin.

For *daughter* does not exist.

There have been too many upsets, Miss Hirshfield says, laughing sharply, too many evictions, too many middle-of-the-night decamp-ings, too many escapes from creditors, policemen, outraged "investors": and now Miss Hirshfield's heart has turned to stone: has turned in fact toward God. "For surely He will not betray me, Katrina, will He?—being pure spirit, and 'He' only by custom."

God the Father.

God of *her* father, the Reverend Thaddeus L. Hirshfield of Rackham, Pennsylvania, whom she betrayed (and is betraying still, if he lives) by eloping with Abraham Licht . . . and vowing to love him forever, and to follow him wherever he wishes to go, and to be a true Christian mother to his children.

So *mother* instructs *daughter*.

So *mother* catechizes *daughter* as they kneel together in prayer.

". . .'And in those days shall men seek death, and shall not find it; and shall desire to die, and death shall flee from them.' Do you understand these words, Millicent?" the laughing woman asks, gripping Millie's tiny shoulders, shaking her, "—do you understand? Or are you too young?"

Yet there are reconciliations. There are unexpected hours of happiness, even of calm. For Abraham Licht cannot be resisted—when he chooses not to be resisted. When he chooses to court his Morna again, to adore her again (his narrow-cheeked golden-blond Siennese madonna), to ignore the evidence of her thinning hair and tense mouth. She can be made to weep again in his arms, as he weeps in hers, for he *is* her husband, she *is* his wife . . . when he so chooses.

And between them, supremely *of* them, is pretty little Millicent.

Who learns early the value of being *pretty* and *little*.

Who learns early the need to keep secrets.

Millicent, my child, where are we?

Is this Hell?

A kingdom at the bottom of the world, where no one can follow.

Yet, here is a steeple—blessed by God!

And a churchyard ripe and rotting with the anointed dead.

In the drafty kitchen Katrina lights the wood-burning stove, coughing so that her eyes fill with tears. Is it possible—stiff-backed Katrina, of all women, has become humbled by want? Losing pride, her stubborn country-bred strength? Telling the children tales of the marsh to frighten them; tales of the miller's son who fell in love with a demon and lost his soul, and of Miss Mina Harwood the Governor's daughter who lost her soul as well . . . and disappeared into the marsh. And, oldest of all, young Sarah Wilcox, or was she Sarah Hood? *Not a Londoner*

*by birth, very likely not even English by birth, you could hear it in her voice.
The princess who died (yet lives still) in old Muirkirk.*

In the marsh. Deep, deep in the interior of the marsh.

Where you would not wish to follow. Would you?

For now it is summer and the air so damp, so warm, as an exhaled
breath, moisture gathers itself in clumps like gnats brushing against
one's face. Mother whispers to daughter, Morna to Millicent, she cannot breathe and fears she will suffocate, Oh my child, my darling little
girl, shall I bring you with me, Millicent?—or are you too much *his*?

If Mother had a rowboat with a bottom not rotted she would row
them to safety across the broad weedy pond, the pond large as a lake,
past tall nodding pampas grass and whispering scrub willow, past part-
submerged fallen logs, past a glittering scrim of dragonflies into the hidden heart of the marsh. *Daughter* and *not-daughter*, will you come with
me? To that place where no one from the other world dare follow?

Is this Hell? Or our salvation?

Where no one dares follow.

And then suddenly, overnight, the wind shifts. A harsh cleansing
wind out of the northeast. The sky opens to torrential rain, and all is
changed.

Business flourishes! There is a much-heralded "boom" in the economy!

One flurried day Father moves them again to the city—but which
city?—not Vanderpoel, not back to elegant Stuyvesant Square, where,
it seems, certain debts remain unpaid—but they have a carriage and a
hired driver, Thurston and Harwood find themselves enrolled in a private school for boys "of good family" and Elisha is being tutored by a
young Irish seminarian and Millie, vivacious Millie, *daughter* and *not-
daughter*, has a French governess and a charming little silk-and-organdy
sunshade and the Licht family attends church services in a massive
whitely gleaming Episcopal church where the angelic choir sings with
such passion Millie must crouch and press her hands against her tender
ears *Is this Heaven?—their Heaven?—I hate it!*—even as she's smiling,
laughing, like her vivacious glittery-eyed Mother in the company of
new friends, Father's new friends and business associates and in an
emerald-green dogcart pulled by two handsome grinning German shep-
herds across the mayor's sloping lawn little Millie and the mayor's nine-

year-old son bask in the adoration of their elders knowing how they are beloved, and blessed. And yet—hardly a day later, Father rouses the family at dawn, out in the street a carriage awaits, they must hurry, they must flee, ask no questions, no tears, please!—for they are returning to Muirkirk to the old stone church to Katrina who greets them with no discernible emotion save irony inquiring how long this time will they be staying?

And what has happened to Father's boisterous good humor? And why does Mother weep, bitter tears etching her cheeks?—she will only make herself ill, Katrina warns her, and die before her time.

And Mother says, calmly *How is it possible to die before one's time? God ordains; ripeness is all.*

And now begins the God-season, for Abraham Licht has gone away again from Muirkirk. This frantic God-season Millie will remember with dread for the remainder of her life.

For she, who is Morna's daughter, that's to say Miss Hirshfield's daughter, is the one to be disciplined, and not her rowdy wayward brothers who are not Miss Hirshfield's sons. Millie's crinkly-wavy hair braided up so tightly (by Mother herself, not trusting Katrina) that the very corners of her eyes pull upward, and 'Lisha teases her she has *Chinee blood*; her tender skin must be scrubbed, or chafed, cleansed of all impurities; her private parts must be especially cleansed, with harsh lye soap, a necessary procedure, Miss Hirshfield has decreed, where there is the likelihood of sin.

And Millicent alone of the children must kneel in prayer, being daughter. Being so pretty, so charming, so crafty; a daughter of the Devil's, indeed.

Now Millicent who has been given no food but watery oatmeal since yesterday morning must kneel in the drafty old church without squirming and without tears, overseen by agitated Miss Hirshfield she must recite verse from Saint Matthew, a water-stained Bible held in the woman's trembling hands, held close to her glassy blinking eyes,

And Jesus said unto them, See ye not all these things? verily I say unto you, There shall not be left here one stone upon another, that shall not be thrown down. . . .

And as he sat upon the mount of Olives, the disciples came unto him privately, saying, Tell us, when shall these things be? and what shall be the sign of thy coming, and of the end of the world?

And Jesus answered and said unto them, Take heed that no man deceive you.

For many shall come in my name, saying, I am Christ; and shall deceive many.

And you shall hear of wars and rumors of wars: see that you be not troubled: for all these things must come to pass, but the end is not yet.

For nation must rise against nation, and kingdom against kingdom: and there shall be famines, and pestilences, and earthquakes. . . .

And all these are the beginning of sorrows.

Her bare knees numbed with pain against the hardwood floor, her head ringing with hunger and fatigue and wonderment. Is that the hickory cross floating before her?—is that contorted piteous figure her Savior, Jesus Christ?—but what is a "savior," and who is "Jesus Christ"?—she dares not ask for there is Mother, there is Miss Hirshfield close beside her, always close beside her, whispering urgently to God to save them both.

For this is Mother, and this is Daughter, and this is the consequence of sin.

For this is the consequence of turning away from God, to follow an earthly, carnal love.

Father is angry. Father is furious. Learning from 'Lisha of Millie's religious "conversion"—Millie's enforced "indoctrination"—for that woman Morna has done it to spite *him*, knowing how he fears and loathes all fanatics of Holy Writ. Taking the child forcibly from the embittered mother, lifting her into his arms, Father carries her into his study and kisses away her tears and gives her delicious "tar-balls" to eat, molasses and ground almonds, perching her on his knee and assuring her there is no God, there is no Savior, there is no Hell, or Heaven, or Sin; yet she might consider herself fortunate that her mother forced her to learn Bible verses, for one day, when she is independent and moving about in the world, such verses will surely be of use. "For it is impossible, dear, to overestimate the value of Holy Writ as it comes rolling and artless off the tongue, as if from the very heart of the speaker," Father says with a smile, and years later Millie discovers this to be true; for when she's away at school, or assisting Father with a business venture, it's often very helpful to quote the Bible; and to speak with reverent familiarity of Our Savior Jesus Christ.

"And so my poor deranged mother prepared me for life after all," Millie thinks, "never knowing whom she served when she imagined she served God."

IV

. . . sometime in the early autumn of 1898 . . . when *daughter* was six years old . . . and Father was away . . . and a heat-haze lay over Muirkirk for days on end and would not lift . . . and Mother complained to Katrina that she could not *breathe* . . . pressing her bony hand to her chest, her eye sockets enormous but her eyes small, narrow, moist, watchful, blinking . . . that gaze fixed upon *daughter* . . . the dry lips blistered, the voice nearly inaudible, *cannot breathe, cannot breathe* . . . when Father was away, had been away for weeks (in love again? preparing, like a young bridegroom, to wed again? but no one in Muirkirk knew of Miss Sophie Hume yet!) . . . and Katrina said it was hopeless to summon Dr. Deerfield because the townspeople hated Abraham Licht and his household and wished them ill . . . and Katrina *knew* . . . and a day and a night passed, and the heat-haze did not lift . . . and in the morning *daughter* was told: "Your mother has left us. She has walked away and left us."

. . . leaving behind her worn frayed clothing, her much-laundered bed linen, her books, her Bible . . .

. . . leaving behind *daughter* who did not grieve and who promptly, at Katrina's urging, began to forget.

"For *he* will quickly forget, I assure you," Katrina said.

And so Miss Morna Hirshfield betrayed them all by disappearing.
And leaving no note behind.
And leaving no *regret* behind.
(Unless, thinks Millie, she died. And is buried in the Nazarene cemetery; or in the marsh. Does it matter?)

For she was easily supplanted in Muirkirk by Father's new young wife: so very new to them all, and so *very* young and lovely. . . .

(Does Millie, now a young woman of eighteen, dwell upon such matters?—*she does not.*

Except: that windy excitable May morning, when, having risen before dawn, "Miss Mina Raumlicht" cunningly strapped the pillow to her stomach, securing it tight against her pelvic bones, that it might not be jostled loose when she walked, or sat down abruptly, or, perhaps, fainted away . . . she was struck by a sudden vision (though why? for there was no connection) of the doomed woman who had been, in another lifetime, her mother . . . that is, little Millicent's mother: doomed *mother* to a doomed *daughter.*

Mina's small childish teeth bared themselves in a sudden smile.

For now she had no mother, and could come to no grief; but was herself (in a comical manner of speaking) a *mother-to-be.*

For none of it mattered.

For nothing, *nothing* mattered: only The Game, never to be played as if it were but a game.)

V

"Millie!—don't be sad any longer!—*I am a dead man!*"

So Thurston murmurs, smiling happily, his frank boyish gaze precisely as Millie remembers, the grip of his fingers, warmly squeezing hers, and suddenly, though they are in the courtroom, under the very eyes of the Law, there is no harm in acknowledging that they are brother and sister: children of Abraham Licht.

She wakes, and her heart hammers in terror, and the voice yet sounds, gentle, comforting, the very voice of her tall fair brother: "Millie!—don't be sad any longer!—*I am a dead man.*"

VI

For on the morning of 22 March Thurston's appeal was denied by the New Jersey State Supreme Court; and on the morning of 23 March Gordon Bullock was angrily dismissed by Father.

And that night Millie dreams she is back in the courtroom again, attending her brother's trial which is (evidently) still in session . . . and, suddenly, to her astonishment, Thurston rises to his feet and approaches her; takes her hands warmly in his; his smile Thurston's smile; his manner of stooping to kiss her cheek, Thurston's; his eyes as she delights to recall, and his brotherly joy in *her*. His wrists are unmanacled, his head is high, he is so transported with the ecstasy of his secret he comes very close to lifting Millie in his arms, as, in childhood, he had frequently done.

But his words, ah! his words!—*these*, Thurston would never say.

And equally upsetting is Elisha's stiff response when Millie tells him of the dream.

Indeed, *is* this Elisha?—'Lisha who has always been so charmed by her, and so patient with her moods and spells and premonitions? Not meeting her eye, nor taking her trembling proffered hand, he says: "You know that dreams rarely mean anything, Millie. Why trouble to repeat this one? Father would not like it."

"But Elisha," Millie says, hurt, "it was so very real. Thurston stood before me, as close as you—*closer* than you—"

"Nonetheless it was only a dream," Elisha says, "by definition a fancy of the dreamer's, and not to be taken seriously by anyone else."

"But if it is true—if his words are true—"

"Of course it cannot be *true*," says Elisha impatiently, baring his teeth in a smile, "—since it is only a dream."

"But like no other dream I have ever had."

"Well! As to that—'like no other dream,' indeed!" he says. "*That* has the ring of mere rhetoric."

Poor Millie stares, perplexed. Can it be? Elisha has turned against her?—as indifferent to her, now, as the brute Harwood? And when she glanced at her mirrored reflection, before running to him, her beauty had fairly blazed out at her . . . or so it had seemed. "Rhetoric? Mere rhetoric?" she says faintly. "What do you mean?" But Elisha will not meet her eye. He stands in a patch of mottled sunlight, his skin exuding cold, it seems, and no hint of the old brotherly warmth to which Millie has been accustomed.

"What you say strikes the ear as false," Elisha says with a shrug of his shoulders. "And in any case it is *only* a dream."

"But why are we quarreling? I had come to you for—"

" 'We' are not quarreling, Millie," Elisha says. "There is no 'we' in this matter." Then, seeing her look of childish injury, he says, more reasonably: "Dreams cannot be intelligently discussed because they cannot be shared. They are nothing but vapor, after all—mere wisps of idle thought."

"But if that were true!—*I am a dead man!*—poor Thurston!" Millie whispers.

Elisha makes a gesture as if to silence her; but freezes, and does not touch her at all.

Now passes a long strained moment, during which the two agitated young people stand, unspeaking, staring at each other, scarcely knowing where they are, or what has arisen between them. Millie, greatly distressed, sees in Elisha's eyes that curious startled look she saw there, or imagined she saw, some months before . . . when, in Contracoeur, in the midst of a crowd of pedestrians on Commerce Street, he appeared suddenly, miraculously, alongside her . . . Elisha, her brother, yet so very wonderfully *not* Elisha! . . . but a stranger, a Negro, in eyeglasses, bowler hat, and prim dark clothing . . . powdered-gray hair and somber whiskers that do not disguise the fact that the man is hardly middle-aged, but bold, brash, defiant . . . and secretly exulting in the subtleties of The Game, to which only *he* and *she*, in all of Contracoeur, are privy.

Why, it is Elisha, her tall dark-skinned brother, *her* 'Lisha, yet not *hers* at all, but a dashing stranger of the "black" race: just as she is Millicent, yet not Millicent, in a dusty traveling cloak, and demure braided hair, her expression yet sickly and pious, and her eyes reddened from weeping.

And what it is that passes between them at that moment—Millie is to remember only haphazardly afterward.

Now, months later, they find themselves alone together in the parlor as they were alone together on Commerce Street. Unexpectedly, secretly alone. From an adjoining room come the bright sharp persistent notes of Darian's spinet, a brilliant cascade of arpeggios. From somewhere outside, the less melodious, rougher sound of Harwood's whistling punctuated by the rhythmic *thwack!* of his ax as, for sport as much as practicality, he splits logs. Elisha says coolly, "Why do you stare at me, Millie? Is something wrong?"

And Millie licks her numbed lips and whispers, "Only my dream."

"Nigger!"

It was seven weeks to the day before Christopher Schoenlicht was scheduled to be hanged, on a raw windy April morning in Muirkirk, that Elisha and Harwood had their terrible quarrel, never to be satisfactorily explained.

Seven weeks to 29 May; and Thurston languishing in prison, and Father away, and the entire household under the strain—*Is he to die?—He cannot die!*—and it was winter still, snow on the ground in pocked and stubbled patches, and the marsh still frozen over, and the sky still a hard cold winter sky, so fierce a cobalt-blue one's eyes were pierced with light. *Will nothing ever change? Will we be locked in winter forever?*

Except: Elisha observes his brother Harwood packing his valises, bound for Leadville, Colorado, where Father is sending him for six months; whistling thinly under his breath; his soiled golfing cap set sportily on his head, hair in lank greasy quills, a clumsily knotted tie bulging out of his vest coat. Elisha observes in silence, drawing his thumbnail slowly across his plump lower lip: Harwood, his brother whom he does not love and who has never loved *him*, bound for the West and a new career (but the Lichts are always beginning new careers, there is nothing remarkable about that), Harwood dapper and sly with his new pencil-thin moustache, his air of watchful gravity, his sense of *purpose* (but the Lichts have always been fired by purpose, there is nothing remarkable about that), yet alternating with his old "nervy" "prickly" manner, so that the household is never quite settled when he's home: and everyone, even Father, has been waiting for him to leave.

Yet it's odd, Elisha thinks it extremely odd, that Harwood won't be in the East when Father requires help (surely Father will require help from both Elisha and Harwood is freeing Thurston?); that Harwood, with an excuse of illness (he who is never ill) failed to attend a single session of Thurston's trial; and seemed uneasy, even annoyed, when informed of its progress.

Harwood, who'd once sneered at Elisha when they were boys the mysterious ugly-sounding epithet "nigger" . . .

Nigger? What's that?

By this time Harwood is aware of Elisha watching him. But stubbornly, defiantly, he won't turn. Continuing with his slow, awkward packing as if such an activity, involving folding, stacking together, a certain measure of gentleness and order, was new to him and untrustworthy. Harwood with thick neck and shoulders, torso solid with muscle, skin the hue and seeming texture of lard; snoutish nose, small resentful eyes; worried forehead; bristles of hair in ears; cheeks bunching upward in an unconscious grin or tic . . . the young man is shorter than Elisha by perhaps two inches but heavier by at least thirty pounds so Elisha thinks *He will hurt me* Elisha calmly thinks *He will take pleasure in hurting me* still more calmly, with resignation *Yet it can't be helped.*

Saying bluntly what he'd wished for months to say, in a level, easy voice, "Thurston would not have committed such an act but *you* would, *you* did, yes?" And Harwood, whistling, misses but a beat or two, a strand of hair slipping across his forehead, he makes no reply, and Elisha says, thumbs hooked in his belt in a casual swaggering gesture, "Then why are you going away now? why *now?*" and this time Harwood grunts a reply, not quite audibly, head ducked, securing the first of the valises, and then the other: they are expensive new purchases, handsome russet-brown leather, small brass buckles and trim, just to draw one's finger along the smooth hide, just to carry one in each hand, the weight, the splendid odor of the leather, the assurance, the excitement: how Elisha envies his hateful brother, who will walk so calmly out of their lives, and out of their grief—!

Harwood is loading up a buggy in the front drive, Harwood is moving methodically, taking his time, Harwood is careful to give no indication that he is troubled by Elisha's presence, annoyed that Elisha follows him outdoors, asking in a voice that has begun to tremble, "Why now? why is he sending you away now?"—to which Harwood mutters a vague quick reply over his shoulder that has to do with the copper mine in Colorado, one or another "partnership," "no time to waste"—as Father has said. Elisha sees that his brother is edgy, resentful, perhaps even frightened: for Harwood of late is always frightened: since Thurston's arrest, since the trouble in Atlantic City, Elisha has noted that Harwood is always frightened: so he says again, softly, now slightly short of breath, daring to pull at his brother's sleeve: "Thurston would never have done it but *you—you* would!"

Being touched, Harwood is galvanized at once: he drops the valises in the snow, leaps away, turns crouching, head lowered and jaws working, eyes narrowed and mean: saying, as if the word gives him pleasure, as if he has been waiting to say it for a very long time: "*Nigger.*"

So they fight.

So it begins.

Suddenly the brothers are at each other, grappling, shoving, striking with fists—bare fists on bare flesh—shouting profanities—epithets of the sort the household has never heard—Elisha wild, rangy, aggrieved, Harwood slower and more calculating—Elisha is no fighter, hasn't been trained, hasn't any instinct, Elisha swings and misses, swings wide and misses, Elisha is thrown off balance as Harwood waits, knees bent, shoulders raised and hunched—*he* is cunning, a fighter by instinct, knows he can depend upon his weight, his strength, his entire body enlivened by the need to *hurt*, the ecstatic delight in *hurting*, for every fight is a fight to the death. Why otherwise does his fear so rapidly drain away, and this splendid manly strength suffuse his being?

The fight is no contest, as any sporting gentleman would see at a glance, for one of the young men is fighting out of emotion, and the other is fighting simply to do injury; one of the young men imagines the struggle a matter of justice, a means by which justice will be exacted out of pain, and the other young man knows that the fight, like all fights, is simply about fighting: the very word an incantation: *fight*.

To do injury, to give hurt.

In theory, to kill.

(But one must not allow oneself to go that far: at least, not in the presence of witnesses.)

(For Millie has run up behind them, screaming for them to stop.)

(And old Katrina is somewhere in the house. And little Darian and Esther.)

A blow to Elisha's jaw so powerful that his body is thrown back like a rag doll, his eyes roll in their sockets, blood springs from his mouth—immediately there's a second blow, harder, crueler, with the force of a sledgehammer, against Elisha's unguarded chest, to his heart. A blow so hard that Harwood winces, his knuckles cracked.

And Elisha is down, half-sitting in soiled snow, bleeding from his torn mouth yet more profusely and alarmingly from the chest—for a surface artery has been broken. Harwood picks up his valises and strides jauntily to the buggy saying, through a mirthless twitchy grin, "Goodbye, *nigger*."

In this way Harwood Licht departs Muirkirk, for the vast open sky and windswept spaces of the West.

What of Elisha?—never in his life has this self-confident young man felt such physical *shock*; for Harwood, within minutes, has driven him into a place beyond pain, so numbed, so much in a state of visceral astonishment, he hardly feels pain; though knowing that, yes, *pain will come—soon*. Sprawled gracelessly in snow, panting through bloodied mouth like a dog, hardly aware even of Millie's cries, Elisha Licht, a.k.a. "Little Moses," thinks bemused *Why, I am not a god after all, it seems.*

What of Millie?—an equal shock overcomes her, for even as Elisha is being pummeled by Harwood, falling to the ground, handsome face no longer handsome but contorted in childlike fear, rich dark skin no longer dark but ashen, and bright blood soaking his stylish wing-collar shirt and close-fitted woollen trousers and sprinkled like dirty raindrops on the snow—even as these horrors occur, quite apart from Millie's sisterly wish that the brothers cease fighting, and her cries of "Stop! *Stop!*" she realizes suddenly that she loves Elisha, not as a brother, for Elisha is *not* her brother, but simply as Elisha, 'Lisha, a stranger she must no longer deceive herself she knows.

In that instant the old Millie, the child-Millie, dies.

In that instant the young woman Millie, seeing her beloved is fallen, and bleeding, and in need of aid, hurries to him, wasting no time in stifled little cries and screams; mature, deft and determined as never before in her life Millie tears open Elisha's shirt and rips a strip from her cotton petticoat and wads it and presses it against the mysterious wound with as much force as her strength allows; kneeling beside him in the snow, comforting him, partly embracing him, her arm cradling his head against her shoulder, her voice rapid and soothing, trying to show no alarm, for now such intimacy is allowed, now such intimacy is needed, when the wadded cotton is soaked with blood another must be quickly torn, and pressed against the broken artery, and Elisha, frightened Elisha, with none of his Negro swagger now, none of his coolness in her presence, trembles in terror murmuring, "Don't let me die, Millie!—don't let me die!" and Millie grasps him tighter and says, as if scolding, "Why, it's nothing, the bleeding will stop soon, *he* has not the power to hurt *you*."

Secret Music

Something is wrong, gravely wrong, but when Darian wakes early one morning, before dawn, to a sound of wild geese flying overhead, he forgets the sorrow of the household—forgets that *something is going to happen, something to change all their lives*—and lies trembling with excitement. He will not open his eyes, he wants to keep the sound pure, a music that wakes him from sleep, unbidden, mysterious, fading even as he strains to hear: wild geese, Canada geese, their queer faint honking in the sky, why such sudden beauty, why any world at all, *this* world, and not simply—Nothing?

To express the life, the certitude, the quivering happiness that courses through him at such times—this, Darian thinks, must be what is meant by God.

But he will not tell anyone, he will keep his secret to himself, this *is* God, trembling in his very body.

Such somber children, Darian and Esther!—forgotten children, perhaps, appearing younger than their ages; even Katrina feels sorry for them, is drawn into the parlor to listen to Darian playing the piano (but how odd, the compositions that child invents!), sits for an hour at a stretch with little Esther in her arms, in the window seat watching rain falling into the marsh.

"No one will ever come back, will they, Katrina?" the child asks drowsily. She is not agitated, not even curious, such questions have been asked many times before, they are a child's questions, not to be taken seriously. "And *he* will never come back, I know," Esther adds, after a confused pause, having forgotten (for she is so very sleepy suddenly) the name of her eldest brother.

Years later Darian is to recall: they are told that Thurston is away, traveling, on business for Father; he is in Mexico, he will be going to Cuba; returning home sometime in the summer . . . or a little later.

Darian was too small still to sit at the piano so Father hoisted him onto his lap, gripped his hands firmly in his, Darian's stubby fingers enclosed in Father's big fingers, and they played at making music, *Like this*, Father said gaily, *and like this! this!* striking chords haphazardly up and down the keyboard. (Darian's hands began to smart, in the morning they would be bruised.) In a loud full baritone voice Father sang fragments of a song ("Gott, der Herr, Ist Sonn' und Schild") while Darian, baby Darian, picked out the melody, frowning in a concentration so intense that droplets of perspiration appeared on his forehead. "Ah, can you do it? *Can* you?" Father cried. "As well as I . . ." With a flourish he tried to play as he sang, striking notes hurriedly and carelessly, the ring on his smallest right-hand finger clicking against the keys, his fingernails tapping, clicking, as well, everything rushed and frantic, until his two-year-old son squirmed in displeasure, and wrenched himself away. For this was not right, this was not the way it should be, the wrong notes and the wrong rhythms cut through him like a knife blade.

On Mondays and Thursdays Darian walks into the village to take his music lesson with Reverend Woodcock, but his happiest times are alone, alone with the piano, hour upon hour and day following day, he is suspended at such times, Darian and not-Darian, he sits at the piano though his fingers are stiff and the nails blue with cold, outside the freezing rain pelts against the windows, against the roof, clattering against the chimney, the sound of the rain is constantly modulated by the wind, as the piano's notes, struck with different degrees of force, acquire mysteriously different textures and meanings: how happy he is! what peace! as if something has closed over his head protecting him from *them*.

There are flights of music that spring up, Darian has no idea how, out of the rain drumming on the roof, the thin howling wind, the harsh staccato cries of birds in the marsh . . . certain brittle strands of Bach, delicate turns of Mozart, the Civil War marching songs he has heard the band play in the square . . . the gospel hymns he has sung at the Church of the Pentecost where he is Darian and not-Darian simultaneously, clapping his hands, his heart swollen with joy, as Reverend Bogey strides about leading the congregation in song. And there is the sound of Millie's airy insincere laughter, the pretty twist to her lips, the anxious flash of her eyes . . . the sight of Elisha trying to sit up in the snow, blood streaming from his chest (his very heart?), soaking his white, white shirt, splattering onto the ground . . . and the ferocity of Father's embrace, the way he grips Darian beneath the arms, lifts him, kisses him, hard, his hot damp thrusting lips against Darian's mouth: ah, he has been away so long, so very long, it is his fate, it is Fate, he cannot bear it that he is required to be away so very long. . . .

Flights of music interrupted by muffled blows, queer arrhythmic runs, sudden halts and starts . . . flights of music of such uncanny beauty Darian knows they are not *his* . . . though they stream through his aching obedient fingers, as sunlight shatters on a pool of standing water, transforming it without touching it. And, more precious, most secret, the music that has the power to draw Darian's mother Sophie to him . . . gliding silently through the rooms of the rectory . . . appearing in the doorway at his back . . . and he must continue playing, he must not hesitate, or miss a note, or turn his head . . . for if he makes a mistake she will vanish . . . he sees her by way of the music, he sees her through his fingertips, the girl with the riding crop, is it? the haughty young woman of the portrait, dark level gaze, the head tilted slightly to the left, and not the wan dying woman amid the bedclothes smelling of sickness . . . that wasted hand extended . . . Darian? Darian? the blistered lips, the eyes glazing over . . . not *that* woman, never *that* woman but the other, Darian's true mother, the handsome girl in the painting who nods in time with his music, who knows his music beforehand, who *is* his music.

He must continue to play without making a mistake, he must never become frightened, or excited, he *must* not turn his head, as Sophie advances . . . advances . . . to stand behind him, silent, for long ecstatic minutes at a time. . . . How happy, Darian thinks, God is everywhere but God is *here*! . . . and sometimes she will brush her fingertips against his hair or the nape of his neck, sometimes she will stoop to kiss . . . and then he cannot help his reaction: he shivers violently, loses the thread of the music, strikes a false note, and, when he turns his head, he sees that she has vanished.

But Darian knows she has been with him: so very close, her lips had touched his burning skin.

The Desperate Man

Though sentenced to be *hanged by the neck until dead* on 29 May 1910 at the State Correctional Facility at Trenton, New Jersey, surely "Christopher Schoenlicht" who is Thurston Licht, Abraham's eldest, beloved son, will not be hanged; nor will he be incarcerated for the remainder of his life.

"Preposterous!"—Abraham snorts in derision.

"Preposterous!"—Abraham fumbles to relight his stumpy Cuban cigar, which maddens him by so frequently going out.

How many weeks, how many months has Abraham pursued the challenge of how to save his son. It seems like years by now, as 29 May 1910 rapidly approaches. *He will be saved, must be saved—but how? As if a glass were steamed or scummy preventing me to see through. Preventing my vision.* A sensation hitherto unknown to Abraham Licht, like Odysseus the man of twists and turns, the man of cunning, and calculation, and duplicity, this sensation of paralysis: his fierce mental powers flash like lightning in one direction, and in another, and still another—but to no avail. He will deny it to Katrina and Millie, but his health has been affected; he's lost weight, obviously; his face bears the look of an elegant Roman bust struck by a hammer and threaded with hairline cracks, about to crumple into pieces.

Yet, alone, in his study with the door shut against his family, he contemplates his image in a mirror and finds his spirit, if not his appearance, unchanged. Eyebrows shaggy as steel wool, gaze cold, level and unflinching, the hastily shaven jaws adamant. *So long as I have breath, strength, genius, and cash—I cannot go down in defeat.*

Strange how Abraham Licht's talent for invention seems to be hindering him: for he hasn't too few ideas, but too many. "If only I could settle upon a strategy. If only—" Too excitable to remain seated, pacing in his study with the door shut against the others, clutching at his head, sighing, muttering to himself, angrily sucking at the damned cigar that has again gone *out*.

His first move was naturally, through (generously paid-off) connections in the Democratic party to apply to the Governor of New Jersey for clemency; for a commutation of Christopher Schoenlicht's sentence to life imprisonment. (With the possibility of an "executive pardon" in a few years when it would no longer arouse local interest.) Negotiations along these lines were going smoothly well into February, when an agent of his named "Albert St. Goar" met with the Governor in secret, at the Governor's private estate in Princeton, to pledge no less than $5,000 to the Governor's upcoming campaign, plus a scattering of smaller donations to "charitable institutions" throughout the state. The Governor, robustly shaking St. Goar's hand, all but gave his word that Christopher Schoenlicht would not hang; a commutation of sentence was "a definite possibility." Nothing was said of plans for the young man's escape from prison, of course; for it was very likely that the Governor would disapprove.

Then suddenly, without warning, word came from the Governor's closest aide that the understanding was cancelled. And no further conversations between the Governor and Mr. St. Goar, or between Mr. St. Goar and any of the Governor's men, were to be arranged. "What has happened? How can this be?"—so Abraham Licht protested. Only belatedly learning that the *Trenton Post*, one of the state's "crusader" papers, was investigating the Governor's business connections since stepping into office; and what had seemed to Abraham Licht a fait accompli was rudely erased.

"And I'd already handed over twenty-five hundred dollars of the payment. God damn me for a fool, and him for a knave!"

Only in his memoir would Abraham Licht confess to having been so swindled. It was not a fact he could bring himself to share with any living person at the time.

Next, even as Abraham spent long insomniac nights, with Elisha, poring over plans of the fortresslike prison, and a map of the city of Trenton, and consulted dozens of firsthand accounts going back to medieval times of successful prison escapes, he was arranging through an intermediary for meetings with prison officials: the underwarden, the resident physician, several guards, the Mercer County sheriff and deputies, even the county coroner. In addition, as Abraham lacked solid contacts in the New Jersey underworld, he was obliged to go in person, that's to say as Timothy St. Goar, a Manhattan businessman, to speak with several high-ranking criminals. His plan, increasingly desperate, was to apply for help both outside the prison and in, in the matter of freeing Thurston from his fate.

How friendly these gentlemen! To a man. Accepting "preliminary moneys" from me—in cash. Yet vague about future meetings. For, as the sheriff himself confided to Abraham, the prospect of freeing a man from both a sentence of death and "The Wall"—as the Trenton prison was known—was a daunting one. Not only had it never been done in the more than one hundred years of the prison's existence, it had never been attempted.

The Chautauqua earnings reaped by Abraham and Elisha were now nearly depleted. So much money, so quickly! "I can hardly believe it, Father," Elisha said, blinking tears from his eyes, "—we had more than four hundred thousand dollars. It was *ours*." Abraham tried to console him, pointing out that no amount of mere money, in the hope of saving Thurston, was wasted. He did resent, though, being fleeced by enforcers of the law—"Hypocrites! Trading on a father's grief." Elisha said passionately, "We must get more money, then, Father. *Tell me what to do, and I will do it*."

But Abraham Licht wondered: Could he ever again risk one of his children in any desperate plan? At Chautauqua, he'd arranged for

Elisha to carry a pistol; for purposes of practicality, the pistol had been loaded. What if—? Another person, or a police officer, had intervened with a gun—?

Abraham shuddered, as if he'd witnessed his beloved 'Lisha, his precious Little Moses, drifting, as in a dream, near the precipice of death.

Tormented by visions. The massive fifteen-foot wall, made of coarse stone and mortar. The labyrinth of inner walls and passageways. The gatehouse. The bare expanse of the yard. Sentry stations, guard boxes, turrets. Hidden rifles on all sides, at all heights. The broad central chimney from which thick black smoke rises. Cellblocks A, B, C, D. The dismal row of cells of the condemned: distinguished from other cells by a certain rank, brackish odor that was said to waft about, all but visible in the air. Beyond were the warden's private quarters, a cheerless four-room apartment. And there was the kitchen, and the laundry room, and the infirmary. And the morgue.

How like a riddle, this labyrinth. How to break it, master it?

Escape by way of—what?—a tunnel. Yes, a tunnel. The most plausible would be from the outer wall to the infirmary, a distance, according to one of the maps, of about fifty yards.

The gallows platform, said to be a weatherworn grim structure, was even closer to the wall, probably less than twenty feet.

In a dream calling my son's name. As, wrists shackled, he ascends to the gallows. But when the fair blond young man turns to me it isn't Thurston but a stranger. Christopher Schoenlicht. Fixing me with a dead man's stare.

II

It is mid-April, it is the final week of April, suddenly it is 29 April; and nothing has been accomplished.

A great deal of money has been spent; and nothing has been accomplished.

Night after night, locked away in his room at the rear of the house, Abraham Licht and Elisha study the plans of the prison . . . the maps of the surrounding area . . . the pencil sketches that Abraham has made, of the prison and of the gallows.

(If Elisha has a secret of his own, a secret worry mounting to obsession, he hides his thoughts from his father. For his love for Abraham Licht and for his brother Thurston is such, *his* emotions count for very little at the present time.)

One night Abraham moans almost inaudibly, "It cannot be done. He cannot be saved." A pencil slips from his fingers and rolls across the floor and a moment later, pricked by a sudden thought, Abraham snatches up the pencil again and says, to Elisha's relief, *"Unless . . ."*

The English Reformer in America

In early May of 1910 there came to the States the celebrated Englishman Lord Harburton Shaw, president of the Commonwealth Prison Reform Society, and author of numerous controversial books, monographs, and articles on the subject of penal reform. (Lord Shaw's zealous five-part series on inequities in the law and the "barbarism" of capital punishment, which appeared in the *Edinburgh Review* in 1908, stirred considerable debate in the British Parliament, and earned him both enemies and fervent supporters; of the several books of his which were published in the States, *Criminal Justice and Criminal Injustice*, of 1903, aroused the most controversy, and gained Lord Shaw a substantial following among like-minded American reformers.) It was Lord Shaw's hope that he might be allowed, during his brief three-week visit to the States, to speak with prison officials and prisoners alike, at a number of representative American prisons—among them, the New York Tombs, Blackwell's Island, Sing Sing, Rahway, Trenton, and Cherry Hill (in Philadelphia). While the famous reformer could not expect to travel incognito, he had requested that news of his arrival be kept from the papers, so far as it was possible, for he feared, with justification, being besieged by well-intentioned admirers, and having no time for the primary purpose of his journey.

Lord Shaw impressed his American hosts, including the flamboyant reform mayor of New York City, William Jay Gaynor, as an agreeably modest, soft-spoken gentleman; well into his sixties, yet fired with youthful vigor; white-haired, clean-shaven, somewhat hard of hearing in one ear; like many Englishmen, even of wealth and family, given to careless, or in any case indifferent, habits of grooming—as if, set beside the idealism of the inner man, such matters as fresh linen, well-scrubbed fingernails, the relations between gray Donegal tweed and brown gabardine, etc., were of little account. The ladies thought Lord Shaw "droll" and "a character—though charming." As Mayor Gaynor's guest at dinner the Englishman ate sparingly, and drank not at all; declined to be baited by opponents; never spoke intemperately despite his strong-held opinions; and comported himself, as even the Hearst papers acknowledged, like a true English gentleman—and not a public-minded American in whom zealous virtue might be confused with noisy egoism.

Though Lord Shaw was rumored to be extremely wealthy, he chose to travel with but a single servant, an Indian secretary-valet of no more than twenty-five years of age (a gracious young man from Calcutta, educated at Cambridge at Lord Shaw's expense), whom he treated rather more like a companion than a hireling; and he declared his preference, early on, for hotels of "modest" pretension, and not the palatial hotels in which his hosts wished to book him. In Manhattan, during his first several days, he quite won the hearts of those men who had resented his arrival, by discussing in detail his new philosophy of reform: this, to begin at the top and the bottom simultaneously, the conditions of jails and prisons being radically improved, capital punishment abolished, etc., and the salaries, living arrangement, bonuses, sick leaves, pensions, etc., for prison officials, being scaled upward as well. "For it has long been a disgrace," Lord Shaw told his avid listeners, "that the very persons who give their energies—indeed, very often their lives—to prison work, should be taken for granted by society, and carelessly classed with the prisoners whom they 'serve.' "

It was Lord Shaw's contention too (an item that particularly struck the ear of Mayor Gaynor and his aides) that elected and appointed officials both be granted salaries proportionate to the highest-paid men in business: for by this measure they would be encouraged to remain in politics, serving the commonweal, and not deserting to more lucrative pastures; and, most importantly, they would be immune to bribery and corruption—long the scourge ("in England if not, perhaps, in America") of government.

Asked where such munificent salaries would derive from, Lord Shaw replied without hesitation, *taxes*.

The United States was the wealthiest nation on earth, after all; and here the rich were extravagantly rich. Had Lord Shaw not chanced to read, to his disgust, that there was an enormous estate in Philadelphia, staffed by ninety servants, where the silver plate alone was valued at *five million dollars*; and were not the objets d'art in the Fifth Avenue mansion of the Vanderbilts worth an estimated *one hundred million dollars*? The wealthy citizens of America would have to be severely taxed, and soon, if the nation was to avoid a complete overthrow of its government; and the taxes would have to be distributed to those men who had distinguished themselves as public servants. "Take from the rich and give to the politicians, as they and they alone have the nation's welfare at heart," Lord Shaw said, his British accent becoming steadily more clipped and pronounced, and a faint blush of indignation rising to his cheeks.

Was it any wonder, then, that this English gentleman was praised at once by his hosts; declared a true aristocrat, in his scorn for material self-interest; heralded as a saint; and invited to visit any prison or house of detention he might wish, during his three-week stay in the country?

Lord Shaw's schedule was gratifyingly crowded.

On Blackwell's Island he and his young Indian servant were allowed to visit the lunatics' wing of the prison hospital, and to interview those inmates whom it was possible to interview without running the risk of personal injury; at the experimental Cherry Hill prison they were privileged to interview several long-term prisoners in their solitary cells, with no guard or bailiff in attendance. At "The Wall" in Trenton, by general consent the grimmest of the state penitentiaries, they were treated with unusual courtesy by the warden, who, having heard of Lord Shaw's radical ideas for reform, insisted upon inviting both him and his secretary-valet to dinner to discuss the matter in greater intimacy. (For by this time, in mid-May, it was known that Lord Shaw planned to write a series of articles on his American visit, singling out prisons and prison officials most deserving of financial largesse.)

At Trenton, where executions were routinely held, Lord Shaw was

made welcome to visit with the public executioner, the prison physician, the attending clergyman, etc.; to examine the gallows; and to
spend as many hours as he wished among the condemned, interviewing
the unhappy men sequestered there ... at this time seven convicts
ranging in age from approximately twenty-five to sixty-two. The next
execution, Lord Shaw was told, would be on 29 May: one "Christopher
Schoenlicht," convicted for the murder of his mistress, was scheduled
then to be hanged.

Several of the condemned men, as it turned out, were clearly insane;
a state of affairs Lord Shaw vigorously protested, as it was a sign of
barbarism to put a madman to death. Yet, the warden's answer was a
simple one: the men had not been insane at the time of sentencing—
only after.

Of young Christopher Schoenlicht Lord Shaw hesitantly inquired,
"Does the lad show remorse for his crime?" and the warden said, "Not
in the slightest, sir—nor remorse for what lies ahead, at the end of the
noose." "But does he seem in full possession of his faculties?" Lord
Shaw worriedly asked, peering in at the haggard prisoner through the
bars of his cell; and the warden replied, with a cruelly hearty laugh, not
minding if the condemned man heard, "As full a possession as he will
need, sir, in twelve days' time."

It was Schoenlicht, of the seven condemned prisoners, whom Lord
Shaw decided he would like to interview.

Did the prisoner object?

He did not.

Did the prisoner seem to *care*?

He did not.

So, with little ceremony, Lord Harburton Shaw and his Indian servant were escorted into the young man's dank cell, and the heavy door
locked behind them; and, so very suddenly, so easily, they were alone
at last ... Thurston Licht and his father Abraham and his brother Elisha ... standing for a long moment in silence, as the guard's footsteps
slowly retreated.

The cells in this part of the prison were in four tiers, one above the
other; ceilings were formed by two large, heavy stone slabs, which were
of course floors of the cells above; communication between one cell to
the next would be difficult indeed, except perhaps by way of the "soil"

pipe that ran along the wall through the cells—yet, even so, Abraham Licht lifted a warning finger and whispered, "Thurston: *say not a word; make not a move*."

How astonished Thurston was, staring from the snowy-haired Lord Shaw to the turbanned Elijii, and back to Shaw again, like a man in a dream struggling to wake.

Poor Thurston had grown gaunt and stooped since being incarcerated; his skin had a jaundiced cast, and his hair, once so thick, had become thin and matted with filth, a dull pewter-gray; and his eyes!—not those of a youth in his mid-twenties but the narrowed, sunken, damp eyes of a man of twice that age.

Trying to speak, his lips moving numbly, inaudibly.

Could it be possible, he saw what he believed he was seeing?

Or were these dream figures: Abraham Licht in the guise of an elder Englishman, with built-up putty cheeks and a subtle realignment of ivory-white, bushy eyebrows; and Elisha with eyes outlined in black, his skin tinted a warm olive-magenta-brown and a dazzling white turban wrapped about his head . . . he, too, lifting a warning finger to his lips, that Thurston say not a word.

Thurston stared. Stood paralyzed. Perhaps his instinct was to rush moaning into his father's arms—or to shrink back against the damp windowless wall, in terror of such apparitions. The elder Englishman Shaw was addressing him in a clipped, formal voice, extending his almost-steady hand that Thurston, the condemned prisoner, might shake it, saying, "Mr. Schoenlicht, thank you for agreeing to be interviewed. We have come to speak with you on a matter of extreme urgency, son—life, and death. *Yours*."

The Condemned Man

I

Neither Abraham Licht nor Elisha can bring himself to consider *Have they arrived too late to save him? Is he lost, his mind shattered?* For more than an hour in the squalid, dim-lighted cell, trying to communicate with Thurston, Thurston-no-longer-Thurston, as a domesticated dog, injured, or terrified out of its senses, is no longer *dog* but a feral creature, its brain altered, even its eyes altered, like Thurston's eyes strangely dilated, the iris near-black. Thurston, or is it Schoenlicht, a man condemned to death, and a man reconciled to death, scratching frenzied at lice visibly crawling on his neck and arms, scratching with blackened, broken nails, his breath fetid, his unwashed body giving off a stench as strong as the diarrhetic waste clogging the soil pipe.

Patiently the snowy-haired Englishman asks, Do you understand, son? *Do you understand?*

And will you follow the plan?

I command you, son: to follow the plan.

(A fleet, furry creature with bristling whiskers scuttles along the edge of the oozing wall.)

(One of the lunatics in the cellblock begins to howl.)

. . . The potion, Katrina's medicine, "enchanter's nightshade" it's called . . . here in this vial: take it, son! . . . to be hidden away (in this crevice in the wall, in the shadows) and taken on the morning of 29 May . . . precisely a half hour before the execution is scheduled. Yes? Do you hear? Do you comprehend? Nod your head, son, if you comprehend. You will take this vial, hidden here, see where I've hidden it, and on the morning of the execution you will swallow its contents a half hour before . . . before *it* is scheduled to occur . . . so it will seem, as they march you into the yard, and you come into sight of the gallows, you will be struck down into a comalike state, and beyond into a mimicry of death . . . your breath and heartbeat too faint to be detected . . . your blood pressure so low, all your bodily warmth will be secreted deep inside you . . . your fingers and toes stiff and icy-cold . . . your skin giving off the clammy radiance of death.

And our enemies will believe you have been frightened to death.

And disappointed to be cheated of their pleasure in watching you die a hideous death at the end of a noose!

For the attending physician, an old fool, pompous but affable, with whom "Elijii" and I have become acquainted, *will pronounce you dead, of cardiac arrest.* For we will require his unwitting cooperation in our plan.

For now you are no longer alone—a "condemned" man.

For now it is us, your family, against them, our mortal enemies.

For now it is the strategy of The Game: our stakes are your life: we will triumph!

Do you doubt, children? You must never doubt.

Unknown to Abraham Licht and Elisha, the prison chaplain, an impassioned, excitable, garrulous elder man not unlike Abraham Licht in the power of his person, has been "ministering unto," as he calls it, the condemned sinner Christopher Schoenlicht, for weeks; leading the youth in tearful, groaning prayers and verses out of Jeremiah vehement in their confusion, and seductive: *A noise shall come even to the ends of the earth, for the LORD hath a controversy with the nations, he will plead with all flesh; he will give them that are wicked to the sword, saith the LORD.* And beyond that, the rhapsodic prophesies of Saint John the Divine in which madness and poetry conjoin yet more seductively.

For it is given.

For it is just.

To die as God bids.

To die as God and the State of New Jersey bid.

Mute, his brain numbed by terror, exhaustion, sleepless nights and inedible food, food crawling minutely with maggots, his body torn by explosive bouts of diarrhea, vomiting, fever and convulsive chills, that he is, or was, a Licht, has become remote to him as a rapidly fading dream, for is all of life not a dream? a hallucination? a vision arrayed before us by Satan, God's perpetual enemy through time? So the sinner murders, but it is sin that murders. So the soul ravages itself, but it is in the service of salvation. *For the meek shall inherit the earth. For the first shall be last, and the last first. Verily I say unto you.*

Christopher Schoenlicht, sinner. Mute in his own defense. For there is, or was, nothing to say. He would not speak the name of the true murderer, for he could not. And knowing, sensing, despite his confusion, and his naïveté regarding the law, that both he and the true murderer would be tried for the death of the woman, for there would have been no distinction between them: brothers by blood, brothers by the soul.

And there was sin. His spirit encrusted, festering with sin.

Even as his earthly, sin-ridden father proclaimed there can be no sin yet Christopher, once Thurston, knows *there is sin.*

For what is The Game but sin?

For what is The Game but Satan's strategy, to blind the sinner from his salvation?

He lapses into a waking sleep. He shouts, springing to his feet to grasp the bars of the animal cage, and shake them—but they are unmovable, as if set in stone. His body is on fire with the bites of demon-insects. A flaming snake is coiled in his bowels, writhing and thrashing. His eyes bulge out of his head, rivulets of tears and sweat conjoined. Then, by a miracle, the chaplain is beside him, not shrinking from kneeling with him on the filth-encrusted floor, for here is a man of God, here is a true believer (fondly mocked by prison guards and by the more hardened of the condemned men) defiant in the face of mere earthly disgust. Grasping Christopher Schoenlicht by his shoulders, shouting into his face, *Verily I say unto you! With men it is impossible, but not with God: for with God all things are possible.* The man of God and the condemned sinner shouting together, singing, laughing. *Hallelujah. Hallelujah!*

II

And in this way he became, he exulted in, as a snake may be said to exult brainlessly yet luxuriantly in its skin, the murderer of . . . but he has forgotten the seductress's name.

A whore, like any whore of Babylon, Noph, Tahpenes, those wicked cities of the plain that have broken the crown of Thy head.

Clutching at him, his young maleness. Kissing him freely and lasciviously in the secret and forbidden places of his body. The whore, the female. The woman old enough to be his mother. The lewd drifting eyes, the mouth hungry for his maleness. And the repulsive hairy mouth between her fattish legs that snatched hungrily too: squeezed, plunged, bit: drawing him, his name unknown, down to sin.

Whether Christopher, or Thurston.

Thurston, or Christopher.

Did it matter which of them? it did not, for Satan named them both.

He accepts this fate. Yet weeps, racked with agony. Kneeling and clutching at his hair, yanking it out in handfuls. Enraged suddenly, pushing away the woman's caressing hands, his strong forearm suddenly locked beneath her chin, her piercing cries, her panicked struggle, now the moment of bringing his arm back, jerking it deftly back, as he'd once seen his brother Harwood snap the neck of a mangy dog that had been trailing them about and would not go away and what a sensation to feel the delicate bones snap and to feel Death convulse in his arms.

So, it was I.

Was it?

Abruptly, three days before his execution, the condemned man refuses to allow the prison chaplain back into his cell. *For I am saved, as much as I will be saved.*

Christopher Schoenlicht, the most "publicized"—"notorious"—"notable"—of the half dozen condemned inmates. Is this young man something of a mystery, even to the veteran guards? Even to the veteran warden? And to the prison physician, required by law to examine him or to make a pretense thereof, to declare him, as the morning of his death rapidly approaches, in "fit condition" to be hanged?

Tall, cadaverous, bearded youth. He's silent, or sullen. Or struck dumb. Never entirely well, his stomach shrunken and his skin the color of aged ivory, always a fever, always mucus glistening at his nostrils, yet he's spared the waves of pneumonia, malaria, Asiatic cholera, bloody flux that periodically rage through "The Wall" and eliminate, as in a dramatic display of Darwin's famed principle of survival of the fittest, of

which, in days long ago and only faintly remembered, Abraham Licht
spoke approvingly, the weakest of the men. And God saw that it was
good, and *it was good.*

The condemned man's age is given as twenty-five. The file for him
will note that he has no (known) family, no (known) past record, no
(known) history. A possible victim of amnesia, one observer has speculated. No, declares another, a victim of mental illness. But no, insists
another, simply a hardened criminal, a subspecies of human being, caring no more for his own worthless life than for the life of the woman he
murdered.

And God saw that it was good, and it was . . . *good.*

The Game is never to be played as if it were merely a game: but what
The Game is, or was, he no longer knows.

Are you listening closely, Thurston?
Will you follow my instructions?

. . . taken to the prison morgue . . . and from there, by arrangement,
to a Trenton funeral home . . . for Lord Shaw will see to it, you won't be
buried in a pauper's grave . . . then to Manhattan where you will be
given clothes, money, identification papers, all that's required . . . to get
to the Canadian border near Kingston, Ontario.

The snowy-haired ruddy-cheeked English gentleman continues to
speak, now daring to grip Schoenlicht's unresisting hand, squeezing the
fingers tight to bid him *hear, understand, obey.* Even as his mind shakes
itself free. Beating and thrumming. Moths' fluttering wings, the scut-
tling of rats and giant hard-shelled beetles here in the sewer pipe; the
marsh, acres of swampland, marbled clouds reflected in a pool of standing water, a face suddenly reflected . . . a boy's face . . . but whose? . . .
he can't see, eyes blinded by tears.

Thurston?
You will follow my instructions?
And we will be united again in Ontario, no later than June 4.

Tall, swaying on his feet, breath shallow and panting and eyes sunk in
fatigue, this *is* Thurston, isn't it? . . . allowing Abraham to grasp his hand
in parting, allowing Elisha, eyes bright with tears, to embrace him . . . for
they *are* brothers, unlikely as it seems. *For what is a man's mere skin, set*

beside his soul? Thurston's fingers have closed about the precious little vial but his eyes evade Abraham Licht's fierce gaze.

I will, I must. Renounce Satan and his ways.

Murmuring aloud, "Yes, Father."

He doesn't come to the cell door after the guard has locked it, to watch his visitors walk briskly away.

The Guilty Lovers

(But, as they are not precisely *lovers*, need they feel *guilt?*)
Millicent, bold and reckless, pretty spoiled Millicent, would inform Father of their love at once, because it is so pure and noble a love; and beg his permission for them to be lawfully wed. Elisha, less certain of Abraham Licht's response, and made rather more subdued than elated by the discovery of his love for Millie, cautions her repeatedly to wait.

At least until Thurston is free, and safe in Canada.

At least until Father is himself again.

In this precarious spring, as May rapidly flies past, they walk together a great deal, in secret, but rarely allow themselves to touch. Kisses are forbidden now, except in certain circumstances: chaste greetings, ceremonial farewells. If they are observed speaking together in low urgent whispers in the manner of plotting lovers they are not in fact speaking of *that* (which is to say, their alarming desire for each other) but, perhaps, about Thurston and what will become of him in Canada . . . or what Elisha might recall of Millie's mother ("Tell me anything you remember," Millie begs) . . . or what Millie might recall of her early childhood in Muirkirk, when Elisha was away . . . or the fortunes of Harwood, the prospects of the youngest children, the likelihood of Father's marrying again ("Though in actual fact I doubt that he has ever been married *at all*," Elisha says).

Regarding Thurston—Elisha is confident, or seems so, that the plan will work: for Father has seen to every detail, and will even be present at the "execution," as Lord Harburton Shaw. But Millie, drawing slightly away from him, will say only in a faint voice, "Oh Elisha, my darling—my dream has prepared me for the worst."

The Ingrate Son

I

CONDEMNED MURDERER STRUCK DEAD BEFORE GALLOWS AT "THE WALL"

Witnesses Reported "Shocked"

This, the banner headline for the *New York Tribune* for 30 May 1910. Tall lurid black letters like a shout.

For it happened that, before a small crowd of witnesses including the distinguished English prison reformer Lord Harburton Shaw, the young man convicted of having murdered Manhattan socialite Eloise Peck apparently fell into a swoon at the very sight of the tall ugly gallows at the State Correctional Facility, and died within minutes despite the attempt of an attending physician to revive him.

What a spectacle! What guilty horror passed through the gathering! The execution ritual was hastily aborted and all witnesses save prison authorities were ushered out of the yard and urged not to make further inquiries. It would subsequently be reported in a terse statement by the prison warden that the convicted murderer Schoenlicht had died of "severe cardiac arrest"; for the first time in the history of the notorious prison at Trenton, a man had cheated the gallows minutes before he was to be hanged. As an indignant Lord Shaw told New York reporters,

"Witnesses were more shocked and shamed, it seemed, that the means of 'punishment' was so cruel as to frighten a man to death, than they would have been had the poor lad been hanged." For some weeks a controversy raged in the *Post* and other New York and New Jersey newspapers over the "cruelty" or "justice" of hanging, or of any form of capital punishment. Lord Shaw was a hero to some, an interfering foreigner to others; in his zealous wake, a campaign for execution reform was begun by several Christian organizations to which Lord Shaw was rumored to have contributed generous sums of money. He was said, too, out of pity for the young murderer who'd died of fright, to have arranged for a private burial for him, to spare him "the final ignominy" of a pauper's grave in the untended cemetery behind the Trenton prison.

Unfortunately, the idealistic Englishman departed the United States to return to England, unless to sail to Australia, in pursuit of his cause, in early June; and disappeared from the controversy.

II

"What? What do you mean—*vanished?*"

"Only, sir, that he—it—is *not here.* As you can see."

"But he—it—*must be here.* A corpse cannot rise out of his coffin and walk away, surely. I insist that you and your assistants search the premises more thoroughly."

"Sir, you can be sure that we've done so. More than once, from bottom to top, sir. But he—it—the remains of 'Christopher Schoenlicht'— is *gone*; and good riddance, we say. And this was left behind, sir, pinned to the satin lining of the casket—"

An envelope upon which the name LORD SHAW was hastily scrawled in pencil.

With shaking fingers Lord Shaw took the envelope, strode out of Eakins Brothers Funeral Home on South Street, Trenton, and, in the street, where his valet Elijii awaited him behind the wheel of a small truck with an open, tarpaulin-covered rear, read aloud this enigmatic message:

"Thurston & Christopher—forgive.
I am neither now.
I renounce Satan & his ways.
Farewell."

From out of the truck Elijii called anxiously, "Lord Shaw? What is it?" seeing the elder man stricken in the grimly pale metallic-smelling Trenton half-light. "Where is—Thurston?"

The elder man's face was draining of blood; yet ruddy spots remained on his cheeks, as if in mockery of manly vigor and good spirits. For a long moment he did not speak, until the Indian servant climbed from the vehicle to stand before him; then he said, feebly, though with mounting anger, "He is 'risen'—and he has, it seems, 'ascended.' At any rate, it seems he is gone."

"What? How?"

"Presumably, he walked away. He has, he says"—waving the scrawled message in Elijii's face—" 'renounced' us. And has *gone*."

The young Indian, his showy white silk turban so tightly wound about his handsome head that his forehead appeared compressed, gaped at his master in astonishment. Lord Shaw's elegant British accent had abruptly disappeared and in its place was a harsh, choked American accent, the flat nasal vowels of upstate western New York colliding with the clipped consonants of New York City. Seeing that no one was near, Lord Shaw roundly cursed, "Hell! Damnation! Son of a bitch—*his* lineage!" swinging himself up into the passenger's seat of the truck, saying, "And we, too, will be *gone*. Elijii, don't stand there like an idiot. I've had enough of Trenton, New Jersey, and of the folly of ingrate sons, to last me a lifetime, and more."

PART II

By Night, by Stealth

I

If you cry your tears will turn into fiery red ants and eat away your eyes.

If you cry your tears will burn rivulets into your cheeks.

If you cry poison thistles will spring up where your tears have fallen.

If you cry our enemies will hear and rejoice.

Never cry except in solitude. *But never cry if you can laugh instead.*

Now that her brother has been sent away to school, now there is no one except the girl who knows of the woman who comes in the night, the woman who smells wet and cold and sharp like night, the smiling woman stepping out of the hill of old bones, lifting her skeleton hand to touch . . . Lifting both her hands, her skeleton-hands, to take hold . . .

The girl is said to have caused the woman's death but no one blames her because she was only a baby at the time because she cannot remember the time. Nor does her mother blame her, smiling, whispering, My *baby? you are my baby! you love me!*

The slanted crumbling lichen-covered grave markers, the burdocks and thistles and chicory, the dandelions that blossom bright yellow and turn to fluff in days, the smell of hot sunshine, the smell of patches of fog, running too fast in spongy soil you can turn your ankle and fall heavily and cut your silly forehead *but never cry if you can laugh instead.*

Because that woman has no power to hurt! because her eyes are stuffed with dirt! the eye sockets empty and stuffed with dirt! any door or window can be locked against her, you can burrow to the foot of the bed to escape her, you can press the pillow hard, hard, over your head to escape her, you can press into Katrina's arms, Katrina will hide you, the woman is nothing but old bones ground down fine as dust, old bones that are gritty white powder, the eyes are not eyes but empty holes stuffed with dirt, they are not *staring* they are *empty*, and that is no voice, that whispering you hear, because she never had a voice.

My baby?
But she is no one's baby.
A tall gawky shy child, nine years old, ten years old, long-legged, clumsy, lank brown hair Katrina keeps thinned and cut short (otherwise it will snarl beneath and hurt, oh, how it will hurt bringing tears into her eyes), small puckered mouth, small deep-set somber eyes, a startled expression, a frightened smile behind the raised fingers, forehead just a little too wide, jaw too thick, feet too long, *and she is only eleven years old*, joining in the boys' laughter as they toss dried clumps of mud and cow manure in her direction, as the hard green pears from the Mackays' orchard fly past her ducked head, her secret is that she loves them all, her secret is that she makes her way by stealth along the back lanes and alleys of the town, at night, she is a red-winged hawk, she is a barn owl with glaring tawny eyes, she spies on them all, she hates and adores them all, how do people live? how do people in other families live? what are the things they say to each other when no strangers can hear? at dusk, at night, behind their partly drawn blinds, behind their filmy gauzy lacy curtains, by lamplight, by the warmth of a wood-burning stove, how do they look at one another? how do they smile at one another? by the high thin tolling of the church bells, as the wind shreds the clouds overhead, what are their secrets we cannot hear?

She escapes them by flying above the marsh, turning away toward the mountains, where Mount Chattaroy catches the evening sun, she is dipping and circling, soaring, slow, lazy, perfectly in control, her wide wings scarcely need to move, only the sleek dark feathers ripple in the wind, her beak is made for jabbing, ripping, tearing, but she will do no injury ... she will do no injury because she is good ... because she wants only to be a slow gliding shadow, there in the water, to be *seen*, to be *feared*, to be *admired*, to be *known*.

She escapes them by turning into a shining copper-colored snake and disappearing into a hole in the ground! ... she is one of the giant orange butterflies ... and sometimes a horse, a young colt, silky black mane and tail, black stamping hooves, only the eyes gleaming white, only the teeth flashing white, as she gallops noiselessly along the road ... in stealth, at dusk, by night, along the road ... down the long dusty hill and across the narrow wooden bridge that rattles as if the planks are going to fly up into the air as if the rusted girders are going to break but she is not frightened *she* is not frightened, her powerful muscular legs driving hard, hard, her mane wild, her tail black and silky and wild, her enormous hooves pounding in the earth, she is no baby any longer, there is no need for her to be frightened any longer, the fresh wet smell of the night fills her nostrils, her lungs expand in joy, is that the taste, the acrid gritty taste, of last year's leaves? is that trickling the sound of the Muirkirk Creek, the shallow rivulets making their way around the great bleached boulders in the creek bed?

II

All that you need to know, Father once whispered, gripping her tight, tight, her tiny ribs aching in his embrace, is that I love you. You are Esther, my daughter, and I love you.

III

Father returns suddenly, Father is home again, after the terrible quarrel with Harwood when Harwood is sent away forever (to Canada? to Mexico? to South America?) he remains in Muirkirk for nearly six weeks, and sometimes he locks himself away in his bedroom and no one dares knock on the door and sometimes he leaves the house before dawn and is gone until midnight and sometimes he glances in Esther's direction without seeing her and sometimes he glances in her direction and *sees* her . . . and it is clear that he loves her, he adores her, too tender to scold if she blunders in her recitations, if she strikes the wrong notes on the piano, if she hasn't Darian's talent, or Millicent's beauty, or the trick of holding his rapt attention as 'Lisha does. . . .

Love is enough, Father murmurs aloud, why isn't love *enough?*

Come here, Esther, little one, Father whispers, his breath smelling of whiskey, oh, don't bother me, Esther, please don't hang on me like that, you aren't a baby any longer, *don't stare into my face.*

To Darian he says suddenly, It may be *time*, mysteriously he says, It may be time now for *you*, and Esther is jealous for a week as Father plans (in defiance of Reverend Woodcock) a campaign to introduce Darian to the music-loving populace of the State . . . beginning, if all goes well, with his début in Carnegie Hall. Which pieces should he play? Which pieces best demonstrate his remarkable piano technique, his *virtuosity*, unparalleled in any child his age on this side of the Atlantic? (There is a Mozart rondo in which Darian's fingers flash, there is a "Minute Waltz" of Chopin's that dazzles the eye no less than the ear, and one or two of the boy's own compositions are impressive if rather discordant. . . . It is so difficult to choose, perhaps they will require the services of a professional manager after all.)

If only Darian were younger, if only Father had not waited so long! . . . for it is difficult to bill the boy as a prodigy when, clearly, he is no longer a child, despite his slender frame and thin-cheeked face, he is twelve years old, is he? or nearly? but might well pass for a child of ten, if dressed appropriately. It might even be a possibility (so Father muses aloud, pulling at his chin as if it were bearded, and fixing Darian with a bright calculating eye) to present him as a *girl*, for the music-loving populace might well prefer a *girl*, up there onstage, seated at an enormous concert grand piano, playing those astonishingly difficult pieces, Chopin, Mozart, isn't there something of Czerny, and Liszt, and . . .

Darian sulks, Darian dares whisper No, all the household is in a turmoil because Darian has whispered No, and Millie and 'Lisha seem to have taken his side (though they do not risk Father's anger by saying so aloud), and Katrina adds to the upset by telling Father it is a very poor idea indeed, doesn't he know that Darian's heart isn't strong, he tires rapidly, in the winter months in particular he is susceptible to all sorts of colds and flus and congestions, can it be that he, Darian's father, has actually forgotten?

Boldly the old woman says, Do you want to lose your youngest son, as you have lost your eldest?

And Father has no reply.

And Father retreats, and says no more about Darian's debut at Carnegie Hall, and is gone from Muirkirk, taking Millie and 'Lisha with him, within a week.

IV

And Father is gone, and within a few months Darian is gone, to boarding school in Vanderpoel; and Esther falls in love with Dr. Deerfield who is so friendly to her when he sees her in town, no she falls in love with Dr. Deerfield's son Aaron, no she is in love with no one, she hates and adores them all, at dusk she prowls the lane behind the old mill, she cuts through the Mackays' cow pasture, makes her way in stealth in silence (as a red-winged hawk, as a barn owl, as a galloping black colt) along the unnamed dirt road that parallels Main Street, staring into windows, puzzling over lives, glimpses of lives, behind gauzy curtains, behind partly drawn blinds, How *do* people live in a family? the girl wonders, What are the things they say to one another, what are the things they don't need to say?

You cannot run wild like this, Katrina scolds.

Katrina grips her shoulders, Katrina scolds, You are a *Licht*—don't you know who you are?

By day the men and women of Muirkirk who have occasion to know Esther Licht know her as a sweet child, a friendly child, despite her strange ways, her painful shyness, that high startled laughter, she is a well-mannered child too despite her clumsiness, and intelligent if you can get her to talk, if you can get her to look you in the eye, attractive too though not pretty, the poor thing will never be pretty, not as her sister Millicent is pretty, but does it matter? The Woodcocks are fond of Esther Licht, the Ewings, the Mackays, Mrs. Oakes, Mrs. Kincaid, her tutor Mr. Ryan, Dr. Deerfield speaks of her with surprised pleasure, her interest in doctoring, nursing, medicine, "making hurt things well. . . ." Esther is so plain-featured and graceless, there *is* something appealing about her, she hasn't the charm of her sister Millicent, the older Thurston and Elisha, certainly she doesn't strike the eye or the ear as Abraham Licht's *daughter*, which is why they like her.

(Not that Abraham Licht isn't liked, or anyway admired. Not that Muirkirk isn't grateful for his intermittent interest in the town—he has donated money to several of the churches, to the library, even to the temperance organization in which, as he has said, he doesn't *altogether* believe. Not that many of the Muirkirk gentlemen don't envy him, indeed, and speculate on the sort of life he leads elsewhere, the financial coups, the beautiful women, the excitement. . . . The problem is simply this: no one trusts him. Even as he speaks warmly, and graciously, and *convincingly*, even then, by some mysterious sort of magic, he fails to *convince*!)

How sad, that lonely child! Motherless since birth; and fatherless much of the time as well; glimpsed wandering by herself in the fields and woods and marshy pastures outside town . . . or, in town, along Main Street, in the square, in the vicinity of the public school, or Dr. Deerfield's white-shingled house on Bay Street . . . observed in the high-ceilinged reading room of the new library (a gift of Mr. Carnegie's, the pride of Muirkirk: a magnificent limestone building three stories high, turreted, with an oak-walled gymnasium, nickel baths in the basement, even a tile pool open to all residents of Muirkirk). She has few friends her own age . . . she seems to know few boys and girls her own age . . . but she has recently joined Mrs. Clay's Temperance Choir, which meets twice weekly in the Methodist Church Hall, and heartily sings such temperance favorites as "King Alcohol"—

King Alcohol has many forms
By which he catches men.
He is a beast of many horns
And ever thus has been!

and "Ten Nights in a Barroom" with its heartrending chorus, which never fails to bring tears to all eyes:

Hear the sweet voice of the child,
  Which the nightwinds repeat as they roam!
Oh, who could resist this most pleading of prayers?
  "Please, father, dear father, come home!"

V

On snowy or rain-lashed days Katrina can be prevailed upon to tell her old tales . . . of Robin the miller's son, and Mina the governor's daughter . . . and the great white "King of the Wolves" who dwells on Mount Chattaroy . . . and the little girl who disobeyed her grandmother and turned into a turtle . . . and the little boy who disobeyed *his* grandmother and turned into an ugly giant bullfrog, condemned to croak in protest for the remainder of his life: and a hideous long life it was!

But most disturbing of all the tales, Esther thinks, is that of the king's son and the king's daughter which (so Katrina says crossly) Esther isn't old enough to understand.

Yes I am, says Esther, shivering—yes I *am*.

No you're not, says Katrina, because the king's son and the king's daughter fell in *love*, and you don't know what *love* is, and you don't know the kind of *love* that is forbidden between brother and sister, don't pretend you do! —Anyway the story took place long ago, a very long time ago, though the marsh was as it is today, the marsh never changes, and the flowers and plants and trees and animals that grow in it, none of them ever changes, they were there at the beginning of the world and will be there at the end, and long ago, when this story took place, there was a certain black fruit, a sweet juicy black fruit, like peaches, like apples, like black currants, and it was known to be a poison fruit, but an elixir might be made of it, a medicine, a potion, to be used to make people fall in love, for instance if a man loves a woman and she doesn't love him, or a woman loves a man and he doesn't love *her*, do you understand? well no I don't suppose you do, how can a child your age understand? but anyway the king's son fell in love with his own sister who was the most beautiful princess in the world, and he was bitterly jealous of her many suitors, and vowed no one would marry her but he, and one day he went into the marsh and met an old woman, a very old white-haired woman, and he asked her for a special medicine to give to his sister, that she would love no one but *him*, and the old woman gave him a juice made of the black fruit, and warned him of its terrible power, and told him it could not be undone except by death, and he snatched it from her without thanking her, he laughed to think that he might ever wish the potion undone, he was wild with love for the princess and cared not at all for the rest of the world, not for her, or their father the king, still less for her suitors, in truth he wished her suitors all dead, for his *hatred* was as great as his *love*, so wicked a young man was he.

He then returned to the castle, and gave his innocent sister the elixir to drink, telling her it was a delicious liqueur an old woman had given him back in the marsh, it was made of peach brandy and black currants and molasses, and his unsuspecting sister drank of it, and declared it delicious indeed, and smiling upon him bade him drink of it too, but he declined, saying there was no need, he had had his share beforehand, and even as they spoke the princess fell in love with him, her eyes blazed, her heart leapt in her breast, and there was no help for it, the poor child fell in love . . . and very soon she and her wicked brother became lovers . . . and loved each other in secret . . . and the princess's love was greater than the prince's . . . and nothing would do but that he love her every minute of the day, and every minute of the night . . . and he began to fear she would suck all his strength from him for her love was so very powerful, there was no end to it, there could never be any end to it, even when the prince grew weary and the princess became great with child . . . but this little Esther does *not* understand, does she! *don't pretend!* . . . and finally the princess grew so jealous of the prince, she berated him for not loving her, and wept, and tore at her fair skin, and wished aloud that they both might die, and sink to the bottom of the marsh where no one would know them, and the princess's beauty was faded now with anguish, her lips were parched and blistered, her eyes rolled in her head, with love, with love so terrible it could never be undone, never except by death. . . .

So one day, not a year after he had given his beloved the elixir to drink, the wicked prince, fearing his sister would betray him to the king, lured her into the marsh and killed her: strangled her with his bare hands: even as the wretched girl caressed him madly in love of *him*.

And, seeing that his beloved was dead, and that the world had no meaning for him any longer, the wicked prince soon died: and there was no one to lament him in all the kingdom.

So it was, the king's son and the king's daughter died for love of each other, and were buried at the bottom of the marsh, long ago, long before you were born, in this very place.

Esther, earnest plain-featured Esther, Esther who stares too hard and listens too intensely, why does she sit hunched over, two or three fingers jammed into her mouth, her child's forehead vexed with thought. . . . She says, O Katrina, it will not happen to Millie and 'Lisha, will it? and Katrina turns from the stove and looks at her, and says carefully, What do you mean, Millie and 'Lisha? and Esther says, Because I saw them together, Katrina, her voice faltering, not wanting to say that she had seen them touch, hadn't she, in a strange way, she had seen them kiss, for it *was* a kiss, wasn't it, a strange sort of half-angry biting kiss, Millie and 'Lisha, blond Millie and dark-skinned 'Lisha, stealing away in the beech grove on the far side of the church-yard where no one would see them . . . except their little sister of whom they took no notice; for no one did.

What do you mean, like Millie and 'Lisha? Katrina asks, her voice rising, her eyes gray as steel wool, and Esther sees something in her face that frightens her, and all she can murmur is, O Katrina please it will *not* happen, will it, before she rises clumsily to her feet and runs out of the room.

VI

Unsuited for The Game, Father has said, sadly, with finality, but what, wonders the girl, is The Game for which she is unsuited . . . ?

VII

By stealth, by night, making her way along the deserted country road . . . down the long hill by the cider mill, across the bridge that rattles . . . the creek below, the vaporous sky above, a moon made of bone, something fierce and wet and sharp rising from the grass . . . and now she gallops noiselessly past the darkened rear of the livery stable . . . past the darkened rear of the icehouse . . . and here is the Methodist church and here is the pharmacy and here is the school to which she will be going in the fall and here is the new Woolworth's five-and-dime with the magnificent red and gold signboard, the magnificent show windows ("any article in this window 5 CENTS") and here is the library with its noble portico and broad sprawling steps and here is the Congregational Church and here the houses of the men and women the boys and girls whom she hates and adores, whom she envies so that her heart lurches in her breast, the lamplight behind the thin gauzy curtains, the glimpse of an arm, a profile, a blurred movement, how do these people live, what are the secret words that pass between them, do they know of The Game, do they know they are doomed never to play The Game, what are the things that pass between them when no stranger is close at hand? The clapboard houses of lower Main Street, the tall brick houses of Muirkirk Avenue, the houses of High Street, Elm Street, Bay Street, the Woodcocks' residence behind the gray stone Lutheran church, the Ewings' house, the Oakeses', the Deerfields' corner house on Bay, white shingle board, black shutters, a veranda with four elegantly carved white posts, one brick walk leading to the front door and one brick walk leading to the doctor's office at the rear, the rusted wrought-iron fence Esther's fingers idly brush, the crooked little gate that can be closed but not locked, a half dozen windows facing the street, lamplight within, firelight within, through the filmy curtains it is possible to see figures inside . . . yet not to be seen by them, never to be seen by *them*: the doctor in his shirtsleeves, the doctor's son (whom Esther does not love because she loves no one), the doctor's wife in the very act of slowly drawing the blinds shut.

By night, by stealth, noiseless, invisible, *here* and *not-here*, now stamping her hooves in the wet grass, now flying drunken and elated into the night sky, no one can see her at such privileged moments, no one can name her. *My baby?* the dead woman had whispered but she is no one's baby now.

The Society for the Reclamation & Restoration of E. Auguste Napoléon Bonaparte

I

In Corvsgate, in Allentown and in Bethlehem, Pennsylvania . . . in the more affluent suburbs of Philadelphia . . . in New Jersey, in Far Hills, Waterboro, Paterson and the better residential neighborhoods of Newark and New Brunswick . . . there appeared in the winter of 1912–13, a Mr. Gaymead, a Mr. Lichtman, a Mr. Bramier, solicitors as they called themselves for a Wall Street brokerage firm authorized to represent, in North America, the secret Society for the Reclamation & Restoration of E. Auguste Napoléon Bonaparte.

"E. Auguste Napoléon Bonaparte"?—the illegitimate son of the great Emperor, born 1821, the year of the Emperor's death. And the lost heir to a great fortune.

Which fortune has grown a thousandfold, as one might imagine, since 1821, until at the present time, in the autumn of 1912, it is estimated to be in excess of $300 million—according to a confidential report of the prestigious New York accounting firm Price, Waterhouse.

Messrs. Gaymead, Lichtman and Bramier were all three gentlemen of robust middle age, with muttonchop whiskers (Gaymead), flashing pince-nez (Lichtman) and a pencil-thin moustache (Bramier); each dressed like a Wall Street banker, in conservative three-piece suits, though Bramier sometimes sported a pink carnation in his buttonhole and Lichtman sometimes wore a checked silk Ascot tie. One wore a

signet ring on his smallest finger stamped with the coat of arms of the
House of Bonaparte; another wore a gold watch chain; one cleared his
throat officiously; another was in the lawyerly habit of gravely repeating his sentences, as if for a stenographer's ear. All three were completely devoted, above and beyond their salaries, to the (secret) Society
for the Reclamation & Restoration of E. Auguste Napoléon Bonaparte.

Inclined, perhaps, to be rather overpunctilious regarding such matters as birth certificates, genealogies, legal records, deeds of ownership
of property, life insurance policies, savings accounts, and the like, these
three solicitors could not resist now and then revealing their natural
sympathies ... for though the Society's negotiations were a matter of
the highest confidentiality, and would, in time, provide descendants
of Auguste Bonaparte with considerable sums of money (hundreds of
thousands of dollars for some, as much as $1 million for others), it was
nevertheless the case that Mr. Lichtman could not always resist informing a client about irregular steps being taken by certain not-to-be-
named relatives of his, in advancing *their* claim to the inheritance; and
Mr. Gaymead, though stiff and disconcertingly "British" in his manner,
might sometimes break into a delighted smile, when surprised by a
client's especially perceptive remark.

Good-hearted Mr. Bramier, never one to raise false hopes, felt that
he would rather err on the side of doubt than inspire in his clients an
unreasonable hope that the lawsuit might be settled soon. Authorized
to pass along the president's words, in effect, Mr. Bramier would tell a
small roomful of his clients that the legal situation in which the Society found itself was unparalleled in the history of inheritance claims.
"But we will not rest until Napoléon Bonaparte's rightful heir is restored to his legitimacy, and the hundreds of millions of francs—that is,
dollars—honestly divided among his descendants; not for purposes of
crass mercenary gain, but for reasons of honor. 'Honor is the subject of
my story'—as the great Bard has said," Bramier would declare, stroking
his moustache, and fixing his steel-gray eyes upon his listeners' faces.
"Yet I must state sub rosa that the French are no less duplicitous at the
present time than they were in 1821, when so many efforts were made
to murder the infant Auguste, by agents of the 'legitimate' son and
Louis Napoléon alike; and it is hardly a secret that their civilization
has, in the past century, lapsed into extreme decadence ... which only
war, I am afraid, and this time a cataclysmic war, will purge. Their Gal-

lic pride and honor are at stake in this matter, yet, even more, their infamous Gallic greed, for it would be disastrous to their national treasury if upwards of $200 million dollars were taken from them ... especially if it were surrendered to citizens of North America, whom, you know, they scorn as barbarians. The difficulty is, our own government, led by an unholy coalition of Democrats and Republicans, in aiding the French government in its suppression of the case, doubtless because certain high-ranking politicians are accepting 'fees' for their trouble. Already, gentlemen, the Society has been hounded, and threatened, and denounced on the very floor of the Senate, as being *not in the best interests of French-American relations!*" (At which outburst the little audience would exclaim in surprise and perplexity. For things were so much more convoluted than anyone might have thought.) "Thus, our need to remain entirely underground," Bramier said severely, "pledged to secrecy; indefatigable in our efforts to legitimize the lost Auguste, and his many descendants; and faithful to the death in our willingness to underwrite the lawsuit. For though it *is* proving costly, only think, when it is settled, what rewards will follow: for Auguste's honor will be restored, after so many years; *and all his living descendants will be wealthy men.*"

The historical facts were: the great Napoléon Bonaparte, exiled on St. Helena after the defeat of Waterloo, sired, in the final year of his life, an illegitimate son with a woman (of noble birth, it was believed, though unrecorded national identity) many years his junior; though the love affair and the subsequent birth were clandestine, the child was eventually baptized in the Catholic faith, as "Emanuel Auguste," sometime in the autumn of 1821; and, as the mother rightfully feared for his life, he was taken away immediately following his father's death—to reside, in secrecy, in one or another Mediterranean country. (Speculation had it that the Emperor's last *inamorata* was a surpassingly beautiful girl of scarcely sixteen years of age, of richly mixed ancestry—Spanish, Greek, Moroccan.) In exile, so to speak, the boy grew to his maturity, being aware of his parentage yet resigned to a bastard's fate; until at the age of twenty-one, he dared venture to Paris, under an assumed name, where he learned that Napoléon had provided for him in his will, and very handsomely too; but that it would be his death to pursue the issue. (For all of France was united by this time under the stern rule of Napoleon III, the late Emperor's nephew.) Being a youth of some equanimity, ill-inclined to greed, Emanuel Auguste resolved to forget his patrimony, and to seek his fortune in Germany (1844–1852), and in England (1852–1879), where he died in a London suburb, known to his neighbors and associates as "E. August Armstrong," a well-respected gentleman in the business of cotton imports. Following his death it became known that, since leaving France, he had taken on a number of pseudonyms, out of necessity—among them Schneider, Shaffer, Reichard, Paige, Osgood, Brown, and of course Armstrong. Thus, the record of his progeny, and his progeny's progeny, was complex indeed.

For many years following Auguste's death in 1879, he and his mysterious patrimony were forgotten and his inheritance remained untouched in the vaults of the Bank of Paris. The original sum was said to be $43 million in francs; with the passage of decades, by way of investments, interest and the like, under the canny manipulations of the officers of the bank, this prodigious sum gradually increased tenfold. How long the fortune would have remained unclaimed no one would have known except for the dramatic intervention of a gentleman named François-Leon Claudel, an American citizen of French extraction who was himself a Manhattan broker and who, following his discovery of a blood relationship with E. Auguste Napoléon Bonaparte in 1909, decided to organize the Society. An elder, wealthy man, Claudel could afford to hire a small army of lawyers, historians and professional genealogists to ascertain the identities of Auguste's descendants throughout the world; and to initiate a legal suit against the Bank of Paris under terms of international law. "It isn't for the sake of mere gold that we undertake this campaign," Claudel was quoted as saying, "but for the lost honor of our ancestor Auguste. We, his blood descendants, his heirs, are obliged to claim our rightful patrimony *in his name*—else we're dishonored indeed."

It was no surprise to the idealistic Americans that the Frenchmen who harbored the fortune proved immediately hostile to their efforts. Though Claudel was gratified to be told by way of French informants (friends, as they identified themselves, of the "late wronged heir") that there had long been a tale of a forsaken inheritance locked away in the Bank of Paris and guarded by bank officials, as closely bound up with the sacred memory of the Emperor. The task of tracing the many North American heirs was less difficult than Claudel had feared, for, recognizing the altruistic impulses behind his effort, people were eager to cooperate.

By the winter of 1912, approximately three hundred heirs had been located in the United States and Canada, and it was estimated that another one hundred remained. For E. Auguste had, it seemed, sired many a child himself by way of numerous wives and mistresses, under his several pseudonyms. "It's neither curse nor virtue," Claudel commented wryly, "that we Bonapartes are a little lustier than our neighbors." At the start, Claudel wanted to restrict the Society to those individuals directly descended from Auguste, but, in time, as more eager parties took up the cause, membership requirements were relaxed somewhat, though all were sworn to absolute secrecy and all were required to forward dues, legal fees and various surcharges, payable in cash, by messenger (and not the U.S. Mail) to Claudel, as president of the Society, or to his authorized agents. It was carefully explained to the legitimate heirs as they were individually interviewed in their homes, that the Society, which eventually grew to more than three thousand members, was composed not only of blood relations like themselves but of parties sworn to pursue Justice; these were primarily well-to-do gentlemen of the law, religious leaders and historians who were inspired by François-Leon Claudel's mission. As the legal struggle that lay ahead would demand great sacrifices, these gentlemen were willing to donate their time, money and encouragement, though when the suit was settled, in 1915 perhaps, or 1916 at the latest, *they would not receive a penny of the fortune*.

Authorized as agents for the Society, for the Mid-Atlantic sector, were Messrs. Gaymead, Lichtman, Bramier and others, all men of the highest personal integrity with excellent legal and financial backgrounds. It was their task to contact the missing heirs and to lay out before them the various documents (genealogical maps, birth and baptismal certificates, facsimiles of legal records, etc.) pertaining to E. Auguste and to themselves; and to present them the opportunity of joining the Society under its necessarily severe terms of absolute secrecy, $2,000 payable within thirty days, and regular dues, fees, surcharges, etc. of various sums (depending upon the progress of the lawsuit) from time to time.

Of the numerous heirs who were interviewed by Society agents, all but a few skeptical individuals were enthusiastic; more than enthusiastic, elated; for the salient facts were very convincingly presented. The altruism of François-Leon Claudel and his professional associates was seen to be extraordinary; and the somewhat faint or smudged daguerreotypes of Emanuel Auguste (as a babe in arms, as a toddler, as a haughty young gentleman of perhaps twenty-one) never failed to excite special interest. (Indeed, it was remarkable how citizens in such diverse regions of the Mid-Atlantic sector as metropolitan Philadelphia, southeastern New Jersey, and the remote reaches of the upper Delaware Valley were struck by family resemblances between the lost heir, as Auguste was frequently called, and themselves or relatives. Again and again young Auguste, though pictured nearly in profile, and with his hooded eyes turned arrogantly away from the camera, was realized as the "living image" of a cousin, an uncle, a grandfather, a father, a child: and poor patient Mr. Gaymead, no less than his colleagues Lichtman, Bramier, Hynd, and Glücklicht, had to endure many a lengthy session, seated on a sofa, being shown a copious family album, with much animated commentary to the effect that the "royal blood" of the Bonapartes had always been evident, though unrecognized as such, in the client's family. It might be a look about the eyes—or the shape of the nose, the ears, the chin—the set of the jaw—the cheekbones, the bones of the forehead, etc.—but the visual evidence was unmistakable.)

"Yes, it is so," Mr. Gaymead or one of his colleagues would say, studying a photograph, or the facial bones of a living child presented blushing before him, "—yes, I believe it *is* so. I wonder that your family did not come to the conclusion, some time ago, that you were not quite of common clay like your neighbors; but clearly possessed of an exceptional history—and a no less exceptional future."

II

A curious predicament: that Abraham Licht's passion for any of his business ventures was in precise *disproportion*, as Elisha had long ago learned, to its *success*.

For where plans proceeded smoothly, and clients were persuaded to surrender gratifying sums of money to his pockets, passion quickly waned; and it seemed to the restless entrepreneur that, for all his genius, for all his willingness to risk safety, he must not be playing for high enough stakes. He frequently confided to Elisha, alone of his children, that difficulties—challenges—obstacles—outright dangers— were what most stirred his spirit, and provided a fit contest for his powers, whose depths (he believed) had not yet been plumbed.

So it happened that "Little Moses" was forced into retirement earlier than seemed absolutely necessary (for Elisha quite delighted in the masquerade, knowing himself, though disguised in the skin of a "darky," *not a Negro at all*). Similarly, "The Panama Canal, Ltd.," closed its doors to further investors, after so wondrous a six-month showing Abraham Licht halfway feared J. P. Morgan would want to buy him out; likewise "X. X. Anson & Sons Copper, Ltd.," and "North American Liberty Bonds, Inc.," and "Zicht's Etheric Massage" (whereby the afflicted patient, suffering from such ailments as rheumatism, arthritis, migraine, stomach upsets, and mysterious illnesses of all kinds, lay upon a table, in absolute darkness, to be massaged by the "magnetic etheric waves" produced by an "osteophonic" machine of Dr. Zicht's invention); and, not least, the enterprise of the astrological sportsman "A. Washburn Frelicht, Ph.D.," who had triumphed at Chautauqua, and was talked of, still, in racing circles. (It was a measure of Abraham Licht's indifference to past success, or his actual generosity regarding fellow entrepreneurs, that he cared not a whit that tout sheets, or tipster sheets, were now sold openly at American racecourses; and that their indebtedness to the pioneering *Frelicht's Tips* went unacknowledged.)

Of course, not all of Abraham Licht's enterprises were successful; and the comparative, or outright, failures, no less than his half dozen embarrassments with the law, rankled still.

For instance, at the tender age of fifteen he had been ill used by a kinsman named Nathaniel Liges, of the Onandaga Valley, who had hired him as a lottery ticket salesman—and failed to inform him when the news broke, rather suddenly, that the tickets were counterfeit; he had scarcely fared better, when, a few years later, now self-employed, he made the rounds of the Nautauga region as a Bible and patent medicine peddler—in the very wake, ironically, of a notorious Dutch peddler from downstate who offered the same general brand of goods, and resembled young Abraham as a father might resemble a son!

He confided in Elisha one day that, as a brash young man of thirty-two, he had agreed to run for state congress on the Republican ticket, in one of the sparsely populated mountain districts north of Muirkirk; but found the campaigning so loathsome an activity, and the prospect of a tame, respectable, *legal* employment so enervating, he soon lost all spirit for the contest, and quite outraged his backers. Moreover, his Democratic opponent was so clearly a self-promoting fool, it seemed an insult to Abraham Licht's dignity to trouble to compete with him. Like Shakespeare's Coriolanus, with whom he closely identified, he felt despoiled by the mere activity of seeking public acclaim in this ignominious way. Here, The Game was of a much lower mettle than he was accustomed to; the prospect of winning over an ignorant elec-torate excited him as would the prospect of seducing a woman who was both ugly and brain-damaged! So Abraham soon began to mock his opponent, and the oratorical style of campaigners in general (whether Republican, Democrat, Populist, or other); and finally betrayed his backers by dropping out of the race and disappearing from the region altogether a few weeks before the election.

Even so, he told Elisha that he would not rule out the possibility of a political career someday for *him.* "You are worth much more than a mere backcountry congressional seat, of course; your superficial racial component—or attribute—or 'talent,' whatever—cannot help but be an asset in the proper circumstances."

Elisha was deeply struck by this remark; yet could not resist assuming a playful tone. "Shall I run for Governor of the state," he asked, "or, perhaps, for President of the country? Might I be a fit candidate one day for the 'White' House? It would allow my fellow Americans a display of democratic sentiment, to elect a 'darky' to such an office!"

"Don't make light of my proposal," Abraham Licht said severely. "The time is not now; but the time may come. 'Covet where you wish; but never in vain.' "

As with the women Abraham Licht had won, seemingly, and then lost—his "wives" as he eventually came to call them—so with the busi-ness ventures he had never entirely brought to fruition. They haunted; they rankled; they picked and stabbed at his very soul.

Among these was the "E. Auguste Napoléon Bonaparte" enterprise, first dreamt into being when Abraham Licht was a young man in his twenties, but, owing to limited resources, and exigencies of the moment, never satisfactorily launched. What appealed to Abraham in his maturity was the prospect, regarding the Society, of its *infinite possibility*: once a person came to believe that royal blood flowed in his veins, and he was a potential heir to a great fortune, how far could his credulity be tested? No sooner had the Society's roster of heirs fulfilled their obligations for one step of the lawsuit (allegedly being fought in the Court of Paris, behind closed doors, by a barrister of international reputation) than the Society would be forced to assess them still more, for there was a mare's nest of hidden fees, taxes, attorneys' retainers and so forth, with no end in sight. It seemed quite likely that a lawsuit of such complexity would drag on for years, as a consequence of French corruption. And in the early spring of '13 a new development arose, forced upon the Society's president François-Leon Claudel by several of his associates who were gravely concerned that Claudel had by this time invested so much of his own money, nearly $700,000, while standing to realize as only one heir of Emanuel Auguste no more money than any other heir; so it was voted by the Society's board of governors that members should invest directly in the inheritance itself rather than merely underwriting the lawsuit. Which is to say, according to the prestigious firm of Dun & Company, auditors for the Society: if an individual invests $1 in the inheritance, he will realize at least $200 when the estate is settled; if an individual invests $1,000, he will realize $200,000. And so forth.

Now, the race was on.

Abraham Licht was forced to hire a half dozen agents to deal with the increase in business. Families mortgaged their homes and property or sold them with imprudent haste; insurance policies were cashed in; a minister in Penns Neck, New Jersey, borrowed $6,500 from his church without informing them; one member of the Society, by the name of Rheinhardt, secretly took out an insurance policy on his wife for $100,000 with the intention, as he naively told Mr. Gaymead, of investing the entire sum in Emanuel Auguste "as soon as the old woman dies." (Gaymead had the presence of mind to inform him on the spot that the board of governors, just the previous day, had passed a ruling to the effect that no member could invest more than $4,000—which after all would reap a magnificent $800,000.)

By February of 1913 post office inspectors for several cities suspected that something was afoot, yet as no one had complained to police, and members of the Society were scrupulous about sending their payments (preferably in cash, though checks were also accepted) by way of a messenger service, and never through the U.S. Mail, where was the harm? Members were cautioned repeatedly on this score, for the postmaster general of the United States was himself in the pay of the French, and prepared to open and destroy any of the Society's correspondence. (So strict was this ruling, members were told that any letter sent by way of the U.S. Mail would not be opened, and the sender's membership would be revoked.) For purposes of security too the Society's address was frequently changed, being now on Broome Street in lower Manhattan; and now on East Forty-ninth Street; and now on the Upper West Side; then again, abruptly, in Teaneck, New Jersey; or Riverside, New York. In a single week in June 1913 such quantities of cash were received in denominations ranging from $5 to $100 that Abraham Licht and Elisha laughingly wearied of counting it, giving up after having reached $95,000; and sweeping it into a burlap sack with their gloved hands to be deposited, under an agent's name (Brisbane, O'Toole, Rodweller, St. Goar) in one or another Wall Street investment house (Knickerbocker Trust, American Savings & Trust, Lynch & Burr, Throckmorton & Co.) Abraham had chosen. He suspected that, by this time, a number of persons in the financial district were watching his activities closely, but in the bliss of triumph he cared not a whit.

He was Abraham Licht, after all—though not known by that name *here.*

III

"If as Jonathan Swift believed mankind is to be divided into fools and knaves," Abraham Licht told Elisha and Millicent, "—is there any greater delight than to be assured of a steady income by the former, as the latter look on in envy?"

Through the long summer of 1913 membership in the Society for the Reclamation & Restoration of E. Auguste Napoléon Bonaparte continued to grow, until by mid-August, shortly before the entire enterprise had to be abandoned, there were approximately seven thousand members in good standing—and an estimated fortune of $3 million. Both Elisha and Millie were dazed by their father's success, yet apprehensive as well, for were things not going too smoothly? . . . was there not an air, very nearly palpable at certain times, that they were being scrutinized on every side, yet never approached? Owing to the rapid increase in business, Abraham Licht had had to hire twenty-odd employees—"solicitors," "agents," "messenger boys," "accountants," "stenographers." These persons, though not in full possession of the facts regarding Emanuel Auguste, were yet experienced enough, and canny enough by instinct, to know that they must not disobey their employer's directives. ("One false step," Abraham Licht cautioned each in turn, "—and the entire house of cards falls. And some of you may deeply regret that it does.")

At this time the Lichts' principal residency was a luxurious eight-room suite at the Park Stuyvesant Hotel on Central Park East, though Abraham and Elisha were frequently away on business and Millie was enrolled as a student in Miss Thayer's Academy for Young Christian Ladies on East Eighty-fifth Street. (Of course, Millie didn't always attend classes faithfully at Miss Thayer's, caught up in the bustle of Manhattan and in the flattering attentions of young gentlemen admirers whom she treated with playful coquettish ease—since her heart, in secret, belonged to Elisha.) When things went smoothly and the Society's demands weren't distracting, Abraham Licht enjoyed nothing better than to treat his handsome children to a Sunday excursion on the town: an elegant brunch at the Plaza, a leisurely surrey ride through Central Park, afternoon at the Metropolitan Museum of Art on upper Fifth Avenue, high tea at the sumptuous Henry IV on Park Avenue. For the elder children Millie and Elisha, amid a small party of social acquaintances, there might be an evening of grand opera at the palatial Met—for, besides Shakespeare, Abraham Licht revered opera as the very music of the gods. (In a single heady season the Lichts attended performances of *The Magic Flute*, *Rigoletto*, *Madam Butterfly* and the American premiere of Strauss's *Der Rosenkavalier* during the course of which Abraham fell in love with Anna Case in the role of Sophie.) These lengthy evenings were often followed by suppers at the Park Avenue or Fifth Avenue homes of Abraham's new friends, or supper at Delmonico's, where Abraham, as a lavish spender, was known and admired.

"How happy we are! And how simple it is to be happy!"—so Millie whispered as if in wonder, giving Elisha a hasty kiss when they were alone together; and Elisha, the more agitated of the two of them, tried to see how this could be so, within a year of their brother Thurston's disappearance. Regarding Millie's bright, feverish face and shining eyes, Elisha couldn't have said if he was "happy"—if indeed Millie was "happy"—or if Abraham Licht, despite the current success of his business ventures, was "happy"—or what, in fact, "happiness" meant. When Millie was gay, irrepressibly gay as an ingenue in a Broadway operetta, Elisha believed he should try to be gay in return; yet, when Millie was gay, perhaps she was testing him to gauge whether such gaiety was, after all, appropriate?

All Millie knew of Thurston's disappearance was that, when Abraham and Elisha went to rescue him from a Trenton funeral parlor where his "remains" had been delivered from the prison, her brother was gone. He'd left, he'd walked away, he'd vanished—without a trace. And no message left behind. "But how could Thurston have done such a thing?" Millie asked, incredulous and hurt, and Abraham Licht told her tersely, "We will not speak of the ingrate—a 'Christian convert' it seems. He has gone over to the camp of the enemy and good riddance." Millie protested, "But, Father—" and Abraham said, "I have told you, Millie: we will not speak of the ingrate ever again."

And so it was. For Abraham Licht was not to be disobeyed.

The tale told generally within the family was that Thurston and Harwood had each ventured forth to seek their fortunes. Thurston was in Brazil exploring possibilities in the "rubber trade" and Harwood was in the West exploring possibilities in "the mining of precious metals." The younger children had no interest in Harwood but begged their father to make a journey to South America so that they could visit with Thurston soon. "At Christmastime, Father! Thurston will be lonely without us."

Abraham laughed briefly, surprised; but said, in that tone of voice that indicated a subject was finished, and would not be revived, "Your brother is accustomed by now to 'loneliness,' I am sure."

("And was there really no note, no message to explain, or to apologize, even to say good-bye?" Millie asked Elisha, in secret; and Elisha lifted his hands in a gesture of bafflement, assuring her, as gravely as their father had done, "No, Millie. As Father said, there was *not*.")

IV

Strange, the careening happiness of that swift season in Manhattan. Affecting Abraham Licht in contradictory ways.

For instance, how frequently he expressed a vague yearning for Muirkirk—"For peace." Yet of course he dared not leave New York until things were more stabilized. He didn't trust his hired employees— what employer, in such times of turmoil, did? He complained half seriously to Elisha and Millie that he would have no trouble building a financial empire to rival the Carnegies and the Harrimans if he could only staff his office with blood relatives. (His kin, the Barracloughs, the Sternlichts, the Ligeses, had, it seemed, proved untrustworthy. So Elisha had reason to believe. And why did Abraham never mention Harwood? Were they in communication at all?)

Then again, perhaps the Society was growing too quickly? Perhaps it would be prudent to limit membership? Even to introduce a new development . . . things being so snarled in Paris, the French courts so mired in corruption, a mistrial had been called and an entirely new case would have to be prepared . . . for presentation in, say, January 1914. This was entirely convincing; and met with strong approval (and relief) on Elisha's part; for Abraham Licht was by this point in his career several times a millionaire, as O'Toole, Brisbane, Rodweller and St. Goar, and could afford to relax. His fortune was in safe hands in the most reputable Wall Street investment houses and would eventually double, or triple, if the economy continued to thrive.

And Abraham Licht, for all his vigor and optimism, wasn't so young as he'd been even a short year before.

Then, abruptly, after a breakfast of skimming rapidly through the usual New York papers and reading, for example, of the lavish wedding of Miss Vivien Gould, granddaughter of the infamous Gould, to Lord Decies of His Majesty's Seventh Hussars at Saint Bartholomew's Church on Fifth Avenue, how could he be satisfied with the meager millions he'd earned?—"It's preposterous for me to think that I'm a wealthy man, set beside these people." For the Goulds were so rich, their empire so enormous, it was noted without comment in the papers that two hundred twenty-five seamstresses had labored on the bride's trousseau for more than a year; the wedding cake alone had cost $1,000, decorated with electric lights and tiny sugar cupids bearing the

Decies coat of arms; the bride's father presented her with a diamond coronet estimated at $1.5 million; and other gifts from such members of the gilded set as the Pierpont Morgans, Lord and Lady Ashburton, Mrs. Stuyvesant Fish, the Duke of Connaught, the Astors, the Vanderbilts, and numerous others, were of similar value. "No, Abraham Licht is a pauper by comparison," he mused, "—he hardly exists, in fact. And what shall he do about it, at the age of fifty-two?"

So that day and for days following he might be caught up in a fever of planning: he'd hire more employees, wooing them away from their "legitimate" firms; he'd begin a fresh campaign in Virginia, North Carolina, South Carolina and remote, mysterious Georgia where blood descendants of Emanuel Auguste surely dwelt, awaiting discovery. ("The farther South, the greater the fools"—so Abraham had been assured.) Restless, he'd summon Manhattan's most prestigious architect to his home to discuss the Italianate villa he hoped to build on the corner of Park and East Sixty-sixth, but a stone's throw from the Vanderbilt mansion.

And one day soon, if all proceeded smoothly, and Abraham Licht and his family ascended to the highest echelons of New York society, he would march as proudly up the aisle of Saint Bartholomew's as had Mr. George Gould, with a far lovelier daughter on his arm to be given away in holy matrimony to a lord, or a count, or a duke—"If not a prince."

V

By the end of the summer of 1913, however, Abraham was forced to conclude that the Society for the Reclamation & Restoration of E. Auguste Napoléon Bonaparte had become too successful; and would have to be curtailed soon or abandoned entirely. (For Abraham *could not* trust his employees, in precise proportion as they were sharp, canny young men not unlike himself at their age. Also, he'd begun to discover disturbing news items in the papers having to do with rumors of an "international scandal" involving an illegitimate son of a Hapsburg duke, an illegitimate daughter of the late King Edward VII, several great-grandchildren of Napoléon Bonaparte and, most tantalizing to inhabitants of New York State, a direct descendant of the Dauphin, King Louis XVII, who had, according to legend, escaped France and hidden himself away in the wilds of the Chautauqua Mountains north of Mount Chattaroy.)

"How Americans, priding themselves on their democracy, yearn for 'royal blood'! It's to be pitied, more than condemned."

Yet such rumors were alarming, obviously.

It seemed necessary, therefore, to call a special meeting of the Society's shareholders, in the Sixth Regiment Armory in Philadelphia, soon after Labor Day. Several thousand heirs of Emanuel Auguste crowded into the building after having identified themselves at the closely guarded doors and paying an admission fee of $5, to help underwrite the expense of renting the armory. (In truth, the armory had been made available to the Society for a token $100, by way of a Philadelphia broker who'd invested $4,600 in the inheritance. So the evening's "gate" was in excess of $15,000—an uplifting figure.) The atmosphere was expectant and as highly charged as a Wagnerian opera, since members had been alerted that they would at last be introduced to their president, François-Leon Claudel; and informed of the latest, somewhat disturbing news regarding the Parisian lawsuit; and, as a bonus, would be presented with *a full-blooded descendant of Emanuel Auguste,* who'd arrived in the States only the previous week.

The Sixth Regiment Armory was a plain, utilitarian space made attractive by strategically placed posters of Emanuel Auguste as a babe in arms, as a toddler, and as a handsome young man—familiar likenesses, of course; though the enlargement process had coarsened and darkened the images. On stage beside the lectern were an American flag and a peacock-blue flag bearing the royal coat of arms of the Bonaparte family; placed about the stage were floral displays of white lilies, carnations and irises, donated by a Philadelphia funeral director who was also a shareholder of the Society. The crowd, beyond three thousand individuals, consisted primarily of men, with a scattering of women, and exuded an air of excited anticipation mingled with suspicion. For all beneath this high vaulting roof were blood relations, however separated by accidents of birth; yet, each having invested in the Bonaparte fortune, wasn't he in a sense a rival to all the others? Could he, indeed, trust the others?

Reasoning that the murmurous, excitable audience would be grateful for a familiar face, Abraham Licht opened the meeting in the guise of the brisk, affable Marcel Bramier with his signature moustache and pink carnation in the lapel of a conservatively cut sharkskin suit. In a ringing voice Mr. Bramier commanded that the doors to the armory be locked by security guards, since it was 8:06 P.M. and no more latecomers would be tolerated. This stern measure was greeted with waves of applause from the nervous heirs, many of whom had been waiting since early afternoon for the armory to be opened. In his welcoming address, Mr. Bramier spoke of the Society's history: its ideals, its fidelity to Emanuel Auguste and the loyalty, generosity and high moral courage of its members; he concluded by vowing that no one in the hall would leave that evening without a "heartwarming vision engraved upon his soul." Thunderous applause followed this poetic declaration. Mr. Bramier then introduced a Mr. Crowe, a founding member of the Society, tall, deep-chested, with the full-toothed grin of President Teddy Roosevelt in his prime, who spoke with equal vigor of the Society's aims and ideals. ("Crowe" was played by an out-of-work Broadway actor-friend of Abraham's. An interim of some minutes was needed for Abraham to leave the stage, change his costume, makeup, etc., before reappearing in his next, more crucial guise.)

Next, greeted with ecstatic applause, walking with a cane and frowning loftily was the esteemed president of the Society, François-Leon Claudel, upon whom several thousand pairs of eyes avidly fixed. An aristocratic figure, frail with age; filmy-haired; impeccably dressed in a dark suit and gray silk vest; with a stiff, priestly air; hollowed cheeks; tinted spectacles; and, strangely, a skin so dark-complected one might almost have imagined him of an exotic race. Yet all doubts were assuaged when once the applause died away and Claudel began to speak, for it was immediately clear, and reassuring, that by his accent he could be no other than Caucasian.

Claudel differed significantly from the speakers who preceded him by wasting no time in winning over his audience. As he said, there was urgent business at hand—"Time and tide, my friends, wait for no man." He stirred the membership by affirming their unity in a common cause for justice; all were blood relations, if only to an infinitesimal degree; they were obliged to trust one another as they trusted their closest and dearest family members—though, he had to warn, there were rumors of informants in their midst in the pay of the government of France. "Of course," Claudel said, an ironic ring to his voice, "—these are but rumors, and not to be fully credited." Next, the aristocratic gentleman spent several minutes passionately assailing those members of the Society—"Some of whom have the gall to be seated among us, at this very moment"—who were behind on their dues. Poking the air with a forefinger, Claudel chided such slothful and unworthy descendants of the great house of Bonaparte and went on to criticize as well those individuals who'd tried to bribe certain officials of the Society, including that paragon of virtue, whose morals were wholly above reproach, Marcel Bramier, into allowing them to invest, under assumed names, more than $4,000 in the inheritance. By this time Claudel's aloof manner had given way to the vehemence of an American campground preacher as he paced about the stage crying, "What do you think would happen, my friends, if certain of your greedy comrades invested five thousand—fifty thousand—one million dollars in the inheritance?" He paused dramatically, staring into the sea of rapt, frightened faces. "I will tell you, gentlemen: *there would not be enough money for the honest investors, when the lawsuit is settled.*"

A panicked hush fell over the gathering.

However, François-Leon Claudel assured them, no member of the Society would stoop to bribe-taking so there was no danger in that quarter. "We are not, after all, members of the United States Congress or inhabitants of the White House," Claudel could not resist adding, to yelps of laughter and vigorous applause.

Next, Claudel read a cable from the Society's Parisian barrister to the effect that the meticulously constructed case for the claimants had been undercut by "subversive" elements, probably from within; that the highest judge of the highest court in the country had confided in him, privately, that it would be in the best interests of the Society for the present suit to be dropped and a new suit initiated after 1 January 1914 to insure a court "free and clear of jurist prejudice." These words were read in a ringing voice, one might have said a Shakespearean voice that revealed how deeply the president of the Society was moved by this development. (There was, midway, a fearful pause during which the old man seemed about to burst into tears, fumbling to extract a handkerchief from his pocket.) Quickly, however, he recovered, to tell the gathering in a voice heavy with irony that such news would delight the *saboteurs* in their midst yet would not, he swore, be a source of despair to *him*; though at his age it wasn't reasonable any longer to expect that he might live to see Emanuel Auguste restored to his lost honor.

"Yet having waited so long we can't object, I suppose, to waiting a few months longer—yes? Do you agree? For Rome, as they say, 'was not built in a day. And required millennia for its fall.' "

At this point a scattering of individuals spaced through the armory began to applaud zealously, as if inspired; within a few seconds, they were joined by the remainder of the enormous crowd, uncertainly at first, then with more vehemence, so that wave upon wave of applause filled the hall, and cheers, whistles and shouts of "Bravo, our president!" brought tears to a proud old man's eyes.

It was all Claudel could do to quiet the crowd and continue.

Thanking them humbly for their "sacred vote of confidence" and reiterating his statement that a six-month delay in the lawsuit would not be a source of despair to him, even at his age, and should not therefore be a source of despair to any of them; calculating that the suit would "certainly" by settled by the end of 1916 at the latest; and that, with interest compounded daily, the fortune would by that time be somewhere beyond $900 million according to the most recent estimate of the conservative Wall Street accounting firm Price, Waterhouse.

At which point more applause ensued, tumultuous as before.

You must lead them like sheep—gently. For sheep will stampede.

You must allow them to think that you are one of them, and your fate linked to theirs.

You must honor their profound wish to believe. Even as, with a smiling countenance, you slash their uplifted throats.

The surprise of the evening followed immediately: the appearance of the only "pure-blooded living descendant of Emanuel Auguste Napoléon Bonaparte"—a native-born Moroccan by the name of Jean Joliet Mazare Napoléon Bonaparte, twenty-five years old, only just arrived on these shores. Would the membership please welcome their privileged visitor, with the spirit that only Americans can summon forth?

So, applause began; individuals at the rear and extreme sides of the vast armory rose to get a clearer view; until at last all were on their feet, more than three thousand eager kinsmen; but, what a surprise, what consternation, when, in a crimson velvet suit with knee breeches and white stockings, and a rakish plumed hat, a gilded dress sword at his side, *a young Negro appeared!*—as assured, insouciant and feckless as if he were not only of royal blood but superior to the Caucasian race itself.

At this point an absolute silence fell over the hall. All who had leapt to their feet to cheer stood paralyzed, staring.

Negro? . . .

Taking no notice of his audience's alarm, a smiling François-Leon Claudel graciously drew the young man forward and introduced him, with the zealous aplomb of P. T. Barnum introducing one of his prized exhibits: "Monsieur Jean Joliet Mazare Napoléon Bonaparte, the purest-blooded of all Emanuel Auguste's descendants!" He embraced the handsome young man with great warmth; as if such behavior, between men, were commonplace to these shores, he kissed the young man smackingly on both cheeks. The Negro's eyes and teeth flashed dazzling white; his skin gleamed and winked as if oiled; in a sweeping gesture of mock humility he whipped his elegant hat from his head and bowed low before his still-silent audience.

How woolly his hair, that fitted his head tight as a cap!

Negro?

Still taking no notice of the paralyzed quiet in the hall, Claudel stood with his arm draped affectionately about young Jean's shoulders and spoke at length of the fact that, according to the most meticulous genealogical charts prepared by the Oxford Authority of Genealogical Research in England, here stood the embodiment of Emanuel Auguste himself; the lost heir's "pedigreed blood" beat fiercely and proudly in Jean's veins as, to varying degrees, it beat in theirs; and how deserved it was, that young Jean would inherit the title of *prince* in France when the estate was settled.

Negro?

As the flamboyant young man evidently spoke no English, his address to the gathering was unintelligible though rapid, charming, and assured. "Messyers ay madamez ici *I am!* Mon freres ay mon sewers voulezvou *thankyou* pour invitee me ici!" He interrupted his cascade of words with childlike giggles; his wide white teeth glared in the stage lights; his hand gestures were flamboyant. Clearly this Moroccan-born black possessed none of the wary, craven air of an American black, for he was of princely blood and not descended from slaves, and so possibly, just possibly, he might be excused for thinking so highly of himself. Yet his audience remained mute, mortified. Here and there one might have seen a face crinkled with repugnance or even revulsion; some were perplexed; others looked from young Jean to the prominently placed posters of their noble ancestor, and back again, taking note too of the dark-complected François-Leon Claudel, whose olive-dark complexion contrasted with his filmy pale hair and his unmistakably "white" manner. *What did such things mean?*

With monkeyish high spirits young Jean began to jabber yet more excitedly in his native tongue, taking up an exotic musical instrument seemingly a cross between a tambourine and a drum and singing, as a beaming Claudel looked on, a ditty even those in the audience who might have known some French could not have grasped:

"*Merdeyvous! Je hais* you!
Tu hais me! *Merdeyvee!*
Ooolala! Ooolalee!
Merdeyblanc! Merdeynoir!
Thankyee vous! Thankyee me!
Blezzeygod you! *Blezzeygod* me!"

Following the young prince's performance, Lemuel Bunting, one of the Society's officers, rose to summarize the "salient points" of the session: the temporary suspension of the lawsuit in the Court of Paris; the temporary suspension of all investments until further notice—"That is to say, no more investing, and, of course, no withdrawals"; above all the need to maintain faith in the Society's aims—and to keep the sacred vow of secrecy.

By this time, however, virtually no one was listening. Many persons were streaming toward the doors, eager to escape; abashed, confused, somber, stricken; not wishing to look too closely at their neighbors, or to be seen by them. In this way, at about 9:20 P.M., what would be the final mass meeting of the Society for the Reclamation & Restoration of E. Auguste Napoléon Bonaparte came to an end.

"Delightful, 'Lisha! You outdid yourself tonight. And, if I dare to say so, *so did I.*"

In triumph, in the privacy of their suite in Philadelphia's most prestigious hotel, Abraham Licht proposed a champagne toast to his son; for
Elisha had never performed before any audience so irresistibly, including, to Abraham's surprise and delight, the delicious opéra bouffe aria
of his own improvisation. He'd deserved more applause than the fools
had given him, Abraham said with a chuckle. "For, like any consummate player of The Game, you knew your audience; you plumbed the
depths of their shallow racist souls."

Elisha swallowed down his champagne thirstily, yet seemed to take
little pleasure in it. He was missing Millie, perhaps: for her praise in his
ears meant as much, if not more, than Abraham's. Yet there was something melancholy in his victory, and he found it hard to fall in with his
father's celebratory mood. "Yes, Father," he said, sighing, "I knew, I
mean I know, the racist hearts of my countrymen well."

Causing Abraham to worry, in his bed that night, whether his most
prodigiously gifted son wasn't becoming sensitive about exploiting his
skin; as if, in his heart, 'Lisha had somehow believed himself *white* after
all. "God help me if I meet resistance from 'Lisha, too," Abraham tormented himself, "—for I am rapidly running out of sons."

Fools and Knaves

A chronicle, pitiless and humbling, to be set down in further damning detail in Abraham Licht's memoir *My Heat Laid Bare*; but,
here, in brief:

5 September 1913. Abraham Licht discovers to his chagrin that approximately $3,500 in door receipts is missing, after the armory meet-
ing, and that one of his accountants is missing as well.

6 September 1913. Abraham Licht discovers in going over the books
in his Broome Street headquarters (in truth, a single near-barren room

over an Italian grocer's) that said "accountant" had very likely been embezzling funds since midsummer; and that even an approximation of the loss is impossible. Thousands of dollars, tens of thousands?

11 September 1913. Sometime in the late afternoon a newly hired bookkeeper operating out of the Society's East Fourteenth Street office (a small utilitarian room above a dry goods store) makes the irrevocable error of sending a letter to a member of the Society in Corvsgate, Pennsylvania, not by American Express messenger service, as Abraham Licht has decreed, but by way of the Post Office Department. (The slip for which postal inspectors have been waiting for months!—the business of this crucial letter being most damning when opened: for "Albert Armstrong" was behind by $200 in his dues and was being threatened with being dropped from the Society unless he paid within ten days.)

12 September 1913. Warrants issued for the arrests of "François-Leon Claudel," "Marcel Bramier," "Lemuel Bunting" and other officers of the Society for the Reclamation & Restoration of E. Auguste Napoléon Bonaparte on several charges of mail fraud.

12 September 1913. Six o'clock at the Broome Street headquarters where Abraham Licht, gloved, sits counting the receipts of the last several days and Elisha, with a mild headache, stands at a window gazing down into the street and sees, by chance, several grim gentlemen in ill-fitting jackets and neckties approaching, with an indefinable yet unmistakable look of being law enforcement officers. *Plainclothes federal agents bearing warrants to serve!* Never has Elisha been present at any "raid" and never has Elisha been interrogated by law enforcement officers, yet, by instinct, he knows; retreats from the window with the monkey-like alacrity of Jean Joliet Mazare Napoléon Bonaparte himself, and says calmly, "Father, excuse me. They are coming for us, I think." With scarcely a moment's hesitation, Abraham Licht rises from his desk, sweeps the remainder of the money into the half-filled canvas sack, tells Elisha to lock the door and barricade it with the filing cabinet— "And make haste, son." Within twenty seconds, before the federal agents are rapping at the door, Abraham and Elisha have stealthily escaped by way of a rear window; to avoid the likelihood of agents stationed below in the alley, they are making their swift but unhesitating way across adjacent roofs; at the end of the block, they descend a fire escape to the street. Panting as much with elation as exertion, Abraham Licht murmurs to Elisha, "Poor 'François-Leon'! Not a very gracious exit."

The canvas sack contains only $12,403 but of course there remain millions of dollars secreted away elsewhere in several impregnable vaults on Wall Street.

1 October 1913. A gentleman by the name of Horace Brisbane, Esq., presents himself at Knickerbocker Trust, 99 Wall Street, with the intention of withdrawing $160,000 from his $780,000 account but is informed after an uneasy wait of twenty minutes that no one by the name of "Horace Brisbane" has an account at Knickerbocker Trust; nor do records show that Horace Brisbane has ever had an account there. Mr. Brisbane is dumbfounded. Mr. Brisbane is incredulous. Mr. Brisbane reels as if struck a blow to the head. Why, does no one recognize him? The senior officer with whom he has been doing business since last April, with such understanding? "It may be, sir," Mr. Brisbane is coolly informed by a Knickerbocker vice president, "that your account is with one of our neighbors. You entered, you see, the wrong building." Following this episode by less than a half hour, a gentleman by the name of Michael O'Toole presents himself at 106 Wall Street at American Savings & Trust, where, according to records, deposit slips, receipts and so forth he has an account of $829,033; yet is astonished to learn that he has no account at American Savings & Trust; nor do records show that "Michael O'Toole" has ever had an account there. "But this is— preposterous," Mr. O'Toole says in a faint Irish brogue, bringing his fist down hard on a marble-topped desk, "—this is *criminal!*" A pause of several seconds; bemused glances between the bank officers; and the manager says, with a smile, that Mr. O'Toole might, then, if he wished, file a complaint with the proper authorities. "Our local Manhattan police might not be up to the effort, so you will want to involve the federal government, yes?"

So too at Lynch & Burr just across the street, a gentleman in a black homburg, one Horace Rodweller, is informed by the unctuous Lynch in person that no one at that establishment recognizes him—no one has done business with him—he has no account—"Not for one million dollars, sir—not for one dollar"; and had better take himself up the block to Throckmorton & Co., for perhaps it was with these rivals he'd plied his vaporous trade. Mr. Rodweller stammers, "Why, I can't believe this! This is unheard of! Why, you are all—*criminals!*" Lynch says with a prim smile, "Why, then, you're well rid of us, Mr. Rodweller, yes?" Though guessing by now that the situation is hopeless, Mr. St. Goar, also in a black homburg, dares present himself at 3:20 P.M. that day in the alabaster interior of Throckmorton & Co., the oldest and wealthiest of the Wall Street firms; only to be informed politely that his entire account of $1,374,662 is lost to him forever—$1,374,662 of his hard-earned fortune! Does the pale, perspiring, shaken St. Goar imagine it, or are numerous eyes fixed upon him?—young men lingering in doorways, craning their necks in his direction?—do even the file clerks and young women secretaries regard him with pitying smiles? None of the senior officers is present, for the hour is late, but the office manager meets with Mr. St. Goar to tell him in a tone of unfailing courtesy that not only does his account not exist as of 1 October 1913 *but that he himself does not exist.* "For we have looked into it, Mr. St. Goar, and there is no such individual as you purport to be. How, then, can such an amount of money as you claim be in your 'account'?"

1 October 1913. 5:25 P.M. In their sumptuous ninth-floor suite at the Park Stuyvesant, speaking as calmly as possible, Abraham Licht informs Millicent and Elisha that the situation "has become somewhat precarious" and that it might be prudent for them to pack their bags as swiftly as possible, taking nothing but essentials and giving no hint to the hotel's sharp-eyed employees that they don't plan to return. (For the family in whose name the spacious suite is registered, the Fairbairns of Boston, haven't settled their bill for the past two weeks.) Though Millie may be frightened, it's in a teasing voice she says, "I hope, Father, we're not going to be arrested!" and Abraham Licht, a fine Cuban cigar clamped between his teeth, says, "Not at all, Millie—if we don't linger."

The Betrayal

I

Is it true, Father, Little Moses asks, that the white folks is devils, and all of them enemies, or is some of them different, Father, like you? and Father sucks his mighty cigar (so strong the tears spring to Little Moses's eyes) and says, Why now look here boy: *I'm not white.*

Not white? says Little Moses, blinking hard.

I may look white, and I may talk white, but I stand outside the white race just like you; and all of the Lichts stand outside the white race; because the white folks is devils, and all of them are our enemies, yes boy each and every one!—and if you don't know it at your age 'Lisha you'll surely know it soon.

But I'm not white? says Little Moses, blinking hard.

No boy you are not.

And you're not . . . white.

No boy I am not.

But you're not black.

Not to look at, am I boy! says Father, laughing and expelling a big mouthful of smoke; and glancing about as if there is (but there is not) a third party observing.

But am I black? says Little Moses, frightened.

Now 'Lisha it's true you *look* black, says Father, but you know that's a necessary part of The Game.

. . . a necessary part of . . . ?

. . . a necessary part of The Game.

Little Moses blinks hard to keep the tears from stinging but the tears sting just the same and run down his cheeks, and he hears himself say, But what is The Game, Father, and Father says expelling another mouthful of smoke, 'Lisha, The Game is what I say it is, and Little Moses says, crying, But how do I know, Father? and Father says, losing patience, You know what I *tell* you, boy, and beyond that you don't need to know: now go to sleep!—as Father has an engagement elsewhere.

... with loathing, such loathing.
... with revulsion: I could see it in their faces.
... (*their* faces! so ugly! so ignoble!)
... But is Jean not handsome? is Jean not of noble blood? ... a brave fine figure, a gentleman of style, humor, wit, sardonic charm, French to the very tips of his fingers, opéra bouffe as Father has said: and what genius!
... (*their* faces! *white* faces! how dare they!)
... yet, with loathing. Sickened loathing. Not even hatred but loathing. For one of what they call *black blood.*

... Yet Elisha is not black, and there's his genius! So Father has decreed. Which is to say: he tricks the eye like a magician: his *inner being* gloats at the confusion generated by his *outer being.*
... And Millie who adores him and will soon be his wife, Millie laughs and laughs at such trickery, for in Love there is neither black nor white, in such secret love, such tenderness, there is only Love, and nothing to arouse loathing and revulsion and sickness, Why there is only Love! and Millie and Elisha will soon be wed.
... (yet, such loathing. I could see it in their faces.)
... (*their* faces! *white* faces! I could kill them all.)

II

Elisha will tell Abraham Licht their secret, at last.
Because it is time.
Because it is well past the time.
Because they are now lovers: husband and wife in the flesh, at last.

Because, since early September, since the night of the armory, 'Lisha has needed comforting. 'Lisha has needed love, and 'Lisha has demanded love, and 'Lisha has frightened Millicent with his anger and his wild laughter and his lust.

For lust too is Love: and no longer to be denied.

"And now do you love *me*?" Millicent whispered, her lovely eyes bright with tears; and Elisha's heart swelled with pride as he answered, "Yes."

The Lichts—Father, Elisha, Millicent—have retreated again to Muirkirk because they are poor; but from Muirkirk Millicent will be going to Rhinebeck, on the Hudson, to stay at the country home of the wealthy Fitzmaurices, as, at Miss Thayer's Academy for Young Christian Ladies, she became acquainted with sweet little Daisy Fitzmaurice, sweet little plain little not-entirely-bright Daisy Fitzmaurice, the wealthiest girl in their class. And Daisy adores her beautiful Millicent, as everyone does. And Daisy is eager to invite Millicent to the Fitzmaurices' country place, where it is "pretty," where they can go for boat rides on the river. And Daisy is eager to introduce Millicent to her family. Including of course (of *course*, says Elisha through his teeth), her handsome older brother who's a West Point cadet, her handsome cousins, all the family—for Mrs. Fitzmaurice has met Millicent and been charmed by that gracious young lady, as everyone is.

And Father urges, "Yes. Indeed."

And Father urges, "Indeed, Millie. Stay as long as the Fitzmaurices will have you."

And Father promises to come visit the Rhinebeck estate—"To see, you know, what's there to be seen. And to be done."

For it's no secret that the Lichts are, this autumn, down on their luck—though Abraham Licht scorns to believe in luck. And since the debacle of the Emanuel Auguste project, *hors de combat* as well— though Abraham Licht has never been out of combat for long, even when wanted by federal agents. But there's no denying that they are poor again, their fortune vanished into the vaults of Wall Street *as if it had never been.* ("Perhaps that is the essence of money," Abraham has mused, "—that it isn't 'real'; no more 'real' in possession than in dispossession. Like the vaporous human soul.") And now the fortune must be replenished; and Mina Raumlicht or Lizzie St. Goar or one of their pretty sisters hopes she will be allowed to help replenish it.

"Only instruct me, Father," Millie pleads, lifting her lovely heart-shaped face to his, "—and I will do it."

Elisha has become unreasonable: he doesn't want Millie to go to Rhinebeck because Millie is *his*.

(And because, though he doesn't tell Millie this, he's smarting still from the waves of . . . physical revulsion? . . . moral repugnance? . . . that washed over him from that crowd of . . . white faces in the Philadelphia armory.)

"But, 'Lisha, why do you care so much?" Millicent asks, startled by her lover's mood, "—what have such people to do with *us*?" She's genuinely baffled; Elisha knows she's correct; yearns to believe she's correct; yet finds himself reacting emotionally, turning roughly away despite Millie's stealthy little kiss on the side of his neck. Now that they're lovers, now since returning to Muirkirk and the enforced intimacy of family life in this remote rural place, at the edge of a marsh, in a region of steep hills, dreamy mountains and stark rushing wailing winds—now, it seems, their feeling for each other is mercurial and unpredictable as flame. Now edging in one direction, now in another. Dangerous. Treacherous.

" 'Lisha, darling—don't you love me?"

"Millie, the question is, don't you love *me*?"

"But why is it more urgent that I love you, than that you love *me*?"

"Because I can trust myself, Millie, but not *you*."

"Yet can I trust *you*?"

"If you loved me, Millie, yes."

"But if you loved *me*—?"

Elisha begins to shout suddenly, "What value am I, loving *you*, if I'm not made worthy by your loving *me*; if I'm deceived, like every other 'admirer' of yours, by *you*!" And moves to exit, with the indignant aplomb of, say, the long-lost heir of E. Auguste Napoléon Bonaparte.

Millie cries after him, "As if everyone isn't deceived by *you*, including, I see now, *me. I never did love you!*"

Elisha leans back into the room, uttering a percussive exit-line, "*Then you were never deceived, girl! Were you!*"

"Yet are we really poor?"—Elisha ponders.

Even as Father's bookkeeper, Elisha isn't entirely informed of Abraham Licht's various bank accounts. And the contents of his safe here in Muirkirk. And the $12,403 in the burlap sack turned out to be almost $20,000 when carefully counted.

And the elegant Willys-Overland automobile with the green plush cushions and spoked wheels and brass fixtures and white kidskin convertible top: does that appear to be the purchase (made in haste in the Lichts' flight from Manhattan) of a desperately impoverished man?

And there are, Elisha stubbornly believes, "treasures" in the old church. Antiques that might be sold, heirloom jewelry and objets d'art that could fetch high prices in a Manhattan auction house, surely. And Elisha has reason to believe that Father is in communication with Harwood at long last, and that there may be a gold-mining project about which he and Millie know nothing.

So Elisha confides in Millie, once they've made up their quarrel. (How many times since returning to Muirkirk have they quarreled, and made up; made up, and quarreled!—sometimes having forgotten, in the midst of a quick, stolen kiss, whether they're officially angry at each other.) So Elisha casts doubt upon Abraham Licht's proposal for Millie to go to Rhinebeck; if they aren't truly poor, if Father is exaggerating their plight as he often does. "But, 'Lisha, if Father wants me to go," Millie says, sighing, "I don't see that I have much choice." And Elisha says, kissing her forehead, "We must stand up to him. For I don't wish you to go, because I love you and because *you are mine*."

The implication being clearly *Mine, and not his.*

At once Millie says, "Then—you must tell Father about us."

"Yes," says Elisha at once. "Yes. I will."

"Tonight."

"Yes. Tonight."

". . . No later than tomorrow," says Millie. "Because he is going away tomorrow."

"Tomorrow is too late," says Elisha.

"But tonight is too soon."

"Tonight *is* too soon," says Elisha, his voice rising in despair, "—but tomorrow is too late."

So they quarrel, they are quarreling again, Esther will hear them, Katrina has already heard them, what if Father hears them?—they must run away into the woods to hide, to kiss, to embrace, to weep together, because they are wretched with love, and ecstatic with love, and Millie accuses Elisha of not truly loving her because he is afraid of Father; and Elisha accuses Millie of not truly loving him because she is afraid of Father. And it is a certainty that by now Katrina knows.

"But will Katrina tell?" Elisha asks in a frightened whisper.

"Katrina will never tell—never!" Millie says. "She would not dare."

Are they quarreling, or are they kissing, hand in hand they're laughing breathlessly when Esther steals up behind them, sweet lonely Esther who adores them, Esther who exasperates them, Esther who's so easily wounded—for why do Millie and 'Lisha draw stiffly apart when she joins them, with the childlike need to press into their embrace, and be kissed, too! And afterward Millie pleads with Elisha to tell Father soon. "If not tonight, tomorrow. If not tomorrow, the day after tomorrow."

Says Elisha in a brave, defiant voice, "Yes! I will."

Millie is so lovely, and Millie is *his*, yet there's terror in his happiness, for he cannot trust her, he cannot trust himself with her, this beautiful sister of his, a sister of the soul if not of blood, Millie with her fair, smooth skin, camellia-skin, so pale, so unlike his own, and her hair so fair and wavy worn in a soft roll, elegantly parted in the center of her head; her small ears covered with a look of girlish modesty; one might say chastity; and a cluster of "kiss-curls" at the nape of her neck. No longer enrolled in Miss Thayer's, Millie need not endure the spinster-teachers' sharp eyes, need not truss herself up in a corset for it is 1913 and not, as she says, 1813, and she will dress, she says, as *she* pleases. Her pretty skirts fall barely to the ankle in the latest style, her shoes are saucily open, often she neglects to tie on a hat, or to adjust her diaphanous veil, except when the sun is very hot and very direct. (For Millie isn't so foolish as to risk her precious complexion for the sake of a rebellious whim.) Millie is so lovely that, thrown together here in Muirkirk in a way they weren't thrown together in Manhattan, Elisha finds himself thinking of her constantly; his head rings with thoughts of her, of her and of *him*; and are they sinful (but Father has taught there is no sin) and are they wrong (but Father has taught it's only mere human prejudice that yields wrong and right) and have they made a terrible mistake, surrendering their virginity to each other like man and wife (but what an unspeakably sweet mistake!); and will Father be angry?

And will Father punish?

It was after returning to Muirkirk that they became lovers—by acci-dent, thinks Millie tenderly; by design, Elisha knows. (For only Millie's love can combat that armory of faces, staring white faces, loathsome white faces, nothing but Millie's kisses, and Millie's slender warm body, and Millie's short fierce sobbing cries, in which, even now, Elisha does not dare believe.) "But I *want* you to be my husband!" Millie said, reck-less, laughing, when he hesitated, "—I *want* to be your wife!—then there will be no going back." He understood that she was in terror of her life as he was in terror of his, yet now there *was* no going back, they were wed to each other forever, no matter how the armory of strangers gaped and stared in revulsion.

Afterward Millie wiped her eyes on the rumpled sleeve of her yellow-checked frock; secured the swelling roll of her hair with a tortoiseshell comb; and said, in a small sober voice, not quite meeting her lover's eye, "Now you must tell him, Elisha, and he will be happy for us." And Elisha, staring at her, said slowly, "I don't think that is possible . . . but I will tell him."

Tonight?

Not tonight.

Tomorrow, then.

. . . The day after tomorrow, in the evening. When he comes home.

III

In retreat, in Muirkirk, the place of his birth; the solace of the marsh (in which one day he will drown himself!—perhaps); the angry com-fort of long uninterrupted days and nights; the gratification of Shame. But it is a convalescence. He has had many such.

For, " 'What wound did ever heal but by degrees?' " is Abraham Licht's defiant query. And: "We are not fools, after all, 'by heavenly compulsion.' "

Thus, he ministers unto himself.

It is a convalescence. There have been many such. The years, the seasons, the balm of quiet, the solitude of the churchyard, the swamp, the locked and shuttered room at the rear of the rectory: with no one as a witness (whether jeering or admiring) Shame will eventually yield to forgetfulness; forgetfulness, to Honor.

For Honor is the subject of Abraham Licht's story.

Fifty-three years old! So quickly!

A life more than half run!

And it cannot be said, can it? that the years have been generous to Abraham Licht; that, despite his love, devotion, industry, and selflessness, he has been provided with a family worthy of his sacrifice.

He requires more children, another son at least, another son very *soon*, for his children have not entirely pleased him.

Of course there is Millicent, who pleases him enormously, and who is bound, he knows, to serve herself by serving *him*; of her absolute fidelity he has no doubt. And there is the incomparable Elisha, the ever-astonishing Elisha, whom Abraham Licht, were he not his stepfather and mentor, might almost envy! . . . a wily young genius, as adept at masquerade and cunning as Abraham Licht himself . . . though a creature of Abraham's, of no worth without his guidance. (And one day, when the time is ripe, 'Lisha's "color" will greatly advance his career; along precisely what lines, Abraham hasn't yet decided.)

Apart from Millicent and Elisha, however, Fortune has treated Abraham Licht perversely.

For, consider: not one, not two, but three women captivated his heart, and, in time, trampled upon it. No matter the ardor, the depth, the eloquence of his devotion. (For, as time passes, Abraham has come to believe that Sophie's illness and her final, deranged behavior was a repudiation of his love, as of all earthly love. *For which, in my heart, how can I forgive her?*)

As for Thurston, his firstborn—he doesn't wish to think of Thurston.

As for Harwood—he doesn't wish to think of Harwood.

(Yet, only a few days ago, there arrived in Muirkirk, addressed to him, a curious letter postmarked Ouray, Colorado; a single stiff sheet of stationery from the Hotel Ouray; and these lines in Harwood's child-like, labored hand:

Ive given thought to my Life Father & am not so angry now with my Brother as I had been. I am not so lonely now. I will be writing again soon Father to seek your advice. I know your angry with me & blame me but *I am not to be blamed*, it was not my fault but Thurstons. I will not return East I swear til my Fortune is made & you will see what a Son I am to you. Or til you bid me come to you Father.

Yr Son Harwood

This letter Abraham hasn't answered, uncertain of the spirit in which it was penned: sober, or drunk; sincere, or mocking; promising well, or ill. *For once a man has spilled human blood he may have a taste for it.*)

Of the younger children, beloved by him, Abraham Licht rarely thinks. For he finds them merely children, who will never mature as the others have matured, lacking a gift for The Game.

Darian may indeed by a musical genius as Woodcock and a few others insist but his talent, in Abraham's unsentimental judgment, is too wayward and capricious to be guided. And Esther, poor dear child— Abraham finds it difficult to listen to the girl's cheerful prattle and to follow with interest her schoolgirl news, her enthusiasm for nursing, or doctoring, "making hurt things well again" as she says. Alone of the family it's plain, good-hearted Esther who seems to have made friends in Muirkirk, quite as normal, ordinary children do; according to Katrina, as bemused as Abraham himself, Esther actually *likes* her classmates and their families and is, in turn, *liked* by them; an unmistakable sign of mediocrity. (Compare this dull child with Millicent at that age, Abraham thinks. Already, aged eleven, Millicent was a practiced coquette, by instinct arousing affection in others without feeling so much as a moment's affection in return. "But then the sensual yet morbidly pious 'Miss Hirshfield' was Millie's mother, a volatile combination," Abraham thinks, "ideal for the stage, if not for life.")

So he muses, broods; through many a long day; too restless to stay in one room, or even inside; hoping to stave off melancholy until it's safely dusk and he can sip bourbon without qualms. How is it possible—he's fifty-three years old, and so quickly?

And my glorious career scarcely begun.

IV

"You 'love' each other—and you intend to 'marry,' " Abraham Licht says quietly, looking from Elisha to Millicent, and from Millicent to Elisha, whose gaze shimmers with audacity and guilt. "I'm not certain that I've heard correctly or that I full comprehend the words I have heard. 'Love'—'marry'—what precisely can you mean? Elisha?"

Elisha says quickly, "Millie and I love each other, Father. We are in love. We have been in love for a very long—"

"—for too long without daring to speak," Millie says.

"—and we want, we must—be married," Elisha says. His voice has begun to quiver. "As people do. As men and women do who love each other."

"Yes, it's all very much as people *do*," Millie says in a bright hopeful voice, "—people who love each other in a—normal manner. There is nothing unusual about it."

"There is nothing unusual about it."

Abraham Licht's declaration hovers in the air, the most ironic of questions.

"There is nothing unusual about it!" Elisha says with a nervous laugh.

"If we are in love, and we *are* in love," Millie says breathlessly, her slender arm tight through Elisha's, holding him fast even as she leans against him, "—and have been so for a very long time, in secret."

"And why 'in secret'?" Abraham inquires.

Again looking from one of the timorous young people to the other with an air of detachment and equanimity. Not taking note of the extreme physical attractiveness of this young man and woman, of their fresh, open faces and striking features, but noting instead, with a clinician's eye, how Elisha's lower lip quivers and Millie's normally placid eyes are unnaturally dilated.

"But why 'in secret'—why the need for secrecy?"

Neither answers; until with an impatient expulsion of breath Millie confesses, "Because we worried, Father, that *you* wouldn't understand; that you'd be unhappy, or object, or—"

"My dear, why would I 'object'?"

"Because—" Elisha begins.

"—you would not *understand*," Millie cries.

"Yet what is there, Millie, and Elisha, to understand?" Abraham asks, lifting his hands in a bemused appeal. "You come to me at this odd hour of the night with a whim of yours that might better wait for the clarity and sanity of morning; you stand there like very amateur actors at an ill-advised audition, yet expect seriousness of *me*, informing me you're 'in love' and want to 'marry'—'as people do'—when the crux of the issue is, you can't be in love, and you can't marry, because you are my children; because you're brother and sister; and, in any case, you can't be 'as other people' because you are Lichts, *and Lichts are not 'other people.'* "

Elisha begins to protest but Millie, alarmed, hushes him, saying, "Father, we're *not* brother and sister—surely we're *not*. 'Lisha is a foundling, an orphan as you've always told us; he is *not* my brother."

Revealing none of the mounting rage he feels, Abraham says carefully, "Elisha is your brother, Millicent . . . and you are his sister. It is not possible for brothers and sisters to love each other in the way you claim to love; still less is it possible for them to marry. That is all I have to say."

"But he is *not* my brother!" Millie cries in exasperation. "Any stranger who glanced at us could tell in an instant!"

"But a stranger cannot know what we Lichts know," Abraham says. "He would be judging you merely by your appearances; by your superficial selves. As for what is inside, and hidden—only *we* know that. As if Elisha is to be known by way of his skin!"

"But Father—" Millie protests.

"What we know is this: that you and Elisha are linked from childhood by ties of blood that are far deeper than the 'love' of which you speak," Abraham says.

"But there is nothing deeper—more beautiful—than the love of which we speak!" Millie says boldly; and Elisha says, "We want only to be allowed to marry—and to leave Muirkirk—because we realize we can't stay here where we'd be misunderstood."

" 'Misunderstood'!" Abraham laughs. "My boy, you would be 'understood' only too readily. For shame!"

As if for mutual support the lovers stand close together, Millie's arm still thrust through Elisha's, and her opened hand, in a gesture of supplication, pressed unconsciously against her agitated breast. How strange that they seem unable to look at each other but only at Abraham, who glowers smiling upon them, baring his teeth.

From somewhere close by in the churchyard a nighthawk cries wanly, a soul in torment.

"There is nothing deeper than the love of which we speak," Millie repeats, in a chastened voice. "There is nothing deeper than . . . our love."

Abraham smiles a hard white fleeting smile, but does not condescend to reply.

Elisha mumbles words to the effect that they want to marry, they *will* marry, but want his blessing; and Millie says softly, "Yes, Father, we want your blessing—*please*."

Yet Abraham will not reply.

He *is* their father, of course. Elisha's no less than Millicent's. They know, they cannot doubt, for, in the beginning, even before their awakening to childish consciousness, was *his* Word, *his* Truth, unassailable. From what reservoir of profane strength might come their capacity to doubt? Already it seems that Millie for all her precocious belligerence is weakening; her lovely eyes are narrowed as if she faces too powerful a light, her smooth forehead is creased with lines of worry and apprehension. And poor Elisha—why does he stare so helplessly at Abraham?

"Oh, Father, we want your blessing—*please!*" Millie whispers.

And now like figures on a brightly lit operatic stage, as if Abraham were empowered with the majesty and cunning of Wagner's Wotan, a role for which, had he only the powerful voice, he might have been born, Abraham takes Millie gently by the wrist, and detaches her from her lover's side, and gazes into her eyes. His large, strong fingers encircle and frame her face; his fingertips stretch the delicate blue-veined skin at her temples; for a long moment father and daughter stare into each other's eyes, as into each other's soul, the fine shivering of Millie's arms the only sign of strain she betrays.

So rapid is their exchange in lowered, urgent voices, like lovers, Elisha might be listening to a foreign language, uncomprehending.

"But you are not yet *his?*"

"Oh no, Father—we're waiting to marry."

Abraham releases the girl who's gone deathly pale with guilt and terror and turns, brusque and smiling, to Elisha, to say, "You and I, Elisha, will talk now in private."

*   *   *

Millie, heartsick and exultant, seeks out Katrina for comfort.

As Abraham leads Elisha to the rear of the house, to shut them to-gether in his study.

Millie, her teeth chattering with excitement, or with fever, presses herself into Katrina's reluctant arms, saying that she and Elisha are in love and will marry, and Father hasn't forbidden it. And Katrina says with a shiver of disgust that of course they can't marry because they are sister and brother—"And because Elisha is not of your race. He is Negro." Millie says, " 'Lisha is not 'Negro'—but only himself." Ka-trina says sternly, "The world sees 'Negro.' " Millie says fiercely, "The world is blind!—mistaken!" Katrina says, "In some matters, Millie, the world's blindness is not mistaken."

At that instant in Abraham's study Elisha has fallen to his knees, sobbing. His handsome face contorted in pain, disbelief, mortification. For no sooner were the two inside the door, and the door locked behind them, than Abraham wheeled on the young man and struck him a sav-age blow across the face with the back of his hand.

Taken by surprise, unresisting, Elisha made no attempt to defend himself; but staggered backward, hurt, dazed, sinking to his knees on the hardwood floor.

"You!—and my daughter! My Millie," Abraham Licht says, in a voice out of the whirlwind and his eyes flashing fire. *"It is not to be borne."*

Accusing the young man of treachery, betrayal and wickedness; for-bidding him ever to approach Millie again; even to speak with her again; not because they're brother and sister (though they *are* brother and sister) and not because Elisha's skin is black (though as any fool can see, Elisha's skin *is* black) but because *it is Abraham Licht's com-mand.* And Elisha protests he can't help it, he had not intended this to happen, he loves Millie, he would die for Millie, and Millie loves him, and they must be married, for they're already lovers, man and wife; and at this point Abraham Licht flies into a greater rage, saliva frothing at his lips, beating Elisha now with both his fists as Elisha, head bowed, cringes before him.

"You lie! You lie!—you black devil."

Is it terror, or pride?—this refusal of Elisha to so much as raise a hand against the older man, for Abraham Licht is Father; and many years ago saved Elisha from the flood; and in his heart Elisha knows, whether there is sin or not, *he has sinned.*

Millie cries herself into a delirium in Katrina's arms, and Katrina sighs impatiently, for it's all so absurd, such tears are so absurd, how grateful she is she's an old woman now and her heart calcified and protected against such hurt. And at last, as she knows he would, Abraham calls to her to bring Millie to him, into the parlor where by the light of a kerosene lamp her father and her lover are waiting. Millie grips Katrina's hand hard, but Katrina pushes her away.

Millie wipes her inflamed eyes, sulkily; seeing that something, unless it's everything, has changed. Father is very angry and has not forgiven them and Elisha is no longer her handsome young lover but a disheveled, shamed, confused young man; a very dark-skinned man; looking too desperately to her for solace.

"Elisha has decided to leave Muirkirk immediately tonight," Father says evenly. "And it's his belief, my girl, that you've agreed to go with him."

Millie blows her nose. Where in another, nose-blowing is a crude, commonplace act, in Millie, as in any stage ingenue, it's an act of sniffy, petulant defiance. Millie says, in a high childish voice, looking at Father and not Elisha, that, yes, she will go with Elisha if that's what he wants—"If that's what he has told you." Elisha says, rawly, that that *is* what he wishes—"And what you wish, too, Millie." Father says, his voice still even, judicious and measured, "If you go away with Elisha, my girl, then you will never again come home to *me.* This, I hope you understand." And Millie doesn't speak, though she's smiling. Dabbing at her nose with her embroidered little handkerchief. For her eyes, too, flash fire; and fire burns. Yet Elisha blunders forward, reaching his hand to her as if they were alone together. Saying, pleading, that Millie must come with him because they are promised to each other; they love each other; how many times they've vowed this. And Millie will—almost—take Elisha's extended hand, for it's a hand she loves, those slender fingers she has loved, swooning beneath their caress, she's kissed and stroked those fingers yet she can't seem to lift her arm, her arm has gone leaden, her spirit has gone leaden, her eyes are swollen and aching and ugly, she has rubbed them so hard the lashes are coming out, for it's wrong, it's unfair, it's cruel of these men to summon her to them as if in

a court of law, putting her to such a test, demanding such a performance of her. And no preparation! Not a single rehearsal! Millie would
whisper *I hate you both!* Elisha continues to speak, growing angry, impatient, but Millie can't concentrate thinking *Hate you both!—bullies.*
Leave me alone I want to sleep. Abraham says nothing, merely smiling
his hard, knowing smile, his eyes glinting like chips of glass; Millie can
see that he is herself in her innermost soul . . . Father *is* her . . . as Elisha, a mere lover, can never be.

And so the scene plays out, until at last Millie sinks in a faint into
Father's arms, at the jarring sound of a slammed door.

V

And so it happens that Elisha Licht departs Muirkirk forever in October 1913 and the following Sunday Millicent departs for Rhinebeck
for an extended visit with the Fitzmaurices.

And so it happens that Abraham Licht will begin to forget Elisha, as
one forgets any disagreeable episode; or, if forgetting is too extreme, he
ceases to speak of Elisha; for, indeed, what's there to say? *The past is but*
the graveyard of the future, as the future is but the womb of the past. And
his thoughts are focused upon Rhinebeck, and the Fitzmaurice clan
about which he will soon know as much information as he can garner.

Millie has ceased her silly schoolgirl tears. Millie has torn up a
packet of letters, and tossed them into the marsh. Katrina never alludes
to Millie's lost love except to lightly scorn it as an attack of nerves such
as high-strung fillies often have, at certain phases of the moon; she
never speaks of Elisha except to assure Millie that once she's away from
Muirkirk and its unwholesome vapors she'll forget him—"As you've
forgotten so much." And Millie laughs a high, startled laughter, a
laughter that seems to pierce her like pain, saying, "Oh, Katrina, I almost wish what you say isn't so; but I know *it is so*; and such is Millie's
fate."

"I Have No Feeling of Another's Pain"

I

"Why—is it myself, transmogrified?"

So thinks the superintendent of the Camp Yankee Basin Mining Company, Mr. Harmon Liges, when, in the late afternoon of 9 April 1914, in the bustling lobby of the Hotel Edinburgh in Denver, Colorado, he happens to catch sight of a stranger, a stocky young gentleman in a brown herringbone tweed topcoat and a matching cap, who closely—indeed, uncannily—resembles *him*. So unnerving is the similarity, Harmon Liges cannot simply pass by; stations himself behind one of the lobby's stately marble pillars, in order to stare at the man unobserved; feels a curious sensation of excitement mingled with repugnance, anticipation mingled with dread . . . for the stranger, apart from superficial differences, might be a virtual twin of his. Or so it strikes Harmon Liges.

Fascinated, even as he's obscurely offended, Liges studies the man in the tweed topcoat to satisfy himself that he *is* a stranger; and very likely a new arrival from the East, on the 4:45 P.M. train from Omaha. Is he traveling alone, as he appears . . . ? Might he be on business? Yet he lacks the self-assured and expectant air of the businessman; seems to be, in fact, ill at ease in his new surroundings, though smiling a nervous, quizzical smile, even as the impertinent registration manager keeps him waiting. ("That is not the tack to take with the Edinburgh staff," Liges thinks impatiently, "—they will only mark you down for a fool.")

Like himself, the man is about thirty years old; of but moderate height, no more than five feet seven inches; thick-bodied; with a large-pored, slightly flushed skin; heavy dark "beetling" brows; and small, moist, pink, curiously prim lips. His head is innocently round beneath the tweed cap, his face moon-shaped, the ears somewhat protuberant; assuredly he is *not* handsome—though, to Liges's practiced and unsentimental eye, he is more attractive than Liges himself, being boyish and vulnerable in his manner, and clean-shaven, while Liges is guarded, and sports a close-trimmed Vandyke beard. (It is remarkable how this beard disguises Liges; how very simple a matter it invariably is, to radically alter one's appearance by way of a minor, though clever, change in grooming, dress, speech, bearing, etc.) In addition, while Harmon Liges is barrel-chested, muscular, and fiercely compact, with a fighter's unconscious habit of bringing his weight forward onto the balls of his feet, the Easterner is plump, harmless, burdened by some thirty or forty pounds of baby fat, and a natural ungainliness in his movements.

Yet more significantly, Liges has cultivated the Westerner's skill of taking in all that is of importance in his surroundings, even as he appears oblivious of them; while the gentleman in the tweed topcoat, though glancing from side to side, and blinking, and smiling his sweet quizzical smile as if expecting a friendly acquaintance to step forward at any moment, very likely sees nothing at all.

"He has not seen *me*, in any case," Harmon Liges thinks.

Since he has a pressing engagement with an agent for the Union Pacific Railroad in the gentlemen's bar of the Edinburgh, Harmon Liges does not linger by the marble column; having in any case learned that the stranger's name is Roland Shrikesdale III, his hometown is Philadelphia, and he intends to stay in Denver for an indeterminate period of time.

("Indeterminate" being, after all, the amount of time most visitors spend in Colorado—or indeed, on earth generally.)

II

Again, at eight-thirty the next morning, entering the hotel's dining room for breakfast, Harmon Liges is given a shock by seeing across the

room his "twin" of the previous day; whom, oddly, he seems to have forgotten in the intervening hours.

(Or had he in fact dreamt of the plump smiling man? Waking toward
morning with a foul taste in his mouth, and an anxious, quickened
heartbeat; and a sensation of arousal in his groin.)

Him—!

Yet again—!

Liges deliberately takes a table close by the stranger, though he
finds the man's very presence disquieting. "*Is* it myself, transmogrified?"
he thinks, watching the stranger covertly, "—or an unsuspected cousin,
or brother? For I have no doubt that Father has sired numberless bastard sons across the continent." This morning the young gentleman,
sportily attired in a suede coat, string tie, and trousers of a casual cut, is
occupied in eating a lonely breakfast and halfheartedly reading the
Denver Gazette, even as his gaze moves restlessly about the room. He
too has an unevenly receding hairline, though his hair is considerably
fairer and curlier than Liges's; his skin is similarly rough, yet mottled,
and pasty-pale beneath, while Liges's is tanned. Indeed, he has the appearance of a man not fully recovered from an illness who hopes to
speed his convalescence by journeying out West where the climate is
supposed to be health-inspiring—in the much-publicized way of Teddy
Roosevelt.

A rich man's pampered son and assuredly not a bastard, thinks Harmon Liges with a thrill of hatred—"Like myself."

Shortly afterward, however, when breakfast is brought to him, Liges
relaxes. Devours with his usual appetite beefsteak, eggs and potatoes;
drinks several cups of black coffee; lingers over his own copy of the
Gazette, though columns of print fatigue his eyes and arouse in him a
vague feeling of resentment and an urge to do hurt; luxuriantly, he fouls
the air about him with a long thin Mexican cigar; quite by accident
glancing up as the gentleman across the way glances toward him . . .
with that faint, simpering smile of the Easterner hoping to be made
welcome. (Apparently the stranger doesn't note the similarity between
himself and Liges, for Liges doesn't look like "himself" these days, having changed his appearance considerably, and practicably, from that of
Elias Harden, who'd run a surprisingly successful gambling operation in
Ouray, Colorado, the previous winter; just as Elias Harden bore but a
superficial resemblance to Jeb Jones, an itinerant salesman for Doctor

Merton's All-Purpose Medical Elixir, previously.) Inspired, Liges smiles warmly, bracketing the cigar; being so clearly a Westerner, he feels it his obligation to be kindly and welcoming to an Easterner. This smile is magic! For Father has said *Smile and any fool will smile with you.* The young man, lonely Roland Shrikesdale, leans forward eager as a puppy, nearly spilling his cup of cream-marbled coffee, and smiles in Liges's direction.

So it begins. And no one to blame.

So Liges and Shrikesdale meet on the morning of 10 April 1914 in the spacious dining room of the Hotel Edinburgh, and Liges invites Shrikesdale to join him for more coffee; the young men talk amicably of travel in Colorado, and of hunting and fishing in the remote Medicine Bow Mountains, where Liges has been; an oddity of their meeting being that, though Harmon Liges introduces himself in a fairly forthright manner as the superintendent of the Camp Yankee Basin Mine, though in fact he's the former superintendent of this ill-fated mine, Roland Shrikesdale introduces himself as—*Robert Smith!*

("Which means that Shrikesdale is a name I should know," Liges shrewdly reasons, "—for he hopes to hide his identity. But it's a name I shall know, shortly.")

III

Yet during the several weeks of their friendship, up to the morning of his disappearance in the foothills of wild Larimer County, the nervous young Easterner continued to represent himself to Liges as "Robert Smith"—a harmless if puzzling bit of subterfuge Liges thought more appealing than not. *Always encourage it when a man will lie to you* Father has said *for, in the effort of lying, it will never occur to him that another might play his game, too.* And it pleased him who had no friends he could trust, in truth no friends at all, to be in the position of warmly "befriending" the incognito Easterner who declined to speak of his family except to indicate that they were "financially secure, yet sadly contentious" and that his widowed mother perhaps loved him "too exclusively"—all this while knowing that he was in fact befriending

Roland Shrikesdale III of Philadelphia, principal heir at the age of thirty-two to the great Shrikesdale fortune. (In Denver, Liges learned within a day or two that Roland was the son and grandson of the infamous "Hard Iron" Shrikesdales who'd made millions of dollars in the turbulent years following the Civil War: their investments being in railroads, coal mines, grains, asbestos and predominantly nails. Roland's mother was the former Anna Emery Sewall, heiress to the Sewall fortune (barrels, nails), a Christian female who'd brought censure and ridicule upon herself several years before by giving more than $1 million to the Good Samaritan Animal Hospital in Philadelphia, with the consequence that the animal hospital was better equipped than nearly any hospital for human beings in the region. The Shrikesdales *were* a contentious lot, quarreling among themselves over such issues as how to deal with striking miners in their home state: whether to use the militia or hire a battalion of even more bloodthirsty Pinkerton's men, and risk public criticism. (The Pinkerton mercenaries were hired.) Roland was an only child, rumored to be almost frantically doted upon by his mother; though appalled by the excesses of his family, particularly the cruelty with which they treated their workers, Roland stood to inherit most of the fortune when she died. Since there were numerous Shrikesdale and Sewall cousins of his approximate age, some of them involved in running the family's companies, it was believed that they would share in it as well—to some degree. Liges's sources concurred that Roland, or "Robert Smith," was generally believed to be somewhat simpleminded; not mentally deficient exactly, but not mentally efficient; a passive, weakly affable, religious young man with little interest in the Shrikesdale riches, let alone in increasing them.)

"And 'Robert' is so wonderfully trusting," Liges thought. "The very best species of friend."

So it happened that Harmon Liges, ex-superintendent of the Camp Yankee Basin Mine, volunteered to show young Robert Smith the West, and to be his protector; for trusting young men traveling alone in those days, and giving signs of being well-to-do, did require protection from more experienced travelers. What plans they made together! What adventures lay in store for Mrs. Anna Emery's sheltered child, whose imagination had been flamed, from early boyhood, by such popular tales of the West as Owen Wister's *The Virginian*, Bret Harte's "The

Luck of Roaring Camp" and "The Outcasts of Poker Flat," Mark Twain's *Roughing It* and Teddy Roosevelt's celebration of Anglo-Saxon masculinity in *The Winning of the West* and *The Strenuous Life*. Harmon Liges had never read these, nor would have wished to, but he took, it seemed, an almost brotherly delight in sharing with his charge plans of camping in the mountains; hunting, and fishing; visiting "a typical gold mine"; visiting "a typical ranch"; riding, by horseback, the treacherous canyon trails "as natives do." In addition there were, here and there, such notorious establishments as the Trivoli Club in Denver, the Hotel de la Paix in Boulder, the Black Swan in Central City, and a few others to which, Liges said hesitantly, he'd bring Smith if Smith wished; though such places were likely to seem vulgar and lacking in dignity to a Philadelphian.

" 'Vulgar' and 'lacking in dignity'? How so?" Robert Smith asked, blinking eagerly. "In what way, Harmon?"

"In a way of presenting females—I mean, women." Liges frowned and stared at his hands, as if overcome by embarrassment. "That's to say—in the way such women present themselves. To men."

It turned out that Smith had never traveled farther west before this than Akron, Ohio, where he, and his mother, had visited Sewall relatives; this trip to Colorado was the great adventure of his life. In fact, he'd left home in defiance of his mother's wishes . . . and he'd left home *alone*, which he had never done before. "So it may be that these are the very persons I ought to meet, if I'm to make a 'man' of myself once and for all," he said, shifting almost uneasily in his seat. "That is, of course, Harmon—if you'll be my guide."

Since the days of Teddy Roosevelt's cattle ranching in Dakota, and his much-publicized hunting expeditions in the Rocky Mountains, Africa and elsewhere, it had become a tradition of sorts for men of good family to distinguish themselves in the wilderness (or, in most cases, as with Roosevelt himself, the quasi wilderness): that they might be declared fully and incontestably *male*, hundreds upon thousands of wild creatures must die. (In Africa alone, Roosevelt killed two hundred ninety-six lions, elephants, water buffaloes, and smaller creatures.) Though Harmon Liges had resided in the West less than five years, he had encountered a number of wealthy sportsmen during that time, bent on bagging as much "wild game" as possible, with the least amount of discomfort and danger; but never had he encountered anyone quite like

Smith. It was usually the case, for instance, that such gentlemen traveled in small caravans, bringing cooks, valets, and even butlers with them up into the mountains, and camping in elegant walled tents, in the most idyllic of circumstances. (One of the most notorious of the luxury expeditions, hosted by Mr. Potter Palmer of the great Palmer Ranch in Laramie, Wyoming, in 1909, involved some fifteen covered wagons, approximately forty horses, and two servants for each of his twenty-five honored guests; the hunters bagged hundreds of wild animals and birds, but ate few of them, preferring the less "gamey" food they had brought with them in tins.) Yet here was the heir to the great Shrikesdale fortune, entirely alone in the West, unescorted, and unprotected—except for Harmon Liges.

On the whole, Liges thought that admirable.

On the whole, he rather liked Smith. Or would have liked him, had he been in the habit of "liking." In any case it was difficult not to imagine himself, in his mind's eye, as a dream-distortion of Smith—coarsely dark where Smith was coarsely pale, muscular where Smith was merely fleshy, given a rough sort of hauteur by his Vandyke beard, where Smith, clean-shaven as a baby, exuded frankness, innocence, and unfailing hope. ("He's the man I might have been," Harmon Liges thought one night, sleepless, a curious pang in his chest, "—if his father had been mine.")

Lingering companionably over the remains of a venison dinner, as Smith sips coffee marbled with cream and sweetened with teaspoons of sugar, and Liges smokes a Mexican cigar, in the zestful, smoky atmosphere of the Trivoli Club, they speak of many things; or, rather, Smith speaks and Liges attentively listens. Smith, like most shy, self-conscious individuals, has discovered that it's easy, wonderfully easy, to talk, if only someone will listen.

Clever "Robert Smith"!—he doesn't once blunder and mention the name Shrikesdale; or Castlewoood Hall—the family estate in Philadelphia; nor does he hint that his family, and he, are burdened with wealth. Yet it wouldn't require an unnaturally sharp-witted observer (and Harmon Liges is sharp-witted, indeed) to gather by way of allusions and assumptions that Smith is surely not "Smith"; an anonymous American; but comes from a most unusual family. A Scottish nanny named Mary Maclean . . . an English governess named Miss Crofts . . .

a Shetland pony named Blackburn . . . Grandfather's house in Philadelphia . . . Grandfather's private railway car . . . a "cottage" in Newport . . . a house in Manhattan (overlooking the Park) . . . a nursery farm on Long Island . . . a small horse ranch in Bucks County, Pennsylvania . . . Mother's gardens, Mother's art collection, Mother's charities . . . the sporting activities (yachting, sailing, polo, tennis, skiing) in which the ill-coordinated youth could not participate, to his and his family's chagrin . . . preparatory school at St. Jerome's and college at Haverford and a year at Princeton Theological Seminary. . . .

"I hope you won't laugh at me," Smith says earnestly, fixing his moist brown eyes on Liges's face, "but it is experience, and experience alone, I crave. *You* cannot understand, perhaps, what it is like to be nearly thirty-three years old, yet never to have lived as a man; never to have gone anywhere without Mother—except to school, and there she visited me as often as possible. (Not of course that I minded at the time, because I was terribly lonely, and homesick, and miserable as a child, and dearly loved *her*: which was ever my predicament—!) When I should have begun a career of my own, perhaps a serious career in the ministry, I did not, because Mother prevailed upon me to accompany her to Newport, or to Paris, or to Trinidad; when I should have cultivated friends of my own, and become acquainted with young women, I did not, because Mother was taken ill; or I was taken ill myself. And so the years went by. And so I have so little to show for them, I am quite frightened. . . . This past winter, for instance, I suffered from a mysterious illness that settled in my chest, and drove my temperature up as high as one hundred and three degrees, and forced me to cancel all my plans for nearly two months . . . during which time I lay abed looking idly through books of photographs of the Rocky Mountains, and dreaming of *this* . . . this trip, this escape, to I know not what! . . . though part of the time poor Mother nursed me . . . insisted upon nursing me, despite her own ill health . . . for she had suffered a stroke of some kind a few years ago . . . though it was never called such . . . a 'fainting spell,' Dr. Thurman called it . . . a 'spasm of the brain' . . . from which she eventually recovered; or so it is believed. In any case I lay weak with fever for a very long time and during that period, I'm ashamed to say, I often exulted in my sickness . . . for I was free to dream of the mountains, and of the deserts, and of horses, and rivers, and hunting, and fishing, and such gentlemen as you . . . though, dear Harmon, I could never have imagined *you*! . . . never. But at the same time I could relax in Mother's care, and take no thought for any of the family problems, and forbid her even to mention the contretemps between one or another of my cousins . . . for, you know, Bertram is always fighting with Lyle, and Lyle is always fighting with Willard, and Uncle Stafford spurs them on as if he glories in such behavior . . . nor is Great-aunt Florence (my mother's aunt) any better. Ah, they are *such* a family! And Mother and I are quite terrified of them! . . . ever since Father's death, when everything began to go wrong. (For that was shortly after poor President McKinley died; and Roosevelt was sworn into office; and the trouble began with Mr. Morgan . . . and was it Mr. Hill? . . . and the Northern Pacific Railroad . . . and the stock market collapse, which *I* never understood; and think it all a disgusting business, in any case, *profit making at the expense of others*.) Despite my illness, however, I wasn't truly unhappy for there was always Mother . . . there *is* always Mother. Are you close to your mother, Harmon?"

Harmon Liges, staring raptly at his friend's face, seems not to hear the query at first. Then he frowns, and replies succinctly—"My mother died at my birth. And my father, too. I mean—not long afterward. End of story."

"Really? You were an *orphan*?"

Liges shrugs indifferently.

"But what does it feel like, to be an *orphan*?"

Again, Liges shrugs indifferently.

"I suppose, to an orphan, his condition seems . . . a natural one. As mine, so very different, seems natural to me," Smith says slowly. He rubs his eyes as if overcome with emotion; perhaps it's pity for his friend, or a sudden pang of nostalgia for Mother. He says, after a moment, smiling, "But how comforting it was, when Mother stayed at my bedside, reading to me for hours as she had when I was a small child! Mother's favorite book of the Bible is Proverbs, which is surely a beautiful book though difficult to grasp. Mother reads so well, one almost doesn't mind that the verse is rather like a riddle sometimes—

'Yet a little sleep, a little slumber, a little folding of the hands to sleep; so shall thy poverty come as one that travelleth, and thy want as an armed man.'

All very poetical; but what d'you think it means?"

Seeing that the plump young Smith takes his own question so seriously, and that his eyes fairly shine with ardor, Liges checks the impulse to shrug again; saying, instead, in as thoughtful a manner as he can summon forth, "The ways of God are inscrutable, it's said. His riddles are not for us to decipher."

IV

How the world is honeycombed with riddles, in fact.

With products of the poetic imagination, fantastical notions and man-made fancies that, to the masses of mankind, yet seem wholly real.

If mankind will agree, to collectively believe.

The value of gold, for instance.

Gold, silver, diamonds—"precious stones."

All mere fancy, if you think of it. Worthless minerals in themselves, yet, as commodities, forms of complicity; delusions worth untold millions of dollars . . . if men will but consent to believe.

And here in the vast West, mankind's very imagination seems limitless. Where in the overly settled, mapped and calibrated East, too many people, among them overseers of the commonweal, make it their business to pry into a man's private affairs.

In New York State, for instance, even in the middle of Muirkirk—there he was fated to be "Harwood Licht." So long as his tyrant of a father guided his life, he was fated to be "Harwood Licht." And, in a deep spiritual sense, he acknowledges that he is, and will always be "Harwood Licht"—for there's no gainsaying the fact of blood inheritance, the potent Licht blood that courses through his veins. *Out of Muirkirk mud, a lineage to conquer Heaven.* So, the temporary impersonation of, say, Elias Harden, Jeb Jones, Harmon Liges or their predecessors Hurricane Brown and Harry Washburn, count for little: hardly more than masks, to be worn and removed at will. Or whim. Or necessity.

This, Harwood's father would understand well. Every action of which Harwood is capable, his father would understand well; and, surely, since the old man's blood courses through the younger's veins, approve.

"One day, I'll make myself known to him," Harwood vows. "I'll make him proud of *me*, one day. And Thurston utterly *gone*."

(For Harwood had the vague notion that Thurston had in fact been hanged, and was of no more consequence to anyone. *End of story*.)

Surprisingly, these past several years, Harwood has become a thoughtful man, at least when idle and not absorbed in the energies of The Game. Like Abraham Licht he sees little profit in brooding on the past unless such mental exertion yields future rewards; but of course there are interludes in a man's life (hiding in the desolate hills above Ouray, for example, or for six days and nights ensconced in the filthy Larimer County jail near-devoured alive by lice) when one has little choice but to brood.

And to plot.

Perfect strategies of revenge.

For all the world *is* the Enemy, as Father taught.

"And I'll certainly never make Thurston's mistake," Harwood thinks, jeering. "To kill a bitch of a woman, a screamer, as he did; and to fail to escape." He laughs, thinking of Thurston swinging on the gallows. His tall Viking-fair elder brother whom women made cow-eyes at in the street, while taking not the slightest notice of him, so much more the virile and stronger of the two. "That's the one unforgivable sin—to fail to escape."

Like Abraham Licht, Harwood is an angry man.

It matters not *why*, or *at what*—his feeling consumes itself, and justifies itself.

Always he feels he's being cheated. This is the American credo—*I'm being cheated!* Somebody else, anybody else, is doing better than I am; deserving no more, but reaping far more than I am; life cheats me, or other men cheat me, or women; I have yet to receive my due, and never will. If liked, I'm not sufficiently liked. If loved, not sufficiently loved. If admired, not sufficiently admired. If feared, not sufficiently feared. Harwood's numerous identities have yielded numerous rewards, it's true, and there have been times when his pockets have bulged with thousands of dollars; but never so much as he expected or deserved. Never so much as another man might have reaped in his place.

I could murder you all he thinks pleasantly, strolling along the bustling Denver streets.

If only you had a single neck, I could murder you all with my hands. The memory of that woman's neck (the woman's name now forgotten, for Harwood is careless about details) twitching in his fingers.

He's twenty-eight years old with the look of a man who's never been a boy. The hooded eyes, sullen mouth, hair like limp chicken feathers, unkempt whiskers and sideburns, musclebound shoulders, the fighter's rolling gait . . . In the casual observer, even another male, Harwood arouses the apprehension one might feel for an aggrieved bison or a coiled rattlesnake. Poor Harwood: even when he smiles, his teeth proclaim his anger; when his linen is fresh it isn't, somehow, fresh; on him, aftershave cologne smells like bacon grease; a purloined gold signet ring edged in diamonds, shoved onto his smallest finger, looks like trash. Yet he has his dignity. He has his pride. He has his plans.

"One day, everyone in the United States will take notice of me," he thinks, "—whatever my God-damned name."

And Roland Shrikesdale III, also known as Robert Smith, will figure prominently in these plans.

For there *is* such a thing as luck, Harwood thinks, though Father taught them to scorn such a belief as the reasoning of weak, puerile men. Luck exists, no doubt of it, and Harwood's luck has simply been bad.

If he wins at gambling (poker, dice are his specialties) he loses within a few days, more than he's won. When he was a salesman for Doctor Merton's All-Purpose Medical Elixir, though he sold a fair number of bottles of the stuff to sickly women, he was betrayed by his supplier in Kansas City, who'd neglected to tell him of the medical complications, including even death in some instances, following in the wake of such sales.

There was his experience at Camp Yankee Basin.

Harmon Liges hadn't been, strictly speaking, superintendent at the camp. In fact, he'd had little to do with the mining operations at all; his position was that of foreman's assistant at the mill; not a very well-paying job but less demeaning at least than millworker. (Though he lacks the air and training of a gentleman, Liges, the blood-son of Abraham Licht, retains the prejudices of a gentleman for whom manual labor is an insult.) Shortly after he arrived at Yankee Basin in the Medicine Bow Mountains, Liges realized that it was in refining mills, and not mines, that opportunities for theft are greatest: the detritus that sifts through the cracks of the machines and collects on their undersides is rich with gold dust, if one has but the patience to collect it and the sagacity not to be caught. So, as foreman's assistant, Liges recruited a team of assistants to help him after hours in packing tubs of sediment taken from beneath the ball mill, and scraping off the thin coating of amalgam on the copper plates, and stripping the copper plates themselves—the most painstaking and rewarding of all such tasks. To the untrained eye such matter may appear worthless: muck, dirt, fine black sand. Indeed, who but a man of imagination might guess that invisible treasure might be salvaged from it, that thousands of dollars might sift by magic into a man's pockets by way of such grubbing? Of course the enterprise was dangerous, for one *could* be caught; involved in clandestine activities, one *could* be punished. Yet wasn't the risk worth it? "The revolt of slaves against masters, and a God-damned good thing," Liges thought. Since his arrival in the West he'd heard wonderful tales of miners who'd made themselves rich by smuggling, day after day, small chunks of "picture rock" out of the veins they worked, and selling it to fences; "picture rock" being a rare ore encrusted and glinting with solid gold, too precious to be delivered meekly over to the mine owners. But his own enterprise came to an abrupt and humiliating end only a month after it began when his most trusted assistant ran off with most of what had been salvaged and another, having breathed in toxic vaporizing mercury while trying to condense some amalgam at Liges's instruction, went berserk believing that God was punishing him and confessed all to the mill foreman. So Liges was forced to flee Yankee Basin on a sway-backed horse with nothing to show for his ingenuity except a leaking sack of black sand which, when refined in Manassa, yielded only $97 in gold, which he lost at poker that night.

Whether such a debacle is fate, or mere luck—"Somebody must pay."

V

Harmon Liges and Robert Smith leave Denver on the morning of 15 April 1914, bound for Adventure. For Smith has shyly revealed that he has a substantial amount of money in traveler's checks, and the promise of more "whenever and wherever I require it."

It is Harmon Liges's general plan that they will travel by rail as far south as El Paso; perhaps, if all goes well, they will venture across the border into Mexico.

It is his plan that they travel as far north as the Bighorn area in southern Montana.

They will hike in the mountains, they will traverse Long's Glacier, they will explore unknown canyons along the Colorado River; they will visit a gold mine; they will visit one of the great ranches (there is the Flying S, east of Laramie, where, Liges says, he is always welcome); they will hunt, they will fish . . . for bear, elk, antelope, mountain lions! . . . for brook trout, black bass, pike! (Liges, not in the strictest sense a sportsman, is vague about the sort of equipment required for such activities, but fortunately his excited companion doesn't notice.)

"And we will camp out a great deal, too, won't we?—when it's warm enough," Smith says.

"Certainly," says Liges. "We will camp out all the time."

So caught up is Smith in their plans for the next several months, so deeply involved in plotting their itinerary on a large map of the Western states, he might very well have forgotten to send off a telegram to his mother, had not Liges thoughtfully reminded him. "Ah yes, thank you!—I should tell Mother not to worry if she doesn't hear from me for a while," Smith says, pulling at his lip. "For two weeks, at least, do you think, Harmon?—or three, or four?"

"Why don't you tell her five," says Liges, "—to set her mind at rest."

So the two friends depart Denver on a spring day so brilliant with sunshine that Harmon Liges is required to wear snow glasses; and Robert Smith is excited as a small child. Already, he declares, he feels "fully recovered from his illness." Already, he declares, gripping his companion's arm tight, he feels "one hundred percent a man."

To which Liges replies with a broad smile, "I should hope so, Robert."

Though Smith has informed his mother that he and a friend are traveling south into New Mexico, Liges announces an abrupt change of plans: he's heard from an Indian guide that trout fishing north of Boulder in the Medicine Bow Mountains is now ideal, and they'd be well advised to go into the mountains instead. Naturally, Smith agrees— "I'm entirely in your hands, Harmon. Anywhere you wish!"

So Liges, with Smith's money, buys two train tickets to Boulder, and the men settle in companionably in their private car, or in the club car, gazing out the window at the scenery, or gazing at each other; and talking together, as men do. It is all very natural, their conversation—it is all very relaxed and casual. Smith confesses that he has never before had a friend with whom he *could* talk openly. "This is all something of a revelation for me," he says shyly. "Not just the West, Harmon, but *you* as well. Especially, you know, *you!*"

Which outburst causes Liges to blush with a curious sort of half-angry pleasure.

On one or another train, in hackney cabs, in rented motorcars, dining together three, or even four, times each day—Liges and Smith become such intimate companions, there is hardly a particle of Smith's soul left unexamined, though the rich man's son is careful never to hint at his true identity. Sometimes it is a task for Liges to detest him, as he knows he should; sometimes it is very easily done. For Smith chatters. For Smith eats in a vague nervous fashion, as if not tasting his food. For Smith perspires even more readily than does Liges; and often pants, after climbing a flight of stairs, or hurrying along the street. Smith's eyes are a clouded muddy brown (while Liges's are a hard stony gray), Smith's skin is pasty-pale, and then sunburnt (while Liges's has the appearance of stained wood). His voice is frequently too shrill and causes people to glance in his direction. He giggles rather than laughs; and giggles too frequently. (Liges must goad himself to laugh at all—for why *do* people laugh?—it's a mystery to him.) There is a fat mole near Smith's left eye that particularly annoys Liges, and he has come to notice that, like himself, Smith has a scattering of warts in his hands. Like himself Smith has pronounced brows, tangled and dark (darker than his fair hair), and a habit of squinting. (Though Liges cannot recall whether this habit has always been his, or whether he has picked it up from Smith.)

Odd, Liges thinks, that Smith has never once commented on their resemblance to each other. Is he too stupid?—has he never dared look fully into Liges's face?—doesn't he *see*?

Still, no one else seems to have noticed either; in public places, so far, the two men have attracted no unusual attention.

"How ugly he is!" Liges sometimes thinks, involuntarily scanning Smith's face. Then again, with a sensation of confused pity: "But I suppose he can't help himself, any more than I can."

"Do you know, Harmon," Smith says suddenly, one morning near the end of April, as Liges is driving them in a rented Pierce-Arrow touring car out of Fort Collins, Colorado, "—I don't always wake up in the morning to God. To faith in God. That is, I *know* that God exists, but I cannot always *believe* it."

To which Liges replies vaguely that he often has the same doubts.

"I'm afraid that I have sometimes sinned against the Holy Spirit," Smith says in a quavering voice, staring sightlessly at the remarkable landscape. "I mean—by falling into despair of being saved. And only the perfect love of Jesus Christ has brought me back to myself."

To which Liges replies that it has often been likewise with him.

". . . Except, out here in the West, in these extraordinary spaces, it seems a very great distance for Christ to come," Smith says. He fidgets in his seat, and glances at his companion, and, grown quite emotional, says, "You see, Harmon, there *is* God—certainly. And there *is* Christ— of that I have no doubt. But sometimes, out here, so far away from everything, I cannot quite understand, you know, what they have to do with *me*."

Indeed, murmurs Liges.

". . . Yet," says Smith, almost aggressively, as if rousing himself, "I must always remember that even if we lose our human faith, that does not affect God. For He continues to exist, you know, Harmon, even if we do not."

"Does *He!*" Liges softly exclaims.

Two and a half days in Boulder . . . a day in Estes Park . . . by touring car up through Passaway, and Black Hawk, and Flint, and Azure . . . to Fort Collins . . . to Brophy Mills . . . to Red Feather Lakes and the Medicine Bow Mountains and the very trout stream that Liges has fished before, he says, many times before, and which has yet to disappoint him.

"What is the name of the stream, Harmon?" Smith asks.

"Oh—it has no name," Liges says.

"What is it near, then? Perhaps I can find it on the map," Smith says.

"You cannot find it on the map," Liges says, rather abruptly. "Such things are not marked on a *map*. . . . When I see it, I will recognize it. Never fear!"

So they make their way up through the foothills, up into the mountains, Liges at the wheel of the smart black touring car, Smith staring out the window. As a consequence of his days in the sun, Smith is no longer quite so pallid; and, in honor of their expedition, he has even begun to grow a beard—at the present time, rather sparse and sickly a beard. ("Perhaps I will never shave again," he says with a wild little laugh. "No matter how Mother begs.")

Of late, Smith is given to uncharacteristic periods of silence; as if brooding, or regretful, or apprehensive. It is very lonely, away from the bustle of the city. It is very strangely lonely. The mountains after all are so very high, the sky so piercing a cobalt-blue—a man's soul is dwarfed. And it is *cold*. Though nearly May, it is bone-chilling *cold*. Back home in Philadelphia, Smith says wistfully, the spring flowers must be blooming.

"And what is that to *us*?" Liges asks.

Shortly past noon of 28 April—a brilliantly bright windy day—they come to the very trout stream Liges has been seeking. It is twenty-odd miles beyond Red Feather Lakes, in a wild region of small mountains, steep sandstone canyons, narrow tumbling brooks whose rocks are edged, still, with ice. At this point the dirt road Liges has been following is little more than a trail; in the canyon sides, enormous scars have been cut in the very rock, by snowslides and avalanches. Here, it is very lonely indeed.

Smith climbs dazed out of the car and stands with his hands on his hips in a pose of supreme satisfaction. His breath steams, his eyes begin to water, his lips move silently. *So this is it.*

He shouts his awkward approval over his shoulder, to Liges, who is impassively preparing their fishing poles, and doesn't seem to hear.

(In Fort Collins the men equipped themselves with fishing gear of the highest quality, at the most expensive sporting goods store in town: twin rods and reels, tough resilient line, a stainless steel gutting knife, a collection of exquisite feathered flies, rubber hip boots, rubberized gloves, hand nets, etc. "All this paraphernalia merely to catch a fish!" Smith marveled; then hastily emended, "But of course it's worth every penny.")

There's a small problem securing the reels to the rods, and looping the lines out clearly; a problem adjusting the thigh-high rubber boots; but by 12:10 P.M., by Liges's watch, the men wade out into the bracing, icy stream, moving with extreme caution, and cast out their lines.

And minutes pass.

And, swiftly, a half hour.

A chill wind whistles down thinly from above. The mountain stream splashes white, and very cold. Liges finds himself regarding Smith with a brotherly sort of compassion. Now, at last, they are here, and peaceful; he's in no hurry; for it's always undignified to be made to hurry, or to act in intemperate haste—snapping that woman's neck between his hands, for instance. Though she would have had to be killed in any case. As he matures, Liges, who is Harwood Licht his father's son, sees the logic of Abraham's philosophy in which crime is dissolved in complicity and much is meditated before the simplest move is played. He knows he's been clumsy in the past but he's learning, and one day soon, perhaps by next Christmas, he will make his tyrant of a father blink in awe of *him*; and Thurston, and Elisha, and even the spoiled bitch Millicent, will be forgotten.

So, as they fish the idyllic mountain stream, Harmon Liges regards Roland Shrikesdale III with a grave little smile. His pudgy child's face creased in concentration, his close-set eyes narrowed against the splashing water as if he's frightened of it; his body taut with anticipation of a fish snapping up his lure and yanking him off balance. (For many are the tales told of fishermen, fallen in icy-cold streams, whose thigh-high boots fill up with water and weigh them down to drown, if they don't die beforehand of hypothermia.) Now that he's begun to grow a beard Smith looks less vulnerable than he had; now that his skin isn't so pasty, and so mottled, he's begun to resemble . . . Harmon Liges.

Poor Roland: poor Robert! Casting out his line again, and getting it snarled; and now the thread is jammed in the reel; and the gaily colored little fly, a bit of red, orange and yellow feathers, is caught in the fabric of his trousers. Smith's face crinkles with an infant's despair as if, were he alone, he might burst into tears . . . but, fortunately, he's not alone, his friend and companion Harmon Liges has been watching him closely, and will come to his rescue.

Yes. It's time. Liges draws the gleaming stainless steel knife out of his waist sheath and makes his way carefully to Smith. "Here, Robert," he says, "—I can fix that for you."

"I Bring Not Peace but a Sword"

I

So mysterious does young Darian Licht seem to his classmates at the Vanderpoel Academy for Boys, with his inward gaze, his dreamy frowning smile and fair light feathery hair, the way like a flame he appears, and disappears, and again appears out of the very air—his suitemate "Tige" Satterlee (of Baltimore, Maryland; father an attorney for the Baltimore & Ohio Railroad) one day asks him in the blunt bluff Brit style affected by the more sophisticated Vanderpoel students *why he is the way he is.*

Breathless Darian, only just returned from the school chapel where he's been playing the organ, turns baffled, blinking, "But—how 'am' I? What do you mean?"

In the room with Satterlee are several other boys—all regarding Darian with quizzical stares. He'd be intimidated by them except why should they want to hurt *him*? Satterlee's soccer teammates.

Satterlee says, accusing, "You're so God-damned *happy*."

"I am?—I don't mean to be."

"God damn, you *are* happy, aren't you?"

Darian looks nervously at the other boys—"Chitt" Chesterson, "Fritzie" van Gelder, "Benbo" Morgan—and sees they aren't smiling. Husky boys with arms folded, facial hair beginning to sprout on their jaws and upper lips where, on Darian's, there's only the smoothest fairest down. *All men are our enemies, as they are strangers.*

Darian stammers, "I don't know," seeing that the unpredictable Satterlee may be in a dangerous mood, "—I don't think about things like that. I was playing my—music."

Has a lighted match been touched to Satterlee, causing him to flare up, contemptuous, grinning—"Your music! 'Your' music! What is this that makes you so happy, some place you go to?—like playing with yourself?—some place that isn't *here?*"

Satterlee stamps his feet, big feet for a fourteen-year-old, and the floor shudders. Here's *here*, and no mistake.

Uneasily Darian says, "Well, I don't know."

"Benbo" Morgan, who's J. P. Morgan's grandson, lurches forward with a threatening grin. "Y'know—you act like nothing touches you. Like you're above it all, Licht."

Darian protests, "But everything touches me."

He's backing off, smiling. They're going to hurt him, not just give him orders. Can he escape? Turn to smoke, so they're striking only the air? Disappear through the single mirror in the room, a gleaming slanted rhomboid atop a bureau? Or transform himself into a few bars of music, cascading treble notes like shattering icicles, flying into his head as his hands wandered over the organ's keyboards too swiftly for him to pause and jot them down—

"Touches you, maybe," Satterlee says in his drawling mid-Southern accent, in which fury and hurt commingle, "but goes right on through. Doesn't it! Eh!"

Shoving Darian back against a table, and the books in Darian's arms go flying, Bach's *Two- and Three-Part Inventions*, Chopin's *Preludes*, Scriabin's *Piano Sonatas*, and Darian freezes and goes inward and he's in his secret place in Muirkirk invisible as musical notes swirl about him as the boys, whooping and yelping, close in upon him.

What is this that makes you so happy and of such happiness he can't speak. He'd never inform on his tormentors, they know they can depend upon him, Darian Licht isn't going to crack like certain of the other targets of their animosity for whom they feel only contempt while for Darian, rumored to be a genius, they feel a grudging admiration, respect if not affection, there's something so . . . strange about him, a light that comes up in his eyes, luminous as a cat's.

Perhaps, he's beginning to think, he's Abraham Licht's son after all: a master of escapes, disappearances. Of things not quite what they seem.

It's a thought that fills Darian with dread. For though he loves Abraham Licht with a fierce, helpless love, he's old enough now and mature enough to know he can't approve of the man. *And certainly I never understood him.*

There's Darian Licht in his navy blue woollen blazer and school tie (dull rust-red stripes upon a dull gold background). Darian whose eyes are watering with a sinus headache. Darian whose heart pounds with excitement as the sonorous old bell in the bell tower tolls calmly and massively reverberating through the chatter of hundreds of boys in the dining hall like the very speech of God, wordless. There's Darian frowning over problems in plane geometry, there's Darian in baggy shirt and shorts trailing after a screaming pack of boys on the soccer field, shuddering with cold and his lips and fingernails purple yet stubbornly or out of futility he continues to run, trot, stagger, stumble actually managing as in a dream of comical implausibility to kick the ball once, twice, a third time . . . and to make a goal. There's Darian silently obeying the commandments of upper-form boys, military-style orders barked in raw adolescent voices *Attention! Sweep up in here, Licht. Attention! Polish my boots, Licht. Attention!* But his attention is elsewhere, that place to which he escapes, Muirkirk, music, the wind in the marsh grasses, the high whistling wind out of the Chautauqua Mountains, the gentle touch of his mother's fingers at the nape of his neck *what is this that makes you so happy so happy* released in the late afternoon from classes running breathless and graceful as a deer across the school's back acre to the gravel road and to Academy Street and so to Twelfth Street where his piano instructor lives upstairs in a tall narrow putty-colored row house, Herr Professor Adolf Hermann, lately of Düsseldorf, Germany, eyes awash with rheumy tears behind gold-rimmed glasses, droplets of sweat easing down his fatty cheeks and neck, he says not a word to any of his (American) pupils of the grief festering in his heart, the hope that Germany will crush her enemies, the terror that Germany *will* crush her enemies . . . and then? What will be the fate of Germans in North America? Darian Licht, his most gifted American student, perhaps indeed the most gifted student Herr Hermann has ever had, sees newspapers scattered about the steam-heated parlor, the war headlines GERMAN SUBMARINES SINK FOUR U.S. MERCHANT SHIPS, WILSON VOWS WAR, the newspaper photographs, averts his eyes and goes at once to the piano and adjusts the stool to his height (still short for his age, he despairs of growing), begins nervously with his warming-up scales, his technical exercises, today it's F-sharp minor, harmonic forms, melodic forms, contrary motion, triads solid and broken. Darian is always nervous, always falters initially, Professor Hermann grunts in sympathy, he quite understands, you are a servant of the piano and of the music that rushes through it, you will never be its equal.

At the conclusion of a feverish hour spent mostly in fragments and repetitions (Chopin's Prelude no. 16, *Presto con fuoco*) Darian is shaking with exhaustion and Professor Hermann, dabbing at his oily face, gives off an odor of angry excitement, or excited anger. *To be equal to such music! To be equal to . . . God!* No other pupil is scheduled to follow Darian, for Professor Hermann's pupils are few, their numbers dwindling, so the lesson continues for another hour . . . or more.

"A pity, my boy," Professor Hermann says, wiping his face with a soiled handkerchief, "—that you didn't come to me until now, when it's almost too late; you, at your age, with your bad keyboard habits; and civilization itself coming to an end."

II

In Abraham Licht's judgment, the world certainly isn't coming to an end but to a new beginning.

War began in Europe on 1 August but Abraham Licht, like numerous others, had been shrewdly anticipating it for weeks, reading all the newspapers he could get to seek out confirmation of his sense of a rich, chaotic Destiny. He tells Darian that the past and the future will be divided; the old, the worn-out, the dead, will rapidly fade into extinction;

those who live now will have the privilege of being reborn, *if they are but strong enough.*

As he himself is strong, and as Darian must be strong.

"We Lichts have been cheated of our birthright in the past," Abraham says, vehemently, "—but the future is ours, I vow."

Yes, it's a very good time; an opportune time; many citizens are gazing hypnotized (with dread, with fascination) across the Atlantic Ocean, and have relaxed their vigilance here. It's an era of plans; almost too many plans; one must narrow one's focus; one must move slowly, cannily, with care. . . . In the autumn of 1914 as a student at the Vanderpoel Academy, Darian Licht has the opportunity should he wish to cultivate it of befriending the sons, grandsons, nephews and young cousins of such illustrious Americans as F. Augustus Heinze, Edward H. Harriman, Elias Shrikesdale, Stuyvesant Shrikesdale, Rear Admiral Robley "Fighting Bob" Evans, Alfred Gwynne Vanderbilt, the Reverend Cornelius Crowan, J. P. Morgan. When Darian protests that he doesn't like these boys, Abraham Licht replies testily that that hardly matters—"Get them to like *you*, my boy."

Tuition is high at the Academy, despite the grim appearance of its neo-Gothic granite buildings and the notoriously combative atmosphere of its classrooms, dormitories and playing fields, for, as Abraham Licht has explained to Darian, the school is one of the oldest private schools in the United States, founded 1721; it's closely modeled upon Harrow, though football rather than rugby is played, and boys aren't required to wear top hats and tails on Sundays; and there are so many distinguished gentlemen (in business, politics, religion) among its graduates, to list them would be exhausting.

The very name "Vanderpoel" (like "Harvard," "Princeton," "Yale") is invaluable, in the right quarters.

"So the cost of the school is hardly an object," Abraham Licht says, "where your education is concerned."

Darian hadn't wanted to leave Muirkirk; he hadn't wanted to matriculate at Vanderpoel, despite its reputation; the very look of the old, dignified, forbidding buildings dampened his spirits. It was a notion of his that, away from Muirkirk, he would lose his mother forever; he would lose his soul; he would, at the very least, be stricken with homesickness. Yet once at school in his drafty, unadorned third-floor room in the dormitory known familiarly as "Fish" (Marcus Fish Hall, 1844), thrown together with a fourth-form boy named Satterlee who's sometimes cruel, sometimes condescending, sometimes unexpectedly friendly, even teasing, Darian has discovered that, much of the time, he's happy after all. *For Muirkirk is my music, to be entered at any time. Even silence is a kind of music.* His classmates seem to respect him even when they don't seem to like him; there's a stubbornness in him that discourages bullies, the banes of such private schools.

"But you must try to make friends pragmatically, Darian," Father tells him, "—and not leave things to blind chance. You must make the effort, son, as we all do." Father raps his fingertips on a tabletop; nicotine-stained fingers with slightly swollen knuckles.

"Yes, Father. I suppose."

"It isn't always easy, you know: you must swallow your natural Licht pride and your inclination."

"Yes, Father. I suppose."

"This 'Satterlee,' he's a rather crude, charming sort . . . though only from Baltimore. What of Mr. Morgan's grandson? What of Mr. Harriman's grandson? . . . the headmaster tells me he's quite a football hero. And there's a chap named Sewall, Roddy Sewall I believe, a nephew of the wife of . . . the late Roland Shrikesdale II of Philadelphia. He, too, they say, is a musically inclined boy, and a bit eccentric. Don't frown, Darian, and look so worried! Your father will guide you in such waters." Abraham pauses, studying his son; smiles sympathetically as if seeing, in Darian's small delicate features, something of his own. "And you must cultivate a personality of your own, and not just drift. You do know what I mean by 'personality'?"

"Yes, Father. I think so."

"Then tell me: what is a 'personality'?"

"A way of—speaking? Laughing? Being happy or sad or . . ."

Darian's voice trails off, baffled. He too taps the tabletop with nervous, unconscious fingers, striking invisible and soundless notes.

"A 'personality' is a ghostly aura one *has*, rather than something one *is*," Father explains. "It's to be shed as readily as one sheds clothing—warm clothes for a cool day, lighter clothes for a warm day. Your sister Millicent is a very devil at 'personality'—she could teach her old father a trick or two! No, son," he says quickly, sensing that Darian is about to ask after Millie, what's become of Millie, why hasn't he seen Millie for

so long, and where are his brothers he adores, Thurston and 'Lisha?—
"Our subject, son, is *you*. For you're lacking skills in what's called human intercourse—social relations—*personality*. The headmaster, with
whom I've shared brandy and cigars, and get on with quite comfortably,
confides in me that you are a 'quiet' boy, a 'forthright' boy, a 'good, polite, intelligent and well-liked' boy but it's clear to me that he can't find
anything else to say about you. You are a person, Darian, lacking a personality. To remedy the situation, observe the most popular boys in the
upper forms. Note how each has cultivated a certain distinctive way of
speaking, of laughing, of smiling, of carrying his body; I know, without
being acquainted with them, that each looks others directly in the eye,
engaging contact forcefully. This you must cultivate. And not look, as
you do, at the floor! As our great American philosopher William James
has said, an individual has as many selves as there are individuals whom
he knows. There isn't the slightest hypocrisy in this, but only pragmatic
ethics. For not all persons are worthy of our acquaintance, and not all
persons require equal time from us. You save your most valuable 'personality' for the most valuable persons you know. And you assemble
your selves with grace. D'you understand, son?"

Darian feels an urge to shout. To shout profanities. To bang fists, feet
in a wild staccato rhythm against the table and the floor. To overturn
his father's stained-glass lamp, to tear at his father's papers strewn across
his desk. Instead, he bites his lower lip, imagines his outspread fingers
crashing chords in both the treble and bass keyboards, music so loud in
his ears he wonders his father doesn't hear. He's hot-faced and miserable staring blindly at the floor.

Abraham Licht sighs. Suddenly he's tired. But lays a warm paternal
hand on Darian's shoulder. "Well, son. Eventually you'll learn. This is
what we mean by 'life.' "

III

"How do you do, sir. *This* is an honor."

Darian can't help but inwardly wince at his father's exuberant public
manner: the way he pumps Dr. Meech's hand, looking the headmaster
in the eye as if they were old, dear friends; the way he raises Mrs.

Meech's gloved hand to his lips and almost—but not quite—kisses it, murmuring *"Enchanté, madame!"* Yet no one takes offense. No one suspects that Abraham Licht might be insincere or might even be mocking them. For he's so very interested in everything here at Vanderpoel, and he's so very charming.

The Meeches who are usually so dignified and stiff; the assistant headmaster Dunne with his narrow joyless eyes; the chaplain, whose anxiety is that the Vanderpoel boys don't adequately respect him; the prefect of studies, the instructors, boys whose usual manner is droll, mocking, juvenile, brash—these persons who differ so much from one another are united in falling under the spell of Abraham Licht, and vie with one another for his smiling attention. Darian doesn't know whether to be dismayed or pleased at the way his father wins over such difficult Vanderpoel personalities as Philbrick, master of Latin; Cowan, master of science, who fancies himself a gentleman; and withered little jaundice-skinned Moseley, master of mathematics, who keeps the boldest boys terrorized with his acidulous wit and his "amusing" comments on man's sinful nature. . . . These men are dry, dull, dim planets given a temporary radiance by the grace of Abraham Licht's beaming sun.

And now, Darian wonders, what will they expect of me?

For already it seems to him that these people glance smilingly from Abraham Licht to Darian, and back to Abraham Licht again, as if detecting a hidden filial resemblance. Where Darian has been seen to be shy previously, now he'll be seen as reticent, self-contained, self-reliant. The strength of the father in the son.

Dr. Meech himself insists upon taking Abraham Licht on a tour of the Academy's grounds: a look at venerable old Rutledge Hall, and a look at the new (built 1896) chapel; a leisurely stroll about the playing fields (where some of Darian's classmates are playing an unrefereed, rowdy game of soccer); even a visit to the dour redbrick infirmary where Darian, with his weak chest, spends a fair amount of time and has been allotted "his" bed by the sympathetic school nurse. Abraham marvels at the dignified yet democratic plan of the school, which seems to him, he says, more practical than that of Harrow, which he'd attended for two years, as a boy; he's appreciative of the newly built Frick Hall, the gift of a wealthy alumnus of his acquaintance from college days at Harvard; he shows a zealous interest in the somewhat shabby dormitories, with a hint of intending to "endow" his son's dormitory

Fish Hall someday in the future; he's cheerful and funny about Darian's and Satterlee's room with its poor lighting, low ceiling and comical beds, or cots, that pull down on springs from the walls—"Not a place, I see, to encourage adolescent self-preoccupation." He and Satterlee exchange quips; he and Satterlee get along famously; he and Satterlee are, you might say, a natural team. *If only such a boy. My son!*—so Darian interprets his father's fond smile, with only a small tinge of jealousy.

Afterward, Satterlee will say to Darian, "You're God-damned lucky, Licht, to have a father like that. My father . . ." His voice fades, his jaws work in mute frustration. Darian murmurs a vague enthusiastic assent. *Oh yes! I know.*

Being such a busy man, Abraham Licht had planned to spend only an afternoon at the school; but so deep is his interest in Vanderpoel and its traditions, and so gracious is the welcome he's receiving on all sides, he's prevailed upon to remain for high tea in the common room, where he engages the fifth-form boys in talk of soccer, boxing and the "grave historical" situation in Europe; and to stay for dinner with the Meeches in their handsome English Tudor residence; even to stay the night in their guest quarters. And, as the next day is Sunday, perhaps Mr. Licht might agree to take the pulpit for a few minutes? There's an old Vanderpoel tradition of guest sermons delivered by fathers, occasionally, on any uplifting subject, for the edification of the boys. "A fresh perspective, a *father's* perspective, does wonders for them," Dr. Meech says. "For you know, some of them—excluding your gifted Darian, of course—lack adequate spiritual guidance from elder relatives. They look to us for what wisdom we can give them in this uncertain world."

Abraham Licht hesitates, for he has pressing business after all—in Boston, or is it Manhattan; then, smiling his warm, winning smile, of course he acquiesces. "Though it's been fifteen years since, as a friend of Archbishop Cockburn of St. John the Divine, Manhattan, I've given a guest sermon at the pulpit—and may be a bit rusty!"

Abraham Licht's subject is "Sacred Values in a Secular World."

The substance is that each boy in the chapel that morning, *each boy without exception*, inhabits both the secular ("America of the present time") and the sacred ("the world of God and of Eternity"), and each must see himself, if he has but sufficient manliness and courage, as a form of Jesus Christ.

A masterfully orated sermon. From the very first the assembled boys and their mentors are roused from the customary Sabbath stupor, for Abraham Licht's appearance at the pulpit contrasts dramatically with that of Headmaster Meech and the chaplain; his voice is subtly modulated, a rich deep baritone now assured, now humorous, now forceful, now quavering with quiet passion. A voice of authority. A voice of genial wisdom. A voice of paternal solicitude. Yet a voice to stir the hairs at the nape. *For what does a man possess if his honor, his very soul, is taken from him? Is life, mere animal life, possible without honor? In Europe today, the story is ever and always the same: after the low Serbian insult of 29 June, Austrian honor had to be defended; German pride, German destiny, must fulfill itself; yet there is English honor, and American honor; and that of France, and Russia and the lesser nations. A tragedy to those whose blood is spilled yet it may be a cataclysm directed by God Himself to cleanse the Old World of its decadence, complacency and blindness to progress. For as our savior Jesus Christ declared "I bring not peace but a sword". . . by which we know that the sword and not mere peace is mankind's destiny.*

This memorable sermon Abraham Licht delivers from the pulpit of the chapel at Vanderpoel Academy on the morning of Sunday, 11 October 1914, soaring inspiring words Darian scarcely hears in a buzz of musical notes that define themselves as heartbeats, as tiny pinpricks of sweat on his forehead and in his armpits, as invisible compulsive twitchings of his toes, a cascade of notes that will save him. *Don't listen! Don't believe! Don't be seduced!* Darian would cry to his classmates and their rapt, approving elders. Yet afterward virtually every boy in the school and particularly the boys of the third floor of Fish congratulate Darian on his father's sermon and assure him he's "God-damned lucky to have such a father"—which, with a quick, wan smile, Darian says yes I know.

IV

So it happens that life in Vanderpoel, which Darian had dreaded, actually passes in a sort of waking dream. *The outer grid superimposed upon*

the inner. Each with its music—in a surprising harmony out of disharmony.
Boys' voices, shouts, stampeding feet, even the flushing of toilets down
the corridor—one day, Darian Licht will incorporate such sounds into
his collage-compositions, to stun and outrage conventional ears, and
intrigue and delight others. *My legacy of the years Father sent me into
exile.*

He's an intelligent, capable boy. His taut nerves can be disguised as
alertness. His penchant for daydreaming can be disguised as serious
thought. He finds that he likes the precisely ordered academic year
with its routine of classes, meals, chapel services, assemblies, sports, ex-
ams and holidays that moves with the ease of clockwork, like a great
metronome. Real enough, yet without spiritual significance.

For, always, contiguous with this bustling outer world yet not contaminated by it there exists a secret inner world, Darian Licht's true
world. There he's free to speak with his lost mother Sophie; he sees her
more vividly than he sees Satterlee and others close about him; he
hears music as it should be played—Mozart, Chopin, Beethoven—and
certain compositions of his own yet to be transcribed. Homesick, Darian can drift like a hawk about Muirkirk, seeing the old stone church
that's his home, the churchyard beyond, the marsh, the mist-obscured
mountains in the distance. Sometimes he sees Katrina so clearly, he
could swear she sees *him*; and what of Esther, growing into adolescence,
a plain-pretty, cheerful girl whose hair Katrina still braids, glancing
quizzically at him . . . surely Esther is aware of Darian? When he speaks
to her, surely she hears?

Like all devoted pianists, Darian has devised for himself a magic keyboard which he plays at will by lightly depressing his fingertips (in
Philbrick's class, for instance, where twenty-six boys with a detestation
of Latin have been engaged in translating Cicero for weeks); when a
real piano isn't accessible he can play his invisible keyboard and hear,
or almost hear, the notes as they're struck. If all goes well, and Darian
isn't called upon in class, he can practice piano for hours every day.

Since the Academy, despite its reputation for excellence, doesn't offer formal music instructions, Darian acquired permission to practice
on the chapel organ; within two weeks of his arrival, he made arrange-
ments on his own to take piano instructions with Professor Hermann,
who lives within a mile of the school, and who was recommended to
him by the chaplain's wife. (These lessons, Darian will pay for out of

the allowance his father sends him—"For luxuries, not for necessities.") Though Mr. Meech doesn't approve of such extracurricular activities, since Darian Licht is the son of Abraham Licht, and known to be an unusually talented lad, an exception has been made. "Mr. Meech, thank you very much. My father will be so pleased"—Darian makes sure his gratitude is clearly, articulately expressed.

Playing organ in the chapel, often in the dark, Darian drifts into one of his trances . . . and his lost mother appears close by, in silence; a diaphanous yet clearly defined figure, with long, unbraided hair; listening, admiring each note he plays; if he plays without error, drawing nearer, and nearer . . . to brush her cool fingertips lightly against his hair or the nape of his neck . . . whispering *Darian. Darian, my son. I love you.* But sometimes the tension is too great, Darian's concentration snaps and he gives a violent shudder and jerks his hands from the keyboard, turns wild-eyed to see . . . no one there at all.

Yet whispering *Mother?* . . .

V

Unexpectedly, just after midterm, Darian Licht is moved to another, loftier and more spacious room in Fish Hall. Though he'd been on cordial terms with "Tige" Satterlee and others in his corridor following Abraham Licht's visit, suddenly he finds himself sharing a well-appointed fourth-floor suite overlooking the green with a boy he scarcely knows, Roddy Sewall, heavyset, frowning, with bitten thumbnails and a squeaking nervous giggle—"Why?" Darian asked the headmaster's assistant, who'd arranged for the move, and was told simply that his father had worried his previous room was too drafty for his respiratory condition.

Roddy Sewall. The name is familiar—isn't it? But Darian, absorbed in other things, quickly gives up trying to recall what, if anything, that name might mean, if not to him then to Abraham Licht.

In that way I passed through their world, untouched.

The Death of "Little Moses"

I

At first he can measure his exile in terms of hours and days, and then it is weeks, and then the weeks blur drunkenly together and it is months, entire seasons, the sun has turned about in the sky, and he has not been well, he has not been *himself*, for a very long time.

It is SPIRIT that has drained from him, it is SPIRIT that has departed, leaving him light-headed and giddy, and sometimes sick in his guts. (For the flesh remains, darkly encasing his luminescent bones. *For the flesh is all that remains.*)

"Father give birth to me," he thinks, without anger, "—and now he has given death to me. *But I will not die.*"

He is not angry. He is not a vessel of wrath.

For pride will not allow such.

For he *is* suffused with pride, even in his tight-fitting livery costume, attending the gentleman of the house, murmuring Yes sir, No sir, Yes *sir* at the proper time, carrying away toiletry items, carrying away stained undergarments, filthy towels, brimming chamberpots, his gentleman's hats (top hat, bowler, straw boater, "derby"), his gentleman's silk-lined cashmere coat, the ladies' furs, walking not with stealth but with dignity, for this is the great Sylvester Harburton home in Nautauga Falls, this is immense Harburton Hall overlooking the river, and he knows himself fortunate to have acquired employment here; against the wishes, it seems, of the pork-faced "Negro" butler who is his superior.

His tenure at Harburton Hall will be brief, and abruptly terminated. Though *why*, he can't comprehend.

He is a model of correct behavior, is he not?—or nearly. He is not angry. He does not tremble with inward wrath. His waking hours are spent at a healthy trot, *Yes sir, yes ma'am, of course sir,* a supple young animal kept in motion, his hours of sleep are primitive and innocent, though sometimes he wakes groaning, near-sobbing, the slap of Father's hand burning on his cheek, sometimes he wakes because his guts have turned to liquid fire and he is in danger of soiling his bed.

Poor Emile—as he calls himself.

Poor Emile—who begins to go strange after two weeks, his soft murmur a (mocking?) drawl, his eyeballs rolling in his head, thick lips twitching as if he has something to say but will not say it, *Yes sir, yes ma'am,* his features impassive when he's observed, his mirth all inward, secret. (For he's light-headed with the horror of a chronological progression of days in which Emile does not have even a minor role to perform at Harburton Hall or elsewhere; a progression of days in which Emile need not exist; for no one guides him, or adores him, or gazes upon him with admiration, awe, *love*.)

SPIRIT has departed, leaving FLESH behind.

Yet it's unlikely that anyone notices, for Emile is far too clever to be found out.

And Harburton Hall is so lively!—so festive!—so resolutely gay!—for despite the War in Europe, it seems to be a time for discreet celebration in certain circles.

They are making money on the war, selling munitions. Selling death.

And out of that income, Emile's paltry salary.

Luncheons at Harburton Hall for more than one hundred guests. Formal balls for more than five hundred. High teas, dinners, evening parties, musical parties, foxhunting soirees, midnight suppers, skating parties, toboggan parties . . . Mrs. Rhea Ludgate Harburton, lady of the house, jealously prides herself on being the outstanding hostess of the Valley; and closely studies the society pages of the New York newspapers to see what her Manhattan counterparts (Astors, Morgans, Fishes, Huntingtons, etc.) are doing. The Harburtons' wealth isn't equal to theirs but Mrs. Harburton is as imaginative as any rival hostess. Where the flamboyant Mrs. Fish gives a dinner party at her Fifth Avenue home in honor of the visiting "Prince del Drago of Corsica" (to her guests' astonishment the "Prince" turns out to be a spider monkey in full evening dress complete with saber), Mrs. Harburton gives a lavish lawn party in honor of the visiting "Princess Kwali de Alibaumba of Ethiopia" (revealed as a large black poodle with frightened eyes and inveterate doggy ways—how Mrs. Harburton's guests laughed!); where Mrs. John Jacob Astor gives a fancy-dress party with an Oriental theme, Mrs. Harburton gives one with an Egyptian theme, appearing as Queen Nefertiti herself—so burdened with a gilt-embroidered head-dress, a gown of silver cloth, a golden scepter and a twelve-foot train carried by two "pickaninnies" in livery, she can scarcely walk. In Man-hattan, the younger Mrs. Huntington shocks society elders by giving a "nursery dinner" where guests dressed as babies prattle in baby talk and eat variants of baby food; in Nautauga, a "servants' supper" in which guests disguise themselves as their own servants, most of them in hilari-ous blackface.

And Emile must serve, moving among them.

Emile must smile . . . must he?

The new craze in Manhattan, however, is "jazz dancing." So there are dances at Harburton Hall each weekend, tea dances, dinner dances, midnight dances, even breakfast dances. Young Emile in his monkey-livery observes with glaring, slightly bloodshot eyes the expensively costumed white women and their partners as they dance, not always very gracefully, such revolutionary new steps as the turkey trot . . . the bunny hug . . . the Texas Tommy . . . the lame duck . . . the half-in-half . . . the Castle walk . . . the jazz-tango, the jazz-maxixe, the jazz-waltz. Possibly one of the Harburtons discovers him staring too intently when he should be serving champagne, his lips drawn back in a smile from clenched teeth as gay drunken couples dance, or try to dance, to the syncopated pace of "Too Much Mustard," "Snooky Ookums," "Everybody's Doin' It, Doin' It, Doin' It."

Emile?—from Jamaica.

Emile who delights white folks' ears with his precise, clipped British accent.

". . . just like a white man isn't he? I mean, his voice. If you didn't, y'know, see him."

". . . like one of those, what are they . . . chimps? On his hind legs."

". . . pitch-black like tar baby. Ugh!"

"Shhhhhhh! Stu, you're ter-ri-ble."

In the end it isn't either of the Harburtons who dismiss Emile but the Negro butler who oversees the Negro staff and whose responsibility it is to keep these servants in line. He and other domestics have been observing Emile as he sits by himself in a corner of the servants' kitchen, his young face creased with thought, his mouth working in silent arguments. They believe his tale of being, not an American black, the grandson of slaves, but a Caribbean black, his original allegiance to the British Empire; they believe him but feel no warmth for him, he isn't a brother to them, he's a stranger with peculiar white ways and an air of reproach as if he's too good for his station. A dangerous man.

So he's given notice. Two weeks' salary.

Pride forbids him to protest. He's contemptuous, departing without a word. *As if he's being watched, assessed, admired* as in the old days of his family who'd loved him, and who'd known who he was.

II

In Barre City, in Norwich, in Niagara Falls . . . in Mount Moriah and Wells . . . in Olean, Binghamton, Yonkers, Pittsburgh. A cultivated soft-spoken Negro gentleman, young, at any rate youthful, presents himself as a candidate for "positions": being qualified, it seems, to be a librarian or a schoolteacher or a tax collector or an insurance salesman or the manager of a small business . . . but none of his interviews comes to anything. Often his very presence, his poise, the dignity with which he speaks evokes smiles.

Not seen, not heard at all.

Emile, or Elihu, or Ezra seeking an interview with a subeditor of the *Pittsburgh Gazette*, yes he has samples of his writing, humor columns he's penned and had set into type, as witty as anything by Mark Twain; he has ideas for advertising campaigns for the paper, and for the establishment of a lottery the *Gazette* might administer, how well he speaks, with what poise, educated speech, pleasing "Brit" accent, deferential yet not craven, clearly not an American black yet American in his energy and eagerness; except he's interrupted in midspeech and told rudely there's no opening for him at the *Gazette*, he might try one of the "colored" papers in the city.

* * *

How then to survive? Being neither black nor white? Trapped inside this skin.

Strange how frequently he dreams of—that man who'd been his father. As frequently as he dreams of Millicent.

Though he's given them both up, of course. In revulsion, in disgust. His Licht blood—"If I could squeeze it out of my veins drop by drop!"

Still, he dreams of that man who'd been his father. His Devil-Daddy. Stooping to save him from the flood, baptizing him Little Moses. *Child, I love you best. Always, I'd loved you best. Don't make me strike you, Little Moses!*

He wakes from such dreams soaked in sweat, his heart knocking against his rib cage. How thin he's become . . . Millie would be shocked. His face stinging from the blows of Abraham Licht's fists and his soul writhing in shame. But he's determined. He won't give up. "You imagine you've given death to me," he accuses their pale, rapt faces, "—but I don't intend to die. Not for a long time."

III

Though Death is growing in him like a malignant tumor.

In Pittsburgh, in Johnstown, in Altoona . . . in Williamsport and Scranton . . . in Newark . . . he's Emile from Jamaica or Eli from Ontario, Canada, whose ancestors, never slaves, fought on the side of the Loyalists in the Revolution; he's Elihu, sullen mute Elihu whose ancestry is unknown . . . working in an icehouse for 50¢ a twelve-hour day . . . working in a livery stable until the stink and exhaustion of the job makes him ill . . . and for a grain elevator operator on the Susquehanna who refuses to pay him his final day on the job . . . and for a brewery where for ten hours daily he loads barrels onto wagons, arm and shoulder muscles throbbing with pain and a nerve burning the length of his spine.

His skin has darkened with fatigue, he believes. Since the expulsion from Muirkirk.

His features have grown coarser. He's losing his 'Lisha-looks. The flat squat nose, flaring nostrils and thick lips. The deep-set bloodshot eyes. A mask that frightens him when he sees it by chance.

"But that isn't me. That isn't me. Not that."

Yet, seeing his mask of a face, others see . . . what they imagine they see. Other Negroes, seeing him, mistake him as one of their own, at least until he begins to speak.

So he begins to speculate: an entire race might mistake him as one of their own if he but knew how to approach them.

But it's true, 'Lisha is fearful of Negroes. Intimidated by them. The men especially. Crude, unpredictable, dangerous when they've been drinking and no whites are around; he's been beaten and robbed several times in the past year. Kicked in the groin, left choking on his own blood. Their speech so alien to him, guttural, crude, he can't comprehend it much of the time, any more than they can comprehend him. They don't speak English! he thinks in dismay. Not as American citizens speak it.

He's afraid, too, that if a Negro looks frankly into his eyes the Negro would discover his secret: Elisha Licht, like "Little Moses," is a fraud.

Through the winter of 1914 and the spring of '15 he resolves to change his fate. Forcing himself to speak with Negroes. His toiling comrades in a reeking tannery on the Delaware River near Easton. Imitating their speech as best he can. Though they have trouble understanding him. Great husky fellows these men are, so much stronger than he is, their arm muscles thick as his thighs, they've been laboring at such jobs since childhood. Still, as Father might advise, smile and any fool will smile with you, smile and "strike up a conversation" complaining bitterly of working conditions, poor pay, the white bosses, white men who own everything, but his voice lacks resonance, he's having difficulty looking into his comrades' eyes for fear they will discover he's a fraud. Or, worse, they'll think he's a spy in the hire of the company. Or a Bolshevik union organizer who'll cost them their jobs . . . and get them beaten until they spit blood.

"No suh thankyuh. No time right now suh."

"Gotta be goin, suh. Sowrry.'

He's hurt. He's devastated. He's angry. Subhuman brutes, long-limbed apes yet they dare to snub *him*.

Walking at the side of the highway leading into Paterson, New Jersey. Where his feet should be, a roaring numbness. He's gaunt with hunger. "Little Moses" with a swollen potbelly. Not ill, yet not well. Is something wrong with his eyes? A glaring nimbus of sun burning his brain.

He sleeps in lice-infested bedding, or out in the open. He sweats like a draft horse. Until he sweats himself dry, and his bowels have emptied out with dysentery. Stooping to drink ditch water like a lapping dog. Splashing icy water onto his face and pausing staring at the face . . . the mask . . . with his eyes. *Yes it's me. Yet no name.*

His several names, he's lost along the roadside. He's lost in sweat. A peculiar peace to it, no-name. Just the skin, and the eyes.

And, at the outskirts of the city he isn't fully aware is Paterson, let alone that he's in the state of New Jersey. That blinding glaring sun. His bloodshot eyes. The handsome couple in the stalled automobile, in the mud. The driver, a white man in his thirties, squatting in the roadway and turning the crank clumsily, failing to start the car; his passenger, a white woman of about his age, with a fleshy pale face and rouged cheeks, a peach-colored cloche hat on her curled hair.

To the rescue! He'll give them aid, and they'll give him aid. He'll ride off with them. And the anxious woman in the cloche hat will recognize him for the person he is and not this . . . mud-splattered creature with jaundiced eyes, sulky lips and protuberant wristbones.

The automobile is a four-seater Welch touring car, cream-colored with chocolate-brown leather interior and trim, flawless brass fixtures (rounded headlights, large horn, prominent grill) and stately spoked tires. When he'd been Elisha Licht—when he'd been "Little Moses"— he'd ridden in automobiles as fine as this, owned by the man who'd been his father; he's even driven such an automobile, a beautiful fair-haired young woman snug beside him, whispering and laughing with him. You wouldn't believe it, these suspicious white folks wouldn't believe it, but—it's so.

"Having trouble, sir? I can help, I think."

"You—?"

"I can try, at least."

In his rags, in his whiskered lice-bitten mask of a face, taking the crank handle in both his hands, trying to get leverage, at last kneeling in the mud, and—"There! There it is, sir." Like magic he gets the sodden engine of the Welch touring car to turn over, and spark into roaring, vibrating life. He squints, wipes his hands on his trousers, tries to rise to his feet but an attack of dizziness slows him, even as the engine drowns out his hopeful words and the gentleman driver in a mud-splashed beige driving costume with flushed face, fatty chin, resentful eyes calls out, "Thanks, boy! You're a lifesaver." The woman in the cloche hat calls out, "Ohhhh thanks! How did you *do* that!" He's on his feet now smiling shakily yet expectantly at the couple awaiting the invitation from them to climb into the rear of the gleaming cream-colored automobile even as the driver carelessly tosses a coin—dime? quarter?—that falls onto the muddy edge of the roadway, and drives off.

IV

Her fierce spicy fragrance makes his temples pound: he's wild, exhila-rated, drunken: wrenched out of his bones for very joy.

A girl with pale blond hair and wide-spaced innocent eyes and fever-ish lips: her skin burning: her laughter choked: for she too, pressing herself into his arms, clutching at him, is drunken with love, with love, with love. . . .

His heart is ready to burst, he can't control himself, he adores her, he would die for her, he *has* died for her, many times: yet she's frenzied, in-satiable: coiling her sweat-slick limbs upon him, writhing violently against him, O Elisha I love you, love you, love you. . . .

O Elisha I love you. . . .

O Elisha I am your wife. . . .

V

And now suddenly seeing them everywhere. Can't hide from the sight, the knowledge. Blacks, coloreds, Negroes, niggers. On the street, at the roadside, in crowded tenement districts, at the northern edge of the Park.

These people who make their way in a world fully conscious of the white man and of one another. While the white man, blind, is con-scious of nothing.

He belongs to neither race. So glancing upon both with Olympian equanimity.

For pride will not allow wrath, and pride will not allow despair.

Long vanished are the days when he might live at the Park Stuy-vesant Hotel in midtown, as the personal valet (as the hotel manage-ment believed) of a wealthy businessman named Fairbairn; long vanished, and nearly forgotten, are the Sunday drives by hackney cab through the Park, Millie's small hand secretly pressing against his, hid-den by the pretty flounces of her skirt. Not fully recovered from his ill-ness but he's strong and buoyant and himself again, or nearly . . . a lanky-legged mahogany-skinned entrepreneur named Emile Gaston, or Dupee Jones, formerly of the Barbados . . . formerly of Mexico City . . . given to fits of coughing, violent brief spasms that break the capillaries in his eyes . . . but all in all a proud figure, a shrewd figure, smart black bowler hat, imitation camel's hair polo coat worn loose on his shoul-ders, pockets jingling with coin . . . from the sporadic sale of 50¢ bottles of hair straightener up in Harlem, skin bleach in putty-colored tubes, lottery tickets printed in various colors, tickets for a Sunday-on-the-Hudson Steamboat Excursion stamped *one-day only* and *non-refundable*. Yes he is himself again! or nearly.

His money is fast running out, however.

And he has made enemies on the street.

In the meantime he comports himself with grace, with a reeling swaying sort of grace, he swallows down gin at midday, never wholly drunk and never wholly sober, not a human being in the world dares approach him to touch him to look him in the eye: *that* not even his enemies would dare.

Twenty-six years old, or is it thirty—but with his thin clipped mous-tache and his hat tilted forward on his head he looks older. With his ravaged skin and hunted ashy eyes he looks much older.

Emile Gaston, Dupee Jones, Elihu Washburn . . .

When he has coins jingling in his pockets he treats himself to meals that stretch his stomach, not minding if he's nauseated afterward, it's a gift he owes himself. He buys a black bowler hat, makes the purchase of an ivory-topped cane. *A man with a cane* says Father *wields power in the eyes of the weak. If he wields it well.* This high-stepping gentleman *wields it well.* In the lobbies of white-man hotels he buys newspapers to read War news: the Pact of London . . . the Allies and the Germans fighting in the Marne . . . Turkish warships, German submarine block-ades, the Allies landing armies at the Dardanelles . . . secret treaties, atrocities . . . the sinking of the British liner *Lusitania* by German submarine, nearly fourteen hundred people killed.

So many! He feels a pang of pity, sympathy. "But they were white—of course. White devils."

He sees them everywhere now, can't not see them.

His kind. His skin. His hunted eyes.

Seeing Little Moses abandoned in the road, bewildered by his fate. An actor who has lost not only his audience but his stage, his purpose for being. The very lights that had illuminated him to himself.

One day in the rain weak from hunger or despair or rage gnawing at his guts he staggers and falls in the street and his polo coat, already soiled, is soiled more—mud, horse droppings, filth—and his smart black bowler hat is snatched from his head by a young boy, brown-skinned, a laughing savage.

He rides the clattering streetcars, he rides the Staten Island ferry, he sleeps where sleep overtakes him unless his pockets jingle with coin. Sometimes he sleeps alone, and sometimes not. Sometimes he shuts his eyes in disdain against the city—against Harlem, *their* city—and sometimes he walks entranced in the streets, eyes stealthy and all-seeing beneath the rim of his dandy's hat. The brownstone tenement buildings like ridges of a natural outcropping, block following block; crowded sidewalks and streets; the traffic on Broadway rising to a din—trolleys, trucks, horse-drawn wagons, fire engines, careening police vans, uniformed police on horseback; shouts, cries, sirens, alarms, horns; the sharp ringing of horses' hooves on cobblestone; powerful smells—sulfurous, rancid, close, feculent, steamy—that seem to rise out of the bowels of the earth and, if he's in a weakened state, go to his head like an inhaled drug.

Harlem. Their city.

My city?

Through which he walks entranced as a new lover, beginning to recognize landmarks, stores and taverns and sidewalk vendors, beginning to understand the music of their speech, until one day he opens his mouth and his speech is identical with theirs, or nearly—he's one of them! Shaking hands with his newfound contacts, friends and business acquaintances—*Why good mornin' Mr. Jones!* comes a sudden happy cry—*How're you this fine day Mr. Washburn!*—wide smiles, gold-capped teeth, gleaming black skin and elegantly trimmed moustaches and starched white shirts and stiff celluloid collars and bow ties neatly clipped in place—*Ain't shaken your hand in a long time, Doctor*—smoke-colored hair shining, glaring, having been heated and creamed and sculpted into a shellacked surface as seamless to the casual glance as the polished shell of an acorn—*Ain't laid eyes on you in a while Mr. Gaston, and you lookin' good.*

And feeling good. At last.

His pockets jingle with coin, his pockets are empty. SPIRIT suffuses him (it's spring, it's a new year), SPIRIT departs leaving him huddled dazed in an alley . . . vomiting rotgut liquor in heaving sobs . . . as close to death as he'll come, and no one's fault but his own. That night in the stifling heat of the United African Baptist Church on Columbus Avenue where buoyant singing and clapping and shouting and the swaying of bodies and wave upon wave of great joy pulse on all sides . . . to pull him down into the tarry-black mud . . . the comforting mud, the muck of Jesus. Black Jesus.

His brothers and sisters are yelling, shrieking, laughing in ecstasy. Clapping, Jesus is in this place with them, Jesus is in their hearts, *can you feel him bro-ther, can you feel him sis-ter*, the sweetly sour smell of flesh, oil-oozing flesh, *Jesus goin to take you home bro-ther, sis-ter Jesus goin' to take you home.*

He's weak with relief, tears streaking his face, he isn't going to die as that man who'd been his father that man who'd been the white Devil-Daddy had prophecized.

Though vowing it won't be Black Jesus who takes *him* home.

Reverend Driskus Price of the United African Baptist Church . . . Right Reverend Slocum Diggs of the Free Evangelical Brotherhood . . . Father Moses of the African Methodist Episcopal Church . . . Reverend T. J. Skirm of the Mount Pisgah African Church of Christ . . . Brother Druse Mohammed of the Bethel African Fellowship . . . Doctor Willard Graver of the Lenox Avenue American-Liberian League . . . Supreme Potentate Douglass Fox of the United Negro Colonization Society . . . Brother Ebenezer King of the First Zionist Church of Christ, Harlem . . .

Commander Diaz Attucks of the Consolidated Free Afro-American Christian League . . .

Some of the preachers urge Jesus onto their flocks, others urge mass migration back to Africa, others believe fervently that Jesus is to be found in Africa, in the Sovereign Free State of Liberia (founded by freed American slaves in 1847), or in the Sovereign Free State of Sierra Leone. . . .

So many preachers, and so much genuine faith: and what difference, brothers and sisters, has it ever made in your lives? . . .

VI

"Little Moses" for all his cunning is to die a *Negro* death after all: shortly past midnight of 7 June 1915, in the neighborhood of Amsterdam Avenue and 140th Street. In the very street, in fact.

He will die of a savage beating by three New York City mounted policemen, "riot" police, in the midst of a six-hour uprising by Negroes occasioned by the rumor (afterward verified) that a seventeen-year-old Negro boy had earlier been beaten to death by police elsewhere in Harlem.

(The boy had been arrested on 134th "fleeing the scene of a crime" . . . manacled and beaten savagely for "resisting and threatening police officers". . . his limp bleeding body, an arm dangling broken, carried away by a speeding police van. More than a dozen witnesses looked on in horror; the incident had taken place across the street from the Afro-American Baptist Brotherhood League.)

In all, eleven Negroes will die in the rioting, nine of them men. A forty-three-year-old pregnant woman, a six-year-old girl.

And among these Little Moses . . . though there will be no official record of his death as there is no record, official or otherwise, of his life.

Except: on the night of 6 June 1915, less than six hours before his death, he debates with a barroom acquaintance (Marcus Caesar Smith, formerly of the Barbados) the metaphysical conundrum of whether a man's identity lies in what he *resembles* to the outer eye, or what he *is*.

For though a man might inhabit a certain shade and texture of skin, that's hardly proof that he must be defined by that skin. And though he resembles other men who inhabit that selfsame skin, it can't be proved that he must be identified with them.

Smith responds, winking at the crowd that has gathered around them, "Brother, look here: if you is talkin' about yourself, or myself, or whoever, say so—without no further ob-fus-ca-tion. If you is claimin' not to be a nigger like the rest of us, then what is you?"

Much laughter, hooting and whistling.

Little Moses, unaccustomed to being laughed at, stiffens; but manages to smile, and winks to draw the crowd onto his side. Saying "Friends, the metaphysics of it is the secret that no ignorant imagination can grasp: some folks is only what they look like by way of their skin and others, only what they *is*."

"Tell it, bro-ther! Tell it!" Smith laughs.

". . . And the two categories stand apart and never can mingle, like oil . . ." Little Moses had been drinking, his tongue slurs his smooth words, ". . . and blood."

"That so, bro-ther? *How* so?"

"Because it *is*," Little Moses says. "And some things is *not*."

Smith plays to the gathering of drinkers saying, "Now you come to your senses, man, and explain to me how come *you* know so damn much and *I* that's older than you and wiser don't know nothin'."

And Little Moses drinks whatever this is he's drinking, orange flame in his throat, searing his eyes, he's confused saying, "Because it's in-side, brother. It's been told *in-side*."

"Howso? Inside what?"

"*In-side.*"

"Look, man—there got to be some outside, like a rind or a husk, that there's an inside of, don't there?—ain't that so?" Smith cries.

"No. There don't."

"Like there's gonna be a, say, catfish—without no skin to keep 'im in? There's gonna be a hog, a cantaloupe, a baby, a flower—and not no outside for the inside to press up against? Not hardly!"

Little Moses removes his wide-brimmed fedora, incensed.

"God-damn don't need to fool nobody," Little Moses cries. "I mean—I don't need to fool *you*. Don't give any God damn, that shit you sayin'."

"Then how come you talkin' to me, brother?—how come you *here*, and sweatin' it?"

"Because I got to be some place."

"Yes man, but how come you got to be *here*?"

"Because it has come to this," Little Moses says, suddenly panicked. "Because—I don't know."

"Now you tellin' us straight, you don't know no God-damn more than anybody else," Smith shouts happily, clapping Little Moses' back so hard Little Moses begins to cough, "—because you is the same as anybody else inside and out. Because you is *me*, nigger, on the inside just as on the *out*side, should anybody investigate innards and guts and kinda stuff. Somebody do autopsy on *you*, my friend, and then on *me*, you think they gonna find much any different? What you think they gonna find?"

Little Moses is leaning against the bar, head lowered, watery eyes squinched up tight. His mouth feels as if somebody has kicked it. "Shit, man—I don't know."

"Louder, man!"

But Little Moses shakes his head, sulky and insulted. If he could retreat somewhere, if he could have some peace and stillness he'd figure out how to reply; but these fools grinning at him, laughing and pointing—it's hopeless.

Smith persists, like a horse that can't stop trampling some poor broken-boned bastard under his hooves, "You think they goin' to find black guts in one, and no-color guts in the other? I *seen* nigger guts come spillin out and the sight ain't pretty, and I sure don't want to see it another time but I'd swear they ain't black any more'n a white man's guts is gonna be white; but maybe *you* got to see it, friend, like Thomas he got to poke his finger in Jesus' side before he get the point. Or you gettin the point now?" Smith generously lays a hot, heavy hand on Little Moses' neck, a hand like a small furry animal. Little Moses shudders at the feel of it. "Say what," says Smith, "we have ourself one more drink and forget that 'meta-whatyoucallit-phys-cal' shit. That stuff, my man, only get in the *way*."

Next evening he's running out into the street cursing paying no heed to a woman shouting into his face, "Go back, they killin' folks out there!"—the night sky is awash with flames, policemen on horseback swinging billy clubs, a girls' head streaming blood, about to fall beneath a horse's plunging hooves and he's shouting he's cursing not drunk but stone-cold sober making a grab at the policeman's reins, a grab at the man himself, trying to wrench him down from his saddle but a second policeman sidles his horse close and strikes him on the shoulder, on the side of the head, on the crown of the head as he falls, he's writhing on the cobblestone pavement trying to shield his bleeding head, his stomach, his groin, as the white-man billy clubs swing in wide arcs like clock-pendulums . . . and the horses whinny and froth in terror . . . bone-crushing hooves strike blindly . . . his right leg, his right arm, his backbone, his unprotected head cracked like a melon.

One of the unidentified bodies. Negro, male, casualty of Harlem uprising.

Venus Aphrodite

I

"**D**oes my hand tremble?—*it does not*. Do I doubt?—*I do not*. Am I an ordinary suitor, fearful of rejection?—*I am not*."

Silver-haired Albert St. Goar, a gentleman in the prime of life (for who would guess that he is nearly fifty-five?—his skin so ruddy, so flushed with good health, and free of lines and creases) regards himself critically in his full-length bedroom mirror, in his apartment overlooking Rittenhouse Square; sees with relief that the disfiguring puffiness about his eyes seems to have vanished; notes with approval the new style in which his barber fashions his hair, brushing it forward in seemingly lush little wings, rather than back, to expose an uncertain hairline; and experiments with several of his most successful smiles—the hesitant, the boyish, the amused, the half-frowning (as if overtaken by surprise), the "sly."

And the lover's spontaneous smile of fateful recognition.

(For Albert St. Goar, despite the maturity of his years, and a certain worldliness in his manner, is in love; and, in the lady's presence, obliged to display the adoration he feels . . . otherwise the lady, being a person of high degree and, perhaps, as secretly vain as he, will mistakenly gauge his feeling as less than it is. "For here we have a case—and it has often been so with me—of being required to 'assume a virtue' even when I have it," St. Goar thinks.)

Slowly, with deliberation, he turns his head from left to right . . . from right to left . . . studying his profile (a just perceptible fleshiness about the jowls, and, yes, some puffiness about the eyes) while he hums Siegfried's joyous surprise at the discovery of Brünnhilde . . . Brünnhilde surrounded by her daunting tongues of flame.

"Am I like other men?—*I am not.* Need I fear, like other men?—*I need not.* Can she find the strength to resist me?—*she cannot.*"

Smartly he slaps his cheeks—adjusts yet again his starched collar, and his black silk four-in-hand—smiles his private Licht smile (rows of strong white clenched teeth)—and declares himself ready for his evening with the wealthy young widow Mrs. Eva Clement-Stoddard.

In the early autumn of 1915, at about the time when, in distant Europe, French and British troops were landing in Greece, and Bulgaria at last declared war on Serbia, all of Philadelphia society was abuzz: for it seemed a distinct possibility that Eva Clement-Stoddard and the cosmopolite Albert St. Goar (formerly of London and Nice, now residing in Rittenhouse Square with his lovely daughter Matilde) might soon announce their engagement . . . and this despite the fact that Eva had vowed, years before, when her husband died, never to marry again; and despite the fact that the handsome St. Goar was more or less a stranger to Philadelphia.

Why otherwise would St. Goar be so unusually attentive to Mrs. Clement-Stoddard's every word, glance, sigh, and nuance of expression? Why would his frowning gaze invariably shift in *her* direction, despite the presence of women (married, unmarried, widowed) of equal or superior attractions, whose fortunes rivalled hers? These were women after all who made some effort to be agreeable to men, and were not by turns capricious and icy-cold, like the unpredictable Eva; nor were they rumored to be, like her, nearly impossible for any suitor to approach.

(Perhaps, it was said, Eva simply did not like *men*.) With her much-lauded "amateur expert's" ear for classical music, and her taste for *haute cuisine*, and her eye for art, architecture, home furnishings, and the like, she took distinct pride in being an exacting hostess; and, as a guest in others' homes, didn't scruple to express her dissatisfaction when things failed to measure up to her standards. "Money cannot buy *taste*," Eva was known to have said, "—any more than it can buy *genius*."

As a consequence of the young widow's imperial, self-absorbed manner, Eva Clement-Stoddard impressed observers as taller than she was, and larger of frame; her natural reserve and shyness were mistaken for disdain. It had long been her custom to wear plainly styled (though costly) clothes of British design; and her lustreless brown hair in so simple a style it might be called "classical." Some observers held her to be an uncommonly attractive woman, with vivid dark eyes, a small straight nose, and a finely sculpted mouth; others were harsh in their condemnation of her odd, angular, narrow face, her "ironic" eyes, her slightly faded skin, and, most of all her habit of seeming to smile *yet not smiling at all*.

Her husband died when she was only twenty-nine, leaving her two trust funds (worth approximately $3 million, as Albert St. Goar has learned) and various properties in and about Philadelphia, including a thirty-two-room mansion in Greek Revival style on the Main Line, and a cottage in Newport; she'd developed an enthusiasm for art of the Flemish Renaissance, and had begun to collect paintings under the tutelage of the redoubtable art dealer Duveen (a gentleman whom Albert St. Goar envied); she owned any number of extraordinary pieces of jewelry, including a famed Cartier necklace of twelve emeralds spaced along a rope of one thousand diamonds, worth, it was said, more than $1 million . . . though such vulgar displays of wealth, such conspicuous "icons," as Eva called them, she naturally scorned to wear.

It was whispered by members of her husband's family that Eva's secret tragedy, of which she was too proud to speak, was simply the fact of her being childless; and knowing herself, for all her air of brittle self-assurance and superiority, not fully a *woman*. How else to account for her rapid shifts of mood, her obsessive interest in an infant niece or nephew, and then, so very suddenly, her contemptuous withdrawal of interest? Though she was only in her mid-thirties she was acquiring a reputation for eccentricity: she mourned her husband for a full week each year, on the anniversary of his death in early December; she attended a different church service each Sunday, contending that "all Gods are equal—equally true and equally false"; she spent a highly intense six months studying what she called Law, and another six months studying what she called Medicine; with a desperate sort of fervor she even took up spiritualism—pronouncing it, in the end, "far too *hopeful* to be plausible." She commissioned portraits of the deceased Mr. Clement-Stoddard, but rejected them all; she commissioned original works of music, "symphonic poems" being her particular passion . . . but these too failed to please. Like most members of her circle, she and her husband journeyed to Europe each summer, but following his death, and her own "appointment with destiny" as she called it (Eva Clement-Stoddard had been booked to sail on the maiden voyage of the *Titanic* in April 1912, and cancelled her plans at the last minute because of illness), she grew fretfully superstitious, vowing she'd never again leave the civilized perimeters of the United States, or even the environs of Philadelphia.

"For I had rather drown in boredom," she laughingly declared, "than in the Atlantic."

Yet more peculiar was Eva's habit of keeping to herself, like a religious recluse, for weeks at a time, in her Philadelphia house. Declining all invitations; refusing to invite visitors; neglecting her charity work, and her correspondence; steeping herself in material of an uplifting or "purgative" kind. Gibbon's great history of the Roman Empire, the rude rhapsodic lyrics of Walt Whitman, a plunging into the Upanishads one month, and into the Bhagavad Gita the next—how American women of the upper classes hunger for enlightenment! There was a season in which Eva attempted to master, under the tutelage of an Indian sage, the ancient, lost language of Sanskrit—with what success, no one knew. And Eva "kept up" with politics and war news, and loved to debate the men: with Anglophiles she argued that England had brought disaster on herself, and that the United States should not be drawn into fighting out of sentimental ties of loyalty; with the isolationists she argued yet more fiercely that President Wilson, to whom she was related, and whom she'd never liked, was endangering the honor of the United States by trying to keep from declaring war against Germany. "It's as Teddy Roosevelt has charged—the President is a coward. He isn't a *man*."

II

When the gentleman known as Albert St. Goar, formerly of London, first set eyes upon Eva Clement-Stoddard, before even being introduced to her by Mrs. Shrikesdale at a benefit performance of *Così fan tutte* at the Philadelphia Opera House, in September 1915—he murmured aloud, "It's she!"

For he seemed to know the woman already, and to know that she knew him.

For not since the years of his early manhood when he'd been fatally vulnerable to the authority of an image of Woman, had he been so struck by a woman's face and presence of being; and by his conviction that, in her, he would at last be fulfilled.

My dream of a child, a son, to take the place of those who have betrayed me. Whose names I have expunged from my heart.

Yet his dream is primarily of Woman . . . a woman. Of such exceptional qualities, possessed of such powers, he'll be drawn out of himself; he will be obliterated, and resurrected in her. Above all the woman will allow him to forget the injuries inflicted upon him by women in the past. (Heartless women. Ill-deserving of Abraham Licht's love and devotion. There were Arabella, and Morna, and Sophie, who preferred death to her life with him. These were "wives" he'd never officially married and from whom consequently he can never be divorced.)

He will court this woman, overcoming her reluctance. He will marry her—this time. They will indeed have a child, an heir.

"I'm in the prime of life," he tells himself eagerly. "I've scarcely begun my life! My greatest conquests lie ahead."

From the start it's noted, not without jealousy in some quarters, that Eva Clement-Stoddard and the dashing Albert St. Goar are mysteriously attracted to each other. Their conversations are quick and elliptical, like the virtuoso sparring of fencers who challenge one another less with the intent of doing injury than for the purpose of happily demonstrating their skill. St. Goar chances to mention his romantic attachment to Kensington Gardens, for instance, in the very late afternoon of an autumn day; and Mrs. Clement-Stoddard challenges him at once as to *which* flowers and *which* shrubs on *which* paths—for it seems she

shares his fondness for the park, which is bound up with her early girlhood, when her family spent six weeks of every autumn in London. On
another occasion, the lady quotes Tocqueville on the pernicious consequences of Equality ("in democratic ages that which is most fluctuating
amid the fluctuation of all around is the heart of man"), and Albert
St. Goar rejoins with a spirited dismissal of the bigoted French cynic, as
he calls him, who did not understand the American soul; and slandered
all Americans by his sweeping judgments, based, by necessity, on a false
application of *his* principles to *our* condition. "How can we take seriously," St. Goar says, addressing all of the room by way of his particular
attentiveness to the embarrassed Mrs. Clement-Stoddard, "a man who
so little understands our democracy as to say, and I quote, 'The love
of wealth is to be traced, either as a principal or an accessory motive,
at the bottom of all that the Americans do'—? It *is* a slander!—and
indefensible."

While others listen in resigned admiration, St. Goar and Eva archly
discuss the politics of the day—the follies of recent history—the current ambiguous state of the arts; whether culture has fallen into a severe decline since the turn of the century; whether war with Germany
is necessary, or merely, as St. Goar ominously says, "inevitable." For
weeks in Mrs. Clement-Stoddard's circle talk centers upon Henry
Ford's much-publicized peace ship, *Oscar II*, which was being organized
to set sail for Europe with $1 million in gold to be paid to anyone who
could stop the war. ("Anyone," St. Goar wittily observes, "—who
speaks with a German accent.") It is the wealthy automobile manufacturer's boast that *he* would bring the boys home for Christmas (for, by
this time, a goodly number of American men had volunteered to fight
for the Allied cause) where government leaders like Woodrow Wilson
had failed. All of Christianity, Ford declares, must join to stop the useless slaughter. And it is fitting that he, the genius inventor of the
Model A and the Model T Ford car, and the initiator of the controversial $5 daily wage, should negotiate peace. For if the first business of
American businessmen is money, the second will be salvation—of others. Eva Clement-Stoddard declares she's sympathetic with Henry
Ford's cause, though she considers, as do others in her circle, the Detroit billionaire a crude and socially distasteful man; she's contributed
several thousand dollars to the venture; and toyed for a few days with
the possibility of joining the one hundred sixty select passengers in the

Oscar II. Albert St. Goar, however, is unsparing in his ridicule of the project. "Has there ever been a human being so vain, so deluded with self-importance, as this 'Ford' of yours!" St. Goar marvels. "If we didn't know the man's wealth, we would suspect that the *Oscar II* is nothing but a confidence game to play upon the charitable impulses of Christian ladies—of both sexes." So eloquently and wittily does St. Goar speak, Henry Ford and the quest for peace are laughed out of the room, with Eva Clement-Stoddard among the heartiest laughers.

Saying good night to her honored guest that evening, pleasantly warmed and emboldened by wine, Eva remarks, in a moment of rare girlish coquetry, "Not even a goddess of ancient times could 'put anything over' on such a skeptic as *you*, Albert St. Goar!" Which so takes St. Goar by surprise, the gentleman stares at the lady, his expression for once tender, and undefined; and no witty rejoinder at hand.

III

Strolling one Sunday afternoon in elegant Rittenhouse Square, where they are bound to encounter a familiar face, and to be taken up by persons of consequence, Albert St. Goar says causally to his striking daughter Matilde, whose arm is linked through his, "You wouldn't be upset, dear, if I asked Eva to marry me? For it's time, you know, for your father to remarry. In truth," he says, sighing, "—it's more than time." And Matilde, in a smart slope-brimmed hat of black straw, with a patterned blue ribbon tied beneath her chin and a dotted swiss veil hiding her eyes, doesn't miss a beat in her languid gait; saying in a low amused voice, "Provided Eva is as wealthy as everyone says, dear Father, why should *I* object? Who am *I* to object? As you know very well."
Albert St. Goar says, in a hurt, offended voice, "Why Matilde, it isn't for her money that I want to marry Eva, but for Eva herself; for love." "Ah, 'love,' is it, this time," Matilde says gaily. "And 'marry,' is it, this time!—the first time, I believe, in your career, Father?" And St. Goar says stiffly, keeping his voice low, "But you know I'm a widower, dear. You know I haven't wished to marry since your mother's death . . . in the south of France in July of '05." "Ah yes, I had almost

forgotten poor Mother," says Matilde, with a downward twist to her mouth, ". . . murdered in her bed, was she not, by an 'unknown assailant'? Poor Mother! And so much a presence in our lives!" "Your mother died of consumption, Matilde," says St. Goar, reddening, "as you well know." "Yes, of consumption, yes surely, consumption," Matilde says hurriedly. "I had forgotten. For, you know, there are so many deaths these days, it is difficult to keep track of them." St. Goar says, "I don't care at all for your tone, Matilde, if I understand it correctly. You're behaving in a way to deliberately provoke your father." "I am not 'behaving' in any way at all," says Matilde, "—but only as your 'Matilde,' who's indeed your daughter; for she is no one else's." "You've been behaving in a childish way for weeks now—for months," St. Goar says. "Since our arrival in Philadelphia. Since your return from the Fitzmaurices', in fact. I hate the role of a scolding parent for it isn't Albert St. Goar's style at all—yet it might be said, my dear, that it has rarely been *your* role to provoke such scolding. You must adapt yourself to our new life; you must forget the old; indeed, I'm surprised you haven't forgotten—" "Ah but I *have* forgotten!" Matilde interrupts, lightly touching St. Goar's chin with her gloved fingers, "—I have forgotten, Father, far more than I have ever remembered." "In any case," St. Goar says stiffly, drawing away from his daughter, "—I don't like your tone. I don't like your arch mocking 'Matilde' manner. For it is not *my* 'Matilde' but a parody. For *my* 'Matilde' is sweet, and gracious, and always smiling, and quick to sympathize . . . yet shrewd beneath, and hardly anyone's fool. And surely that *is* 'Matilde,' and you *are* she, so why this harlequinade?—for it's done, I know, solely to provoke. I have no doubt that it shocked and displeased the Fitzmaurices, no less than it shocks and displeases me, and I do not countenance it; I do not *wish* it." "Yes Father," Matilde says meekly. "In Mrs. Clement-Stoddard's presence you're quiet to the point of rudeness, and in private, of late, you chatter like a magpie," St. Goar accuses. "*I do not wish it.*" "Yes Father," Matilde says meekly—though a strange little smile hovers about her lips. "There's no reason for you to feel jealous of Eva, surely," St. Goar says. "You are an exceptionally beautiful young woman who will soon have her own life, I am certain, once things get settled. You don't, of course, dwell upon the past?—for that isn't productive." "Certainly not, Father," Matilde says. "Didn't I tell you?—I've forgotten more than I've ever remembered." "You don't, for instance, think of . . . *him?*" St. Goar asks. "Of 'him'? What do you mean, Father?" Matilde asks, lifting her head at a quizzical angle. "Assuredly not; I don't think at all." "You have admirers already in Philadelphia, dear—or would have, if you encouraged them," St. Goar says. "You need hardly concern yourself with the older generation." "Yes Father," says Matilde. "I'm a man in the prime of life, lonely after so many years for female companionship and domesticity," St. Goar says. "Eva won't be easily won and perhaps can't be won, for she's very different from—other women. She's a woman set apart from women even of her class and station." To this, Matilde makes no reply. "Naturally it pleases me she's wealthy—I wouldn't deny *that*—but it pleases me that she's the very age she is, that her face is as it is, her eyes, her mouth, her hair, her superb wit— When one is in love, everything about the beloved pleases; for that *is* love." "Is it, Father?" Matilde murmurs. "Your mother cheated me of the happiness of domestic life," St. Goar says, "—she, and the others. But I will not remain cheated. *I will claim my love before it is too late.*" "Yes Father," says Matilde. "And I hope you will be happy for me, when you see that *I* am happy," St. Goar says, "—and will not continue to displease, as you have been." "It is only 'Matilde,'" Matilde says, tying more securely the pretty blue ribbon beneath her chin, "—and what is she to you, after all? She too might be handily forgotten." "What are you saying?" St. Goar asks. "You know I'm devoted to you, dear. And I'm convinced that, out of my happiness, yours will spring." "Will it, indeed?" says Matilde. "In any case, you know, I hardly need apply to you for permission to marry," says St. Goar, "—any more than for permission to love." "Indeed *not*," says Matilde, laughing. "Therefore I wish you and Mrs. Clement-Stoddard well. Therefore I wish the wedding might be next week. For the more wealth to you, Father, as to our 'Roland,' the less obligation to 'Matilde,' to marry at all."

At this, St. Goar draws sharply away from his daughter; for he *is* offended.

"You must never speak of him in such a context, Millie," he whispers, staring at her. "What are you thinking of!—*you!*"

"'What am I thinking of'?—'*I*'?" says Matilde, smiling innocently, "—why, I scarcely know. Will you tell me?"

IV

"Does she love me as I love her?—*she does*. And will she refuse me a third time?—*she cannot*."

Approaching eight o'clock on the evening of 30 March 1916. He must delay no longer; he *must* leave; for he is due very soon at Mrs. Clement-Stoddard's house, to dine (alone) with her; and to press upon her his final proposal of marriage. (For if pride won't allow the widow to acquiesce, this time, pride won't allow the widower St. Goar to humble himself and ask again.)

He finishes his glass of English sherry, and, frowning, turns his head from side to side: three-quarters profile, seen from the left, is his strongest suit.

"Can she refuse me a third time?" he whispers, "—she *cannot*!"

He first proposed to Eva Clement-Stoddard in November 1915, scarcely two months after they were introduced: a tactical error. Naturally the lady was taken by surprise; stared at her admirer with an expression of genuine alarm. And *no* was her reply, thank you Mr. St. Goar but *no*, murmured in so low and rapid a voice, he had barely heard.

The second proposal, however, made in January 1916, had surely been expected; for during the intervening weeks Eva had given her suitor ample reason to believe that she was coming to admire *him*. She paid him a flattering amount of attention in company; laughed happily at his remarks; casually slipped her arm through his as they walked together; invited him frequently to her house, for small parties as well as large; and didn't seem to mind that they were beginning to be whispered of as a couple. When St. Goar told her that he loved her and wanted to marry her, she blushed painfully, and turned away, and said, stammering, that she was probably "too old and too settled" to think of such things; that, surely, *he* could not want *her*; and that she dared not deceive herself, that he did. St. Goar protested that he spoke the truth: he did love her: he *did* want to marry her: but Eva was too distraught to hear him out. "I must say *no*, Albert," she whispered, drawing away, "—for I cannot allow myself to say *yes*."

And now, tonight—what will be her answer, tonight?

"She dares not refuse me," St. Goar says, unconsciously lifting the empty sherry glass to his lips. "For other women have betrayed me, and cheated me of the happiness of domesticity that is my due; and now it is time for Venus Aphrodite to reward me—as the goddess well knows."

His new black sateen top hat—his fine white gloves—his ebony cane with the smart gold-and-ivory handle; a quick glance at his pocket watch (ah, the hour *is* late!); and St. Goar is on his way.

Ever the considerate father, he calls out a hearty good night to his daughter Matilde; but sulky Matilde has locked herself away in her quarters, having refused her own invitations for the evening (one of them to the Grand Ball at the Philadelphia Academy of Music, for the benefit of the Children's Charity Hospital), that she might bathe, and lie about *en déshabillé*, smoking her forbidden cigarettes and reading her forbidden newspapers: for the defiant young miss insists upon being knowledgeable in the follies of her time, profitless as such knowledge is.

Will you want a carriage, sir, asks the liveried doorman, on so cold and blustery an evening, sir?—but no: St. Goar prefers to walk: for there are grievances in his heart he would air, before meeting his beloved Eva.

"Aphrodite, hear me—it *is* time!"

For he's been cruelly used in his life; aroused to passion, deceived by love, betrayed by the very women to whom he'd given his soul.

There was Arabella Jenkins—that sharp-eyed, sharp-witted beauty; the mother of two strapping boys, and what pride in her gift to him . . . except, in the end, there's a bitter vagueness about the end, she'd abandoned him and run off with another man as in the lowest of stage comedies; there was Morna Hirshfield, the daughter of a man of God, and quite a demon in bed until madness overcame her . . . Millie's fated mother. And there was poor sweet Sophie, the mother of Darian and Esther, whom he can't allow himself to recall except as a name chiselled upon a granite grave marker in the cemetery that belongs to Abraham Licht. *A fitting fate, to lie in "my" cemetery. Would they all were buried there, who've trampled my heart.*

Strange how, once Venus Aphrodite departs from a woman, she becomes merely . . . a woman. You might glance at her in the street and look right through her, where once, inhabited by the radiant goddess, her face and being were a summons to your leaping, exalting heart; and the mere sound of her voice a provocation to joy.

And now, Eva.

Eva Clement-Stoddard, soon to become Eva Licht.

V

Yet—it seems that Venus Aphrodite is toying with him another time, to St. Goar's dismay and displeasure.

Can it be, the woman intends to refuse him a third, final time?

Near-midnight. The end of their evening. They've dined in the most intimate of Eva's several dining rooms and they've attended a performance of *The Mikado* both have found "spirited, but mediocre" and now they're uneasily alone together in Eva's drawing room, which is dominated by a new purchase of hers: a landscape (quaint windmill, river, cloud-ribbed sky) by a seventeenth-century Dutch artist Jan Steen of whom St. Goar hasn't heard except to know that, of late, in New York art-collecting circles, he's become fashionable. Eva, like numerous other widowed wealthy ladies, follows the advice of the Manhattan art dealer Joseph Duveen, who reaps an enviable commission with each sale he makes; St. Goar hears of the man's maneuvers with clenched jaws, and, even as he admires the painting—"Surpassingly beautiful, one of Steen's very finest"—he vows inwardly that once they're wed he, and not the wily Duveen, will supervise each of Eva's art purchases. Indeed, he's looking forward to a confrontation with the renowned Duveen, who dares to suggest to his wealthy, ignorant clients that they must prove themselves worthy of the art they purchase through him; they must work their way up to the Old Masters, for instance, by way of the Barbizon school, or the minor Flemish painters! The wealthy widow Mrs. Anna Emery Shrikesdale was allegedly told she might purchase a painting by Giorgione (which Duveen happened to have on hand), but not a Titian; Pierpont Morgan was told that he might buy, if he wished, a half dozen lesser works of Rembrandt, but was "not yet ready" for one of the monumental paintings; Henry Ford and Horace Dodge, residents of Detroit, Michigan (a city unworthy of great art), were not allowed, for years, to buy any of Duveen's stock at all. ("Duveen must be a genius—for who, including even Abraham Licht, would have thought of *that?*" St. Goar sighs.) It's a fact, that

Henry Frick, the Pittsburgh millionaire, had to leave Pittsburgh for
New York City, and build a mansion on Fifth Avenue, before Duveen
would consent to sell him important paintings; and, not least, though
Eva Clement-Stoddard is hardly a fool, she believes in Duveen unstint-
ingly, and doesn't doubt that, in his hands, her money is perfectly safe.

Finally Eva turns from the paintings, self-consciously, as if anticipating—with dread? with delight?—her admirer's intention; and sits very
still, as, in a voice that falters with emotion, Albert St. Goar tells her
yet again that which she already knows—he loves her—adores her—
respects her above all women—and wants to marry her as quickly as
possible.

Eva sits staring at her beringed hands, too greatly moved to speak.

"I hope I haven't upset you, Eva? But I must speak my heart. But if—
if you wish—if I'm refused—I will never speak in such a way again; I
will, in fact, leave Philadelphia forever."

A brave statement, but sincere. At this moment, achingly sincere.

For truly he is in love with the woman. Her mature sobriety, intelligence, wit; her classical features, the austere plainness of her face and
hair with their look of dignity. For surely the goddess of love might inhabit a woman like Eva, as any younger woman.

St. Goar impulsively kisses Eva's hand. She allows the kiss, even as
she moves to withdraw her hand in a shy, abashed gesture, like that of a
young girl.

Eva says slowly, hesitantly, that perhaps he would not wish her for
his bride, if he knew her better.

St. Goar says, smiling, though startled, that such a notion isn't possible; he can't hope to know her well enough.

Eva says, studying her hands, and the sparkling gems of her rings that
seem incongruous on her ordinary, slightly stubby fingers, that there are
different sorts of knowing.

Yes? And what are these?

Speaking carefully, as if dreading a misunderstanding, Eva tells
St. Goar that one sort of "knowing" has to do with social position and
not sentiment; and that, if he knew her secret, he might feel differently
about loving her . . . and wanting to marry her.

Feel differently! Impossible!

But St. Goar has begun to feel a chill. Hesitantly he moves to take
the lady's hand again; indeed, both her hands—so small, so chill!—that

he might warm them with his own. And he says softly that there could be no secret that would dissuade him from his love for her . . . for, in loving her, he has felt his soul expand to touch hers; he is certain that he knows her from within, more subtly and more powerfully than she knows herself.

And Eva says with lowered eyes that he is kind; very kind; yet his knowledge of her is faulty, if he has believed what people say about her . . . that, for instance, as the widow of a well-to-do man, she is herself well-to-do.

And St. Goar squeezes her hands, gently; and murmurs that it doesn't matter to him, not in the slightest, what her financial situation is.

And Eva says stubbornly that it surely does; it must; for he's a man of the world, and must have expectations—"As scores of 'admirers' have had, over the years"—which would be rudely shattered by the truth.

And St. Goar says quietly, "Why then, Eva dear, what *is* the truth?"

And Eva draws a deep breath, and says quickly, "I will tell you, Albert—and beg your confidence. As my attorneys know, and two or three other persons, I, Eva Clement-Stoddard, have virtually no money at all, but am the mere custodian of my late husband's fortune. Most of the estate will go to a young nephew of his when the boy comes of age in two years. Of course I am to be left with something . . . I will never be a pauper . . . but I'm hardly the woman so many believe me to be. It has been my task to maintain a certain role, out of pride; I confess myself, for all my pretense of integrity, a hypocrite . . . a creature of vanity. . . . This house, and its furnishings, and even my newly acquired works of art are not truly *mine*, you see; I am only their custodian; and when I am exposed, Albert, when all the world knows of my situation, I can hardly expect mercy—for I do not deserve it."

Eva speaks in so low and shamed a voice, St. Goar scarcely understands her at first. *Can it be, this!—the widow's secret! She is only the custodian of another's wealth.* He moves to comfort her, but she remains sitting stiffly; turned slightly to one side; her heavy-lidded gaze lowered, and her lashes bright with tears. She dares not look at her lover for fear that he loves her no longer, yet, if only she would look, she would see how he stares with a queer hungry compassion: how radiant his face is with the certitude of Love. Gently, by degrees, he draws her into his arms, murmuring those word she hadn't dared hope to hear: "Dearest

Eva, my darling Eva, of course what you say makes no difference to me, nor to my love for you. How can you think it! My love," he says, pressing her to his bosom, and cupping her overheated face in his hand, "—if it did not sound unfeeling, I would confess that your lack of a worldly fortune actually pleases me. For now, with my modest annuity, and the earnings from my various investments, I, Albert St. Goar, will have the privilege of 'rescuing' Eva Clement-Stoddard from want . . . if you will allow me."

Half-frightened, Eva says that she doesn't deserve such kindness, as she has been deceiving him these many months; and St. Goar replies that it is hardly *kindness* on his part—it is *Love*.

And, suddenly, Eva gives way to a fit of convulsive weeping.

And St. Goar hugs her close.

VI

As the church bells sound the hour of one o'clock, St. Goar takes his leave of Mrs. Clement-Stoddard, near-drunken with happiness; and wondering now why he had ever doubted his powers. For Venus Aphrodite smiles upon him still; has always smiled upon him; and will reward him richly, for his adoration of *her*.

He is far too excited, of course, to return immediately to Rittenhouse Square. So he drops by the public room of the rowdy Pennsylvania Union Hotel, where his face and his name are unknown, and where he is not likely to meet any of his Philadelphia acquaintances. Standing alone at the bar, he downs a celebratory rye and water—and another—and yet another: for Eva Clement-Stoddard has agreed to marry him, sometime in January of 1917; and all has gone as, in his wildest fancies, he wished.

And does he love her?—*he does*.

And does he believe for an instant that she is truly but the "custodian" of her wealth?—*he does not*.

"Eva is a very poor liar," he thinks, "—doubtless because she has had so little practice. As if I, of all persons, could be taken in by her improbable tale—her shameful 'secret'! Why, little Millie at the age of six could have played that scene more convincingly. . . ."

In a while, perhaps even the next day, Eva will make another confession to him: that she was advised (strongly against her inclination, no doubt) to pretend to be poor, to test St. Goar's love.

And St. Goar will profess stunned surprise.

And St. Goar might even pretend to be somewhat . . . hurt.

But in the end he will of course forgive her, for he loves her just the same; and will always love her.

For Aphrodite has smiled upon him another time; and saved his very life.

A Charmed Life

I

In the hot dry summer of 1914, through the vast territories of Wyoming, Colorado, and, in most concentration, New Mexico, hundreds of notices were posted to the effect that a Philadelphian named Roland Shrikesdale III was missing; having been last seen in mid-April, in Denver, at the Edinburgh Hotel. A $50,000 reward was offered to any person or persons with information leading to Shrikesdale's whereabouts, said information to be delivered to local law enforcement agents, or telegraphed to Mrs. Anna Emery Shrikesdale, the missing man's mother, in Philadelphia. Shrikesdale was described as a gentleman of refined habits—thirty-three years old—measuring five feet seven inches, and weighing approximately one hundred eighty pounds—with brown eyes, a mole near his left eye, and fair brown curly hair. His photograph, starkly reproduced, showed the head and shoulders of an unhealthily plump young man with a squinting smile.

The newspapers took avidly to the story, as Shrikesdale was principal heir to one of the great Eastern fortunes; and great pathos derived from the fact that the missing man's mother was so intent upon finding him she'd embarked westward herself by train, only to be struck down by ill-ness two hours out of Philadelphia. Invalided in Castlewood Hall, Mrs. Shrikesdale bravely allowed rapacious reporters to interview her in the hope that their stories, reprinted across the country, often with like-nesses of Roland (she offered them the use of photographs, chalk draw-ings, even an oil portrait painted at the time of his graduation from Haverford College, by William Merritt Chase) would bring him home. She never doubted for an instant, she said, that her boy was alive—she knew he would be found soon ("For God would not punish us so cruelly, I am sure"); yet feared he'd been taken ill, or was lost or injured in the wilderness. The West was so inhumanly vast!—the state of New Mexico alone, about which one never heard, appeared of monstrous size on the map.

"Yet I am certain—I *know*—that Roland is alive," Mrs. Shrikesdale declared.

In the last letter received from her son, dated 15 April, on the sta-tionery of the Edinburgh Hotel, Roland spoke excitedly of traveling south by train to New Mexico, for "fishing, hunting, and Adventure"; his companion being a Westerner of whom he had grown exceedingly fond, and whom, he said, he would trust with his life. ("Harmon is a gentleman of *Christian* yet *manly* sensibility, Mother," Roland said, "—the likes of which are so rarely to be found in Philadelphia! If ever you two meet, I am sure you will like each other, Mother, but I doubt very much that *he* could be enticed to come East.") In evident haste Roland had added a postscript to the effect that, since he would be off in the wilds for an indeterminate period of time, Mrs. Shrikesdale should not expect to hear from him again for five weeks, until mid-May at the very earliest.

As she had begged her son from the first not to embark upon so fool-hardy a trip (undertaken, as Roland mysteriously insisted, for the sake of his "physical and spiritual health"), Mrs. Shrikesdale was gravely worried at this point; and stirred quite a fuss in the family, well before mid-May, with her proposal that Roland's cousins—Bertram, Lyle, and Willard—be sent to fetch him home. (As Roland's mere existence clouded the happiness of these hot-tempered young men, who stood to inherit a great deal of money if in fact he were dead, this naive proposal on Mrs. Shrikesdale's part was met with extreme resistance.) By the end of May, however, when no word came from Roland, the family at last reported him officially missing; and, not trusting to law enforcement authorities alone, hired a team of Pinkerton's best detectives to go west at once. For Roland was surely alive, as Anna Emery Shrikesdale insisted. *For God would not be so cruel to her, a poor widow, who had always adored Him.*

Thus was launched, with more fanfare than the Shrikesdales might have wished, the search for young Roland, the "Missing Heir," or the "Missing Millionaire," as the press called him; with a great deal of feverish excitement throughout the West, and vigorous competition among law enforcement officers and civilians alike for the $50,000 reward. (Which was, at the desperate mother's insistence, gradually increased to $75,000 by early autumn, when Roland was finally found.) In New Mexico in particular, it was marveled that a new gold rush seemed to have begun, for bounty hunters cropped up everywhere, looking for Roland Shrikesdale III; and men who bore only a glancing resemblance to him were brought forward, often forcibly—sometimes bound and manacled, and thrown over the backs of mules! In Las Cruces, northwest of El Paso, a man led federal officers to a shallow grave in which, he claimed, lay the remains of Roland Shrikesdale III: these being but the bleached bones of someone who had been dead a very long time, very likely the victim of murder. In Central City, Colorado, a female employee of the infamous Black Swan sporting house announced to reporters that she had married the young heir shortly before he disappeared, had a ring (ten-carat diamond in a cheap gold-plated setting) to prove it; *and was carrying his child.* Yet more audaciously, in Pueblo County, Colorado, a bearded ruffian of no less than forty years of age made his claim to the sheriff that he himself was Roland Shrikesdale III!—and demanded that the reward money be handed over to *him* at once.

The search reached a peak of sorts in midsummer, and then began to subside, as a consequence of both the unusual heat and aridity of the season, and the perplexing news from abroad, which began at last to take precedence in newspapers over more local affairs. No one could quite comprehend what was happening in Europe: why, on 1 August, did Germany formally declare war on Russia?—and then, on 3 August, on France? Within a matter of days Germany invaded

Belgium—England declared war on Germany—even Japan, a world
away, declared itself in a state of war with Germany; and President Wilson hastily proclaimed the neutrality of the United States. How was it
possible that all of Europe had gone to war over one or another trifling
assassination, of some obscure Austrian duke or archduke, with a name
no one could remember? . . . What were Americans to make of such behavior? So, when a stranger appeared on the outskirts of Fort Sumner,
New Mexico, on the morning of 8 September, afoot, alone, in a dazed
and disoriented state, his face caked with dried blood and his clothing
badly torn and stained, no one guessed at first that this might be the
missing Roland. He could not speak coherently, even to supply his
name, or to explain what had happened to him; and he had on his person no identification, and no personal effects other than a broken
pocket watch.

A few hours later, however, identification was tentatively made by a
deputy marshal who brought with him the Shrikesdale poster, and all of
Fort Sumner was aroused.

For surely this *was* the missing millionaire: being approximately
thirty-three years of age; of medium height, and stocky—though at the
present time his face was gaunt, as if he'd lost weight quickly; his hair
was indeed brown, and might be said to be curly; his eyes too were
brown, or nearly so (for in certain lights brown and silvery-gray resemble each other closely). If he didn't look altogether like the smiling young man on the poster, being, after all, rather the worse for wear
after his ordeal in the desert, it was remarked that his clothing, though
badly torn and filthy, appeared to be of an uncommon cut; and it
seemed clear that, even in his initial feverish state, when the only coherent word he could utter was *Mother!* he was an Easterner of genteel
upbringing.

Surely it was he, and no one else!

And the reward would be divided up among the half dozen Fort
Sumner residents who had found him!

A shame, some observers noted, that the millionaire's handsome
face would very likely be permanently scarred by an ugly wound running from his left temple to his jaw that had narrowly missed, it
seemed, gouging out his left eye; deeply embedded with dirt and sand,
and badly infected beneath its encrustation of coagulated blood. While
the wound was being drained and treated by a Fort Sumner doctor, the

injured man moaned in pain and terror, and spoke of a landslide—he and his companion trapped—thrown, along with their horses, over the edge of a cliff—pitched down a canyon wall amid a nightmare of rock, dirt, and sand—his friend (the name sounded like Herman, or Harmon) killed immediately—both horses crippled—only he surviving; yet barely alive; and unable to move for hours from where he'd fallen.

How many days ago the tragic accident had occurred, he had no idea; nor did he know where it had taken place. The very name *New Mexico* seemed to mean nothing to him.

Nor did the name *Roland Shrikesdale* mean anything.

(Although the doctor attending him believed that the injured man evinced some peculiar agitation, a distinct fluttering of the pulses, when the name was spoken close to his ear.)

Questioned the following day by local authorities, who were certain by now that this *was* the missing millionaire, he was incapable of collecting his thoughts well enough to answer. Within minutes he began to weep in hoarse gulping sobs; and so squirmed and writhed in his bed, he seemed on the verge of a convulsive fit. In a delirium he cried out "Mother!" And, less frequently, "Harmon!" and "God have mercy!"

Clearly he was a victim of amnesia, brought about by the injury to his head, or sunstroke, or a deadly combination of both; and it was thought purposeless to interrogate him at the present time.

So he was allowed to rest, passing in and out of consciousness, and waking to extreme confusion, as if he had not the slightest idea where he was, or that he was now safe.

(A miracle, Fort Sumner thought, that a lone man, afoot, could have survived for more than a day or two in the blistering desert heat, let alone drag himself free of a landslide.

But of course miracles do happen, from time to time.

And bring with them distinct rewards, for the deserving.)

II

The first Pinkerton detective to arrive at Fort Sumner made a cursory examination of the sick man, studying several likenesses of Roland

Shrikesdale III he had on his person, and declared that this surely *was* Shrikesdale; for one had to allow after all for the man's ravaged state.

The second Pinkerton detective, arriving early the next day, was less certain: for, in his opinion, the amnesiac's eyes were not exactly brown . . . and, even allowing for his present condition, wasn't his forehead rather broad and square, and his jaw strong, whereas Roland Shrikesdale's face was represented as plump and innocently round? Yet, after a few hours' deliberation, the man finally came to the conclusion that of course this *must* be Shrikesdale; for the odds against there being two lost men in this part of the world who so closely resembled each other were unthinkable.

The official identification of Roland Shrikesdale III was made the following week, by Anna Emery's most trusted attorney, Montgomery Bagot, sent out to Fort Sumner to fetch poor Roland home.

And of course it *was* Roland, as Bagot saw at once.

He had known his client's son, after all, since a very young age; and was confident that he could recognize him anywhere, in any state of health.

And it seemed clear to him that the sick man recognized *him*, though, weakened by fever, he could do no more than smile faintly, and extend a limp dry hand for Bagot to shake.

"My dear Roland," Bagot said, deeply moved, "—your mother will be so happy when I cable her the good news!"

"Yet I'm not altogether certain that I *am* 'Roland Shrikesdale,' " the afflicted man told Bagot, fixing him with anxious eyes, and smiling that pale cringing smile Bagot remembered so well—which, in his opinion, now that he saw it once again, was one of Roland's most typical mannerisms, of which Roland himself was surely unaware. "For, you see, Mr. Bagot, *I can't remember*. I remember the roar of a landslide, and a sudden nightmare of rock, pebbles, dirt, sand—I remember the frenzied whinnying of horses—the sensation of falling—being thrown—amid great terror and helplessness—as if God in His wrath had reached down to destroy my companion and me, for what offense I can't know. This horror I remember clearly, Mr. Bagot—but it has blotted out everything else."

So the man Bagot knew to be Roland Shrikesdale repeated during their long railway trip east, speaking sometimes in a favored whisper from his invalid's bed, and sometimes in the high-pitched reedy voice Bagot recognized unmistakably as Roland's. When Roland's physician declared him well enough to leave his bed, the two men sat together companionably by a window of their private Pullman car—which was very like a luxury suite in a hotel of the first rank, equipped with every modern convenience, beautifully furnished and staffed by as many as five expertly trained Pullman Negroes. Bagot scrutinized his young charge with lawyerly tact, noting that Roland's eyes in direct sunshine weren't exactly brown but a steely mica-gray; his hair appeared coarser and a shade or so darker; the distinct mole near his left eye was gone, as a consequence, perhaps, of his injury. Yet the man was Roland— without a doubt. For who else might he be?

Indeed, the self-effacing young heir had always doubted himself since early boyhood, Bagot recalled. He'd been intimidated by his father and babied by his mother and rendered unfit to hold his own in even childish games and competitions like croquet and badminton. The prospect of a debutante ball had more than once rendered him unable to walk, let alone dance. It had been a fear of the dictatorial Elias that Roland would never prove "man enough" to marry, let alone sire a son to continue the noble Shrikesdale lineage by way of him; shortly before his death in 1901 Elias had spoken of breaking up Roland's inheritance and diverting much of it to his brother Stafford's three strapping boys, who would surely marry in time, and would *surely* sire any number of Shrikesdale sons. Yet a minor contretemps over another issue arose between Elias and Stafford, and the matter of the inheritance was abruptly dropped; and at Elias's death the immense fortune remained entire—weighing rather heavily, Bagot suspected, on the inadequate shoulders of both Anna Emery and Roland.

Even as their train entered central Philadelphia, and the Pullman men prepared for them to disembark, Roland told Bagot yet again in a craven voice that he didn't know if he was the man Bagot assured him he was; and Bagot, impatient after so many days of confinement in Roland's company, said curtly, "Then who do you imagine you *are*—?"

To which the agitated youth could give no reply.

III

The legendary reunion of Anna Emery Shrikesdale and her son Roland at Castlewood Hall, after Roland's absence of one hundred eighty-five days, was as ecstatic as newspapers throughout the nation proclaimed; for Mrs. Shrikesdale, though in poor health and handicapped with blurred eyesight, hadn't the slightest doubt that the sickly young man restored to her was her Roland—"For which God be praised."

How ardently she'd prayed for his safe return!—pleaded and bargained with her God! Even before it was self-evident that Roland had fallen into a misadventure out West, Anna Emery had been canny enough to donate $140,000 to a charity home for unwed mothers in the city; by the end of the summer she'd given equal sums to a foundlings' hospital, the Philadelphia Academy of Fine Arts, the International Red Cross, and, not least, the Episcopalian Church. Anna Emery's sense was of Roland—pale, plump, shivering, paralyzed with terror— held hostage by God Himself, that God and Anna Emery might come to terms satisfactory to both.

So, when Montgomery Bagot at last cabled her with the news that the man believed to be Roland was indeed Roland, and that Roland was, apart from superficial alterations, very much himself, Anna Emery was so suffused with joy that she climbed out of her sickbed, to her nurse's astonishment, and, lowering herself to her knees, gave thanks to God for His kindness.

"I had never doubted You," she declared.

Anna Emery Shrikesdale, née Sewall (the granddaughter and daughter of governors of the Commonwealth of Pennsylvania), was just five feet tall, with a small, round, compact figure, not exactly fat (except in her stomach and hips) but tight and rotund, like a fruit swollen nearly to bursting. At the age of sixty-nine she retained a vague girlish manner; was somewhat vain about her appearance—particularly her hair, which had grown too thin not to require the supplement of an elaborately coiffed pearly-gray wig; and suffered from such a variety of ailments, both female and general, her physician scarcely knew how to attend to her. Following Elias's mysterious death (the distraught widow was told only that he had died of heart failure; in truth he'd died of a syphilitic infection of the spine), her nerves had so deteriorated that she started like an infant at ordinary sounds and movements; suffered frequently from hypertension headaches and fainting spells; and could not always control the palsied trembling of her hands. "Ah, you frightened me—!" Anna Emery would exclaim, laughing breathlessly, and pressing her hand to her bosom, when her companion had done no more than make an innocuous remark or gesture, or drawn breath to speak.

It was believed by some Philadelphians that Anna Emery began to lose her health after the ordeal of Roland's birth (Roland being the Shrikesdales' sole surviving child, born when Anna Emery was thirty-eight); by others, more intimately acquainted with the Sewall family, that she had always been a nervous and high-strung girl. She wept easily; laughed easily; feared company, yet pressed herself upon both men and women, chattering with an earnest sort of gaiety. At the age of fifteen she underwent a religious experience of some sort, never satisfactorily explained to her family, and pleaded with them to allow her to convert to Catholicism, and join a cloistered order of nuns; but of course the Sewalls, being a resolutely Protestant family, forbade their daughter to entertain such fantasies. At the age of twenty-four Anna Emery became engaged to a lively young bachelor-about-town who shortly thereafter threw her over for another, prettier, young heiress; and, after a period of intense shame and humiliation, when she scarcely dared show her face in society, she consented to marry the fifty-two-year-old Elias Shrikesdale—a wealthy widower known for his financial coups in the railroad, grain, and asbestos markets, but not otherwise admired in Philadelphia society. Anna Emery suffered several miscarriages—gave birth to a baby girl, who subsequently died at the age of eight months—and finally, after years of barrenness, gave birth to Roland, whom she adored immediately as the redeeming fact of her life. "Now I see why God has made me suffer!" the radiant mother exclaimed, hugging her baby hungrily to her bosom. "Now I see *all.*"

Following this, though Anna Emery's health was never stable, she hardly minded; for she had her son, who loved her nearly as much as she loved him.

Within months of Roland's birth Elias Shrikesdale began to travel more frequently on business. It seemed he was rarely at Castlewood though, as observers noted, he might be glimpsed at one or another of his Philadelphia clubs, or at the racetrack, or in Manhattan, often in the company of an attractive young singer or actress whom he made no effort to introduce to acquaintances. He explained to Anna Emery and the Sewalls that he was simply too busy with his own affairs, financial and political, to concern himself with domestic matters. If Anna Emery and little Roland spent the summer in Newport, Elias might visit a weekend or two; if they went abroad for six months, he might decline to accompany them at all. A man's life, Elias said, couldn't be shared with a woman; at least not the sort of women one found in Philadelphia society.

"We must go, after all, where life quickens us," he declared.

Observers marveled at Anna Emery's allegiance to her husband, no matter his infidelities, his public rudenesses and questionable business practices. She may have believed, like most women of her class and era, that moneymaking was a man's vocation that had no relationship to ethics or even to the law. She refused to hear any criticism of Elias even from her own family; refused to read any newspaper, including the *Philadelphia Inquirer*, that chided him for ungentlemanly behavior in the public sphere. (The most serious charges were brought against the Shrikesdales at the time of the 1902 strike of the newly organized United Mine Workers in eastern Pennsylvania, when Elias and his brother Stafford hired a small army of mercenaries to break the strike. A number of miners were killed, many more were injured and several of their houses burnt to the ground in mysterious blazes. Following the breaking of the strike, however, the Shrikesdales enjoyed their most profitable years, and stock in the company rose to new heights.) After President Teddy Roosevelt forced negotiations on the anthracite mine owners in Pennsylvania who'd refused to discuss contracts with the union, or to listen to union requests at all, Elias and Stafford jested angrily of ways in which Roosevelt might be "cut down": there being the recent excellent example of Mark Hanna's flunkey McKinley shot in the fat belly as he reached out complacently to shake his assassin's hand, and the example of Old Abe, or Old Ape, shot in the back of the head in Ford's Theater—"Better late than never." As the Shrikesdale brothers retained a powerful security force, such jests were perhaps half serious. Certainly they spoke of possible stratagems for "the perfect assassination—to be credited to Bolshevik terrorists" in the presence of others, even at formal dinner parties at Castlewood; yet, oddly, Anna

Emery took no note of them, retaining the dignity of her station as a Philadelphia grande dame for whom the ways of men are inscrutable and not to be questioned, still less challenged.

After Elias's death, however, Anna Emery rarely spoke of him. As if, dying at the advanced age of eighty-four, he'd cruelly abandoned her and was to be blamed for her financial predicament, as she called it, though as Montgomery Bagot and other advisors insisted, Anna Emery Shrikesdale was one of the richest women in the Northeast. Still it was her nervous complaint, made to relatives and friends, that she and Roland were "at the mercy of fortune—unless God intervenes."

This, despite the fact that, at the time Roland disappeared into the West, and reappeared as a battered amnesiac, Anna Emery was earning by way of Shrikesdale holdings, investments and income more than $7,000 an hour.

Eccentric as Anna Emery Shrikesdale became in her seventh decade, she wasn't unlike a number of Philadelphia dowagers of her circle who worried obsessively about money, no matter the size of their fortunes. They were fully capable of giving away enormous sums to charity, or, upon impulse, paying as much as $400,000 for a painting promoted by Joseph Duveen; then they reacted by cutting their household budgets to the bone, or going without buying a single new item of clothing for a full season. Anna Emery took a sort of grim pride in the very dowdiness of her attire; she refused to heat many of the rooms in Castlewood Hall (including the servants' quarters); guests at her infrequent dinner parties were dismayed to confront fish, butter, sauces, and linen of less than the highest degree of freshness. Young Roland, his mother's son to his fingertips, behaved in much the same way—dressing unfashionably, procuring the cheapest seats at the theater, showing a prim sort of disdain for the usual diversions and sports of his class, like polo, yachting, and horse racing—but in Roland such parsimony had philosophical underpinnings. If spending money could add a cubit to a man's height, he said severely, we would be surrounded by giants and not, as we are, by pygmies.

Had Roland allowed it, Anna Emery would gladly have spent a good deal of money on him. But he cared only for books, evenings at the theater and concert hall, and occasional retreats, as he called them, to "lonely and unexpected" parts of the world where his name and face were unknown. So, the ill-considered trip to Colorado in the spring of 1914, made, as Roland declared, for the sake of his physical and spiritual salvation.

"If you leave me now, Roland, I am afraid we will never see each other again on this earth," Anna Emery said; and Roland, hardening himself against her tears, said, "If I do not leave now, Mother, I will not be able to tolerate *myself* on this earth."

No expense was spared in Anna Emery's effort to locate her missing son, whether she paid out extraordinary sums for the design and printing of the soon-famous poster, and its distribution everywhere in the West; or allowed her private detectives unlimited expense accounts. (One of the detectives dared submit a tally sheet for $11,000 in expenses alone, for the single month of July; which sum Anna Emery promptly paid.) Bagot, whom Anna Emery believed an old friend, as well as one of the shrewdest lawyers in Philadelphia, was paid $8,000 simply to go out to Fort Sumner, make the crucial identification, and bring poor Roland home.

And of course it *was* Roland—as Anna Emery saw at once when Bagot led him into the room, though her poor heart was pounding, and her eyes had misted over in tears.

Her Roland, after so many days away!—her boy!—one side of his face grotesquely bandaged, and his hair darker and coarser than she recalled; his lips less moistly pink and soft; his very figure thickened, and given a fearful simian cast by all he'd endured. Anna Emery had been warned that Roland suffered from a temporary amnesia, could not recall his name or anything pertaining to his circumstances, etc., yet it amazed her to see for a brief flickering moment how he stared at her, eyes narrowed in that old squinting habit, yet luminous, with dread, exaltation, and wonder.

"Mother—?"

In the next instant he was crouched beside her bedside, weeping in her embrace. "My darling Roland, my baby, God has sent you back to me," Anna Emery cried. And so it was.

IV

Sharp-eyed old Stafford Shrikesdale saw within seconds of their meeting that this "amnesiac nephew" of his, talked of obsessively through Philadelphia, and heralded in the national press, was an imposter. Yet so stunned was he, so thrown off balance by the audacity of the man's game, Stafford could do no more than stare at him and stammer a faint, faltering greeting and, to his subsequent chagrin, *shake the bastard's hand.*

Which was cool, moist and clammy yet momentarily hard in its grip as never in the past, that Roland's uncle could recall.

And the squinting flash of the imposter's eyes, nothing like Roland's watery gaze.

Yet: there was poor Anna Emery, radiant and quivering with joy, clinging to her boy's arm and clutching at Stafford's as if to bring the two into an unlikely embrace. It was as everyone said: Anna Emery was convinced that this man was her lost son Roland, and who would wish to quarrel with her, at least at such a time? She was urging the stranger, "Roland, dear, try to remember your uncle Stafford, please! Your late father's brother. *Do try.*" The thick-bodied young brute gave every appearance of trying, staring at Stafford Shrikesdale with narrowed eyes, his mouth working mutely as if . . . *as if he were genuine.* And when he did at last speak, *it was in Roland's very voice.* "Y-Yes, Mother. I will *try.* If but God will help me."

So sharp-eyed old Stafford Shrikesdale went away from his first encounter with his "amnesiac nephew" both knowing that the man was an imposter and shaken in his conviction. *For what if? . . . Couldn't an ordeal in the Southwest, great physical hardship have altered Roland Shrikesdale?*

Stafford's sons, who were Roland's cousins, and never very close to the pampered, petted sickly creature, found themselves, as usual, in sharp disagreement. For each saw what was *obvious*; and was filled with contempt for anyone who disagreed.

Said Bertram, "He isn't Roland. Any fool can see."

Said Lyle, "But he must be Roland—how could he deceive so many people, and Aunt Anna Emery most of all?"

Said Willard in his ironic, lawyerly voice, "The man's way of speaking, the nervous little inflections and his squinting smiles and sighs, the way he wriggles his shoulders and buttocks like a female, and carries him-self, and *is*—it's Roland, God damn him. Yet at the same time if one looks carefully, as I've done, studying him from the rear, and the side, from a distance and at close range—it seems to be our cousin in the form somehow of another man, a stranger a few years older than he, or as we remember him."

"Willard, are you mad? What are you saying?" Bertram interrupted. " 'Our cousin in the form of—' What?"

"—not so fleshy as Roland but more muscular," Willard continued, irritably, "—with a slightly different mouth and chin—and those eyes. Yet the expression of the face, that sort of droopy doggy hopefulness—"

"I would have said he looks younger than Roland. Than Roland would have been."

"Younger? Surely older."

"I mean—for one who's endured such an ordeal. How many days wandering in the desert? And those injuries . . ."

"His eyes are darker than Roland's."

"Lighter, I should say. Steelier."

"I believe he knew *me*. I could have sworn—it *is* our cousin."

"Aunt Anna Emery is a silly old woman, and half-blind. You know everyone laughs at her."

"—pities her, I should have said."

"If *I* went away, and was lost, and suffered injuries, and almost died, and returned to Philadelphia—you would wish, I suppose, not to know *me*," Lyle said hotly, "—in order to defraud *me* of my position—yes? Is that it?"

"You, Lyle? What has this to do with you?"

"It has to do with us all. If Roland can be dismissed—so can we all."

"But that's absurd. *You* are not Roland. *You* are not an imposter."

"This man's head is larger than Roland's, I swear. His forehead squarer."

"Yet he's wearing Roland's hats, it seems. You saw him."

"His neck—it's thicker, obviously. Like a young bull's."

"Yet this might be Roland, toughened and made 'manly' by the West."

"No longer a virgin."

"Roland? Impossible."

"*That* man—? Certainly, possible."

"Yet I was thinking, God help me—I like him much more than I did, when we were boys."

"*This* Roland, or—?"

"His ears don't stick out so much as they did. But the points are sharper."

"Hairs in his ears. Like my own."

"His eyebrows are more gnarled—"

"The man's presence somehow more *real*. More of a physical *fact*."

"As poor Roland never seemed a *fact*."

They stood for some time smoking their cigars, pondering.

At last Lyle said impatiently, "He *must* be Roland. No one has said he isn't."

"Except Father. And us."

"*I* haven't said it isn't Roland, not exactly," Willard said.

"Well, *I* have," said Bertram. "*I know the man is not Roland.*"

"Look, it's inconceivable that a stranger could deceive so many of us, beginning with Bagot. Bagot is no fool. Many of the relatives have seen him, and granted some of them are idiots like Aunt Anna Emery, yet they would sense if Roland weren't Roland; the Sewalls were all so fond of him. The servants at Castlewood appear to accept him—not that they matter greatly. But—there is Bagot. How d'you account for Bagot?"

"A fellow conspirator," Bertram said bitterly.

"Not Bagot!"

"Surely. The man isn't to be trusted, he has never been on our side."

"Father spoke at length to Bagot—"

"And Bagot was, Father said, rude."

"To Father?"

"To Father."

"Well, he'll regret *that*."

"They will all regret *that*."

"In the meantime—"

"What of the man's handwriting? A sample—"

"It was that, partly, Father saw Bagot about."

"And—?"

"This Roland's handwriting is very close to the old—allowing for a certain shakiness. He isn't well, after all; they say he nearly died in New Mexico."

"*He* may have died—but this one lives."

"And he will live to regret it. If, of course, it is *not* the right man."

"—an imposter, a brazen criminal, hoping to deceive the Shrikesdales, of all people—"

"*That* would be intolerable."

"—inconceivable!"

"*Not to be borne.*"

"Yet," said Willard, breathing harshly, "—perhaps it is Roland after all?—and we are the ones who have somehow changed in our perceptions. For it isn't likely, nor would any jury be inclined to think so, that a man's very mother—"

"Anna Emery is *not* this man's mother," said Bertram.

"She is Roland's mother—that is in fact all that she *is*."

"No, you are speaking carelessly. She *is* a woman of advanced years, susceptible to all sorts of sickly fancies, on the verge, if she has not already crossed over, of senility, as any forceful attorney might argue."

"But simply to erect so preposterous a case, with the man's very mother testifying in his behalf—"

"—we would be laughed out of court, we would *never* live it down—"

"Anna Emery Shrikesdale is not this man's mother. She is Roland's mother; and this man, as I keep telling you, is not Roland Shrikesdale. *He is not our cousin.*"

"Then who is he?—and how can it be humanly possible, that he so closely resembles Roland?"

Said Bertram contemptuously, "That's your idiotic notion, that the man resembles Roland. Father and I see clearly he does *not*."

"I hope, Bertie, you won't embarrass the family by trying to demonstrate that Aunt Anna Emery doesn't know her own son," Lyle said curtly. "The wisest course of action is to stop thinking about this; to continue with our lives as if nothing were wrong."

Willard said, with lawyerly aplomb and disdain, "On the one hand, I counsel extreme caution. On the other, if the man is an imposter, this is doubtless what he wishes. Consider the fortune that's at stake: more than two hundred million dollars, as Father calculates. Of our money!

And it's intolerable that a criminal should inherit Castlewood Hall and our name, without our putting up a fight. Yet—"

"Yet—?"

"—the prospect of an open legal disagreement, a lawsuit dragged through the civil court, terrifies me. As a man of the law, I know what we might expect. For the defense would be formidable, if not unshakable, with poor Aunt Anna Emery testifying for 'Roland' as her beloved son, and the Sewalls, and Bagot, and the Pinkerton men—their testimony would weigh heavily in the court. I'm afraid it's all but hopeless. Unless—'Roland' reveals himself by accident."

"Certainly 'Roland' will reveal himself," said Bertram. "I'll see to that."

"But how? Without tipping our hand?" Willard said. "The man must be devilishly clever—in fact, he frightens me."

"Ah, then you side with me!" Bertram said.

"I don't necessarily side with you," Willard said stiffly.

"You admit the possibility, however."

"There is always a 'possibility'—in the law. Yet another possibility remains that this man *is* our cousin and that his memory will eventually return—queerer things have happened in the annals of law, believe me. And we Shrikesdales would be committing a grave injustice if we took action against a blood relative—"

"That brute!—he's no blood relative of mine," Bertram said angrily. "And two hundred million is at stake, at the very least. Our aunt is sure to die within a few years—"

"No, no—the Sewalls live forever. Like that ghastly race of Struldbruggs of which Jonathan Swift wrote, who never die but only live and live, in total senility. She will outlive us all."

Lyle said, exasperated, "The man *is* Roland, I'd swear to it. I've seen in him the very person we'd pitied and disliked. You want to imagine that that weak, ineffectual, overgrown baby is someone other than our cousin; you're simply too eager, brothers, to want to believe that our cousin is dead."

Again they fell silent; sucked at their cigars; stared at the floor.

After some minutes Bertram said, with a sly sidelong smile at his brothers, "If he's died once, y'know—he can die a second time."

And Willard, the eldest and most responsible, wheeled upon Bertram, giving his upper arm a hard blow, as if they were boys. "God damn

you for a fool, Bertie—you must never say that sort of thing where anyone else, even a servant, might hear."

V

Roland Shrikesdale III was recovering his health by degrees, painfully and haltingly. But everyone agreed that he *was* recovering.

By early winter he was strong enough to dress, and to take most of
his meals downstairs at Castlewood; to walk about the grounds unescorted; to attend church with his mother; to sit, nervous, smiling, but
for the most part silent, at small social gatherings that did not overtax
him. He ate heartily, which delighted Anna Emery; he slept very well
indeed—"like a baby"—being capable of staying abed for twelve hours
at a stretch, until Anna Emery herself gaily roused him. Despite the fre-
quency with which they received invitations—for Roland Shrikesdale
III was one of Philadelphia's most eligible, and wealthy, bachelors—
Anna Emery and Roland condescended to accept few invitations to
dine out; they much preferred the theater or the concert hall, where, as
Roland said, he felt his spirit quicken and vibrate, as of old.

Ah, what joy, what balm, to listen for hours to the music of Mozart,
or Wagner, or Beethoven!—to give himself up to the caprices of *Rigoletto*, as he'd done of old! There, seated close beside his mother in the
Shrikesdale family box, leaning forward to drink in, with quivering intensity, every note—that was the pale, stocky, ravaged young Shrikesdale heir, oblivious of the attention he drew on all sides; so immersed in
the music, it was as if he'd never left the safety of Philadelphia to suffer
his mysterious adventure. (Indeed, it remained mysterious, for Roland
was incapable of remembering save in jagged and incoherent fragments; and no trace was found of his companion, who must have died
somewhere in the wilds of New Mexico.)

"He's Anna Emery's boy as he has always been," observers noted,
eyeing him covertly, "—though he *is* much changed."

By degrees, the scar tissue on the side of Roland's face acquired a less
painful, and a less startling, appearance; where once it had ached violently, Roland now confessed it was numb. And, too, was not some-

thing gone now from the corner of his eye, that he dimly recalled was ugly?—a birthmark, a mole?

Anna Emery snatched his hand away from his face, squeezing it hard, as one might do with a small child; partly to reprimand and partly to comfort. She told him it had been a mole; but it had not been at all ugly; for there was nothing ugly about him—neither now nor in the past.

Ah, but the warts scattered across his hands!—Roland said with a fastidious shudder. Surely these *were* ugly—?

At this, Anna Emery flinched; for, it seemed, she too had warts on her hands—they were a family affliction of the Sewalls, vexing but harmless.

"You have had them all your life, dear, and have not often complained," Anna Emery said, hurt. "Indeed, I remember you speaking of them as a minor sort of curse, as curses go."

Roland showed some embarrassment at his rudeness, and tried to make amends. He stooped to embrace his trembling mother; kissed her cheek; and said earnestly, "Yes, you are right, Mother—I believe I remember now: a minor sort of curse, as curses go."

It began to happen that, in the presence of marveling witnesses, Roland Shrikesdale was struck by flashes of memory—whole episodes out of his former life resuscitated by way of a stray word or gesture, or an accidental combination thereof. Ah, what an experience, to see the amnesiac waking, as it were, from a part of his eerie trance—!

For instance, in January of 1915, at a small dinner party given by a friend of Anna Emery's, at which Stafford Shrikesdale happened to be a guest, Roland astonished everyone by suddenly clutching at his head, when his hostess happened to speak of Admiral Blackburn. He grimaced, as if he were in fearful pain; and rocked in his chair; saying finally in a hoarse, halting, yet elated voice that the name "Blackburn" stirred such a memory!—if memory it was, and not a child's dream—of a sweet-tempered pony, a Shetland with long shaggy mane and tail, liquid-bright eyes, a black hide streaked with gray—*his* beloved pony Blackburn!

Then, as everyone listened in great excitement, Roland shut his eyes, and, speaking slowly and dreamily, yet deliberately, proceeded to recall not only the Shetland pony, but the green-painted pony cart in which he had ridden at the age of six ... the "big farm" out in the country (in fact, in Bucks County) ... a young black boy, a favored stable hand named Quincy, who had been allowed to supervise little Roland's play ... and a dignified elderly gentleman with snapping black eyes and white, white hair who must have been ... *must* have been ... Grandfather Shrikesdale himself, dead since 1889.

Poor Anna Emery could contain herself no longer; but began to sob helplessly; and had to be comforted by Stafford Shrikesdale, of all people—who'd begun to tremble himself, hearing Roland's remarkable recitation.

On another occasion, hardly less dramatic, at a reception at the home of Mrs. Eva Clement-Stoddard, Roland lapsed into an extraordinary fugue state, as if he had been hypnotized, when the name "Maclean" was mentioned—for this triggered a memory of a Scots woman of that name who had been little Roland's nanny at Castlewood; which in turn triggered a memory astonishing in its visual and tactile detail of the nursery in which Roland had spent his first eight years. The stuffed toys with which he played, and slept ... the floral print of his bed quilt ... the view of the old rose garden and the fountain from his window ... poor Miss Maclean who spent a great deal of her time weeping and sighing, for what reason the child Roland did not know ... and, most vivid of all, most poignant of all, Mother with her hair loosed on her shoulders, rocking him, crooning to him, kissing him ... reading to him his favorite fairy tales in her sweet melodic voice ...

At this halting recitation, made as Roland swayed on his feet, his head thrown back, his eyes shut, and his lips gleaming with spittle, not only Anna Emery Shrikesdale but a number of ladies were reduced to tears; and all the gentlemen close by were powerfully affected. An astonishing feat of memory, indeed, for anyone at all—let alone a man suffering from amnesia! It seemed that Roland's unconscious mind was stimulated to such a degree by these chance associations, the memories came unbidden to his consciousness, and possessed an extraordinary potency. Evidently Roland could not initiate them, nor, once begun, could they be stopped; they must simply run their course; leaving the perspiring young man drained and exhausted, and his skin, already sallow, turned a sickly grayish-yellow hue.

The Philadelphians who witnessed such heartrending trances could

hardly doubt that Roland was Roland; and if, now and then, from de-
cidedly queer sources, they heard whisperings that the Shrikesdale heir
was not quite the man one supposed him to be . . . such idiotic rumors
were irritably dismissed at once, as the speculations of the yellow press.

"He *is* a remarkable case, is he not?" Dr. Thurman, the Shrikesdales'
physician, said proudly. "When he's fully restored to his health I shall
make a name for myself—and, of course, for Roland as well—by writing
up his story. *The medical world will scarcely believe it.*"

VI

In the spring of 1915, when newspapers were filled with stories of the
barbarous sinking of the British liner *Lusitania* by German submarine,
and reports of President Wilson's uncompromising response, there was
delivered to Mr. Abraham Licht of Muirkirk a most curious telegram,
indeed—

ALBERT ST. GOAR ESQ. IS HEREBY INVITED TO A CHARITY FÊTE HE WILL
NOT FAIL TO FIND AMUSING CASTLEWOOD HALL PHILADELPHIA SUN-
DAY MAY 15 2 PM TWO TICKETS RESERVED IN HIS NAME SHOULD HE WISH
TO BRING A COMPANION ("COMPLICITY?")

Astonished, Abraham Licht read it several times over, rapidly; and
showed it to old Katrina, who could make nothing of it; and even,
later—though father and daughter happened not to be on the most
cordial of terms at the moment—to Millie, who likewise read it several
times, and turned a frightened face toward him. "But who knows of 'St.
Goar' here at Muirkirk!" she whispered. "It must be a plot of some
kind."

Abraham smiled suddenly, though not, precisely, at Millie; and said
as if brooding aloud, "Yes, it *is* a plot of some kind—to whose advantage, we must discover."

So it happened that Abraham Licht drove himself and Millie down
to Philadelphia, in his newly acquired Packard touring car (plum-
colored, with creamy-white upholstered interior and gleaming chrome
trim); and, on that splendidly sunny Sunday, joined a slow procession

of carriages and new-model motorcars through the gates of Castlewood Hall, and up along the quarter-mile gravelled drive to the house. As Albert St. Goar and his daughter Matilde, he had acquired at the gate two tickets priced at $300 each—the proceeds of the afternoon's fête to go to the United Hospitals Charity Association of Philadelphia.

A double row of plane trees lining the drive . . . a gently sloping lawn, or meadow, of several acres . . . azalea, rhododendron, and lilac in gorgeous blossom . . . Castlewood Hall itself: a mansion of eclectic American design (eighteenth-century Gothic the predominant style) of pale gray stone, with an immense curving portico, and too many windows to be counted. Baring his teeth around his cigar, Abraham Licht exclaimed: " 'This is Heaven, nor can we wish to be out of it!' "—in so ingenuous a tone, it would have been impossible to judge whether he spoke sincerely, or in mockery. Beside him, her gloved hands clasped tightly in her lap, Millie stared at the house—the lawn—the handsomely dressed ladies and gentlemen strolling about—and said nothing at all. She had in fact been silent for much of the drive; it was her conviction that they should not have come.

"I can think of only one person, Father, who might have sent us that telegram," she had said, after much thought, "—and he does not wish us well."

"Of course there is only one person who might have sent the telegram," Abraham Licht said irritably, "—and of course he *does* wish us well."

St. Goar's automobile was taken from him at the front entrance of the house, and driven off by a liveried servant to be parked elsewhere; leaving father and daughter feeling suddenly exposed, and on their own. Still, as they strolled through the crowd, very few persons glanced their way; they knew no one, and, it seemed, no one knew them. "How long must we stay, Father?" Millie asked, looking suspiciously about. "I think it must be a hoax." To his disappointment Abraham Licht, or, to be precise, Albert St. Goar (formerly of London, England: a gentleman "retired from business") soon discovered that there were no beverages stronger than lemonade, iced tea, and cranberry juice to be had at the fête; and, like a fool, he'd left his silver flask behind, locked away in a compartment in his car.

"We will stay, Matilde," St. Goar said severely, "—until the scene is played out, and we know its significance."

They made their questing way through the crowd of chattering strangers on the flagstone terrace; they made their way, Matilde's arm through St. Goar's, into a garden of topiary shrubs, statues in stained white marble, and gently splashing fountains; they allowed themselves to drift into the nimbus of ladies and gentlemen gathered about one of the refreshment tables, beneath an immense red-and-white striped awning; they exchanged greetings, vague yet animated, animated yet vague, with people who drifted past. St. Goar was fashionably dressed in a dove-gray costume of lightweight wool, with an embroidered silk vest, and a flowing white silk shirt; he wore a straw hat not unlike the hats worn by the majority of the other gentlemen, and a white carnation in his buttonhole, and gray mohair spats; and looked, on the whole, quite handsome and assured. His beautiful daughter Matilde (who had attended schools in Switzerland and France, until the outbreak of the War) wore a spring frock of the sheerest cotton, arranged in many layers of robin's-egg blue and pale cerise, with a cerise sash that showed her tiny waist to artful advantage; and a skirt designed to show a surprising amount of ankle, and the silky gleam of transparent stockings. Her blond hair, smartly bobbed, was, for modesty's sake, perhaps, very nearly hidden by a hat with a wide scalloped brim, and a veil of dotted swiss.

Yet something chill and haughty in the young woman's expression discouraged gentlemen from approaching her; and, in any case, there were a number of extremely pretty young women at the fête, known, no doubt, to Society.

"Strange that our host doesn't come forward to identify himself," Albert St. Goar said, surveying the crowd with a pleasant if abstract smile, "—for I have the sense that he watches us, perhaps with amusement."

"With no amusement," Matilde said curtly, disengaging her arm from her father's. "You forget—he is a creature without a sense of humor."

With this, Matilde drifted off; and St. Goar, following slowly behind her, found himself, within a few minutes, in a curious conversation with a small, bald, irritable gentleman of approximately his own age (although he, St. Goar, looked a full decade younger) on a subject not easily grasped: the political situation? the perfidy of the German-Americans? the price paid by the gentleman's wife for her horoscope? ("You would agree, sir, that $25,000 is too steep a sum, would you not?

What is your opinion, sir?") It was St. Goar's instinctive understanding that this mousey little man, this person of such evident inconsequence, must be in fact a very wealthy man; and an important contact, perhaps, for St. Goar; yet, though St. Goar fell in vehemently with his denunciation of astrology and astrologists, or was it the German-American spies in our midst, his heart wasn't truly in the exchange, and his attention continued to be focused upon his daughter as, in a pose of insouciance, she strolled through the crowd of strangers, twirling her parasol on her shoulder. The filmy layers of her dress rode the breeze, lightly; her step was graceful; her manner, to the casual eye, intensely feminine—in the old-fashioned sense of the word. Yet, how strong her will; and how her father was growing to fear it—!

It was then that St. Goar chanced to see a stocky young man in a Panama hat, pushing someone in a wheelchair, brush, by accident, close by Matilde; saw how Matilde glanced around, startled; and how, like a small rude child, she knew no better than to stare, and stare— and stare. Even as St. Goar made his way to her, he saw that she was swaying, as if about to faint; she pressed a gloved hand against her throat; and drew away from the young man who, with some clumsiness, yet gallantry, made an effort to take hold of her arm, and steady her. "Very odd, very very odd," St. Goar thought angrily, "—it isn't like a daughter of mine, to be so odd!"

When he hurried to her, however, he saw, through a sudden vertiginous blur, the cause of her incredulity: for the husky young man in the Panama hat, who, smiling and blushing, was nervously introducing himself as Roland Shrikesdale, and the woman in the wheelchair as his mother, Anna Emery Shrikesdale ("your hostess, you know, for this afternoon") was no one other than . . . *Harwood.*

. . . who was also, evidently, unless Abraham Licht had suddenly lost his senses, the son of the squinting old woman in the wheelchair; even as the old woman must be Elias Shrikesdale's widow, and the proprietress of Castlewood Hall.

Precisely how the remarkable scene was managed, and whether, as St. Goar, he acquitted himself respectably, Abraham Licht could not afterward remember: for his brain was adazzle.

Harwood!—*his* Harwood!

After so many years!

Yet he was Harwood no longer: and darted quick warning glances at St. Goar and his daughter, not to stare too raptly.

As to who he *was* . . .

Plump, nervous, his skin sallow, a queer strip of scar tissue running down the left side of his face; his thick hair brushed flat, and severely parted; his mouth smaller, pinker, more moist than it had been of old. Not quite manly, perhaps; boyish, shy, sweet; inclined in certain situations to stammer; yet clearly intelligent and well-spoken; and unfailingly gallant to his mother—leaning now over Mrs. Shrikesdale's wheelchair, and holding her lace-gloved hand in his as if to steady its tremor. (One could see at a glance that they were mother and son: their squinting smiles were identical.)

Herewith, some minutes of bright brisk nervous social chatter, on Roland's part primarily, as he explained to his guests the tradition behind the May fête (held each year in Philadelphia, and held every six years or so at Castlewood, depending upon his mother's health); and to Mrs. Shrikesdale that he had met Albert St. Goar and Matilde some years ago, in London . . . when Matilde had been a schoolgirl . . . and Albert had been involved in antiquarian books . . . and they had enjoyed one another's company enormously; but had, unfortunately, lost contact over the years.

"It was naughty of you, Roland, not to bring them to meet me, then," Mrs. Shrikesdale said, in a faint, breathless, yet coquettish voice, fixing her watery gaze upon Albert St. Goar; and Roland, his cheeks lightly flushed, murmured in her ear, in some embarrassment, "But Mother, I'm afraid, you know, I *did*—one beastly rainy afternoon—to our suite at Claridge's. You enjoyed our little tea with them so much at the time—and now, dear, you seem to have forgotten it entirely!"

St. Goar and his daughter now recalled the visit with evident pleasure, despite its having been some years ago; which threw poor Mrs. Shrikesdale clearly into the wrong. She begged their forgiveness; called herself a silly old feather-brained fool; and, extending her trembling hands to them both, she insisted they come soon—*very* soon—to dine with her and Roland at Castlewood.

"Why, we shall be happy to do so, Mrs. Shrikesdale—we shall be delighted," Albert St. Goar said in a voice of quiet elation.

VII

Following this lucky meeting, it transpired naturally that St. Goar and his daughter frequently visited Castlewood; were introduced by the kindly Mrs. Shrikesdale and her son to a number of extremely interesting Philadelphians; and even made the decision by midsummer to move from their home in upstate New York to an apartment on fashionable Rittenhouse Square, which Roland helped them acquire. Mrs. Shrikesdale was thoroughly charmed by St. Goar, who knew, it seemed, all about music, and history, and poetry, and painting—almost as much, indeed, as Joseph Duveen himself. ("He is so cultured a gentleman!—he may even be a genius, to hear him talk! Might not he and Eva Stoddard make an ideal pair?" Mrs. Shrikesdale asked, suddenly, one evening, in schoolgirl excitement; and Roland said lightly, "I had already thought of that weeks ago, dear.")

As to Matilde St. Goar—why, being so blessed with beauty, was the young woman so singularly melancholy; and, when not melancholy, so disagreeably bright, and brittle, and arch—her very laughter like shattered glass?

Roland confessed that he didn't know, as he'd never been on intimate terms with either St. Goar or Matilde; but word was, poor Matilde had suffered a broken heart, about which she would never speak out of pride.

As to Roland Shrikesdale himself—despite the efforts of any number of parties, he rarely showed any interest in the opposite sex, at the various social events to which he escorted his mother; nor was he, for the remainder of his life, ever to regain his full memory. Yet, by degrees, his health returned—in fact, as Dr. Thurman remarked with some perplexity, Roland's health *more than returned!*—for the new Roland, having survived his ordeal in the desert, was becoming far more fit than the old.

Also, to the delighted surprise of people who'd known him since boyhood, and had known something of his father's wishes for him, Roland began to show a tentative interest in horses, both in breeding and in racing; as, of course, Elias had done through *his* life. And, in his shy way, he began to express an interest in traveling abroad, or even back West—though hastily promising his mother that he would never,

never go without *her,* this time. "When you're feeling more yourself, dear, we shall go by rail to the Rockies," Roland said cheerfully. "For they are one of God's great spectacles, and must not be missed."

To Bagot Roland also expressed some childlike curiosity, for the first time, about the Shrikesdale fortune; and some distress, that, within the next few years, as a thoughtless relative had happened to mention, Roland would be obliged to sue for power of attorney over his mother's estate. "It's true that Mother is failing week by week," Roland said in a quavering voice, his eyes aswim in tears, "—but I cannot believe that there will be a time when she is not fully herself; I cannot believe it. And, do you know, I have but the dimmest notion of what *is* meant by 'power of attorney,' Mr. Bagot—will you explain it to me?"

These various developments, along with the sudden arrival in Philadelphia of the mysterious gentleman "Albert St. Goar," didn't go unnoticed by Stafford Shrikesdale and his sons. Yet the four quarreled bitterly as to what steps to take with the fraudulent heir; and whether, even after so many months, he might not be Roland after all—their cousin, as Lyle stubbornly argued, though transformed.

("Identity is not that ambiguous," Bertram said. "A man is either the man he was born—*or he is not.*" "But if we make a mistake?" Lyle said. "And if the mistake is fatal?")

Having been present at one of Roland's feats of memory, Stafford Shrikesdale claimed in disgust that the entire performance was fabricated; very well done, to be sure, the way a professional actor might do it—but fabricated nonetheless. Willard, however, was present on another occasion, when, in a state of trance, perspiration streaming down his face and his eyes rolled whitely upward, Roland recited a good deal of the Book of Proverbs; and Willard confessed to being powerfully moved . . . and almost persuaded, for a few hours, that Roland *was* Roland. Then again, Bertram's arguments for fraud were extremely convincing; and Aunt Anna Emery was easily duped; and, from time to time, even Lyle grew doubtful of his position, and spoke gravely of the seriousness of the crime if Roland turned out not to be Roland . . . "For might this not mean," he asked, "that the real Roland, our cousin, has been murdered?"

St. Goar, they believed, was a clue to the puzzle, since no one seemed to know anything about him, except Roland. So they hired a private investigator, Mr. Gaston Bullock Means, of the William J. Burns National Detective Agency (which frequently did classified work for the Justice Department in Washington); but Means, after an exhaustive ten months' investigation, claimed that he could find no information about St. Goar at all—not even a birth record, or a history of employment.

"If ever a man does not exist," Means reported, "—it is 'Albert St. Goar.' "

The Shrikesdales observed that Roland remained Roland when he was in company; but that, at other times, he was beginning to grow negligent.

For instance, he was glimpsed drinking now and then.

For instance, he was glimpsed smoking—both cigarettes and cigars.

For instance, he, or someone closely resembling him, was rumored to have visited a South Philadelphia bordello upon several occasions; and to have identified himself to the madam as "Christopher."

For instance, in Newport, in August, aboard the family yacht *Albatross*, Roland fell by accident over the side into fifteen feet of water; yet, to the amazement of all, he swam easily and confidently to safety, before he could be rescued—Roland, who had never before swum a single stroke in his entire life, and had been, since boyhood, terrified of water! ("Where did you learn to swim so beautifully?" his relatives asked him; and Roland said, somewhat evasively, "I think it must have been out West—I really don't remember.")

That same month, in Newport, having inveigled the unsuspecting Roland into walking with them along the beach, his cousins reminded him of how very much, as a boy, he had enjoyed wrestling with them in the sand . . . wrestling with Bertram most of all . . . surely he remembered? "I'm afraid I don't remember anything of the kind," Roland said carefully, edging away. "But you *must* remember, cousin," Bertram said, following him, "—you were the one who always wanted to play!" Lyle and Willard laughed as Bertram pretended to stalk Roland. It was a sunny windy day, an afternoon of boyish high spirits and levity; a sumptuous two-hour luncheon behind, and a yet more sumptuous four-hour dinner scheduled for the evening. "Now you know you did, you *know*,"

Bertram said in a high-pitched child's voice, feinting in Roland's direction, "—you *know* you were the one! Always springing on us from behind, and grabbing us in a wrestling hold, and rolling and tumbling about in the dirt, in the sand, in the briars—why, little Roland was *quite* a terror, in his youth." "This I find difficult to believe," Roland said nervously. He was panting; agitated; so very warm, he removed his Panama hat for a moment, to wipe his damp brow. " 'This I find difficult to believe!'—what a fussy old nanny we've become, afraid to get our linen soiled!" Bertram said, baring his teeth in a grin. As Willard and Lyle looked on, amused, smoking their cigars, Bertram sprang at Roland; seized him crudely about the head and shoulders, in a "hammer" lock; yet, within seconds, before anyone quite realized what happened, Bertram was himself thrown down flat on the sand—with such violence, the breath was knocked out of him, and, for several minutes, he lay as one dead.

As Lyle and Willard crouched over him, trying to rouse him, poor Roland hovered about, wringing his hands and apologizing. He hadn't known such a thing could happen, he claimed. Why, he didn't even know what *had* happened—he was quite innocent of any intent to harm. Bertram tried to sit up, clutching at his head. His trim brown moustache was sprinkled with sand and his skin had gone ashen. As his brothers comforted him, he began to vomit; choked; coughed spasmodically; vomited again—a thin white substance, like gruel; all the while poor Roland hovered nearby, apologizing, and insisting that he didn't know what on earth had happened. Their own expressions somber and blank, Lyle and Willard eyed Roland without comment: noting how, for all his agitation, he yet held himself in a slight defensive crouch, his sinewy legs bent at the knee; noted how muscular his shoulders suddenly appeared—how the cords in his beefy neck stood out—how, through a slash in his shirt, dark curly hairs bristled like steel wool. His straw hat had been knocked off in the scuffle and without it the curious breadth and squareness of his forehead were pronounced. Above all, his eyes—so steely-cold, darting from face to face, sobering to see.

"I must have learned to defend myself out West, you know," Roland said earnestly, "—and forgotten all about it, in my illness. Do forgive me, Cousin Bertram!"

But Bertram was not to forgive; still less was Bertram likely to forget.

When, after Labor Day, the Shrikesdales prepared to depart Newport, Bertram chanced to brush near Roland (who was busying himself with preparations for his mother's traveling comfort), and said in a lowered, furious voice: "You lead a charmed life, cousin!—but only so long as Anna Emery lives."

For a half second it seemed that Roland *might* err, in looking his accuser full in the face, and speaking too abruptly; then, with impeccable restraint—of the sort, indeed, that caused St. Goar so to admire him—he simply said, in Roland's very voice: "But my mother, you know, is still young—just at the start of her eighth decade. If God is just she will outlive us all!"

"Pathétique"

I

The eighth of December 1916. A benefit recital for the United Church Fund of Vanderpoel, New York, held in the newly built Frick Hall on the campus of the Vanderpoel Academy for Boys. The evening has been sold out; an audience of more than five hundred people has been warmly enthusiastic; and now as the final item on the programme the Vanderpoel student Darian Licht, sixteen, who has accompanied most of the soloists this evening—a violinist, a mezzo-soprano, an Irish tenor and a string trio—is playing the first movement of Beethoven's Sonata no. 8 in C minor, popularly known as the "Pathétique." How childlike the pianist appears, seated at the keyboard of the great gleaming Steinway, his body taut as a coiled spring, fair brown hair in soft flamelike wings, his narrow, long-jawed face putty-colored in the bright stage lights—yet how powerful his hands on the keyboard, as if he were entranced, mesmerized by the music he himself is creating.

The end of childhood. Which I'd imagined in my vanity had ended years before.

Because the Beethoven sonata is too long and too demanding for this audience, Darian is playing a foreshortened version worked out with Professor Hermann. "It is never wise to test the limits of the music lover's love of music," the elder German has warned Darian, "—especially at the very end of a musical evening." Each movement of the great sonata is represented, yet each has been ingeniously edited; though Adolf Hermann is present in the audience this evening, no doubt hunched forward in his seat, staring at his pupil and listening with painful concentration, pinpricks of oily sweat glistening on his fleshy face, Darian plays as if he's entirely alone. In this stark brightly lighted place the figure of his lost mother Sophie will not appear.

Darian Licht. A fifth-form boy who has established for himself a reputation for independence, aloofness, arrogance. His classmates regard him as they might an adult set in their midst: with grudging respect yet without warmth. Though he has made a few friends—he believes. Misfits like himself, disfigured by eccentric talents (for chess, for poetry, for advanced math, for long-distance running) as by acne. Darian knows from his sister Esther's letters that he's disappointed their father by standing only twelfth in his class of ninety boys and by having failed to "cultivate" important friends like his suitemate Roddy Sewall. How much more disappointed Father would be, how angry, if he knew that Darian neglected his academic studies because he cared only for music; and that Darian had made no effort at all to befriend Roddy or any of the rich men's sons. In fact it's Darian who avoids Roddy as Roddy lingers in their common room as the bell sounds for meals. (In the dining hall the older boys' talk is of war: the United States should declare war against Germany, it's as Roosevelt says, pacifists are just cowards, their hope is that fighting won't end before they can get to it.)

Strange that Darian Licht should snub rich boys. The rumor is, Darian's tuition hasn't been paid for the fall semester. Not a penny paid of course for the spring semester. Headmaster Meech called Darian into his office to speak with him in confidence, taking care not to embarrass the boy (for Meech remembers with pride the extraordinary guest sermon Abraham Licht made in the chapel and the hint he'd given of one

day endowing a trust fund for the school); delicately he asked Darian if
he knew anything of his father's financial situation, for the school had
emergency funds which might be tapped if necessary. *No I don't. I don't
know. I'm sorry, sir. May I be excused, sir. I know nothing of my father's
private life.*

Esther wrote to Darian, and sometimes Katrina added a postscript.
Every few months, Millie sent a postcard that made Darian's heart leap
with anticipation and dread; for Millie's gay, slanted handwriting was a
riddle to record, and sometimes all Darian could be certain of were
Dearest Darian and *Love, your sister Millie.* Abraham Licht was living
now in Philadelphia but had an additional post office box in Camden,
New Jersey, across the river. From Esther, Darian learned the surprising
news that their brother Harwood was back East—but where he was living, whether he was reunited with Father, wasn't clear.

Of Thurston there was never any news. He'd traveled to South
America "on business" and hadn't returned, so far as Darian and Esther
knew; nor was there word of him; yet how strangely Abraham Licht de-
flected questions about his eldest son with a shrug of his shoulder.
Thurston? Who? Ah yes. But no. So much time had passed since Darian
had last seen Thurston, he'd begun to wonder if his tall fair handsome
genial brother had been . . . a dream of his. A vivid heartrending phrase
of music.

It was hours after the awkward meeting with Headmaster Meech
that the shame of it hit Darian like a wave. His father hadn't paid
his tuition! *Making of me a beggar. A criminal accomplice.* He'd been on
his way to the chapel to play organ and turned at once and ran back
to the headmaster's residence to ask, breathless, if there was something he might do to repay the money he owed? Work in the dining
hall, or on the school grounds? The older man regarded him with pity
and exasperation. "You must know by now, Darian, that such a thing
is hardly in the Vanderpoel tradition. You would be embarrassing
your classmates, too." Beyond Headmaster Meech's grave, grizzled
head were busts of Shakespeare and Milton in stark, poreless white
with blank white eyeballs and utterly serene expressions. The Vanderpoel insignia, what appeared to be a flaming scepter, was engraved
on a bronze plaque above the script *Monumentum aere perennius*, the
school motto. Darian wondered what it might mean to these long-
deceased men, to know that in some way incalculable to them they'd

become immortal; even as, in the most obvious way, they were simply . . . gone. Dr. Meech was about to send Darian away when a thought struck him: the upcoming recital. The United Church Fund would be using Frick Hall, though the evening was not under the auspices of the Academy; perhaps if Darian would like to participate in the recital, there might even be a modest fee involved. "Yes?" Darian said hopefully. "I would like that very much, Dr. Meech." He'd spoken impulsively, and would have time afterward—days, weeks—to wonder if he'd done the right thing. To perform in public, when his musical abilities seemed to him so raw, so far short of perfection, so often a source of extreme anguish to him . . . surely this was a mistake? He'd been sleepless with the prospect of stage fright.

His fee for the evening, as accompanist and soloist, would be $35.

Adolf Hermann was both bemused and annoyed that Darian was participating in the recital. "They asked me first—of course. They have hired me, if 'hire' is the adequate term, from time to time for this event." Professor Hermann paused, fixing Darian with a gloomy stare. A sickened thought came to Darian—was his piano teacher resentful of *him*? "These are not serious music lovers, these Americans. You must beware their influence. They are 'nice' people—seemingly. They will want 'nice' music from you. They will pay you—as modestly as they dare. In return, all they will take from you is your soul."

Darian said, with a smile, "I've never earned thirty-five dollars in my life, Professor Hermann. It isn't much but—there it is! And I'll be given a 'cold supper' afterward at the Frick residence in the city, in the company of the other performers." *And I will invite my father to the concert. And Millie, and Esther, and Katrina. My family!*

Professor Hermann muttered that, as Darian Licht was his protégé, he hoped that Darian would not sell himself cheaply to such people who knew nothing of music and so did not deserve music. For long minutes the elder man spoke ponderously, vehemently, as Darian sat with increasing restlessness at the piano, his fingers twitching to strike the yellowed keys of the old, stained, yet still beautifully resonant Bösendorser. What did he, a sixteen-year-old, care of an old man's fretting, when there was music to be played? And what music: Beethoven's "Pathétique." He'd been preparing it for weeks and had only just begun to feel he was gaining ground. But Professor Hermann, wiping his damp face, persisted in speaking of the "tragical" situation in Europe which might well poison the entire civilized world; the insane belligerence of the great German nation against weaker, neutral nations; the distressing nature of anti-German sentiment in the States—"For all Germans, it seems, are now barbarians and huns." It was difficult for Darian to determine, listening to his piano teacher's ranting, in a heavily inflected Teutonic accent, whether the man's rage against Vanderpoel citizens was based on their presumed dislike of him as a possible traitor in their midst, or his dislike of them, as Christian bigots. To all this Darian murmured a faint assent, while knowing he wouldn't change his mind about playing in the recital.

My music I will play for its own sake and not for others' ears.

For music is born by way of our fingertips, it passes through us. We don't hear, we overhear.

"Darian, you must have your pride," Professor Hermann said, laying a heavy hand on Darian's shoulder as he too often did, with a wheezing, humid breath against the boy's face. "*We* must have our pride—for you are Adolf Hermann's pupil. Of all things, don't sell yourself cheaply!"

"Yes, sir." Darian frowned at the piano music as if about to begin playing, positioning his fingers above the keyboard.

"—For once they guess how eager we are to please, and would lower ourselves to their brute capitalist level for mere money," Professor Hermann continued, "then we are lost, and the sacred cause of music is violated. Do you understand, *mein Kind?*"

I am not mein Kind. I am no one's Kind.

Even Bach, Mozart, Beethoven sold their music. Even a great genius must eat.

But Darian said nothing, and hurriedly fled into the opening measure of the great sonata.

Soon after this, Darian Licht began earning small sums of money by way of music. He gave elementary instructions to several children of Academy teachers, including the Meeches' grandchildren; he played organ on Sundays at the Free Baptist Church of Vanderpoel; he was even hired for a wedding, at which he accompanied a busty local soprano who sang "Make Me No Gaudy Chaplet" from *Lucrezia*, though he'd never set eyes on the piano music before. How easy it was to please an audience, to make people smile; yet how tempting, to strike disharmonic chords, to play for their appalled fascination Chopin's enigmatic first Prelude, or an arrhythmic, cacophonous little composition by Darian Licht! Yet he resisted. He was too needful of goodwill, and of the cash gifts that accompanied such goodwill. *I will pay my own tuition, I will astonish Dr. Meech. I will astonish Father who has abandoned me.*

Really, Darian didn't believe that Abraham Licht had abandoned him. Not yet.

It greatly helped Darian's reputation in the Vanderpoel area that he was a polite, sweet-tempered and delicately attractive youth, with distinct "feminine" features; his eyes in particular, which were dreamy, thick-lashed and large as the brooding, mystical eyes of certain pre-Raphaelite portraits of androgynous beings of exotic beauty. Though he didn't believe himself shy, and was, in his heart, rather arrogant, he did give the impression of being shy; modest; uncertain; a youth with whom women might identify, and whom they might "advance." There was no need for Abraham Licht to have told his youngest son what Darian knew by instinct, that women will advance a young man to the degree to which he's "talented"—that is, attractive to them, and no evident threat.

And none of this mattered, in any case, once Darian Licht sat down at the keyboard. Piano, organ—it didn't matter. A Steinway grand or a nameless American-made upright; the costly pipe organ in the Academy chapel or the wheezing foot-pedal organ at the Baptist church. Once Darian began to play, another more forceful personality took over. Is it I, Darian, or the music that speaks at such times? But what is "I" apart from the music? Even when he played his own peculiar, gnarled compositions, it seemed to him that he was the mere instrument by which the music was given life; that it existed elsewhere on another grid or plane of being, frozen into silence as a statue is frozen; doomed to silence except for the accident of Darian Licht!

Of such paradoxes he'd have liked to speak with Adolf Hermann but in the past half year, since the *Lusitania* and the deepening of anti-German sentiment in the States, the older man had become increasingly doubtful about Darian's prospects for the future. As if Darian's future had anything to do with Germany's, or with Professor Hermann's own!—Darian bristled at the assumption. "There is nothing for people like us except music," Hermann would say, sighing, "yet can there be 'music' without 'civilization'?"

Darian's impulse was to cry boldly *Yes.*

It wasn't any secret that Adolf Hermann's piano students were disappearing. Their parents, once so deferential and flattering, now cut him in the street. Even his neighbors who'd known him for years had turned cool, if not rude; the pharmacist, the local stationer, the greengrocer—of English descent—were openly hostile. An anonymous prankster desecrated his doorstep with HUN in black tar, and one afternoon while Darian was having his lesson, boys threw stones against the parlor windows, breaking several panes. Vanderpoel police weren't helpful, for they too were bigoted against all Germans, as Professor Hermann charged. What to do? Where to flee? Vanderpoel was his home, the United States was his country, for he'd broken all ties with Germany and was sickened to his soul by his homeland's war tactics, and *could not countenance war in any guise most of all for imperial gain.* "My only hope—the only hope for civilization—is that the war will end soon and that Germany will make amends for all she's done, and be forgiven—"

The previous year, Adolf Hermann had been in a fever over the issue of Henry Ford's much-publicized peace ship, *Oscar II,* which had set sail for Europe in early December with the goal of paying $1 million to anyone in Europe who could stop the war. This was a proposal so insane, so vainglorious and childish in its assumptions and expectations there was, as Herman acknowledged, a kind of purity about it—"A native American spirituality." For weeks Darian had to listen to Hermann's commentary on Henry Ford and the *Oscar II* and the absurdity of meddling with such an imperial world power as Germany; yet when the venture failed, and the *Oscar II* merely returned with its $1 million untapped and the great Ford himself sick, it was gloatingly reported by newspapers, with a severe head cold, Professor Hermann sank into a depression. "I might have given aid to the cause instead of belittling it," he said. "I might have volunteered to go along as a German-speaking American citizen—but now it's too late. Darian, it's too late."

More distressing, Professor Hermann was growing increasingly eccentric as a piano teacher.

Because of his ranting monologues, when he finally roused himself to teach, it was late; and so the lessons ran later, and later; beginning at midafternoon, they might stretch into evening; and Darian would miss dinner. Sometimes the older man would insist upon Darian playing the "Pathétique" from start to finish, no matter his errors; sometimes he'd slam a fist down on the keyboard and lecture the frightened boy on the spot, when Darian's playing displeased him. For there was a way in which Beethoven's sonatas must be played, and numerous ways in which they must not be played. It was Adolf Hermann's belief that a Teutonic sensibility was required to fully comprehend Beethoven; no Frenchman, for instance, could play Beethoven correctly. So it infuriated Hermann when Darian played Beethoven, or Bach, or Mozart, or Schubert, in a style *not* Teutonic; in any case in a style that differed from Hermann's own, which he demonstrated for Darian. "Are you not 'Licht'? Are you not one of us, boy, despite your 'American' birth?" he once cried.

There were days when Darian could do nothing right, and days when his playing moved the elder man to tears. "So beautiful. So delicate. And the thrumming power beneath. And yet you'll betray me one day, Darian—I know." And the warm heavy hand cupped Darian's shoulder in fond, clumsy reproach.

It was Darian's belief that a musical composition even by the greatest of composers could be interpreted in any number of ways by any number of performing artists. Depending upon any number of factors: chance, intuition, the hour of the day, the weather, the whim of the performer and the whim, even, of the instrument . . . he'd imagined a composition to be titled "Broken-Stringed Piano & Warped Fiddle." A technically complex piece, yet it would make listeners laugh! (Though not Adolf Hermann. He wouldn't be quite the ideal listener.) Dreaming in his classes, gazing out whichever windowpanes were in view, Darian theorized that music need not be solemn just because "serious" music has usually been solemn; why couldn't it be as robust, as hearty, as noisy, as rousing as military parade music, or the untrained Baptist choir, or the blacksmith shouting at a horse, or the blacksmith's very bellows? There was a hissing pneumatic sound of the steam radiator in his bedroom that fascinated his ear; and the *drip-drip-drip drip drip-drip-drip* of a faucet, both rhythmic and unpredictable; the slow, then accelerated *tap-tap* of Abraham Licht's fingers on a tabletop that betrayed his private feelings even as his smiling mask of a face hid all. America was a lively symphony of automobile horns, horses' whinnies, roosters' crowing, laundry flapping in the wind; what a stifling tradition to expect that every note of a composition must be played in the same sequence, or at the same tempo, or even in the key in which the composer had written it. "And what of silence, the white margins at the edge of the notes?" Darian wondered, thrilled with his own audacity.

To Professor Hermann, however, there were two ways of playing music: correctly (that's to say, the way he played it) and incorrectly.

So with the "Pathétique." Darian was to play it at a rapid, even, measured clip; with a thunderous passion as marked; abrupt pianissimo as marked; a not-overly-slow adagio cantabile; a precisely measured tempo throughout so that the dazzling runs were perfectly executed. It was necessary to maintain absolute evenness of tempo just as the metronome on the Bösendorser kept perfect time with never a hairsbreadth of a variation. Idiosyncratic variations in rhythm and tone were *verboten* though an innocent wrong note now and then didn't greatly matter. (In fact when Professor Hermann played, Darian noticed that he struck any number of wrong notes without pause or embarrassment.)

"Why can't there be more freedom in music, Professor Hermann?" Darian once asked, "—I mean more *play* in the matter of music?" and Professor Hermann said with a snort, "Because music is *not play*."

These long, exhausting lessons left the older man too weary to see Darian to the door. So Darian let himself out of the dim-lit house after having fetched a bottle of schnapps for Professor Hermann from the sideboard in the parlor. "*Mein Kind*, you've drained all the strength from me," Hermann said with a wheezing sigh. "It is my pleasure, and my curse."

A few days before the recital, Darian played for Professor Hermann a new composition, a miniature sonata as he called it, titled "Worship." (He didn't tell his teacher but the piece was dedicated to his mother.) An eight-minute variation on a theme out of the final movement of the Beethoven sonata, it consisted of muffled chords, single notes struck and held high in the treble and low in the bass while a thin, hesitant, trickling sort of melody, an inversion of Beethoven's, made its way slowly across the keyboard like something overheard. With a bowed head, his chin creased against his chest, Adolf Hermann listened to this without comment; then, with a shrug of his shoulder, commanded Darian to play the piece another time. This, Darian did. The second time through, his fingers were more assured. He felt a thrill of excitement, anticipation. True, the "miniature sonata" didn't follow much of a formal structure; it slipped in and out of the key of F-sharp minor; and didn't resolve itself but faded out mysteriously into silence, in such a way that a listener might not realize it had ended. At the conclusion of the second playing of "Worship," Professor Hermann said with a cruel smile, "Darian. A tour de force. An 'American Pathétique'—ja? Wonderfully compressed and brief—but not brief enough."

Darian flushed with hurt. He would have risen from the piano and gathered his things and left, but Professor Hermann said quickly that he was only joking—of course. A boy composer shouldn't be so thin-skinned.

"Tell me what has led you to compose such a thing? Such a—bold and experimental piece of music? Will you?"

Darian said tonelessly that he'd written "Worship" the other night, when he'd been unable to sleep; he'd been thinking of the Beethoven sonata almost ceaselessly, and was beginning to feel stage fright about Sunday. In a state of nerves, excitement rather than worry, he'd jotted down this composition for piano which was meant to suggest the singing of a boy and his younger sister in memory of their lost mother. The scene takes place in midsummer at dusk, in the country, at the edge of a vast marsh. Sometimes the boy sings alone, in the bass; sometime the girl sings alone, in the treble. They can't be heard distinctly because of the intervention, through memory, of the Beethoven sonata, and because they're singing across distance and time. A wind is rising. Already it's autumn. Their voices are blown away. Tall grasses are rippling, a stream runs nearby. All these sounds are part of the worship. Because the lost mother is dead, she can't reply; though she tries to reply, hearing her children singing. "Her silence, though, is a special silence," Darian said. "It isn't just emptiness. It can be heard." At the piano, he played several full, deep chords; left the keys depressed for a beat of several seconds; then slowly raised them.

Almost, she might be beside me. Even here.

Touching my hair, my neck. Darian, I love you.

There was a commotion out on the street, raised voices and a dog barking, and Adolf Hermann tensed, looking toward the window. But the danger, if it was danger, passed.

"That, too, could be part of the 'Worship,' " Darian said. "The dog barking especially—I like that."

Adolf Hermann shifted his bulk in his chair and declared the lesson finished for the afternoon.

That was all: finished for the afternoon.

He told Darian please to see himself to the door, after fetching for him, from the sideboard, the bottle of schnapps and a fresh glass.

II

Harmony and disharmony. Assonance and dissonance.
Why not both?: Why not everything?

Darian foresaw that his piano lessons with Adolf Hermann must soon end. But he wouldn't be prepared for the terrible way in which they ended two months later.

On the morning of 4 February 1917, the day after President Woodrow Wilson was to sever diplomatic relations with Germany, and hardly a week after Germany declared unrestricted submarine warfare in neutral waters, Adolf Hermann would be found hanging by his neck from a beam in the cellar of his house; his face so distorted, it wouldn't appear human but bestial; his reddened eyes bulging from their sockets in a look of astonishment and horror. His suicide would be more a vexation and an outrage than a tragic, or even a pitiable, event, for his landlord and the other tenants of the row houses would be shocked and disgusted by it, and feel little sympathy for the dead man. A neatly written note in German, left on a nearby table, would be torn to bits by the landlord, whose misfortune it was to discover the body.

Why had he torn up the note?—Darian Licht would ask the man, stricken with grief; only to be told that, since the note was "unreadable, in some sort of code," it might be dangerous.

The rumor was, through Vanderpoel, that Adolf Hermann of Düsseldorf, Germany, had been a secret sympathizer with the German war effort, possibly even a practicing German spy.

III

"Bravo! Brav-vo!"

On the evening of 8 December 1916, in Frick Hall, Adolf Hermann rises to his feet (ironically? sincerely? in a spirit of play? in a gesture of boldness?) to lead the enthusiastic applause for young Darian Licht, who has performed Beethoven's "Pathétique," or a shortened version of it, with much feeling and precision. If he hasn't struck many wrong notes, if he's maintained a perfect tempo throughout, no one except a very few individuals knows; but everyone agrees he's a brilliant pianist—"And so *young*."

Adolf Hermann, though invited to the soirée to follow, disappears into the crowd with the alacrity and grace of, not a heavyset middle-aged man in a bulky overcoat, but a cat. Abraham Licht has never appeared at all, so far as Darian knows.

Though he'd sent a card and flowers to Darian at the school, delivered the previous day and signed by both *Your loving Father* and *Your loving sister Millie*.

Darian tells himself *I didn't expect them to come of course*.

Darian chides himself *How could you imagine, you fool!*

Finding himself dazed with fatigue and exhilaration trundled into a motorcar outside the chapel, driven across town to the home of the Joseph Fricks, it's Mrs. Frick who is their hostess, for Mr. Frick is away—"How Joseph would have admired your playing, Darian Licht! His favorite composer is Beethoven." Darian doesn't hear most of what is said to him; most of what is said to him is repeated, and repeated; how brilliant his "rendition"; how "handsome a figure" at the piano; is his family here?—"How proud they must be."

An elegant, enormous dining room. A buffet table so long its end can't be seen. Servants in livery, impassive and deft. Glasses of sparkling champagne, cut-glass goblets and silver trays. The mezzo-soprano advances upon Darian to tell him he's brilliant, and a handsome figure at the piano. Women friends of Mrs. Frick cluster near for they've been told (is it true? they don't dare inquire) that the brilliant young pianist is an orphan, a charity pupil at the Academy. But won't he eat? *He must eat. He's far too thin.* Won't he have a glass of champagne? Just one! Darian isn't hungry, Darian's nerves are tight as a piano's strings, he can't stop shivering, swallowing down a glassful of the surprisingly tart liquid that stings his nostrils, he recalls his sister Millie advocating *Champagne! Champagne! for all the ills of the world, from the pocket to the heart to the brain.* In a passionate voice that will tolerate no disagreement the mezzo-soprano praises young Darian Licht as a brilliant pianist in the style of the great Franz Liszt; there's applause; Darian finds himself seated at his hostess's piano, a gorgeous Bechstein that seems to float upon the rich wine-colors of the Indian carpet underfoot, his fingers aren't stiff after the ordeal of the Beethoven sonata but come to life leaping along the keyboard in a merry rendition of "Chirping Crickets" complete with interventions from Bach and certain delicate passages of the "Pathétique" several ladies find so achingly beautiful they begin to feel faint; trailing off into allegro agitato, a whirlwind of notes improvised by Darian on the spot, the giddy confluence of a sixteen-year-old's first taste of champagne and his first Bechstein and his first public applause that quite goes to his head. *Smile and any fool will smile with you!* Father cynically advised and it's true, for Darian Licht has a sweet, shy smile, the ladies are taken with his smile, the way his fair brown flamelike hair glides forward across his brow, part-obscuring one of his eyes, the way he moves his slender, sinuous arms along the keyboard. *Bravo! Brav-vo!*

Suddenly, Darian has had enough. He ceases playing. Rises from the beautiful piano. He isn't rude, but he hasn't time to be courteous. Must escape. These strangers with their glittering jewels and eyes pressing near. Can't breathe, must escape. They draw back as he plunges past them not seeing them. *Smile and any fool . . . Play piano to please the ear of any fool . . .* "But no. No. I don't want to play for fools. I will not."

Darian makes his way blindly through the crowded, festive rooms. Finds himself in a corridor, walking swiftly. A maze of a house. How can one escape? And how many miles is he from the Academy? Can he find his way back alone, in the harsh damp December wind, in the night? His eyes adjust to the dim light of the corridor and he finds himself studying what must be Frick family portraits; he's staring at a portrait of . . . his mother? The name on the gilt plaque is SOPHIA ELIZABETH FRICK, the dates are 1862–1892. This young woman died eight years before Darian was born.

"It's her."

His lost mother not quite as he remembers her, of course. Though this is certainly the woman in the Muirkirk portrait locked away in Father's room. Darian would know those large, lovely eyes anywhere that fix him with an expression of mock sobriety. Her dark hair is arranged in a fussier, more feminine style than in the Muirkirk portrait; here, instead of a smart riding habit, she's wearing a white silk gown with a feather-fringed cape gracefully draped over her shoulders. Strands of pearls, white gloves to the elbow. Ivory-pale skin. Eyes given an eerie glisten by the artist—two tiny dots of white on the irises. *Are you my son? Am I your mother? Who has told you so? What do such things mean—"son," "mother"?* Sophia Elizabeth Frick who died in 1892 regards Darian Licht born in 1900 with love, pity, recognition.

It must have been, Darian thinks, that they'd disowned her. Their daughter. She'd eloped with Abraham Licht, she'd repudiated their world, they disowned and declared her dead.

"My daughter."

So mesmerized is Darian by the portrait on the wall, by this woman who is his mother yet unknown to him, he hasn't noticed Mrs. Frick beside him until the elderly woman speaks. "Isn't she lovely? My daughter Sophie. Lost to me." Mrs. Frick tells Darian that her daughter died of typhus traveling in the Greek Isles with her married sister and her family, what a tragedy! what waste!—"Sophie was an extraordinary girl, so sweet, warm, quick-witted, intelligent; a devout Christian; a lover of horses since girlhood; gifted at the piano—though nothing, of course, like *you*. She'd been courted by a dozen outstanding young men yet she was determined, she said, to remain independent. And then . . ."

Darian is expected to speak, he supposes; yet can't speak.

Darian hears the woman's voice through a roaring in his ears.

Darian is being led . . . to another portrait of Sophia Frick, a smaller, more intimate painting of a girl of perhaps sixteen in a blue velvet riding jacket, a plumed hat on her head, and a riding crop held in her gloved right hand. *Darian. My love. If I'd but known you when I was thus, and you as you are.* Darian tries to listen to his hostess's voice but the roaring and rushing in his ears overwhelms him. His legs are weak, his senses go out like a candle flame, he falls heavily to the floor at the feet of the astonished Mrs. Frick, who stares down at him, the brilliant young pianist she'd been so eager to invite to her home, too shocked at first to cry for help.

Music is speech for those for whom speech is inadequate.
The silence surrounding music is the secret soul of music.

"The Lass of Aviemore"

I

Lovely Millicent prepares for yet another dinner dance, beautiful Matilde fusses over her gleaming silk-blond bobbed hair, and there is Mina, cunning Mina, who adjusts the bodice (snug!) of the pretty flounced dress; and Marguerite (Mr. Anson's beloved daughter, sweet, simpering, who nonetheless learned to smoke cigarettes on the sly) sees to the charming arch of the eyebrow and the near-imperceptible blush of the ceramic cheek; and Moira (born in New Orleans, honey-soft and feline but a shameless liar) . . . Moira sings "It Is Better to Be Laughing Than Crying" (as indeed it *is*) while regarding herself in profile in the mirror . . . in the mirrors reflecting mirrors . . . and declares the vision, or visions, complete.

And God saw that it was good.

And all these are the beginning of sorrows.

II

"Meet Me Tonight in Dreamland" is being played in the glass-enclosed poinsettia-bedecked ballroom, Matilde St. Goar may be observed consenting to dance with a handsome young gentleman in white tie and tails, the graceful circling, the near-weightless sweep, of a long flounced skirt, chiffon in filmy floating layers (white upon black upon white upon black), near-transparent sleeves falling loose to the elbow, the poreless doll's face, the small measured flawless smile not quite covering the white, white teeth: just as Millicent, lazy sullen Millicent, stretches and yawns and rings for the maid to draw her bath (the *purple* bubble-soap this afternoon, smelling of plums, please), and lights up the first cigarette of the day, holding her sleep-stale breath for the pleasant little jolt, that agreeable sensual little *zing*, when the powerful smoke hits her pink-tender lungs. (Has Father breakfasted already?— but what time *is* it?—and has he, yes of course he has, the perfect brute, hidden away the newspapers?—so of course Millicent must send out for more on the sly, the New York City papers in particular, being greedy, quite shamelessly greedy—sweet Millie, yawning in the midst of a childish smile—greedy for news of history.)

In narrow panels amid the glass there are gold-flecked mirrors in which the dancers may observe themselves swaying, and turning, and dipping, if they so wish, one might count as many as ninety-eight dancers if one so wishes, an equal number of attractive ladies and an equal number of attractive gentlemen, now the orchestra is playing a medley from *Babes in Toyland*, a smashing success of a bygone season, and now there are gleaming silver trays brandished aloft by liveried Negro servants (all male: but Matilde never looks), there are Venetian glasses glittering with French champagne, one may as well accept what one is offered.

Naughty Mina, who would tease by downing her glass in one great mouthful: assuredly forbidden *here*.

And Moira taps a high-heeled white-kidskin foot, the prettiest little foot imaginable, and allows her escort a glimpse, a fleeting glance, a mere soupçon, of silky ankle to flash: also forbidden.

And Marguerite the tease puckers her lovely lips as if . . . to kiss? . . . to whistle? . . . no, merely to whisper in the gentleman's ear something vague and melodic about being *tired*, being *weary*, of the foxtrot, which, it very often seems, she has been dancing *since the onset of Time*.

Poor sensitive creature! for it has become well known in Philadelphia society among the younger set in particular, that the mysterious daughter Matilde of the mysterious gentleman Albert St. Goar is so high-strung, a single ill-considered word or gesture tears against her nerves like a nail against raw silk.

Millie, not minding that her new Japanese kimono has slipped open, screams at the maid because the bathwater is too hot, too damned hot, too hot too hot too *hot!*—and another five minutes will be required for it to be adjusted.

Millie, silky pale hair falling in her face, cigarette slanted in the corner of her lips, paces about, barefoot, while the frightened girl allows water to run out of the enormous tub in approximately the same proportion as water (cold) rushes in.

And where are the newspapers?—the New York City papers in particular?

But is the orchestra *still* playing Victor Herbert tunes?—Matilde has heard them all innumerable times, Matilde has danced to them all innumerable times, she must be excused if she drifts off to the ladies' reception room . . . to do something delicious but very very forbidden in mixed company.

III

Mina who is daughterly and jealous can't resist observing by way of a mirror-panel how that much-discussed couple Albert St. Goer and Eva Clement-Stoddard dance in the midst of the other dancers, as light on their feet, as graceful, yet far more stately than most. The gentleman is handsome if rather too flushed (is his tie too tight? his starched collar? does he wear a corset?—there *is* something painfully tight-to-bursting about the man's figure); his silvery hair neatly brushed; a white rosebud in his buttonhole; his smile serene. The lady too is smiling, even rather coquettish for a woman of her age, tilting her head, sparkling, glittering, scintillating, enchanted as any young girl in love, not minding, evidently, if the world now sees: for the engagement is no longer a secret and what matters the gaping world? Eva is a handsome woman, even sharp-eyed Matilde can't deny it.

What is love except the intoxication of being wholly deceived?

Millicent orders the maid out of her sight and with trembling fingers arranges the newspapers on a table beside the tub. Lights up another cigarette—she hates it when they burn down to stubs. Throws off the kimono.

No man has looked upon her, no man has touched her. Since.

Her happiest time: sinking into a warm bath, sweet fragrant soap bubbling and winking and popping around her like champagne.

* * *

Matilde's mother long ago taught her her catechism. That madonna of stern blond beauty. *Kneel beside me, Millie. Pray with me. Deliver us of this bondage of love. Deliver us of this earthly delusion. Pray to Our Lord constantly and you will be saved.*

"The Game is our only happiness," Matilde observed the other evening to her manicured nails, "—but The Game isn't happy, is it?"

Of course the engagement has been informally announced to the couple's many friends; but on the evening of 21 December 1916, the winter solstice, it's to be formally announced by Eva's great-uncle Admiral Cyrus P. Clement at a party at his estate, Langhorne Hall.

Clearly the stellar social event of the Philadelphia season.

And when will be the wedding?—in May.

And what will Matilde St. Goar do, when her father becomes a bridegroom?—why, marry someone herself; or swallow a bottle of laudanum.

Matilde tries not to pity Eva Clement-Stoddard. Eva wants no female sympathy with her father's bride-to-be.

Taking offense that, lately, Albert St. Goar has become sentimental, speaking of a wish to have a son; a son "who might please me as much as my Matilde." A son to continue the St. Goar name and tradition? Matilde shakes her head perplexed, for—is Eva in agreement with this mad hope? This folly? (Might a woman of her age bear children? Matilde has made inquiries and has been told to her surprise and disapproval that if nature cooperates, a woman can bear children into her forty-fifth or -sixth year. And Eva Clement-Stoddard is said to be thirty-seven.)

That slightly sallow face . . . that air of vivacity . . . a splendid new Empire-style gown of robin's-egg blue . . . and looped around her throat, at the request of her fiancé, the fabled Cartier necklace of twelve perfect emeralds spaced along a rope of numerous diamonds.

For St. Goar has said he doesn't find such riches vulgar, exactly; it's within the scope of his democratic principles to find such riches . . . rather jolly.

IV

Talk is of Bucharest, which the invincible German army has just captured; and talk is of Admiral Clement's grand party—with what anxiety, what fainting eagerness, invitations are being awaited! But Millicent, in her bath, indifferent to the fact that her just-curled hair is getting wet, is reading avidly of Harlem's Prince Elihu, Prophet of the World Negro Betterment & Liberation Union.

Prince Elihu, born in Jamaica, West Indies. Prince Elihu in spotless white linen caftans in summer and spotless white woollen (and sometimes fur-trimmed) caftans in winter.

Prince Elihu in gold braid and crimson velvet with a ceremonial ruby-studded sword at his hip, preaching of the inevitable downfall of the white race—the Race of Cannibal-Devils—and the inevitable rise of the black race—Allah's Chosen People. Tens of thousands cheer Prince Elihu, Prince Elihu is the revolutionary new Negro leader who has alarmed and outraged white officials from the mayor of New York City to the President of the United States with his exotic, tireless preaching: Prince Elihu has set a record for nonstop preaching, at seven unflagging hours. *I bring not peace but a sword. I am he who am come to you who await me. I ask only that you give me your love. In return I will give you back your souls. Your souls the cannibal-devils have stolen.*

Matilde laughs, splashing her toes in the bath. Oh, delicious!

Matilde laughs, chokes . . . a sharp pain in her eyes.

In *Harper's Weekly* she reads of the controversial "prince" who rose suddenly to prominence in the past several months, out of agitation in Harlem among Negro leaders unable to agree upon the most politic attitude for their people to take regarding the War in Europe. The most prominent Negro spokesmen, friendly to whites, argue that the United States, and as Woodrow Wilson repeatedly insists, Democracy, must be defended at all costs; issues of race must be set temporarily aside. Others, younger, more marginal, more rebellious, argue that the War is "a white man's war" fought not for Democracy but for the sake of racist imperialism in Africa and elsewhere. Prince Elihu, Prophet of the World Negro Betterment & Liberation Union, is the fiercest of these new leaders, having become famous, or notorious, virtually overnight, after a rally in Central Park in which he spoke contemptuously of certain of his brothers as "white men's black men"; accusing such men of preaching subservience to whites out of cowardice and expediency. But Prince Elihu preaches rebellion: the world unification of all Negroes: a collective refusal, tantamount to treason, to enlist in the United States Army or even to register for the draft.

Death Before Humility is Prince Elihu's command to his followers.

For some time in secret Millicent has been reading of this exotic Prince. Soon, she will go to Harlem to see him with her own eyes; she will disguise herself; or, better yet, she will not disguise herself; boldly attending one of his rallies in which, it's said, gospel music is mixed with electrifying speeches and thousands upon thousands of black men, women, adolescents and children are moved to a single thunderous wave of affirmation. Prince Elihu preaches a Black Africa; Prince Elihu preaches a Black Elysium Colony, to be established in North Africa by 1919; Prince Elihu preaches an absolute end to slavery—including wage slavery; Prince Elihu warns that the Negro God is the Absolute God, All-Conquering Allah, and that the white God is but a pagan remnant.

As far as Jesus Christ is concerned—"If he was crucified, he had got to be black," Prince Elihu declares.

Harper's Weekly repeats what Millicent has read in the New York papers: that this charismatic young Negro leader is so gifted, so hypnotic a speaker, he has the demonstrated power of persuading thousands of men and women with little money to contribute considerable sums to the World Negro Betterment & Liberation Union of which he is Prophet, Regent and Exchequer.

Yes. Millicent, or rather Matilde St. Goar will soon make the journey from Philadelphia to Harlem, to see the remarkable Prince Elihu with her own eyes.

And if he spits in my face as a white devil, that will be his privilege.

V

The orchestra is playing a melody with a lively syncopated beat. The younger set is energetically dancing the half-in-half—or the lame

duck—or the newest jazz version of the waltz. Out of breath, her color
high, Matilde St. Goar flies across the floor in her partner's arms, never
seeming to lock eyes with Albert St. Goar, who glances in her direction. He's seen the papers, too—of course. The New York papers with
their two-inch headlines PRINCE ELIHU DEFIES "WHITE DEVILS" he'd
hoped to hide from his daughter for as long as possible.

As the dancers spin and dip, their heels making a staccato music
against the gleaming floor, two dozen brightly colored Australian finches
have been released from white wicker cages to fly panicked against the
glass skylight in an effort to escape, in vain. Champagne is being
served—again. Matilde St. Goar's escort in black tie and tails, a smooth-
chinned, thick-nosed, frank-faced young man with hopeful eyes, goes
to fetch her fan but, returning, can't find her . . . she's sequestered in a
grotto in the northeast corner of the grand ballroom (the theme of the
Admiral's party appears to be Roman gardens) in the company of
Roland Shrikesdale III. The convalescent young heir has never learned
to dance but has been urged by his mother to request a slow, unde-
manding waltz from St. Goar's charming daughter Matilde, for Anna
Emery has got it into her head that her only son must marry; must fall
in love as young men do with a sweet young girl of the proper sort, and
marry; and should God so grant, present her with a grandchild—"That
I may embark upon eternity with a smile."

So there's shy, bashful Roland approaching the rather arch, high-
strung beauty Matilde. Though he's large enough to hulk over the girl's
slender figure, he has the ability to make himself shrink and cringe;
you'd believe him a tongue-tied lad of fourteen, hardly an adult man in
his mid-thirties. "Excuse me, Miss Matilde—would you be so kind as to
join me in this dance?" Roland asks in a cracked voice, his face mottled
with embarrassment; and Matilde murmurs with a cool, poised smile,
"Why, Roland, thank you. But I'm rather warm, I believe I'd like to
wait this one out." Roland heaves an audible sigh, relieved. He and
Matilde are both facing forward, and seem to have nothing to say to
each other. Until Roland mutters in a lowered voice, for Matilde's ears
only, "A pity, isn't it, the finches don't sing. All they've done so far is
shit on a number of us."

Matilde smiles half in anger. Whispering, "But not, dear Roland, I
hope, on *you*."

"Nor on *you*, dear Matilde."

Matilde St. Goar in her airy chiffon gown with its layers of mauve and white flounces glances down at her voluminous skirts with a look of trepidation. A number of observers watch: will Roland, dare Roland, *can Roland* overcome his fatal shyness, and succeed in getting the girl to dance with him? Poor Roland! A virgin at the age of—is it thirty-five? And he'd survived, if only barely, an adventure in the West that few if any of his Philadelphia acquaintances could have survived. The heir to so many millions, it makes one's head spin to calculate the mere interest rate per annum.

Yet St. Goar's daughter scarcely seems to tolerate him. So very different from the father, who'd cut to the chase within weeks, capturing one of the prizes of Philadelphia, Eva Clement-Stoddard, who'd vowed (it was said) she would never, never marry again, her heart having been broken past repair.

Matilde walks swiftly away, to an outer alcove where, on the sly, she can smoke one of her bitter little cigarettes under the pretext of needing to breathe fresh air. Roland surprises his sympathetic observers by following in her wake, limping only just slightly. Mrs. Anna Emery, seeing the "young lovers" moving off the dance floor, feels a thrill of excitement. Nothing would thrill the old woman more, despite her failing eyes, kidneys and bones, than to cradle in her arms little Roland Shrikesdale IV.

Matilde, snatching up a half-filled glass of champagne from a table, drinks it down and says to Roland puffing up behind her, "I wonder you can stand it—you. For it's a prison here, isn't it? It's death."

Roland assumes a suitor's gaping, besotted look. In case anyone should be watching; and surely someone is. He says, slitting his eyes at her, and lighting up a cigarette of his own, "You're wrong. Death is dirt in the mouth, and never any music."

"Is that where 'Roland Shrikesdale III' is?—in the dirt?"

"Shut up."

"Why?—no one can hear. Not even Father."

Roland begins to speak in Harwood's gravelly voice. Smoking his cigarette in short, quick puffs as if he wanted to get it out of his hand. "He's worried they've hired a detective. Evidence is being unearthed." There's a pause, Roland laughs, chokes off his laughter with a fist against his mouth, says soberly, "—Not that evidence, I hope."

"The actual corpse? Of the actual heir?"

Matilde, that's to say Millicent, is trembling with emotion; whether hatred of her brute brother, or terror of him, or the simple exhilaration of her own daring she couldn't have said. She would flee him now and return to the ballroom din of music and laughter except, daringly, he grasps her thin wrist between forefinger and thumb and retains her. Saying, again in Harwood's voice, "I have Father's permission. His blessing. You're in with us. And there's a kind of . . . I wouldn't have guessed . . . sport in it. Such as a man feels on the back of a bucking steer. So long as you don't get thrown and trampled, you'd think you were the steer; the steer, and you, can trample anyone in your path. This, I wouldn't have guessed."

Millicent wishes she didn't understand her brother and for a moment pretends she doesn't. Then says, "It's a trap, Harwood. Even for you it's death."

But Harwood, that's to say Roland, only laughs, a high-pitched giggle. "Who's 'Harwood'? Never met him."

Millicent stares at her brute brother in black tie and tails, starched white shirt, his coarse hair trimmed and brushed and oiled and half his face disfigured by a vertical scar like lacework; his mica-glinty eyes are smiling; he exudes an air of . . . sincerity? Innocence? *For what if he isn't Harwood any longer, exactly; but under the influence of the man he murdered?* Millie feels the blood drain out of her face. Millie would seek a place to sit, to overcome this spell of faintness, but Harwood, that's to say Roland Shrikesdale, continues to grasp her wrist between his forefinger and thumb strong as an iron ring.

Yes, a trap. And, yes, sport. The Game.
And God saw that it was good.
And all these are the beginning of sorrow.

VI

On the subject of Prince Elihu, the scandal-subject of this Sunday's *New York Herald Tribune*'s front page, Abraham Licht declares in a voice to preclude discussion, "He is no one we know, or have ever known. You're being irrational, Millie—too much champagne last night, as I've warned you." And Millie says calmly, "Father, I hardly need be 'rational' to recognize Elisha when I see him." And Abraham Licht says, bringing his fist down softly upon the breakfast table like a Broadway actor for whom each gesture, beneath lights, has become so stylized it need not be completed, "Millie. My dear. You have not seen this 'Prince Elihu'—you have only seen his photograph in the papers."

On the subject of "Roland Shrikesdale III"— Millie would like to speak with Abraham Licht seriously, for is it true that a private detective has been hired? And what is this, Anna Emery Shrikesdale is urging Roland and Matilde to . . . become a romantic couple?

Initially, Abraham Licht refuses to discuss the matter.

Not for Matilde to worry about, he says.

Nor even for overly inquisitive Millicent.

Then, next day, in an ebullient mood following a seemingly profitable game of poker at the most exclusive gentlemen's club in Philadelphia, to which Albert St. Goar has recently been admitted, Abraham Licht confides to Millie that, yes, there was a detective making inquiries after St. Goar some months ago; and after Harwood as well; and no doubt after her. "But as my own informants have assured me, this man, 'Gaston Bullock Means' of the Burns Detective Agency, has given up the case as hopeless. He is of no threat."

"No threat! If old Stafford Shrikesdale and his sons suspect Harwood, they suspect him; and they suspect us. We may be in danger."

"Danger, Millie? Never."

"Father, please. You underestimate our enemies."

"In such matters, it's as well to think of 'enemies' as 'accomplices' in a unified effort. I'm well aware of Stafford Shrikesdale's suspicion of Roland, and of Bertram, Willard, Lyle—and others. But they're stymied, you see. They don't dare accuse 'Roland'—they would never initiate a lawsuit. Philadelphia is too proper, my dear, for such scandal. And you might, you know, even 'marry' Harwood—I mean, Roland. To consolidate our history, so to speak."

" 'Marry'! My own brother! That brute! That—murderer!"

"Millicent! Hush!"

This time, Abraham Licht brings his fist down hard on the table, and cups, saucers and silverware go flying.

Millie persists daringly, "He *is* a murderer. Twice over. You know, and I know. He killed that poor woman in Atlantic City, for which Thurston was blamed; and he killed Roland Shrikesdale III—obviously. Yet you seem to forgive him. You seem not to *remember*."

"Memory is not an American predilection. Where it cripples action, it's wise to forgo the past. For what is the past but—"

" 'The graveyard of Future.' Yes. But it may be a blueprint of Future, too. For people repeat themselves in action; a man who murders once may murder twice, and a man who murders twice may murder a third time. It will be on your head, Father, if—"

"Millie, I don't at all like your tone. This isn't a Broadway melodrama, that you can stand there, bristly as one of those little yapping Pomeranians the Philadelphia ladies adore, and speak to your father so—arrogantly. In so masculine a style. What if someone overheard? We must always assume that our own servants may be spies in the hire of the Shrikesdales; just as one or two of theirs are spies of Albert St. Goar."

"Father, really? Is that so?" Millie smiles, for this is news. "Who is it? And since when?"

"Since the day it became clear to me, seeing Gaston Bullock Means in Philadelphia, with dyed hair and moustache, that the Shrikesdales were in pursuit. Months ago. Exactly who, which of the male servants, you needn't know; except to bear in mind that in the matter of spying and bribing, you must always hire men, not women. For a man—any man—is open to hire; but even a sensible woman may be handicapped by loyalty."

At this, Millie laughs; goes away shaking her head, and laughing; as if the original subject of their conversation however grave, worrisome, profound has been quite banished by Abraham Licht's good humor.

For perhaps Father is wisest after all. Perhaps we would all do well simply to trust in him.

VII

What an attractive couple!—and so unexpected.

Yet both seem shy of each other. Even she.

Aloof with other young men yet agreeably, modestly shy with Roland. Surely that's a sign?

Only a quiet young woman could appeal to Roland. The more a young woman "charms"—the more terrified he is, and retreats like a turtle into its shell.

Poor boy. All he's endured. So brave. So good. Anna Emery prays for him even now, you know—"That he marry, and have children, and become one of us."

It seems that Matilde St. Goar and Roland Shrikesdale III are continually being thrown into each other's company. By the design of Philadelphia dowagers in Anna Emery's circle, as well as the enterprising Anna Emery herself; she's one of those older women who under the guise of self-effacing solicitude possess a will stronger than a stallion's. One day after Anna Emery's repeated invitations, Matilde reluctantly agrees to accompany mother and son on a drive along the Delaware River north into Bucks County, that they might all "rejoice in the beauty of fresh air and nature"—for it's a gloriously bright blue Sunday in winter, and much of the world fresh-coated in snow; and Roland has only just acquired a remarkable new imported car, a lemon-yellow Peugeot sedan with steel-spoked wheels, mahogany fixtures and cream-colored leather interior. Of this expensive car, Anna Emery herself is rather girlishly vain—"It quite suits Roland, doesn't it? So handsome."

Matilde *is* impressed, that Roland does indeed look unusually fit—for Roland—in a belted motoring coat of Scottish brown tweed and a brown leather cap with goggles and chin straps and gauntlets that give him a military air; even Anna Emery, near-blind, near-deaf, with a myriad of medical complaints and a perpetual head cold, looks quite striking in furs, seated plumb in the center of the Peugeot's backseat. And here beside young Shrikesdale in a splendid ermine coat of her own with matching hat and muffler, a Christmas gift from her father, is Matilde St. Goar with ivory-pale skin and small fixed smile . . . having very few words to utter to Roland, as he has few to utter to her, for most of the two-hour excursion.

Is Mrs. Shrikesdale disappointed, that the "young lovers" are so stiff
with each other? So reluctant, it seems, even to look at each other,
even as she chatters, chatters, chatters to the backs of their heads? If
so, she disguises it; she's a well-bred, that's to say stoical woman; a
Philadelphia lady. Only when Roland swings back into the city to
bring Matilde home to Rittenhouse Square, in the late afternoon, does
Anna Emery murmur, "I had thought the day was beautiful, and so
promising . . . ," but neither Roland nor Matilde makes a reply.

At the St. Goar residence on the northeast corner of the elegant
square, Roland parks the Peugeot at the curb and politely escorts
Matilde into her building. Propriety dictates that he should take her by
the elbow, but Matilde shudders at his touch. She says in an undertone,
"You must not, you know—please, Harwood." In his low gravelly voice
he says, " 'Must not' what?" She says, "Do away with her. That poor
well-intentioned silly old woman." He laughs. He squeezes her arm between thumb and forefinger so forcefully that, through even the thick-
ness of the ermine, she feels a jolt of pain. "No need, I'll soon have
power of attorney. Father so advises."

Perhaps someone is watching in the opulent overheated foyer:
Roland with a shy suitor's smile fumbles for Matilde's gloved hand, in a
gesture of farewell. Yet again she shudders, and clumsily shrinks from
him. "Murderer!" she whispers. Baring his teeth around the ten-inch
cigar her escort whispers in turn, "Nigger's whore!"

VIII

Sly little Mina slits her eyes, and Moira's breath grows short with the
danger, but it's not to be avoided: haughty Matilde St. Goar in waves
of gossamer white, pink-translucent pearls about her neck, must grant
a dance to that tall cousin of Roland's with the angry bristling moustache and knowing eyes, Bertram. "Bertie" to his friends—but the St.
Goars are not his friends. *I was sailing along on Moonlight Bay . . . singing
a song . . .* but neither Matilde nor her stiff dance-partner is listening to
the words of the new, popular song for it's clear, Millie thinks, *this man
knows.* And his breath is a dog's breath, hot and damp; and the nostrils
of his aquiline nose quiver; and he says not a word to Matilde nor does

Matilde say a word to him; yet in the dance, the two are locked together in understanding; an almost erotic bond.

The dance ends. The dancers step back from each other unsmiling.

Bertram Shrikesdale bows, murmuring, "Thank you, Miss St. Goar, for a most enjoyable and edifying turn on the dance floor."

Matilde St. Goar makes the barest semblance of a curtsy, murmuring, "Thank *you*, Mr. Shrikesdale."

And yet Millie thinks afterward *am I imagining it?*

For one of the hazards of The Game, she has come to realize, is that one may imagine too much. Or too little.

This morning at breakfast studying the hazy girl's face reflected in a table knife smeared with raspberry jam as Father, whistling a strain of *Don Giovanni* under his breath, rapidly skims columns of newsprint making pencil checks beside certain stock market listings. Abraham Licht is in one of his good, mysterious moods. He's been chuckling over the news that Henry Ford has leapt into the "war profits" fray with plans to manufacture airplane motors, submarine equipment and other military items—"Having given up, it seems, on peace." (Abraham Licht has never forgiven Henry Ford for his great success with the Model T and Model A automobiles, for a quarter century ago Abraham had hoped to manufacture a vehicle patented as the "horseless quadricycle," an open sleigh-like chassis with four-cycle engine and thin wobbly bicycle wheels; this effort, predating Millie's birth, she's heard of only elliptically, and thinks must have been very silly indeed. Bicycle wheels! Yet Abraham Licht firmly believes that Henry Ford cheated him of his rightful fortune, as of his rightful place in American history.)

Millie says suddenly, as if she's only just now thought of it, "You seem to be forgetting, Father, that you should be giving warning to Darian and Esther to expect a new stepmother soon. And you should bring them to Philadelphia to meet Eva, you know."

"No, dear. I am not. Forgetting, I mean."

Abraham Licht doesn't glance up but continues to make checks against stocks.

"Well—are they to join us? For the wedding, and the rest?"

"No, dear. I don't believe so."

Millie stares at her father, maddening in his ambiguity.

"Excuse me, Father: do you mean you've told them about Eva and the wedding, or you have *not?*"

"So many questions, Millie! This isn't an audition for a fluffy Broadway comedy, you know. You need not be arch and brittle with me."

Millie pouts, Millie lets the table knife fall with a reproachful thump. It worries her that Father may be sharing more of his plans lately with Harwood than with her; not that Millie's pride has been wounded, though of course it has been wounded, but that Father may be misled by Harwood, and bring them all to a disastrous end.

Millie thinks of Darian and of Esther . . . though it's an effort. Her young brother and sister whom she loves, or would love if she could spend time with them; if life in Philadelphia weren't so . . . consuming. Only the other day she received from Darian a copy of a song he'd written "For Millie's Voice Alone Alone"—she took it to the piano and tried to peck out the tune, but there didn't seem to be any tune. A queer composition, so many sustained notes above high C "in an angry elegiac tone." Did Darian seriously expect her to sing this song? She had yet to reply to his preceding letter, or letters; she hoped he would forgive her. Guiltily she asked Abraham Licht if he'd sent flowers as he planned for Darian's concert debut, and if he'd remembered to pay Darian's tuition for the semester, and Abraham Licht said, annoyed, "*I* am the boy's parent, Millie. *I* hope I fulfill a parent's responsibilities."

Nor has Millie taken time to thoroughly reply to Esther's letters, which are of even less interest (to be truthful) than Darian's. Esther writes, writes, writes about Muirkirk as if Muirkirk were the hive of the universe and not a dreary backwater village of no significance; her letters are churned out in a breathless schoolgirl hand, filled with allusions to people who've become, to Millie, no more than names: the Deerfields, the Woodcocks, the Ewings, the Mackays . . . and many more. The last time Millie saw Esther, she'd been surprised by her sister's size: the girl is taller at twelve than Millie at twenty-three. (Both are a year older now.) Unlike poised, practiced Millicent, Esther is shy and yet talkative; rawboned and eager; graceless, gawky and well-intentioned, but not what one would call charming. "A female lacking in charm must have a good heart," Abraham Licht once said, in another context; yet he might have been speaking of his own younger daughter. Esther has wavy dark hair inclining to coarseness, like a dog's fur; her eyes are warm, intelligent, hazel-brown, of no special distinction; her frame boyish, with long gangling limbs and lean hips. Esther had shocked Millie by saying she wished to turn eighteen as quickly as possible and join the American Red Cross volunteers in France. "Why Esther," Millie responded, "—how can you say such a thing? The mere thought of blood is repulsive. And we're not yet in the war." Esther said eagerly, "Oh but there're many American girls and women working for the Red Cross, Millie, just as there're many American men who've joined up with the Allies. The innocent victims of war need our help, you know, whether the United States has formally declared war or not." Millie saw the logic of this; yet still the prospect of working with bodies, let alone wounded bodies, let along the dying, made her feel faint. Esther went on to tell Millie that, through church, she knew a woman who'd done volunteer work with the Red Cross Children's Bureau in France, and another woman volunteer at a refugee hospital in Beauvais; and yet another woman who'd been near the front lines to work with the wounded and disfigured. There was a Red Cross unit in Paris attached to a clinic where artificial limbs and faces (metal masks of paper thinness) were fitted to mutilés, as they were called. "Only imagine, Millie, being allowed to do such work!" Esther said with shining eyes. "And there's so much of it to be done."

Said Millie, "I'm sure, yes, there is."

Esther begged Millie to intercede with Father, so that she might begin her nurse's training as soon as possible in Contracoeur, but though Millie vaguely promised her she would, she hadn't said a word. It made her feel faint just to think of . . . mutilés. Poor stricken men (and women?) fitted with metal masks for the remainder of their lives.

Abraham Licht calls Millie back to herself by saying, in a more normal voice, the stock market listings set aside amid toast crumbs and congealing bacon grease, "To answer your original question, Millie: I've decided that it's wisest to keep news of the wedding from Darian and Esther for the time being. All news, I mean, of their having a stepmother."

"Oh Father. Isn't that . . . extreme?"

A frown. Abraham Licht rises from the breakfast table rather abruptly.

"I mean, Father . . . won't you ever see Darian and Esther? With Eva? They aren't to be forgotten, are they?"

Still Abraham Licht frowns, glowers; as if confronted with a singularly slow-witted daughter.

"Oh! I see," Millie says, embarrassed. "It's Eva you don't want to know about *them*. One stepchild, Matilde, is more than enough. *I see.*"

"Indeed, yes," Abraham Licht says, in a better mood now that Millie hasn't disgraced herself, and on his way out of the room, "—one is more than enough."

IX

The wind bloweth where it listeth, and thou hearest the sound thereof, but canst not tell whence it cometh, and whither it goeth: so is everyone that is born of the Spirit.

A tattered dream, a remnant of the previous windblown night. She'd been a child again in Muirkirk in thrall to her mad, vengeful mother. A child again, conceived in sin. A wretch whom only Jesus Christ might save.

Your mother was a religious lunatic, Father has said.

Your father is the only savior you require. Reason, sanity and strategy.

Standing at one of the tall windows of her bedroom in the sixth-floor apartment of the Rittenhouse Arms staring at the snowy square below: the crescent walks, the frozen fountain at the center, the great leafless elms. *Having given so much pain to the woman who was my mother it's fitting that I endure pain for pain's very sake.*

Still, Millie's frightened. What will become of her after her father marries Eva Clement-Stoddard? Must she marry, too? And . . . whom?

X

At a festive though crowded soirée at Longue Vue, the country estate of the Marcus Van Hornes, Albert St. Goar draws his daughter away from the circle of young bloods that has surrounded her, to whisper in her ear: "Do you see, Matilde, that woman across the way, chat-

ting with Roland and his mother?—in the green crêpe de chine dress—
her hair that flaming chestnut-red? Yes: she is the one I mean. She's
Senator Collis Swift's wife Lucille—so we were introduced, a few minutes ago—she and her husband, up from Virginia, are houseguests of
the Van Hornes—yes, a reasonably attractive woman, for her age. Now
what I should like you to do, dear," St. Goar says, speaking now rapidly,
and gripping Matilde's arm, "—what I should beg you to do, is not to
meet her—not to be introduced, as such—but, as soon as the lady
strolls away from Roland and Mrs. Shrikesdale (which will not be long:
they are so boring, those two), position yourself close by her, and, looking gaily past her, as if to a far corner of the room, call out the name
'Arabella'—keeping a resolute gaze *past* her; and we will see what her
response is."

St. Goar is staring at the lady in question as if transfixed; as agitated
as ever Matilde has seen her dignified father in public. Yet he doesn't
allow her to interject a question; he has no time. "Be off, be off, my
dear!" he whispers, "—and we will see what we will see."

So Matilde cheerfully obeys; she's always happiest obeying Father
when the task is easily executed, and tinged with an air of mystery.

And when she stations herself close behind the lady in question
(who *is* handsome, though slightly stout, and heavily rouged), and calls
out in a light though piercing soprano voice, "Arabella!—oh, *Arabella!*" while making a pretense of waving gaily at someone on the far
side of the room, Senator Swift's wife responds in a manner most striking: she doesn't turn toward Matilde—doesn't so much as glance in
Matilde's direction—instead, she stands rigid, her expression frozen,
as if a current of electricity pulsed through her body; and it's clear to
the keen-eyed observer at least that the lady in green steadfastly refuses
to turn—that all of her muscular strength, and the strength of her
will, goes into the act of *not* turning.

Then a moment later all has changed; and Matilde has swept past;
and Senator Swift's wife has the opportunity to glance around, covertly,
casually, yet with an air of vague relief, to see that this "Arabella" was
hardly meant for her; and that there can be no reason in this company,
in the year 1916, that it *might* be meant for her.

XI

Suddenly, with no warning—for how could there have been a warning—on the evening of 18 December, at a dinner dance hosted by a couple whose names Millicent has temporarily misplaced—suddenly, there comes her Savior.

Calling out, in a startled voice: "Mina—?"

And she who has been cavorting among the mirrors in the Gold Room, by no means drunk (for she has had only two or three glasses of champagne) yet not, perhaps, entirely sober (for it is so very tedious to remain sober), whirls about, not very gracefully, and sees—but whom is it she sees?

A young man of about thirty, a stranger; yet alarming in the eagerness with which he bounds up to Matilde, and the boyish delight with which he addresses *her*.

Yet in the next instant the young man is apologetic and deeply embarrassed, for of course this isn't "Mina Raumlicht" whom he has so rudely accosted but "Matilde St. Goar"—who confusedly offers him her hand and in violation of proper etiquette dares to introduce herself.

And the blushing young man introduces himself—"Warren Stirling, of Contracoeur. More recently of Richmond, Virginia, where I've joined an uncle's law firm."

(*Warren Stirling.* Does the name strike a chord, evoke any response? You would not think from Matilde's composed face that, yes it does.)

". . . very sorry to have upset you, Miss St. Goar," Warren Stirling is saying, still holding Matilde's delicate gloved hand, and speaking passionately, "—but you so much resemble a girl I once . . . knew. 'The Lass of Aviemore' I called her—a romantic fancy of which she knew nothing just as, I should make clear, she knew nothing of *me*. You might be sisters, Miss St. Goar—you might almost be twins. Though years have passed . . . we are all a bit older now."

"And what was the name again?" Matilde asks carefully.

Warren Stirling repeats the name. Reverently.

Matilde says, "Mr. Stirling, I am sorry to disappoint."

Following which, things happen swiftly.

In three hours and forty-five minutes, to be exact.

And in the course of several hastily arranged meetings for the following day, the next day and the next.

For Warren Stirling's devotion to the lost Mina Raumlicht is readily transferred to the living Matilde; and Matilde, dazed and shaken and forgetful of her hauteur, is irresistibly drawn to him. ("He loves me," she thinks. "Isn't that argument enough, that I am to love him? And Warren Stirling is *good*.") In a burst of tears and candor at their third rendezvous, in a tearoom on Rittenhouse Square, she confesses to Warren Stirling that her name isn't Matilde but Millicent, or Millie; "Matilde" being a caprice of her willful father's following the death of her mother, whose name was Millicent, when Millie was twelve.

" 'Millie'—a lovely name. 'Millicent.' It suits you perfectly," Warren Stirling says, gazing upon her with tender eyes.

"My father, you see, is a strange man," Millie hears herself saying, "—a powerful and even cruel personality. For me to feel affection for any other man, any man not *him*, would be interpreted, I'm afraid, as a betrayal of him."

Warren says, squeezing Millie's gloved hands, "Why, I wouldn't wish you to betray your father, Millie, in becoming my—bride," and Millie says, suffused with happiness, "Nor would I, Warren—but what must be, must be. 'As above, so below.' "

"The Bull": L'Envoi

Poor Anna Emery Shrikesdale: though she was only in her midseventies her bones had grown so light and brittle, her left thighbone snapped of its own while Roland was helping her to walk; and so ravaged was she by the subsequent pain, and so generally demoralized by the predicament of being yet again bedridden, the poor woman never recovered, but lay for hours in a delirium, during which time she wept, and raved, and prayed, and begged for Roland to remain close by her; and abruptly, in the early morning hours of 19 December 1916, passed into a comatose state—from which her physician said it was "highly unlikely" that she would recover.

"Do all you can to save my mother," Roland said, agitated. "Yet do not, you know, dare to exceed the boundaries of 'natural law'—do not extend the poor woman's suffering by a single minute!"

For hours Roland maintained a strict vigilance by Mrs. Shrikesdale's bedside, as all the household staff noted; stroking her limp hand, speaking to her in an encouraging, boyish voice, even for some heartrending minutes singing to her one or another lullaby which, long ago, *she* had sung to *him*. Then, growing restless, he called for newspapers—for a bite to eat, and several bottles of ale—and went so far as to light up a cigar in the very sickroom!—being distracted by his worry for Mrs. Shrikesdale, no doubt, and not entirely possessed of his usual good judgment. (However, Roland meekly put out the cigar when reprimanded by Mrs. Shrikesdale's physician.)

Following which, it was afterward estimated that, between the hour of midnight and one o'clock (of 20 December), Roland slipped away from his mother's bedside, and from Castlewood Hall itself—never, to the astonishment and horror of all of Philadelphia, to return.

It was a discreetly kept secret at this time that Roland Shrikesdale III, while a loving and dutiful son to his mother, and a pious churchgoing Christian, and in society a gentleman famously ill at ease with women, had yet acquired since his return from the West a very different sort of repute in one or another of the Philadelphia sporting houses: being known, for example, not without affection, and some awe, as "The Bear" (owing to the prodigious quantity of hair growing on much of his body) at the Clover Street establishment of Mrs. Fairlie, and "The Bull" (owing to his prodigious sexual powers) at the Sansom Street establishment of Madame de Vionnet. Rather more as a gesture of good breeding than out of an actual intent to deceive, Roland customarily gave a false name at such places—"Christopher," "Harmon," "Adam," etc.—and so accommodating was the atmosphere, so diplomatic the persons with whom he was likely to come into contact, only a very few members (all, of course, men) of Roland's own set knew of his double identity.

(For such is the expression—"double identity"—crude and sensational, indeed—to come into play, after that tragic event which newspapers throughout the East were to headline as *Roland Shrikesdale's Second Demise.*)

It was directly to Madame de Vionnet's brownstone that Roland drove that night in his Peugeot; it was in the favored Blue Room on the second floor that the grieving young man spent several recuperative hours in the company, as was his custom, of two of Madame de Vionnet's most attractive girls—who afterward testified to The Bull's undimmed ardor and prowess. That poor Roland didn't give a hint of the distress he obviously felt for his dying mother was in keeping, Madame de Vionnet said, with the rich young man's good manners; for he wasn't one of those tedious gentlemen of whom, alas, there are many, who insist upon bringing their troubles with them to the very place where such distractions are to be overcome.

Following this interlude Roland said good-bye to the girls and to Madame de Vionnet, tipping her handsomely. He left the brownstone by a side door to make his way through the softly falling snow to his lemon-yellow Peugeot parked close by. Yet, about to unlock the automobile, suddenly, so suddenly he didn't have time to think, he was accosted by two, or was it three men, of his approximate size and weight, who bore quickly upon him and whose faces he couldn't see as they pinioned his arms to his sides and yanked his hat down over his eyes. "Mr. Shrikesdale," said one, in a falsetto voice, "—we've been sent by Anna Emery to fetch you to her at once." Roland, struggling, protested, "But—I'm fully capable of driving home myself—I'm on my way to her at this very moment." A second man, drawing a brawny forearm beneath Roland's chin so he was forced onto his toes, choking and sputtering, unable to breathe, said in a similarly high-pitched, jeering voice, "Mr. Shrikesdale!—we have been sent by your long-dead father to fetch you to him at once, with the greatest dispatch."

"Albert St. Goar, Esquire"

"Is't so?—to 'bestride the narrow world like a Colossus'—!" speaks Abraham Licht softly to his mirrored reflection as at a quarter past five on the afternoon of 21 December he at last completes his exacting toilet. "Indeed yes: it's so."

By way of a hand mirror he spends some minutes critically examining himself from all sides, and finds the vision gratifying—though certain gray-grizzled hairs and the creased forehead, in this light, show glaringly; and it's as he feared, a slight excess of weight has had a deleterious effect upon the Roman line of his jaw. Yet as always formal attire, in this instance white tie and tails and a prominent French collar, enhances his natural aristocratic bearing and gives a spark, of sorts, to his spirits.

A spark or a smoldering flame?—within the hour the bridegroom-to-be will have dropped by Eva Clement-Stoddard's house to escort her out to Langhorne Hall; and all of Philadelphia will begin assembling there to celebrate the engagement of Mrs. Clement-Stoddard to Albert St. Goar, Esq.

At which time Admiral Clement will announce the date of the nuptials: 30 March 1917.

"Am I content?—very nearly. Am I fulfilled?—very nearly. Have I conquered all?—very nearly."

And I love the woman.

The deep-set eyes, the winking secrets, the smile, it *is* a genuine smile, Abraham Licht's smile, superimposed for a dizzying moment upon the smile of Albert St. Goar.

And God saw that it was good.

And at this moment the doorbell to the apartment sounds and St. Goar's manservant hurries to answer it.

*   *   *

So excited is Abraham Licht at the prospect of the evening ahead—
the apotheosis, or nearly, of all he has yearned for in his lifetime—
he has decided to be lenient in the matter of his daughter's strange
behavior this past week. He attributes Millie's frequent absences from
the apartment and the flurried distraction of her manner to the fact
of his imminent marriage. (For of course Abraham knows nothing of
Warren Stirling, not even the young man's name; nor of the couple's
plans rapidly taking shape for a wedding—or a secret elopement—of
their own.) "Millie is jealous, Millie is frightened of the future—poor
girl, I quite understand. As if I, her father, would abandon her. Never!"
He's decided, too, not to vex himself right now with anxiety over Darian . . . from whom he received just that morning a startling, impertinent letter.*

"I shall deal with Darian in good time," Abraham Licht thinks uneasily, "—and only hope the lad will have the tact not to spring his
nasty surprise on poor Esther."

Of these distressing matters Abraham Licht doesn't think, for it begins to seem to him that the glimmering earthly globe *is* but the size of
an apple to be snatched up in hand, and devoured!—and the days,
months and years of warfare leading to this consummation are as
nothing— "Mere chaff in the wind." Even if he wished, he couldn't
summon back that terrified child of six or seven who was discovered exhausted and starving one day along a country road near the great
Muirkirk marsh; he couldn't summon back the boy he was, the hungry
young man he'd become, the lover, the father. . . . As for the many

---

* Darian's letter, astonishing from a son who'd seemed so long obedient and reasonable,
was a harsh, unwarranted attack upon Abraham Licht as a "deceitful father." Darian
charged him with causing the death of his and Esther's young mother Sophie and, following her death, seeking to erase her memory. Darian's letter was scribbled in anguish, and
obvious haste, covering four sheets of notebook paper and concluding:

> You cheated us of our Mother so I will cheat myself of all that is Father. I
> swear I will never see you again. I will never speak with you again. I will
> never be a son to you again SO LONG AS I LIVE.

> P.S. I have arranged to pay my own tuition for the term at Vanderpoel & will
> not be returning next year.

>   Darian

women in his life, upon whom so much of his passion has been centered, he refuses to recall them. They disappointed him: but Eva
Clement-Stoddard will not.

There's the hope, too, that he and Eva will have a child together. A
son?—but even a daughter would do! To replace those who've been
faithless.

So jubilant is he, so pleasantly enlivened by a glass of sherry he's
been sipping during his lengthy and exacting toilet, Abraham isn't concerned at first over the mysterious, heavy packages which have been
delivered by messenger to ALBERT ST. GOAR, ESQ.—wrapped in stiff silver paper with gilt ribbons and bows and numbering at least one dozen;
of odd sizes—one appears to be a hat box, another is cylindrical, others
are long and narrow like florists' boxes, the rest are rectangular. If
there's an edge of mockery to the accompanying card,

SALUTATIONS & CONGRATULATIONS
HAIL & FAREWELL
"ALBERT ST. GOAR, ESQ."

Abraham isn't in a mood to take note. Instead it seems to him in
the celebratory mood of the day that out of nowhere these handsomely wrapped presents should arrive, and that they should be sent
anonymously.

"Damn! I have so little time," Abraham thinks, glancing at his gold
pocket watch, one of Eva's heirloom gifts. "But I can't resist opening
one or two of these now; maybe they contain something that will
amuse my darling."

So, briskly, whistling a favorite aria from *Don Giovanni*, he unwraps
one of the moderate-sized packages, noting its peculiar heaviness. Not
clothing, clearly—an objet d'art?

In fact it's a tin stamped with the familiar heraldry of Fortnum's Food
Shop, London. ("That's right: Albert St. Goar is formerly of London.")
The lid has been hammered securely down so he has some difficulty
prying it loose; has to use a butter knife, for leverage; then, staring inside, astonished he sees—a hunk of raw meat? Leg of lamb? beef? *covered in dark, kinky hairs?* He feels a tinge of nausea. Why would meat
from the butcher's shop be delivered in so crude a manner—the inside

of the tin reeking with fresh blood, and bone marrow, gristle and torn flesh hideously exposed?

"How disgusting," Abraham exclaims. "And in Philadelphia of all places."

With shaking hands, yet with that stoic fortitude that has characterized his entire life and career, a sense that *we must proceed to the end even if the end be bitter*, Abraham tears off the wrappings of another tin, and pries it open to discover—dear God!—*a bloodless-white naked human foot with misshapen toes and nails ridged with grime, attached to the remains of an ankle.*

From this, grimly, teeth clenched, Abraham proceeds to a smaller tin containing *several pounds of intestines heaped together in an unspeakable slippery mass.*

Indeed it's a pity as Abraham Licht would one day note in his memoir that, imagining himself a lucky man he'd been in truth luckless, a pawn of the gods, for had he begun the unwrapping with the hat-box package containing Harwood's head *I would have immediately comprehended the horror of the situation and would have been spared proceeding further.*

PART III

There is no conclusion . . . There are no fortunes to be told and there is no advice to be given. Farewell.

—*William James, at the time of his death, 1910*

A Blood-Rose!

. . . **W**hispers the dying woman in amazement, a woman no older than Esther, look! a blood-rose! . . . though she's staring at the ceiling and unable to see the black blood spreading about her thighs in a soft sighing explosion, soaking into the mattress, O God help me, a blood-rose! . . . in a fever delirium, in a parched heat so powerful that Esther's fingers burn touching her skin, trying to steady her, as the older nurse works to staunch the flow of blood: and the room's four walls press suddenly close.

So suddenly, Death. And Esther staring, numbed, unprepared as if the reversal of Life were a mistake of her own which, if she but knew what she'd done, she might rectify.

Afterward it's said of the dead woman (aged nineteen, mother of three young children): What did she expect, doing a thing like that? And if she had three children already, why not four? why not five? six?

Had she lived, criminal charges would have been brought against her, but not against her husband, no longer living with his family.

A blood-rose, thinks Esther, appalled, fascinated, pressing her forehead against the windowpane of the dormitory room, while the other student nurses chatter behind her; and Death hovers about her, a thin

coating of panic, sweat sticking to her skin. Standing here, her back to
the crowded room, she can barely see—for it's nearly dusk—the fine
chill mist that rises in the valley each day at this time, blown in opaque
little clouds, hurtful to breathe. On cold nights it freezes and the tall
grasses in the field behind the hospital are covered unevenly in frost
and in the morning Esther's heart aches with thoughts of Muirkirk and
home . . . for she has come a very great distance, it seems to her, and
perhaps, as Katrina has warned, there will be danger in going back.

Standing with her back to the lighted room, staring out at the gathering dark, at Death, Esther begins to see in the glass her hazy image,
taking form. It is strong, it is defiant, it is her own.

A *blood-rose,* Esther whispers.

A *blood-rose,* she writes in her letter to Darian, telling him of this,
and of other spectacles now commonplace, now daily, spectacles past
imagining if one were to fully imagine (though Darian might write the
music to express them: only *he!*) but words fail her as if, with clumsy
fingers, she were trying to hold a pen too small, whose point broke
when pressed against paper. Now there is so much to say, so much! but
she cannot speak! the words turn to tears in her throat and she cannot
speak! trying to describe for her brother (so many hundreds of miles
away he will never hear, he will never understand) the quality of her
life as a nursing student, one of three hundred girls, at the nurses' training school attached to the Port Oriskany General Hospital. But there is
the restraint of paper, pen, ink, words. How very painfully they shape
themselves, *words,* awkwardly held in the mouth, a tongue grown oversized. Esther would tell Darian about the young mother who hemor-
rhaged to death the previous day with no doctor in attendance but
doesn't the word *hemorrhage* make distant and clinical what was so real,
Esther's own first experience of Death, the astonishment of Death, that
blood-rose blossoming so very suddenly in an ordinary room. . . . Esther
would tell Darian of the strange angry strength that rushes through her
in waves to leave her sick and numbed and exhausted . . . yet exulting.
Esther Sophia Licht living away from Muirkirk for the first time in her
life, enrolled at the Port Oriskany School of Nursing, in her starched
white student's cap, her nursing uniform and pinafore, her white stockings, white shoes.

For white is the hue of purity. Of idealism.

Esther's secret, which she would tell Darian alone of all the world: *Past terror, there's happiness. I am on earth to serve, not to be served.*

Zealous Esther, impulsive Esther, Esther who's so good-hearted and naive writes also to a young man named Aaron Deerfield, away taking premedical courses at the university in Albany. Aaron she's adored since eighth grade; Aaron who's embarrassed by her attention and loyalty yet allows her to love him though he can't, as he's painstakingly explained, love her in return.

Yet, Aaron has made a vow that if he ever loves any young woman (which maybe he can't, he *has* tried) it will be Esther.

Which fills Esther with a hot embarrassed pleasure. As if, indeed, she were already loved.

To Aaron Deerfield, Esther writes several lengthy letters a week, not minding that he replies no more than once a month, and then briefly. It's her privilege to write to him describing her nursing classes, her routine at the hospital, her more interesting cases, providing sharply detailed little sketches of the doctors on the hospital staff, the older nurses, her instructors, her nurse-classmates who are emerging as "characters"— as it's her privilege to love him. But she won't embarrass him by making such claims. Concluding her letters not with *Love* but *As always.*

Most of her fellow nurses have boyfriends. Fiancés of one kind or another. Lovers. And some of the older, prettier girls—so excited rumors wash about, spilling and splashing as they will—are said to be involved with doctors at the hospital.

Married men.

(And what are the results of such affairs, sometimes?)

(Of such matters, Esther doesn't write Aaron Deerfield.)

Yes Esther is happy, yes she's privileged. It's human beings that fascinate, more than disease and accident; though these are the means by which she, as a nurse, might come into intimate contact with them.

A fascination of flesh. Examining anatomy-text drawings, photographs. The extraordinary drawings by Leonardo da Vinci reproduced in a portfolio-sized book she'd purchased for $8 in a secondhand-book store in the city. The revelations of the dissection lab, that initially shock, disgust, terrify; then excite and illuminate. For how natural the body is, how . . . ordinary. Yet the amazing subtlety of flesh, its variations in thickness, solidity. How inadequate, mere words: to say of an individual's skin *white, black, colored.* And how strange that we're encased in flesh from birth to death.

Our first obligation is to serve the flesh. Others' flesh.

To relieve pain, to restore health. To allow the spirit to shine forth.

Not to punish by withholding all we can do.

Not to judge, not to moralize, not to punish. Not to give aid to Death.

Esther's head rings from twelve hours, fifteen hours on her feet. Sleepless hours of being commanded to hurry here, to hurry there, do this! do that! and promptly. The hospital is a vast ship at sea amid unpredictable weather, its captain is an elder doctor and his officers a hierarchy of doctors, exclusively male; below them a hierarchy of nurses and nurses' aides, exclusively female. Esther doesn't yet question this double hierarchy for it seems to her as to everyone else, including the elder, head nurses who are so much more experienced and capable than the younger doctors, that this is the very principle of the universe, inviolable. It's true, in high school, Esther Licht and Aaron Deerfield were both A students and possibly Esther was more imaginative in biology class than Aaron, but neither of them would have thought that Esther, and not Aaron, should go to medical school. Esther's father, and her sister Millie, even Katrina have expressed disapproval of Esther going to nursing school. *Ugh. Blood and bodies. Excrement. How can you soil your hands?*

There's the concern, too, unspoken—*Who would wish to marry a nurse?*

Yet Esther's happy. No matter she's frequently sick with the flu that passes continuously through the nurses' residence hall and the hospital. Fevers, infections, racking coughs that kill the weaker of the patients, even if they've been hospitalized with other ailments. Such are the facts of medical life, not to be helped. Or so it seems in 1918. Or so Esther wishes to think, in love with her destiny.

In the end, Esther's father agreed to her request, seeing how passionately she wanted to become a nurse. Seeing, perhaps, that like Darian she was stubborn and self-determined, and *would* become a nurse with or without his blessing. Making a show of taking out his checkbook with a flourish—"And how much is a semester's tuition? Or better yet, a year?"

Poor Father. He'd returned to Muirkirk just before Christmas of 1917, exhausted and ill; he'd had a breakdown like the one he'd suffered when Esther was a little girl, many years ago; once again he was forced to abandon his business and retreat to Muirkirk, where Katrina and Esther nursed him back to health.

He'd been sick for nearly three months. He'd lost weight, and aged; what most frightened Esther, as she wrote to Darian, was *He has aged in his soul. Something has happened of which he will never speak.*

Abraham Licht was enough himself to be annoyed that a daughter of his should "wear her heart on her sleeve so openly" for a neighbor's son, Aaron Deerfield; and should admire in such schoolgirl fashion Dr. Deerfield, who was an ordinary village doctor—"A sawbones, as I believe his ilk are called." Abraham's scorn was rejuvenating to him; as Esther shrewdly saw, her father took heart when there was someone to oppose, a presumed adversary or enemy. It worked out well for her, as she overheard Abraham remarking to Katrina, "Let the girl go to nursing school, if she wants. Away from Muirkirk and the pernicious 'Deerfield' influence. A daughter of mine in love with such a dolt!"

The days, the weeks, months . . . at the start, Esther kept a meticulous diary but soon fell behind for there wasn't time, never enough time; losing count of all who'd died (and each death so precious, unique) . . . of the babies born (and each birth a miracle, beyond comprehension) . . . and the many letters written in head-on haste and emotion to Aaron Deerfield and others . . . Father, Millie, Darian, Katrina . . . who fail to reply to her in the spirit in which she writes to them, or fail to reply altogether. *Am I too eager with love for them? Do I repel them with my hunger?*

At the nursing school, Esther's energy, stamina and idealism are spoken of with awe, admiration, exasperation, in some quarters mockery and envy. To no one's surprise Esther Sophia Licht will graduate first in her class of seventy-three students.

Yet one day in early spring rapidly climbing three flights of stairs to her airless, cramped room, shared with three other nursing students; in a basin of tepid water she washes her face, dries her eyes, pressing a towel against her eyeballs she sees suddenly the blood-rose illuminated in fire where previously it had been dark; and shocks herself by beginning to cry; she, Esther Licht, who never cries, unable to stop crying for many minutes though by this time she's accustomed to Death and, as she tells herself, happy, very happy.

The Wish

I

"I am not ill—I am well."
      "I am not *ill*—I am *well*."
"I am not ill—I am well."

This mantra the patients of the Parris Clinic, Annandale-on-Hudson, New York, are instructed to chant one hundred or more times a day; silently or together in a swelling communal orison; with eyes open or tightly shut. The discipline is known as Autogenic Self-Mastery, the discovery of Dr. Felix Bies, cofounder with Dr. Moses Liebknecht of the Parris Clinic. Here, the infirm are taught that as the physical being can be cured of affliction by way of elixirs, diet, hot baths, hydrotherapy, herbal medicines and the like, so too can the spiritual being be cured of its more insidious afflictions by way of Self-Mastery. It's an Eastern discipline descended from ancient yogic practices and Buddhist teachings yet as Dr. Bies and Dr. Liebknecht insist it's a discipline uniquely suited to North America—"Where *will* and *destiny* are one."

Paralysis, cancer, nervous disorders; feebleness of intellect and of personality; anemia, otalgia, migraine, multiple sclerosis, myxedema; senility, aging—these are but symptoms of spiritual disequilibrium that can be treated at the Parris Clinic; with the contractual understanding beforehand, fully documented and notarized, that only by way of the patient's "active volition" can a true cure be effected. Among the permanent residents of the Parris community are an eighty-seven-year-old woman cured of glaucoma and ileitis; a ninety-three-year-old woman once crippled by arthritis and now capable of hiking on the Clinic's fifty-acre grounds, and of playing lawn tennis; an eighty-six-year-old man wounded in the chest in the Battle of Bull Run and subsequently subject to numerous ailments—heart trouble, dyspepsia, fatigue, asthma—until recently, by way of a strict diet, hot baths and Autogenic Self-Mastery, he declared himself one hundred percent cured, and a candidate for remarriage. The Clinic's most renowned patient is an elderly man said to be one hundred nineteen years old who suffers intermittently from the usual infirmities of age (arthritis, gum disease, vertigo, etc.) but as a result of Autogenic Self-Mastery and other Parris disciplines, he not only recently married for the eighth time but sired his twenty-first child, a healthy baby boy—an event written up in the New York newspapers. The Clinic's former patients include a chess grand master, a youth of nineteen who'd once suffered from extreme melancholia; numerous veterans of the Great War now entirely cured and returned to active life; and numerous women—neurasthenic, hysterical, melancholic, amenorrheic, abnormally willful or will-less—also cured to various degrees and returned to the world as well-adjusted daughters, wives and mothers.

The Parris Clinic was founded in 1922, by way of a generous gift from a convert to Dr. Bies's teachings, an elderly woman named Mrs. Flax-man Potter who willed her estate, including a spacious Georgian house and numerous outbuildings, to the controversial physician-researcher. There have been numerous other gifts from cured, grateful patients; for the servicing of the physical dimension of being (the maintenance of the forty-room mansion, the grounds, the baths, etc.) is recognized as no less necessary than the maintenance of the spiritual. It is the promise of the Parris Clinic's directors that none who enter through its wrought-iron gate will come to grief from any mortal affliction including age itself; yet such are the vicissitudes of natural and human frailty, a certain percentage of patients do occasionally fall short of this goal and come to unfortunate ends, with the result that the Clinic is often being sued, or is threatened with lawsuits, by relatives of the deceased, disinherited children, former physicians and the like. In addition, the goodwill of county and state officials is frequently costly. Financial solvency, therefore, is required—that's to say a healthy cash flow. The

Parris Clinic, despite the idealism of its directors, can't open its doors to
all who have need but only to those who can afford its high fees.

In spring 1926 when a Wall Street investor named Arthur Grille
arranged for his neurasthenic daughter Rosamund to be admitted to the
Clinic, on the eve of his departure for Naples with his new bride, he
was initially shocked by the price quoted by Dr. Bies; yet came around
to the doctor's position as in such matters where health and peace of
mind are concerned, money should be of secondary significance. Mr.
Grille was a recent widower who'd come into prosperity like so many
investors and speculators following the Armistice; he'd seen an investment of $400,000 in various stocks soar to $2.3 million in a whirlwind
eighteen-month period in the early 1920's, and was now a millionaire
many times over. Yet it was his tragedy that, simultaneously, he lost his
wife to a premature death and his only child Rosamund to numerous
mysterious ailments—fainting spells, tachycardia, migraine, anemia,
loss of appetite, chronic melancholia and the like. Rosamund was an
ethereal girl with a fondness for poetry, professing a morbid obsession
with the work of such poets as Keats, Shelley, Chatterton, Byron—
poets who'd all come to tragic or shameful ends. Between the ages of
sixteen and twenty Rosamund experimented with poetry of her own,
so caught up in writing verse that the family was forced to intervene
and forbid her to continue, to prevent a complete mental breakdown;
which provoked the rebellious girl to burn her poetry in a roaring blaze
on the front lawn of the Grille estate on Long Island, and to lapse into
a near-catatonic state afterward. Rosamund's coming out at the Cotil-
lion Club was cancelled, to her mother's grief; and the New York City
débutante season of 1920 passed her by gaily and indifferently.

Eventually, when Rosamund emerged from her lethargy to try her
hand at sculpting small figures in clay under the tutelage of a prominent society sculptor, she again became so involved with her work, as
she called it, that she had to be chastened a second time, with more extreme results, for now the unstable girl broke out of seclusion with a
manic zeal, attending jazz parties in Manhattan where drinking, only
just prohibited by federal law, took place, as well as dancing of a wild,
abandoned, lascivious kind; she became engaged to a young entrepreneur of whom the Grilles disapproved and, after breaking up with him
in a tumultuous scene at the Plaza Hotel, she became engaged to a

young tap dancer and Broadway actor whom the Grilles liked even less; at the height of her hysteria, as her condition was diagnosed by the family physician, Rosamund frequented such notorious Manhattan speakeasies as the Marlboro Club, the Stork Club, and Helen Morgan's, where she was once swept up and arrested in a police raid. And all her antics were performed, as observers noted, without pleasure; indeed, in defiance of pleasure.

As if the new generation sought pain, humiliation, defeat and even death through the forms of "pleasure"—to spite their elders.

In his interview with Dr. Bies and Dr. Liebknecht, Arthur Grille explained that his daughter had been inclined since infancy to a certain degree of willfulness; but beyond the age of thirteen, when her mother first took ill, she became very difficult indeed. "All that was sweet in my little girl curdled; all that was soft and yielding turned hard, cunning and stubborn; she gave the impression of being *stalled*—caught up in the maladies and malaises I've told you about from which, as she said, striking terror into the hearts of her mother and me, 'Only Death could release her.' " Following this, Rosamund was never well. She often threatened to do injury to herself, setting afire her beautiful black hair or raking her skin with her nails or, like Ophelia, who was one of her morbid heroines, drowning herself in a stream. She wasn't loved by anyone, she charged; or she was loved too much, and didn't deserve it. She despaired of God and of being "saved"; then, abruptly, declared the idea of God "supremely silly" and announced herself content to be the descendant of African apes. After her mother's death, when Rosamund was, in her own words, an old maid of twenty-four, she took to her bed and slept in a fevered state for as long as eighteen hours at a time; she ceased speaking except in sibylline utterances—"Where tragedy would ennoble, farce intervenes"—"Eternity despises the productions of Time"—which puzzled and angered her grieving father. Mr. Grille took her to specialist after specialist, admitted her to clinic after clinic, begged her, and commanded her, to behave in a manner suitable for a young woman of her rank and family background; and all without success.

For she *was* ill, beneath her hysteria and histrionics—seriously ill.

Following the advice of a Wall Street associate, Arthur Grille made the decision to commit Rosamund to the care of Doctors Bies and Liebknecht, before sailing for Europe on his honeymoon. (In despair of his life, Mr. Grille had suddenly fallen in love with a young woman twenty years his junior, whose soldier husband had died in France.) Dozens of physicians had failed with her; perhaps they would succeed; in any case, he told them somberly, since his daughter was more troubled now at the age of twenty-seven than she'd been before in her life, they could hardly do her harm. "If I were a superstitious person, which I am not," Mr. Grille told the doctors, "I might almost believe that a . . . demon of some kind inhabited my poor girl."

"A demon! What a laugh. Rather more, the absence of a demon. *There's* the loss."

Rosamund Grille was a willowy, fine-boned, alarmingly thin young woman who looked more seventeen than twenty-seven. She had damp green gemlike eyes narrowed in playfulness one moment and mistrust the next; an aquiline nose with a charming little bump—where it had been broken, as she explained, in a speakeasy raid; a sullen, but very pretty mouth; and a grainy skin that looked as if it were rarely exposed to the sun. The insides of both her forearms were scarred with tiny nicks and scratches—"Hieroglyphics," as she called them. "Signifying nothing." Her hair was fine and filmy, a smoky-black threaded with dead-white hairs; at the time of her admission to the Parris Clinic she'd carelessly bobbed it with a scissors, and refused to go to a hairdresser to repair the damage. Her manner was both skittish and lethargic, sometimes within the space of a few minutes. As Dr. Bies examined her (though he placed little emphasis upon the physical being, he knew it was necessary to consult it) she held herself stiff as a rod, resisting her impulse to recoil from a stranger's, or a man's, touch. Her elegant head high, her greeny eyes partly closed, Rosamund Grille gave no evidence of hearing the questions Dr. Bies asked, and no more cooperated with the physician than a dressmaker's dummy would have done. Dr. Liebknecht, looking on sympathetically, his pince-nez pressed against the bridge of his nose, asked the young woman questions of his own, "Do you comprehend, Miss Grille, that it's your own Wish turned against you that has made you 'ill'?"—and appeared more annoyed than Dr. Bies when she ignored him. *A stubborn creature, as her father warned. Not to be easily cured, if cured at all.*

Afterward, when they were alone, Dr. Bies observed in a languid voice to Dr. Liebknecht, unscrewing the top of his silver pocket flask,

"We must hope for two things: that the wench doesn't do herself in too quickly and that the second Mrs. Grille doesn't spend her husband's money too quickly." Dr. Liebknecht, who'd removed his pince-nez and was thoughtfully rubbing his eyes, sighed, and shrugged, and made no reply, as if he didn't trust himself, at the moment, to speak.

II

"I am not ill—I am well."
"I am not *ill*—I am *well*."
"*I am not ill—I am well.*"
Rosamund bites her lower lip to keep from laughing, and draws blood. Rosamund is racked with silent tears. Rosmund's clenched fists fly striking any available surface, causing such a disturbance in the Ladies' Sulfur Bath that a therapist will lead her back to her room.
"*Don't* touch. I can't bear it!"
Trying to explain that she can't continue, it's no one's fault but she can't continue, yet she's fearful of "crossing over" into the void, and so must continue; out of cowardice, not even pride.
"*I am not well—I am ill.*"
Her heart trips. On the verge of running wild. It can beat as many as two hundred fifty times a minute and her doctors have warned it might beat her to death if she didn't make an effort to calm herself.
Autogenic Self-Mastery does seem to her, despite the obvious charlatanry of the Parris Clinic (a haven for wealthy neurotics, misfits and failures), a basically sound idea. She accepts that her malaise is a malaise of the soul and that it creeps upon her from within. To master the malaise, she need only master the "self" that causes it—but how, precisely, is this done? Reciting the mantra *I am not ill I am well, I am not well I am ill* is like saying a rosary, numbing, hypnotic, silly, shameful. Laughter shades into a fit of coughing. Coughing shades into choking. Choking shades into heart palpitations. Heart palpitations shade into a fainting attack. And her swollen belly and bladder ache from the abnormal quantity of mineral water they've urged her to drink—twelve pints a day.
An insensible body sprawled in the hottest of the baths. Damp black

hair in clots spread like a spider's legs across the chipped marble rim. Bruised eyes shut. In a chamois smock that clings to her thin body, her prominent collarbone and small hard breasts with nipples like berries. Roughly she squeezes these breasts not out of sensuality but to determine if she's *there*. "*I* am not ill—*I* am well. Am *I*?" Thinking of Bies and Liebknecht, a vaudeville team. The one vague, false-fatherly, clammy-fat weighing beyond two hundred fifty pounds at five feet nine; sausage-neck tight to bursting; small squinting red-rimmed eyes; a bald dome of a head, tufts of gray hair in a cupid-fringe. A legitimate doctor, Mr. Grille ascertained, with a degree from a respectable medical school and a number of publicized cures, generally of wealthy patients, to boast of.

Liebknecht, whom Rosamund fears, is Bies's opposite: tall, lean, dry, watchful; quicksilver eyes that bore into Rosamund's skull (one of the female patients shivering in the bath declares Liebknecht has the power to read thoughts); cheekbones severe and ascetic as if the flesh had eroded away; an air of angry sorrow, of pain, of loss. It's believed among the Parris Clinic patients that Liebknecht has a tragic background—he's a figure of romance, in his early sixties—perhaps a veteran of the War?—perhaps a Jewish emigre?—not a doctor of medicine like his fattish partner but a doctor of psychology, or is it psychotherapy—he's reputed to have studied with the controversial Sigmund Freud and to have been a major participant in the International Psychoanalytical Congress at The Hague in 1920. (Freud! Rosamund, like the brightest young people of her circle, had read scattered essays by Freud and helpful resumés of his work, avidly accepting the mysterious unknowable Id as the volcanic source of libido, and the Ego, or "self," as the seat of both identity and anxiety, and the Superego as internalized conscience—the dull, dreary, suffocating voice of authority. Less avid was Rosamund's acceptance of Freud's theory of sexuality in which, in short, the female compensates for her castration or anatomical deficiency in three possible ways: sexual anxiety and withdrawal, rivalry with men/lesbianism, or by shifting libido from her mother to her father, changing the object of her sexual interest from female to male and hoping for an infant, ideally a male infant, as a substitute for the lost penis. "But I don't want an infant," Rosamund protested. "I don't even want a penis . . . what a burden!") If Liebknecht is a Freudian he has said nothing to Rosamund of his beliefs but has only

reiterated, in a kindly, commanding voice, one of the mantras of the
Parris Clinic:

> *"It is your own Wish turned against you that*
> *has made you ill, and it is your own Wish*
> *that will make you well."*

Rosamund sees Liebknecht when he isn't present, for, as the other
patients claim, Liebknecht has the power to see with eyes like X-rays
and the power to read thoughts at a distance. Where Bies is a heavyset
perspiring presence, Liebknecht is a mysterious absence. On weak days,
too exhausted to rise from bed, or from the enervating bath, Rosamund
cringes as the man appears to her, with his expression of severity;
though her trembling eyelids are closed, he stares at her with knowledge of her; her voice rings in her head. *It is your own Wish, Rosamund.*
Yours.

III

April, and Easter, and Rosamund wakes from her long languid
drowse to find herself . . . herself. Her father has abandoned her and she
has no relatives or friends she recalls with affection; her lovers have
passed through her body like mild jolts of electricity, leaving no
memory; soon she will be twenty-eight years old; a voice ringing in her
ears *I am not ill, I am well! not well, ill! not ill not well! I am not I!* In the
day room there's Mrs. Harold Bender of the Manhattan Benders with
her rouged face beaked like a parrot's, a low wondering boastful voice
for she is dying (of some sort of wasting disease) even as she claims she
is well! is well! is well! and will be returning home soon in time for
the contract bridge tournament in May, in which in previous seasons
she's performed brilliantly. These eyes snatching hungrily at where
Rosamund who looks so youthful for her age stands, a willowy apparition in white. There's the Captain, palsied, aged, a turtle's head and
sleep-dazed lidded eyes squinting up at Rosamund with the jest that
he'd once been a tall dashing officer of the United States Army in
charge of one of the post-War military districts in the South under the

Reconstruction Act, his cousin was Thaddeus Stevens of Congress whose power had exceeded President Andrew Johnson's—for a time. Hadn't he known Rosamund, many years ago? Or had the woman been Rosamund's mother, or grandmother? Nature had played quite a trick on him, the Captain laughed, for once he'd been young and now he was old; once tall, and now a virtual midget—"And yet, you know, dear, this isn't truly *me*." And there's a plump sighing woman in her mid-thirties, spinster daughter of one of President Warren Harding's disgraced cabinet members who has, it's rumored, tried to kill herself several times, with overdoses of aspirin and alcohol; she never speaks above a whisper, and never raises her eyes. And there is elderly "Tia" Flanner who'd once been a dancer with the New York City Ballet and a lover of numerous wealthy men, now crippled with arthritis, her face a creased sack, fingers like claws, nearly blind yet chattering of the Discipline that has made her well and restored her youth. And there is the quivering skeleton David Johnson Brown, New York's most prestigious architect in the heady days of the 1890's when the great houses of the wealthy were being built on Park Avenue, Fifth Avenue and vicinity, gazing with death's-head yearning at Rosamund asking if she has seen his houses? his artwork? (yes, Rosamund has, in fact she's lived in a Sixty-sixth Street brownstone built by Brown) would she be his bride? for he's very wealthy, a man of powerful connections, and knows how to make a woman *happy*.

To avoid these apparitions in steamy Hades Rosamund finds herself running through the English garden; there's a stand of juniper pines at the foot of a hill; she stands trembling at the edge of a pond staring, dreaming, swaying on her feet breathing in the scent of brackish water, ripening vegetation, algae, she moves out into the surprisingly warm water, water to her waist, arms too heavy to lift in an appeal, a partly naked woman quivering in the water beneath her, rippling, shivering, the sky beneath her too, veined and pale, light on all sides. "Rosamund. No."

Dr. Liebknecht has spoken, softly, commandingly. Rosamund looks around but can't see anyone. She's panting like an animal, clutching at her small hard useless breasts. Soft muck beneath her toes, the pressure of water against her belly, her pelvis. "But why not! Why not! If it's my Wish." She begins to cry out of anger, resentment. Liebknecht in shadows at the edge of the pond, or hidden in the stand of juniper pines, or watching her from one of the myriad windows of the house flashing with the wan, dying light of sunset—"Rosamund, no. Come back at once."

Rosamund laughs, but obeys. Only a fool would try to drown herself in three feet of water clogged with lily pads and water irises.

It's May, and June; a reluctant chilly spring; Rosamund wakes, and Rosamund sleeps, and Rosamund lies comatose in the bath, and Rosamund whispers *I am not ill I am well, not ill well, I am I and not-I* until a fit of childish laughter overtakes her, and she's yawning over the postcard of Florence, her jaws ache with yawning, and she recalls suddenly how she'd loved her cousin Timothy who'd died in the War, his plane shot down over Colombey-les-Belles in May 1918, she has a photograph of Tim in his dashing aviator's topcoat with its broad fur collar, Tim in his helmet, goggles pushed back onto his head, that glamor-stance, a boastful smile, what are War and Death but glamor and boastful smiles yet Rosamund vowed she'd never smile again after word came of his death (and the poor body burnt to ash amid the plane wreckage) but she refuses to tell Dr. Liebknecht of this secret because it will lessen her in his eyes: she's shallow and worthless like the rest, in love with her own infirmities and imminent deaths. Rosamund tears the postcard into several pieces and scatters the pieces in the air. Caring not for her father and new young stepmother, truly she doesn't care whether they regard her with affection or suspicion, whether they return from Europe or remain forever, whether they live or die, truly Rosamund doesn't though Dr. Liebknecht has suggested that she cares very much, she's consumed with rage, why not admit it.

"D'you know, Dr. Liebknecht—if 'Liebknecht' is your name—I don't like *you*. That, I will admit."

"That, Miss Grille, is your privilege."

"And please don't call me 'Miss Grille' as if I were some sort of North Atlantic fish. If you must call me anything—'Rosamund.' "

Dr. Liebknecht smiles. Even as the man insinuates himself into her soul. "Yes. 'Rosamund.' A fetchingly *feminine* name—and excellent disguise."

Poor Mrs. Bender it's whispered at the noonday meal can no longer raise her head from her pillow, she's desperate to play bridge in her bed, her estranged family has come to fetch her home but she refuses to leave for the Parris Clinic is her home now, Dr. Bies and Dr. Liebknecht have given her hope where there's been no hope. Everywhere else, she tells Rosamund, is Death.

Criminals, Rosamund thinks spitefully.

She'll telephone her father's uncle Morgan Grille who's a judge of the state supreme court, she'll report criminal activities at the Parris Clinic, Mrs. Bender's talon fingers digging into her arm and the woman's terrified eyes, can *will* and *destiny* be one? can we ardently wish what will obliterate us? Quick, before it's too late! (The rumor is that Mrs. Bender has left $1 million to the Parris Clinic though in her final days she'd despaired of maintaining the Discipline and pleaded to be forgiven by her doctors she'd adored, for disappointing them.)

"You shouldn't pass severe judgment on yourself, Rosamund," Liebknecht informs her, "for being unable to love. For, to love, we must love someone—an object. But who is a worthy object? In this chaotic world, where? It's your excellent instinct that guides you, forbidding you to love insignificant people who don't deserve your love."

Rosamund laughs harshly, and fumbles to light a cigarette. Dr. Liebknecht doesn't assist her. "But I won't love *you*. Worthy as you are."

Midsummer. The nocturnal insects sing of Death, of Death, yet new patients arrive at the Clinic: a tremulous white-haired woman in a wheelchair, an obese youth ostentatiously carrying a volume of Swinburne's poems, twin sisters of fifty years of age perky as young partridges, bangs in a fringe on their foreheads. *I am not ill—I am well. I am not ill— I am well.* The prayerful chant arises from the cloistered sick as from a galaxy of nocturnal insects desperately singing against the end of time.

The muted voices of America, Rosamund thinks. *I am not ill—but make me well! Help me to live forever.*

How many casualties of the War. This new desperation not to die.

As for Rosamund: she's airy and transparent, rising above the surface of the earth like mist above the Hudson River in the early morning. She's hard, hot, sharp as an ice pick, an instrument made for jabbing and drawing blood.

"I can't love you. You're too old. Older than my father. And I don't trust you. Worthy as you are."

Yet it's her own Wish that has made her ill, so it is her own Wish that will make her well.

And make her his.

She complains of melancholia, fatigue, dizziness and loss of appetite, she's torn up the postcard from Rome signed with both her father's and stepmother's names, she's torn up the copies of her quarterly bills at the Parris Clinic she receives (which are marked PAID IN FULL, for of course her father pays for everything), she's stunned when Dr. Liebknecht prescribes for her what no other doctor has ever prescribed: muscular labor, exertion. "Rosamund. Stand up. Go out of here, and hike to the top of that hill. Bring me a handful of wildflowers from the crest of that hill. Now, before the sun is too hot. Hurry." Clapping his hands at her as you'd urge on a dog.

Rosamund laughs, shocked. Rosamund refuses.

Yet within the hour on her feet, eager, excited, in sturdy walking shoes, a long-sleeved shirt to protect her arms, trousers comfortable as a man's, Dr. Liebknecht's panama hat on her head and her sleek black hair caught back in a careless chignon. Lean-hipped, flat-bosomed, she might be a young man. She's walking fast, in dread of being joined by another patient. She's half trotting. Hurrying. Swinging her arms. Smiling with the exertion. Beginning to pant. Trickles of sweat beneath her arms. Her head throbs, her blood pulses hard, bright, blinding. She hikes one mile, two miles, nearly three miles in hilly terrain, much of the way steeply uphill. The farthest distance Rosamund has ever hiked. She's happy! She's never been so happy! If her heart bursts it will be the doctor's fault. If she collapses and has to be carried back to the Clinic on a stretcher by attendants it will be his fault. Breathing the sharp scent of pine needles she's never breathed before, like this. Sun-heated grasses. Murmur and buzz of insects. The high sweet cries of birds. At the crest of the hill she picks Queen Anne's lace, blue heal-all and wild asters, tough-stemmed flowers to bring back to Dr. Liebknecht as a love-offering. For of course she loves him.

Shading her eyes gazing over the wild land falling beneath her to the wooded banks of the great river. How happy she is, how free! Her legs ache, she isn't used to such exertion, yet how happy she is knowing she can do this at any time, hike to the top of this hill, or any hill. From this perspective the buildings and grounds of the Parris Clinic that have been the entire world to her for months are hardly visible.

She leaves the ragged, already withering bouquet in a jar in tepid water on the doorstep of Dr. Liebknecht's residence. And avoids him for the remainder of that day, and all of the next day, and the next.

In the privacy of his office (dim slatted sunshine, a rustling of amorous birds in the ivy outside the window) he speaks suddenly from the heart, as Rosamund has never heard any man speak before, or any woman.

He loves her, he says.

And he believes that she might love him.

Rosamund, stricken, claps her hands over her ears. "No. I don't want to hear this."

Shall she confess: in the night she embraces herself with a lover's ardent arm that is his arm; his head on the pillow gently nudges hers.

Shall she confess: she is bitterly jealous of all his life that isn't this single moment.

She whispers, "No. It's too late for me."

He tells her she must listen to no one except him. She must believe no one except him. For she knows that he loves her, and will make her his bride—"For this is our common destiny, Rosamund."

In the privacy of his office (the blinds drawn, a sudden silence outside the window) he rises to take her hands in his; to restore warmth to her hands that have gone cold; her eyelids flutter, she doesn't dare look up at him, where his face should be there's blindness, an intensification of light; she stammers, protesting it's too late, she isn't worthy, if he knew her innermost soul he wouldn't love her.

But he seems not to hear. Gripping her hands to quiet her, he stoops over her and presses his lips against her forehead.

"I tell you, Rosamund—it's so. We love each other, and we will be wed. This is our destiny."

IV

I will not, thinks Rosamund.

I will *not*, thinks Rosamund. Her heart tripping on the edge of running wild.

But now she encounters the man everywhere on the grounds of the Parris Clinic. Walking swiftly in the early morning mist she sees him ascending the hill before her so she has no choice but to follow. Miles away beside the rapidly moving, vast river she sees him farther along the tangled bank, beckoning to her. *No I will not. Yes. I don't believe in destiny!* In the slightly shabby English garden among the topiary hedges, along the graveled front drive between rows of stately poplars she sees him . . . turning quickly aside before he summons her to him. For now suddenly the man is everywhere. Close beside her in her bed, and in the hot lulling bath where, helpless, she can't escape. "I love you, Rosamund. For only I know how you've suffered. How your soul devours itself. How, yearning to die, you yearn to live. And we will be wed—you have only to consent."

But no she will not consent. For the man is too old: in his early sixties. And it's wrong of him, unprofessional, unethical, to speak in such a way to one of his patients. To touch, to kiss, to make his claim. To cause murmurous, excited talk among the other patients, a number of whom are in love with him . . . their envious eyes snatching after Rosamund. As a young girl she'd stealthily entered her parents' bedrooms (which were joined by a common door, never in Rosamund's memory open) and in their absence she'd dared to explore their lavish clothes closets, their numerous bureau drawers and even their bedclothes . . . now and then discovering an item that mystified and intrigued her like a rosary of exquisite carved ivory beads amid her mother's lingerie, a small gold snuffbox engraved with a stranger's initials in a pocket of one of her father's coats, a dog-eared copy of Kate Chopin's outlawed novel *The Awakening* amid the piles of mostly unread books on her mother's bedside table. So too in Moses Liebknecht's office which Rosamund boldly entered late one afternoon, finding it unlocked, and empty, she'd hurriedly examined desk drawers, shelves, a cabinet, searching for precisely what she didn't know and coming away disappointed for the man had few possessions apparently, little to identify him save a supply of meticulously wrapped Cuban cigars and a small black notebook of codified inscriptions in pencil covering page after page; and, on the bookshelves behind his desk, the *Collected Works of William James* . . . Rosamund paged through two or three of these volumes, risking discovery by Liebknecht, her heart pounding buoyantly with the audacity of her behavior, yet deciding not to care, for a book is meant to be public property surely, to be shared even with the ill. Many pages were annotated, in pencil; in the margins were exclamation points, question marks, and stars; at the front of a volume titled *The Will to Believe* there was an inscription in ink *Truth is the "cash-value" of an idea. Truth is a process that "happens to an idea."*

Could this be so? Was this devastating cynicism, or simple American wisdom? Rosamund returned the volume to the shelf in exactly the place it had been, smiling. How much easier life, if one could believe so. Choosing beliefs for any weather, as one chooses hats, gloves, wraps, boots. As one chose's one's destiny, and did not wait to be chosen.

Having had no word from Arthur Grille in weeks, Rosamund begins writing him. Cascades of letters, repentant and chagrined. *I am "cured" at last of my hateful maladies. I am ready to re-enter the world.* She writes to her father and to other relatives, copying passages from one letter to another as if transcribing poetry. *Will you ever forgive me? I am ashamed of my behavior these many years. I can't explain now that I am well why I so clung to my sickness as if my sickness were myself.*

The letters are signed, sealed, carried by Rosamund to a mailbox at the end of the gravelled drive. She doesn't trust any of the servants at the Clinic. (Yet can she trust the mailman?) Though she sends a dozen or more letters, she receives no replies; except an envelope addressed to MISS ROSAMUND GRILLE, sealed but with no stamp, which she opens quickly in the privacy of her room—

Dearest Rosamund,
You have only to consent. I am waiting.

L.

In early September, Rosamund insists upon speaking with Dr. Bies, though Dr. Liebknecht is her therapist. She takes a good deal of time with her toilette, fashioning her hair into a passably neat chignon, dab-

bing powder onto her pale face, selecting attractive clothing and jewelry. Wondering, with a stab of shame, how she'd ever been indifferent
to her appearance.

Telling the heavyset turtle-eyed physician that she wasn't ill, she was
well—exactly as she'd been promised. "And I want to be discharged
from the Clinic as quickly as possible."

Dr. Bies smiles politely, as if he's heard these words many times before. "Miss Grille, I'm afraid that isn't possible. We are accountable
solely to your guardian. You've been, you know, *committed.*"

"A voluntary commitment," Rosamund says, trying to remain calm.
"Surely that makes a difference?"

"Your father will be contacting us soon, I'm sure. Perhaps we can
speak with him on the phone. Unless he's still in Europe, traveling."

"But—how recently have you heard from him? I haven't had a letter
or a card in weeks."

"Naturally the Clinic issues monthly reports, quite detailed reports,
on its patients," Dr. Bies says, "and naturally it's our hope and our expectation that guardians *will* respond, apart from merely meeting their
financial obligations. But we rarely receive personal letters, if that's
your question. And never from gentlemen as busy as Arthur Grille."

"But what do you tell Father in your reports?"

"Our reports, as you must know, Miss Grille, are confidential. But
very thorough and responsible."

"May I see mine?"

Dr. Bies lifts his hands in a gesture of helpless gallantry.

"Impossible, Miss Grille! As you must know. For, as I've explained,
our Clinic is accountable solely to your guardian."

"And if my guardian has abandoned me?" Rosamund asks, her voice
rising. "If everyone in the outside world has abandoned me?"

"*Your* guardian hasn't abandoned you, Miss Grille. Please don't
worry. Mr. Grille's financial accountant in Manhattan has never been
late with a single payment, and raises no questions at all."

Rosamund sits quietly. A pulse beats at her temple. She tells herself
of course she isn't trapped in this place, if she wishes she can escape . . .
can't she? From time to time patients more disturbed than she, more
desperate, more rebellious, have slipped away from their residences, disappeared into the woods . . . only to turn up again a day or two later,
subdued, drowsy with medication . . . looking as if they'd never been

away, nor had had a thought of being away. She says, matter-of-factly, as if they weren't physician and patient but equals, "You see, Doctor—I am not *ill*, I am *well*. As you and Dr. Liebknecht have promised. It seemed to have happened suddenly, but I suppose it may have happened by degrees. I *am* well, and I was well all along. There was a kind of veil over my eyes, like spite. A wish to hurt the person closest to me—myself. But now I see the truth of my situation—the truth that has happened to me. For my Wish was turned against myself, and now—as you've promised—my Wish has made me well. And so I want to be discharged. I insist upon being discharged. You must write to my father, to inform him."

"I shall note it on your September report without fail, Miss Grille."

"No more quickly than that? If you could locate Father, you might telegraph him. Obviously he must be in touch with his financial advisors. His broker, his banker. His accountant. For, as I've explained, I'm well now; I don't want to remain with sick people. My life is passing rapidly by!"

There's an ebony-handled penknife on Dr. Bies's desk amid a scattering of envelopes and papers. The stiletto-like blade glitters invitingly. Dr. Bies's languid turtle-eyes observe the knife, and the distance from it to Miss Rosamund Grille as she sits perhaps three feet away, beginning to rock in her seat; he's a shrewd fellow, deceptive in his bulk. "I would not, my dear, if I were you," he confides, lowering his voice as if another party might be listening, "—for then you would be put back into restraints, and suffer a relapse."

"But my life—"

"Why yes, it's true for all of mankind," Dr. Bies says, with an air of finality, "—life rapidly passes by. 'The fact of having been born is a bad augury for immortality'—as George Santayana, at one time a patient of mine, has said."

Rosamund says, rising unsteadily to her feet, "Dr. Liebknecht would agree that I'm well. Ask him. He might write to my father. And of course I'll write. I have written."

"Yes."

Dr. Bies is standing, Buddha-like, behind his desk; he makes a nearly imperceptible signal to one of the burly male attendants who's been standing a respectful distance behind Rosamund, waiting to escort her back across the quadrangle to her residence. From somewhere close by,

a bell is ringing. It's time for the midday meal. An enormous meal, formally served in the dining room, which will last for well over an hour.
Rosamund feels a sensation of nausea, repugnance. She has to resist the
impulse to clutch at her head, loosen her hair. She has to resist the impulse to shove and scratch at the attendant who, gently but firmly, unmistakably firmly, has taken hold of her forearm to lead her away.

"I am well, and I was well. All along! I'd deceived myself. It was my
Wish—as you've said. But now—my Wish is to be well. *And I am well.*
Please, Dr. Bies—"

Earnestly, hands clasped at his midriff, Dr. Bies says, "It's helpful of
you to write letters, Miss Grille. As many as you like, and to whom you
like. The Honorable Morgan Grille of the state supreme court in Albany is a relative of yours, I believe? His elder daughter was a patient of
ours too, some years ago. Letter writing, like the keeping of a journal, is,
for women, excellent therapy. It will keep your mind active, and fill up
the hours. And, you know, Rosamund—we'll be delighted to mail your
letters for you. It's no trouble at all."

By night she tries to escape the Clinic's vast grounds. In a hooded
coat, in rubber-soled boots, a scarf tied tightly around her head she
tramps the woods for hours, in panic, in delirium, *It is my own Wish that
confines me, it will be my own Wish that sets me free,* in the end exhausted, lost, circling back toward the Clinic which rises like a ruin
out of the darkness, like a nocturnal animal panting at the edge of the
lawn seeing, in Dr. Liebknecht's residence, a solitary lamp burning. She
wonders if he, her lover, examines her letters too, or only Bies; or if her
letters are read at all or merely disposed of.

He sends her his thoughts. Kindly, yet persistent.

You have only to give your consent, Rosamund. I pledge to love you forever.

She has no choice but to think of the man as her lover. Though he's
nothing like her previous lovers.

She discovers gifts from him: a silken cord tied in an elegant, complex knot, left on her pillow; a bouquet of violets in an ink bottle filled
with water, on her windowsill; a volume of verse by Christina Rossetti
titled *Goblin Market*, which Rosamund reads avidly, with delight and
incomprehension; and an emerald ring in an antique silver setting,
which, waking one afternoon in the languor of the hot-sulfur bath, she
discovers on the third finger of her left hand. As if it had always been

there. "But whose ring has this been?" Rosamund vexes herself, wondering. "A former Mrs. Liebknecht? A mother. A grandmother? A daughter?"

For she's young enough to be Liebknecht's daughter of course.

Almost, she has to inquire: *Is she this man's daughter?*

She walks in the woods, at the edge of the marshy pond. It's autumn now, an exhilarating taste to the wind, though cold, making tears stream down her cheeks. Marsh grasses, cattails, Jerusalem artichokes grow in profusion, making a high keening melodic sound in the wind. Moses Liebknecht observes her from a short distance, vigilant to see that she comes to no harm. Tall and erect and courtly he stands, handsome for a man of his years; his clean-shaven face slightly flushed as if heated; eyes silvery-bright with alertness, expectation; his hair, graying, shading into white, brushed thick against the crown of his head. Rosamund calls to him, "I see you, Dr. Liebknecht. You aren't hidden from me. I respect you and I honor you but I don't love you. I don't want to love any man."

Dr. Liebknecht doesn't reply. When Rosamund looks up, squinting—there's no one there.

Yet in fact you do love me, Rosamund. Your Wish is for us to be one: man and wife: a destiny you dare not resist.

She runs from him, she's not a woman to succumb to fantasies, hallucinations. She's an intelligent young woman! She's of the new generation of young women who have come of age in the early years of the twentieth century, she's attended college . . . until growing bored with books, lectures, routine . . . she isn't her mother and she certainly isn't her grandmother and yet . . . who is she, exactly? *Venus Aphrodite guides us in such mysteries, and Venus Aphrodite is never to be comprehended.* So Moses Liebknecht's voice assures her. She protests, "But—my father will object." He says, dryly, *But "Father" will always object. It is the curse of being "Father."*

V

. . .Which day is this so strangely warm in the sun, biting-cold in shade, a fierce autumn sky and sepia light suffusing the tall juniper pines through which she runs like a dream gliding in and out of consciousness; in stealth making her way to the marshy edge of the pond, and into the pond, cold numbing water to her knees, to her thighs, she's wearing flannel trousers, rubber-soled boots, a suede jacket and no gloves, bareheaded, and now the water rises to the pit of her belly, how fresh how chill how clear the surface of the water after days of November rain washing away debris floating in the pond and now the water is to her waist ... she's stumbling, her feet sinking in the mud, *I am not ill I am well, I am not ill I am well*, she is determined to escape her lover, she is determined to escape love, unworthy of love, a mutilated woman like all women seeing beneath her a half-woman cut in two at the waist, reflected in the pond's surface glaring as a black mirror, a woman with no face, a woman with no eyes, rippling and quivering reflected in the depths of the sky, and everywhere the blinding blaze of sunshine so powerful she must shut her eyes. *It is my Wish that has made me ill, now it is my Wish that has made me well, and made me free.*

"And the Light Shineth in Darkness"

His head, his head!—jammed with broken glass, slivers of memory!—and his soul of which he'd been so absurdly proud in constant danger now of dribbling down his elegantly tailored pants leg, an old man's shameful urine.

From which she will save him.

She, who's young. A remarkable woman. His creation, you might say. As a god might fashion out of mud, sticks, pebbles, minerals a shapely figure and breathe life into it, and suddenly—It lives! And he'll suffuse her with strength, where there's been weakness. And he'll impregnate her with children, where there's been barrenness. Children to replace his lost children. Children to replace the children who've betrayed him. And the miracle will happen again.

"For Nature is never exhausted," Abraham Licht thinks. "It is only we who wear out—some of us. Through a failure of imagination."

But *he* hasn't worn out. Despite the bitter shocks, disappointments and trials of recent years.

For only consider: he has boldly reentered The Game though on all sides of him, in these vertiginous 1920's, other, younger men are embarked upon The Game in their various uncharted—unconscionable— ways. On all sides there are fortunes to be reaped, and destinies to be claimed. Suddenly there are so many more Americans . . . so many more competitors . . . yet also customers, clients, patients. A vast seething sea of hungry souls. Ever more waves of immigrants from Europe and Asia; ever more waves of babies, from out of the inexhaustible void; and, wonder of wonders, older men and women living longer— and demanding to live longer, and ever longer. Mortality isn't a consumer product but health, beauty, longevity are.

The ultimate consumer product which affluent Americans (of whom there are more and more, with each passing month) will clamor to buy.

Like Abraham Licht himself who, a few years ago, unknown to even Katrina and Esther, traveled to Manhattan to the office of the renowned urologist Victor Lespinasse and arranged for a sensitive, and very costly operation; an operation that has resulted, Abraham Licht thinks, in a rejuvenation of body and spirit; for as Dr. Lespinasse says gravely, "A man is as old—or as young—as his glands."

It may even be, a man *is* his glands.

He's a follower of William James, America's home-nurtured philosopher. He'd have liked to meet James up at Harvard, and shake the man's hand. For to what purpose is it, he's always wondered, to inquire after origins? "original sin"? out of what unfathomable pit of Medusa-serpents an idea, a sentiment, a passion, a belief arises? We ask only *What are the results?* Our gaze is resolute, *Not backward but forward.* Not thought *but the fruits of action.*

And once more he's succeeded in winning the love of a beautiful, desirable, mysterious woman; a woman who's his intellectual equal, or nearly; a woman with no brothers or sisters, the heiress daughter of a Manhattan millionaire. Once more, drawn to Venus Aphrodite in the flesh of a mortal woman. "This time, unmistakably, a woman deserving of my love and devotion. A woman of the New Era, yet a woman, still; wounded as a woman is invariably wounded, and seeking her fulfill-ment in a man." The nervous hooded eyes moistly green, the thin, sen-sual mouth in a fixed smile. *No man can love me, I can love no man.* Yet from the first he'd known they were fated for each other, he's a man of romance, a man born to that terrible American decade the 1860's, he believes in fate even as he believes that we make our own fate, and call it what we will.

But no denying how his pulses, including the thick sinewy pulse in his groin, stirred, that morning in Bies's office. *Rosamund* he prays, not entirely jesting *O Rose of the World have mercy on an ardent lover in an aging man's body.*

II

By autumn of 1926 it can be confirmed, as Abraham Licht confi-dently notes in his memoir, that he's well again; fully recovered; though at times, admittedly, his head aches as if it's filled with broken glass which the slightest movement can unsettle.

But he's well. Himself again. In the person of Dr. Moses Liebknecht (of Vienna, Zurich, Paris, London) he carries himself both elegantly and forcefully; a man of mysteries, yet a man aligned with science; a psychotherapist, yet (it's sometimes hinted) a man who'd begun his career as a biologist, or perhaps a physicist, in Vienna in the 1880's. A man of mature years—in his early sixties. (In fact, Abraham Licht is sixty-five years old. A face he contemplates with perpetual dis-belief, like a man gazing into a mirror and seeing two heads.) And the monkey-gland transplant has worked out very well . . . indeed.

Unfortunately, he and Dr. Bies have been quarreling often.

For though Moses Liebknecht owns only 37 percent of the Parris Clinic and isn't precisely a cofounder, he's certain that his ideas about running the establishment and about mental health in general are superior to Bies's. *He* would screen prospective patients far more scrupulously not only in terms of health and finances but in terms of family background: there's an obvious advantage to admitting primarily patients without immediate relatives. (For relatives invariably cause trouble. The more relatives, the more heirs; and the more heirs, the more trouble.) In principle, Bies agrees; in practice he's become careless and greedy. Business is all that absorbs him, making the most money in the shortest period of time; and unhealthy quantities of food and drink. (Now that Abraham can drink only sparingly, he's disapproving of his partner's excesses.) There's a rumor among the staff that Dr. Bies injects himself with morphine . . . but Abraham, that's to say the rather taciturn Moses Liebknecht, isn't the sort to bring up so private a subject.

Like most business partnerships, this one has had seasons of relative health, and decided unhealth. In early 1924, when Abraham Licht made the decision to invest $42,400 in the Parris Clinic, at that time in debt, Bies had been extremely eager to oblige him. Giving over to him the largest office in the former mansion, with floor-to-ceiling bookshelves and a view of the English topiary garden; assuring him he wouldn't make any decisions without consulting him; flattering him by declaring that, with Licht's business sense, and his own medical-professional background, they couldn't fail to become millionaires within a few years. "It's only a matter of time, 'Moses.' The right patients, and a good, reliable staff of therapists, masseurs, nurses, aides— the Clinic will practically run itself. For Autogenic Self-Mastery *is* the cure to most ills. Of that, I'm convinced." Dr. Bies spoke with such smiling confidence and boyish idealism, Abraham found himself believing . . . wishing to believe. (Hadn't he read that most psychological ailments cure themselves, in time? So long as the Clinic didn't admit seriously ill patients like schizophrenics, manic-depressives, paranoids and the like; and as few patients as possible with organic, medical ailments.) Abraham had checked out the background of Felix Bies, M.D., and confirmed that the man had a medical degree from the Medical School of Rutgers University, in New Jersey; he'd been a resident at the University of Pennsylvania Medical Center; he'd even studied psychiatry in Edinburgh. (At least, Abraham thought uneasily, a man named "Felix Bies" was so trained.)

Bies knew of Abraham Licht from the flamboyant era of the Society for the Reclamation & Restoration of E. Auguste Napoléon Bonaparte; one of Bies's in-laws had invested, and lost, a considerable amount of money in the scheme, to Bies's amusement. He'd much admired the mastermind behind the Society, he told Abraham when they first met, and knew that, one day, they must meet—"Our paths would cross, and we would know each other. Yes!"

So it was of the utmost importance, Abraham Licht insisted to Bies, in these later, more difficult days when they found themselves in frequent disagreement, that, as partners, but more importantly as friends, they speak the truth to each other at all times. And Bies vehemently agreed. "As if, 'Moses,' one so clumsy as *I* should hope to deceive *you*."

Yet it seems to be happening that Bies more and more often ignores Liebknecht's recommendations. Or doesn't consult him at all. His prescribed treatment for some patients is, in Liebknecht's judgment, negligent; he has admitted near-moribund men and women to the Clinic who clearly haven't any chance of recovery. A ninety-year-old blind man, dazed and sputtering, delivered over to the Clinic by a brusque son in his sixties, whose Rolls-Royce idled in the drive; an obese woman in a wheelchair, wheezing and gasping for breath, suffering from the delusion that she was awaiting a "train for home" in Pennsylvania Station, delivered over by a glamorous woman in mink and tinted glasses identified only, on the official admitting form in Bies's office, as "Daughter-in-Law"; a wizened, prematurely aged child of nine brought to the Clinic by a sullen nursemaid who claimed that the child's parents, wealthy residents of Tuxedo Park, had instructed her to "enroll" him here and to remain with him "for the duration"; a rail-thin woman in her thirties, wife of a prominent Manhattan attorney, so nervous her teeth chattered, and her eyes bulged in her skeletal head, under the delusion that she was at a clinic "to have my baby" . . . "Surely it's bad judgment and bad for the morale of all, to accept so many hopeless patients at the same time," Moses Liebknecht said worriedly, but Bies, sighing expansively, shrugged and said, "Ah, they will outlive us, 'Moses.' And if they don't, where's the harm? As the great Santayana, who was once my patient, has said, 'There is tragedy in perfection, because the universe in which perfection arises in itself imperfect.'" " 'Perfection'! Where, hereabouts, do you see 'perfection,' Felix?" (Between Liebknecht and Bies there was a feud of sorts, playful at the start but lately fairly hostile, for the former much admired William James, the very essence of native American philosophy, and the latter admired, or claimed to admire, the Spanish-born George Santayana, James's antithesis.) Bies smiled at the wincing expression on his partner's face, and offered him a drink—"The smoothest Scotch whiskey, lovely as death"—from his silver flask, unpleasantly warmed by the heat of his fleshy body. Liebknecht politely declined.

Am I being stricken by conscience, so late in The Game?

God help me, if it's so.

Lately the partners were inclined, too, to disagree on the composition of the "Parris elixir." This was a secret medicine to be administered solely at the Clinic under the aegis of Felix Bies, M.D., who had patented it in his name in 1921; it was prescribed to patients in carefully modulated doses, for it was a powerful and potentially addictive formula consisting of blackstrap molasses, oil of coconut, finely ground thyme, almonds, dried seaweed and tincture of opium in varying degrees. (In truth, the precise nature of the elixir depended upon the whim of Dr. Bies's assistants, who created the elixir in large steaming pots on a kitchen stove.) Moses Liebknecht, sympathizing with the infirm who so unquestioningly and hopefully drank down the elixir, convinced of its magical powers, argued that the elixir should contain a fixed amount of nonaddictive matter and a minimum of opium; he'd had some experience (of which he spoke evasively, for Dr. Liebknecht wasn't one to share intimate secrets even with his partner and friend Dr. Bies) with opium addiction, and knew how malevolent it could be. "Above all, the elixir shouldn't smell and taste repellent, which is sometimes the case—it's a discouraging sight to see patients gagging on it even as, with tears in their eyes, they proclaim its magical powers." It seemed inevitable that certain of the patients as they grew sicker and weaker and less certain of their surroundings begged for heavier dosages of the elixir even when, in the most literal sense, they couldn't stomach it. Dr. Liebknecht, that's to say Abraham Licht, recalling Katrina's herbal medicines, which had helped restore his health more than once, had been experimenting with a rival medicine: it would be called the Liebknecht Formula, consisting primarily of sweet, heavy cream into which cherries had been ground to create a smooth, blood-tinctured texture intended to stir in the patient's unconscious idyllic memories of nursing at his mother's breast; there was no practical way to avoid tincture of opium, but Dr. Liebknecht made sure that only delicious ingredients were ground into the formula—cinnamon sticks, brown sugar, pistachio nuts, cocoa, Swiss chocolate, and so forth. In some patients the Liebknecht Formula acted as a gentle soporific, in others as a stimulant; in others, a powerful emetic; in one patient, Mrs. Deardon, the neurasthenic wife of the Manhattan attorney, it had an alarming aphrodisiac effect resulting in Mrs. Deardon's pregnancy after only five weeks at the Clinic. (As there were no provisions for pregnant patients at the Parris Clinic, Mrs. Deardon was obliged to hurriedly depart. The father, or fathers, of the unborn child were not named by Mrs. Dearborn, and did not come forward to identify themselves; but Mrs. Dearborn was reportedly very happy with the pregnancy, speaking of it as an autogenic conception involving no crude sexual "act" for which she might be blamed.) Bies, normally indifferent to the atmosphere of the Clinic, began to take exception to the fact that a number of patients were choosing the new medicine over the old; while others insisted upon having both, with sometimes unfortunate results. So, the Liebknecht Formula was causing division at the Clinic where tranquility of mind was necessary, if Autogenic Self-Mastery was to retain its potency.

Half in jest, yet half seriously, Moses Liebknecht observed to Felix Bies one day that the distinction between the new elixir and the old was that the new might well have curative powers—"I'm taking it myself in experimental doses. And I must say, Felix, I've never felt so—healthy, and happy." Bies regarded him with searching eyes, and a sly spiteful smile, saying, "Yes? There is a sort of luminous glow about you. As there is about our patient Miss Grille. Is she, too, taking the Liebknecht Formula? Like Mrs. Deardon?" Liebknecht flushed at this remark with its lewd innuendo, and would have departed Bies's presence in dignity, except Bies added, quickly, as if to placate him, "Moses, do you think the Liebknecht Formula would work for me, too? I am in need of some sort of—restoration."

Moses Liebknecht smiled politely, and laid an assuring hand on the other man's shoulder. "Dr. Bies, recall the words engraved over the entrance to Hades: *Caveat emptor.*"

III

Full of scorpions is my mind.
And who will purge it?
After Abraham Licht's nervous collapse in Philadelphia in December

1916 he didn't plunge of his own volition but fell helpless and terrified to the bottom of the marsh; to the rich slimy-black bottom of the marsh; where Katrina grown old now, gaunt and altered, her once-firm skin finely creased as an eggshell with myriad cracks, and of that pallor, nursed him for many months; Katrina, and Esther his youngest child whom he scarcely knew; until by Katrina's judgment he was well— "And fit now to return to the world of Time."

In Katrina's mouth these words had the effect of a statement of health that was simultaneously a kind of curse. For the "world of Time," to Katrina, the world beyond Muirkirk, was no paradise.

But for those months, in her care, Abraham Licht thought nothing of the world of Time, nor even of Philadelphia society which, he'd had every reason to believe, he had conquered; instead he slept like an infant again in his mother's breast; slept, and woke; and slept again; and took sustenance from sleep, as from Katrina's vigilant care; no matter that Katrina's smile slipped cruelly from her gums and her eyes in their deep sockets blazed with an unearthly light; waking, Abraham might see that in the shadows only a few feet from him there crouched a wizened featherless bird, sharp-beaked, of about the size of a sparrow hawk: he wanted to cry out in terror, but could not. He wanted to whisper her name but could not. He wanted to shut his eyes to dispel the vision but could not. *Help help help me I am not fit to die. I have not fulfilled my destiny on this earth.*

In such fever-states Abraham was certain he could remember his lost mother across a space of . . . could it be six decades? Six? Recalling not the exact image of the woman but the aura, the radiance of her abiding love.

Waking another time, to see Katrina quite ordinary, an aging but still capable woman, a woman to whom one might babble of nightmares; Fortnum & Mason tins crammed with flesh, blood, body hairs, the ooze and reek and shame of it, *a body that was Abraham's own* served up to him like one of those hideous cannibal-feasts of antiquity; a son of Abraham Licht's prepared as for a holiday meal in tinsel-wrapped packages with crinkly bows. And Katrina seemed to listen, and to humor him; saying, as she pressed a cool damp cloth against his burning forehead, that it was only a dream, and dreams are to be forgotten.

And Abraham raged to Katrina of his daughter, his beautiful angel-daughter whose name he could no longer speak, his daughter who'd betrayed him at last as her mother had done, eloping with a man Abraham Licht scarcely knew, eloping and marrying without Abraham Licht's blessing, and now the girl was dead; and her name must never again be uttered.

And Katrina said, more somberly, that this too was only a dream, and dreams are to be forgotten.

All these follies you must forget for the Past is but the graveyard of the future; and no place for Abraham Licht.

IV

So it happened that Katrina, with young Esther's help, saw to it that Abraham ate when he hadn't the appetite, and slept when he protested his thoughts raged too wildly for sleep; and had nothing to do with Muirkirk, nor the great world beyond.

Protesting only mildly, Abraham gave in to her; slept as many as twelve hours at a time; made an effort to eat all the food she prepared; and, when he was feeling stronger, contented himself with walking in the marsh, or through fields, or along deserted country roads where he wasn't likely to meet anyone who knew him. (Even those older inhabitants of Muirkirk who'd known Abraham Licht in the prime of his young manhood, as the city-dweller who'd galloped into their midst to buy, at auction, within minutes, the derelict Church of the Nazarene, seemed not to recognize this gaunt, longhaired man in seemingly good-quality but soiled and rumpled clothes, a battered fedora on his head so slanted to partly hide his eyes, with a bristly graying-white beard sprouting on his face like lichen.) If Abraham saw another person approaching—usually a farmer driving a horse-drawn wagon, or boys on foot—he quickly retreated and hid in the woods; in this way giving rise in the course of his eighteen-month sojourn in Muirkirk to a number of rumors and tales. The most persistent was that of a supernatural marsh creature, half-man, half-demon, who couldn't bear the gaze of a human being but had to flee back into the marsh.

A cryptic tale that endures in Muirkirk to this day, though Abraham Licht has vanished long ago.

*   *   *

By degrees, regaining his health, he regained as well his old zest for reading. *Don Quixote* ... the dialogues of Plato ... *Home Cures & Emetics* ... *A History of the Chautauqua Region* ... *P. T. Barnum's Illustrated News* (for August 1880: featuring the sultry Zalumma Agra, "Star of the East," a lovely "Circassian" girl who quite distressed Abraham Licht by so closely resembling, despite her brunette coloring, his lost daughter Millicent) ... and volumes of the *Encyclopedia Britannica* whose mildewed pages he turned in nervous haste as if seeking a revelation that might alter his life. He reread the great tragedies of Shakespeare— *Hamlet*, *Macbeth*, *Lear*, *Othello*—which he'd first encountered years before in the wretched isolation of a county jail (though which county, and for what reason he was there incarcerated, he couldn't now recall); he studied Milton's great poem of paradise lost to man by way of God's cruelty; he discovered, to his delight, the melancholy wisdom of Schopenhauer—

Suicide, the wilful destruction of the single phenomenal existence, is a vain and foolish act, for the thing-in-itself—the species, and life, and will in general—remains unaffected by it, even as the rainbow endures however fast the drops which support it for the moment may chance to fall.

"As I've always surmised," Abraham thought, slowly closing the book of yellowed and torn pages, as if he feared it might crumble to dust in his hands, "—suicide is pointless! One must be the rainbow, and exult in its prismatic ever-changing colors, that live forever, and cannot be destroyed."

V

It was a happy omen, which both men laughingly acknowledged even as they shook hands like old friends or brothers—Abraham Licht and Gaston Bullock Means were each wearing a Palm Beach suit, a white shirt with gold studs, and a straw hat that gave off an air of cheery affluence; and white shoes only very slightly scuffed. Abraham Licht's bow tie was a conservative jade green, while Gaston Bullock

Means's bow tie was red and green polka dots. "Ah, Abraham, I am so relieved to see *you, here*," Means said, gripping his old friend's hand and gazing, with rather protuberant red-veined eyes, into Abraham Licht's face, "for so many men are flooding into Washington these days, and so much is happening every day—every hour!—we desperately need someone in our office whom we can trust."

The year was 1919; the month, June—a half year already since the signing of the Armistice, and the restoration of peace to Europe; and Abraham Licht, by way of his renewed contact with Gaston Bullock Means, was being hired by the Burns Detective Agency as a "special consultant," a position he would hold until August of 1923, the month of President Harding's death. With the passage of time Abraham Licht's official duties were to vary widely, and, like numberless gentlemen brought to Washington during these heady years, he would make a good deal of money; yet, if the truth be told, his work for Burns, Means, the Justice Department, etc. never greatly excited him, or aroused in him any feelings of pride. For whether he operated as an agent for Attorney General A. Mitchell Palmer (under Democrat Woodrow Wilson), or Attorney General Harry Daugherty (under Republican Warren Harding), or worked with Means on special assignments for the Prohibition Bureau (where considerable sums of money routinely changed hands, as prominent bootleggers paid their fees for immunity from federal prosecution), Abraham Licht was rarely in a position to immerse himself in a project of his own but was accountable to other men, and their projects. (And, under Harding's administration in particular, the schemes they devised were so transparent, so lacking in subtlety, originality, and grace—a matter, really, of simple theft from public funds— he saw very little point to it, and gradually lost interest in his career. "Why, they are mere pigs at the trough, nothing more," Abraham Licht realized, one day in 1922, "—and what pleasure is there for a gentleman, in competing thus?")

Initially, however, he felt extreme excitement, and a renewal of his old powers. How good for the soul, to be immersed in the world of men again, steeped in Time!—and to be here, in Washington, D.C., at the very heart of the nation, where his talents might at last come to fruition. Moreover, it quite dazed him that Gaston Bullock Means, with whom he'd never been close in the past, welcomed him so openly and genially; even slung an arm around his shoulders, and gave him a manly sort of hug, repeating several times that he was most relieved to see Abraham Licht in the flesh, *here*, and *now*.

"For now at last *we* are coming into our rightful inheritance," Gaston Bullock Means said expansively, signaling the black waiter for two more whiskeys, "—and no one is to stop us, ever again. Wait and see, brother, if you doubt."

The two men were seated comfortably in a leather-cushioned booth, in the dim-lit gentlemen's bar of the Shoreham Hotel, to which Means had brought Abraham Licht, direct from the railroad station. (Abraham's temporary residence was to be the elegant Shoreham, until such time as he might find adequate lodgings in the city, preferably close by the Burns Detective Agency. He was gratified to learn that, in the meantime, the United States Justice Department would underwrite all his expenses.) For several hours, over whiskey and cigars, Means outlined Abraham Licht's general prospects as a special consultant or secret agent in the employ of the Burns Agency; and spoke, in a voice alternately lowered and exuberant, of his own remarkable adventures in the hire of the U.S. Government, and his plans for the future. "There has never been a time like *this*," Means said, hunching his big shoulders over the table, and fixing his gaze firmly to Abraham Licht's, "—for, you know, life, and liberty, and the pursuit of one's fortune."

Abraham Licht's initial confusion about who his employer actually was, and of what his duties would consist, was quickly laid to rest: for though his workplace would be the Burns Detective Agency on Wisconsin Avenue, his employer would be the United States Bureau of Investigation, under the aegis of the Justice Department. Like Means, he would be a confidential agent; his title, Special Employee of the Department of Justice. He was already on the payroll and in the morning, when he dropped by the office—10:30 A.M. was early enough: the detectives kept late hours—he would be sworn into his duties and equipped with a badge, telephone, official stationery, secretarial service and the like. "I've advised that you be issued a firearm," Means said, dropping his voice dramatically, and opening his coat so that Abraham could glimpse inside the polished handle of a pistol, snug in what appeared to be a gleaming leather holster. "For the Bolsheviks are sly sons of bitches," Means said, laughing, "—once they know you are onto their game."

"The Bolsheviks—?" Abraham Licht asked.

Abraham was aware, wasn't he, Means inquired, lowering his voice yet more dramatically, that thousands of enemies of the State had been arrested, and jailed, during the War? The Espionage Act of 1917 and the Sedition Act of 1918 had netted quite a catch, in all: German-Americans (who could be counted on to be pro-German); pacifists of various persuasions (who were either in the hire of the German war machine, or its dupes); Socialists, Anarchists, and Black Nationalists (Eugene Debs, "Prince" Elihu of Harlem, etc.); critics of the War, or of Woodrow Wilson's policies, or, indeed, of Woodrow Wilson and his administration in general. Yes, quite a hodgepodge of felons!—and some of them put away for a long, long time. Neither President Wilson nor his Attorney General, A. Mitchell Palmer, was likely to forget a political insult, or forgive an enemy; and the sentiment in Washington among both Democrats and Republicans was that the Armistice should not encourage a relaxation of vigilance at home, against subversives, would-be traitors, Socialists, radicals, union agitators, etc. The fight, Means said, sighing in pleasure, and rubbing his immense hands briskly together, was only now beginning.

"For we are secretly launching an undercover campaign," Means said, "to identify, and round up, *every single dissenter in the country*: very likely by the end of the year, if Mr. Palmer's scheme holds. Which is one of the reasons that *you* have been hired; though I have other plans for the two of us, as well. But first things first! *Waiter!*"

So secluded a life had Abraham Licht led during his convalescence in Muirkirk, he'd followed only vaguely the progress of the War, and knew even less of the home-front war: mass arrests of striking pickets, radical speechmakers, German-born subversives, and the like. He asked carefully about the arrests of Eugene Debs and "Prince" Elihu of Harlem, and was told by Means, indifferently, that so far as he knew, both men—"the Socialist and the nigger"—had been sentenced to ten- or fifteen-year terms in the federal penitentiary in Atlanta. Since the Armistice, the administration had had to release hundreds, possibly thousands of "subversive" prisoners; but it was Woodrow Wilson's vow that so long as he remained in office, neither Debs nor Elihu would be pardoned.

"The President *is* a tough old buzzard, for being a schoolmaster from

Princeton," Means said, grimacing and shaking his head in admiration. "*I* would not want to mix with him."

Abraham's vision misted over. He felt an ache of profound sadness and loneliness. Little Moses!—poor child! To think of him locked away in a federal penitentiary in Georgia, *a nigger among niggers,* and all because of his betrayal of Abraham Licht's fatherly love . . .

"Is anything known of this 'Elihu' at the present time?" Abraham asked Means. "He had a sizable following among the Negroes of Harlem and elsewhere, didn't he? You'd think Wilson wouldn't want to offend them."

"Offend niggers?" Means asked, staring at his companion. "How d'you mean?"

"Why, in the usual way. 'Offend.' "

"A nigger?"

"Well—a 'nigger' *is* human, isn't he?"

Again Means stared. Then he began to laugh, as if seeing that Abraham was joking. "Hell, the coons have forgotten him by now," he said, when he could draw breath again. "They forget easily, and forgive. They're nothing like *us.*"

The conversation then shifted to other topics: Means's wartime service (he had, he said mysteriously, operated as "German Agent E-13" in the Washington–Baltimore–New York City region); Means's current affairs (he was involved in negotiations with a certain millionaire "cereal king" who'd made a tidy profit during the War by cheating the government in bulk cereal sales, and was now bargaining with Means about the purchase price of the files pertaining to him in the Bureau of Investigation); and Means's vague but rhapsodic plans for the future (with the imminence of Prohibition, and the inevitability of a clandestine market for alcohol, what might *not* be at hand?).

"A new era, Abraham, a new dawn," Means said, his voice catching as he gripped his companion's arm tight. "*And you have arrived only just in time.*"

Abraham Licht agreed; but thought it queer that he failed to feel as much exhilaration and zest as he should. Perhaps it was because he hadn't eaten a meal for many hours, and, under Means's influence, had had too much to drink. (In Muirkirk, away from the company of other men, Abraham had lost interest in drink altogether.) Moreover, Gaston Bullock Means's company was more overbearing than he recalled: for

Means was in the habit of talking virtually nonstop, interrupting himself with little wheezing asides and spasms of mirth, in a manner now blustering, now deferential, now sly, now merry, now rather brutal—a sudden startling reminder of the man's past, in which, as a convicted confidence-man, swindler, and outright thief, many years ago in Albany, he had assuredly not worn white costumes of the cut of his Palm Beach suit, nor entertained a friend in the luxurious twilight, aglimmer with tall bottles, glasses, and mirrors, of a gentlemen's bar like the Shoreham. He had newly acquired a habit of dropping his voice low, as if he had reason to believe he was overheard; then, when his companion leaned forward, cupping his hand to his ear, he was likely to explode in a guffaw, and finish his remarks in a boisterous near-shout.

Though in height and coloring Means resembled Abraham Licht, he was a few years younger; forty pounds heavier; with an unusually round head, shaggy gray-brown hair, and a dimpled, even cherubic smile. His close-set eyes flashed and beamed with masculine good humor; he *was* the sort to immediately inspire confidence, Abraham Licht conceded—feeling in that instant suddenly old, and not prepared to return to The Game.

Means, however, took not the slightest notice of his companion's change of mood, but, briskly ordered another round of drinks, continued to chat of his contacts in the Justice Department, and in the Senate, and in the House; and of confidential investigative work he was doing, without Burns's knowledge, for the Bureau of Special Reports, or was it the Alien Custodian Bureau, or the Bureau of Internal Revenue, or the Secret Service, or the Bureau of the Budget. . . .

At the end of the long evening, Means slung his heavy arm around Abraham Licht's shoulders again, and leaned his head close, and winked, saying: "What is it about? *What* is it about? Honor, I say: honor! And again—*honor*. D'you understand, my friend? *You* understand, my friend, don't you!"

(Yet wasn't there something about Gaston Bullock Means that Abraham Licht should remember?—that, in the privacy of his sumptuous hotel suite, he half-remembered?—having to do, perhaps, with the unspeakable disaster in Philadelphia. But no: he was convinced that Means hadn't recognized him then, or poor Harwood; or, if he had, surely he wouldn't have revealed their identities. "Otherwise it wouldn't be possible for the man to be so friendly and forthright with me now," Abraham thought, undressing with slow leaden motions for bed.)

VI

The Great Red Raid, as it was afterward called, opened with commendable dramatic effect on 1 January 1920, when two hundred suspected subversives, cited by the "Fighting Quaker" Attorney General Palmer as being in violation of the Sedition Act, were seized in their homes by government agents in several American cities, and thrown into jail. And, before the enormity of the event could be fully grasped by patriotic Americans, there followed, on 6 January, the arrest of *two thousand subversives*, in thirty-three cities!

"That's odd," Abraham Licht observed to Gaston Bullock Means, as in the privacy of Means's office at the Burns Detective Agency, the two men were glancing through newspapers, "—where did Palmer come up with the extra names? I don't remember there having been more than eight hundred on our list."

For a moment Means too looked puzzled, though as he readily confessed he himself had added a few names taken from the telephone directories of such cities as Chicago, Boston and New York (notorious hotbeds of Anarchist and union agitation, owing to their large immigrant populations); then the obvious explanation occurred to him— since the administration took the stand that anyone who protests the arrest of a Red and visits him in jail is naturally a Red himself, the logical step for law enforcement officers is to arrest him or her too, with no delay. "It's a matter of security," Means said. "And very practical. For within twenty-four hours our Attorney General has doubled his list of subversives, and it *is* most impressive, isn't it? Palmer may well run for President himself. Such headlines! Such publicity!" Means smiled in admiration.

"Yet—where will it end?" Abraham mused. "For if friends and relatives come to visit these additional people, they'll be arrested too, and within a few days our jails will be overflowing. A Malthusian predicament!" He tossed down a newspaper and picked up another which displayed on its front page a blurred photograph of a dozen stunned-looking men and one or two women being herded by uniformed police into a van. (One of the men, tall, broad-shouldered, husky, fair-haired, grimacing as a stream of blood ran down his face from a head wound, looked very like ... but Abraham did not wish to acknowledge *My firstborn, my lost son*; and so would not think of Thurston who had broken his heart, from whom and of whom he hadn't heard since that tragic farce in Trenton, New Jersey, long ago. Ridiculous!) Saying, cynically, "Though I suppose there's no problem: any armory, warehouse or cattle pen could be commandeered."

As it turned out, Gaston Bullock Means and "Gordon Jasper Hine" (Abraham's assigned name) were hardly the only investigators working in strictest confidence on plans for the raids. Yet it seemed to Attorney General Palmer that *we two were the most ambitious of the agents, and the most enthusiastic; he commended us in private and apologized for the fact that, due to the secrecy of the Burns connection with the federal government, he and President Wilson couldn't offer us public citations.* "And what will be the fate of the 'Reds'?" Abraham asked Palmer, out of curiosity, perhaps; and Palmer surprised him by saying with simple gentlemanly frankness, "Of course some of us would like to hang the leaders, like Debs and the Harlem rabble-rouser—hang 'em high for all the world to see. But there are obstacles to that, Mr. Wilson concedes, at least under our present Constitution."

As Special Employees of the Justice Department, Abraham Licht and Gaston Bullock Means had spent months traveling about the country; usually by Pullman car, though sometimes in a chauffeur-driven limousine. They stayed in the finest hotels, dined superbly, yet as it happened they *did* work hard—for in some cities they were confronted with a scarcity of Reds, and in others, a fertility that seemed doubtful. So, the list for New Orleans had to be improvisationally expanded; the list for Detroit, judiciously edited. Virtually no old-fashioned detection work was required, however, to Abraham Licht's relief, for as it turned out, his partner was blessed with contacts everywhere—reliable police informers, editors of Republican newspapers, conservative politicians, members of the organized underworld, veterans of the War—who were eager to provide them with names for little payment, or none. "It is impressive isn't it," Means more than once exclaimed, "—the degree of *volun*tary patriotism in America!" So there was never any fear of Means and "Hine" returning to Washington without a bulging caseload of evidence.

Acting upon whim or perversity *or my knowledge that all men were my enemies but particularly Woodrow Wilson and his administration,* Abraham Licht began to amuse himself by idly crossing out some names and, like his mentor Means, copying others from the telephone directory. He thought it incumbent in any case to gratify the Attorney General with a few surprises—men with upstanding Anglo-Saxon surnames, members of the Protestant clergy. Who was not after all a traitor to his country in posse?—confronted with the torturer's rack, for instance; or the right amount of cash.

With the passage of months, however, the campaign against the Bolshies widened to include an alarming diversity of citizens. Newspapers were shut down, and their editors charged with sedition; the Justice Department arranged, with a great deal of publicity, to deport two hundred forty-nine immigrant undesirables to Russia; strikers in Chicago, West Virginia, Indiana, and California were beaten and wounded by police; zealous War veterans smashed Socialist offices, and even, out in the State of Washington, lynched and castrated a member of the I.W.W. So it was, both Abraham Licht and Gaston Bullock Means were relieved when the Democrats were thrown out of office, and Harding and his Republican pals from Ohio arrived in a cheerfully disorderly sort of triumph. Farewell to Wilson, and memories of War, and the ill-fated League of Nations! Welcome to Warren Harding and "normalcy"!

An unprecedented victory for the common man? Abraham Licht was moved rather to amazement than envy; for it was never any secret among Republicans and Democrats alike that Warren Harding had no qualifications for the office of President other than a dauntless bonhomie, and a genuine enthusiasm for speechmaking.

Yet more important, the new Attorney General was a political hack from Ohio, Harry Daugherty, who'd been Harding's wily campaign manager. He had none of Palmer's crusading zeal or patriotic pretensions; he had no ideas at all; he wasn't cruel, and he wasn't kind (except to his friends); he slipped into his new office as an undersized man slips into clothes too large for him, yet comfortable nonetheless. *To the victors go the spoils.*

At the clamorous inaugural reception in the White House, to which both men were invited, Abraham Licht and Gaston Bullock Means exchanged a glance of recognition after having shaken Daugherty's hand: "He is one of *us*."

VII

Yet the Harding years, from 1921 to summer 1923, proved keenly disappointing *as I could not have anticipated.*

For Abraham Licht, even as Gordon Jasper Hine, began to feel an aesthetic revulsion for thievery so gross and undisciplined it resembled a "shark feed" in the ocean; or, indeed, hogs grunting about a common trough. Where was the subtlety, the ingenuity, the sport? The Game had become mere plunder! It was true that as Gordon Jasper Hine he made a good deal of money, both from his salary as a government agent (for he and Means were immediately hired full-time by Harry Daugherty) and from various fees, gifts, loans and so forth provided by uneasy citizens who were being investigated by the Bureau, or threatened with that possibility. Like Means, "Hine" was nearly always on expense account, had a chauffeur-driven Packard limousine at his disposal and a suite of six rooms in Chilchester House, K Street (an elegant English-style hotel with high tea in the afternoons, the finest-quality bootleg liquor and handsome brass spittoons). His vanity was flattered that the Harding circle sometimes included him in their boisterous poker evenings, whether upstairs at the White House or at the Little House on H Street, as Daugherty's residence became known. (Yet how noisy and slapdash the poker evenings were!—Abraham lost nearly as much money as he won, and came away with violent headaches as a consequence of the heavy cigar smoke and the clumsy shouted repartee of Harding and his companions.)

So perverse is man, as Schopenhauer well knew—the anguish of struggle yielding to the ennui of success—Abraham Licht began to feel it a wearisome sort of life, to trade in explicit *deals* where his aesthetic instinct urged him to create secret *plots*; and to be approached by gentlemen fearing prosecution from the Justice Department, before he or Means got around to approaching them. Means thrived, week by week, and grew ever more swaggering and confident; Abraham Licht

assumed an enthusiasm he did not invariably feel, and came to understand the President's odd, even compulsive, habit of placing quick side
bets (at poker, at craps, on the golf links)—such tactics aroused a brief
sensation of risk, of *being alive*. (One night, during a typical poker game
at the White House, Harding negotiated an off-the-cuff bet with Abraham Licht on some small matter in the game: a diamond stickpin of
Harding's against a diamond stickpin of Abraham's. "Aren't they identical, Mr. President?" Abraham asked; and Harding, his heavy sweat-
stained face agleam, said genially, "No matter! No matter!" The result
of the bet was that Abraham Licht came away with two diamond stickpins, each worth approximately $3,000.)

He couldn't have guessed at the degree of his aristocrat's sensibility, before he discovered himself offended, upon several occasions, by
Mrs. Harding (a supremely brash, squat, ugly woman, older than Harding, whom Harding had married for her money, known with sniggering
affection as the Duchess); and revulsed by the President's mistress Nan
(a coy, simpering, fleshy Ohio girl decades younger than the Duchess,
who professed to adore her "Warren," and to be faithful to him unto
death: no matter that her portly lover had no more gallantry than to
copulate with her on the floor of the clothes closet in his very White
House office, with any number of ushers, couriers and secretaries close
by). Accustomed, perhaps, to the degree of sophistication and wit possessed by (ah, he hardly dared think of her!) Eva Clement-Stoddard,
Abraham Licht found himself disgusted by the coarseness of men like
Harding's Secretary of the Interior Albert Fall (who scarcely made it a
secret, from the start, that his office was open to "bids" from private
parties, in the matter of leasing oil-rich public lands), and Colonel
Charley Forbes of the Veterans Bureau (who had somehow finessed a
budget of a half billion dollars yearly, and was busily involved in the
sale of "surplus" and "damaged" medical supplies left over from the
War), and Daugherty's constant companion Jess Smith (big-boned,
shambling, flabby, asthmatic, yet rewarded with a mysterious connection to the Justice Department, and to its files and influence, though he
was never officially on the payroll); and, indeed, the pugnacious Daugherty himself. (Both Abraham Licht and Gaston Bullock Means resented
the fact that Daugherty blew hot and cold—to use Means's expression—
with his Special Employees at the Bureau of Investigation. Clearly, he
wanted them to spy on all his enemies in Washington, and on all his

friends with the exception of Jess Smith and Harding; he wanted detailed reports, though not in writing; and not at any prescribed time. When one or another of the Bureau's special deals fell through, or was in danger of being discovered by the opposition press, Daugherty shouted abuse at them over the telephone, and threatened to fire them; when a deal went very well indeed—Abraham Licht labored for weeks, for instance, to arrange a nearly legal means by which unsaleable whiskey stocked in warehouses might be shipped to foreign countries, with a generous "surcharge" split between the Prohibition Bureau and the Bureau of Investigation—Daugherty boasted of the coup as if it were his own.)

In order to repay hundreds of political favors, Harding had appointed friends, or friends of friends, or reliable party hacks, to nearly all the federal judgeships; and to such offices as the Alien Custodian Bureau, and the Public Health Bureau, the Bureau of Special Reports, the Bureau of Engineering, the Bureau of Internal Revenue, the Bureau of the Budget, the Bureau of War Risk Insurance, et al. Unqualified but faithful Republicans were named as Governor of the Federal Reserve System, Superintendent of Federal Prisons, Governor of Puerto Rico, Alien Property Custodian, Chairman of the Shipping Board . . . and, to Abraham Licht's amazement, his old kinsman "Baron" Barraclough was named Comptroller of the Currency, and the wily Jasper Liges, of whom he hadn't heard in years, was named Commissioner of Indian Affairs! (When Abraham inquired of one of the President's men what the duties of the Commissioner of Indian Affairs might be, he was told with a broad smile: "Oil leases and real estate.")

Most astonishing of all: Harding would have appointed Jess Smith Secretary of the Treasury if there hadn't been protests from all sides.

"Why, the world has been turned upside down," Abraham Licht thought in despair, "—and where is *my* place!"

VIII

Yet, as he fully intended to make clear in his memoir one day, *all* was not disappointing during his Washington years: for, as Gordon Jasper

Hine, he commanded uneasy (if not occasionally resentful) respect about town; he traveled where and when he wished, under the auspices of the Bureau; and it pricked his gambler's curiosity, as to how long the Harding administration could last, before the house of cards came tumbling down.

"Why, we will go on forever—who will stop us?" Gaston Bullock Means asked, staring. "The people *love* Harding."

Which was true, at least initially.

No matter the passionate vacuity of his public addresses, no matter the childish nature of his "bloviating" (as he himself called his speechmaking talents), or the laughable presumption of his beliefs ("I do not think any government can be just if it doesn't have somehow a contact with Omnipotent God"), crowds everywhere applauded him with unstopped enthusiasm: for, at the start at least, Harding *looked* like a President.

Of course Abraham Licht bitterly envied Warren Harding. He felt the crude injustice of Fate, that *he* should be but an anonymous federal employee, under the capricious thumb of Harry Daugherty, while a bumptious fool like Harding was President of the United States! Daugherty was said to have groomed Harding for public office and to have worked over the years to assure his nomination, *solely on the basis of Harding's appearance*; the irony being, that Abraham Licht was every bit as attractive—as noble, as stately, as "sincere," as Presidential. Why had he thrown away his political prospects, as a greenling youth! Was he himself to blame? It didn't bear thinking about, Abraham Licht counseled himself; that way lay madness.

When he first rose to national prominence Harding was a statelyappearing, silver-haired, rather ordinarily handsome man in his midfifties, with a strong profile, prominent brows, and a winning smile. His heroes were Caesar, Hamilton, and Napoleon, so far as he knew of them; he carried himself with an air of purposeful dignity, as, perhaps, they had done in their times. (Was the Harding line tainted by Negro blood, as vicious, unproved rumors would have it, originating in his hometown?—those who wished to vilify Harding claimed to see "Negroid features" in his face; others professed themselves incapable of seeing any such thing.) Harding had been for years the editor of a small Ohio newspaper and his sense of the world's complexity derived from that experience: what was significant might be presented in a column or two of type; what could not be fitted into that space could not be significant. Once in the White House he had neither the time nor the concentration to read newspapers carefully, and of course he never read books; even an interview with a "specialist" (in taxation problems, in European affairs, for instance) wearied him. He was too small for the office of President, he smilingly complained to his friends, who waved aside his remarks impatiently: for, after all, were not *they* prepared to help? Apart from poker, golf, infrequent trysts with Nan, and drinking with his companions, nothing so delighted Harding as addressing crowds in large, open, public places; and afterward mingling with the people and shaking hands. If only the Presidency could always be thus—!

With his sharp eye for imperfection Abraham Licht noted early on a certain unmistakable air of doom about the President: dapper, and congenial, and resigned: but doom nonetheless. Perhaps Harding sensed that his friends were betraying him on all sides; that he wouldn't live out his term of office; and that, following his death, every aspect of his Presidency would be contemned. (Even Nan, dear sweet silly Nan, would boast to the world of their liaison, selling their "true love story" to the press!) At times it seemed to Abraham Licht that Harding must know of the corruption practiced by his friends, and was giving his tacit consent; at other times it seemed clear that the poor fool knew nothing, and wished to know nothing.

"Shall I be the one to tell him?" Abraham mused. But then, sighing, "Ah, but *why*!"

Yet Harding was deteriorating rapidly, and with so queer, stoic and wistful an air, Abraham Licht came to pity him.

The President's weakness for bootleg whiskey, wienerwurst and batter-fried chicken took its toll; by degrees he grew bloated. His fleshy jowls puffed out even as his eyes retreated beneath the heavy patrician brows. His voice, once blandly well modulated, now quavered when he stood before the most innocuous of well-wishers; microphones unnerved him. He sweated in public. His luck, of which he'd once innocently boasted, now deserted him at both poker and golf; if he won bets, they were frantic off-the-cuff wagers for a pittance, or items of jewelry. (Though one memorable evening he infuriated the Duchess by gambling away an entire set of exquisite Wedgwood White House china which, as the Duchess charged, was not his to barter.) To his male companions he joked crudely—yet wistfully—of having a "monkey-gland" operation to restore his virility. Though beginning to be criticized by sharp-eyed foes of tobacco, largely female, Harding chewed his Piper Heidsieck tobacco compulsively, hacking and spitting in a way some observers found offensive. Yet, Harding pleaded, he required chewing for his health: he simply couldn't get through a morning without it!

It became an affectionate anecdote among the President's circle how poor Harding infuriated the Duchess by sneaking several plugs of Piper Heidsieck into his mouth while sitting on the dais at the Princeton University commencement ceremony of 1922, where with great pomp, drenched with sweat in his woollen cap and gown, he was awarded something called an "honorary doctorate"—indeed an honor for a man of Harding's modest educational background and yet more modest intellectual ambition.

Like all Presidents, despite his innocent good nature Warren Harding drew threats against his life, whether by those seriously intending to do him harm or by mere crackpots (of whom the nation's capital enjoyed a good many in the twenties). So Secret Service men accompanied the President everywhere, as in a children's game, even to his hotel trysts with Nan (where, to the amusement of those in the know, they waited discreetly in the corridor outside the room) and to the Gayety Burlesque on lower Pennsylvania Avenue (where the President was privileged to sit in a special box screened from view of the lowlife audience). By degrees he found no relaxation and virtually no happiness anywhere except in the groggy uproarious midst of his circle of friends—who, perhaps, were not truly his friends.

One evening at the Little House on H Street, to which Abraham Licht had come after midnight in formal evening attire and tall silk hat (having attended a performance of the *The Flying Dutchman*, which magnificent tragic music never failed to excite him), Harding chanced to remark to Abraham, in a wistful tone, that when he was awarded the honorary degree of Doctor of Laws at Princeton it was said of him he "stood in the tradition of Lincoln"; but somehow, he didn't quite believe it, himself.

At this, Abraham professed to be puzzled; and said, with a gracious smile that if at Princeton they told him he was in the tradition of Lincoln, and one of the nation's greatest leaders, then certainly he must be—"For who would know better than the administrators at Princeton?"

Harding leaned over to spit a silver-dollar-sized clot of tobacco juice into the brimming brass spittoon at his feet. Weakly he said, "Yes. I suppose so." Again he paused, to chew and spit. He turned to Abraham Licht as to a newfound friend and said, with a sudden frank smile, that he'd come a long distance from Blooming Grove, Ohio, and would be returned in one way only. "And do you know what that way must be, Mr. Hine?"

Abraham Licht felt a stab of recognition. *He is a form of myself only not schooled in The Game. Knowing like a fated animal that his doom is upon him.* Though afterward Abraham would regret not having spoken to Warren Harding in equally frank, brotherly tones, at the time, in the clamor of the poker setting, he could only stroke his goateed chin and look perplexed and reply emphatically, "Why, Mr. President, I certainly do *not.*"

One of the very few controversial acts of Harding's term of office was the pardoning, in his second year, of a number of political prisoners whom Woodrow Wilson had charged with wartime sedition.

There were twenty-three remaining alive in federal penitentiaries by this time; all men; among them the notorious Socialist Eugene Debs and the yet more notorious Negro "revolutionary" Prince Elihu of the World Negro Betterment & Liberation Union.

Which of these "enemies of America" was the more dangerous had long been an issue in the conservative press. President Harding, to the astonishment of all his staff, decided that neither was an enemy, and must be freed at once.

No one was more furious than the Duchess. "Not only a traitorous *Red* but a traitorous *black!*—Warren, I put my foot *down; I will not allow it.*" Unspoken between them was the old, slanderous charge that Harding had "Negroid" ancestry; his opponents would take up the cause again, more cruelly than ever.

Harding yet held his ground. Saying, to the press, that he could not comprehend his predecessor's hatred for "political" foes—the United States, after all, under its sacred Constitution and with its special connection to the Omnipotent, is the only place in the world where freedom is guaranteed.

"I will pardon them because it is the right thing to do. That is the only reason to do any thing, I think," Harding said tersely.

When Debs and Elihu were brought by special car to the White House to be photographed in the Oval Office with the President, Abraham Licht made certain he was among the small gathering of witnesses; and felt quite moved by the sight of the legendary Debs—tall and gaunt, with the look of a man uncertain of his surroundings; and Prince Elihu—who did indeed look princely though he was wearing not one of his flamboyant caftans but an ordinary brown gabardine suit, and his hair, formerly wild and woolly, was trimmed close to his head.

(Abraham felt a stab in his heart. For a weak moment, he worried he might faint. How greatly changed his 'Lisha! His Little Moses!)

(But clearly this man *was* Little Moses, grown up, a being not even Abraham Licht with his prescient powers could have imagined.)

As Prince Elihu, the sole Negro in a crowd of Caucasians, he stood in a pose virtually sculpted, knowing himself on display, and, even in his belligerence, basking in such attention. His arm and shoulder muscles, Abraham saw, had grown hard; his torso was nearly as well formed as Harwood's had been, though Elihu possessed a grace his crude stepbrother had never had. His nose was broader than Abraham recalled, yet his mouth, corners tucked downward, appeared thinner; his gaze was shrewd, watchful, restless; his hair touched lightly with gray. Prince Elihu's age was a matter of conjecture in the press, ranging from thirty to above forty years, but Abraham knew the young man was but thirty-three—yet, one had to admit, so very changed! Mature, and transmogrified.

As President Harding stumblingly read off a prepared speech honoring the occasion, and reaffirming the sacred rights of Freedom of Speech, Freedom of the Press, and Life, Liberty and the Pursuit of Happiness, Prince Elihu alone seemed scarcely to be listening. His hooded gaze darted restlessly about the room; skimming the unfamiliar white faces; lingering nowhere . . . not even upon Abraham Licht, whom, as Gordon Jasper Hine, Special Employee of the Justice Department, it would have required extraordinary powers to recognize: with his graying chestnut-red hair, neatly trimmed goatee and thick-lensed pince-nez firm upon his nose.

Yet I might have winked at him. Made a gesture if only a gesture of pain.

Eager to finish the ceremony so that he could retire upstairs and get free of his tight clothes, and pour himself a needed drink (the White House during Prohibition was provided with only the finest Canadian whiskey, through the altruistic effort of Jess Smith), Harding smiled awkwardly at the "political prisoners" before him, and took no notice of the insult, if insult was intended, of Prince Elihu's aloof manner. With an air of nervous jocosity, as the ceremony concluded, Harding remarked that he was certain that President Wilson in his ill health and anxiety about the War had possibly misunderstood their intentions—"You had not meant, after all, to commit the actual act of sedition." To this, Eugene Debs smiled and seemed to agree; but Prince Elihu said, in an arrogant voice lowered so that only a few persons might overhear, "I doubt Mr. Wilson was such a fool, Mr. President."

IX

Warren Harding died suddenly on the evening of 2 August 1923, in San Francisco, following an exhausting and ill-advised "Voyage of Understanding" (speechmaking through the West and Alaska); but by that time, when the house of cards *was* at last tumbling down, Abraham Licht had been gone from Washington for several months. With bank drafts for considerable sums of money, and small valuable items (the diamond stickpins, for instance) in his suitcases, he checked into the Waldorf-Astoria in Manhattan; consulted with Dr. Lespinasse; underwent the mysterious "rejuvenative gland transplant" operation (which was always to remain mysterious, as Dr. Lespinasse never divulged, even to the medical profession, the secret of his technique) in Mount Sinai Hospital; and afterward recovered from the mild trauma of the experience in the resort town of White Sulphur Springs in the Catskill Mountains . . . where, by chance, even as he was casting about for a fresh business venture, he learned of Dr. Felix Bies and Autogenic Self-Mastery and the Parris Clinic.

"There it is! Just the thing!"

He had always intended to try his hand at medicine: at healing.

Also, Abraham couldn't shake off a feeling of having been contaminated by his many months in Washington, amid that carnival recklessness, and things-spinning-out-of-control; and daily contact with such crude persons as Harry Daugherty, Jess Smith and Gaston Bullock Means.

In the end, in fact, Abraham had become frightened of his partner, who brandished his pistol too freely, and boasted, when drunk, or high on cocaine, of his ingenious plan to make a million dollars in a single deal (by quashing an indictment pending against U.S. Steel, perhaps); and to take Jess Smith's favored position with the administration.

"But how will you do that?" Abraham Licht asked uneasily. "No one is closer than Smith and Daugherty: you would have to kill Smith, I am afraid, to get rid of him."

Means sucked energetically at his cigar; and, pretending their conversation might be overheard, he winked, and said, in a voice heavy with innuendo, "Oh as to *that*—however might *that* be managed!" even as, with a crude swipe of his elbow, he indicated the gun strapped about his spreading middle.

Abraham had reason to believe it was Means himself who'd sent death threats to the White House months before with the idea that, should the President request extraordinary security, *he* might be singled out for the task. But nothing had come of it; Harding had not taken the threats seriously, or had not cared a great deal about dying.

(Abraham himself had been issued a Police Service revolver, and a smart leather shoulder holster in which to carry it; but his gentlemanly scruples were such, he really couldn't bring himself to strap the foolish thing on. The revolver he kept locked in his desk at the Bureau, where it remained when he left in June of 1923.)

As it happened, a few weeks following Means's conversation with Abraham Licht, Jess Smith was found dead in his apartment, an apparent suicide: clad in pajamas and dressing gown, a bullet through his head, and a revolver on the floor close by his person. (Which revolver was to disappear during the police investigation.)

Anxiously, with sweat beading his face, Means assured Abraham Licht that Smith's death was but a coincidence—one of those odd, queer, fantastical things that seemed to be happening all the time now, in Washington—and that *he* had not a thing to do with it. "No more than Harry Daugherty himself," as he said, with a ghastly grinning stare.

At which Abraham Licht winced, and made no reply.

And, within a week, resigned his position at the Bureau as the industrious "Gordon Jasper Hine," fleeing the nation's capital forever.

X

Venus Aphrodite!—pray for me.

For where Abraham Licht loves, he must be loved in return: where he would surrender his soul, he *must* be granted a soul in return: otherwise The Game is wicked indeed.

And he will not be cheated again: not another time!

And though his manly prowess has been restored to him he can't deny that the years are flying by quickly now, and that, if he wants another son, or even another daughter, to continue his name, it must happen soon.

Venus Aphrodite!—have mercy.

It is known that one's Wish guides one's Destiny yet the patients at the Parris Clinic don't always thrive: which is an embarrassment indeed, and necessitates a good deal of hurrying about, and telephone calls made, and tidying up.

(Though it has become the usual procedure now, that, when a patient passes away, the body is kept in a sort of quarantine until after dark; at which time a special band of attendants, who can be trusted to keep their work confidential, loads it into a van and carries it to the county morgue twenty miles away, where, in the morning, the coroner—hardly a stranger to the Parris Clinic's routine, by this time—makes a discreet examination; signs the death certificate; and releases the body for delivery to a nearby funeral home. Beyond this, matters pertaining to the body's disposal rest with relatives of the deceased, though Doctors Bies and Liebknecht continue to be helpful, up to a point.)

Patients don't always thrive but business thrives: no doubt it has to do with the fact that prosperity, in 1926, is at an all-time high; yet will rise, and rise, and rise!—as a variation (as philosophers of the economy have speculated) of the Law of Evolution.

Business thrives; and also disease.

But Abraham Licht has become restless yet another time, for, despite the fact that the Clinic is making a fair amount of money, and his experimental investments in the stock market (in the most conservative of commodities) have yielded a healthy return, he finds that he can't bear the company of "Felix Bies" (if indeed that is the man's name); and, since he has fallen in love with Rosamund, he begins to think that he must leave . . . he *must* leave, and begin another life.

For he quarrels too frequently with the charlatan Bies, whom he can no longer respect. Only a few years ago the man had struck him as clever, even rather brilliant in some of his notions; now alcohol has rotted his brain, and he has become as slovenly in his reasoning as in his person.

For what does it profit a man to excel at The Game, when his heart is no longer in it; when, indeed, his heart shrinks in revulsion from all that lies about him?

Venus Aphrodite, he thinks, excited as a young swain, and, like a young swain, confident that he *will* win his beloved—*pray for me.*

XI

And now. This dreamy autumnal morning. The enthralled lover Moses Liebknecht sees the woman standing as in a trance on the grassy shore of the pond; her eyes shut, her beautiful face framed by untidy blackly gleaming hair to her shoulders. She is wearing a gray smock of the kind women patients wear to their hydrotherapy sessions; her legs are bare, and very white; and her feet.

Why has the woman led him here, out of sight of the Clinic?

Why has the woman led him here, where no one but he, her lover, observes?

As she steps into the pond he feels a quickening in his soul, as in his groin; he calls out her name, gently yet forcibly—"Rosamund!"—to awaken her, that she will at last surrender to the authority of his love.

As she will, and does.

For which Venus Aphrodite be praised.

"The Lost Village"

I

A balmy evening in May 1928, and at Carnegie Recital Hall on
Fifty-seventh Street, Manhattan, a small group of musicians and
several singers, men and women in their twenties and looking *very*
young, are presenting to a gathering of less than one hundred puzzled
individuals a strange composition by the young composer Darian Licht—
who happens also, with odd contortions and lurches of his lanky body,
to be conducting. The title of the work is *Esopus, the Lost Village*. The
printed program describes it as a "tone poem with variations" but to the
trained and untrained ear alike it appears to consist of a bewildering number of movements—stops and starts, really—and a bewildering
number of tempos, one or two of which frequently detach themselves
from the predominant tempo and in the form of a flute, oboe, or soprano voice, or what sounds like (in fact is, as the program notes confirm) the grating of pebbles in a wooden box, veers off in a direction
rhythmically and tonally unpremeditated. How is it possible, a piece of
music in which performers drift off into reverie-like solos, independent
of the others?—so that the effect is one of random sound, or noise; to
which at intervals the audience's responses (restless coughing and murmuring, stifled laughter, expressions of incredulity, distaste and even
anger) contribute yet another layer, or layers, of distraction?

This, the boastful "world premiere" of a work by an instructor at
the Westheath School of Music, Schenectady, New York: chimes; sighs
and explosions; a hint of church bells; the intrusion of a too-hearty
march as it might have been played, circa 1880, by a marching band; an
intonation of water? rain? flood? deluge? so faint it can scarcely be
heard; an abrupt caterwauling of a trombone, a clarinet and a single

old-fashioned E-flat cornet; a hint of piety (an allusion to "Gott, der Herr, ist Sonn' und Schild") countered by the rattling of the box of pebbles; a suddenly beautiful, but short-lived Kyrie from the singers—three young women and two young men who, as they sing, stare out bravely beyond the audience. A beat, two beats; an instrument that appears to be a long-necked glass beaker of the kind used in chemistry laboratories is earnestly blown into by the trombonist: it produces a queer high-pitched cooing, both eerily beautiful and comical, that arouses muffled hilarity in the audience; another beat, and an intonation again of wind, rustling grasses, muffled voices; and, abruptly, silence.

Silence! The most difficult music of all.

Conductor and performers freeze, like sculpted works. As the silence in the recital hall is too silent . . . apart from murmurings and rustlings and the commotion of patrons rising from their seats to slip, or to stalk, out . . . forcing one to listen to silence *and how arduous silence is, how fraught with terror if one isn't accustomed to it.* So earnest, so strained, so dazed and yet hopeful are the faces of the youthful performers and the conductor-composer Darian Licht, it seems evident that *Esopus, the Lost Village* is not meant to be a parody or a comical work, but a serious composition.

Sympathetic well-wishers, very likely relatives and friends of the performers, begin to clap, tentatively—for surely the piece is over?—but conductor and performers remain frozen for several further beats, and then, with remarkable aplomb considering the mood of the audience, the young Licht, face covered in a film of perspiration, longish hair damply straggling into his eyes, gives a swipe of his baton and the musicians begin again: brazenly, it would seem, in the slipping, sliding, dissonant tone that marked the opening of the piece; yet reversed, or upside down, so that the melodic lines emerge as if glimpsed in a mirror *or in the broken, rippled surface of a body of water.*

II

"What trash!"

"How dare he!"

"Who is this—'Darian Licht'! And the 'Westheath Ensemble'!"

"Under the patronage of—can it be Joseph Frick's wife?"

"How dare they! Any of them!"

Harsh angry laughter. Rude mutterings. A woman complained to a companion that the music "stung her ears." Another patron, an elderly gentleman, spoke of being "nauseated." By the end of the forty-five-minute composition entire rows had emptied out, though disgruntled patrons remained in the foyer wanting to share derisive opinions. There had been only polite, scattered applause; a few hisses and boos; overall, a nasty combative mood from which Darian Licht's musical companions wished to shield him, even as they hurriedly left the stage themselves. But Darian, hurt, puzzled and beginning to be angry, stood at the edge of the stage, baton in hand, hair in his face, gazing past the lights. A man's voice rose from the rear, "You ought to be ashamed! Desecrating music!" and Darian Licht said, stammering, "I—I should not be ashamed—*you* should be. You haven't listened, and you haven't heard. You—" Other voices rose in a kind of chorus, both male and female protesting they had heard, they'd heard more than they wanted, this was a desecration of music, hurtful and hateful to the ear; and Darian Licht protested in turn, "Why should I compose music that's already been composed? Why do you want to hear again, and again, and yet again, only what you've already heard? Always Mozart, and Beethoven, and—" but they shouted him down, "D'you think you're superior to Mozart? Beethoven? *You?* What a joke!"

So it ended, the premiere of *Esopus, the Lost Village*: the début of Darian Licht, composer, at Carnegie Recital Hall, 23 May 1928.

Except there remained, after most of the audience had gone away, a tall fair-haired man of youthful middle age, with an equally tall, though starkly black-haired female companion, who applauded loudly in the silence of the now lighted hall. "Such strange music! Like nothing I've ever heard. Yet, y'know—*I* know so little of music—it seemed to me the very voice of Our Lord—so unpredictable, I mean." This individual spoke so genially, in so frank and somehow tender a voice, Darian Licht stared at him in wonder. For wasn't that voice familiar, and . . . that face?

"Thurston?"

"Darian!"

Darian hurried down from the stage, and the tall fair-haired man came to embrace him heartily, as his companion, unmoving at the rear of the hall, looked on in silence.

Darian stammered, "But—Thurston? Is it *you*? You're—*here?*"

"In truth I'm not 'Thurston'—he's been dead and gone since 1910. And I'm not truly here, in Manhattan I mean; Sister Beulah Rose and I are bound for Florida, and have not really time to linger. Yet I wanted to see you, brother; and to shake your hand, and bless you; for, being your father's son, as I am, you will need the blessing of the Lord—the true Lord."

Much of this was lost on Darian, who stared at his brother, and at his brother's face, in shock that he was so altered. Not so much time had altered Thurston, it seemed, as some violent act: his broad, open, still-handsome face looked as if it had been broken vertically from the left temple to the jaw, and healed only partially. His eyes were unevenly aligned and his bristly eyebrows were scarred like lace. His once-blond hair shone an eerie metallic silver and his asymmetrical smile showed broken teeth. Yet he continued to smile as he spoke, introducing himself as "Reverend Thurmond Blichtman of the New Church of the Nazarene" and shaking Darian's hand so firmly, Darian feared his bones would crack. This was Thurston; yet not-Thurston; a youthful, vigorous, ebullient individual in cheaply smart clothes, whose entire being seemed to radiate *a yearning to love and to be loved* that was nearly overpowering. Yet, all the while, at the rear of the hall in the aisle stood the tall, Amazonian woman, with a face blunt and impassive as a trowel and eyes inexpressive as stones. "Sister Beulah Rose"—such stark, lustreless black hair, in a braid down her back, Darian was reminded of those Iroquois Indians who'd recently taken residence, under government coercion, on a reservation not far from Schenectady, in the rocky foothills of the Adirondack Mountains. Not a single word would Sister Beulah Rose utter, yet you could tell she had her own thoughts and passed her own judgment.

No sooner had Thurston, that's to say Reverend Blichtman, introduced himself to his astonished brother than he was explaining how he must leave, for there was an urgent ministry awaiting him in Miami, Florida—"Not in material form yet but in a vision. Sister Beulah Rose and I have had the identical dazzling vision, of a pink-stucco church with strange, striking roofs, a kind of undersea green; so we must make our pilgrimage southward, to realize it." Already Thurston was striding up the aisle, and Darian hurried to accompany him. "But, Thurston— so soon? This is terrible! Can't you—" In alarm Thurston smiled, pressed a forefinger against his lips, and with a gesture of his head indicating that Sister Beulah Rose didn't perhaps know of "Thurston Licht" and should not know. "—'Thur-mond,' " Darian said quickly, clutching at his brother's elbow, "—can't you stay for an hour? We have so much to learn from each other." "Ah, I wish! I wish that was possible," Thurston, or Thurmond, said with a look of pain. "You are—a music instructor? In Schenectady? Not married, I believe? And estranged, Millie has told me, from Father?—like others of us." But already Darian's eldest brother was detaching himself from Darian, as his silent, impassive female companion fell into step with him exiting the hall. Like the Reverend Blichtman, Sister Beulah Rose wore cheaply stylish, attractive clothes, loose-fitting trousers and a man's jacket in a vivid fawn color; both wore white shirts open at the collar, workingman-style. Darian noted that both wore sleek, shiny black-polished boots of simulated leather. Ignoring Darian, Sister Beulah Rose shivered as a horse shivers, in anticipation of open spaces; clearly, she yearned to be gone from the airless recital hall. Her companion glanced smilingly at her and told her she might run ahead and fetch the truck and bring it around. Without a word, nor certainly a farewell glance at Darian, the handsome woman strode off and was gone. "Is she—'Sister Beulah Rose'—your wife, Thurston? I mean—Thurmond?" Darian asked, and Thurston laughed and said, "Sister Beulah Rose is her own woman, and not any man's." Out on Fifty-seventh Street, where traffic was passing in a continuous stream, Thurston said, "Darian, farewell. Though I no more understand music than an ox, like any Christian I thrill to 'make a joyful noise unto the Lord' and am happy that, in your own way, you have done so." Like an anxious puppy, his face still gleaming with perspiration after the ordeal of his début, Darian followed his brother along the sidewalk, in the direction of Seventh Avenue. He stammered, "But, Thurston—Thurmond?—you are a minister? You are ordained? 'The New Church of the Nazarene'—has it any connection to the church in Muirkirk?" His brother said, as if these words gave him pain, "Brother, I do believe! I believe in the truth of the Gospels as preserved for us in the Bible. I believe that Jesus Christ is my savior and the savior of mankind. Surely He saved me from death—not once but numerous

times. And yet—" He was striding along the crowded sidewalk, crossing the wide, windy avenue as Darian hurried to keep up. "—and yet,
Darian, at the same time I stand detached from my belief like a man
observing his own hanging and I wonder if it isn't as unlikely and
ridiculous as any superstitious nonsense. Like the Fiji Islanders who
worship their own ugly man-eating gods or the Eskimos—God knows!—
a polar bear." Thurston, or Thurmond, laughed suddenly and harshly.

Darian shivered, staring at his brother's handsome ruin of a face.
That laughter so like mine, inhabiting my own heart.

By this time an open-backed truck the size of a hay wagon, in poor
repair but painted a luridly bright green, had made its rattling way
along Fifty-seventh Street and was idling close by at the curb. Well-
dressed pedestrians glanced at it, smiling, and at the tall figure of ambiguous sex behind the wheel. Preparing to climb into the truck,
Reverend Blichtman hugged Darian with such zestful affection Darian
winced, fearful his ribs had cracked. "Don't let narrow-minded fools
dictate to you how you should feel about your own music," the elder
man said passionately, "—so long as *you* know your vision, Darian, that
will suffice. All is ordained for us—'As above, so below.' If you are a
musical genius—or if you are not—who among mere earthly ears can
judge? God be with you, brother; and may Jesus Christ dwell forever in
your heart." With these words, Reverend Blichtman, beaming, swung
his large body up into the cab of the truck, managed to shut the door
after two attempts, and raised his hand through the opened window
in farewell. His lips quivered as if on the verge of a wide, maniacal grin
(for perhaps Reverend Blichtman's parting words echoed dubiously in
his own ears) that was the final vision Darian had of his long-lost eldest
brother, as, running after the truck for a half block, drawing the attention of pedestrians, he shouted, "Good-bye! Good-bye!" and frantically
waved.

*Not having known how much I'd loved Thurston, till then. Till knowing
there was no longer any Thurston, but only my memory. That ragged hole
in the heart that music must fill—yet never fills.*

The truck driven so capably by Sister Beulah Rose sped east on Fifty-
seventh Street in the direction of fashionable Fifth Avenue, vibrating
and rattling, exhaust spewing out its rear. Darian would have an impression afterward of words, Bible verses probably, in glaring red letters
on its sides.

Its rear license plate, attached to the truck by wires, was caked in mud, unreadable.

III

Yes I was brazen, and will remain so.
No I have no shame as you know shame. And want none.

So with the passage of time Darian Licht would tell himself. Yet on the evening of his disastrous début as a composer, he feels little such confidence. At the age of twenty-eight he is a very young man, virginal in most respects: his pride has been stung as by a swarm of angry hornets.

Worse yet, Darian will have to return to the Westheath School knowing that those senior faculty members who'd disappoved of his Carnegie Hall début, under the sponsorship of elderly Mrs. Frick, would believe their judgment vindicated. To his face, they'd wished him well; but made excuses for being unable to attend the recital in Manhattan. "Of course, it's but the début," they told Darian with seemingly sincere faces. "Your *Lost Village* will surely be played many times, in America at least!"

In his rented apartment in an old mansion in Schenectady there are numerous such compositions, several of greater ambition than *Esopus*; which Darian in despair that his vision ("If vision be the word, and not rather madness") will ever be realized. Not even his two or three musical friends know how many pieces of music Darian Licht has attempted since early adolescence. More than twenty are formally complete, like *Esopus*, and await performance; dozens remain in sketchy form—sonatas, string quartets and quintets, miniature symphonies ("Silence: Dusk" is eight minutes long); elegies, marches, nocturnes, madrigals, cantatas; "letters"—"impressions"—"reveries." The compositions are scored for all variety of musical instruments and many instruments (pebbles, glass beaker, crackling flame, washboard) not ordinarily considered musical. There is an opera for forty-eight voices, including the voices of children, animals and the dead, untitled and uncompleted after fifteen years, which would present the life of a village (like Muirkirk) for an intense twenty-four-hour period.

All that I'd lost was not lost. Wayward motions of the soul. Like wood smoke rising, our lives . . . our music.

At the time of his notorious Manhattan début, Darian Licht is in his third year as "visiting instructor" at the Westheath School of Music in Schenectady, a school of regional distinction and ambition under the aggressive directorship of a former musical prodigy and composer named Myrick Sheffield. Among his circle of friends and admirers, Sheffield is considered an American musical genius, unfairly unrecognized in New York City; his compositions are lavishly romantic, in the flamboyant style of his master Franz Liszt; as a pianist he's a dynamo of keyboard virtuosity, ponderously sentimental, showy and imprecise. The very antithesis of Darian Licht: yet Sheffield hired Darian with the shrewd knowledge that for a low salary, and no contract from year to year, he could acquire a brilliantly talented young music teacher with little thought of academic achievement and financial security. "Attractive to women as he is, Licht is blind to his own attractions. His sex is all in his head: his music. He will never marry and will never need much money. He neither knows nor cares of his own worth. And I will be the judge of that worth, to Westheath"—so Sheffield has publicly boasted. Though he's fond of the younger man, too; perceiving him as a rival, yet a worthy rival to be bested. (Sheffield would be more jealous of Darian Licht if he knew how the more advanced Westheath students have made a cult of Darian Licht and his musical theories which, while incomprehensible, and perhaps mad, have the force of being contrary to most of what is taught at the school.)

It's true that Darian is blind to his own attractiveness, and therefore blind to the attractiveness of women. Where one can't take seriously the objects of desire, desire itself has little force; or, if it has force, its potency has burrowed underground, like certain fires that burn undetected, beneath the surface of the earth, for years. And there is the model, the monster-model, of Abraham Licht the lover of women, pitiless and absurd seeker of Venus Aphrodite in mortal women; that voracious and insatiable appetite Darian can't think of without a shudder. "Do I hate the man, still?" Darian asks himself, twisting his lower lip between thumb and forefinger hard enough to hurt. "But why should I, Darian, hate him now?—we're nothing to each other, now."

Darian keeps up his contact with Esther, of course; for Esther is an avid letter-writer, and devoted to him. Through Esther he has news of Millie (whom he last saw in 1921 when Millie and new husband Warren Stirling were visiting in Boston, at the time Darian was briefly hired to teach composition and piano at the New England Conservatory) and Katrina (who remains in Muirkirk, a keeper of the old church-residence, now empty of Lichts). Always he will remain estranged from Abraham Licht—he's certain. And Abraham on his side has made no attempt to contact Darian since December 1916.

What's past but the graveyard of future. And no place to dwell.

Yet sometimes, in those feverish insomniac states that make the writing of music so exhausting, if exhilarating, Darian lapses into a waking dream at the keyboard and sees Father approaching him, all smiles and stooped for an embrace; Darian is a child again, yearning and dreading Father's rough, smothering hug; the heat of his hard kiss; the warmth of his tobacco-whiskey breath. Hearing Father's ringing words that are a summons to his soul, the sweetest, most piercing music *Where will ye fly little birdies, Old Sir Ebeneezer Snuff knows y'r name, Old Ebeneezer Snuff sees all in Heaven, and Earth, and the Darksome Regions Beneath with his one almighty eye.*

IV

Since childhood he'd been told he had a weak heart but who had told him this but Father? He doubted it was true.

Though sometimes he *was* short of breath. A stranger's chill hand, fingers spread, pressing against his chest.

Yet he was physically fit: not strong, not muscular but lean, lithe, hardy, stubborn. His best musical ideas came to him while hiking, for miles in the rock-strewn foothills; tramping through winter fields, freezing gusts of air whining about his bent head. After he'd quit the Vanderpoel Academy Darian had wandered for months . . . years. Northward, westward through New York State and looping around, in a southerly direction, below the Great Lakes; working variously as a Western Union messenger boy, a printer's assistant, an icehouse employee (until his breathlessness forced him to quit), even as a handyman in a boardinghouse in Oxard, Ohio, in which he roomed for $7 a week. He offered himself as an itinerant music teacher, his speciality piano and organ; he was a choir director for a Presbyterian church in Flint, Indiana; he tried his hand at piano-tuning. He hitched rides with travelers headed west; risked injury riding the rails, in boxcars in the company of homeless, sometimes desperate men. In Needham, Minnesota, he remained for nearly a year, working in the post office and living in a cheap hotel near the train depot and giving much of his spare time to Colonel Harris's Needham Silver Cornet Band under whose spell he'd fallen hearing the vigorous playing of these sixteen men one summer evening in the town green. *What music is this? Who is calling to me?* Back in the East he'd fallen temporarily under the spell, knowing it was a malevolent spell, of Arnold Schoenberg, whose *Five Pieces for Orchestra* had penetrated his soul; only hearing Colonel Harris's band had cleansed his head, or so he would swear. Can one fall in love with a band? a music? a sound? This brass band was composed of men between the ages of twenty-two and eighty-one who played with an extraordinary degree of enthusiasm and energy such instruments as the E-flat cornet, the B-flat cornet, the alto, the tenor, the baritone, the tuba, the bass drum, the snare drum, the slide trombone and the mighty sousaphone. Darian lacked sufficient wind as well as training to play any of the horns, but the Colonel gave him a snare drum which he played when he marched with the band, shyly at first, then with more confidence. "Don't be afraid of *making noise*, son," the Colonel advised, "—to get people to listen to good music you first have to capture their attention."

The hardy little band marched as frequently as well-wishers and admirers would have them, or perhaps more frequently. They were a legend of sorts in Needham, a small city otherwise not known for musical ambition. Of course, the Colonel, long retired from the U.S. Army, was the driving force, the soul of the band; either you were an unquestioning instrument in his imagination, or you were not likely to remain long in the Silver Cornet Band. Military marches, quicksteps, polkas, schottisches, the national anthem, "The Battle Hymn of the Republic" . . . "All Quiet Along the Potomac" . . . "Tenting on the Old Camp Ground" . . . the Colonel's transcriptions of "Carry Me Back to Old Virginny," "The Band Played On," "Peg o' My Heart" . . . even "Adieu! 'Tis Love's Last Greeting," "Gaily Through Life I Wander," "The Angel's Whisper." Darian, marching with the men, banging on his drum until his arms and hands ached, felt a thrill previously unknown to him, that music might be performed in the *open air*; that music might be greeted with noisy, hearty applause, cheers and whistles, by men, women and children who would never have tolerated a concert of "serious" music. And most of all the music moved through both space and time: you didn't sit, nor even stand, you *marched*.

And wasn't Darian drawn to the band, and to the strong personality of Colonel Harris (brisk, stout, genial and quarrelsome by turns, with a drink-flushed face and white tobacco-stained drooping moustache) because *here was a version, not wicked but benign, of Abraham Licht. Father not-Father.*

In the end, though, Darian left Needham, Minnesota. For even happiness can wear out; even happiness is not the quest.

V

"But you *are* happy?—you look happy," Millicent said with a half-accusing ring to her honeyed voice. "You haven't changed," she said, smiling as she lied, "—nearly at all."

Darian laughed. "I can't believe that," he said.

"That you're happy—?"

"That I haven't changed."

"—When *I* have, so greatly, you mean to say!" Millicent brightly exclaimed.

And reached across the tea things to rap at his hand with her pretty lacquered fingernails. Darian caught, not for the first time since she'd removed her gloves, a flash of her rings.

This beautiful woman in the silver cloche hat, thirty years old, lips subtly colored, her steely-blue eyes fixed upon his with a disconcerting intensity—was she really Darian's sister Millie whom he'd once adored?

Millie teased, asking him another time if she'd changed—"For the better, I hope?" All the while, her eyelids quivered as if she might be fighting back tears.

(Millie had already wept at their meeting, in Darian's boarding-house as her husband looked uneasily on. Darian, resisting emotion, had embraced his perfumed sister fondly, yet slightly stiffly. *What is it we want from each other, what do we imagine we can give?*)

Now that Millicent had made what appeared to be a very good marriage, and had moved away to live in Richmond, Virginia, she was, as Esther had warned him, a woman of the South; of superior breeding and culture; so assured of her background and her present social status she could afford the mild self-deprecatory airs Darian had noted in those classmates of his at Vanderpoel who were from the most legendary old families. (Though Millie's husband Warren wasn't a Virginian by birth, Darian gathered, but was in fact from upstate New York.) Edgy, chattering, alternately sipping tea and lighting up one of her cigarettes (her brand was Omar, a "Turkish" tobacco), she seemed, even as she asked Darian about himself, to be drawing back; maintaining a vigilance he'd assumed would disappear when they were alone together, out of Warren Stirling's company. Almost wistfully she asked him another time if he *was* happy, so far from home, among strangers; and Darian said, annoyed, that there was no reason for him *not* to be happy. He wasn't a child any longer: he was twenty-one years old.

"And aren't we all, the *Lichts*, happiest among strangers?" Darian asked.

Millie stared; said nothing; after a moment stubbed out her cigarette, and reached into her beaded handbag for another.

Against a stately background of palm fronds, wicker and black marble and ceiling-high mirrors, Mrs. Warren Stirling's blond enameled beauty shone to dramatic effect. She was wearing a fashionable smock-like dress in crimson jersey wool with a satin waistline dropped to the hips; the silver cloche hat, fitting her head tightly, seemed to be compressing it, into a stylish and hurtful sort of innocence. By contrast with his glamorous older sister Darian knew himself shabby in a mismatched jacket and trousers and a tieless shirt, open at the collar. While Millie who was Mrs. Millicent Stirling seemed fully at home in the elegant tearoom of the Hotel Ritz-Carlton, though the place was as new to her as to Darian, he felt ungainly and unwanted, like a homeless drifter who'd wandered into the wrong setting. He devoured too many of the tiny crustless sandwiches and slopped his English tea into his saucer. Saying, enigmatically, "Yet we are brother and sister, y'know, Millie—I mean, we have the same father. Or had."

Millie stared at him, startled. "Why do you say that? Why say such a thing?"

Darian shrugged. What he meant, damned if he knew.

Millie pretended that nothing was wrong, that her reunion with her youngest brother was proceeding with the bright brisk animation of a reunion scene in a bittersweet melodrama; there was emotional strain, but all would turn out in the end. In her role as affluent older sister, a much-loved married woman with life brimming in the wings, she plied Darian with questions until he grew more and more taciturn. Why had he broken off relations with Father; how had he come to be on the staff at the New England Conservatory—"Which Warren's aunt says is very prestigious"; did he visit Muirkirk; did he miss Muirkirk; did he approve of Esther's nursing career; did he truly believe he might make a living in music—teaching, performing, composing? Thoughtfully she said, as if the words pained her, "Darian, what a precarious life! The world sees only 'stars' and knows nothing of the gifted, even inspired musicians, actors, artists who try, and try, and try—and fail. Because there are too many of us." She laughed, exhaling bluish smoke. "I mean—of *you*."

Darian shrugged, slopping more tea into his saucer. His heart pounded in dislike of his newfound sister.

As if there were too many Darian Lichts.

Next, Millie asked him if he'd ever been in love, or if there was anyone whom he loved now—"I mean, you know, in a romantic sense." Her voice was conspicuously Southern by now. Again Darian shrugged, not liking so personal a question; and embarrassed, and resentful, not knowing how to reply. He hoped never to succumb to mere romance. He hoped he was superior to childish, primitive cravings. "Possibly," he said. "If ever I become that bored." Millie laughed, uncomfortably. Darian was recalling why he'd felt resentful of Millie, even as he'd missed her: he'd written several songs for soprano voice, for her, as a part of his Muirkirk opera cycle, and sent them to her by way of Esther, but she'd never responded. He'd known that she'd received them because she'd told Esther she had. Like Thurston, like Elisha—Millie had gone away, and forgotten him.

Like a magician Millie was extracting from her silver lamé purse a packet of photographs which she passed over to Darian. Most were of her baby—"Maynard Franklin Stirling. Your nephew, Darian." Darian found himself moved by the baby's sweet, quizzical face and startled expression. He didn't want to think the baby resembled, ever so slightly, his mother's father. Millie said defiantly, "*He's* something!—he's *real.*"

Darian acknowledged, yes it was so. Nothing more *real* than a baby created out of one's mortal flesh. "You're happy, then, Millie. You've crossed over."

"Yes." Millie spoke with satisfaction, taking the photographs back from Darian and checking them, severely, as if she feared one might be missing, or in some way altered; then dropping them into her purse and snapping it shut. There. That's that! Darian sensed how she'd been preparing to ask a question long contemplated, and now plunged into it, more nervously than she wished—"You've lost contact with Elisha, I suppose. You never hear of him or from him—I suppose."

Darian shook his head, sadly.

There was an awkward pause. Darian, not looking at Millie, could hear her quickened breathing; he imagined her close to breaking into sobs. Her grief wouldn't be pure but a grief of loss and anger.

Like a spoiled Virginia matron Millie called to the waiter to bring more hot water for their tea. Even with the tea cozy, their tea had become lukewarm.

In a honeyed voice saying to him, as if this were an old quarrel, and Darian quite the crank for failing to come round to common sense, "I s'pose you haven't respect for composers like Verdi, Rossini, Bellini . . . and who was it wrote *The Bohemian Girl* . . . Gilbert and Sullivan? And Richard Wagner." She pronounced the name with the precise German inflection, "Rick-ard," as Abraham Licht had done.

"Wagner, certainly," Darian said shortly.

"And the others are—old-fashioned? Too easy, too pleasurable to the ear?"

"Too boring, I would have said."

"Well! Boring is in the ear of the beholder, *I* would have said."

"And so you have. And very clearly."

Millie's bee-stung, perfectly painted lips twitched in a smile. He knew she was feeling the sting of discovering her shy young brother not so young any longer, and not so shy. She said, pouring more tea for them both, with a frowning sort of concentration that marred her smooth forehead, "But you must, you know. Eventually. 'Love'—'fall in love.' You may scorn romance, but your music, without it, will be super-

ficial." When Darian refused to rise to this bait, Millie changed the subject, and asked after his finances. "Are you poor as your clothes, your
haircut and that rooming house suggest, or are you, like the proverbial
bohemian artist, indifferent to material things? The way you've devoured these little sandwiches! If you need money, Darian, I'll be happy
to . . . lend you some. That is, Warren will. I know you're too proud to
accept an outright gift. But—" She made a movement to open her silver lamé purse again, but was deterred by Darian's look of disdain.

"Millie, thank you. But I don't need your money."

"Ah! I've offended you."

"Not at all. I think I've offended *you*."

Millie who was Mrs. Warren Stirling with her flashing rings and
bright, knowing smile said accusingly, "Darian, you loved me once, in
Muirkirk. When *he* was our father. Is that it? But now—everything has
changed. *You* have changed, and I suppose that I have. And so you've
ceased to love your 'pretty'—'doomed'—sister."

" 'Doomed'? Why?"

Millie laughed. Adjusting the smart cloche hat on her head, with a
small violent gesture. Darian saw her gaze fixed beyond his shoulder
and, following it, caught sight of his sister's floating oval face in a wall
mirror a short distance away. And there was his own face, narrow and
blurred as a face glimpsed from the window of a speeding train. Had
Millie been watching herself all along, in a pretext of watching him?
"Damned, maybe," Millie said. Darian looked at her uncomprehending.
"Your 'pretty'—'damned'—sister, I might have said."

Soon it would be time to leave. Darian seemed to know beforehand
how he would miss Millie; how he would rage at himself for letting this
opportunity pass, without taking his sister's hands in his and telling her
he loved her. He said, fumbling, "D'you ever hear of Thurston?" and
Millie quickly shook her head, no. "He *is* alive, isn't he?" Darian asked,
and again Millie shook her head, this time to indicate she didn't know.
She shivered; she was warming her hands on the teapot, in a gesture
Darian remembered from many years ago in Muirkirk, when tendrils of
wind came whistling through cracks in the windows and skeins of frost
glittered on the panes in blinding, yet freezing sunshine. Darian said
stubbornly, "I believe that Thurston *is* alive. And that we'll see him
again—someday." Millie shrugged, and wiped at her eyes. In the doorway of the tearoom Warren Stirling stood hesitantly, looking in their

direction. Millie had asked him to join them after twenty minutes or so and now, uncertainly smiling, he approached their table; a tall, slightly stocky man of youthful middle age. He'd served as an Army colonel in the Great War and had been wounded in northern France; he'd nearly died of exposure and later of infection; he'd told Millie that in a state of delirium he'd seen her face—that is, the face of the "Lass of Aviemore" he'd confused with hers. "As if I, Millie, who knew so little how to save her own life, could have saved his"—so Millie had confided in Darian, with an expression of half-shamed wonder.

Quickly, before Warren came within earshot, Millie seized Darian's hand, caressed the long, powerful pianist's fingers and murmured in a thrilled undertone, "Thurston *is* alive. Only no longer 'Thurston.' He came to visit Warren and me in Richmond, and gave us his blessing. But Harwood—is dead."

"What? *Dead*—?"

It was a taut dramatic moment, precisely timed. For Darian's gentlemanly brother-in-law was pulling out a chair to sit at their lacquered table, and such confidential exchanges must cease. "May I join you? You're sure you don't mind?"—Warren Stirling smiled at Darian. A genial, kindly man, an ideal husband for Millie and an ideal father for her children, who no more knew her than he knew Darian. The expression in his warm mud-brown eyes as he gazed at beautiful Millicent in her cloche hat and pretty clothes told all: to be the object of another's adoration is to be blessed.

So: Harwood was dead! Cruel Harwood Licht.

When Darian's half brother had died; and how; and where; whether of natural or unnatural causes; whether deservedly, or undeservedly—Darian Licht in his innocence was never to know.

VI

The twenty-third of May 1928. Near midnight. Darian Licht has returned alone to his room at the shabby Empire State Hotel on Eighth Avenue, where a number of his fellow Schenectady musicians are also staying, when there's a loud rap at the door; and Darian, in his shirtsleeves, hurries to answer thinking it might be Thurston—though knowing it can't be Thurston, of course. "Yes? What?" Darian cries. He pauses to stare at himself in a scummy mirror; irritably brushes his hair out of his face, an alarmingly flushed, mottled, haggard young face, and makes a stab at adjusting his clothing. Since the nightmare recital and the shock of meeting Thurston, and at once losing Thurston, Darian has dropped by several taverns on the way back to the hotel and has had, for him, an inordinate amount to drink, if only beer. He hasn't eaten since breakfast that morning on the train; he supposes he'll eat again in the morning on the train, returning to Schenectady with his musician friends. (He dreads seeing them. Their eyes. Their embarrassed smiles. At the Westheath School, none of his colleagues will speak to him of *Esopus, the Lost Village* except to assure Darian vaguely that his music is too difficult and unconventional for ordinary ears; none will speak to him of the critical notices that appeared in several New York papers, the kindest in the *Tribune*, beginning "A career other than musical composition is urgently advised for the youthful, earnest but painfully talentless Schenectady resident Darian Licht. . . ." Nor will Darian make any inquiries.) The loud rap is repeated, and Darian opens the door, and sees—who is it?—a couple in evening attire, so handsomely glittering they might have stepped out of the society pages of the Sunday rotogravure.

"Darian? Darian Licht? Is it you?"

"No. Yes. I'm not sure. Who are *you?*"

"You don't recognize me, son? Of course you do."

A silvery-haired gentleman in his early sixties, it seems; in black tie, and carrying a silk top hat; a much younger woman at his side, in an ankle-length deep-purple velvet gown, staring at him with dark shining eyes he'll recall afterward as too intense. Who are these strangers? Well-wishers? Musical connoisseurs? In the very wake of defeat and humiliation Darian Licht is vain enough, or naive enough, to believe that, yes, someone took notice that evening of his genius.

The silvery-haired gentleman steps forward into the room, uninvited. His gloved hand extended. His smile somewhat forced, yet confident. "Of course you recognize me, son. Even after so many years. And here is my wife Rosamund. . . ."

Darian is deafened by a roaring in his ears like Niagara Falls. As in a distorting mirror he sees a familiar-unfamiliar face leering at him, and the mouth moving soundlessly. And the woman's face, no one he has ever glimpsed before, a hard chiseled beauty he seems nonetheless to recognize. "Father . . . ?" he manages to say. "Is it . . . ?"

Abraham Licht, hardly changed. Or if changed, in the shock of the moment Darian Licht hasn't the capacity to see.

"We're aggrieved, Rosamund and I, to have missed your concert," Abraham Licht is saying, "—but we were held up at an impossibly long, dull cocktail reception at the Astors' over on Fifth Avenue—the usual thing at that house, I've been told; my error, for which I'm deeply apologetic and chagrined, and hope you'll forgive me. Son!" In Darian's hotel room which is scarcely larger than an old-fashioned claw-footed bathtub, the elegantly dressed smooth-shaven Abraham Licht and his new wife take up so much space, Darian is forced back against the iron bedstead, panting. A few hours previously there was Thurston; and now Father; is he on the verge of death, and his life flashing before his stunned eyes? He has all he can do to keep his balance. The new Mrs. Licht reaches out to steady him with a gloved hand and he shrinks, cat-like, from her touch.

A woman no older than Darian. With greeny-glistening eyes. Her fine wavy black hair, just perceptibly streaked with gray, brushed back from her angular face and fashioned into a sleek French twist. There's a charming little knob near the bridge of her nose and her lips are perfectly sculpted, darkened to crimson. Maybe Darian imagines it but isn't there, in the new Mrs. Licht's face, an expression of . . . startled recognition?

How could you do it, marry this man! You, so young and so beautiful, to marry a man old enough to be your father!

And her green eyes flash defiantly *Because I love him. Because he loves me. What right have you to judge us?*

Darian hears himself stammering words he won't recall afterward, a fumbling faltering performance. It's like the aleatory moments in *Esopus* that so baffled and outraged the audience. Abraham Licht cuts Darian off, aggressively praising him though he didn't attend the recital and hasn't heard any music of Darian's in more than a decade, presenting him to the new Mrs. Licht as a "musical genius of a son"—a "musical prodigy"—a "will-o'-the-wisp" whose whereabouts are often unknown even to his family. Darian protests laughingly, "Father? What family?" but Abraham Licht takes no notice; nor does Rosamund seem to hear;

as in a performance of a play in which not all the actors are equally familiar with the script or equally well rehearsed, Darian is confusedly aware that something is happening of which he hasn't any control yet can't resist; must not resist; there's a momentum of what might be called *audience expectation* . . . a sense that, beyond the blinding footlights, in a vast, undefined space beyond this room in the Empire State Hotel, a gathering of witnesses is waiting. With a part of his mind Darian would like to open the door and shove the beaming Abraham Licht out into the hall, with the new Mrs. Licht; yet he stands paralyzed, staring and smiling at his visitors like a fool. Abraham Licht is saying, in a voice of fond reproach, "You might, y'know, son, have notified your own father about your premiere. Here in Manhattan, at Carnegie Hall! Only imagine—a child of mine, making his début at Carnegie Hall! And yet I knew nothing of it until yesterday; it was my darling Rosamund who happened to see the item in the paper. Our name—'Licht.' "

Darian manages to protest, mildly, "But—how would I have known you were here? We've been out of touch for—"

"No, no," Abraham Licht says quickly, with a look of alarm, "—we must put the past behind us. Where is your coat, son? Here? *This?*" Abraham has taken up the formal jacket with its silly split tail which Darian wore as conductor, and which Darian had tossed onto the floor. "Something less formal, I should think, would be appropriate for the hour. Ah, here—this will do better." Abraham has discovered another jacket, which Rosamund takes from him and brushes, for it's dirty from the floor; it seems that Abraham Licht and his new young wife are going to take Darian out on the town to celebrate the world premiere of *Esopus, the Lost Village*—Abraham has made reservations at the Pierre, a short carriage ride away up on Fifth Avenue by the Park. "But, Father, I'm drunk; I'm exhausted, humiliated, broken—I want only to sink into sleep and into oblivion—please!" Darian protests laughingly but again no one listens. There's no elevator in the Empire State Hotel so Abraham Licht, Rosamund and Darian descend the stairs, several flights of poorly lit, gritty stairs, Darian finds himself gripped by the arms, protected from slipping and falling, there's much laughter, good-natured jesting, for both Abraham Licht and his beautiful young wife have been drinking this evening, though assuredly they're not drunk, such glamorous demigods never get drunk, it's poor Darian Licht visiting

Manhattan from Schenectady, New York, a visiting instructor at the Westheath School of Music who's likely to get drunk, yet in the open air Darian revives, or almost, managing after two attempts to climb up into the horse-drawn carriage, the driver in tails and top hat grinning at this handsome trio of revelers, he's hoping for a generous tip, the elder gentleman in evening attire looks well-to-do and magnanimous, crying, "To the Pierre, my man! Posthaste!" in a commanding baritone voice.

The jostling carriage ride causes Darian's head to rattle as if pebbles are being shaken inside it. He begins to cry—tears are streaking his face. *Where am I being taken, who are these people, Father why did you forsake me for so long!* But it's Rosamund who slips her fingers through his, her gloved fingers through his, to steady and comfort. Darian is seated between the new Mrs. Licht and Father, squeezed upright between them, the ride is jolting, hilarious, the driver wields his whip, the dapple-skinned horse whinnies with excitement, or with pain, as he's whipped, careening along Eighth Avenue north toward Central Park.

How to resist, you cannot.

After more than a decade's estrangement Darian and his father are reconciled. Late next morning when Darian wakes from his comalike sleep, having missed the train to Schenectady, he'll be unable to recall why he'd ever vowed *not* to be Abraham Licht's son.

VII

"The island is finite, its promise infinite."

Abraham Licht confides this wisdom to his youngest son Darian who's so unworldly, he'd been drinking the "Manhattan" his father had prepared for him as if it were merely beer, to be swallowed quickly down. Even Rosamund laughs at him, with sisterly mock-censure. "Oh, Darian! *Do* go more slowly."

Since being taken up by Father and Father's new young wife, Darian Licht has been, you might say, careening . . . wild crashing chords up and down the keyboard, hands crossed over so the left is pounding the treble and the right, the bass. *Am I in love? Or just drunk?*

Though trying to remain sober. Trying to remain . . . Darian, the skeptic. Caring for nothing but his music, which is to say his solitude; the solitude required for the composing of . . . music.

He hears his own laughter, often. A harsh raw boyish laughter as of a violin long out of tune, half its strings broken.

Abraham Licht is in a mood to confide. He's forgiven his youngest son, apparently, for ten years' estrangement—"The stubbornness of youth, I suppose necessary if analyzed in Darwinian evolutionary terms." He has forgiven Darian, and Darian has evidently forgiven him. ("Why did we ever quarrel?" Darian wonders, genuinely baffled. He believes it may have had something to do with the Vanderpoel Academy . . . what a difficult adolescent he must have been, tormented by emotions as by acne. "But no more!")

Almost, it's a litany that might be put to music. In fact it is a litany that might be put to music. Darian envisions kettledrums, a B-flat cornet, a baritone voice in Gregorian-chant style. *Bethlehem Steel. Mexican Seaboard Certificates. Pan American Western Corporation. Cole Motors, Indianapolis. American Telephone & Telegraph. Fleischmann's Yeast. New York Central. Fisk Insurance. Standard Oil of New Jersey. Kennecott Copper.* "All very conservative stocks," as Abraham Licht says. "For, despite his exemplary broker's tips, 'Moses Liebknecht' is too cautious to gamble his hard-earned money." Exactly who "Moses Liebknecht" is, Darian isn't sure though he's been told; both by Father and by Father's new young wife, laughingly. "When we'd met, it was 'Moses' I first loved," Rosamund says, shaking her head in wonderment. "Little did I know that 'Abraham' was guiding us both."

Apart from the stock-market profits which, Darian gathers, are considerable, in this careening season of summer 1928, Abraham Licht and the beautiful young Mrs. Licht are beginning to make a fair amount of money from the sale, increasing weekly, of Liebknecht's Formula. "At the outset, I'd marketed it as an 'elixir of health'—that sort of thing. But, y'know, there are many competitors; too many; what's wanted is a specific property. It was staring us in the face all along: fertility."

Darian isn't sure he has heard correctly. " 'Fertility'—?"

Abraham says, smiling happily, "Human fertility, Darian. Babies—to be blunt. Some couples are unable to conceive. It's a medical predicament of which few persons wish to speak—at least at this time—yet of course it exists, and women are aggrieved at being 'barren,' and men at

having failed to 'sire.' One can't blame them, for it's a biblical injunction *Increase and multiply!* 'Liebknecht's Formula' is being promoted as a
fertility elixir, manufactured and distributed by Easton Pharmaceuticals
in Pennsylvania. It *is* something of a wonder drug, I would swear to it."

At this, Rosamund begins laughing like a young girl, and has to
leave the room; Darian hears the sharp tattoo of her high-heeled shoes
on the parquet floor, and her melodic voice raised at the rear of the
brownstone (she must be speaking to the housekeeper); in a minute or
two she'll return, giddy and flush-faced, for she's never out of Abraham
Licht's presence for long, and possibly she's drawn to Darian as well.
Am I in love, certainly not. My own father's wife. What a joke! Darian too
begins laughing, and coughing; Father slaps him between the shoulder
blades; telling him of a whim of a bet he'd placed the previous Sunday,
on a filly running at the Preakness, odds 5 to 1, he'd had a hunch
she might win for her name was June Hardy and the month is June
and some years ago—"Someday, son, I will tell you in full"—Abraham
had been a dear friend of the former president Warren Harding, a good-
hearted soul for all his failings and his deeply American ignorance;
and so, with such stars in collusion, Abraham had known the filly
would win.

"Only imagine, Darian—your madman of a father sneaking off without telling me, and placing two thousand dollars on a horse, and returning with ten thousand! And in cash, in all his pockets," Rosamund
cries, nearly faint with laughter, pretending to be thrusting her hands
into the pockets of Abraham's velvet smoking jacket as he laughingly
fends her off, "—commanding me to search him! Till all the carpet
here was covered in hundred-dollar bills. But I don't, y'know, approve
of gambling. I *don't.*"

"Yes, Rosamund is of old, censorious American-Puritan stock. Her
ancestors arrived on these shores in 1641—imagine! Some years preceding our own." Abraham grows sober suddenly, as if his words have
awakened a disturbing memory; but the mood of the evening is such,
sobriety can't endure for more than a few seconds. At once Abraham is
on his feet mixing another round of this delicious new drink, new at
any rate to Darian—"The 'Manhattan.' Smooth as silk going down,
yes?" Rosamund brings Darian his drink, their fingers brush as he takes
the exquisitely shaped crystal glass, never in his life has he so much as
lifted such a glass to his lips, never exchanged such a glance, such a

smile from a beautiful young woman so clearly fond of him. ("Am I your 'stepmother,' Darian dear? I should have rushed to get well, instead of languishing like a ridiculous old prude, all those years.") Abraham is informing Darian that he's invested nearly $1 million in Manhattan real estate. This three-story brownstone residence (at East Seventieth Street and Fifth Avenue); a similar brownstone on East Sixty-third; and a commercial building on Broadway and Forty-fifth. Prices in Manhattan are steep but will continue to rise; in another five years, if all goes well, the price of these properties will have *trebled.* "You have only to contemplate the stock market to see how prices will rise, rise and rise—like a spouting fountain."

For, yes, as Abraham is fond of saying—*The island is finite, its promise infinite.*

And its corollary—*Manhattan today, all of America tomorrow.*

Still, Abraham Licht's plan isn't to remain in Manhattan for long. He and Rosamund are going to make a major purchase sometime before the fall, a horse ranch in the Chautauqua Valley—"That most beautiful region to which I yearn to return, with my bride." Both are great admirers, it seems, of Arabian horses; Rosamund rode when she was a girl out on Long Island, and Abraham has long been interested in (hadn't Darian known? surely yes) breeding Thoroughbreds for racing. "Not at all for money," Abraham says sternly, "—but for the aesthetics of the sport. For nothing, y'know, is quite so splendid as an Arabian in his prime."

"Or her prime," Rosamund murmurs.

"Certainly, yes. Or her prime."

Husband and wife exchange an intimate smoldering glance. Just to witness it is to feel the danger of combustion.

Darian takes a large, improvident swallow of his Manhattan.

Abraham Licht is musing how in the Chautauqua Valley, not many miles from Muirkirk, they might lead a secluded and idyllic life; precisely the sort of life suited for their imminent situation.

Imminent situation?

No. Yes. Of course. Rosamund is pregnant . . . that explains much that has passed between husband and wife; and Darian, being an adult of nearly twenty-nine, was expected to have understood without having been told explicitly. *My father, again a father. And I, another time a brother.*

Rosamund, seeing Darian's startled glance, blushes. A faint lovely rose rising from her slender throat into her angular, rather narrow face. Her skin is of the hue of ivory; despite her vivacious manner, which may be fueled by alcohol, she's an abnormally thin woman; shivers often, though perhaps in excitement, nerved-up, as Katrina would say high-strung as a filly in heat; except, being pregnant, Rosamund is assuredly not in "heat." She has draped a white crocheted shawl over her slender shoulders; her loose-fitting dress is of sea-green silk, falling fashionably to midcalf; not bobbed or shingled in the fashion of the day, her glossy black hair is parted this evening in the center of her head and gathered back in a Grecian twist at the nape of her neck. The proud mother-to-be. Darian would cry, "Congratulations! To you both." But instead takes another swallow of his drink.

Over a cold supper of oysters Rockefeller, filet mignon, creamed potatoes, Stilton cheese and glazed apricots, served by a Filipino woman in black, Abraham Licht takes up the subject, perhaps a familiar one to him, though unfamiliar to Darian, of the philosophical consequences of physiological experimentation in identity. "Whether, that is, an individual being identical and fully present in either half of his brain might be 'divided' into two separate individuals to be housed in two separate bodies. As William James believed, we are as many 'selves' as there are individuals who know us; so it may be that . . ." Darian nods, trying to follow his father's abstruse logic; yet distracted by Rosamund's presence, her daughterly attentiveness to Abraham as if every word of his were sacred, to be committed to memory. Darian feels a pang of jealousy; of loss; that Abraham and Rosamund hadn't attended his recital . . . for, surely, Rosamund would have found something to admire in *Esopus*; Rosamund would have recognized Darian's heartfelt yearning, the very music of his soul, beneath and beyond the playful experimentation of sound. *My music was written for you. Will you hear my music . . . someday?*

Abraham is musing on the paradox that identity seems to reside in the head; in "consciousness"; yet we don't really identify with our physical selves—"For this, we say, is 'my' hand, implying that it's a mere possession, and we're possessors. 'My' arm, 'my' head; even 'my' brain.' Isn't it paradoxical that we're in the habit of referring to 'my' soul as well?"

Darian, aroused by wine and by Rosamund's presence, laughs nervously; saying he doesn't know, he's never given much thought to it, if you're a musician you're immersed in music night and day, day and night, hour following hour, like a lover obsessed with his beloved. "And possibly, Father, it's only just a convention of language, peculiar to English."

"No. Hardly peculiar to English. 'Moses Liebknecht' is both psychologist and linguist, a polyglot in fact, and informs us that such patterns of speech indicate a universal human habit, of separating, as Descartes did so methodically, 'mind' from 'body.' What interests me is why we resist identifying even with our souls."

"Assuming, darling, that we have souls," Rosamund says. "For perhaps not all of us are so burdened."

But Abraham Licht, brooding upon his own thoughts, pays her no heed; nor notices how his long-lost Darian is gazing at him, and at her, with an expression of infinite yearning.

Shortly afterward, Rosamund excuses herself to retire for the night; and Darian's father persuades him to stay another hour, in fact to stay the night—"We can finish this bottle of burgundy. There are so many things we need to speak of, son!"

And naturally Darian consents. Though he'd planned—vaguely—to return to Schenectady on the earliest train out of Penn Station. (Already he's delayed returning by two days; has missed classes at the Westheath School, with no explanation or apology to Myrick Sheffield; the past forty-eight hours have sped by in a dream.) What pleasure in Abraham's—and Rosamund's—company! What riches! It's as if the humiliating "premiere" at Carnegie Hall had never occurred, nor had ever been envisioned by an arrogant young composer. When Father focuses his attention so exclusively on Darian, Darian can feel his heart swell; his "ailing" heart; and knows himself far stronger than he'd imagined. *For so Zeus might breathe the spirit of life into a mere clay vessel. The first music of all is breath.*

So Darian remains for another hour in the handsome brownstone on East Seventieth Street, tempted to stay, as Abraham has invited him, the night; yet wanting to maintain some measure of independence . . . some distance from Abraham Licht and his young pregnant bride, despite the dreariness of the Empire State Hotel. Eagerly he listens to his father's conversation, which is as usual one-sided; Darian would like to ask Abraham how he and Rosamund met, how long they've been mar-

ried, what are the circumstances of Rosamund's life . . . but he's too shy
to interrupt. All too briefly Abraham remarks that Rosamund is a remarkable woman whom he loves deeply, far more than he's loved any
other woman; as he believes she loves him—"For it's her conviction,
Darian, that I saved her life. Which perhaps I did."

"I hope to play some of my music for her soon. If only you had a piano here. . . ."

"We'll buy a piano. Tomorrow morning. Well—tomorrow afternoon! There's a Steinway showroom on Park Avenue, close by. And
Rosamund, I know, loves piano music." Abraham Licht smilingly snaps
his fingers. Almost, Darian can see the magnificent gleaming piano ma-
terialize in the adjoining drawing room.

Following this, Abraham begins to make inquiries, tactful enough
but edged with paternal concern, about Darian's present circumstances.
Abraham has to confess he's never heard of the Wheatsheath—the
Westheath?—School of Music; nor does he know anything of Schenectady, New York. "To speak bluntly, son: have you much of a future in
such a place? Will you perhaps be moving on to a more prestigious
school—like Juilliard, here in Manhattan?"

Darian, giddy from wine, says carelessly, "To hell with Westheath—
and Juilliard, too. I want to compose, Father. I want to alter the sound
of American music." Yet in his own ears how childlike these words
echo; a mere proposal, and not a statement of fact.

"Do you, son? I wish you well." Abraham raises his wineglass in an
oddly restrained gesture, and drinks.

Darian feels himself subtly rebuffed.

He doesn't believe me. He has no faith in me.

Long ago pronouncing me unfit for The Game.

The evening is fast waning. Darian will not stay with his father and
his father's bride but must return to the Empire State Hotel; and fall
into bed, and sink into another oblivion. He's both relieved and disappointed that Abraham hasn't asked him more about his life, especially
when Rosamund was still at the table. What tales Darian had to tell,
long prepared to be told in such a way, to Abraham Licht, of riding the
rails in the Midwest, shabby, unshaven and reckless as any hobo; of
scraping together a living however he could, as he had reason to think
Abraham had done as a young man; of Colonel Harris's Needham Silver Cornet Band . . . and many more. "Well, there will be other

evenings," Darian thinks. "Many more." It is only relief he feels that Abraham hasn't inquired after Millie or Thurston; assuming no doubt that Darian hasn't heard of them or from them in years.

Abraham offers Darian a cigar, which he unwisely accepts; the men smoke together in thoughtful silence for a few minutes; Darian, who has only smoked cigarettes in the past, and few of these, knows he must not inhale the powerful smoke but isn't quite sure how to smoke without inhaling. He begins to cough, and his head begins to swim. Abraham, fortunately, doesn't notice; he's speaking dreamily of his plans to move to the Chautauqua Valley, and to raise the finest Arabian horses to set "records of the future"; there's a possibility, Abraham confides in Darian, in a lowered voice as if he fears being overheard, of his purchasing the renowned stallion Black Mars who'd won last year's Kentucky Derby, sired out of the 1925 Triple Crown winner Crescent, in turn sired out of the great Midnight Sun of years past. "If only I can realize this dream," Abraham says, exhaling smoke in a bluish vaporous cloud. "What prizes, what glory for my wife and my family!"

Darian listens, fascinated. Or would be so except his head is swimming.

"For I am 'family' too, am I not?" he thinks.

Darian rises to leave, and stumbles; but rights himself, with a thrill of pride, before his father can assist him; for he won't have it said (in jest, even if in affection) by Abraham to Rosamund that poor Darian was incapacitated in the slightest. Another time Abraham invites Darian to stay the night, and another time Darian politely declines; Abraham promises to telephone him in the morning, before his train leaves; and promises to keep in touch with him, in Schenectady; even to visit, soon—"For we won't miss another of your concerts, Darian, I vow." (Darian is confused: hadn't Abraham planned to buy a piano the next day, so that Darian could play it for Rosamund? Or had Darian misunderstood? He blames the cigar for his muddled head and discreetly lays it aside.) Then they're out on the street, and strolling arm in arm in the direction of Fifth Avenue, where Abraham will hail a cab for Darian, to take him to his hotel. When they part, Abraham embraces Darian impulsively. "Bless you, son!"

"And you, Father. Bless *you*."

VIII

Next day, Darian can't move from his bed until early afternoon.

He has never been so sick . . . so deathly sick. As if his insides, from his lungs to his bowels, were crammed with a corrosive substance like lye. And his head filled to bursting with broken glass.

No telephone call comes from Abraham Licht.

When Darian tries to telephone Abraham Licht, he's informed by an operator that "no such party" is listed in the directory.

When Darian is well enough to venture forth, in the early evening, he takes a cab to the brownstone on East Seventieth Street, or is it East Seventy-first Street . . . he can't quite remember. The brownstones resemble one another, very like brownstones on East Seventy-second and East Seventy-third. When he rings the doorbells at two of these residences, no one answers; at the third, a soft-spoken woman in a uniform, possibly Filipino, opens the door to inform him that "Mister and Missus" are away. Darian asks if Abraham Licht resides at this address, and the woman shakes her head wordlessly, and quickly shuts and bolts the door.

"Wait!" cries Darian. He stumbles down the steps, and out into the street, in order to see the upper stories of the handsome house more clearly. He cups his hands to his mouth—"Father? *Father!* It's me, Darian." But the upstairs windows are darkened. No face appears.

Next morning, he takes the train north to Schenectady. Praying that his "visiting instructorship" still remains at the Westheath School.

Sitting alone in the day coach staring dry-eyed out the window hearing no music in his head, scarcely even the thump! thump! thump! of the train wheels and the intermittent melancholy whistle; seeing nothing of the majestic landscape along the Hudson River. *Could I console my idiot self thinking I am headed home except Schenectady is not my home. I have none.*

. . . A vast featureless Silence against which elliptical patterns of Sound define themselves: overlapping, drawing apart, rippling, shuddering, running together as wayward currents of water join in a larger stream, rushing together at varying speeds; the rising of voices (of the lost souls of Esopus, of all of the dead) displaced in Time; a gradual fantasia of broken melodies, incan-

*tations, children's voices, chants; and always the beat, the blood-heavy beat,
the relentless primitive blood-heavy beat, hardly discernible until the final fading unresolved notes.*

"Prophet, Regent & Exchequer . . ."

I

When Prince Elihu speaks all of the world, white no less than Negro, is obliged to listen: for it is Elihu's teaching that Africa is
the birthplace of all civilization, and black and dark-skinned peoples,
descended from Ham, are the origin of mankind; of whom the white
man is but a fallen, diseased, and doomed specimen, who, by an ironic
reversal of history, has come to assume a temporary sovereignty. And
Africa, and the black and dark-skinned peoples of the world, shall rise
again, to reclaim in righteousness the lost grandeur of that civilization—whether with the cooperation of the white race, or no.

(For the Caucasians are but a tribe of vicious cannibal-devils, as the
recent World War made clear; and within a decade or two, according to
Elihu's calculation, there will follow yet a second world war waged by
Caucasians, against Caucasians, which will destroy their degenerate
civilization entirely.)

Thus, speaking as the Prophet, Regent & Exchequer of the World Negro Betterment & Liberation Union, Prince Elihu commands that the
United States Government prepare to deliver to the Negro people
within its territorial boundaries either a portion of land (of the size of
Oklahoma), including a waterfront; or restitution of no less than $5 bil-
lion as indemnity for the outrage of slavery, that the entire Negro popula-
tion of the North American continent might one day migrate en masse
back to Africa, to colonize a pure black republic . . . and to prepare for

the eventual overthrow of the white-controlled regions of the entire
continent.

Liberty or Death! was the watchword of the martyred Gabriel Prosser,
a twenty-two-year-old slave tortured to death in 1800 by his white
captors—*Die silent as you shall see me do.*

So with Prince Elihu, it is *Liberty or Death;* and *Death Before Humility.*

And: *Brothers by blood are brothers by the soul.*
And: *All white men are our enemies, then and now.*

It is whispered through Harlem that Prince Elihu is possessed of immortal powers: that he was born with the gift of voodoo-telepathy; of
mesmerism; of slipping out of his skin and entering another's, by way of
the secrecy of Night. Though born in Jamaica, or Haiti, or, perhaps, the
Windward Islands, some forty years ago, he is nonetheless believed
to be the avatar of the ancient African king Elihu (himself related to
Egyptian and Turkish nobility)—he who, according to legend, arose
out of the fiery flood of a volcano's eruption, and led his people to military glory as conquerors of the region now known as the Ivory Coast.
Thus, though numerous attempts have been made on his life, by both
Negroes and whites, *he cannot be killed.*

Yet he carries a bone-handled stiletto strapped to his left leg, with
which, it is said, he has killed a white man (a white policeman, in some
versions of the account); and, when attacked by a crazed fellow prisoner in the Atlanta penitentiary (a Georgian Negro whose brains had
fried from chain-gang work in 110-degree heat), he managed to overcome his assailant, and hold him powerless on the ground, *without so
much as laying a hand to him.*

(Of such feats Elihu says carelessly, that, as the eyes of the cannibal-
devils are fixed upon him, he is obliged to be a god, that they not mistake him for a beast.)

In Paterson, New Jersey, in March of 1917, while leading a rally to
protest the deaths of three young Negroes savagely beaten by police,
and to promote the cause of the World Negro Betterment & Liberation
Union, Prince Elihu was fired upon suddenly by white-hooded men: yet
so fierce were his powers that night, so impenetrable the aura he had
cast about himself, the clumsy fusillade of bullets spared him utterly.

And not long afterward, following his arrest on charges of sedition ("Having incited both by language and conduct actions directly in defiance of the authority of the United States Government . . ."), Elihu, though making no attempt to resist his captors or to escape, was nonetheless handcuffed by federal agents, and subjected to a beating of many hours in the Manhattan interrogation chamber of the Bureau of Investigation: which beating had not the power of weakening his proud defense, and his disclaiming of all authority of the United States Government over *him*, at the time of his public indictment.

And, in the hellish Atlanta penitentiary, amid diseased, mentally deranged, and vicious persons, of his own race no less than the Caucasian, the noble Prince withstood any number of physical assaults upon his body; and soon developed a power of second sight that allowed him to know beforehand if he was in danger . . . nor did this remarkable faculty ebb when Elihu was pardoned by the publicity-seeking Warren G. Harding, but, rather, intensified, as the Negro leader continued fearlessly to travel about the country, *even into the deepest South*, seeking members for his revolutionary organization, and making investigations into lynchings, rigged trials, rapes and various assaults, etc., directed toward Negroes by their fellow Americans.

Many a time the Prophet, Regent & Exchequer of the World Negro Betterment & Liberation Union was fired upon by cowardly white men, in ambush; many a time was a bomb attached to his car, or thrown into a meeting hall or church in which he was speaking. Yet his powers were such, not only he but those standing close to him were spared; in most instances, at least. (For it must be admitted that numerous tragedies have occurred during Prince Elihu's campaign to awaken his fellow blacks from their delusion of believing themselves *American*, when in fact they are *Negroes*: a truth, Elihu tells them, the white man knows, and acts upon covertly or otherwise at all times.)

Also, it's whispered that Prince Elihu did indeed succumb to Death, in the palace of the President of Liberia (whose privileged guest he was at the time): being stricken suddenly with a violent malaise that threw him into convulsions, and then into a coma, or a trance, for twenty hours: from which finally, he emerged—by way of his own princely will. And it is said that he alone survived the "accidental" crash of the six-

passenger biplane, the *Black Eagle* (newly purchased for the World Negro Betterment & Liberation Union); and the "accidental" sinking,
one hundred miles south of Long Island, en route to Miami, of the
ocean liner *Black Jupiter* (newly purchased for the purpose of trade with
Negro businesses in the West Indies and Africa) . . . though very little
is known of the actual circumstances of these misfortunes. (For they
were reported but tersely on an inside page of the *Negro Union Times*.)

Yet more sensationally, it is whispered that Prince Elihu overcame a
crude attempt on his life in the fall of 1928, at a secret meeting with
white leaders (among them Mayor Jimmy Walker, Anglican bishop
Henry Rudwick, a scattering of wealthy businessmen, and, not least,
the Imperial Wizard of the Ku Klux Klan), when he unknowingly swallowed poison in a glass of wine . . . or a piece of fruit . . . yet managed,
by a supreme effort of his noble will, to shake off the effect of the powerful draft.

And so on, and so forth: for as many persons who have glimpsed
Elihu, let alone have had occasion to speak with him, come away with
tales about him; which, while being never wholly true, are yet perhaps
never wholly false.

Elihu is not a man but a Destiny, the Prince himself has said—*and Destiny must run its course.*

Less to his liking, however, it is said that, despite his pose of celibacy,
he has in fact numberless wives: a virtual harem of dark-skinned
women!—many of them sequestered on the topmost floor of his private
brick residence on Strivers Row (the most exclusive block in all of
Harlem); others scattered through the city. Indeed, in every part of the
United States, in every foreign country in which Elihu has had occasion to travel since the formation of the World Negro Betterment &
Liberation Union in 1916—among these, Liberia, Sierra Leone, Ethiopia,
Central America, the West Indies, Brazil and Argentina—Elihu has
aroused such desire in women, or by voodoo-telepathy has summoned
them to him, that not King Solomon in all his manly glory (possessed
of seven hundred wives and three hundred concubines) is more to be
marveled at. How shameless these women, and how desperate!—
aflame, as they confess themselves, with love of the mahogany-skinned
Prince (most dazzling in his immaculate white caftan and white, white

trousers, flaring just perceptibly at the ankles, with, upon certain ceremonial occasions, a bit of gold braid, a bit of crimson velvet, a ruby-
studded golden sword carried almost sportily at his side): whom they
attempt to approach after his speeches and rallies, crowding about,
weeping, nearly hysterical, kept at a discreet distance by Elihu's guards,
though, surely?—the more attractive among them are summoned afterward to meet with Elihu, that their frenzied passion be absolved. For
even lust may be counted holy, when in the service of the race. (Indeed, it has been the claim of hundreds of Negro women, during the
years of Prince Elihu's ascendancy, that the "call" comes to them in
their dreams: a vision of their Prince appearing to them by night, sum-
moning them to him, that he might get them with child . . . to maintain the purity of the Negro race, much despoiled in the past several
centuries by the white devil's seed.)

And it surely follows, then, that Prince Elihu *has* fathered numberless sons and daughters, in these many parts of the world; each marked
by his strong bold features, the near-black eyes flecked with micalike
glints of hazel, the long broad nose, the haughty upper lip; marked too
(as their mothers boast) by *his* wild spirit.

For Prince Elihu is no ordinary man; but fired with the zealous virility of an African king, of ancient times.

The Prince and his most trusted ministers, however, respond with
impatience at such tales; for after all Elihu has pledged himself to
chastity, celibacy and manly virtue, as have the most devoted of his followers; all passion to be directed toward the triumph of the World Negro Betterment & Liberation Union, and the eventual reclamation of
the great lost civilization of Africa. (This to be done within the next
decade; for, by Elihu's calculation, the second of the cannibal-devils'
wars will begin by that time, in Europe.) So when distraught women
crowd about the platform following one of Elihu's rallies, or appear
drunken and weeping at his doorstep on 138th Street, pleading to be
admitted, his guards are instructed to turn them away courteously yet
forcefully; and to discourage them from further such shameless and degrading behavior. It is their sacred duty to wed and to bring forth black
progeny with men of their own sphere, that the race maintain its vigor.
For, as Elihu has said, *the eyes of the cannibal-devils being fixed upon him,
he is obliged to be a god, that they not mistake him for a beast.*

II

Yet to many observers, his fellow Negroes no less than his adversary whites, Prince Elihu is neither a god nor a beast but a common charlatan: indeed, a common criminal—too wily, at the present time, to trip himself up.

But Elihu is as swollen with pride as the legendary peacock, isn't he?—and Pride goeth before a fall.

For, murmur his enemies, only consider: since the formation of his World Union in 1916, he has drawn into his net an estimated eighty thousand to one hundred thousand Negroes in the United States and abroad, each paying dues of 35¢ per month; and contributing a good deal more. (In the official publication of the World Negro Betterment & Liberation Union, *Negro Union Times*—a brisk new rival to such publications as *The Crisis* of the National Association for the Advancement of Colored People, and *The Guardian* of the National Rights League—reports of the Union's progress and financial state vary from week to week. Sometimes it's proclaimed that the membership is climbing toward its goal of 1 million members by 1930; sometimes it is lamented that the membership is stalled—the consequence of "old-time Negro cowardice." Occasionally a news item will proclaim that Prince Elihu's followers are generous in their contributions; at other times, that they are falling behind in their dues. In general, however, the tone of the *Negro Union Times* is one of formality and dignity, at least in those editorials written by Elihu himself; for it's a principle of Elihu that one cannot boast of worldly success without lapsing into vulgarity. When the Negro revolution is complete, and Africa reclaimed by her exiled sons and daughters, then will begin the new age, the Black Age, when human worth will no longer be equated with mere money. . . .)

But as Dr. W. E. Burghardt Du Bois of *The Crisis* has charged, Is not one of Prince Elihu's goals the accumulation of money?—and power, and fame, and the installation of the fraudulent "Prince" as the reigning monarch of the colored world?

To which crude accusation the Prince himself has declined to reply except obliquely, at his Harlem rallies: "It is not given to one of low propensities and despoiled vision to comprehend the high."

* * *

As the fiery Elihu, springing, it seemed, virtually out of nowhere—the eruption of a holy volcano, perhaps, in the very midst of Harlem's streets—drew from the first the active hostility of white adversaries ranging from the New York City police to the Attorney General of the United States, so too, and perhaps not altogether innocently, did he arouse the hostility and deep resentment of other Negroes. For, after all, each Negro who chose to join the World Negro Betterment & Liberation Union, and to pay 35 cents per month for the privilege, was very likely choosing not to join such Harlem-based organizations as the NAACP, which had been founded in 1909; or the National Rights League; or the National Urban League; or the Liberty League of Afro-Americans; or even the aggressive Socialists of Harlem. These organizations, closely bound up with Negro churches and businesses, and headed by intellectuals, drew Elihu's lofty scorn from the very first. Their leaders, he charged, lacked the "tragic eye of History": they suffered from the blindness of false optimism; the inability to comprehend, as one of noble blood did, that the purity of the Negro race can only be contaminated by association of any kind with the white cannibal-devils . . . who must be delivered from the Christian delusions of certain of their spokesmen, pressing upon them the injunction *Love thy neighbor as thyself* when such an action, for the white cannibal-devil, is an impossibility.

"They do not love themselves," Elihu says scornfully, "—how, then, can they love their neighbor?"

No: the goal for Negroes cannot be integration with their enemies, still less with a race as debased as the Caucasian; it can only be the establishment of a colony-state on this continent, prior to a mass emigration to the continent of their origin, Africa. Begging former slaveholders for crumbs (stable wages, decent working conditions, a federal lynching law) is unworthy of a noble race; it is *demands* that must be made—for a sizable portion of land, fronting on the ocean, within the territorial United States; or restitution of $5 billion as indemnity for past abuses. ("Though it is ten billion that is deserved," as Elihu has said.) To dwell amid a degenerate race, particularly one that in its mental derangement imagines itself superior, is intolerable for all Negroes. Thus the aims of existing Negro "betterment" organizations are null and void from this time hence.

Little wonder then that Prince Elihu has accumulated countless enemies among his neighbors; and that bookmakers both Negro and Caucasian began as early as 1925 to make book on how long he might live.

The earnest, well-spoken, proudly Christian and educated gentlemen of the NAACP, for instance, find it intolerable that a transparent charlatan like "Prince" Elihu (avatar of an African king, indeed) has been able to draw the enthusiastic, even ecstatic, support of large masses of Negroes to whom they have made little appeal—*they*, who are so reasonable, and pious, and patriotic, they might be white men but accidentally trapped in black skin! The much-publicized goal of this organization is equality for the colored in all phases of American life; and where possible *integration* of the races—the very ideal treated with such contempt by Prince Elihu.

Then again, the Socialist Party is scandalized by Elihu's repeated assertions that race, not class, determines destiny; that the Negro worker has very little in common with the white worker, save being the object of his especial hatred, should an economic recession occur. The Socialist publication in Harlem, *The Emancipator*, stresses the ideal of world unification of all workers against the imperialist class, but Elihu insists that all whites without exception, including Marx and Lenin, constitute an imperialist class—"For it is the very soul of the Caucasian that is degenerate, not merely his rung on the ladder of society," Elihu says with withering scorn. Those Socialists, Communists and Anarchists who preach a natural brotherhood of man, regardless of skin color, are as deluded as their imperialist adversaries who believe the dark races marked by their Christian God as inferior, and fit solely to be enslaved.

Also, says Elihu contemptuously, "There can be no *classless society*—not even in the grave."

It's no surprise that the Christian ministers of Harlem are allied in righteous opposition to Prince Elihu, who ridicules their churches for being childish versions of the white cannibal-devil's church, and their theology for aping the white cannibal-devil's theology; and who speaks lightly of the Savior, Jesus Christ ("*If* he was crucified, *then* he is bound to have been black—but where are the black Christs?"). The Christian God is never evoked by Elihu in his speeches, though he makes a glancing reference now and then to Allah; his emphasis is primarily upon History, Destiny, Fate; yet the "free volition" of the Negro race to alter its present condition.

For Heaven, should it exist, is *African*; *Africa itself*.

Black businessmen who want only to make as much money as possible in the interstices of the racist society, and who fear and loathe the poorer Negroes among them, are frightened of Elihu's aim of a separate state or African colony; those businessmen whose specific trade turns upon Negro self-hatred (their products being skin bleaches, greasy pomades, hot combs, etc.) are frightened that Elihu's preaching of race pride will injure their sales. (For the Negro race *is* the origin of mankind, Elihu insists, and the white man is but a fallen, diseased, and doomed specimen: thus it surely follows that white features—skin of a certain pigment, hair of a certain texture, etc.—are hardly to be emulated.)

Naturally black politicians hate Prince Elihu, in whom they see a dangerous rival for the fickle love of the masses; black "numbers" bosses and bootleggers hate him, for his pose of self-righteous purity, and his frequent admonitions to the people that they give to the World Negro Betterment & Liberation Union the money usually wasted on gambling, whiskey and other dissipations. Elihu has also warned that when he and his followers come into power, all Negroes who emulate Caucasians in preying upon their own kind will be "severely punished."

More mysterious is the official action of the Republic of Liberia in declaring Prince Elihu persona non grata following his tour of the country in winter 1926, and barring the black revolutionary from returning. The Liberian ambassador to the United States has declared that Elihu, Prophet, Regent & Exchequer of the World Negro Betterment & Liberation Union has tried to interfere with domestic Liberian affairs (daring to suggest economic and land "reforms" while a guest of the President himself); and his intention to make war against other sovereign African states by proclaiming that Black Africa has the "moral obligation" to free those Negro peoples enslaved by the colonial rule of the English, Dutch, Belgians, etc. For these reasons, Prince Elihu will not be permitted to cross the border into Liberia again *under pain of death*.

"If I am the declared enemy of criminals and murderers, am I to be ashamed, or rather proud?"—so Prince Elihu has issued his sole public statement on the Liberian affair. He has told his associates at Union headquarters that, on his side, diplomatic ties are henceforth severed between his society and the black African states that have betrayed them. "And when millions of Negroes emigrate from North America to the continent of their origins, it will be to another sort of Africa, I promise—perhaps the southern tip which is said to be so beautiful, and so rich in natural resources—and not the treacherous West Coast."

Beyond these black enemies there lies of course, as Elihu makes no secret of declaring, the vast world of white privilege, white censure and white murderous rage: in short, the United States of America. For this cruel white nation, private citizens no less than government officials, is secretly dedicated to the eradication of the black race; and of Prince Elihu in particular.

So Elihu jokes, "Those persons who don't wish Elihu dead are simply those *who haven't yet heard his name.*"

III

He draws his bone-handled stiletto out of its sheath and, gripping his opponent tight—a muscular forearm slung across the man's chest, arms pinned against his sides—he saws the razor-sharp blade rapidly back and forth across the naked throat.

And lo!—how the red blood flows.

And how, being red, is it *white* blood? And how being red as his does it differ from his, accursed as *black?*—this, Elihu's dying opponent won't be able to explain, having fallen, with a look of profound astonishment, at Elisha's booted feet.

(Yet: wouldn't the results be bloody? disgusting? For Prince Elihu is a king, a god, yet also a man of nervous and highly refined sensibility.)

Elisha can summon back by way of his newly acquired powers that miraculous birth out of the raging flood (the Nautauga River, *not* the Wabash), but the years between are blurred and blinding as a cascade of water in brilliant sunshine.

Blurred, blinding, the long reign of the Devil Father, until Elisha's awakening in a Harlem street, when the true nature of the world was revealed.

Elihu's name: which means *The Lord is God.*
Or: *God is God.*
Or: *Elihu is God.*
Elihu is of course the fully awakened one, the supreme conscious-ness, as potent in this age of the Devil Father as in the bygone age, where the blood of mortal black men mingled freely with the blood of gods. Elisha is the part-awakened one, aware of the long sleep of twenty years . . . when he was hypnotized as to his true nature, taught that his skin is nothing when of course it is *all* . . . yet susceptible at times (when alone, when ill, when drifting into sleep) to the old spell; the lu-minous chimeras of the marsh; that vast swamp in which he wandered lost, powerless to save himself.

True, he could not save himself. A child. Too young. Weak-witted, weak in body.

He *could not* save himself and so was saved by another; carried aloft, a triumph, a sickly prize, on the shoulder of his tall fair brother . . . whose name, in the name of Elihu the Awakened One, he has forgotten.

(But even this must be a lie. For the tall blond boy could not have been Elisha's true brother—except under the spell of the Devil Father.)

Crime? whispers Father.
Then complicity.
Complicity?
Then no crime.

Prince Elihu, born of the fiery flood, born of rubble and paving stone, born of his own spilled blood and mutilated flesh, brings not peace but a sword: the gift to his people (as he has said in his April 1916 *Procla-mation of Rights as Propounded by the World Negro Betterment & Libera-tion Union*) of a margin of Promise and Hope: a way of seeing with the inner eye that is bound neither by the finite nor by the cannibal-devil's "infinite."

For they who have been slaves are in truth gods, cast low by the vi-cissitudes of History.

For they who have been scorned as ugly, and bestial, and accursed by

God, are in fact blessed by their own God Allah: His sons and daughters, god-mortals, in whom His spirit breathes.

For the secret is, they cannot die. He will die in their place.

Prince Elihu is falsely accused by his many Harlem enemies (including any number of pious "white men's black men") of being swollen with pride; yet, as befits a true son of Ham, he is in fact humble in the face of his destiny. (Thus Elisha thinks a half dozen times a day, *I am not I but another; that is, the bearer of another.*)

The envious among both Negroes and Caucasians stop their ears against the power of his speech, murmuring *Fraud! Hypocrite! Charlatan! Con man!* when the Prince addresses a vast crowd of followers; or when they see him being driven along Broadway in his splendid Rolls-Royce with dark-tinted windows, gleaming white, gleaming chrome, a uniformed Haitian chauffeur, two husky black lieutenants-at-arms on guard. The envious profess to scorn the Prince's fastidious attire—spotless white fine-spun linen in summer, exquisite white cashmere in winter; his white gloves and white kidskin boots; they dare to ridicule in such journals as *The Crisis, The Guardian, The Emancipator,* the eighteen-inch ostrich-plumed helmet and the ruby-studded gold sword he wears upon ceremonial occasions. As they can't conceive of Prince Elihu's miraculous birth out of the elements of fire and flood, they dare to mock his formal, studied, accentless diction, charging that he's nothing but an American-born Negro (if not a former field nigger!) like the rest of them: not a West Indian, and certainly not a native African. Having been at a loss to account for Elihu, and embarrassed at the impoverishment of their files on him, the Bureau of Investigation lists Prince Elihu's official birthplace as Harlem, and the arbitrary date of his birth as 11 June 1889. *This Negro is known to be subversive, seditious, unpredictable in his behavior and should be considered dangerous at all times.*

The envious question Elihu's motives in spending a rumored $50,000 for the English Thoroughbred Ruby Blood, registered in the name of the Negro World Betterment & Liberation Union and boarded and trained at James Ben Ali Hagin Farms, Kentucky; just as, a few years before, the envious questioned his motives in purchasing the oceangoing ship *Penelope* (rechristened *Black Jupiter*) and the sport biplane *Black Eagle.* For, knowing but a low earthly pride, the pride of mere mortals, they can't conceive of the *race pride* of a son of Ham.

And the envious are at a loss to account for Elihu's courage, if the man *is* a fraud: for why would a fraud voluntarily return to the United States as Elihu did, in 1918, from Central America, to answer to sedition charges and be jailed; and why would he risk his life countless times as Elihu has, publicly declaring that no threat of physical injury can dissuade him from his mission?

The envious speak of seeing Elihu one day dead but very few are bold enough to speak of killing him.

Elihu and Destiny are one says the Prince in his formal, coolly ironic public voice; in which, if even the envious listen closely, they might discern a note of sorrow.

"Elisha that *was*, and Elihu that *is*."

So Prince Elihu sometimes murmurs to himself, in the midst of his newborn life.

So 'Lisha, the white man's puppet, has vanished entirely. The white girl's plaything. Little Moses, strangely, will emerge in weak moments, in solitude before a mirror—

"Weel about and turn about
 And do jis so
 Eb'ry time I weel about
 I jump Jim Crow!"

—the Prince lurching, flailing long arms and legs, jumping with a ferocity of joy, making faces at himself in the mirror, wide white grins.

Yet perhaps 'Lisha does survive. As Elihu lies perspiring and insomniac between sheets of the most expensive linen in his narrow celibate's bed with the brass headboard; in his bedroom on the third, topmost floor of the stately brick residence on 138th Street, Harlem (of which the envious have much to say, for whose money has paid for this expensive, heavily guarded house?), listening to the noises of the nighttime city that penetrate even the leafy calm of Strivers Row.

"They will not bring me to earth, here. I am safe, here."

He rises early, at 4 A.M. to pray to Allah (in whom he can't believe) that he will be strong enough to endure Elihu's terrible spirit for another five or six years at least.

He prays that he won't shrink before Elihu's tragic destiny.

"For I know, I accept: Prince Elihu will be assassinated one day."

And he prays too that his health won't suddenly deteriorate . . . for Elisha suffers from certain medical problems of which Elihu in his pride knows not.

(His skull once fractured by a policeman's billy club; all the fingers of his left hand smashed. Rheumatoid arthritis in the joints of his knees and thighs, a result of the unheated Atlanta prison. A weak stomach, prone to ulcerous inflammations. Migraine headaches, wavering vision. The aftermath of malaria and a sinister parasitic blood fluke, acquired in his West African pilgrimage. These and other maladies are secrets to be kept from even his most trusted aides in the Union.)

Where Elihu is defiant of all physical infirmity, Elisha carries himself with the caution of a much-kicked dog; where Elihu is a paragon of Negro manhood, robust and still young, a dashing black man whom women turn to watch in the street, Elisha is after all nearing forty— "And not a young forty." The Prince is six feet tall, supple, muscled, light on his feet as a panther, supremely self-confident; poor Elisha is undernourished, with ribs straining against his slightly jaundiced skin and, perversely, a slack, soft little potbelly. (For there are few foods he can eat and the malarial fevers, striking at will, sweat him dry.) The Prince is a renowned master of rhetorical outrage, in his ostrich-plume and ceremonial attire in particular, but of course he's never angry— "For to be angry is to be *small*"—while Elisha is becoming increasingly short-tempered as he grows older. (Behind his back, his most trusted aides refer to him, not without affection, as "the Hornet.") The Prince is cavalier enough to tolerate flatterers and fawners and hypocrites while Elisha recoils in disgust; the Prince is shrewd enough to accept donations from virtually any source, for money is but money and is needed for the cause, while Elisha is apt to turn on his heel with a look of nausea and stride out of the room—"There is some shit a man will not even *smell*."

Yet both the Prince and Elisha hold themselves aloof from the numerous hot-eyed women who claim that Elihu has summoned them by night to be his brides, and the bearers of his sacred issue. (For Elisha is certain there can't be any truth in the legends relating to Prince Elihu's remarkable virility. . . .)

Though Elihu is proudly innocent of such knowledge, Elisha is well aware of the fact that his own people spy on him. And carry tales about the city, even to the cannibal-devils who pay them for their information. It is fate, it is destiny. *I am not I but another. The bearer of another.*

IV

The massed dark-gleaming faces, the eyes uncannily prominent, even to the shadowy rear of the hall: rippling, surging, sighing pulsing life: *theirs,* and *his.* Unexpected words spring to Prince Elihu's lips by way of these people; without them he would be mute. So it is wicked of his enemies to accuse him and his organization of exploiting the poorest Negroes when it is they who speak through him: they who have blessed him with divinity.

It is not so much Prince Elihu's strategy as his instinct, that he begins in slow, formal, incantatory tones; then speaks more quickly, by degrees; more forcibly; at last vehemently, his magnificent rich voice raised nearly to a shout. All that he utters at such dazzling moments is holy; and true, because holy; else why would the people shout in agreement with him, why would they adore him so powerfully, so ecstatically? For he tells them precisely that which they already know.

Our love for America has not been returned, brothers and sisters, though we have given of ourselves virtually all we can give, though they have taken from us virtually all they can take, it must be realized at last . . . today, now, at this very hour . . . that the Negro's love for America has not been returned: and cannot be returned.

And why can it not be returned, now or in the future? . . .

Because, brothers and sisters, there can be no love when the agent of love is accursed; when the agent of love is diseased, degenerate, doomed; a creature of the Age of the Machine, damned by History.

Because, brothers and sisters, the Caucasian is but a subspecies of the great original tribe of the children of Ham; a subspecies that drifted, many millennia past, from the sun-blessed birthplace of mankind . . . to regions of geography and climate inimical to life . . . and to the soul. Thus, the depth and richness of their spirit were bleached out in them as, by degrees, the pigment of their skin was bleached, to the sickly pale pigment it now possesses.

And, thus, Prince Elihu is the only man to dare name them what they are: white cannibal-devils!

And to decry, for all the world to hear, their crimes against us! Which are unforgivable, and not to be forgiven!
Which dare not be forgiven!
Which will not be forgiven!
And never, never, so long as Prince Elihu draws breath, to be forgotten!

Thinks Elisha, in a virtual trance of certitude, The Game is now given over to *us*: and we must be cruel, as we have been taught.

V

True, perhaps, that Prince Elihu and his staff sometimes give the impression of boasting, in public, of the fact that the World Negro Betterment & Liberation Union is the fastest-growing organization of its kind in Negro America—indeed, in the world.

And of the fact that they are tireless in their campaign to improve the lot of the Negro people: there will be, for instance, a forty-page Land and Indemnity Bill presented to Congress on or before 1 March 1929 seeking restitution of $5 billion from the United States Government as well as a sovereign Negro state; the First Negro Confraternity Rally will be held in June 1929 in Madison Square Garden, which rally is expected to draw more than one hundred thousand men and women from all over the world; negotiations are in process for the purchase of a second oceangoing ship, *Black Jupiter II*, and to launch Prince Elihu's proposed Black Jupiter Line (for trade between Negro parties and for the eventual transportation of North American Negroes to Africa). Also, purchases have already been made of an eight-passenger Cessna plane, *Black Eagle II*; and the two-year-old Thoroughbred Ruby Blood, one day to be the pride of the Negro sporting world, and the envy of the white; and certain properties in Harlem, Jersey City, Newark, Philadelphia and Baltimore, to be renovated by way of contributions from the membership for the establishment of Negro schools and colleges and centers for medical welfare, legal counseling and recreation. (True, these properties are in states of advanced dilapidation and disrepair at the present time, and heavily mortgaged; but Prince Elihu and his staff insist that, within a few years, all will be restored to their for-

mer conditions if not improved.) Thus, the acquisition of such properties may be seen as a shrewd investment in preparation for the mass
emigration to Africa.

Because a number of these purchases are partly financed by the selling of stocks and bonds, Prince Elihu's activities have aroused the hostile attention of the Manhattan district attorney, to whose grim office
in lower Manhattan Elihu has been so frequently summoned it's beginning to be charged, even by Elihu's Harlem detractors, that he's being
persecuted yet again by the United States Government.

Yet, since Prince Elihu and his staff are scrupulously honest in their
Wall Street dealings, and can present remarkably detailed financial
records and reports, the white racist officials are powerless to act. At
least at the present time.

(Elisha knows that he and the World Union are being continuously
investigated by city, state and federal agents; that Prince Elihu's file in
the Justice Department in Washington must be enormous by now; that
it's only a matter of time before . . .

"But what does *that* matter," Elisha murmurs, critically contemplating his yet fine-boned face in his favorite mirror, examining his veiny
yet still alert eyes; and his damned upper gums which were bleeding
again during the night, staining his white linen pillowcase. "What does
any of *that* matter?" he says, with a careless smile, "—for The Game is
never to be played as if it were but a game when it is in fact *life*.")

VI

Of course, Prince Elihu must marry. Prince Elihu must father sons to
carry on his name and his sacred work.

But there is no woman in all of Harlem for him.

Visits with an affable smiling well-to-do black physician, a neighbor
here on Strivers Row, the man's bamboo cane has a brass bird for a handle, his left eye has a merry gleam, but his shy plump daughter of
twenty gives off a regrettable odor of starched cotton and dank fruity
sweat; and Elihu cannot love her.

Visits with the family of his minister of finance, ebony-black Jamaicans, gay, watchful, proud, and he sees that the daughter of the household is beautiful, wide-spaced dark-lashed eyes bright with secrets, thin plucked eyebrows curved in crescents, and lips ripe for biting; for love. But Elihu cannot love.

Next, he is brought to meet a handsome widow of thirty-one, mother of a ten-year-old girl, she tells him her husband died for his country overseas, in France, she too is proud, nervous, tight-cinched waist and heavy melonlike breasts, melonlike hips, she wets her lips with a quick pink tongue and Elihu feels the stir of manly desire but his heart remains unmoved, he cannot love.

Next, they bring him to a laughing young woman, part Puerto Rican, gold-glinting teeth, hair straightened to a smooth stiff thick-textured sheen, lips rouged, ripe for love, for Prince Elihu—his muscular shoulders and thighs, the promise of his hungry mouth—but though he stares at her entranced he cannot, cannot love.

And, last, there is a sweet plump too-young girl named Mina, her parents' boastful chatter distracts him, why is she so young? why have they lied about her age? Mina? Mina? why does the name so upset him? shy, stammering, lips pursed over big white teeth, eyelashes beaded with tears of childish shame; and of course Elihu is polite, Elihu is icily polite, for perhaps after all he's too old for marriage, for carnal love.

His ministers inquire worriedly—Will he give up the search? Is there no Negro woman anywhere to please him? Elihu passes a hand over his face, for a terrible weak moment he and 'Lisha are one, the throb of pain behind the eyes that have seen too much, the malaise of the gut that has endured too much, "Yes," he says, "—I mean no," he says stiffly, "—it's just that, my friends, Venus Aphrodite is a strong proposition."

VII

A small-boned girl, white, very blond, in an old-fashioned traveling cloak . . . the hood lifted from her face by a sudden gust of wind . . . her lower lip caught in her teeth and her eyes narrowed in the savagery of The Game, that single glance a razor blade, a lighted match . . . beside her, keeping a jaunty comical flirtatious mocking pace, some yards away but beside her, surely, it cannot be a coincidence, a tall, thin, middle-aged Negro with a goatee, impeccably groomed, graying, rather stoop-shouldered, with a ministerial look: rimless glasses, smart black bowler hat, a cane beneath his arm *just like white folks.*

Whispers 'Lisha, How did you do?—*did* you?

Whispers the girl, Shut your mouth till we get by ourselves!

Whispers 'Lisha, Ain't you a proud little beauty!

Whispers the girl, lovely eyes narrowed to entice, to tease, to play (for she is only a child after all), Wait'll you see!—just wait!

And 'Lisha struts with his cane, preening-proud, now keeping a discreet eyes-ahead, a discreet distance betwixt him and the little white minx, her laughter tinkling like breaking glass in another room, O sweet Millicent the sinful companion of his soul whom one day he *will* love, as Devil Father cannot foresee.

Elisha who *was,* long ago in Muirkirk; Elihu who *is,* in the great clamorous kingdom of Harlem; yet, at certain helpless moments (indeed, hours), Elisha who *is,* gaunt and trembling with rage behind the Prince's imperturbable face.

The Prince neither knows nor cares about skinny white women, white she-devils with dry sickly skin like the underbellies of crawling things, silly rolled stockings, boys' hats, tiny dresses that show the inconsequential outlines of their undergarments; lips darkly bee-stung in the manner of Clara Bow, or is it Gilda Gray with her feathered shimmy, or ugly Theda Bara posed with a giant snake's tongue protruding toward hers? The Prince has no memory of the Devil Father, let alone of Millie, or Muirkirk, or the lie of white brothers; the Prince would recoil in disgust, for to him all whites *are* diseased, and the thought of sexual intercourse with a white woman is wholly repugnant.

Elisha remembers, at times; Elisha is condemned to remember, so long as he has any memory at all; but in truth, with the passage of years—the tumultuous years and days of his second birth!—he cannot remember very clearly or coherently; and has even stopped hating his young white bride.

The issue of Devil Father, she was; contaminated by his greed.

She whom he loved, and adored, and so wildly desired, under the

Devil's enchantment: that 'Lisha and the others were as *one*; and the color of his skin made no division between them.

For only brothers by blood are brothers by the soul.

And once that truth has been beaten into one's very flesh, it is never to be denied.

In any case, thinks Elisha, it's purposeless: continuing to hate Millicent.

"For she too was under his spell; and diseased, like him, in the way of her race. For where there can be no love there can no longer be hate. And it *is* ended," he says aloud, in a flat, hard, certain voice, "—it *is* no more."

VIII

One of the more persistent of the legends told of Prince Elihu, to be endlessly embellished following his death, has to do with an attempt on his life by prominent white citizens in fall 1928.

According to this story, the Prince was given poison; but by way of his immortal powers managed to overcome the effect of the draft and escape back to Harlem—in the magnificent white Rolls-Royce driven by his faithful Haitian chauffeur and protected by his husky uniformed lieutenants.

(For the record, nothing of the kind occurred in Manhattan. The sole poison attempt on Prince Elihu was made in the Republic of Liberia in May 1926, following the Prince's shock and outrage at having discovered that the Liberian ruling class, the descendants of freed American slaves, had enslaved certain of their tribal peoples.)

What precisely happened to Prince Elihu on the afternoon of 5 October 1928, in the sumptuous cherrywood-panelled library of Bishop Rudwick of St. James's, Park Avenue, was mysterious indeed; and never, to the Negro revolutionary's satisfaction, comprehended. For, though he prided himself upon his pristine control in the presence of his enemies—though he prided himself upon being, to his very fingertips, an avatar of a great, even godly personage—in the midst of a secret conference with several prominent white men (among them Pierpont Morgan, John

D. Rockefeller, Sr., Charles E. Mitchell of the National City Bank, and Bishop Rudwick himself), Prince Elihu became, suddenly, so overcome by sheer animal loathing that, for some minutes, he could not continue with his presentation; and felt so powerful a desire to unstrap his stiletto from his leg, and kill one of his enemies before he was stopped, he scarcely allowed himself to breathe.

"They *are* repulsive," he thought, staring with widened eyes at one after another of the gentlemen, "—it is true, it is *true*."

For it seemed to him that the white men, not excluding even his host, the gracious Bishop Rudwick (who made so elaborate a pretense of sympathy with the plight of the American Negro), were physically grotesque; their eyes in particular were small, hard, glassy, more like reptiles' eyes than humans'; and didn't they emit, variously, queer stale papery or dusty odors? If Elihu gazed too long at the elderly Rockefeller, for instance, he felt the panic rising in him, in his very bowels, that he *would* behave rashly; thus he looked quickly away, to the more benign Mitchell—who, after a few seconds, began to seem subtly hideous, the creases about his mouth, made by decades of smiling, deep enough, Elihu thought, for tiny parasites to burrow into and lay their near-invisible white eggs. . . .

As Elihu, or Elisha, had arranged for this historic meeting himself, and had plotted his course in some detail beforehand, he was frightened by his own response. For had he not, in the old days of his youth, in the reign of the Devil Father, adroitly bent to his will men and women whom he secretly detested? . . . persons whose only relationship to *him* was as mere objects of The Game?

Do you doubt?—you have already lost The Game.

("But I do not doubt!" Elisha thought. "For I am not I—but the bearer of a sacred mission.")

The subject of Prince Elihu's meeting with this group of wealthy and influential gentlemen was nothing less than the partial funding of the World Negro Betterment & Liberation Union in its plan to establish an American, and then an African, colony, to which all American Negroes would emigrate within the next decade. For there had begun to arise certain difficulties of a financial nature, in regard to selling enough stock in the Black Jupiter Line, even to pay off debts owed on the initial ship; and Elihu had discovered, to his bafflement and chagrin, that large sums of money (membership dues, contributions, advertising revenue for the *Negro Union Times*) appeared to be missing . . . as were two or three of his most trusted associates; and the district attorney's office had issued him yet another summons, the eighth in a single year; and, most distressing, the Harlem congressman with whom he had been working closely in the matter of the historic Land and Indemnity Bill had informed him but the other day that in his opinion the bill was doomed . . . for if white Americans voted to pay $5 billion owed to black Americans it would be revealed to all the world that they *did* owe the money, and this they would never accept!

So it occurred to the ingenious Prince that, since all Caucasians including the presumably liberal, Christian and humanitarian secretly despised Negroes ("As any normal Negro despises them"), and if negotiations were kept confidential, wealthy whites might be willing, if not eager, to help finance the mass emigration back to Africa.

"Gentlemen, we understand one another completely: we are mirror images of one another, and race-loathing is our common bond. So, may I speak openly?"

A murmured pretense of surprise, among a few of the gentlemen; while the remainder, to Elihu's relief, put aside the usual masks of hypocrisy and condescension, and bade him speak frankly.

For the first hour of the conference, Prince Elihu did speak frankly; with his usual clarity of purpose, and rather less of his usual flair for words. He could see that he quite impressed his white companions with his knowledge of both white and Negro (that is, slave) history of North America. Succinctly, without a trace of rancor or sentiment, he limned for them, as if such might be new to their ears, the wretched lot of Africans brought chained to the New World when New York City was but a wilderness inhabited at one end by the Netherlands colonists; he spoke of early, naive hopes for "African reclamation" by freed slaves in Rhode Island and Philadelphia in the eighteenth century; and of the support of the philanthropic American Colonization Society—which had funded the experiment of Liberia in 1847. ("And what is your opinion of Liberia, Mr. Elihu?" Bishop Rudwick asked earnestly; and Elihu, not to be diverted from his argument, said coolly, "I am not a man of mere 'opinions,' Bishop.") Should they require statistics, Prince Elihu was in possession of statistics; should they require a distillation of white promises repeatedly made and then broken to the Negro—most recently, Woodrow Wilson's promises to Negro veterans of the Great

War—he was in possession of these. Also, should the white gentlemen, who were shrewd businessmen after all, require precedent for their involvement in what might be termed domestic Negro politics, he could point to the Tuskegee Institute, to which Andrew Carnegie had given a tiny portion of his money (which is to say, millions of dollars): an organization of gross paternalist racism, yet a gesture of charity nonetheless.

On their side, the white men knew to ask the right questions ("What guarantee have we that you will use the money properly, if we give it," "Who will provide the cheapest manual labor, if all Negroes emigrate," "Should you establish a sovereign African state, would *we* be granted special privileges in regard to trade," etc.); and it soon became evident that, for all their pose of geniality, Prince Elihu had read their sentiments correctly. As he said, with a flashing smile, "It can hardly be denied that, in your hereditary nostrils, we dark-skinned peoples *stink*: and there is no more natural desire than to wish a *stink* as far away as possible."

This incidental remark was met by the white gentlemen with pained, and then abashed, expressions; and only the embarrassed bishop made an effort, faltering and unconvincing, to assure Prince Elihu that this was not so.

Discussion was resumed; and, after some time, a light meal was served around the table (rich-veined Stilton cheese, bread, several kinds of fruits and nuts, dry white wine, mineral water), which most of the gentlemen fell upon with appetite. Elihu, paying little heed to what he was doing, expertly pared for himself a sweet fruit of some dark, pulpy, unfamiliar sort (neither an apple nor a plum, though possessing the qualities of both; but rife with masses of soft slimy seeds), and swallowed a few mouthfuls . . . following which (but surely there *was* no connection) he began to feel uneasy; vaguely sick; light-headed. A sweaty chill of animal panic overtook him as he looked, and for the first time actually saw, the men seated about the polished mahogany table, gazing at *him* . . . unspeakably ugly, vile, "diseased," indeed! The most offensive was the arrogant Pierpont Morgan with his small beady eyes, enormous misshapen nose, and puckered mouth: he had been staring at Prince Elihu from the very start as if he were a species of exotic trained monkey.

Yet all were frightful; grotesque; repellent—the very pigment of their skin curdled in any number of sickly hues, ranging from ashen-white (the ninety-year-old cadaverous Rockefeller) to a mottled beefy red (the fat-bellied bishop). And how curiously and morbidly their skins were blemished: moles, warts, broken capillaries, liver spots and discolorations inscribed deep in the flesh, like rot.

And I saw that I despised them in the flesh, and not merely in theory.

And knew that I would exult in killing them with my own ravenous hands.

And then . . . the most extraordinary development of that day:

For suddenly Prince Elihu ducks his handsome head in a comical loll . . . widens his thick-lashed eyes till they nearly pop . . . Elihu the descendant of African kings, his face distended by the white glistening grin of affable idiocy, softly intoning:

> *"Weel about and turn about*
> *And do jis so*
> *Eb'ry time I weel about*
> *I jump Jim Crow!"*

So unanticipated is this cheery outburst, so wholly inappropriate to the setting, it seems for a moment that the unspeakable has at last been uttered, and cannot be retrieved. Yet more mysteriously, no one in the Bishop's library could have said, *not even Prince Elihu himself*, whether the feckless little rhyme has been sung voluntarily, or no.

And how exquisitely Prince Elihu sings the words, with what infectious zany good humor he sways in his chair, lolling head, comical bulging eyes, his tongue darting busily about: who would have guessed that he, of all Negroes, could cut such hilarious monkeyshines?

> *"I'm a rorer on de fiddle,*
> *An down in ole Virginny*
> *Dey say I play de skientific*
> *Like massa Pagganninny!"*

As if he can't restrain himself another moment, Prince Elihu in his flowing white caftan leaps to his feet, and cavorts, and flails his arms about, and, rolling his eyes, shouts:

> *"De way dey bake de hoe cake,*
> *Virginny nebber tire!*

Dey put de doe upon de foot
  And stick im in de fire!"

The disoriented white men can't determine whether Elihu, who had seemed so congenial earlier, and so straightforward in his remarks, is now joking; or "entertaining"; or mocking them in so vicious a way, it dare not be acknowledged. (For surely it *is* a peculiar thing, to hear a favorite minstrel ditty sung not by a white man in blackface but by an actual black man . . . in his own face.)

The Prince continues dancing for another few minutes—squatting, wriggling, shimmying, clapping broadly as if to expose the pinkish palms of his hands—

"Weel about and turn about!
  And do jis so!
  Eb'ry time I weel about
  I jump Jim Crow!"

—until suddenly he's drained of energy, and simply stops.

There's a brief, frightened outburst of applause; a few nervous chuckles; and unctuous Bishop Rudwick rises stiffly smiling as if to confer a blessing upon the meeting . . . and the historic secret conference is adjourned.

So it happened that Prince Elihu failed in his mission to extract from the white enemy money to finance the Union's great project; and retreated, in a trancelike state, back to his shaky kingdom in Harlem.

Yet, en route to Union headquarters, Elihu, that's to say poor Elisha, began to feel sick again; sick in his guts; and, not wanting to despoil the luxurious plush interior of the Rolls-Royce, commanded his driver to stop. And so the whitely gleaming vehicle, familiar to Harlem eyes, came to a stop at 120th Street; and, shielded partly by a rear door, the renowned Negro revolutionary stooped, and retched, and vomited into the gutter while his burly twin lieutenants, stricken with shame, looked resolutely away.

The Enchanted Princess

Like one of Katrina's old fairy tales it's all coming true: her heart's most secret, stubborn wish: the prayer of many a foolish lost hour.

And, like one of Katrina's cruel tales, it teaches that one's wish is not after all one's *wish*.

Says Aaron Deerfield, But I had always thought . . . that we *would* marry.

Says Esther Licht, But my life is different now, *I* am different now.

Says Aaron Deerfield, Then we can't be married? We won't be married? And again he repeats, smiling, bewildered, staring at Esther's tense face, It's just that I'd been led to believe we had an understanding, all these years. . . .

Says Esther, But you never spoke of it to me.

. . . all these years, until we were ready.

Until you were ready. Until you made up your mind.

No, of course not. . . . I suppose it might have looked that way to you, Esther, I mean from time to time; but you must have *known*.

Says Esther, I had hoped, but I didn't know.

Says Aaron, If you had hoped, then . . . ?

Says Esther, choosing her words with care, Because I am different now. My life has changed.

That night Esther writes a letter to Darian in Schenectady, taking care not to seem boastful, let alone vindictive (for in truth she still loves Aaron, and would marry him if circumstances allowed), telling him that, at age twenty-six, she feels like a princess awakened from a long enchanted slumber . . . or was it a lifetime of having been bewitched as a frog, or a toad, or a dun-colored little bird? . . .

If I regret my decision, she concludes, at least it has been *my* decision.

* * *

But is that too smug, too self-assured? too boastful after all?
Esther doesn't mean it to be!

Thus, in a postscript, written the next morning: *It is one of Katrina's cruel old tales, where the wish comes true but it is no longer the wish . . . and it's no longer true.*

"The First Annual Universal Negro Confraternity Rally"

I

"Why . . . ? Because it's his 'game,' Maynard," Millicent whispers, suffused with a queer exhilaration, as her nine-year-old tugs at her gloved hand in an annoying little spasm of fear. "He won't fall as you would, in his place."

"But why, Momma?" the child persists.

"Because it's *his*; because it's what he does."

"But—"

"Do be quiet, sweetheart: you ask too many pointless questions!"

Forty dizzy feet above Richmond's Rialto Theatre there sits, on a rubber-covered seat, atop a flagpole newly erected for this very purpose, the great "Shipwreck" Kelly himself—champion flagpole sitter of North America, man of mysteries and amusing little foibles (he will play only "Peg o' My Heart" on his harmonica, for instance, and is said to have refused a Hollywood contract because his filmed self would replace his true self in the hearts of his fans). Shipwreck refers to himself as "the luckiest fool alive" and it appears to many that this is so: hotels and movie theaters have bid for his services across the United States, paying him a goodly sum of money simply to climb atop a flagpole and *sit*.

And now he's come to Richmond, Virginia, to the splendidly gaudy

Rialto Theatre on Main Street, and is in his fifteenth day of sitting—a
lone triumphant figure against a changing sky, cheery, stoic, much admired and debated-over (for is he mad, or is he merely very shrewd?),
the focus of all local attention, white and Negro alike. People of widely
divergent ages and social classes have sent Shipwreck small gifts; several young women have proposed marriage (for he *is* handsome, and
only thirty-two years old); a number of local businesses have joined up
with the Rialto Theatre, pledged to pay for bonus days beyond the first
two weeks. There is even a lottery—not altogether legal, but very
popular—which will pay $500 to the person who guesses closest to the
day, the hour, and the minute of Shipwreck's descent (voluntary or
otherwise) from his solitary perch.

How does he do it, is a question far more commonly asked than *why*,
for the answers are relatively straightforward. Shipwreck makes no secret of his use of a well-cushioned seat tightly strapped to the flagpole
ball (the seat is examined beforehand by local authorities, its photograph published in the newspaper); he has trained himself, as he says,
to sleep with his thumbs anchored into holes bored into the seat and
his ankles firmly clasped about the pole. During his vigil in the air he
eats only fluids (broth, milk, fruit juice, and "gallons of black coffee, to
keep awake") hoisted aloft by a pully; his bodily wastes are lowered by
way of the same pully, in a discreet tin bucket. (Shipwreck, being a
gentleman for all his vanity and clownishness, takes care to relieve
himself only at night or when he is reasonably certain that no one is
watching.)

When it rains and storms, even when lightning flashes, why then
poor Shipwreck must endure it: for such is the price of his profession,
and his coast-to-coast fame. On mild days (like today) he sits bareheaded, softly playing his harmonica (*is* the tune "Peg o' My Heart"?—
the breeze blows much of it away into the sky), his legs jauntily crossed.
Seen through a pair of binoculars (which Millicent has brought along,
as much for her own use as her son's) he appears in high spirits, quite
darkly tanned. As he plays the harmonica his eyebrows wriggle and his
eyelids droop with a sort of languid pleasure, comically inappropriate to
his perch in the sky. Peering through the binoculars' lenses Millicent
realizes she is half awaiting the impossible: that the "luckiest fool alive"
will suddenly chance to see *her*.

Millicent offers to pay 50¢ so that she and little Maynard might climb to the roof of the Rialto, in a long straggling line of sight-seers, for a closer look at Shipwreck Kelly; but, to her surprise and annoyance, the child refuses to go. "What if the man falls, Momma," Maynard says, in the hurt whining tone Millicent particularly dislikes, "—what if he falls and hurts himself, I don't want to *see!*"

Millicent says, "He isn't going to fall, don't be silly."

"I don't want to *see!*" the boy whimpers.

"And even if he fell," Millicent continues, angry, inspired, "he wouldn't hurt himself, like you or me. Or Daddy."

But little Maynard is clearly frightened and now wants only to be taken home, though, for many days, he begged Millicent to be taken downtown: all his friends had seen the flagpole sitter, only *he* was left out. Warren had no interest, naturally, in journeying downtown on so supremely childish an outing (he has to conserve his strength, in any case); and six-year-old Betsey's nerves are such, her mother would never consider bringing her along. ("She's too much like myself," Millicent thinks uneasily. " 'Myself,'—at that frightening age.")

So the little excursion on a mid-May afternoon comes to an abrupt end. Millicent *is* rather bored, herself. Around her on the sidewalk, necks craned, eyes shielded from the sun, a number of men and women stand peering at Shipwreck Kelly so prodigiously high above them, waving frantically, shaking little flags and banners, calling out loud cheery greetings ("How's it goin', Shipwreck!" "How's the weather up there!" "You ain't goin to fall, are you!"), and laughing with an edgy, pointless gaiety, for after all Shipwreck might slip to his death virtually at any moment . . . he might, the wind being right, fall at their very feet.

Millicent leads the trembling little boy away without a backward glance. Flagpole sitting is after all a lowlife activity, to put it mildly; as Warren warned, she'd likely run into white trash, mainly, if she took their boy to see it.

Still, the daring!—the foolish bravado!

So mad a display of self-esteem!

So reckless a Game, played out in the very sky!

And will I come to him, humble myself before him? I will not, I dare not, I am a wife and a mother . . . a white woman.

That night her sleep is agitated; she dreams not once, but repeatedly, shamelessly, of her lost lover; waking with the decision that, yes, she will arrange to travel to New York, and soon; she will, at last, after these many years, arrange to meet with 'Lisha whom she still loves. ("For there is only one first love. As, they say, there is but one first death.")

This decision made, Millicent feels enormous relief. As, they say, the decision to die can release long-withheld sensations of joy.

II

Beautiful Millicent Stirling breaks hearts, but can it be her fault?— she doesn't force men and women, even an occasional mooncalf college boy, to adore her, or even to take her seriously. As there is no Game there must be numberless games, of varying degrees of intensity, for golf and tennis and mahjong and bridge and dancing and amateur theatrics and light opera cannot absorb all of Mrs. Warren Stirling's nervous energy . . . any more than being a wife to an ailing aging husband, and a mother to two beautiful children, and the mistress of a splendid house overlooking the Richmond Country Club golf course can absorb the ferocity of her concentration.

By now Millicent Stirling has acquired detractors amid the "youngish older" country club set to which she and Warren belong, disillusioned admirers primarily, and of course those (all women) who are jealous of her conquests: yet detractors as well as friends commonly report themselves dazzled by her . . . even perplexed by her . . . for how has she time, let alone the physical strength, to do all the things she does, and to do them, for the most part, so well? Acting, and singing, and even a bit of spirited dancing in such productions of the Richmond Players as *A Trip to Chinatown*, *H.M.S. Pinafore*, *The Sunshine Girl*, *Watch Your Step*, *The Mikado*; chairwoman of committees of the Women's Auxilary of Grace Episcopal Church, the Friends of the Richmond City Orchestra, the local branch of the Virginia Historical Society; one of the most popular hostesses in the city; and a highly competitive, if somewhat temperamental and uneven, player of bridge and mahjong.

Depending upon her mood Millicent Stirling is even rather good at golf, for a woman who seems to have come late to the game.

And how striking a vision on the club's tennis courts, in her stylish white costume with the short pleated skirt, her hair tied back by a vivid red scarf—though the ferocity with which she plays, the way she slams the ball out of bounds or into the net or directly at a startled opponent has cost her friends.

"Darling, it's only a game," Warren says, concerned that she becomes so emotional so easily. "Why be upset?" And Millicent says calmly, with her sweetest smile, "Because it *is* only a game, and not worth the effort I give it."

Thirty-two years old . . . thirty-five . . . at last an unimagined thirty-eight. *And I, Father's fairy-daughter. Destined for what prince?* Millie must concede with a shrug that she's no longer the youngest, prettiest and most fashionable woman in any gathering; she's the mother of two growing children; the wife of a good, decent, distinctly middle-aged (and aging) man whom she loves . . . or in any case respects. "Warren is so much better than I deserve," she thinks, almost bitterly. "To give him up would be a mistake. And yet . . ."

Never once has Millicent Stirling succumbed to one of her romantic friendships or allowed herself to be persuaded by a passionate admirer that they should consummate their love, let alone elope together. In this giddy Jazz Age in which it suddenly seems everyone is getting divorced (from "Peaches" and Daddy Browning of the tabloids to millionaire Rockefellers and McCormicks), Millicent Stirling is terrified of the very thought of divorce . . . though it's an open secret in the social circle to which she and Warren belong that she's bored with him. (Since Betsey's birth six years ago the Stirlings have slept in separate bedrooms and Millicent quite enjoys her independence as a virginal wife. Certainly, Mrs. Stirling isn't the only virginal wife in Richmond.) Her challenge is simply to keep Warren believing that she loves him as he loves her . . . she adores him as he adores her . . . no matter that by degrees their marriage has become increasingly formal. *Seeing him sometimes gazing at me with that look of boyish yearning seeing in me another person a young girl perhaps, a stranger.* And Millicent envies her husband for *to love* is so much more joyous than *to be loved.*

Thinking then, indifferently, "But what does it matter? I'm sure love is only a species of game, in any case."

(But has Elisha ever married? Millie thinks not. She subscribes to New York papers where she reads greedily of Prince Elihu and never once has his name been linked with that of any woman.)

III

Thirty-eight years old. Yet in her innermost heart no more than seventeen.

When first he'd dared touch her not as a brother but as a lover.

Not this anxious woman with the skin so thin, dry, bleached of healthy color; white creases by her mouth; hollows beneath her eyes; a woman who must labor now at beauty where once she scarcely played and who has become cautious, this past year, of which of the household mirrors she looks into.

Would he recognize me now? Love me . . . now?

Of course. He has promised!

He would die for me he said.

The Game! What pleasure in it, if there's no one with whom to share the smallest victory?

Millicent Stirling has become an artist of the lie-not-precisely-a-lie. You might call it "inventing"—"romancing." With wide-eyed innocence she concocts misunderstandings among her friends and admirers, her Stirling relatives, the members of her Episcopal congregation (in which Warren is a much-respected deacon) and even her household . . . her staff of devoted Negro servants. Discreetly not blaming Tabitha for something that Roslene has done; expressing hurt that Rodwell has failed to complete a task as he'd seemed to promise, or had it been Jebb who'd promised; or had they all promised their elegant Mrs. Stirling and had they all disappointed her? It stirs her icy heart to hear a Negro woman sob for a Negro woman knows how to sob; to hear a Negro man curse, imagining no white folks near, for a Negro man knows how to curse. On a whim, she "lets go" one of the girls; on a whim, she hires her back the following Monday. She's sharp-eyed noting which of the women is gaining weight in the hips and breasts . . . which of the men is swaggering, the sexual glisten in his face and his body so alive she feels faint that she might accidentally brush against him . . . how easy that would be! And irrevocable.

Yet knowing, to the black servants she's merely the *white lady*. She's *Mr. Stirling's wife*. Even if she fires them and breaks their hearts their hearts will quickly mend, they will be hired elsewhere by another white lady. Sometimes she imagines she's the only white person in Richmond to know a secret: that the many Negroes in their midst are not in fact "Negro" but . . . what?

Father says our skins are neither white nor black.
As "white" and "black" are ignorantly understood.
Father says we stand outside the "white" race . . . and the "black." For all men are our enemies.

Yet it's Elisha's dark skin she loves, she cannot help loving, for Elisha's skin is Elisha; as his brown eyes are him, his lanky restless body, his long slender fingers and toes. She'd kissed the inside of his hands: so pale! pale as her own skin! They'd laughed at such markings. For in young love, there's much laughter.

In these fever dreams of her thirty-ninth year Millie is herself yet subtly altered. Naked, and sprawled in a stranger's bed. In a sexual delirium as her lover comes to her, hot-dark-skinned, more forceful and blunt than he'd been in Muirkirk. There, he'd been a shy, trembling, reckless lover; here, he's impatient. *'Lisha?* she whispers, *'Lisha?* she begs but the mouth is hard and greedy against hers, sucking her breath away. The act of love is swift, impersonal. Her arms close desperately about him, her face is buried against his neck, for this time she must not lose him, she must not surrender him; waking in shuddering, voluptuous waves of sensation, sobbing, frightened. For long minutes she lies exhausted unable to grasp where she is—what room is this, so prettily decorated? smelling of fresh-cut flowers, and her own sweet perfume?

"Why do you hurt me, 'Lisha? When you know that I have never stopped loving you. And if you are 'black'—and if I am 'white'—what is that to *us*? What is Father's curse to *us*?"

IV

Since the Philadelphia days as St. Goar's beautiful, mysterious daughter, Millie has been aware of the career of Prince Elihu, the radical Negro revolutionary of whom it was predicted he wouldn't live for more than a year—how many years ago. Her father refused to discuss Prince Elihu with her, as he'd refused to discuss poor Thurston, but Millie hadn't needed Abraham Licht to confirm what was clear to her through studying newspaper and magazine photographs minutely. "There couldn't be two young men like 'Lisha. So like 'Lisha. Impossible!"

And what of this teaching of his, that the entire white race is damned and only the colored races of the world will be redeemed?

Millie believes it an artful variation of Father's grand scheme: the Society for the Reclamation & Restoration of E. Auguste Napoléon Bonaparte. Here, the scheme is the World Negro Betterment & Liberation Union, boasting more than one hundred thousand members, whose plan it is to emigrate back to Africa by the year 1935. Elisha can't be serious, it must be a scheme. A brilliant game, though dangerous.

Yet it seems that many people, white as well as Negro, do take Prince Elihu seriously, whether as a savior or a madman; or a traitor to his country. Millie had read with astonishment of how Prince Elihu voluntarily returned from Central America to surrender to federal authorities in San Francisco, to answer to absurd charges of "wartime sedition" and to receive a harsh sentence of twelve years in prison with no possibility, as Attorney General Palmer insisted, of parole. (Though in fact President Harding pardoned Elihu anyway—to the consternation of Millie's Stirling in-laws who are, like most Richmond whites, genteel Christian racists.)

How could this be? Millie wondered. Had 'Lisha failed to heed Father's admonition not to be seduced by The Game?

Millie has long worried that something may have happened to 'Lisha in the intervening years. A blow to the head, severe illnesses . . . (She'd read, greatly upset, of his three-month tour of Africa during which time he'd been dangerously ill.) For it's impossible to comprehend how the 'Lisha she knew so intimately, closer than any brother, could believe such cruel nonsense—that Caucasians are fallen, diseased and doomed;

but a degenerate subspecies of the original Homo sapiens who were Negro. Quite apart from the doubtful science of this belief, which Millie has seen refuted in such journals as *Atlantic Monthly*, it's a fact, isn't it, that Millie, whom 'Lisha had vowed to love forever, is *white*? "How can he then believe that 'whites' are inferior to 'blacks'? In love, we were equal. He knows that."

Going squirrelly is one of the colorful catchphrases of this colorful era, prevalent in popular songs, comic strips and jokes. Millie laughs, to think that *going squirrelly* may be à la mode, and Prince Elihu is riding the crest of the mode. The more absurd the lie, the more easily it might be believed.

"But I would be more desirable to him," she tells herself, "than any Negro woman, as I *am* white."

Yet: would Millie leave her children behind? Yes she would leave them if 'Lisha insists. Or—might she bring them along? "If we eloped to Europe, for instance. He is said to be a wealthy man, and I have saved money of my own. The children could come . . . if they wished. For a while." She paces through the upstairs of the gracious old house plotting, rehearsing. What she will say to Warren. What she will say to 'Lisha. What she will say to her children.

Yes she will go to New York. But no—"Ridiculous! I would not drive across Richmond to throw myself at any man's feet."

Then one morning in early summer idly skimming the Richmond Sunday paper, the decision is made for her as if she'd rolled dice: on page 2 there is an article headlined HARLEM LEADER ELIHU TO SPEAK AT RALLY, and on page 19 there is an article headlined MIAMI EVANGELIST PLEDGES MILLION-DOLLAR MINISTRY. Millie reads these seemingly unrelated articles in tandem, with mounting excitement. The first reports that Prince Elihu will preside over the First Annual Universal Negro Confraternity Rally in Madison Square Garden, Manhattan, on 19 June 1929; over one hundred thousand participants are expected. The second reports that Reverend Thurmond Blichtman of the New Church of the Nazarene, Miami, Florida, has received more than $1 million in donations as a result of an intensive tour through Florida earlier in the year, and that he'd had a vision from God of exactly the church he would cause to be built on a "sacred piece of property" on Biscayne Boulevard overlooking the bay. The focus of the slightly scandalous article is Reverend Blichtman's newly emergent fame, or notoriety, in Florida; evidently the man is a mesmerizing preacher who recites the Gospels in an impassioned voice that provokes men and women to break down in tears and rush forward to be "saved." Rival preachers and ministers complain bitterly that this "Northern carpet-bagger" has been stealing their congregations from them—"That man knows no shame," a Baptist leader has charged. A prominent Methodist minister has accused Blichtman of "satanic powers of seduction." Blichtman refuses to reply to his critics except to say he prays for them; in the meantime he's amassed an undisclosed amount of money from donations for the construction of a New Church of the Nazarene in Miami. Millie is initially drawn to the article by the accompanying photograph of a strongly built man of middle age, fair-haired, hand-some, with something damaged about his face. He's kneeling on the ground, hands clasped at midchest in prayer. *Thurston!* Millie thinks.

Peering through the magnifying glass Warren uses for close reading, she studies the grainy photo, breathless with excitement. *Reverend Thurmond Blichtman. New Church of the Nazarene. My lost brother. Can it be?*

Something slips off the edge of the wrought-iron table (they're break-fasting on the terrace, this warm May morning) and shatters. Tabitha comes forward quickly to remedy the harm. "Millie darling, why are you so—nervous?" Warren asks in his kindly, exasperating way; and Millie, thrusting the newspaper from her, yawns and stretches and de-clares she isn't nervous at all—"Only restless! Richmond is so *finite.*"

It's Reverend Thurmond Blichtman who has made up Millie's mind for her. Like her eldest brother, she will bravely seek her destiny.

Speaking to Warren of her longing to see her brother Darian and her sister Esther in upstate New York in such a wistful way that Warren will imagine it's he who has thought of a train trip north for Millie—"To revive your spirits." Millie will travel to Schenectady to visit Darian, and travel on to the west to visit Esther in Port Oriskany where her sister has become involved in what Richmond citizens would decry as an "immoral" movement . . . nurses, welfare workers, volunteers, nearly all female, crusading for a newly founded organization, the American Birth Control League. (Since becoming a well-to-do Richmond ma-tron, Millie finds this title so coarse, so crude, she'd be embarrassed to utter it aloud in mixed company. Birth control! "Though it's a very good thing of course, for the lower classes. And yet—think of the inno-cent children who would never have been born!")

At the Richmond station, Millie kisses her adoring husband, and Betsey and Maynard, good-bye. She'll be gone, she promises, only two weeks. "Already I miss you, darlings," Millie hears herself say, a lilting soprano voice, her eyes shining with happiness and audacity and some-thing like terror; as if, stepping up into the train, gaily waving at her family only a few yards away, she has already stepped into a void, and will never return.

Imagining as the train speeds relentlessly north *he might be, he must be sensing my approach. My arrival. My return to his life.*

In Manhattan, Millicent Stirling loses no time checking into the Waldorf-Astoria, which is the only hotel she knows, the hotel in which she and Warren have stayed previously; next evening, she takes a taxi to Madison Square Garden for the rally, or rather to the vicinity of the Garden, for there's so much traffic in the streets, so many vehicles and pedestrians, and mounted policemen shouting into the crowd, the driver can't bring her within two blocks—"This is as far as I go, ma'am." Millie smiles to see the man frowning and shaking his head in the rearview mirror. *He wonders who I am, a white woman; wonders why I have a special invitation to such an event.*

This rally of 19 June 1929 will be, as newspapers promise, a "his-toric" event. Never have so many Negroes gathered together for such a purpose, in the very heart of a white metropolis; only Prince Elihu, leader of the World Negro Betterment & Liberation Union, could draw such a crowd. Millie has costumed herself for the occasion, quite clev-erly she thinks: to disguise, as best she can, the color of her skin, she's wearing a stylish tunic dress of dove-gray silk with long sleeves, and a high lace collar; her stockings are of a matching hue, though sheer silk; she wears white eyelet gloves and a flat-crowned hat of Spanish style, made for her by the leading Richmond milliner, in glazed black straw with a black dotted swiss veil—"Both ladylike, Mrs. Stirling, and *very* 'sexy,' " as the milliner has said. Now Mrs. Stirling, on foot, as rarely she's on foot in such a place, wide city streets, avenues, an unfamiliar and inhospitable atmosphere, is breathless with excitement, like a young girl embarked upon an adventure unknown to her elders; finds herself carried along by the throng of noisy people, black faces on every side, pushing into the interior of Madison Square Garden by several doors. The marquee boasts FIRST ANNUAL NEGRO CONFRATERNITY RALLY. Everywhere are six-foot posters of PRINCE ELIHU, a fierce, handsome youngish Negro in a white caftan, wearing a helmet with a white ostrich plume, an amazing costume, a quite effective costume Millie thinks, like Prince Elihu's fine, fierce, intelligent eyes, his clenched jaws, that expression both noble and truculent—"It *is*. 'Lisha." Millie would know her lover anywhere, as he would know her, even in disguise.

As Millie stumblingly ascends a flight of steps, jostled by the hurrying crowd, she hears someone shout, "Ma'am? Ma'am!"—and turns guiltily to see, about ten feet away on the sidewalk, a helmeted policeman, white, eyes hidden by a tinted visor; but Millie pretends she hasn't heard, and escapes inside.

Inside, the air is far denser and warmer than in the street; for there are too many people; too many; the smells are beginning to define themselves to Millie's sensitive nostrils; where she'd halfway imagined a kind of path cleared for her, as Mrs. Warren Stirling of Richmond, Virginia, a white woman known to Prince Elihu, even while knowing such an expectation was nonsense, she's confused that she's so . . . anonymous, even in her white skin.

In the foyer, long lines press forward to the ticket counters, for there are many who haven't purchased tickets beforehand, like Millie; the interior of the great, high-ceilinged building is dizzy with the ring and echo of thousands of voices; an air of intense excitement, expectation; here and there are pickets, enemies of the Negro Union?—pamphlets thrust rudely into Millie's gloved hand, and Millie is too polite to refuse—*All-Race League Protests Negro Zionism*—*Manifesto of the NAACP*— *Black Socialists Unite!*—*Why Did Jesus Die for You?*—*"Prince Elihu" Traitor to Race & Nation*. There are raised voices, arguments; sudden scufflings and struggles; moments of eerie stillness when everyone in Millie's vicinity freezes, to see what is happening; giant Negroes in uniforms sweated through beneath the arms, bearing the insignia of the Negro Union, are engaged in hauling protestors away, walking, or dragging, them swiftly and deftly against the incoming stream of people which parts to let them through.

Millie's beautiful, costly Spanish hat has been knocked askew on her head, and the veil, heated and dampened by her quickened breath, clings to her face. Millie adjusts the hat, blindly using her three-inch ebony hatpins; she imagines eyes glancing upon her, more curious than startled or disapproving. *A white woman, a white lady—here?* Millie has begun to think that she's in foreign territory though still in the United States; perhaps she should have planned her strategy differently . . . a telegram to 'Lisha, notifying him of her arrival, instead of this planned surprise.

Tickets are $1. Millie pays with shaking hands, her eyelet gloves already mysteriously soiled.

Inside the vast hall, however, the atmosphere is less frantic. Earnest young Negro boys and girls, in navy blue suits and white shirts, are ushers; they pass out pamphlets titled *The World Negro Betterment & Liberation Union: Salvation Here & Now,* with the glorified likeness of Prince Elihu on the cover. From somewhere out of sight a brass band is playing loudly, quick-stepping military music. (Millie recognizes one of 'Lisha's old favorites—"Tramp! Tramp! Tramp!") Millie is escorted to a seat many rows from the stage, and a hard, uncushioned seat it is, so very different from seats in the Richmond Opera House; she's imagined she came early to the rally, and might sit in the first row center so that, once she removed her veil, Elisha might notice her; but clearly she hasn't come early enough.

" 'Lisha has become a master of The Game," Millie thinks, glancing uneasily about.

And what a variety of men, women, children: some of them dressed as if for Sunday, in colorful pastels, with snap-brim straw hats, patent leather shoes, vests, ties, enormous flowered hats, elbow-length gloves; others, the majority, in more ordinary workaday clothes, though clean and well groomed, like the reliable, devoted Negroes of the Stirlings' household; others visibly poor, with mismatched clothing. Here and there Millie sees, not wishing to see, an obviously deranged person; one of them, an obese woman, sits only a few seats away, angrily fanning herself with a pamphlet and singing what sounds like "There Is a Fountain Filled with Blood"—a hymn Millie has heard Tabitha sing in the kitchen. And here and there in the crowd Millie sees a Caucasian face—except, when she looks more closely, she decides that the individual is only just very light-skinned, in some cases creamy-skinned, with fair brown hair, or red hair; Caucasian features mixed with

Negroid features; a ghost-blend of races that seems to her beautiful, haunting.

Had we had a child together, 'Lisha and I, he would have looked like that.

And yet—is it too late? Millie is not yet forty, and women have been known to have babies well into their forties. And how youthful, how young she is, scarcely changed from the girl she'd been twenty years before when she and 'Lisha were first lovers.

The rally is scheduled to begin at 8 P.M. but the military band plays until 8:20 P.M. when the first of the speakers, the minister of state of the Negro Union, appears to welcome the throng. Following him is an impassioned minister of the treasury, and a Negro with the title of vice-regent; at last, as anticipation in the Garden has grown, at 9:10 P.M. there appears Prince Elihu himself—striding into the spotlights, magnificent in his white costume, gold braid, helmet and ostrich plume, his jewel-studded saber at his side. One hand is raised in triumph and the other extended to the cheering, screaming multitudes in a gesture Millie seems to recognize, the Buddha's promise of peace? love? sympathy?—the palm of the hand open and the fingers outstretched. Yet how *electric* Prince Elihu is, charged with energy as a wild animal.

Millie stares greedily. She has removed her hat, no matter if her white skin draws the attention of people around her, in fact no one notices her, for all are captivated by Prince Elihu as Millie is, captivated and dry-mouthed wondering *Is this my 'Lisha . . . this fierce stalking angry Negro?*

Millie sits too stunned to move as on all sides people leap to their feet in a frenzy of welcome; awkwardly she tries to stand, but sinks back into her seat staring hungrily, desperately at the prancing figure on the stage. *Prince Elihu? 'Lisha?* His skin is much darker than she recalls; the set of his jaws harder, and the eyebrows more severe; his hair lifts in a fine dark woolly aureole; he's taller, more muscular, though lean-bodied like a snake, with a quivering, flamelike energy. So tense! so angry!—why is this man, beloved by so many thousands, angry?—why doesn't he smile to welcome them, instead of standing with booted feet apart, his clenched fist raised above his head and his handsome face uplifted, waiting with barely restrained impatience for the rapturous ovation to subside?

Yes, it *is* Elisha; yet, simultaneously, this rabid furious Negro who has swallowed 'Lisha up. In his blinding white costume it's almost hurtful to look at him. Yet Millie, too, gamely claps; raises her gloved hands to clap, that Prince Elihu might see her; until her hands smart with pain, and she's obliged to give up.

After how many prolonged minutes, the waves of noise begin to fade. And Prince Elihu begins to speak, with theatrical abruptness, his voice raised, raw, or raw-seeming, trembling with emotion; he will address the gathering for ninety minutes, nonstop, in an atmosphere ever more highly charged, and commingled with odors of hair, flesh, sweated clothing, rank animal passion. *The Negro's love of America has not been returned, my brothers and my sisters* Elihu begins his chant. *The Negro's love of America has not been returned.* At first Millie can't make out Elihu's words, she absorbs only the man's ecstatic rage, and begins to feel a sense of helplessness and panic, as on all sides men and women murmur, moan, sob, sway their bodies in sympathy with his chant which they seem to know, words wholly alien to Millie.

What is the tragic history of America cries Prince Elihu motionless as a pillar in the bright burning circle of light *but the history of BROKEN PROMISES. Of LOVE NOT RETURNED.*

Of enslavement of BODY AND SPIRIT.

Of enslavement to this day by FALSE FREEDOM.

Of Negro women scorned as dirt by the white cannibal-devil BUT EVER VICTIMS OF HIS UNCONTROLLABLE LUST; and Negro men EVER THE VICTIMS OF HIS DEVIL-HATRED OF HIMSELF.

And now, by way of Prince Elihu's message, A TEARING ASIDE OF THE VEIL.

A speaking-out of that WHICH HAS ONLY BEEN WHISPERED.

And woe be to those WHO LACK COURAGE.

And woe, woe! to OUR ENEMIES.

For he who is fearful and holds back BETRAYS HIS RACE. And the sacred undeniable AFRICAN BLOOD BEATING IN HIS VEINS.

For he who shrinks from acknowledging his kinship with all dark-skinned peoples, and his enmity toward all whites, BETRAYS HIS RACE. AND THE SACRED UNDENIABLE AFRICAN BLOOD BEATING IN HIS VEINS.

He who withholds his soul's fullest strength, in craven worship of the false gods of the white man, JESUS CHRIST and MAMMON, will not be forgiven; nor will he have a place in AFRICA GLORIFIED.

He who aspires to a BLEACHING-OUT OF THE SOUL *in denying the* WISDOM OF THE FLESH *must come to a tragic end.*

For there are numberless kinds of EVISCERATIONS, *my brothers and sisters, numberless kinds of* LYNCHINGS . . . CASTRATIONS . . . PUBLIC STONINGS . . . LIVE CREMATIONS . . . FLOGGING . . . TARRING . . . HANGING . . . DEATH. *Numberless kinds of* DEATH, *my brothers and sisters, numberless kinds of* DEATH.

Fed screaming through a rock grinder in Bowman, Georgia, while a gathering of the Klan and fellow whites stand by, like a Negro male named Dale Scoggins in March of 1926, O my brothers and sisters THIS IS NOT THE ONLY OUTRAGE OUR RACE MUST ENDURE: DO YOU KNOW? DO YOU KNOW? DO YOU KNOW WHAT ELIHU TELLS YOU?

For history is nearing its fiery conclusion; a second War is close at hand, to be fought by the white cannibal-devils in Europe, and very likely in America; and the long reign of DISEASE AND WICKEDNESS WILL BE OVER.

And no black man must submit to the yoke of soldiery this time: THE LIE THAT THE WORLD IS TO BE MADE SAFE FOR DEMOCRACY. *For we have seen, my brothers and sisters, since 1919 we have seen,* ALL THAT DEMOCRACY IS, IS WHITE PRIVILEGE, WHITE POWER, WHITE INJURY, WHITE LOATHING OF ALL DARK-SKINNED PEOPLES. *For we have seen, since 1919, in the decade following the Negro soldier's return from the European War, ever more atrocities toward our race. A decade of* BLOOD VENGEANCE AGAINST OUR VERY PATRIOTISM. *A decade of* RAGING SCORN AGAINST OUR VERY NOBILITY. *A decade of* SHAME, *my brothers and sisters,* SHAME THAT WE DARE NOT RISE TO STRIKE THE MURDERERS DOWN. *In East St. Louis in the summer of 1919, forty Negroes massacred by a lynch mob . . . and no justice following. In Springfield, Illinois . . . in Los Angeles and San Francisco and Seattle and Philadelphia . . . the rise of the Ku Klux Klan . . . the privilege of the white lynchers . . .* BEATING AND RAPING AND MURDERING AS THEY WISH. *In Texas, nine Negro veterans hanged* AND BESIDE THEM THE PREGNANT WIFE OF ONE OF THE VETERANS. *In Macon County, Georgia,* A LIVE FETUS RIPPED FROM THE WOMB OF A NEGRO WOMAN AND TRAMPLED UNDERFOOT BY WHITE-HOODED MEN. *And no justice following. In ballparks in Louisiana, Alabama, Mississippi, North Florida . . . in public fairgrounds . . . squares . . . before the very court-*

house . . . *LIVE CREMATIONS OF NEGROES FOR THE ENTER-TAINMENT OF WHITES: PUBLIC HANGINGS . . . EVISCERA-TIONS . . . FLOGGINGS . . . TARRING AND FEATHERING . . . CASTRATION BLOODY AND FOUL. . . . And no justice following. And no justice ever to follow. And the rise, my brothers and sisters, of the Klan: and the many admirers of the Klan.*

For the Klan, now five million strong, is America: AMERICA HOODED AND TRUTHFUL IN ITS ANONYMITY.

For the Klan shouts the truth that ALL NEGROES MAY HEAR; while the white cannibal-devil, unhooded, tells lies THAT NEGROES MAY BE DECEIVED.

In West Virginia . . . in the Carolinas . . . in Ohio (boasting more than four hundred thousand members) . . . in New York State and New Jersey and Delaware and Maryland . . . in Illinois, in Michigan, in Indiana, in Tennessee and Kentucky and Arkansas . . . the rise of the Klan . . . AMERICA HOODED AND TRUTHFUL IN ITS ANONYMITY. Five million Klansmen, my brothers and sisters, but behind them wives and children, families, fellow citizens IN SUPPORT OF THE KLAN AND THE KLAN'S AVOWAL TO DESTROY THE NEGRO. Five million Klansmen, my brothers and sisters, and not yet one million Negroes in support of Prince Elihu WHO PREACHES RACE SALVATION AND AFRICA GLORIFIED. In Beaumont, Texas, where a twenty-two-year-old Negro named Willie Shelton was tied with barbed wire and dragged from the bumper of an automobile UNTIL SCREAMING IN AGONY HE DIED not five months ago to this day there is A KLANSMAN MAYOR . . . A KLANSMAN DISTRICT ATTORNEY . . . A KLANS-MAN EPISCOPAL MINISTER . . . AS WELL AS MANY THOU-SANDS OF KLANSMEN AMONG ALL SOCIAL CLASSES . . . and no justice for Negroes: NO JUSTICE TO FOLLOW. And when Dale Scoggins was murdered in March 1926 in Bowman, Georgia, begging for his life, screaming and struggling in terror, fed in unspeakable agony through a rock grinder TO THE CHEERS AND ANIMAL DELIGHT OF MORE THAN ONE HUNDRED WHITE MEN AND A SCATTERING OF WHITE WOMEN was justice to follow: Is justice ever to follow? A KLANSMAN GOVERNOR OF GEORGIA . . . A KLANSMAN STATE ATTORNEY GENERAL . . . A KLANSMAN SUPREME COURT . . . A KLANSMAN COUNTY PROSECUTOR . . . A

KLANSMAN SHERIFF: *each and every one of them dedicated to NE-
GRO ANNIHILATION.*

While Prince Elihu is dedicated to NEGRO SALVATION; *and* AFRICA
RECLAIMED.

While Prince Elihu cries aloud the TRUTH THAT CANNOT BE
DENIED: THE NEGRO'S LOVE OF AMERICA HAS NOT BEEN
RETURNED.

For the Democracy of America, for all dark-skinned races, DOES NOT
EXIST; AND HAS NEVER EXISTED.

And those Negroes who believe that it has, or will, ARE SELF-
DECEIVED VICTIMS.

*For the Communists, Socialists, and their kind, who promise equality of
the races in the class struggle, deliberately lie in declaring that* THE VERY
WORKINGMAN WHO BELONGS TO THE KU KLUX KLAN
WILL BE YOUR BROTHER; *and the Christians who preach of love, and
charity, and the redemption of sin, and forgiveness of enemies, and the re-
ward of Heaven, deliberately lie in exhorting that* CHRISTIANITY IS A
BLACK FAITH: FOR IT IS NOT: IT IS BUT A SNARE AND A
DELUSION: THE MOST CYNICAL OF GAMES.

*For, only consider, in this Christian nation, in the decade following the
War: the systematic reversal of government policies on the hiring of Negroes
for civil service positions, public teaching positions, etc.,* BY SPECIFIC OR-
DER OF THE RACIST WOODROW WILSON. *And this, after num-
berless speeches by Wilson and his fellow Democrats promising reform and
equality of rights* IF THE NEGRO WILL BUT SUPPORT THE WAR
AND ENLIST IN THE ARMY (WHERE THE ARMY WOULD
HAVE HIM). *For the Negro's love of America has not been returned. For
all white men are our enemies, then and now.* FOR AMERICA, FOR US,
HAS NEVER EXISTED.

*Only consider: the refusal of Congress to pass a lynching law; the refusal
of Congress to pass civil rights legislation; the refusal of Congress to honor the*
LAND AND INDEMNITY BILL *sponsored by the only organization to
pride itself upon being* WHOLLY BLACK *and* WHOLLY DEVOTED TO
THE RECLAMATION OF BLACK NOBILITY.

And the rise, in this past decade, of the KLAN.

The rise, my brothers and sisters, of THE WHITE CANNIBAL-
DEVILS SWORN TO DESTROY US.

Five million Klansmen, thus ten or fifteen million Klansmen in spirit. Five million, ten and fifteen million, how many more million in the Kingdom of the Damned: eleven Klansmen governors . . . yet more senators . . . numberless congressmen, from every district . . . mayors . . . councilmen . . . sheriffs, policemen, federal agents . . . lawyers . . . millionaire businessmen . . . clergy of the so-called Christian faith . . . schoolteachers . . . workingmen: LOYAL MEMBERS OF THE KLAN SWORN TO DESTROY US.

So it is my brothers and my sisters on this historic night of 19 June 1929 upon this great occasion of the FIRST ANNUAL UNIVERSAL NEGRO CONFRATERNITY RALLY sponsored by THE WORLD NEGRO BETTERMENT & LIBERATION UNION, I, Prince Elihu, declare to you that we must unite that THE NEGRO RACE BE SAVED; and AFRICA RECLAIMED; and COLONIAL DESPOTISM OVER-THROWN; and THE WHITE CANNIBAL-DEVIL DEFEATED.

For all that we HAVE BEEN, we WILL BE AGAIN.

For the FUTURE IS OURS.

FOR HONOR IS THE SUBJECT OF OUR STORY.

FOR I SAY TO YOU MY BROTHERS AND MY SISTERS: HONOR IS THE SUBJECT OF OUR STORY.

Thus, the First Annual Universal Negro Confraternity Rally of 19 June 1929, which would also be the last such rally; and at its conclusion past 11 P.M. Millicent Stirling is too exhausted and distraught to rise from her seat, she's been crying silently for a long time, the front of her stylish silk dress is damp with tears, her black straw hat has fallen, or has been knocked, onto the floor; she has given herself up as years ago she'd given herself up to the nightmare of childbirth, a roaring in her ears, a roaring in all her veins, she's given herself up to grief, to shame, to the anguish of love, her heart is broken, this throbbing boiling pain is her heart, she will give herself up henceforth to sorrow, to middle age and eventually old age and death, she's scarcely aware of her surroundings, or even that Prince Elihu gleaming with perspiration like an oiled idol has left the stage, and the stage lights have been lowered, and the lights in the hall have been raised, she doesn't notice how she's being worriedly regarded by several of the neatly dressed young Negro ushers, for by this time most of the Garden has emptied out and Millie remains, a hunched broken figure in her seat—*What's wrong ma'am? What you cryin' about ma'am? You need some help there ma'am?*—but in her dove-gray silk dress and matching stockings, in her white eyelet gloves and her white, white skin, the pride of her white skin, its shame, its outrage, its horror from which there can be, so long as she lives, no salvation, she doesn't hear.

In Old Muirkirk

I

Am I defeated?—*I am not.*
    Do I smell of mortality?—*I do not.*
Will I return to my former triumphs?—*I will. I will.*

At last in a fierce-howling March 1932 Katrina dies. If Abraham Licht could blame Katrina's death on the infamous Wall Street Crash of some years previous he would, he would!

Katrina has died, and is buried in the village cemetery but Abraham Licht, an aging (yet not-old) man himself—ivory-pale filmy-floating hair grown past his ears, though papery-thin across the crown of his head, eyes sharp with suspicion and mouth quivering with irony—knows better. He knows the household will never be rid of the old woman.

"Listen. There she is, Katrina scolding me again," Abraham says, cocking his head as wind, or winds, whistle in the chimney and tear along the eaves like shrieking bats. Abraham shakes his head in disgust. "Katrina, dear: *do* leave us alone! We must get on with our lives, you know." Is Abraham joking, or serious, often it isn't clear; as, now, it isn't at all clear; for Rosamund pauses to regard her husband with fond, worried eyes; and little Melanie, playing on the floor with a rag-lynx that Katrina sewed for her, stares blinking and smiling up at her father, perplexed. Darian, entering the kitchen, feels he's entering a scene that has all but played itself out and he doesn't know his lines or what is expected of him. Then, hearing the wind, the perpetual wind of Muirkirk, and seeing the expression on his father's face that is both mock-grave and genuinely alarmed, he supposes it's Katrina again, or in any case the subject of Katrina. "Y'hear, Darian?" Abraham asks, a forefinger upraised. "That old woman scolding. Laughing. At us. At *me*."

They hadn't parted on the most civil of terms, it seems. For Katrina hadn't approved of Abraham Licht marrying a "girl younger than Millie" and she certainly hadn't approved of Abraham Licht fathering "a daughter who should be a granddaughter" and most of all she hadn't approved of Abraham Licht's most recent bankruptcy—no matter that, as he'd explained dozens of times, *it was not his fault but the fault of certain wealthy manipulators of the stock market.*

Darian, like Rosamund, chooses to interpret Abraham's jesting about Katrina as simply that, jesting. Sometimes the cry is clearly the wind, sometimes it's the cry of a hawk, an owl, a wild creature in the marsh, sometimes it resembles a baby's cry and sometimes, yes, you might say it resembles Katrina's voice lifted in annoyance, but at the moment the sound is obviously the wind—isn't it? At any rate, it's growing fainter.

"She's retreating for now, back into the swamp," Abraham says thoughtfully. "But we'll never be rid of her—never."

II

A chill windy evening in April 1932 and Darian is experimenting with his "echo-chamber piano," an instrument of his own invention, in his high-ceilinged music studio at the rear of the old Church of the Nazarene, and he hears a light footfall behind him; not the child's, for Melanie always runs head-on into "Uncle" Darian's studio no matter how many times she's been reprimanded; and surely not Abraham Licht's—for Abraham would have made it a point to knock formally on the door, in ironic acknowledgment that, patriarch of the family as he is, and owner of the property, he might not be welcome in his eccentric composer-son's studio.

Not Melanie, and not Abraham. Darian turns, calmly. "Yes?—oh, hello."

Darian speaks calmly. A calm smile. Though so nervous he has botched an intricate passage of crossed triads he's been playing, fortunately this composition for echo-chamber piano isn't the sort of music one can easily judge is botched or played with perfect command, and it's natural for him to lift his eyes to his father's wife's face, and smile. Though this is the first time (rapidly he's calculating) since he came here to live eighteen months, three and a half weeks ago, that Rosamund has entered his studio alone or uninvited.

Strange how, even now that Katrina has died, and the house is relatively empty, Darian and Rosamund are rarely alone together. And, alone together, rarely do they speak.

Now the woman's image floats in a cloudy mirror propped against one of the pews Darian dragged into the room, and Darian at his keyboard observes it calmly. Rosamund facing him, yet in the mirror in profile. His fingers return to the keys, plucking out delicate, subtle notes, less strident now, for these notes are being struck like harp strings, even the strings' vibrations are music; even Darian's slightly faltering, thrown-off playing is part of the composition, the instrument, the music itself. *Notation: music may be interrupted at this point. An air of calm surprise!* Rosamund stands motionless for a beat or two, listening. Darian wonders what she hears. He knows what he hears, but what does another person hear? As all composers must wonder.

Darian's father's wife. A city-bred woman, a woman born to affluence, yet a woman, as Darian has learned, not to be swiftly summed up, or understood. Now she's a country wife, a Muirkirk wife, the mother of a three-year-old, she lets her smoke-colored hair loose to her shoulders, sometimes tied back by a scarf; she wears men's trousers, wide-legged slacks and oversized sweaters, several of Abraham Licht's formerly white, starched cotton shirts that billow about her like maternity blouses. Since her pregnancy she walks solidly on her heels as if still balancing a swollen stomach on her thin frame; there's a boyish raffish air about her, a habit of smiling quizzically, though sometimes, like now, she's strangely still, even solemn. In the kitchen, at Katrina's ancient iron stove, Rosamund has been baking sourdough bread, the house is filled with its warm yeasty delicious smell, and Rosamund's already soiled apron is splotched with flour. Darian murmurs again,

"Yes?" and Rosamund smiles that quizzical smile, and says, "I thought you called *me*."

Calmly regarding each other across a space of approximately six feet, now that the echo-chamber strings have ceased their vibrating, in exquisite silence.

III

All defeat not extinction Abraham Licht records in his journal *is but temporary.*

His journal, his voluminous memoir. A ledger whose pages have been covered in handwriting and in coded hieroglyphics, into which loose sheets of paper have been inserted. *Once the victim identifies his enemies he is no longer a victim. For revenge is the final act.*

True, Abraham Licht has retired "into the country" but he has not retired from business. In his seventy-second year he's never felt more vigorous, more energetic; his brain swirling ceaselessly with plans, plots, bold new ventures.

"Once I regain some of what I've lost, I will begin again."

Abraham needs to regain only a fraction of what he has lost, and he tells himself this is crucial. The merest 1/2000 of those lost millions, which would give him more than $12,000 to purchase a partnership in a cider mill in Paie-des-Sables ("apple cider" being but the mill's official, legal product) or an investment in a Thoroughbred horse ranch in Manitowick or laboratory equipment that would allow him to manufacture Liebknecht's Formula himself—which, given its tranquilizing effect, would prove hugely popular in this troubled, anxiety-ridden nation. If only the elixir could be manufactured in sufficient quantity, distributed, marketed, advertised, sold . . . he'd be a millionaire again, many times over! Of course, the small pharmaceutical company in Easton, Pennsylvania, that had been selling the elixir went bankrupt shortly after 29 October 1929, without having paid Abraham Licht more than $75,000 owed him.

"If I had but that $75,000 . . . like Archimedes with a lever, what might I accomplish!"

Brooding these ever-lengthening spring days upon a new business enterprise . . . a legitimate variation of The Game; legitimate in the sense of not being illegal. For since marrying Rosamund whom he loves beyond his own life, and since the birth of beautiful little Melanie, Abraham can't bear the thought of even the possibility of being sent away to prison or indicted to stand trial. (How close he'd come, back in '28! On the very eve of his wedding to Rosamund, in fact; when the Parris Clinic was under investigation by the New York State attorney general, and that fool Bies reluctant to pay the proper "fine.") This new invention, however, as he's tried to explain to Rosamund in their bed at night (for some reason, Abraham prefers to speak to Rosamund about such matters when they're lying peacefully in the dark and when the sharp-eyed woman can't see his face), would involve the manufacture not of a mere "product" but of the idea of a product; the fleeting, glistening, inviolable image of a product; to be sold to businessmen and politicians for their private use, who might then broadcast it to the American consumer who would then purchase, or vote for, not the product itself but the *idea*. "For why not systematically and scientifically manufacture those idiosyncratic notions fools have in their heads?—why allow them to remain haphazard or but partly controlled?" Abraham mused grandly. Rosamund murmured she didn't understand, could he please explain more clearly? Abraham told her that the germ of the venture first came to him during his stint as a government agent in Washington when it came to be cheerfully known that Warren Harding had been elected President of the United States only because, by the merest comical (or cynical) chance, the man had the appearance of a "Roman senator"!—not that the American voter had the slightest idea of what a Roman senator might have looked like.

"The essence is, public opinion can be manipulated at will," Abraham said, "provided of course there's enough money to invest in advertising, in the right quarters."

Rosamund laughed, or may have sighed. "But where is the satisfaction, Abraham, in that sort of thing? How could one take pride in accomplishing something 'unreal'—and under such circumstances— making money, being elected to public office—"

Abraham cut her off impatiently. Rosamund was an intelligent woman, yet often not a very smart woman. "Pride, my dear," he said, "is in our *technique.*"

Until the last breath is drawn, Abraham Licht writes, *the last blow has not been dealt.*

In his memoir he's making a list of enemies: the men whom one day he will boldly and publicly name as the manipulators of the so-called Crash of 1929, in which billions of investors' dollars were lost. He, Abraham Licht, will compile a dossier against them and file a complaint with the Justice Department! (Though he's learned to his surprise that an old rival of his and Gaston Bullock Means's is now director of the Bureau of Investigation—J. Edgar Hoover.) These men are Richard F. Whitney of the Banker's Pool; Charles E. Mitchell of the National City Bank; the officers of the House of Morgan; the directors of the Federal Reserve Bank; John D. Rockefeller, Sr.; the "Aluminum King" Andrew Mellon, Hoover's Secretary of the Treasury; and the Republican President Hoover himself, who maintains three years after the catastrophe, that nothing serious has happened to the economy.

Abraham confides in Rosamund, and more recently in Darian who has come to live with them following the bankruptcy of the Westheath School of Music, that he will not be silenced, and will not be bought off or bribed; nor will he slink away in defeat— "Or blow out my brains like so many of my brother victims."

For indeed, a number of Abraham Licht's Manhattan associates have killed themselves. Or sunk into such dissolute habits of drinking bootleg liquor, it has come to the same thing.

Am I defeated?— *I am not.*
Do I smell of mortality?— *I do not.*
Will I return to my former triumphs?— *I will. I will.*

In his secret mirror, of which even Katrina knew nothing: a noble countenance from which, through suffering, all excess flesh has burned away . . . a forehead stark, ridged with bone beneath the papery skin . . . skin drawn tight across the cheekbones (not creased and flabby, repulsive, like that of others his age) . . . the eyes shrewd and ever-watchful, clear as washed glass. And, framing the face, a floating halo of hair suddenly white, purely white, very fine, very thin, diaphanous as milkweed pollen. Why, he has passed through the Fire; he *has* passed through; and the "fainting-spell" (or brain seizure, or stroke) he suffered in 1929 hasn't touched him at all.

"Fate, do your worst! I am no craven coward."

IV

I thought you called me.

Not I. My music.

Yet your music is you.

Impulsively he'd seized her hand, a warm rather grubby-floury hand, and would have pulled her to him, to kiss her, or to try to kiss her; but, with a childlike squeal, as if this were but a game and not achingly, heartrendingly real, his father's young wife managed to turn, an elbow in his ribs, it's an accident, they're panting and laughing and little Melanie rushes into the studio laughing, shrieking—"Uncle Dar-yn! Play for us like you were! Don't stop!"

Darling I will never stop. My music for you, and for your mother, never will I stop.

His elderly father's wife. His elderly father's daughter.

Can I? Dare I? Must I?

"Like this, Melanie!—no, sweetheart, not so hard! Like *this*."

Rosamund stands barefoot beside the kitchen table, little Melanie in the crook of one strong arm, balanced on her hip, mother and daughter absorbed in the proper playing of the "icicle" Darian has made for Melanie (a musical instrument of his own invention, several lengths of silver attached to a silver ring of about four inches in diameter, that, when shaken, gives off lovely delicately varying notes) . . . not conscious of how Darian stares . . . yearning, anxious, greedy . . . defiantly happy . . . not conscious (or is she? has she been, since the other day?) of how warmly and urgently his blood pulses, his very heart swells, and the sinewy-ropy vein of his groin.

Look at me. I love you.

I won't look! Melanie and I are making music.

Darian laughs, and shrugs, and walks out of the kitchen. Abandoning them to the icicle. Listening from the threshold of his studio to the chiming, rippling notes, a music in code? But whose code? And what does it mean?

On one of his mysterious journeys Abraham Licht acquires a second-hand telescope with which, as he says, he will study the stars.

For long ago in another lifetime he knew a good deal about the constellations: how the conjunction of certain stars, planets, moons, influences human life, both on the level of the individual and in the aggregate. Now, unfortunately, he's forgotten nearly everything.

In time, when she's old enough to comprehend, he will teach his daughter (his only remaining daughter) the wisdom of the Heavens. That, in turn, she may teach *her* children.

For now that Time begins to accelerate there's suddenly so much to *know*, and to *do*.

The challenge is to calibrate precisely the positioning of all the Heavenly bodies on the morning of 3 September 1929, when the market (and Abraham Licht's fortune) was at an all-time high; and to calibrate their positioning on 24 October, when the Crash, as it was afterward to be called, began.

And if he doesn't live to fulfill the task, then Melanie, blood of his blood, spirit of spirit, must take over.

An ambitious project, a major work of economic theory. Yet there are others.

For his brain is buzzing these days, and these nights, with ideas.

While his young wife sleeps a thin, disturbed sleep in the next room. A door locked between them, for all in this room is secret as he's tried to explain to her. Abraham Licht seated at his noble ruin of a rolltop desk calculating the return he'd realized by 1935 if he invests $12,000 in the Paie-des-Sables cider mill (for though Prohibition has been repealed there's still a fortune to be made in such enterprises provided shipping and distribution are in one's own control, and not that of organized crime) compared with the return he might realize if he invests in the beautiful derelict Manitowick ranch. And of course, there's Liebknecht's Formula which is perhaps the most promising of the ventures provided the Food and Drug Administration doesn't throw up obstacles. (For America has changed so much since the days of Abraham

Licht's boyhood and youth, how many decades ago, such a grid now of
absurd confining punitive laws, regulations, "standards," requirements!)
Abraham calculates too the amount of money at 3 percent interest
since 1 November 1929 owed him by his enemies Whitney, Mitchell,
Rockefeller, Morgan, et al. and drafts letters, petitions, briefs in which
he sets forth his claims as succinctly and irrefutably as possible.

Copies of these, he will very likely send off to J. Edgar Hoover as
well. "The man will remember me, I hope. I will sign myself 'Abraham
Licht, formerly Hine.' "

*Control, control and yet again control. For otherwise we are but beasts of
the field.*

Through the rainy spring and into the abruptly hot, damp and
insect-ridden days of summer Abraham Licht, sleepless much of the
night, is aware of Katrina hovering close by. That woman the villagers
whispered was his mother yet who was not his mother yet plagues him
from the grave behaving as if she *is.*

"Woman, let me be! Mercy, please."

He'd been stunned, and deeply mortified, to bring his beautiful
young bride and their year-old daughter to such a place. From their elegant residence on Fifth Avenue to this shabby domicile in Muirkirk at
the edge of a marsh; this building part church and part house out of
whose rotted raingutters foot-high saplings and lichen were growing.
Inside, the ceilings were splotched with raindrops like tears and the
floors were tilted as if, close beneath, rocks and wild vegetations were
pushing up. "My darling, this will be only temporary," Abraham promised Rosamund; and Rosamund said, with a surprising, robust laugh,
"Why, Abraham—all life is temporary. Let's be happy while we can."
As at the Parris Clinic she'd been most resilient when at her most
despairing.

In the midst of his calculations Abraham pauses, hearing a screech-
ing close outside the window; the flutter of feathery wings; he catches a
glimpse of red-glaring eyes, a sharp beak, scaly legs and talons. . . . Perhaps he's been asleep: he forces his eyes open wider, thrashes his stiffened legs and to his chagrin wakes the woman sleeping beside him; for
he isn't at his rolltop desk (is he?) but in the big old brass bed; one of
his wives (but which wife?) startled beside him. "Abraham? What is it?
You've been having a nightmare." There's a child fretting in a crib,

kicking at its blanket. Which child this is, his firstborn Thurston, or tough little Harwood, or angel-Millie, or . . . is it Darian? Esther? the newest, youngest baby whose name he's never been told? *Why, Abraham. All life is temporary. You must have known.*

"Do I 'mind,' Father? Of course not. A little manual work is good for me, I think."

Darian, the breadwinner of the Licht family. With his scattering of jobs in Muirkirk and vicinity: he isn't just choirmaster of the Lutheran church, piano instructor to a dozen talentless pupils, substitute teacher at the high school, he's a seasonal employee at the canning factory and, on weekends in summer, an orchard picker. Bronze-tanned and his fair hair bleached in streaks by the sun, his eyes light in his genial face; this tall lanky son who'd once been so anxious and uncertain, Abraham had gazed upon him with annoyed pity.

Darian, Rosamund and little Melanie laughing together in the kitchen. Fooling with one of Darian's absurd musical instruments. Falling silent as Abraham pushes into the room, their eyes glancing guiltily in his direction.

"An unusual position for *me*. Bringing no income into my household."

Darian even pays for the gasoline in Abraham's 1927 Packard touring car which, fortunately, Abraham doesn't drive very often any longer. There's an ominous rattling in the engine and he's fearful of being marooned somewhere in the countryside miles from home.

Darian himself walks into town, or rides his bicycle. He and Rosamund on bicycles speeding like truant schoolchildren along the Muirkirk Pike.

Moreover, Abraham is fast losing patience with Darian's musical compositions. His ridiculous experiments. That clanging, plucking, thumping, ka-booming in the young man's so-called studio. (Which addition Darian built himself with unfinished pieces of lumber, strips of insulation and beaverboard nailed in panels in front of which he'd cleverly hung the most attractive curtains, drapes and tapestries out of Abraham's store of "antiques." The roof is a mad amalgam of lumber, hammered tin and pieces of slate—"Almost one hundred percent waterproof," Darian boasts.) Abraham complains to Rosamund of how, when Darian was a young child, his health— "His heart condition"— ruled out a career as a musical prodigy; he'd had the talent, but talent alone isn't enough. Now when money is needed so badly for Abraham to purchase the cider mill, or the horse ranch, or equipment to manufacture Liebknecht's Formula, it's maddening that Darian squanders his time writing music no one will ever hear let alone applaud or pay for. "If Darian wants to squander his time," Rosamund says, "—surely it's his time to squander."

Abraham tries to reason with Darian. Pointing out that there's a fortune to be made in popular song writing. "Why can't you apply your skill to writing tunes like 'Home Sweet Home,' 'Sweet Georgia Brown,' 'Look for the Silver Lining'? Even today when no one has any money people will buy sheet music; hundreds of thousands of people with simple, childlike tastes. The more inane and repetitive the ditties— 'On the Sunny Side of the Street' for instance—'Tea for Two'—'My Blue Heaven'—the more popular. Why can't you, Darian, my son, compose songs as catchy and idiotic as these?" To which Darian coolly replies, "My idiocy isn't of the moneymaking sort, Father." Worse yet, Darian is continually inventing musical instruments: the "icicle"; "glass-winds" of old bottles, goblets, Venetian wineglasses; a thirty-string lyre that sounds like a cat in heat; a woodblock marimba with bamboo resonators; various sorts of drums and percussive instruments; a miniature violin; an "echo-chamber" piano; and a quarter-tone piano . . . so that, as Darian has excitedly explained, he can play microtones and actually hear the music he's been composing for the forty-three-interval scale. ("And you'll be the only person who will hear it, probably," Abraham remarked.)

Rosamund warns he'll be driving Darian away from Muirkirk if he isn't careful. Abraham says hotly the fool is his son, to drive away if he pleases.

V

Gradually it comes to light that someone is spying on Abraham Licht.

His enemies, the Wall Street manipulators. That's to say the professional agents, very likely Pinkerton's detectives, in their employ.

Footprints are discovered one morning in the rain-softened earth close by the rear of the house. And strangers' voices, murmurous, derisive, are frequently heard in the distance, borne by the caprices of the wind. One night Abraham is astonished to discover that his cosmological notations are missing; there's a hairline crack in the lens of his telescope. Another night he's terrified by a ghostly face at the bedroom window as Rosamund in her nightgown is turning down the bed; which hellish vision vanishes when Abraham shouts and throws one of his shoes through the window.

Another night, in the humid heat of midsummer, as Abraham, Rosamund and Darian are sitting at dinner, with Melanie in her baby chair, there's a crackling noise outside as if someone or something is crashing through the underbrush. "*That* is not Katrina," Abraham says ominously, chewing his food. "*That* is a stranger."

In his journal (kept locked in his rolltop desk) Abraham notes in a steady hand *I have scorch'd the snake not killed it.* Though he can't comprehend how Rockefeller, Mellon, Morgan and the rest learned of his secret plans to bring them to justice since he hadn't yet written to J. Edgar Hoover nor had he ever spoken of his plans to Rosamund. Unless . . . their Pinkerton spies have broken into this room, read the most recent pages in the journal, and reported to their employers. Unless . . . in Muirkirk chatting with someone, Darian unwittingly let drop information.

Until the last breath is drawn the last blow has not been dealt.

So it happens that Abraham returns from one of his mysterious journeys with a double-barreled 12-gauge Winchester shotgun with silver trim, and several boxes of shells. Rosamund, never having seen such a weapon before at such close quarters, is frightened; and Darian simply blinks and stares in silence. "You needn't worry," Abraham tells them in a voice heavy with sarcasm, "—I haven't spent a penny of Darian's precious earnings. This gun came to me honestly in a game of stud poker over at Paie-des-Sables."

VI

Locally it's begun to be whispered, as Darian learns from his friend Aaron Deerfield, that Abraham Licht has "millions of dollars" buried somewhere on his property. That, before the banks closed, he'd managed to withdraw his fortune.

"His 'fortune'!" Darian laughed sadly. "Well. Father would be proud of such tales, if he knew."

VII

When the market initially began to drop on 24 October 1929, that infamous day later to be known as Black Thursday, Abraham Licht in the company of four other investors from Manhattan was in Miami contemplating investment properties on the ocean and on Biscayne Bay. He and the others flew back north immediately in their privately chartered Cessna to find that things weren't nearly so bad as news bulletins had indicated . . . since a sizable sum of money, $240 million it was afterward confirmed, had been pooled by Wall Street's wealthiest men, meeting secretly in the House of Morgan, to keep stocks afloat. The next day, only half as many shares were traded; the general mood was less grim, if not wholly optimistic; Abraham Licht counseled himself not to worry, though each of his stocks was down: AT&T by eighteen points, Bethlehem Steel by twenty-three, Kennecott Copper by thirty. His most recent acquisition, Electro-Vision, an electronics research company located in Rutherford, New Jersey, which was rapidly developing a brilliant new form of broadcasting to conjoin radio and visual images, as on a movie screen, "one day to be beamed into every American household for enormous profits to shareholders," had tragically plummeted and would disappear within weeks, causing the suicide of its visionary executive; but Liebknecht's Formula, on the market as simply Liebknecht, Inc., had held its own. "If I refuse to panic as a coward would, and sell short, if I wait for the market to rally and rise, as it's sure to do, I will be untouched." Already it was being announced in the newspapers that the crisis was past. The federal government had issued a statement that there had been in fact no crisis, only a "hysteria" of selling provoked by an unknown cause. And fools with no financial expertise were the ones rushing to banks to withdraw their savings. . . .

A day, and another day, of reassuring calm in Wall Street; cautious optimism; Abraham's stocks were holding steady or, as in the case of

Standard Oil, rallying. The secretary of the treasury declared that "the economy had never been in healthier condition" . . . John D. Rockefeller, Sr., and his son were pictured busily buying common stock . . . Abraham's Manhattan business acquaintances, by this time fortified by whiskey, declared they were all "holding fast."

And then came Sunday: a vast relief throughout the city, as the damned market was closed.

But then, unfortunately, Monday morning . . . when Abraham Licht, having decided to sell three million dollars of his holdings, found himself in a stampede with virtually everyone else in the country: nine million shares sold on the Exchange, four million on the Curb, losses of more than ten billion.

Ten billion—!

"It can't be," Abraham Licht repeatedly said, to his anxious young wife and alone, to his ghastly mirrored reflection. "*It can't be.*"

Like many another investor, Abraham had frequently daydreamt of a financial catastrophe in which he and a small number of shrewd thinkers walked away unscathed, with more profits than ever; he had never daydreamt of a catastrophe in which he was but one of hundreds of thousands, swept away by a demonic flood.

And the following morning, Abraham's worst fears came true: there was pandemonium, outright terror; a true Panic—searing the eyeballs, coating the tongue with slime, loosening the bowels; the most extraordinary of all waves of selling in the history of the world: sixteen million shares on the Exchange, seven million on the Curb, *thirty billion dollars lost within a few hours.* Kennecott Copper disappeared. Cole Motors fell off sixty points, seventy points, ninety points. Westinghouse, in which Abraham had invested only the month before, dropped to one-third of its former value. And AT&T and Bethlehem Steel, Mexican Seaboard Certificates, Fleischmann's Yeast, Pan American Western, Liebknecht, Inc. . . . . " 'Licht' is extinguished," Abraham laughingly declared, making his way like a somnambulist through a throng of yelling, jeering, perspiring, weeping strangers on the floor of the stock exchange. "*It's as if 'Licht' had never been.*"

Yet he was spared the indignity of collapsing in the street like so many others.

And when he did collapse, early in the morning of the following day, it was in his wife's arms; and Rosamund, like one steeled in disaster from a previous lifetime, as a woman to whom Death had frequently, seductively beckoned, telephoned for an ambulance at once to take the stricken, ashen-faced man, the father of her infant daughter, to Columbia Presbyterian Hospital.

IX

Midsummer. Abraham Licht in smart oyster-white linen suit and Panama hat makes a day's journey to Manitowick, $800 in his pocket to show his good faith, his firm resolve to raise more, but, when he arrives, he learns to his horror that the horses are all dead! . . . burned alive, all nine of them, in a fire that took place a few nights before, when lightning struck the stable. (In Manitowick, the fire is considered "suspicious in origin," since the horses were heavily insured.) But Abraham Licht is appalled. The horses are dead? Nine beautiful English Thoroughbreds, dead? . . . And not one was rescued or survived? . . .

When he returns to Muirkirk he shrinks from the embrace of his young wife, for the sickening smell of burnt animal flesh, burnt animal hair, the terrible smell of animal agony, has seeped into his clothing.

The $800 he returns to his son with trembling fingers.

"Too late, Darian! I came too late to save them!"

Midsummer.

Which is Eternity.

Mist rising in slow tendrils over the swamp. The random joyous shrieks of unknown birds. Heat that begins at dawn, heavy, damp, hypnotic . . . Shall we go hunting? Shall we shoot us a pretty-feathered bird? Or an ugly scrawny bird with a bald head?

In knee-high rubber boots, in an old candy-striped shirt, now collarless, stuffed into trousers that hang from his wasted frame, the soiled Panama hat set jauntily on his head, shotgun under one arm, little Melanie, shivering in delight, perched high on his shoulder, Shall we go hunting, dear? My sweet precious dear? My only pretty one?

But Rosamund, spying from the kitchen garden, calls out sharply. No. No. *No.*

* * *

Late summer.

That heavy sulfurous season rife with secrets.

For though they would steal away his notations (now carefully codified), or hide them amid the many thousands of pages of his memoir, or scatter them beneath the desk where they can scarcely be retrieved, they cannot penetrate his thoughts; his powerful thoughts; his private cosmology.

For though their hired agents would peer at him through their telescopes, and record every one of his movements, every one of his words, it is only by day they dare approach; the night is his.

The night: which is rife with secrets.

Soon, very soon, when *she* is asleep, he will take his daughter to show her how the sky is a great living ocean . . . black yet translucent, lightless yet pricked with light . . . stars beyond counting and beyond all imagination save Abraham Licht's.

For the sky, dear Melanie, is a navigable sea upon whose earthy shore we stand upside down; on our heads. The sky is a sea in which fools drown, lacking the proper maps.

A bone-bright Moon, making shadows.

Vague red Mars, hovering over the tallest peak of the church's roof.

The Big Dipper, with its confused message; great Taurus, with a warning (is it a warning? or a command?); the Pleiades clustered and winking, oh, the sky is rife with secrets, like the night, like the long marsh summer which is Eternity.

X

Suspecting that his wife is pregnant but daring not to confront her— "Did you imagine I could be deceived, the child is *mine*?"

But no, it's a scene he knows beforehand he can't play except mawkishly, most amateurishly.

Barely able to sit still on the back porch, in the late-summer twilight, as Darian plays "Melanie Is Four"—a song for Melanie's fourth birthday— on marimba, "icicle" and miniature violin; and, a surprise for Abraham, who's after all this child's father, Melanie herself sings . . . For she,

Rosamund and Darian have planned this, evidently. "D'you like my song, Dad-dy? Uncle Darian wrote it for me." Abraham smiles, kisses the child, perhaps she's his child and perhaps she isn't, how like Millie's sweet wavering soprano at that age, but perhaps Millie wasn't his child, either. "No, my dear. I don't like your birthday song. But who am I, to matter?" Abraham mildly inquires, rising, with mock-elderly dignity, to make his exit as Darian, Rosamund and the astonished child stare after him.

This, the final year of what the vulgar world would call my "life."

Shouting!—panicked!—an enormous bird is trapped in the parlor, flying from window to window, striking the glass, recoiling, frantic pumping wings, death throes in midair, it must have blundered down through the chimney, only a starling but it seems to Abraham Licht the size of a vulture, with a vulture's jabbing beak, of course it's Katrina playing another of her cruel jests, he's striking his hands together *Out! out! out! Back to hell where you belong you evil old woman!* Stomping so hard he breaks several of the weakened floorboards, his handsome ruin of a face distorted in fear and anger and Rosamund tries to reason with him, it's only a bird, a frightened bird, maybe we can capture it in a pillowcase, but Abraham turns on her blind, shoving at her, where's his shotgun? where has she hidden his shotgun? and Rosamund rushes into the kitchen to snatch up Melanie and run with her outside, out onto the Muirkirk Pike where by lucky chance it's Darian who comes bicycling along and not a neighbor— "Help me! Help us! Oh God anything, to get her away from *him*."

It's the first time that Rosamund has so spoken. It's the first time that Darian has held her tight as she holds him—tight, tight!

The poor trapped starling dies of a broken neck. Its limp, black-feathered body lying harmless as one of Melanie's rag dolls on the carpet. No need therefore for the hefty 12-gauge double-barreled shotgun Abraham Licht has oiled and primed for emergency use, hidden away in his locked study.

"And if Father had used it . . . ?" Darian thinks, sick with worry. "And if I hadn't been there . . . ?"

In secret Darian discusses his father with Dr. Aaron Deerfield, who tells him to bring Abraham in for an examination, but of course Darian can't convince his father to come with him, nor can he convince the suspicious old man to allow Deerfield to visit him at home. "Why, Deerfield the sawbones must be one hundred years old by now," Abraham says scathingly. "The man was ever incompetent in his lifetime, now in the boneyard he must be non compos mentis indeed." Darian explains that Aaron Deerfield is Dr. Deerfield's son, Darian's own age, but Abraham stalks off chuckling as if it's all a joke, but a joke that's gone far enough.

Rosamund cautions *We can't hurt him. Not even his pride.*

Rosamund, weeping, says *We can't provoke him into hurting us.*

And: *He did save my life, Darian. I can't betray him.*

In town, after choir rehearsal at the Lutheran church, Darian drops by Aaron Deerfield's house for a drink, and counsel. "It's the aftermath of the stroke, probably. Or maybe he's had another mild stroke. And there's what is called 'senility.' ... I'm sorry, Darian." Darian can't think of any reply. *He* is sorry, too; yet feeling sorry isn't quite enough; he's heard of elderly and not-so-elderly men in the Chautauqua Valley who've gone on rampages with sledgehammers, ice picks, rakes, axes, you don't need a 12-gauge shotgun for slaughter.

It's this evening that Aaron casually asks Darian how his sister Esther is; and Darian says so far as he knows Esther is fine . . . well, Esther is a busy, energetic woman, to be truthful Esther has been involved in picketing, protests, demonstrations and she's been in jail . . . crusading in western New York, Ohio, Indiana and Illinois with the National Birth Control League, Margaret Sanger's people; she's a friend of Sanger's, a trusted aide; mostly women, though a few men, who've pledged themselves to what they call direct action (meaning angry, dangerous mobs, arrests and police brutality, jail sentences, lurid publicity in all the papers) in violating state laws that forbid the dissemination of any and all birth control information.

Aaron Deerfield refills his guest's glass with ale, and his own. He sighs. He's still unmarried, in his early thirties: he'd been engaged to a local girl, and is now unengaged; Darian knows some of his friend's personal history, but not much. One of only a few general practitioners in Muirkirk and vicinity, Dr. Deerfield is a busy man; a tired man; an affable man; a lonely man; prematurely balding, with thick-lensed glasses (so like his father, now dead, to see him in the street is to see his father,

an unnerving apparition); a man accustomed to telling others what's
wrong with them, and how to remedy it; yet now baffled, staring at his
clean, short-clipped fingernails. "I'd always thought, y'know, Darian,
that Esther and I . . . might marry," Aaron says. "She would be my
nurse, at least until children came." Darian, embarrassed, wants to ask,
Yes but did you love her? did you ask her to marry you? but only murmurs that might've been a good thing. (Though thinking, why? His sister a doctor's wife, and not an independent woman? Confined to
Muirkirk for life?) "I can't comprehend how Esther who was always so
sweet . . . could behave so recklessly. With that female Sanger. The lot
of them, y'know, are Communist atheists who would tear down the
very fabric of society, don't you think?" Aaron asks anxiously; and Darian, draining his glass, says with a neutral smile, "My friend, I'm just a
musician, what's it matter what *I* think?"

XI

Dares not confront her. Or them. Though keenly aware of her small
swelling breasts, her hard swelling belly with its bluish pallor, sin pulled
tight as a drum's.

Spying on them, the lovers. Though they must be aware of him for
how innocently they behave: never so much as touching, not even fingertips, while he's a witness.

To Darian's astonishment, and the surprise of the Lutheran congregation, Abraham Licht turns up one Sunday for the ten o'clock service
in snappy red suspenders, a yellow scarf knotted about his old-man wat-
tled throat, in handsome if soiled homburg and those fine hand-sewn
leather shoes promised to last a lifetime (as they will); to hear the
twenty-member choir sing choruses and arias from Handel's *Messiah*,
with creditable results. Abraham, aficionado of grand opera, a musical
elitist, finds himself moved by this country-church choir and has to
suppose that, yes, his son has had something to do with the beauty of
their combined, thrilling voices. Yet abruptly he slips away before the
service ends for a pulse has begun beating in his head *Then shall the eyes
of the blind be opened, and the ears of the deaf unstopped, then shall the lame
man leap as a hart, and the tongue of the dumb shall sing.* An unmistakable

message for the elderly husband of a young wife pregnant with another's seed.

A prolonged rainy-windy October. Shall we never survive October.
The insult of the banker Carr (Vanderpoel Trust) still fresh in Abraham's memory, refusing to lend him $1,200: a mere fraction of $12,000.
Nothing is but what is not Abraham writes in a careful hand across the
top of a clean sheet of stationery.

The well water, always so clear, and so delicious, now has a flat
metallic taste. Its purity lost, contaminated by toxins. Yet when Abraham slyly invites Darian to sample it in his presence, Darian drinks a
full glass of the stuff; and calmly denies to his father that there's anything wrong with it.

Abraham bursts into laughter. "My boy, *you* should have gone onto
the stage, not me. How brave, how reckless—to drink that poison
down without flinching."

"Father, there's nothing wrong with our water. I'm sure."

And, "Abraham, there's nothing wrong with our water. *I'm* sure."

(Mrs. Licht, hair tied back in a rag of a scarf, in a much-laundered
old white bag of a shirt and a pair of formerly glamorous wool-silk
slacks, must contribute her two cents worth from a corner of the
kitchen. Her forced, anxious smile. Those eyes glazed with guilt.)

Abraham, chuckling, drifts away. Checking the Winchester in his
study closet: well oiled, but beginning to pick up minuscule bits of grit
and dust. He stares into the twin sockets of the barrels. Eyeless. If an
emergency comes, old Katrina flying down the chimney another time,
or government agents crawling through the marsh in their ingenious
rubber suits (he'd been issued one, involved in surveillance for the Bureau), he won't have time to load the shotgun and so must keep it
loaded. *A gentleman does not soil his gloves.*

In addition, unknown even to the household, adulterous spies, Abraham has acquired a second firearm: a .38-caliber handgun, Smith &
Wesson, nickel-plated with a handsome mother-of-pearl handle, surprisingly heavy, purchased in a sporting goods store in Innisfail, in a
back room. A "debt collector" the storekeeper called it. This, too,
Abraham keeps loaded at all times; and since it's small enough, no
problem to slip it into his coat pocket when he leaves the house.

Once an enemy is dead, however, he's dead; and nothing can be collected from him. A principle of British common law.

He'd had a law practice once. A flourishing practice. In Philadelphia. The Shrikesdale woman had been his client, seeking her lost son. And though he'd found her son for her, the woman had repudiated him. "And now all is lost. Ridiculous!"

He wonders: if his enemies are dead, who is spying on him from the outside, as surely they are; ransacking his documents, perusing his journal so he's obliged now to write exclusively in code.

Starlings, grackles, red-winged blackbirds calling excitedly to one another in the old Nazarene graveyard. A flocking of birds—how like a flocking of men. And old Katrina disguised as one of the birds, wide wings flapping close to his (shade-drawn) window. *It's those closest to us in blood-kinship who return to haunt us. Most urgent then their corpses must be buried deep!*

He has yet to experiment with either the handgun or the shotgun.

He fears their explosive power. Once detonated, set loose upon the (guilt-ridden) world.

Frankly he confronts Rosamund and in astonishment she denies she's pregnant. As she'd denied she has Arthur Grille's money secreted away in an account in Vanderpoel Trust.

(It's Rosamund's claim that Abraham invested all her money years ago and that it was lost with his.)

Yet she's his wife. "Lawful wedded."

"In sickness and in health."

"Till death do us part."

If she carries another's bastard in her belly, this child will be Abraham Licht's under the law. Does she know that?

Denies it. Denies it.

. . . Approximately $2 million in securities and property out on Long Island, Abraham is certain, moving the kerosene lamp so that he can see his wife's tense face more clearly. (Perhaps to spite him, who so dotes upon female beauty, Rosamund has allowed her hair to become shapeless, a wavy mop of silvery-brown; she now wears schoolgirl wire-rimmed glasses, with the excuse that she's nearsighted.) I remember our joint surprise, that your father hadn't disinherited you after all.

But you invested it, Abraham. I signed it over to you that day. Father's lawyers were witnesses don't you remember. Please remember. You invested it, it was lost with everything else.

The woman lies, lies. Yet not at all as Millicent lied, for she lacks Millicent's dramatic talent as she lacks Millicent's classic beauty. A country-wife slattern, in men's rubber boots clucking as she scatters kernels of corn for the chickens, a noisy brood of red hens lacking a rooster; and a bad influence upon the little girl in thrown-together clothes and bobbed hair showing the tips of her ears, allowed to play with neighbors' brats up the Pike where talk is of Abraham Licht brought low, Abraham Licht a ruined man. In the sacred privacy of the marital bed there must never be lies, Abraham warns the woman. Tell me where the vault is, where you've hidden the money, a wife's property is her husband's property under the law. Tell me. Why you no longer love me.

"Abraham, no! *Please!*"—hiding her guilty face, beginning to weep.

Now when she disrobes she'll have something to show her lover: a kidney-shaped bruise on her upper arm, a peach of a bruise beneath her eye, and those ugly wire glasses bent. *Don't tempt me farther* Abraham whispers.

XII

At dusk of a November day there comes Abraham Licht to his son's window, in a jocular mood; thin cheeks overgrown with stubble, eyes playful, a grimy green cap found on the road pulled down low on his forehead; raps on the pane, and is admitted by the makeshift door to declare, "My boy, you're making a fool of yourself in the world's eyes. I know what people are saying, though I scorn gossip. You should marry before it's too late. You can't know what joy it is to have a wife and a child of your own."

A not-subtle emphasis upon the words "of your own."

Darian, just returned from an eight-hour stint at Muirkirk High School (where this half year he's a full-time teacher of something called social studies and music and helps out with boys' gym), stares at his father without comprehending. Decides to make a joke of it— "True, Father. I don't know. But life isn't so easily arranged."

Glaring about the cluttered room, at the madman pianos and other instruments, stringed, of glass, bamboo, God knows what—tin cans, baling wire—Abraham says sneering, "Life is never arranged 'easily,' Darian. It's arranged by force."

XIII

As if I had never been.
Licht—extinguished!
(For where one can pun, like Shakespeare's Falstaff, in fact one hasn't yet *gone out*.)

Though by degrees he's swinging away from Time. Its wearying cycle of caprices. Who has just captured the Presidency of the United States with the ridiculous promise of a New Deal; who is lost and consigned to oblivion.

That marshy oblivion in which enemies, like lovers, like one's own children, are swallowed up.

Mere bubbles on the scummy surface. Silence, once the birds' shrieking ceases.

He's lucid. He's calm. He's in excellent physical condition.

His eyes . . . his eyesight. A wavy, wavering brightness. Sunspots. Cataracts? He's explaining to Deerfield, a fattish young man with thick-lensed glasses, that he wouldn't trust Vanderpoel General Hospital to operate on an ingrown toenail of his let alone his *eyes*. Telling Deerfield he doesn't wish to be examined with a stethoscope thank you. His heart, lungs, inner organs *listened to. No thank you.*

(Deerfield had driven out to the house under the pretext, an absurdly transparent pretext, of having been called by Rosamund to examine Melanie. Abraham just laughed, his wife and his son were so crude in their connivance.)

Much of the daytime he must surrender to his enemies. But the night remains his, the night has always been his. If only Melanie will understand. . . . Why does she shrink from her father when he wants only to reveal to her certain precious secrets: where Past, Present and Future are one, in the Heavens. "Melanie, darling, it's all for you. These charts, these graphs, these constellations cracked open like nuts . . . how bright-glowing Sirius affects our happiness, how the dance of the Pleiades is our own, the moons of Jupiter that float in our dreams, the bright star of Aries that rises in our blood with the claim of honor."

But the child shrinks from his whiskery embrace, and runs to her mother.

XIV

I will kill the old man!

Seeing that Rosamund's eyes are swollen, her mouth soft and hurt and trembling. Knowing the old man has struck her, surely he's threatened her, though Rosamund refuses to speak. "What is it? He's jealous? He's angry? Why? At you? At me? When there's nothing between us?" Darian asks. "What should I do, Rosamund? Tell me. Don't turn from me. *What should I do?*"

Rosamund pushes past him, out of the room; her eyes averted, her expression stubborn and fixed. Hiding her bruises, her soft battered flesh as if these were signs of grace. So Darian calls after her, "Then go to hell! Both of you."

Having heard the muffled voices in the night. The thumping sounds, the thud! thud! thud! as of a body being slammed against a wall or the headboard of a bed. Having run from his own bed to knock on the door and twist the (locked) doorknob demanding What is it? What's wrong? Father? Rosamund? Open this door, please. But Darian hasn't the right to make such demands as Abraham Licht, panting on the other side of the door, allows him to know. Nothing. No one. Go away. *You* know nothing.

Impulsively Darian follows her. The old man has driven off in the Packard and left them alone; Melanie is napping beneath a feather comforter; even the mailman has come and gone along the solitary Muirkirk Pike; Darian pulls gently at Rosamund, then more forcibly; grips her face in his hands and kisses her; a raw angry yearning kiss, denied for too long.

Don't, Rosamund whispers.

Darian I can't.

Darian . . .

In the last month of Abraham Licht's life, his wife and his son become lovers.

And Darian, dazed, exulting, tries to console himself. *It's just love. People do this all the time.*

XV

(Like all lovers whispering, conspiring. When did you first know, Rosamund asks, and Darian confesses it was the first night he saw her, in his hotel room, the Empire State, remember?—Abraham brought you, in your purple velvet gown, you'd missed my recital, remember? and Rosamund laughs, Rosamund wipes her eyes saying but that woman wasn't me truly, not me as I am now; and Darian says, Yes but the man was me: always it's been me, in regard to you. Their surprise, which is the surprise of all lovers, is with what ease their bodies at last join, the urgency, yet the grace, as if these many months, these years, they'd been celibate yearning for only each other; miserable, yet elated; knowing it must happen someday; and so they'd been lovers without needing to touch. Darian isn't the man he'd been only a few hours ago. Darian the lover, lanky long-limbed Darian now a woman's lover, vowing he'll love her always, he'll love her and Melanie always, he'd kill for her if necessary, it's right, it's just, it's Nature, it's necessary, it's what people do. He will save her and Melanie both, he will protect them from all harm.

Some days later confiding in her, lying in each other's naked arms, a strand of her wavy hair across his face, their breaths and their heartbeats synchronized as if they were two fine-tuned musical instruments, he tells her he's heard (from Aaron Deerfield) that in town it's been believed that they've been lovers for years and that he, and not Abraham Licht, is Melanie's father; and Rosamund says sighing, I know, I've guessed.)

XVI

Short-tempered as a hornet, eyes bright with antagonism, he dismisses this "miraculous" election: the triumph of Franklin Delano Roosevelt, the defeat of Herbert Hoover, the New Deal for the Forgotten Man. "Fools and knaves. Speak to me not of the 'glib and oily art' of politics."

But, Darian argues, Roosevelt is different.

Yes, Rosamund agrees, daring to oppose him, Roosevelt *is* different.

With dignity he rises from his chair; with dignity, manages to maintain his balance; his thin cheeks, hawklike features, the stain of old ivory, a fleeting elderly beauty . . . now his heart's laid bare, for greedy daws to peck at.

Stumbling in the marsh where they'll find me, but he isn't hurt, nor even short of breath; refuses to allow them to drive him into Muirkirk so that Deerfield can check him over. No no *no.* I am the custodian of these bones and will not consent. Though his eyesight has deteriorated. Cataracts, and maybe glaucoma. Though there's a warty growth on his throat just below the left ear. Though his old-man's piss emerges in sullen dribbles, sometimes trickling down his leg. And his head, his brain, aswirl, abuzz, a flood of stars winking in Canis Major have bored through his castle wall and farewell king! farewell.

Yet he will not consent.

Saying coldly, even as they half carry him back to the house, "Abraham Licht is in perfect health for his years, his circumstances and his suffering."

Do you think he knows? the guilty lovers whisper to each other as all guilty lovers whisper, frightened and yet exulting in their adultery. *Do you think he . . . senses? Poor Abraham!* Kissing, tongueing each other, wishing only to press together so there's no separation between them; not even the separation of thought. Knowing they're in danger should the old man guess their adultery yet unable to resist loving, their bliss, their greed, what are they to do, what is the right thing to do, the decent thing, the moral thing, the ethical thing, the pragmatic thing, for they must make love for they love each other so, it's anguish to be denied their love, their bodies' urgency, after so many years of denial, they no longer think of Abraham Licht except to torment themselves *Do you think he knows? And, if he does . . . !*

What must happen, must happen.

XVII

Prowling the leafless forest and marsh, at least the outer edges of the marsh where the earth is frozen; crusts of ice like broken teeth beneath his booted feet; his nostrils like a stallion's flaring steam— "Who's that? Who?" The woman singing to him; humming; combing her long pale hair in the mist, he doesn't hear, he ignores her, like Odysseus he'll stop his ears and will not hear, it isn't time; the heavy shotgun slung beneath an arm for Abraham Licht, Esquire, is a country gentleman, a gentleman-farmer, a hunter, seeking in the idle diversion of sport some replication of The Game, for The Game is both hunter and prey, prey and hunter; in herringbone tweed trousers baggy at the knees, a stained cashmere topcoat, rakish old homburg propped on his head like Jimmy Walker. In the three-way mirror in the dressing room at Lyle's Gentlemen's Clothiers, Lexington Avenue, Abraham Licht modeled to perfection this coat, fitting his broad shoulders snugly yet comfortably, $740 was not too high a price for such style and beauty, $7,400 might as easily have been tossed down for he was a millionaire in those halcyon days. AT&T up. Standard Oil, up. Cole Motors, up. Westinghouse, up. And Liebknecht, Inc., steadily rising.

Still the woman sings, teasing and seductive. If his eyes were better he'd see her . . . but maybe he doesn't want to see her. He stalks away, swinging the shotgun at his side. It's loaded but he hasn't yet wished to test its power; he knows the detonation will be deafening; Darian will hear, and make a fuss; Rosamund will hear, and make a worse fuss. Ice veins have formed in the creases of his face, like burning wires.

Some days, clear-frost days, Melanie begs to come with him.

"Daddy, can I? *Daddy* please!" Smiling up at him, the pink knitted cap already on her head though crookedly since she'd pulled it on herself. "Momma won't know."

"Yes, darlin'. If you hurry."

But Momma does know, Momma always knows and calls her back.

For the shotgun terrifies Momma. "Abraham, for God's sake. Don't."

"It isn't loaded, Mrs. Licht. What's to fear from an unloaded gun?" he teases. "If your conscience is clear."

The child is his child after all. That, he knows.

Clambering outside, calling as if it doesn't matter to him in the slightest, "Coming with your Dadda, puss? Or no?" and Melanie laughs, and dashes after him; and her mother calls sharply, "Melanie, *no*," and the child is rooted to the spot, already her little nose is running, laughing she'll run to Dadda's side, no she'll turn and hurry back into the house, he relents, he forgives her, he understands, it isn't yet time, go back to the house darlin' and comfort your momma, running like a frightened cat back to the opened door where, breath steaming, winter sunlight flashing in her eyeglasses like flame, her mother calls her name.

"Melanie. *Melanie!*"

Thirty-three years old and it's the first great passion of his life, and will be the only great passion of his life for he'll marry the woman after his father's death, let all of Muirkirk buzz with scandal. Never has Darian been so *inspired*; never so *crazed*; even away from his studio he's composing music, even in his sleep, wild ecstatic music of love fulfilled, of love so ravenous it can't be fulfilled; forbidden love; guilty love; the love of sister and brother; transcendent love; ordinary love, *what people do all the time*. He's on fire with ideas! Can't transcribe them quickly enough, his fingers are aching! A symphony for voices . . . a trio for flute, cello and echo-chamber piano . . . wordless oratorios . . . a sonata in which aleatory sounds complement the piano . . . a four-hour piece for chamber orchestra, special instruments and chorus to be titled *Robin, the Miller's Son: A Tale of Destiny* . . . which will eventually be performed when the composer is forty-two years old, as irony would have it on 10 May 1942, at Carnegie Hall, by the New York Philharmonic Orchestra, such a long time to wait! the composer's admirers marvel but Darian Licht isn't a bitter man, Darian Licht's a man perpetually on fire, perpetually in love.

Or so his music proclaims.

* * *

Don't let Father know. I will call you soon.

Millie, from whom Darian hasn't heard in more than a year, has sent a packet of clippings to Darian, guessing he doesn't read the New York papers, indeed the world of politics and racial strife is distant from him, and not very real; now that he's music director of the Muirkirk Consolidated School District, a position he accepted for the salary exclusively (though it isn't much of a salary, as Abraham Licht allowed him to know), he's too busy to read any newspaper; Millie has sent clippings PRINCE ELIHU SHOT DEAD IN HARLEM the headlines read NEGRO REVOLU-TIONARY ASSASSINATED BY UNIDENTIFIED NEGROES. An ugly account of a black leader shot down in the street outside his fortresslike house, but Darian's perplexed what this has to do with him. He studies the accompanying photographs . . . but this isn't his brother Elisha, certainly; he assumes Millie means him to think that "Prince Elihu" is Elisha, for otherwise why would she send the clippings and warn him against letting their father know? But this angry-looking Prince Elihu, identified as African or Jamaican, is no one Darian has ever set eyes on in his life, he's sure.

Darian destroys the clippings, not wanting Rosamund to discover them, either. His older sister has had a "drinking problem" for some time, Darian knows, for Warren Stirling has so hinted to him; Darian thinks he'll call Millie soon, yes he should call Millie soon, except he's so damned busy, and what will they talk about?

Better to wait for her to call him. If she ever does.

XVIII

It's an accident, yet they blame him.

The mailman's low-slung car is stuck in mud out on the Pike, his tires spinning helplessly so what's he do but climb out of the car of course and go to knock at the Lichts' door, he's an acquaintance of Darian Licht, went to school with Darian in fact, but Abraham Licht peering from a window doesn't recognize him, Abraham Licht's eyes are bad and he's had a bad night, a succession of bad nights, he's convinced that his enemies have come for him, federal agents have come for him as long ago they came for him and 'Lisha, and they got away across rooftops barely escaping with their lives, bullets flying past them, bullets grazing their heads, and this is a special order of the secretary of the treasury since Abraham Licht knows the inside story of what happened in October 1929, he rushes for his shotgun, locked in his study and in perpetual readiness for just such an emergency; he means only to frighten away the intruder (he will swear afterward) but somehow one of the barrels is discharged, the explosion is deafening, buckshot shatters a window and sprays glass everywhere and the kick of the gun knocks Abraham backward onto the floor, and there's Darian white-faced entering the room, *Father? My God, all you all right?* and Rosamund behind him staring and Abraham is on hands and knees crawling to pick up the gun for there's another barrel remaining to be discharged, but Darian rudely wrestles the gun from him, *Father, no! God damn it no*—struggling with Abraham Licht whose shoulder is dislocated, yet he feels no pain, he's ashamed, repentant, a fool in the woman's eyes, he manages to get to his feet and runs from the house by a rear door before anyone can stop him, he's bareheaded, in his shirtsleeves and stocking feet, he runs into the marsh, without boots or shoes he runs into the frozen marsh where like a cagey wounded old beast he eludes his son and his wife refusing to answer their desperate calls, hiding in the marsh burrowed in icy mud and underbrush for the remainder of the long day.

And when he returns at dusk the shotgun is gone.

And never again will anyone in the household speak of it, including Abraham Licht.

As if I never was.

Stooped over the hot flames, poker in hand. Tears gathering in the creases of his face, in whiskers and eyelashes; both whiskers and eyelashes singed; but he's determined to destroy all incriminating evidence; all evidence that involves Abraham Licht; he must erase Abraham Licht; every document, every financial record, every worthless share of stock in every extinct company, Liebknecht's secret formula, his most recent cosmological speculations and coded journal entries and as many as two thousand pages of the memoir titled *My Heart Laid Bare*, the work of sixty years and the labor of his life.

Except Rosamund is knocking frantically at the door, begs him to unlock the door, the house is filling with smoke, what is he doing? what is he burning? in the fireplace? but the chimney is clogged as he must know; but Abraham pays the woman no heed, he has broken off all relations with her and with his son, he feels only a lofty scorn for the adulterous conspiring lovers, Abraham please what are you doing? won't you unlock the door? striking her fists against it, she's a powerful woman for one so young, so slender and well-bred, like all of Abraham Licht's wives she's a well-bred woman and yet she has betrayed him, he pays her no heed, he's mesmerized by the fire, by clouds of smoke emerging from the fire, flames leaping and crackling greedy for all he can feed them, a notarized document pertaining to the Santiago de Cuba Company bursts into flame and vanishes within seconds, several yellowed copies of *Frelicht's Tips*, stationery bearing the letterheads of the Panama Canal, Ltd., and X. X. Anson & Sons Copper and the Society for the Reclamation & Restoration of E. Auguste Napoléon and here's a scented love letter from a woman named Eva (whose heart he broke, she's accusing him) and here a packet of unopened letters from Millicent (who having broken *his* heart was never to be allowed to mend it) and here a semi-illiterate letter from one "Felix Bies, M.D." threatening litigation and here in a cascade the myriad papers of his memoir and coded speculations on the ligatures between distant constellations and the most immediate human actions, speculations on Past, Present and Future burning as one; for he understands that he must die soon in his sleep or (better still) in the marsh, in the wintry marsh where no one will find him.

So he pays no heed to the woman's raised voice. Or to a child's crying. And by the time his son returns home the task is completed, everything destroyed, or nearly; only blackened scraps and wads of paper remaining; fireplace, hearth, the cluttered room itself filthy with ash.

The .38-caliber handgun. A weight in his jacket pocket. He intends to throw it far into the marsh. Where with spring and the melting of ice it will sink from sight. Where it will never be found or if found linked to him *except I refrained from using it, I might have used it yet did not, four bullets were all I would have needed yet I did not, remember me with kindness.*

The Pilgrim

The place where sunlight ages and withers to Night, the place
where the trees are Night, where the woman walks in the mist,
where the woman brushes her long pale-golden hair and sings, the air
winks and glitters with cold, suddenly he's young again, on young
springy legs he's running, he's flying, his feet barely skim the surface of
the broken marsh grasses, to the East where no one knows him, to the
West where no one knows him, to the North where ice clusters are
blinding, the winter winds are deafening, someone is whispering his
name, someone walking in mist knows his name, it's time she says, it's
peace she promises, it's solitude, it's oblivion, it's the place of Night,
the place where his children are waiting, where the world's voices con-
verge to one, deafening, and the light blinding, she draws him to her,
she whispers his name, his hair is grown long and filmy-white caught in
the tallest branches of the spider-trees, lichen grows in patches on his
skin, his feet are tangled in the cattails, his fingers are tendrils and
roots, the breath that has steamed and panted so hotly turns now to ice
particles, the flaring stallion's nostrils are coated with ice, these clutching fingers that are ice, she promises Night, she promises sleep, eyelashes stiffening with ice, the curve of the eyeball hard with ice, the
lungs coated with ice, the spinal column that's ice, the veins that are
ice, a tree of ice, a constellation of ice, not the most fierce of winter
suns can penetrate such trees, not the most fierce of winter winds can
melt such trees, such a place of icy sleep, such Night.

· A NOTE ON THE TYPE ·

The typeface used in this book is a version of Goudy (Old Style), originally designed by Frederick W. Goudy (1865–1947), perhaps the best known and certainly one of the most prolific of American type designers, who created over a hundred typefaces—the actual number is unknown because a 1939 fire destroyed many of his drawings and "matrices" (molds from which type is cast). Initially a calligrapher, rather than a type cutter or printer, he represented a new breed of designer made possible by late-nineteenth-century technological advance; later on, in order to maintain artistic control, he supervised the production of matrices himself. He was also a tireless promoter of wider awareness of type, with the paradoxical result that the distinctive style of his influential output tends to be associated with his period and, though still a model of taste, can now seem somewhat dated.